Michael Dobbs

Michael Dobbs' books make an impact, not simply because they are superbly written but also because they have an uncanny knack of being totally timely. His award-winning *House of Cards* trilogy foreshadowed both the downfall of Margaret Thatcher and the increasing turmoil within the Royal Family, while his *Goodfellowe MP* novels showed how a small band of highly motivated men could bring a great city to its knees. The bestselling hardback of *Winston's War* was published just as the nation was voting for Winston Churchill as the Greatest Briton.

He has been an academic, a broadcaster, a senior corporate executive and an adviser to two Prime Ministers. He was at Margaret Thatcher's side when she walked into Downing Street, and with John Major when he was kicked out. As *The Times* has said, 'he certainly knows where all the skeletons are hidden'. He has also, perhaps less kindly, been described as 'Westminster's baby-faced hit man' and 'a man who, in Latin America, would have been shot.'

He is now working on a second novel featuring Winston Churchill – *Never Surrender*.

WINSTON'S WAR

'An intriguing blend of fact and fiction. Dobbs memorably conveys his hero's almost superhuman charisma. *Winston's War* is a vivid dramatization of a thrilling passage in British history. This is a novel about the vanity, cowardice and corruption of ambitious men. And it is Dobbs' instinctive feel for insider politics that keeps you turning the pages.'   *Mail on Sunday*

Further reviews overleaf

WHISPERS OF BETRAYAL

'Dobbs has given us a splendid diversion, one that makes it worth chucking the TV set out of the window and settling down with a book.' *Sunday Express*

THE BUDDHA OF BREWER STREET

'Parliamentary intrigue, political scandal and government treachery . . . Dobbs demonstrates why he is the master.' *Times Literary Supplement*

GOODFELLOWE MP

'Goodfellowe is a modern hero with all the welcome weaknesses we expect . . . The fun (and there's plenty of it) comes from watching honest Tom struggling with his own frailties and battling against the massed ranks of base politicians.' *Sunday Express*

THE FINAL CUT

'Triumphant . . . the action is unflagging, the characterization razor-sharp, the satirical barbs unfailingly accurate.' *Sunday Telegraph*

TO PLAY THE KING

'This thriller will delight anybody who relishes intrigue . . . a model of its kind and impeccably timed.' *Daily Mail*

HOUSE OF CARDS

'This blood-and-thunder tale, lifelike and thoroughly cynical, certainly carries the ring of authenticity . . . a great triumph.' *Independent*

By Michael Dobbs

THE TOM GOODFELLOWE SERIES

Goodfellowe MP
The Buddha of Brewer Street
Whispers of Betrayal

THE FRANCIS URQUHART TRILOGY

House of Cards
To Play the King
The Final Cut

OTHER TITLES

Wall Games
Last Man to Die
The Touch of Innocents
Winston's War

MICHAEL DOBBS

WINSTON'S WAR

HarperCollins*Publishers*

This is a work of fiction.
Apart from well-known historical figures and events,
the names, characters and incidents portrayed in it are
the work of the author's imagination. Any resemblance to
actual persons, living or dead, events or localities is
entirely coincidental.

HarperCollins*Publishers*
77–85 Fulham Palace Road,
Hammersmith, London W6 8JB

www.**fire**and**water**.com

This paperback edition 2003

First published in Great Britain by
HarperCollins*Publishers* 2002

Copyright © Michael Dobbs 2003

The Author asserts the moral right to
be identified as the author of this work

ISBN 978-0-00-649800-1

Typeset in Meridien by
Palimpsest Book Production Limited,
Polmont, Stirlingshire

FOR SANDY AND EDNA SAUNDERS,
AND EDNA DICKINSON.

Much loved aunts and uncle.

AUTHOR'S NOTE

This is unashamedly a novel, not a work of history. Yet if it inspires its readers to dig more deeply into the events and personalities of that extraordinary time, and to decide for themselves not only what happened but *why* things happened, then both the truth and Mr Churchill will have been well served.

MD, May 2003

'How horrible, fantastic, incredible it is that we should be digging trenches and trying on gas masks here because of a quarrel in a faraway country between people of whom we know nothing.'

Neville Chamberlain, speaking about Czechoslovakia, hours before flying to Munich to negotiate the deal with Hitler that surrendered to Germany large parts of Czechoslovakia. The Czechs were not invited to the negotiations.

PART ONE

Blessed are the Peacemakers

ONE

London, Saturday 1 October 1938.

A story has to start somewhere. Ours begins on a disgruntled day in autumn, in the unsuspecting year of 1938.

It could have begun a generation earlier, of course – in 1914, as the British Expeditionary Force whistled its way off to war with the Kaiser. Or 1918, when the few that were left dragged themselves back. There again, we could have started a century earlier when the hooves of the Emperor Napoleon's cavalry turned the continent of Europe into a muddy dying place that stretched from the tumbling rivers and mountains of Spain to the gates of imperial Moscow. Extend the imagination just a little and we could go back – why, a thousand years, to that day on a hill overlooking the coast of Sussex when King Harold raised his eyes to view his enemy in full retreat, and got nothing but an arrow for his efforts – or another thousand years still, to the time of the great Julius and his invasion fleet as they landed a little further along the shore. We could go back to almost any day, in fact, and still it would be the same. Johnny Foreigner was a pain.

But this story starts on the Bayswater Road, and not with a King or an invading Emperor but an undersized figure named McFadden. He is a gentlemen's barber, and a good one. One of the best, in fact. A man with a sharp eye for detail and a soft hand, a punctilious sort of fellow both by his nature and by his trade. Yet McFadden is late, which is unusual for him. And he shouldn't be late, not today, for this is the day he has agreed to be married.

He has dressed as best he can in the circumstances, but it doesn't quite work. The heavy wool jacket is meant for someone at least ten pounds lighter and the button at his belly keeps coming undone. The rose in his buttonhole also refuses to co-operate. It has slipped away from its pin and is threatening to jump. McFadden mutters a dark spell under his breath and makes running repairs, hastening on his way, which isn't easy with his pronounced limp. We haven't mentioned his limp, but he has something badly wrong with his hips, which are out of line, and when he hurries he has to swivel his entire body in order to propel his right leg forward. So McFadden never likes to hurry. This isn't working out as he had hoped.

He had planned to make the journey by underground train from his home near the Piggeries in North Kensington to the register office at Caxton Hall, but when he turned up at the station he found nothing but an untidy notice pasted on the gates – 'closed for urgent structural repairs'. A minor deception, so far as official pronouncements went. The whole of London knows the truth. The station roofs are being reinforced so they can be used as bomb shelters.

Ah, but there isn't going to be any bombing.

4

They have the Prime Minister's word on that. He has flown back from Munich just the day before to announce that he has brought with him 'peace with honour, peace for our time'. Mac doesn't believe him, of course. Another *cholemi*, goddamn lie. Ever since the *mohel* had turned him over on the kitchen table and assured him that it wouldn't hurt, moments before cutting the end off his prick, he has known that the System always lies. (Not that he can remember anything about his circumcision, of course, but his elder brothers Yulek and Vovek never spared him the more gruesome details. He had screamed for hours afterwards.) Mac knows about lies. Lies have followed him like a shadow wherever he has gone and were usually there to greet him when he arrived – in Poland, in Germany, and particularly all those years in Russia. Now he is in England, and the only difference in Mac's mind between Mr Neville Chamberlain and the psychopath Stalin is that the Englishman went to a proper school and has learned not to scratch his balls in public – although, come to think of it, Mac has never seen photographs of Stalin holding his own umbrella, there is that difference, too.

His leg is hurting like hell. It's always giving him gyp – he can't remember a time when the bloody thing wasn't on fire – and the damper it gets the more it burns, deep inside, right to the marrow of the bone. So Mac decides to take a short cut across the park. Not one of his better decisions. The flat expanse of Hyde Park is usually serene and calm, but something has happened. Instead of green acres, Mac is greeted by a bubbling chaos of mud. Like

Judgement Day. On all sides the earth has been torn open where workmen with pickaxes and mechanical shovels have hacked a chaotic maze of holes into the thick London clay. Trenches everywhere. 'Air Raids – Public – For The Use Of' – hah! These bloody holes can't offer protection from the rain let alone from fat Goering's bombs. They aren't finished and already they've begun to fill with water, sullen and brown. Typical English idiocy. Treating war like a game of cricket. Something to be called off if it rains. *Tzibeleh!* They grow like onions, these English, with their heads stuck firmly in the earth.

The spoil from the newly dug graves is beginning to cling to Mac's shoes and find its way onto the legs of his trousers, even though the trousers, like the jacket, are conspicuously short. That's why they had been cheap, from the pawnbrokers on the Portobello. It's his only suit. And the rose in its lapel is wobbling once more.

McFadden isn't his real name, of course. Jewish boys born in Poland just before the turn of the century had names like Kleinman and Dubner and Goldberg. He'd been born in the small market town of Wadowice at the foot of the Carpathian mountains, in an airless upstairs room next to the women's ritual bath-house and on a hot summer's day that had hung heavy with the dust from the harvest. He was one of six children and had been nothing more obvious than a schoolboy who spent his spare evenings as a part-time tailor's assistant, someone who was of no interest to anyone other than his parents, but that was before they had decided that they needed a new type of System in Europe and tore the old one apart. Mac had belonged to a small class of friends, eighteen in total, and every one of them had been swept up in the madness, conscripted, forced to fight for the Kaiser as part of Auffenberg's Fourth Army. But the Fourth Army had lasted only weeks and Mac's unit had been cut to pieces in front of the river town of Jaroslaw. Literally, cut to pieces. It was amazing how high a boy's screams could rise more than a year after his voice had broken. But still Mac hadn't escaped the System, for those few of his class who remained alive had been captured and questioned, then stood against a crumbling farmyard wall beside a filthy chicken coop and told they had a choice. *The System was giving them a choice!* Either they could fight for the Tsar or, if they preferred, they could be shot. Not much of a choice when you're still a few months short of your seventeenth birthday. So for the remainder of that awful year they had fought for the Russians against their old German comrades until the Revolution had come to rescue them from the madness and at last Mac had been able to throw away his rifle. But by then only he and Moniek, the doctor's son, were left. Still, they were alive, they felt special and they rejoiced. It was the last time Mac could remember being happy.

He had celebrated the peace along with all the other soldiers, until the Bolsheviks had discovered that he and Moniek weren't Russian at all and so didn't fit into the Brave New System and its world of miracles. They knew it was truly a world of miracles, not only because the guys with the boots and rifle butts told them so but because their rabbi had always taught them that miracles would be beyond

7

their comprehension. And nothing made sense any more. It was important in this new world to be internationalists, they were told, but apparently it was more important still to be Russians. Which they weren't. So the angels with the boots and the rifle butts placed them once more in the service of the System and sent them off to labour camps, the gulags – Kolyma, Knyazh-Pogost, Sretenka, Yertsovo, Pomozdino, Shchelya-Yur, Solikamsk. An endless world of little miracles, often at thirty degrees below, filled with angels who in the morning would scream instructions – 'anyone unconscious come out now or be left behind to freeze!' – and saints who refused to distinguish between the living and the dead. They were all expected to work. They were herded from camp to camp, crammed into a metal-sided Stolypin rail carriage with room for twelve but often stuffed with thirty or thirty-five for days and even weeks on end. Mac remembered one carriage so filled with prisoners that for three days his feet hadn't touched the floor. He had remained suspended between earth and heaven, hovering on angel's wings, fighting for every breath, until an inspection had allowed them to sort the dead from the slowly dying and lay them on the floor of the carriage so that those who were left could complete the journey standing on the bodies. Pleas to offload the corpses were received with nothing but a beating. The paperwork had said that the Stolypin had started its journey with so many bodies, so that's how many it must finish with. The journey lasted fifteen days.

Another time he had been thrown into a carriage of women, mostly withered old veterans but one or two with flesh still clinging to their bodies and so closely crowded that he'd had a continuous if inevitably crude form of sex with one of the younger ones for the best part of a week. It was his first time. Oh, what a lot he owed to this new world of miracles.

And so it went on, and on, and on, half starved then half beaten to death until their existence had been entirely forgotten and their names and origins wiped from any record. Nothing but entries on a transit sheet. Then, around the year of 1920 – who could be sure, time meant nothing, only suffering and food had meaning – he and little Moniek had found themselves in the gulag by the sea. Camp No. 3, Fourth Compound, Solovetsky Islands. On the other side of the world above the Arctic Circle. Intended for three hundred but housing more than four and a half thousand. The camp had grown and grown – another miracle. Only the number of latrine buckets had remained the same.

And Mac remembers, relives it all, no matter how hard he tries to obliterate it from his mind.

Moniek has almost died of fever on the endless journey. Mac drags him semi-conscious and rambling from the prison ship that has taken them there from Archangel, but there is no respite. Within hours of arriving they are set to work on the new harbour. Moniek, feverish, rambling in his mind, has never seen the sea before. The gently swelling water seems to him to be the new world he has been dreaming of, peaceful, embracing, infinite. He gives a quiet hurrah of joy, then begins to stumble into the surf. He doesn't seem to notice that it's barely above freezing. Now he turns around, he's looking back like a guilty child, but the guards are laughing and waving him on – fish bait, they shout, go drink the ocean dry – and ignore him as Moniek struggles away from the shoreline, until all that can be seen of him is the back of his dark head bobbing in the distant swell.

That's when the guards decided to lay a few bets as to which of them could give little Moniek a proper parting. A difficult job in the swell, but the fifth bullet had taken off the top of Moniek's head like a ripe gooseberry.

It's strange what a persecuted mind will do, how it tries to protect itself. Mac would always remember Moniek, but when he had finally found his way out of the gulags and obtained passage on a ship bound for anywhere, he couldn't remember his own name. It had gone. Somehow the System had swallowed it up, robbed him of his identity, left him as nothing more than a number. When the ship eventually docked at a place called Tilbury, the official of yet another *mamzer* System had demanded a name from him – didn't seem to care which – so he had called himself McFadden, after the ship's captain. A good, stout, non-Jewish name.

And it's what he still calls himself all these years later. He has long ago learned that being Jewish in this world is an invitation to a beating, or worse – even here in London. It's not so much that he has forgotten he is Jewish, simply that he's put it behind him, like taking off an old coat. Things are so much easier that way.

Now there is to be a Mrs McFadden. She is a *shiksa*, not kosher, but pleasant enough, a widow several years older than he who has been left with her own modest ground-floor apartment in West Hampstead and a desire which borders on the desperate to be married once more. 'It could be war at any moment,' she says, 'and by then it might be too late.' She's right. So Mac has agreed, not because he loves her but for no more solid reason than that he doesn't want to disappoint her. Anyway, as she says, if war breaks out London will be bombed and gassed until nothing is left, so it doesn't make any bloody difference.

But – miracle of miracles – there isn't going to be a war!

Chamberlain has come back from his mission to Hitler waving a little bit of paper 'which bears his name upon it as well as mine' and which promises peace, all in exchange for a chunk of an unfamiliar, faraway land which belongs to someone else. The world has gone quite mad. They believe Hitler. But Mac knows better. He knows dictators, knows the System, knows that the only signature you can trust is the signature they put on a death warrant or transportation order. He sighs. His leg feels as if it's burning to the bone and the mud beneath his feet is now clinging, treacherous. He stoops to grab a sheet of wind-thrown newspaper to wipe the mess from his shoes. The page carries a huge photograph of Chamberlain back from his dealings in Munich and standing triumphant alongside the King and Queen on the balcony of Buckingham Palace. Everything is floodlit, like a huge stage, and the crowd below is almost hysterical with relief and gratitude. Mac scrapes the mud from his feet and wonders if they are celebrating in Prague, too.

But maybe they are right. Perhaps there isn't going

to be a war – in which case he and Mrs McFadden will most certainly repent their marital rashness at leisure. But his nose tells him that war can't be far off, he can smell it, in which case – what's the point? Of hurrying? Of marriage? Of anything?

In the corner of the park he can see the crew of an anti-aircraft gun at their training. They seem to be making a hash of it, judging by the exasperated voice of their instructor. It's rumoured there are fewer than a hundred of these guns to defend the entire capital – no wonder they're praying there isn't going to be a war. But Mac has long since lost any belief in a god. The rain has started again and the mud is back on his shoes, the damp worming its way through the welts. He pushes his aching body forward once more, head bowed, like the slave he once was. As he does so the flower in his buttonhole finally makes its escape and drops back to earth. 'Pshakrev!' He curses and throws away the soiled newspaper in disgust.

Then he turns and retraces his footsteps back home.

Chartwell, Kent.
It was the season of decay and the leaves of the chestnuts that stood guarding the Weald of Kent were beginning to curl at the edges and turn brown. The young man had found the drive down from London exhilarating. His open-top MG had nearly eighty brake horsepower – not the biggest machine on the road, but he was able to stretch it on the empty weekend roads and he had topped eighty-five

past Biggin Hill. The occasional shower of rain had only added to his pleasure, if not to his elegance, but he had never placed much store on elegance. Although he was a radio producer for the BBC he was more likely to give the impression of being a garage mechanic caught in the middle of an oil change, and if others occasionally looked at him askance it only served to add to the risks of life. He enjoyed taking risks. Or perhaps he had something inside him that required him to take risks, like others needed to take drink. Like the Great Man.

As he turned off the road into the short drive that led to the front of the house he found himself scratched by a sense of disappointment. He had imagined a residence that sang of the Great Man's eminence and aristocratic origins, but all he found was a sombre Victorian frontage standing in shadow on the side of a hill, squeezed tight up against a bank of rhododendron bushes that, so long after their season of flowering, were dark and sullen. The front aspect of the house was mean and more than a little dull. He hated dullness. Christ, the Victorians had spawned so many great architects – Pugin, Barry, Sloane – but this one seemed to have failed his inspiration exams and been sent into exile in Kent. The BBC man pulled at the bell by the front door and was answered by a forlorn echo. He pulled again. Nothing. Perhaps the trip had been a waste of time. Distractedly he walked around the side of the house and only then did he begin to understand why the Great Man loved this spot so, for if England had a heart it was surely here. The views seemed to tug at the soul. The house was built into the side of the

Weald and before him tumbled thousands of acres of trees over a countryside that was dressed in the green-gold colours of autumn, stretching away towards Crockham Hill and disappearing into the mists that clung to the south coast some thirty miles beyond. The ground fell away sharply from the back of the house, and below were stream-fed lakes on which swam black swans and where trout rose to ruffle the surface. There were also several outhouses, a substantial walled garden and cottages built of red brick. Beside one of these cottages he could see two figures at work – perhaps he hadn't wasted his time after all. He began to make his way down the steep pathway, slippery in its covering of recent rain, and as he approached he could see that one of the men was a young worker. The other figure was disguised in a thick overcoat and hat, yet the curve of the back was unmistakable, as were the shoulders, hunched like a prizefighter's. There was also a haze of cigar smoke.

'Hello!' the man from the BBC called from a distance.

Winston Spencer Churchill, a man who had filled the offices of Chancellor of the Exchequer, Home Secretary and First Lord of the Admiralty and who had served his country as soldier, statesman and historian, turned from his labours. He had a trowel in one hand and a brick in the other. 'What do you want?' he demanded, with no pretence at goodwill. The mouth was clenched tightly around the cigar, giving his chin a stubborn look.

'My name is Burgess, sir.'

'So?'

'I telephoned . . .'

The Great Man scowled, trying to recall. 'You can see I'm busy,' he snapped. 'The world has decided to destroy itself, so I am building a wall.'

Burgess tried to follow the politician's logic. Perhaps it was a symbolic act of defiance, or nothing more than an outstanding sulk. This wasn't quite the greeting he had expected, or required. 'Guy Burgess,' the young man repeated. 'From the BBC.'

Churchill's eyes were swollen and sleepless, red with anxiety. They travelled across the unexpected visitor, taking in the unruly hair, the crumpled suit, the sorely bitten fingernails. 'You don't look much like the BBC.'

Burgess returned the stare. The old man was wearing an ancient and much-soiled overcoat whose middle button had been ripped away. His homburg looked as if it had just taken part in the Eton wall game and the boots were covered with splashes of cement. 'You don't look much like a great politician, either,' he replied bluntly.

The cigar twisted between the lips as the Great Man sized up this impudent intruder. Then he threw the trowel to one side. 'Perhaps we had better discuss our mutual lack of authenticity inside.'

Churchill led the way back up to the house, stomping impatiently but with remarkable vigour for a man of his age, his balding head bent forward like a battering ram. He threw off his outer garments to reveal a blue boiler suit which strained beneath the thickening waist, then led Burgess up to a study on the first floor. More architectural disappointment. The room was intended to be impressive with a vaulted timber ceiling in the manner of a mediaeval hall, but Burgess found it unconvincing. And isn't that what they said about Churchill – pretentious, posturing, and unconvincing? Yet the windows offered still more magnificent views across the Weald. From here Churchill could see far beyond the gaze of almost any man in England. Some said that about him, too.

'Whisky?' Churchill didn't wait for a reply before pouring.

Burgess glanced at his watch. It was barely eleven.

'You wanted me to perform on some radio programme of yours, is that it?' Churchill growled, splashing large amounts of soda into two crystal glasses.

'Yes, sir. It's called *The Week in Westminster*.' Burgess was waved into one of the wing chairs near the fireplace. Logs were glowing in the grate.

'Without fear of contradiction I can tell you, young man, there's not the slightest damned point.'

'Why?'

'Because –' Churchill refused to sit but paced impatiently on the other side of the fireplace, stabbing his cigar angrily in the younger man's direction – 'you represent the BBC and you have plotted and intrigued to keep me off the airwaves ever since I upset you over India and the Abdication . . .'

'Not me, sir,' Burgess protested, but the other man had no intention of pausing to take prisoners.

'. . . but most significantly because our Prime Minister . . .' – the cigar was trembling, the voice seeming to prickle in despair – 'I hesitate to speak so. The families of Mr Chamberlain and I go back a

16

very long way in politics. His father Joseph was a great statesman, his brother Austen, too. Friends of my own father.' The voice betrayed a sudden catch. Ah, the sins of the father . . . At Cambridge Burgess had been a brilliant historian and needed no reminding of Churchill's extraordinary father, Lord Randolph – the most prodigious and enticing of men, widely favoured as the next Prime Minister, yet who had destroyed himself at the age of thirty-seven by storming out of the Cabinet and into the quicksand of exile, never being allowed to return. He had died suffocated by sorrows, although his doctors diagnosed syphilis. He was regarded as unsound. So was his son. It was an awesome and uncomfortable inheritance.

'Our Prime Minister lays claim to leading the greatest empire on earth, Burgess, yet he has returned from his meeting with that odious Austrian upstart waving his umbrella and clutching in his hand an agreement that drenches this country in *shame*.' As he slipped into the grip of his emotions the characteristic sibilance in Churchill's voice – the result of a defect in his palate – became more pronounced. His words seemed to fly around the room in agitation looking for somewhere to perch. 'I despair. I feel cast into darkness, yet there is nothing I can do. I am an old man.'

'Not as old as Chamberlain.' Burgess had meant to encourage, but already he was discovering how difficult it was to interrupt the Churchillian flow.

'Hitler will give us war whether we want it or not. I have done all I can to warn of the perils, but no one listens. Look!' He grabbed a pile of newspapers

17

from his desk. 'They call themselves a free press, but they haven't a free thought amongst them. Chamberlain controls them, you know, all but writes the editorials for them.' He threw the newspapers into the corner where they subsided like startled chickens. 'What did *The Times* say this morning? I think I can recall them, words that burn into my heart. *"No conqueror returning from a victory on the battlefield has come home adorned with nobler laurels than Mr Chamberlain from Munich yesterday . . .".*' Churchill seemed incapable of continuing with the quotation, shaking his head. 'He has sacrificed not only little Czechoslovakia, but also our honour.'

'Hitler's only got the German-speaking bits of Czechoslovakia.'

Churchill turned on Burgess with fury. 'He has got *everything* he wanted. He demanded to feast upon a free and democratic country, and instead of resisting we have offered to carve it up for him course by course. Some today, the rest tomorrow. It won't even give him indigestion. You know the Czechs had thirty divisions of fine fighting men? Thirty divisions – imagine! Protected behind great bastions of concrete and steel. Enough to give Hitler endless agonies, but instead of fighting they are reduced to raising their frontier posts and waving the Wehrmacht through. The Nazis have been able to occupy half of Czechoslovakia with nothing more threatening than a marching band.'

The cigar had gone out, exhausted, but Churchill seemed not to have noticed. He was standing by the window, looking out over his beloved countryside towards the Channel and the turbulent continent that lay beyond. 'I love this spot. It was once so quiet, so peaceful here, Burgess, yet now there is nothing but the howling of wolves from every corner of Europe. They are growing louder, more insistent, yet there is nothing I can do about it. I am alone.' The old man sank into silence, his body seeming to deflate as Burgess watched. The shoulders that had belonged to a prizefighter now seemed merely hunched and cowering before the blow that was to come.

'Mr Churchill, you are not alone. There are many of us who share your fears.'

'Are there? Are there truly?' Churchill turned. 'Not according to those harlots who infest Fleet Street.' He lashed out with his foot at the pile of newspapers.

It was odd, Burgess thought, for a politician like Churchill who took the shilling of Fleet Street as regularly as anyone in the land to describe them as harlots. Odd, but not incorrect.

'What can I do? I have no armies to command, no powers to turn against the enemy.'

'You have a voice.'

'One voice lost in the midst of the storm.'

'When a man is drowning even one voice can represent hope. Encourage him not to give up, to continue the struggle. And you have the most eloquent voice of our time, Mr Churchill.'

'No one listens.' The head had dropped.

'Fine,' Burgess spat, 'give up if you want to, but you may just as well fall in behind Chamberlain and start practising the bloody goose-step. That's not good enough for me. I'm only twenty-seven and if there's war then I'll be one of the first sent out to get my bollocks shot away while the old men sit around their fires and pretend that this god-awful war was really someone else's fault. Just like they did last time.' He paused, not bothering to hide the contempt in his voice. 'So how old are you, Mr Churchill?'

Churchill's eyes were ablaze, ignited by the insolence. It took many moments of inner turmoil before he found himself able to reply. 'I'm sixty-three, Mr Burgess. But my dear wife often remarks that I am remarkably immature for my age. Would you by any chance have time for lunch?'

They lunched in the dining room at the circular oak table. Churchill muttered apologies – his wife was away in France and there was only one house servant on duty; they would have to make do with cold cuts. They reinforced themselves with a second large whisky and a bottle of claret. Burgess found the atmosphere inside the house stretched, almost painfully quiet. The world outside was on the verge of Armageddon yet at Chartwell time seemed to be standing still. There was no insistent jangling of the telephone, no scribes rushing back and forth with messages and documents of state, no grand visitors at the door requesting an urgent audience, nothing but two lonely men, one old, the other young, both crumpled.

'You see, Burgess, the greatest threats to our island have always arisen in Europe. Our Empire spans the globe, we have helped civilize half the world, yet every time we embark upon an adventure on the continent, instead of grasping glory we end up covered in regret.' Churchill, who was carving, slapped a thick chunk of ham onto his guest's plate. 'At the time, of course, it always seems so different. Europe is like a fine broad stairway of hope, but after a bit the carpet comes to an end. A little further on we discover only flagstones, and a little further on still these break beneath our feet. Now they have crumbled completely and we are supported by nothing more substantial than Mr Chamberlain's aspirations.'

'But we have friends in Europe. Friends who still have great armies.'

'Like the Poles? They have very fine cavalry, Burgess, and as you may know I have a particular love of cavalry. Why, I myself had a part in the last great cavalry charge ever made by the British Army. At Omdurman. Oh, that was a splendid piece. But there we faced an opponent armed with spears, not artillery and machine guns.'

'I was thinking more of the French.'

'You forget! The surrender at Munich was signed not only by Chamberlain but also by Daladier.' He slurped vigorously at his glass of claret. Burgess followed him. It was a fine vintage, better than any Burgess could afford. A little of it dribbled from the glass onto the front of Churchill's boiler suit, which Burgess noted bore the stains of similar encounters. Churchill was not elegant when he ate. There was too much energy bottled up within him, too much impatience to give much heed to manners. 'The French have vast armies,' he continued, 'but that's been true since the time of Napoleon, and yet they have gone down to one miserable defeat after another, as if the habit of losing has become an infection.'

'Do you discount Russia?'

'Ah, the Bolshevists! How I hate them. They are butchers.' A forkful of ham waved in Burgess's direction. 'But I dare not discount them. They exist and by God they put the fear of damnation into all those around them, Hitler and his Huns, too. Stalin's capacity for slaughter knows no bounds, but he's been too busy slaughtering his own to have time or temper for turning against Berlin.'

'They could never co-exist, Russia and the Fascists.'

'Perhaps you are right. Maybe Russia is the answer, but if so it only shows us the terrible nature of the questions we are facing.' Suddenly Churchill's eyes darted across the table like arrows. 'You one of those Communistic types, Burgess? I hear there's a whole nest of 'em inside the BBC.'

'At Cambridge, like so many others. There seemed no other choice if one wanted to stand up to Fascism. But that was a long time ago. People change. I seem to think you were still a member of the Liberal Party in those days.'

'No. I had switched back to the Conservative cause by then. But I take your point.'

'There is nothing worse than a fixed mind and closed eyes. While I was up at Trinity our esteemed Mr Chamberlain came as the guest of honour to our Founder's Feast. He was Chancellor of the Exchequer then, of course, and we put on the full works – college silver, six courses, including the fatted calf. He was exceedingly reassuring. As the port circulated he told us that we need not worry, there was no hunger about, not even amongst the unemployed. Those were his exact words – not even amongst the unemployed. You'll remember the times. Two million in the dole queues and hunger marches the length of the nation. Yet Chamberlain couldn't see them. I almost threw up.'

'Yet you didn't. You look like a man with a strong stomach.' Churchill almost smiled, recognizing a man whose capacity in those quarters might even be a match for his own.

'No, I didn't throw up. Instead I stood up. Started shouting. Called him an ignorant provincial iron-monger. The dining hall at Trinity has an amazing echo. Caused one hell of a scene.'

'Ah, but now the crowd gathers to cheer him.'

'Should've been a lynch mob!'

They had both consumed too much claret for subtle jibes and there was no hiding the vehemence of the younger man's words. Churchill remained silent for a moment, staring intently, and Burgess thought he might have gone too far.

'We have much in common, Burgess, you and I.'

When next the younger man spoke, his voice betrayed a tremble, not of sycophancy but of a passion that sprang from deep within. 'I fear for my country, and I fear for the entire civilized world. There is nothing I wouldn't do to stop the spread of Fascism. And with all my heart I can tell you, sir, that at a time such as this there is no one in whose company I would rather be.'

Churchill's voice crumpled with emotion. 'Then, as you say, I am not alone.'

He was up from the table now, a fresh cigar

between his lips, and gazing out through the windows that stretched from floor to ceiling.

'I had always thought I should retire here, Burgess. Spend my final days gazing out over these fields.'

'I hope you shall. When the time comes.'

'Whenever the time comes, I fear it will not be here.' Churchill sounded as if he were saying goodbye to an old friend. 'It seems that Clemmie and I shall have to leave.'

'For safety?' It didn't take a military genius to recognize that Chartwell sat directly beneath the bombing path to London.

Churchill shook his head sadly. 'It is one of the many ironies littering my life that it is the very *lack* of war that may force me to leave my home, Burgess. It's no state secret that I have been neglecting my financial affairs in recent times – I have been devoting myself to politics, even though politics have so steadfastly declined to devote themselves to me. The vast majority of my income is generated by my writings, but the books and articles that should have been written have remained locked up in my mind.'

'But you said the lack of war . . .'

'A few months ago I was forced to place Chartwell up for sale. It almost broke my heart. I have created so much of it with my own bare hands, I love it without reservation. But as I despaired, another policy presented itself to me. If war were to break out in Europe, the value of everything in this corner of the world would be crushed, while investments in America would rise to ever greater heights. The New World refreshing the Old. It's a policy that appeals to me; as you probably know my mother was American.' Churchill's mother, Jennie, had been a New Yorker who pursued life with a remarkable vitality that had encompassed three husbands and a multitude of more dubious liaisons. The first of her husbands had been Churchill's father, who had been a classic example of ducal degeneracy, and they had both neglected their son as sorely as they neglected each other, yet Churchill clung to the wreckage of their reputations like a man adrift. He was at a side table now, pouring substantial cognacs. 'So I took Chartwell off the market and, in the expectation of war, invested every penny I could raise in short-term stocks on Wall Street. I should by now be sitting on a small fortune.'

'But Chamberlain comes crawling back from Munich . . .'

'An umbrella torn to pieces by the storm. We seem destined to cross each other, Chamberlain and I. He beat me for the leadership of our party, then ignored my claim to office in his Government. He has tried to isolate me, now he may succeed in crushing me.'

'Because there is to be no war.'

'Not soon enough for my investments.'

'What will you do?'

The lower lip jutted forward. 'Comfort myself in the knowledge that he is wrong, and that in the end I shall be proven right. And hope I may still be alive when that happens. Try to find consolation in the thought that – in war – buildings such as this have a value no greater than the pile of rubble they leave behind.' There was an unmistakable dampness in the pale blue eyes.

'We can always rebuild bricks and mortar, Mr

Churchill, but we can't replace your stubbornness and your eloquence.'

'Words, words, words – when we need armies. Weaponry!'

'Mr Churchill, at the moment your eloquence may be the only weapons we've got. You have to go on.'

'One man against the world?' He shook his head. 'Here I am, an old man, out of office for a decade.'

'But with a pride in freedom and a belief in the majesty of a man's right to choose that is the measure of any man I've ever met.' Burgess began to beat his chest. 'Mr Churchill, my passion is as deep as yours, but I don't have your powers. No one does. You give up and you'll leave our sky without its pole star. You must carry on. Your country expects it, demands it. And I know you will listen to them. The Churchills always have.'

The dampness in the old man's eyes now bordered on tears and he turned to gaze out at his beloved Kent countryside. Burgess was at his side, pointing. 'These fields, these blessed fields – a distant corner of the bloody German Reich? Never!'

The old man stood staring for a while, then turned slowly towards his companion. 'It would seem that I cannot give up. You will not let me. And I have come too far to turn back. You are a persuasive man, Burgess – why, you remind me a lot of myself when I was young. Although I think I could afford rather better suits. So . . .' – the eyes were alight once more – 'I shall do as you insist. I shall continue to speak out. After all, I have nothing to lose. And, as you can see, I am too old to learn the goose-step!' He dispatched the cognac in one draught. 'But now I must sleep. I have slept very badly in recent days, and not at all last night.' Churchill held the other man's hand. 'You found me at my lowest ebb, Burgess. I had descended into darkness. You have helped restore me. Words will never be able to embrace my gratitude.' He was propelling Burgess rapidly in the direction of the door. 'So much to do, so little time to do it. And for that I shall need my strength.'

When they reached the hallway Churchill suddenly stopped as though some important memory had tumbled into his mind. 'Pray, sign the visitors' book and wait here for a moment,' he instructed, before scuttling off. He returned bearing another book. 'I have been idle, but my son Randolph has not. He is about your age, Burgess, and has recently published a volume of my speeches, *Arms and the Covenant*. Here.'

He took the pen from Burgess's hand and began to inscribe on the flyleaf of the book: *'To Guy Burgess, from Winston S. Churchill, to confirm his admirable sentiments.'* He dated the inscription, September 1938.

'Read. Enjoy. And if ever you should need me, Burgess, send me this book. I shall remember our conversation, and the debt I owe you.'

They parted, the Great Man and the Arch-Manipulator. It was only later that Churchill read the message left by his guest in the visitors' book.

'From a fellow traveller, belligerent, bibulous – and broke.'

It was written on a page that, many years later, would be torn from the book and destroyed.

* * *

The weather forecast had been discouraging. It had also proved to be entirely accurate, and the young telephonist scurried to work trying her best to shield her new perm from the elements. She had accepted a date for the following day with a dark-eyed travelling glove salesman from Manchester named Norman, and although she knew their relationship could be measured in little more than moments and plumbed the depths of folly, still she wanted to look her best. She arrived in time before her duty started to repair the storm damage and smoke half a cigarette, carefully replacing the unused portion in its packet.

The exchange room where she worked was gloomy, the overhead lighting meagre and inadequate for its task. She settled onto her high-backed stool and confronted the array of switches that were set out with military precision on the board in front of her. At chin-level were posted the Instructions of the Day, printed on a small card. From all sides came the quiet female chatter of operators handling enquiries and connecting calls. It proved to be a busy night at the exchange with much of the country intent on sharing the hard-won pleasures of peace. She listened in on many of the trunk calls in order to ensure that the connection remained clear, at times feeling tempted to join in, to celebrate with them, even to tell them about her Norman. Thoughts of Norman made the night drag. His hands were elegant and remarkably soft, just like a glove salesman's should be, and she wanted it to be tomorrow already.

When the call came up on her board, she knew precisely what to do. The Instructions about this number, Westerham 4433, were clear. She turned to attract the attention of her supervisor, who was sitting at her cubicle in the middle of the exchange floor and who responded with a nod. The supervisor, several years older than any other of the girls on the floor, inserted a plug in her own board and re-routed the call through the Observation Room.

The Observation Room was small, almost sepulchral, without the background chatter of the main exchange. In it sat another young female operator with headphones on, recording tape machine at the ready, and pencil in hand. As the call was connected she noted both the time and the number on her Observation Sheet, and as the voices poured out she began her task of taking down in shorthand every word of the conversation.

It wasn't difficult to tell the difference between the two men's voices. One was ordinary, just a voice in the babble.

The other was quite unmistakable. Sonorous. Distinctively sibilant.

She began scribbling till her fingers ached.

TWO

Alfred Duff Cooper, PC, DSO, MP and many other bits and bobs, was a man of prodigious appetites. He couldn't spend a week without women – many of them – including his beautiful and sophisticated wife, Diana. As a species he found them irritating, yet individually they were irresistible. Neither did he seem able to live without the encouragement of alcohol, although in this he was far from unique within the clubs and corridors of the powerful. He was also a man of considerable intellectual capacity, having written an acclaimed biography of Talleyrand and another of Field Marshal Haig even while he was undertaking his duties as a senior member of the Cabinet. But above all else his appetite was for politics, a game that had brought fame, high office and many beautiful women to his doorstep. Yet, for 'Duffie', politics were to prove the most faithless mistress of them all.

'A trim and a shave, if you will, McFadden. And take your time. I have to look my best.'

'An important engagement, sir?'

'With the executioner's axe.'

'Certainly, sir,' Mac replied, displaying as much emotion as if he had been asked to put out the empty milk bottles.

The politician had walked the fifteen minutes from his office in the Admiralty to Trumper's, the finest gentlemen's barbers in the country, which stood on Mayfair's Curzon Street. It was a walk made by an extraordinarily large number of the grandest men in the land (although in the case of the Palace and Downing Street it was more usual for the barber to pack his small case of necessities and make a house call). McFadden was one of that handful of select barbers who served them. He had joined the firm years before through a combination of good fortune and his considerable ability. Everyone liked Mac because he was totally undemanding. Nobody needed to bother getting to know him. He arrived, he worked, he cleared up and he left. Now the First Lord of the Admiralty was reclining in his chair within a highly polished wood-panelled cubicle, one of many that stretched into the depths of the shop.

'I'm sorry to hear you're going to die, sir. Any particular reason?' Mac enquired as he prepared the hot towels. The announcement of this great politician's imminent demise had seemed to require some sort of response, but Mac was always careful not to appear too interested or to become emotional about any of his customers' concerns. They came here to relax, to put aside the troubles of their day, and they found it much easier to accomplish this with someone like Mac who simply didn't matter. It was bred into them, the tendency to display in front of a servant the range of thoughts and emotions you'd never dream of sharing with a friend or your wife. It also helped that Mac had a slight accent and a limp and appeared to be a little stupid and slow, not a complete man, conforming to a certain notion of the working man that made him the safe recipient of confidences, if not of the vote.

Duff Cooper closed his eyes and allowed a slow exhalation of breath. 'I'm not dying literally, for God's sake. It's worse than that. This afternoon I have a very important speech to make to the House of Commons. My resignation speech.'

'A sad day, sir.' Mac slowed down his preparations for the shave. The client clearly wished to share a confidence with him, which he would find difficult through a swathe of hot towels.

'God, but I've loved my job. I've sat in the Admiralty and sent the mightiest navy in the world to every corner of the globe. More power and privilege than most men could ever dream of. Yet by tonight I shall be an outcast, despised by people who yesterday hung on my every word and called me their friend. All because of . . .'

'Lift the chin for me, will you, sir? Thank you. Because of what, sir?'

'Damn it, McFadden! We won the bloody war. Never again, we said. Then Hitler comes along and starts building his squadrons of panzers and fighter planes – purely for defence, he assures everyone, and we believe him. Even when he marches into the Rhineland we believe him. Two years later he's trampling all over bloody Austria, and now he's ripping Czechoslovakia to pieces. And still our Prime Minister says he trusts him!'

His client was tense, his moustache a-bristle. Mac reclined the chair even more to help him relax.

'Tell me, McFadden, what do you think of our beloved Mr Chamberlain?'

Mac didn't care for such direct questions. All his adult life had been spent in the mentality of the gulag, never openly complaining, always seeming to conform, never risking a row. Perhaps that's why he had agreed to marry, not so much to avoid disappointing the lady but more because it was the simplest way to fit into the flow of things. Yet there weren't any simple ways open to him any more. The time had come when even barbers had to take sides.

'I think Mr Chamberlain wears his hair too long,' the barber replied softly.

'God, but what would I do to get near him with a razor,' the politician spat.

'Doesn't go with the image, it doesn't. That hair – and the winged collar and tail coat. Out of date, if you ask me.'

'A man out of time.'

'Will any of your colleagues be joining you, sir?' Mac made it sound like an invitation to sit down and dine. As he applied the first towel, the politician offered up a soft moan and for a moment Mac thought he had applied it too hot, but it soon became clear that the pain came from an entirely different source.

'They promised, you know. Walter Elliot, and others. We'll be there with you, they said, right at your side. Munich was one goose-step too far. But where are they now? Elliot waffles on about how he can be of more use working from inside the Government than being a leper on the back benches. *Leper*. That's the term he used. The day before he was talking about honour, now it's become some sort of disfiguring disease. The bastard. And the others keep drivelling on about there being an election around the corner and how it would be suicide to resign now, how party headquarters would make sure they never got another job again. What sort of job do they think they'll have when the Wehrmacht comes marching down bloody Whitehall, for Christ's sake?'

Mac held back on the final towel. It was as though the politician was pouring out all the anguish and pain of betrayal he would never be able to display in the House, needing somehow to get to grips with the wreckage that only hours ago had been a grand life.

'I despair. What's become of my party? I thought we were a league of gentlemen, but only Eden telephoned. And Winston, of course. In tears. Sentimental old bugger. By God, if tears could drown Hitler, Winston would've finished him off before a single jackboot ever trod on Vienna.'

Mac hobbled around the chair to apply the final towel. Before his face disappeared, Duff Cooper muttered the words that Mac had heard so many times from this chair. 'Not to be repeated, of course, McFadden. Shouldn't really be telling you this but . . . Just between the two of us, eh?'

The politician wanted a sounding board and who better than a slow, stupid Jew-boy barber? Mac dropped the towel and at last the politician was silent.

Mac held a simple view about politicians. He loathed the lot. He'd been governed by Tsars, by Kaisers, by Kings and by Bloody Chaos. He'd seen both imperialism and communism up close – too close – and he had a pretty clear idea about Nazism, too. They were all the same. They were politicians. They sat behind vast desks in their vast palaces and moved vast armies backwards and forwards across the map – until the armies were no longer vast but had been destroyed and the game was over, for a while. Lives of millions of men sliced to pieces by arrows on a map.

This one was scarcely better than the rest. He wanted war and he'd get it, in the end, if not over Czechoslovakia then over some other god-forsaken patch of Europe. At some point someone would draw a line in the sand and soon it would run red and be so drenched in tears that eventually the line would be swept aside. Vanish. That's what happened with lines in the sand. The soldier's boot, the storm, the downpour of tears. Then the line would disappear, leaving everyone except old women struggling to remember where – and why – it had ever been.

Duff Cooper, of course, would stand in his place that afternoon and insist he was defending the cause of the common man, but Mac was about as common as they came and he'd burn before he saw any sense in it. If Cooper was defending freedom, as he claimed, why hadn't he done so in Spain, and why not in Austria where Jews were already being rounded up and sent on their railway journeys to nowhere? What was so special about fucking Czechoslovakia?

No, for the politician this was nothing more than a glory hunt, a game of ambitions and advancement, a game pursued from the day he had been shoved out of his nursery and sent to learn the rules of the sport on the playing fields of some English public school.

The shave and trim were finished, the moustache back in its proper place. The politician was ready to face the enemy. 'Have a good day, sir,' Mac said at the door, holding out his client's freshly brushed hat.

The soon-to-be former great person barely heard. In his mind he was already on his feet making one of the most memorable resignation speeches of the age, a speech which might yet rock the Government, even bring its house down. He tried to ignore the worm that had been wriggling deep inside all morning and telling him that he should come to his senses, be realistic, understand that the most he could hope to achieve was to sway the House enough for the door to swing open and allow him back in.

'I'll be back,' Cooper barked.

Mac declined to offer an opinion.

Guy Francis de Moncy Burgess woke badly. It was not a good place in which to wake badly. His apartment, in Chester Square near Victoria Station, was decorated with a deliberate taste for the grotesque – the carpet was red, the walls a murky white, the curtains and sheets beneath his heavy Italianate bed-head an uncertain blue, and everything covered with a film of nicotine. As he opened his eyes the colours and stale tobacco mounted a co-ordinated assault on him, and he groaned. His mouth felt like the bottom of a bird cage, and very soon he would be late. Again.

He slipped out of bed and stumbled to the window. On his way he knocked over a pile of books on which was balanced a glass of red wine. Fortunately the wine, like Burgess, had been almost completely consumed and the stain would be invisible amongst the rest. He threw open the window and lit a cigarette, coughing as a trickle of fresh air tried to penetrate the room. It was miserably squalid, but as he insisted on telling his friends, if this was squalor it was nothing compared to what you'd find in Guernica or some of the side streets of Moscow. So, you've been to Moscow, have you? they would invariably ask. How was it? Tough, uncompromising, intellectual, unsentimental, he would tell them. He would relate his encounter with a militiaman who had threatened to beat him up for walking on the grass, but that was only half the story. He'd been throwing up over a statue of Stalin at the time.

He flung the cigarette stub out of the window and hauled up a piece of dried fish that he kept dangling on a string from his windowsill, tearing off a piece before throwing the rest back out again. Breakfast on the run. But his mouth was so dry he couldn't chew, not until he'd poured himself two fingers of Jameson's and swilled it round the back of his gums.

'To mastication,' he murmured, raising his glass to the straw-stuffed Regency buck that stood by the wardrobe. It stared back at him in reproach, the glass eyes seeming to follow him around the room. Sometimes it seemed as if the whole world was after him, even the stuffed animals. The apartment was crammed with artefacts, from a frigate in a bottle to an old American harmonium that he occasionally played, nothing of any great value, all garbage really. One day he'd get rid of it, along with the rest of his ludicrous life. He rubbed whiskey with his finger round his teeth to get rid of the sour taste in his mouth. He always seemed to be drinking whiskey, more than he'd intended to, and more still to get rid of the hangover. He would chew garlic to get rid of the smell of whiskey, then drive ludicrously fast to see if he could get rid of all the things that bothered him. His friends said he'd kill himself eventually, and maybe they were right. It was amazing how many friends he had, all things considered.

It would be another one of those days. He would arrive late at Broadcasting House and they would shout at him, so he would shout back and yet again try to get them to use Churchill. He knew they would refuse, because they were under instructions from above. But in all the shouting about Churchill they would forget he looked like a tramp and had been late yet again. So he would have just one more drink to fortify himself and be on his way.

It was at that point that the eiderdown moved. It was piled high on one side of the bed, a tangle of old silk and cigarette burns, and out from beneath it protruded a calf, then a thigh, followed by the most gorgeous arse he'd seen since . . . ? Since last night. Victoria Station, one of his habitual hunting grounds, where if ever he was stopped and questioned he could always argue that he was on his way home, just round the corner, officer. The arse moved. It belonged to a young bellboy from Claridge's. He couldn't remember his name. Which in the scramble last night hadn't mattered a damn, but in the damp light of day seemed – well, unnecessarily rude. So Burgess decided he'd spend a little more time with his guest that morning, give himself the opportunity to find out the lad's name. And if it made him still later at the BBC, what did it matter? The war would wait. That was official.

Brendan Bracken was one of those figures who could be described as many things, but mostly he was outrageous. He would also, soon, become one of the most powerful men in the country.

Bracken was a fantasist. He was also the Member of Parliament for North Paddington. He was Irish by birth but claimed to be an orphan from Australia where his parents had been killed in a bush fire. In fact, his father had been a stonemason and also a member of the Republican Brotherhood, an illegal Irish nationalist organization on whose behalf he would go round blowing up Anglo-Irish walls and buildings. The following day he would appear cheerfully on the doorstep and offer to repair them. Perhaps he passed on to his son the capacity for vivid imagination.

Bracken went through life lying about his origins, about his education – at times he would suggest he had gone to Oxford University – and even about his parentage. When he attached himself to Winston Churchill and worked his way up to become the elder man's indispensable right arm, rumours began to circulate that he was Churchill's illegitimate son. He did nothing to discourage these rumours, and perhaps even started them.

Bracken did more than invent the world around him, he invented many worlds and seemed to be able to move guilelessly from one to another. People knew it was largely nonsense, but the brashness and energy he devoted to his fantasies persuaded others to go along with them. It was so much easier than calling his bluff. By October 1938 he was thirty-seven years of age with a safe parliamentary seat and was being driven around in his own custom-built Bentley. Still he had trouble being taken seriously.

Yet he wanted so desperately to be taken seriously. Which was why, when he entered the Members' Lobby beside the great oak doors leading to the chamber of the House of Commons and was greeted by Duff Cooper, he was deeply confused. For Duffie had been part of the team. Cooper had been Churchill's drinking partner, dining companion and intimate colleague in the battle against Chamberlain and appeasement. It had been an awesome team, one of them inside the Cabinet, the other rampaging freely outside, but now it was all unravelling. Cooper, Churchill's last great ally inside the corridors of power, was gone. Churchill was despondent. Whichever way Bracken looked at it and turned it over in his mind, Chamberlain had won.

'Brendan,' Cooper greeted him, taking him by the arm. 'At last a friendly face. Beginning to feel about as popular as Dr Crippen standing here.'

'Hello, Duffie. Glad I've been able to find you. Wanted you to know that we're all behind you.'

'Ah, words of comfort. Good, because that's what I'd like. Would you come and sit beside me on the benches while I make my speech? You know, moral support. Someone to lean on when the old legs go a little wobbly.'

Instead of replying, Bracken produced a large handkerchief and with some care blew his nose. He was always complaining of sinus trouble. And it gave him time to manufacture his response.

'Be honoured to, Duffie – but you know that's not possible. Got to be on duty beside Winston.'

Churchill always took the same place on the green leather benches of the House, on the front row just a few feet along from where Government ministers themselves sat. Resignation speeches, by tradition, were made from farther back.

'But surely on this one occasion . . .' Cooper began to urge. A thread of steel had wrapped itself around his smile.

'Duffie, you know what Winston's like.'

'My God, it's like being abandoned on a desert island.'

Before he could continue his protest they were interrupted by a penetrating American voice with a distinctive Boston Irish twang.

'Ah, the man of the moment. Not changed your mind, I hope.'

'Your Excellency,' Cooper responded, not even trying to contain his dislike. Joseph Kennedy, the United States Ambassador to the Court of St James's, was one of the least diplomatic envoys ever provided by Washington. His admiration for the efficiency and ambition of the German Reich was as deep-rooted as the contempt he retained for the decaying, chaotic democracies of the Old World, and he took no trouble to hide either.

'Brought along a couple of guests to see the performance. My son, Jack' – he introduced a fresh-faced man in his early twenties, but looking younger – 'and someone you may already know. Captain Charles Lindbergh.' The aviator, the first man to fly the Atlantic alone and famed throughout the world, held out his hand.

'I'm delighted you should think my performance worthy of such an audience, Joe. I'll try not to disappoint.'

'You already have, Duffie. If you'd had your way, you'd already be at war against Hitler. You might as well take a dip in a bath of acid.'

'What did I tell you, Brendan. A veritable Dr Crippen.'

'Look, ask Lindie here. He's been telling me all about the Luftwaffe – and he knows, goddamn it. They can send up ten times the number of planes as you, the French and the Russians put together. His view is that in a shooting war London wouldn't last a week – is that what you want?'

'That's what puzzles me, Joe. Here we are – according to you – totally without any option. And there was me thinking we'd won the last war.'

'That's where you Brits always get it wrong, Duffie. *We* won the last war. America bailed you out in '17. Fifty thousand dead to prove it. Damned if we're gonna do that again.'

'We'd fight alone, if necessary.'

'Fight! What the hell you got to fight with? Hitler's got more planes, more tanks, more divisions, more everything.' His finger was stabbing in the direction of Cooper's waistcoat. 'Hey, you know what happened to your English unemployment this month?'

Cooper, who wasn't following the American's train of thought, shook his head. 'I've had other things on my mind . . .'

'Through the goddamn roof. Again. Nearly two million. Your factories are closing down and producing nothing but cobwebs. Meanwhile the Fuehrer's got his factories working to splitting point. Building the biggest army and air force this side of the Atlantic. Face it, Duffie, you guys've got about as much chance as a cock in a convent. What are you gonna do when the Wehrmacht comes marching down Whitehall? Throw cricket balls at 'em?'

A flush of anger had risen in Cooper's cheeks. 'And what will you do when he's turned Europe into a dictatorship? When the world is dominated by Communism and Fascism? When America is cut off from its markets, without friends? When Hitler can hold you to ransom?'

Kennedy smiled coldly, not rising to the bait. He nodded towards the Chamber. 'You're gonna go in there and make a fool of yourself, Duffie.'

'Stop pulling your punches, Joe.'

'Hell, it's not the time to pull punches with the situation in Europe.'

'My point precisely.'

'Then, as I said, it should be a fine performance. Damn fine. Gotta go claim our seats now. See you around.' Then, in a final act of insult to the former First Lord, he turned to Bracken, who had remained silent throughout the exchange. 'Nice talking with you, Mr Bracken. Come to dinner later in the week. I'll give you a call.'

'That would be splendid . . .' Bracken replied, before realizing how insensitive he must have appeared to his parliamentary colleague. He turned to offer some words of remorse, but it was too late. He'd gone.

Duff Cooper had got it wrong. He wasn't going to be alone on the benches. When he rose to make his resignation speech, the Government whips had ensured he was surrounded by a platoon of loyalists who saw it as their duty to make his moment in the parliamentary spotlight as uncomfortable as possible. By tradition resignation speeches are meant to be heard in silence and *Hansard*, the official record of parliamentary proceedings, is renowned for its inability to hear insults and inappropriate interruptions even if they ring round the ancient rafters. But *The Times* also published extensive verbatim extracts of parliamentary proceedings, and their report was unable to hide the crude treatment Cooper received at the hands of members of his own party.

They surrounded him, intimidated him, jeered and scoffed at him. Destroyed many friendships. Only when he mentioned the name of the Prime Minister did they cheer, then fell into sullen silence when he said that, no matter how he had tried, he couldn't believe what the Prime Minister believed. 'And so I can be of no assistance to him or his Government,' Cooper continued, looking around him, eyes flooded with sorrow. 'I should only be a hindrance.' Growls of agreement began to rise about him like flood water. 'It is much better that I should go.' And Order Papers were waved like a breaking sea that threatened to wash him away. He stood in their midst like a rock, lonely, defiant, mouth dry as the abuse continued.

Yet gradually a hush fell. Perhaps his tormentors grew ashamed, or simply ran out of breath. In any event, Cooper's dignity at last was allowed to shine through, without interruption.

'I have forfeited a great deal. I have given up an office which I loved, work in which I was deeply interested and a staff of which any man might be proud. I have given up association in that work with my colleagues with whom I have maintained for many years the most harmonious relations, not only as colleagues but as friends. I have given up the privilege of serving as lieutenant to a leader whom I still regard with the deepest admiration and affection.'

He was looking directly at Chamberlain, who refused to return his stare.

'I have ruined, perhaps, my political career. That is a little matter. I have retained something which is to me of greater value – I can still walk about the world with my head erect.'

Only then did he sit down. And still the Prime Minister would not look at him.

For a place of such eminence and influence, Downing Street was architecturally extraordinarily undistinguished. Even after the extensive renovations to Number Ten undertaken by Neville Chamberlain and his wife, required in part by the need to shore up floors that were sagging and in danger of collapse, much of the interior remained remarkably dark and cramped. A place of elves and goblins. Two of the most voracious of these goblins were Sir Horace Wilson and Sir Joseph Ball.

Wilson's official title was the Government's Chief Industrial Adviser, which did no justice to his real influence. In practice he was recognized as being Chamberlain's most trusted assistant. He had accompanied the Prime Minister on all three of his flying visits to Hitler in the previous month and had even been despatched to talk with the German leader on his own. 'He is the most remarkable man in England,' Chamberlain had once told colleagues, 'I couldn't live a day without him.' Wilson controlled most of the levers of Government. Meanwhile his close colleague Ball controlled the political machinery. He was the director of the Conservative Research Department, the policy-making body for the Tory Party, and was also the official in charge of publicity and propaganda at party headquarters. Ironically he had turned down Guy Burgess when Burgess had applied to become an employee of the Conservative Party after leaving Cambridge. He thought him too scruffy.

Wilson and Ball shared many things – a background in the secret services (both had been officers in MI5), virulent anti-Semitism, a passionate belief in the policy of appeasement, and above all a devotion to Neville Chamberlain that went far beyond any job description. They were formidable, and in some quarters were justifiably feared.

Now these two eminent servants of the people sat in Wilson's office, a small room that ran off the

Cabinet Room itself. It was already dark, the curtains drawn, the only light provided by two green-hooded lamps placed on desks by the tall windows, lending a conspiratorial atmosphere which both men enjoyed. Ball had just come off the phone from talking with one of the directors of the *Yorkshire Post*. Not for the first time they were discussing the predilections of the editor, Arthur Mann, a persistent man who seemed determined to be impressed by the resignation speech of Duff Cooper.

Phrases like 'personal grudge' and 'loss of grip' had littered Ball's conversation, but he seemed to be making little headway. Mann was a notoriously stubborn anti-appeaser, the director had explained, and he wasn't sure what anyone could do. 'For heaven's sake, Jamie, whose bloody newspaper is it? Why do you let him kick you around like that? For God's sake, get a grip. No sane man wants to reconquer Berlin for the Jews.' Ball mouthed the words slowly, hoping they might sink firmly into the other man's mind. 'This is a matter of survival. And not just the country's survival, your survival as a newspaper, too. Look what's happened to your damned advertising revenues. A summer of war scares and the bottom's fallen out of your market. Down – what? Thirty per cent? Precisely. So long as you encourage cranks like Duff Cooper to go on whipping up war scares you can watch your profits shrivel like a baby in bath water. Nobody's going to buy a bloody thing. Look at the economy in Germany – that's the sort of thing we want here, not blood all over your balance sheet. You want war? 'Course not. But that's exactly what you'll get if you carry on crawling up the arse of Duff Cooper and his crowd.' At last the argument seemed to have struck home, the director promised to see what he could do, and the conversation was resolved with promises of lunch.

It had been a profitable evening's work. Other newspapers had been leant on, too. Ball scratched his stomach, contented. By morning Duff Cooper's obituary would be suitably disfigured.

At that moment there came a knock on the door and a head appeared. It belonged to Geoffrey Dawson, the editor of *The Times*. As always in the dark corners of Chamberlain's Whitehall, he was welcomed like a general returned to his camp. 'Thought I might find you two old rogues here,' he said. 'Need to take your mind.'

'And a glass of sherry, too, Geoffrey.'

The editor made himself comfortable in a cracked leather armchair by the fireplace, wriggling in order to reacquaint himself with an old friend. 'Just taken tea with Edward at the Foreign Office.' The 'Edward' in question was Lord Halifax, the Foreign Secretary, and it was Dawson's custom to meet with him on a frequent basis, particularly when preparing a trenchant editorial. They were long-standing personal friends, their lives intertwined. Both were Etonians and North Yorkshiremen, High Anglicans who worshipped and hunted foxes together.

'He was helpful, I trust,' Wilson prompted.

'As always. Got a pocket full of editorials that'll take me right up to the weekend. But that's not what I'm concerned about. It's my young pup of a parliamentary reporter, Anthony Winn. He's written some god-awful eulogy about Duff Cooper's resignation speech this afternoon, about its nobility, how it was a resounding parliamentary success, its barbs striking home. How it shamed the Government's troops into silence, even. That sort of stuff.'

'Then change it.'

'Steady on, Joey. Editorials are one thing. Chopping a news reporter's copy around is considerably more tricky. A little like kicking cradles. Not made any easier by the fact that, according to my sources, he's got it absolutely bloody right.'

Wilson and Ball glanced at each other uneasily. 'Right only on the day, perhaps. Not in the overall context,' Wilson mused. 'He had to go. Duffie is a man who lives his life on the very edge of disaster. Not a man of sound judgement, Geoffrey – why, just look at his women. Pulls them off the street. Some of them are foreign, with completely inappropriate contacts . . . I sometimes wonder whether his rather lurid liaisons haven't weakened his mind.'

'And *The Times* of all newspapers can't go peddling Jew propaganda, Geoffrey,' Ball added. 'Heavens, it's an organ of propriety and eminence. Of the Establishment, not the revolution. We all recognize your newspaper's special position – just as we recognize your own personal contribution to it.' Ah, the final twist. All three of them were acutely aware that Dawson was the only man in the room who hadn't yet been handed his knighthood. It was occasionally the subject of uneasy banter between them, an honour pledged but a promise yet to be delivered. And while he waited, he would behave.

'That's why I needed your guiding hand. Is the

Duff Cooper story so damned important? Worth the aggravation I'll get if I play the heavy-handed censor and rewrite the damned copy?'

The expressions of the other two men eased. Ball's feet swung up onto the desk. The eminent servants of the people smiled at their guest, and expressed their mind as one.

'Oh, yes, Sir Geoffrey. Please!'

The editor of *The Times* did as he was told. Destroyed the copy as though he were laying siege to a medi-aeval fortress. Then he reconstructed it. *'Emotional gourmets had expected a tasty morsel in Mr Duff Cooper's explanation of his resignation,'* he wrote, *'but it proved to be rather unappetising. Speaking without a note, the former First Lord fired anti-aircraft guns rather than turret broadsides. The speech was cheered by the Opposition, but Mr Chamberlain disregarded it for the moment with only a pleasant word of respect.'*

The copy still went out under the name of Anthony Winn, the paper's parliamentary corre-spondent. The following morning he resigned. He would be one of the first to be killed on active service in the war that was to follow.

And so the House of Commons gathered to debate the Munich agreement. The arguments continued for four days – far longer than the resistance shown by Chamberlain at Munich. It was a debate awash with nobility and bitterness, defiance and servility, with servility by far the larger portion – although, of course, at Westminster it is never known as that, being dressed up in the corridors and tea-rooms under the guise of loyalty and team spirit. Play the game, old fellow! Chamberlain demanded loyalty and dominated his party – those men of mediocrity who gathered around him knew he had the offices of state at his disposal, along with the substantial salaries and residences those offices commanded. Duffie had thrown away his London home and five thousand pounds a year – a small fortune in an era when those who enlisted to die for their country still did so for 'the King's shilling' plus a couple of coppers more a day. Anyway, an election was due at some point, perhaps soon, and disloyalty to the Great and Popular Leader was certain to be repaid in kind. Appeasement was *inevitable*, it was argued, and nowhere more vociferously than in the Smoking Room of the House of Commons, where MPs throughout the ages had gathered in pursuit of alcohol and the secret of everlasting electoral life.

'What's your poison, Ian? Gin? Tonic? Slice of the Sudetenland?'

'Make it a whisky, Dickie, would you?'

'Large whisky coming up.'

A pause for alcohol.

'You ever been to Czechoslovakia, Ian?'

'Not even sure I could find it on a map. Faraway places, and all that.'

'What did Neville say the other night after he came back from Munich?' Dickie imitated a tight, nasal accent. ' *"And now I recommend you to go home and sleep quietly in your beds."* '

'Somebody's bed, at least. Whose was it last week, Dickie?'

'I adhere to a strict rule. In the six months before any election I deny myself the pleasure of sleeping with the wife of anyone with a vote in my constituency. Which includes my own wife, of course. Sort of self-discipline. Like training for a long-distance run.'

'For God's sake, don't tell Central Office. It might become compulsory.'

'It's good politics. I work on the basis that I shall always get the women's vote – so long as their husbands don't find out.'

'Better than leaving it dangling on the old barbed wire.'

'Can't stand all this bloody war-mongering, Ian. Any fool can go to war.'

'Particularly an old fool like Winston.'

'Been at it half his adult life. Look where it's got him.'

Slightly more softly – 'And if war is to be the question, how the hell can Bore-Belisha be the answer?'

Their attention was drawn across the cracked leather of the Smoking Room to where the portly and dark-featured figure of the Secretary of State for War, Leslie Hore-Belisha (or Bore-Belisha or Horab-Elisha, according to taste), was ordering a round of drinks.

'Do they make kosher whisky, Ian?'

'Judging by the amount he knocks back it's a racing certainty.'

'Fancies himself as a future Leader, you know.'

'Elisha? Really? Not for me. Always thought it

might be helpful if we found a Christian to lead us on the next Crusade.'

'Precisely.'

'He's getting even fatter, you know. Strange for a man who proclaims his devotion to nothing but the public good.'

'A genetic disposition to –'

'Corpulence.'

'I was thinking indulgence.'

'Christ. Gas masks to the ready. Here comes St Harold.'

Harold Macmillan, the forty-four-year-old Conservative Member for Stockton, drifted in their direction. He was not often popular with his colleagues. Not only did he have a conscience, he would insist on sharing it.

'Evening, Harold. Dickie here's been telling us that he's a reformed character. He's given up sleeping with his constituents' wives. Saving it all for the party in the run-up to an election. Suppose it means he's going to be sleeping with *our* wives instead.'

Macmillan drifted by as silently as a wraith.

'My God, you can be a brutal bugger at times, Ian.'

'What the hell did I do?'

'Don't you know? Macmillan's wife? And Bob Boothby, our esteemed colleague for East Aberdeenshire? Apparently he's been chasing her furry friend for years – catching it, too. Open secret. Supposed to have fathered Harold's youngest daughter.'

'What? Cuckolded by one of his own colleagues? I've heard of keeping it in the family, but that one takes the biscuit. Why doesn't he . . . ?'

'Divorce? Out of the question. Tied to her by the rope of old ambition. Harold's reputation for sainthood would never stand a scandal.'

'Ridiculous man. Won't fight for his wife yet wants the rest of us to go to war over Czechoslovakia.'

'He'll never come to anything.'

Another drink. 'Neville has got this one right, hasn't he, Dickie?'

A pause. 'He knows more about it than anyone else in the country. Got to trust him, I suppose.'

'Young Adolf's not all bad, you know, knocking heads together in Europe. A good thing, probably. Needed a bit of sorting out, if you ask me. Get them all into line, sort of thing.'

'A united Europe?'

'Going to be good for all of us in the long run. Look to the future, I say.'

'We had to come to terms. It was inevitable.'

'Inevitable. Yes. Bloody well put.'

'What was Winston calling it in the Lobby? "A peace which passeth all understanding . . ." What d'you think he meant by that?'

'I have long since ceased either to know or to care. Never been a party man, has Winston.'

'Always takes matters too far.'

'Anyway, soon over and out of this place. Any plans for the weekend?'

'A little cubbing, we thought. Give the hounds a good run. And you?'

'The wife's still in France. So I thought – a touch of canvassing.'

'Anyone in particular?'

'There's an English wife of an excessively busy

foreign banker who's asked me for a few lessons in patriotism.'

'The nobility of sacrifice. For the cause.'

'But not in my own constituency. You know my rules.'

'Thank the Lord, Dickie. Everything back in its place.'

THREE

It was business as normal at the residence of the American Ambassador in Princes Gate. Not, of course, that business in the household of Joseph P. Kennedy resembled anything that in diplomatic circles would customarily be described as normal, but Kennedy was barely a diplomat. A man who had only just finished celebrating his fiftieth birthday, he was more at home in the clapboard tenements of Boston's tough East Side where he was born than this gracious stucco-fronted mansion overlooking London's Hyde Park, but although Kennedy was intensely protective of his Irish-American roots, they were never going to tie him down.

Kennedy was a man of passion and action, if, at times, remarkably little judgement. His approach to diplomacy in the stuffy Court of St James's was often very similar to his approach to sex – he didn't bother with the niceties of foreplay. He was a man always impatient, pushing and grasping. During an earlier life as a movie tycoon he had bedded Gloria Swanson, the most famous sex symbol in the world during the 1920s. She retained a vivid recollection of their encounter. Afterwards she told friends that Kennedy had appeared at her door and simply stared for a while, before letting forth a moan and throwing himself upon her. He was characteristically direct. She compared him to a roped horse, rough, arduous – and ultimately inadequate. 'After a hasty climax, he lay beside me, stroking my hair,' she recalled. 'Apart from his guilty, passionate mutterings, he had still said nothing coherent.'

It was an approach the British Foreign Office would have recognized. Yet for all his lack of orthodoxy he had taken London by storm since his arrival earlier in the year. In a world of quiet fears and ever-lengthening shadows, an old world coming to its long drawn-out end, his brashness was a joy and his lack of respect for social cobwebs a source of endless entertainment. He called the Queen 'a cute trick' and dashed across the floor to dance with her, scattering courtiers and convention in his wake. His language was borrowed from the Boston stevedores of his youth. He had a natural flair for publicity but perhaps the strongest basis of his appeal was his nine children – 'my nine hostages to fortune', as he called them, ranging in age from Joe Junior and Jack in their twenties to the infant Edward. It was like 1917 all over again; the Americans had sent an entire army to the rescue. So the corridors at 9 Princes Gate were turned into a touch-football field, the marbled patio was transformed into a cycle track while the elevator became an integral part of a vast imaginary department store run by young Teddy. And if observers believed Kennedy was using his self-claimed status as 'the Father of the Nation' as a platform to challenge for the presidency in 1940, no one seemed to mind – except, perhaps, for

President Franklin Roosevelt, who had sent him to London hoping never to hear of him again. It was one of the President's classic misjudgements.

Yet, four days after the declaration of peace in our time, the residence was unusually quiet. There was no sound of children echoing around the hallways, no clatter of dropped bicycles bouncing off the marble, and even the Ambassador's dinner guests were restrained. Churchill seemed burdened, while Brendan Bracken, seated next to Kennedy's niece, appeared uncharacteristically tongue-tied. On the opposite side of the table to Churchill sat the aggressively isolationist correspondent of the *Chicago Tribune*, who was proving something of a disappointment since his mastery of the arts of aggression appeared to be entirely confined to his pen; he had done nothing more than mumble all evening and disappear into his glass. A Swedish businessman named Svensson was courteous but cautious, preferring to listen and prod rather than to preach himself, almost as if he was a little overawed by the company. Meanwhile the Duke of Gloucester at the far end of the table was on his usual form, anaesthetizing guests on every side. This was not the effect Kennedy required. He enjoyed confrontation, the clash of words and wills. The English were so bad at it, but the Irish of East Boston – ah, they were a different breed entirely.

'Mr Ambassador, where are the little ones?' Churchill's head rose from his plate. Kennedy noticed he had dribbled gravy down his waistcoat, but the politician seemed either not to have noticed or not to care.

'Sent most of them to Ireland last week. A chance to search for their roots.'

'Ah.' A pause. 'I see.' So the hostages to fortune had fled. Churchill returned his attentions to his plate, indicating a lack of desire to pursue the line of conversation.

'You don't approve, Winston?'

'What? Of sending the little birds abroad at a time of crisis?' He considered. 'For men in public positions there are no easy choices.'

'But you wouldn't.'

'There is a danger of sending out the wrong sort of signal.'

'You'd keep your kids here, beneath the threat of bombs?'

'There is another way of looking at it. The presence of our loved ones serves as a constant reminder of what we are fighting for. And perhaps a signal to the aggressor that we are confident of victory.'

'But we Americans have no intention of fighting. And as for victory . . .'

'You doubt our cause?'

'I doubt your goddamned air defences.' He attacked his pudding as though he were redrawing frontiers. 'You know what I hear, Winston? Last week as you were all digging in around London and waiting for the Luftwaffe, you guys had less than a hundred anti-aircraft guns for the entire city.'

Churchill winced, which served only to encourage the other man.

'Hey, but that's only the headline. Of those hundred guns, less than half of 'em worked. Had the wrong size ammo, or the batteries were dead. And you know what I found when I chatted to the air-raid guys in the park?'

'Why bother with conjecture when surely you are going to tell me?'

'They didn't have any steel helmets. After all these years of jawing about the bloody war, you think the guys in command might just've figured out that the troops needed some steel helmets? Just in case Hitler decided to start dropping things?'

Churchill seemed, like his city, to be all but defenceless. 'I have long warned about the deficiencies of our ARP,' was all he could muster.

On the other side of the table Kennedy's niece whispered in her companion's ear. 'What's ARP?'

The question caused Brendan Bracken to chew his lip, and not for the first time that evening. He was a man of extraordinary features, his vivid red hair cascading down his forehead like lava from an exploding volcano. He had a temperament to match, conducting his outpourings with a wild swinging of his arms. Yet this evening, in the presence of the Ambassador's niece, he had become unusually subdued. Women – apart from his mother – had never played much of a role in his life, his singular energies having been devoted to making money and climbing the political ladder. And what did women matter in an English Establishment where rumours of homosexuality circulated as freely as the port? Yet Anna Maria Fitzgerald was different. Most other young women he found frivolous and teasing, viewing him either as a potential wealthy match or an object of sexual curiosity, or both, at which point he would hide behind his bottle-end spectacles and invent a new story about himself to suit the situation. But American girls – and Anna in particular – seemed so much more straightforward. He didn't feel the need to put on an act, but since role-playing had been the habit of his adult life he found it difficult to know what to put in its place. So he grew tongue-tied. Now she was whispering in his ear, smelling fresh, not like a tart, with her fingers brushing the back of his hand.

'ARP?' she whispered again.

'Um, Air-Raid Precautions,' he explained. 'You know, ducking bombs.'

'Horrid!' Her fingers remained briefly on the back of his hand. 'I've only just arrived in London, to be a sort of assistant to Uncle Joe, and already they're threatening to destroy it.'

'I hope you'll allow me to show you around. I know all the best air-raid shelters.' It was a clumsy and unintended joke, reflecting his unease, but she laughed it off.

From the end of the table, her uncle finished off his apple pie and slice of American cheese, and decided it was time for the after-dinner entertainment. He had wanted to invite the German Ambassador, Dirksen, but he was engaged elsewhere, so had had to make do with his Spanish Fascist counterpart, the Duke of Alba, instead.

'Tell me, Duke, some people argue democracy's finished in Europe. What do you think?'

Instantly Churchill's head came up. 'Finished?' he growled, cutting across the Spaniard.

Kennedy was already in his shirtsleeves; now he slipped off his braces. Time for a scrap. 'What I mean is, the Brits and the French tried it after the last war, imposing democracy all across Europe, but look around you. It's been shot to hell – or disappeared completely. Germany, Italy, Spain, Austria – now Czechoslovakia. It never even got started in Russia. And what's left is so pathetically weak.'

'Is that the language of the New Diplomacy?'

'Come on, you've been saying yourself you should've picked Hitler's pecker years ago.'

'Democracy is like a great play. It lasts more than one act. You must be patient, Mr Ambassador.'

'You mean, like those ARP guys still waiting for their helmets?'

A cheap debating point, or an intended slur? Churchill ignored it.

Kennedy prodded again. 'But democracy can be a hard mistress, too, you know that, Winston, as well as anyone. And the Germans elected Herr Hitler. You can't dismiss that fact.'

'At which point he promptly dispensed with elections.'

'He's offered a referendum in the Sudetenland.'

'Hah! A referendum simply to confirm that which has already been resolved. Thrust upon the poor Czechs. A peculiarly twisted notion of democracy.'

'But I think you're forgetting, Winston. British politicians like you and Mr Chamberlain got elected with a few thousand votes. Hitler got elected with millions. Makes Herr Hitler more legit than you, don't it?'

'Power is not seized through the ballot box, Mr Ambassador, it is shared. It comes from the people. It is a remarkably infested form of democracy which takes that power in order to enslave its own people.'

'Aw, come on. You telling me it's slavery? Slavery don't get millions of people out on the streets waving banners and torches to give thanks that their country's no longer starving. German governments used to be chaotic, criminally incompetent. You might have called that democracy, Winston, but to the Germans it was a dung heap. They were dying in the gutter. So Hitler's replaced the bread lines with armies of workers building autobahns. Where the devil's the harm in all that?'

'One day, in a very few years, perhaps in a few months, we shall be confronted with demands that we should become part of a German-dominated Europe. There will be some who will say that would be efficient. Others already say it is . . . *inevitable* – a word I do not care for, one that has no place in the dictionaries of a democracy. They argue it will make us all the stronger, that we cannot remain an off-shore satellite of a strong and growing Europe. We shall be invited to surrender a little of our independence and liberty in order that we may enjoy the benefits of this stronger Europe. In a word, we shall be required to *submit*.'

Churchill was into his stride now. He had pushed his plate away from him, making room on the table-cloth as though preparing to draw out a plan of battle. 'Soon we shall no longer be ruled from our Parliament but from abroad. Our rights will be restricted. Our economy will be controlled by others. We shall be told what we may produce, and what we may not. Then, a short step thereafter, we shall be told what we may *say*, and what we may *not say*. Already there are some who say that we cannot allow the system of government in Berlin to be criticized by ordinary, common English politicians. They claim we are Little Englanders, xenophobic, backward-looking. Already we are censored, sometimes directly by refusing to allow us access to the BBC, at other times indirectly through the influence of the Government's friends in the press. Every organ of public opinion is being systematically doped or chloroformed into acquiescence and – step by step – we shall be conducted further along our journey until we find, like silent, mournful, abandoned, broken Czechoslovakia, that it is too late! And we can no longer turn back.'

'Hell, that's democracy for you. The people want to do a deal with Europe, so that's what they get,' Kennedy goaded. 'You said it yourself, Winston, it's the people who get to decide. And you saw how they greeted the Prime Minister. The man of the moment. Cheered him all night outside Downing Street.'

'There was a crowd to cheer him in Munich, too.'

'Doesn't that make you think for one moment you may be wrong? There'll also be a crowd in the House of Commons tomorrow, voting on his policy. You can't deny he's gonna win, and win big.'

'He may win tomorrow. But I shall warn them! And perhaps the day will come when they will remember. Soon we shall discover that we have sustained a total and unmitigated defeat, without firing a single shot in our defence.' He swept crumbs from the table in front of him like imaginary tank divisions.

'Winston, you got whipped 'cos you got nothing to fight with. Face up to it, you're gonna get whipped in any war. That's why you had to run away.'

Two clenched fists banged down on the table, causing every piece of silver to jump. Churchill's wine spilled over the rim of his glass. It spread on the cloth like a dark stain crossing the map of Middle Europe. 'Hitler demanded to feast upon poor Czechoslovakia, and instead of resisting his demands we have been content to serve it to him course by course! At the pistol's point he demanded one pound. When that was given, the pistol was produced again and he demanded two pounds. Finally, Mr Chamberlain waved his umbrella and consented to offer one pound seventeen shillings and sixpence and to make up the rest in promises of goodwill for the future. My country is shrivelled with shame.' There were tears in the old man's eyes. He rose in his seat. 'I apologize. I am too passionate. But the Ambassador should not have spoken as he did. We have passed an awful milestone in our history, Europe is held at the pistol's point, and the Western democracies have been found wanting. But this is not the end. This is only the beginning of the reckoning. The first sip, the foretaste of a bitter cup which will be proffered to us year by year unless we, by a supreme recovery of will and vigour, dash it from the dictator's hand!'

Silence gripped the entire gathering. It was theatre, of course; and Winston always overplayed his role. A candle guttered, dripping wax onto the table cloth where it piled up like a thousand sorrows. Churchill took several moments to recompose himself.

'There is much to be done. And so little time.' His eyes searched around the guests, defiant. 'At Munich the Government had to choose between war and shame. They chose shame. I tell you, they shall get war, too.' He nodded curtly in the direction of Kennedy, a gesture trembling on the brink of scorn. 'Come, Mr Bracken. We must set ourselves to our duties.'

Before he knew what he was doing Bracken, too, was on his feet, muttering apologies to Anna and bidding a hurried farewell to the Ambassador, fuming that once again Churchill had taken him for granted. Dammit, he didn't want to leave, not right now. Churchill always treated those around him as barely better than altar boys, waiting to serve him. They said that about Winston, that he was like Moses, except being more modest he made do with only one commandment: 'Thou shall have no other god but me.'

'Pity you have to run off so soon, Winston,' Kennedy called after the retreating figures, twisting their pain. 'Say hi to Neville for me. And come again. Come for Thanksgiving. That's when we normally stuff turkeys.'

'And don't forget the air-raid shelters,' Anna cried out, innocently unaware.

'Hah! Or your steel helmets. If you can find any . . .'

Burgess knew it was going to be one of those days when he got drunk, very early, and did something completely appalling. Sometimes he couldn't help it, he found himself driven, in much the same way that his heart was forced to beat and his lungs to inflate. A friend had once called it a form of madness but it was simply that he viewed the world with different eyes – eyes that were more open and saw more than mere convention and correctness required – which at this moment wasn't difficult, since convention required the world to be more unseeing and unknowing than ever.

The point had been made most forcefully to him by the Controller of the BBC Radio Talks Department earlier that morning. Burgess had suspected there would be trouble, had even taken the precaution of arriving at Broadcasting House on time and so removing that bone of contention, but punctuality was never going to drain the ocean of irritation that was waiting for him, and neither was argument.

The issue had been Churchill. Burgess had argued quietly, then with growing force, that the inclusion of the elder statesman would add depth and popular appeal to the programme he was preparing on the security problems of the Mediterranean. Admittedly, it wasn't the most grabbing of topics, but all the more reason to include Churchill. The Controller had simply said no, and returned to his copy of *The Times*, leaving Burgess standing in front of his desk like an errant schoolboy. He'd bitten his fingernail and stood his ground.

'Why? Why – no?'

'Executive decision, old chap,' the Controller had responded, affecting boredom.

'But help me. If my suggestion that Churchill be included is an embarrassment, tell me why, so I can understand and make sure I don't make the same mistake again.'

The Controller had rustled his newspaper in irritation, but offered no response.

'Is it because he's an expert in foreign affairs?'

No reply.

'Or perhaps that he's one of the best-known historians of our age?'

The rustling grew more impatient.

'I know. It's because he has a lousy speaking voice.'

Nothing.

'Or are you too pig-ignorant or simply too prejudiced to be able to put an explanation into words?'

'Damn you, Burgess!'

'Oh, I probably shall be, but I'll not be the only one. Because you know what I'm thinking? That the reason you can't tell me why Churchill has been banned is because you don't know – or don't want to know. Those that told you didn't have the courtesy to trust you with an explanation. You've just been told to vaseline your arse and keep him off the air and that's that. Just obeying orders, are we?'

'Rot in hell! What do you know about such things?'

'Enough to know that even you aren't normally this much of a shit.'

'Look, Guy – these are difficult times. Damned difficult. Sometimes we have to do things we don't care for.'

'So not your decision?'

'Not exactly . . .'

'How far up does this one go?'

'Guy, this one comes from so high up you'd need an oxygen mask to survive.'

'Know what I think?'

'Face it, Guy, right now nobody gives a damn about what you or bloody Winston Churchill thinks.'

It was then that Burgess had thrown himself across the desk, his face only inches from the Controller's. The Controller tried to pull away, partly in surprise but also in disgust. He could smell the raw garlic.

'Seems to me it's about time you queued up for your party cap-badge, isn't it?' Burgess spat.

The Controller was speechless, unable to breathe, assailed by insult and foulness.

'*Sieg*-fucking-*Heil*!' Burgess threw over his shoulder as he turned and stormed out of the door, kicking it so hard that a carpenter had to be summoned to repair the hinge.

That was why Burgess decided to get drunk. He'd get drunk, get obliterated, then he'd see what Chance threw his way. But as yet it was a little too early, even for him. He didn't like to get drunk before noon. He briefly considered going to ease his frustrations in the underground lavatories at Piccadilly Circus, but they'd just stepped up the police patrol so there was no question of his being able to get away with it. Too risky, even for him. So instead he'll kill some time. Get his hair cut. At Trumper's.

Which was how he met McFadden.

'You've got good thick hair, sir' – although in truth it was already beginning to recede and looked as if something was nesting in it. 'Nice curl. But you should get it cut more often.'

'There are many things I should do more often,' Burgess snapped.

'How would you like it cut, sir?'

'Preferably in silence.'

Burgess felt suddenly miserable. He'd been unjustifiably rude to the barber, which in itself was no great cause for regret. Burgess had a tongue honed on carborundum and his rudeness was legendary. But McFadden had simply soaked it up, dropped his eyes, shown not a flicker of emotion or resentment. As if he were used to the lash. Which cut through to a very different part of Burgess, for his was a complex soul. Yes, he could be cruel and could find enjoyment in it, particularly when drunk, but there were few men who were more affected by genuine distress. While inflicting wounds freely himself, he would in equal measure give up time, money and his inordinate energies to help heal wounds inflicted by others. And the whole pleasure about insulting people was that it should be deliberate and give him a sense of achievement and superiority, a sort of twisted intellectual game. Kicking a crippled barber was way below his usual standards.

He sat silently, guiltily, listening to the snipping of scissors. Then he became aware of a voice from the next booth, a deep, rumbling voice that evidently belonged to a banker in the City who was coming to the end of a troubled week. 'I probably shouldn't mention this, but . . .' the financier began as, layer by layer, he discarded the burdens of his business, any one of which might have helped a sharp investor turn a substantial profit. But there was no danger, of course, because there was only a barber to overhear him, and other gentlemen.

Suddenly Burgess understood how much like a confessional these cubicles were, with their polished wood, the whispered tones and almost sepulchral atmosphere. You relaxed, closed your eyes, drifted. Yet when you looked up again the face staring back at you from the mirror would not be your own, not the youthful, virile self you knew so well and took for granted. What you saw instead, and more and more with every passing month, was the face of your long-dead father as though from another world, the spirit world. A world of different rules, where there were no secrets, where everything was shared. It sparked his curiosity.

Burgess stirred himself. 'Sorry,' he apologized to McFadden. 'Bad day.'

'That's what we're here to help with, sir,' Mac responded, bringing out the words slowly in a voice that was evidently of foreign origin but not immediately traceable, one more accent in a city which in recent years had become flooded with refugees. 'It is a privilege to be able to serve gentlemen such as yourself. This may be the only time in a hectic month you get to relax. A chance to put aside all those worries.'

'People often shout at you?'

'We have all sorts of busy gentlemen – businessmen, politicians. Sometimes they shout, sometimes it's nothing but whispers. We don't take offence. And neither do we take liberties, of course. We help them relax. Then we forget.'

'You get politicians here?'

71

'Had Mr Duff Cooper in here the other day, when he resigned. Not a surprise, it wasn't, sir. He'd been complaining to me about the state of things for months. Rehearsed bits of his speech with me, so he did, while he was sitting in this chair. But you get all sides,' Mac hastened to add, anxious not to offend. 'Even the Prime Minister has to have his hair cut sometimes, sir. Foreign Secretary, too, and members of the Royal Family.'

'They all have their stories.'

'Indeed they do.'

'And your story, McFadden. What's that?'

'My story, sir?'

'Where d'you get the gammy leg?'

'No story at all, really. A crushed pelvis. Unfortunate, but . . .' He shrugged his shoulders.

'An accident?'

Mac continued cutting, concentrating in silence as though he'd found a particularly stubborn tuft, shifting uncomfortably on his damaged leg. But the eyes told the story.

'So, let me guess. If it wasn't an accident you must have been attacked. Beaten up in some way. Maybe injured in the war?'

'A little while after the war, sir.'

'Where?'

Mac didn't wish to appear impolite or evasive, but neither did he want to lay himself open. This wasn't how the game was played. It was the customer who *kvetched* and prattled, and the barber who listened, not the other way round. Still, English gentlemen were so extraordinarily anxious about displaying their ignorance in front of the lower classes that Mac felt confident

72

he knew how to put an end to the conversation. 'Somewhere you'll never have heard of, sir. Abroad. A little place called Solovetsky.'

'Fuck,' Burgess breathed slowly.

'Beg pardon, sir?'

'The gulags.'

Mac started in alarm and dropped his scissors. 'Please, sir.' He glanced around nervously, as though afraid of eavesdroppers. 'It is a thing I don't care to talk about. And in an establishment such as this . . .'

'You poor sod.'

Mac was flustered. He fumbled to retrieve his scissors from the floor and almost forgot to exchange them for a fresh pair from the antiseptic tray. He stared at Burgess, his face overflowing with pain and a defiance that even half a lifetime of subservience hadn't been able to extinguish. Burgess stared straight back.

'Don't worry, McFadden, I've no wish to embarrass you. I'm sorry for your troubles.'

Mac saw something in Burgess's eye – a flicker, a door that opened for only an instant and was quickly closed, yet in that moment Mac glimpsed another man's suffering and perhaps even private terror. This man in his chair understood. Which was why, when Burgess suggested it, he agreed to do what no barber who knew his proper rank would dare do. He agreed to meet for a drink.

The entrance to Shepherd Market stood just across from Trumper's. It was a maze of alleyways and small courtyards hidden in the heart of Mayfair. Here a hungry man could stumble upon a startling variety of pubs and restaurants, mostly of foreign origin, and if he stumbled on a little further he could find narrow staircases that led to rooms where he might satisfy many of his other cravings, too.

When Mac arrived Burgess was standing at the bar of the Grapes, as he had said he would be. He was smoking, cupping the cigarette in the palm of his hand, and drinking a large Irish whiskey. The barber levered himself up onto a bar stool. Mac was short, wiry, his shoulders unevenly sloped as though to compensate for his crooked leg, with a back that was already bent, perhaps through stooping over his customers. The greying hair was scraped neatly but thinly across the skull, the skin beneath his mouth was wrinkled, as though the chin had tried to withdraw and seek refuge from the blows. He was not yet forty but looked considerably older.

'I thought maybe you wouldn't come,' Burgess offered, but didn't extend a hand. The English never did.

'I thought so too. Particularly when I saw you drinking in the saloon bar. Bit rich for me.'

'It's on me. What's your poison?'

'I'd be thankful for a pint of mild, Mr Burgess.'

Burgess noted the obsequious 'sir' had gone. This was a meeting of equals. Burgess took out a large roll of notes from his pocket and paid for a glass of flat brown liquid. 'You couldn't get that in the gulag, could you, McFadden?'

'We got many things. Brutality and starvation mostly. But there was always plenty of work to fill idle moments.' He drank deep, wiping his mouth with the back of his hand. An old scar ran across the hand, dulled by time, and he had a crooked finger that had clearly been broken and badly set.

'How did you end up in Solovetsky?'

'Who can tell any more? Through a series of other camps, moved from one to another, forgotten about, rediscovered, moved on. I wasn't a criminal, just unfortunate. That was the problem. You see, they'd completely forgotten why I was there, so they couldn't release me, could they? Not without the proper paperwork. If they'd let me free and made a mistake, they would end up serving the sentence for me. Such things have to be handled correctly. So they kept me, just in case. The only reason I can recall Solovetsky above the many others is because of this.' He indicated his leg.

'How'd it happen?'

'We were building a new dock. It was February, I think. Winter in the Arctic Circle. We hadn't seen the sun for weeks. I was ordered to unload a wagon full of heavy timbers. In the dark and the cold, they fell on me.'

'I thought you said it wasn't an accident.'

Their eyes met once more, almost as combatants. 'When it's thirty degrees below, you've already worked nine hours without food, you can't feel your feet or your hands and the entire pile of logs has frozen solid, you've been beaten twice by the guards that day because the work detail hasn't completed its quota, and they threaten they'll go on beating you until the timbers are unloaded – I don't call that much of an accident. Do you, Mr Burgess?'

'You must hate the Russians.'

'Why should I? Most of my fellow prisoners were Russians.'

'The Soviets, the guards, then.'

'Not especially. They simply took over the camps that had been built by the Tsars and didn't know any different. And it was a Soviet doctor who in the end saved my life. I was one of the lucky ones, Mr Burgess. At the start of the war I was one of many friends, yet today I am the only survivor. They all died, every one of them. That wasn't the Bolsheviks' fault. Except for little Moniek, perhaps.'

Burgess offered another drink but Mac was still less than halfway through his pint and declined. Burgess ordered another large Jameson's. 'So whose fault was it?'

'The System.'

'What system?'

'Any System. Happens everywhere. Politicians and rulers who decide, who decree, and who leave ordinary folk like me to pay for their mistakes. At least one thing about the Russian Revolution, Mr Burgess, is that when they shot the Tsar at last they got someone to pay for their own mistakes. It's progress of sorts, I suppose.'

It seemed an excellent time to start playing the game. 'In a way that's why I wanted to see you, McFadden. The System. To ask for your help. Do you know I work for the BBC?'

'No, Mr Burgess, I didn't. I know quite a lot about you, but not that.'

'What the hell do you know about me?'

'That your job involves a deal of writing – judging by the ink smudges on your fingers and the stain on your jacket pocket. It also involves you in a lot of stress – look at your fingernails. And I know you're not married. Nor ever likely to be.'

'What?' Burgess muttered in some alarm.

'An observant barber knows a very great deal about his clients. That collar of yours, for instance. Hasn't ever been near a woman. And if the rest of your wardrobe is like that, you stand about as much chance of getting a woman as Stalin has of becoming Pope. You're an intelligent man, you must see that, yet it doesn't seem to worry you. So I conclude you're not a ladies' man at all.'

'You think I'm trying to pick you up?'

Mac smiled gently. 'No. With the sort of money you just pulled out of your pocket there'd be no need for you to bother with the likes of me. Anyhow, in my experience you gentlemen are perceptive types – is that the right word? You would know from the start that you were wasting your time. You and me, we worship in different churches. But I don't rush to judgements, Mr Burgess, not at all. In the camps, you see, you learned to survive by any means that were necessary. Any means, Mr Burgess, whatever it took. You did, or you died. You understand me?'

'I think so.'

'Not places for moralizing, the camps. So I don't moralize, not even about my customers.' Mac was enjoying himself. He was in control, had the upper hand, so different from being on the end of a boot. That was why he'd agreed to a drink. He'd seen in Burgess someone who was suffering more than he was, and had come out of curiosity.

'So we have established that you're not after my body, Mr Burgess. Then what do you want?'

'Proper bloody Sherlock Holmes, aren't we?' Burgess snapped, but smiling, offering a compliment and at last persuading his guest to accept another drink.

'Understand, Mr Burgess, the best time to get to know a man is when you're polishing his boots – or cutting his hair. That way you get to see all of him, from top to toe. Trouble with most English gentlemen – if I may venture an opinion, Mr Burgess? – is that they never take the time to get to know another man. It's a class thing. An Englishman only ever looks up – and usually up someone else's backside.'

'You don't like the English?'

'A certain type of Englishman. I've got customers whose hair I've cut for years and still they have to ask my name every time they come in. You knew it – wanted to know it – right from the start. Doesn't matter why, it was enough you took an interest, didn't patronize me. So I thought I'd take an interest, too. How can I help?'

Burgess knocked back his refreshed drink in one draught. 'Not sure you can, really, but . . . I work for the BBC. Political programmes. I like the job, it's important – more important than ever right now – yet it's like driving in a fog. The Government tells us next to nothing and what it does say is twisted like a corkscrew. Or it lies, promises peace in our time, yet we're going to war whether we like it or not.'

The barber's deep-set eyes held his own, steady, not agreeing, not dissenting either.

'So I need to understand. If we're going to war I

want to know the bloody reason why. And as I was sitting in your chair it struck me – the people you see every day are the ones who make these decisions. And they talk to you. If you could help me understand what they're thinking, what they're planning, I'd be able to do my job a hell of a lot better.'

'Mr Burgess, I cut the hair of politicians, Cabinet Ministers, all sorts of great men. They entrust me with their confidences because they think I'm slow and stupid and working-class and a little foreign, so they assume I couldn't possibly understand. And you want me to pass those confidences on to you.'

Damn it, but this man knew what he was about. 'I'm not asking you to divulge secrets or anything . . .'

'I have secrets, Mr Burgess? If they tell me, a mere barber, how could they be secrets?'

'I'm sorry, if you find this offensive I'll go . . .'

Mac was sipping his beer, contemplating. Slowly, gulp by gulp, he drained his glass and gently replaced it on the polished counter. 'Offensive? Mr Burgess, I don't find you trying to do your job offensive. I find the gulags offensive, yet what's going on in Europe right now is going to lead to far, far worse than the gulags. I find that offensive. There's something else. Just this morning I was reading in the newspaper – it was left behind by a gentleman, he'd only been interested in Court Circular and the horse-racing news. It was buried inside, a little report. Not of much consequence, apparently. About how in Vienna they were celebrating Mr Hitler's victory in Czechoslovakia by rounding up Jews. They dragged entire families from their houses and made the old ladies sit up in the branches of trees like birds, all night long. It snows sometimes in Vienna at this time of year, Mr Burgess. And they lined up old men in front of their daughters in the street and shaved their private parts, saying it was a delousing programme. Humiliated them, not because they'd done anything wrong, but because of what they were. Then they were told they couldn't go back to their houses, that their homes had been confiscated. If anyone objected, they were told they'd be sent to Dachau. Or worse. An interesting choice of phrase – *Dachau or worse*. What do you suppose they meant by that. Mr Burgess?'

'Truly, I hate to think.'

'But somebody has to think, Mr Burgess. And it's as plain as a maggot in a slice of meat loaf that Mr Chamberlain's not going to think about all that.'

'You're Jewish?'

McFadden shook his head, as though trying to shake off an annoying fly. 'Doesn't matter what I am. Or what you are.'

'Meaning?'

'We live in a complicated world. I don't suppose that cash you've got in your pocket was given to you by the BBC to pay for your haircut, was it?'

Burgess covered his alarm with laughter – God, but this one was sharp. 'Would you believe it if I said I lived off my mother's immoral earnings?'

'We are all held hostage by our past.'

'You'd like payment?'

Mac slowly shook his head. 'No. You can buy me a drink when it suits you, but I won't help you for money. I'll do it because if Mr Chamberlain gets this wrong, a lot of people are going to die. People like me and Moniek. Not people like Mr Chamberlain.'

'Who is Moniek?'

'It is no longer of importance.'

'Have another drink.'

McFadden shook his head once more. 'No, thank you. It's been a difficult week and – like you – I am a single man. I feel I need a little distraction. While such things are still allowed, eh? If you don't mind, I think I'll take a walk around the Market. See what's happening.'

'I'll be in touch, McFadden. Thanks,' Burgess offered as the other man slipped off his bar stool and limped away. He turned at the door.

'You know something, Mr Burgess, at this rate you're going to end up the best-groomed bugger in Britain.'

That evening on his way home, McFadden stopped by the entrance to the synagogue at the top of Kensington Park Road. He hadn't entered a synagogue since he was a teenager, but now he hesitated, troubled by memories of Moniek, things he had hidden away for so many years. He put his hand on the door. He seemed almost relieved when he found it locked.

Churchill spoke in the debate on Munich – or European Affairs, as it was called in *Hansard*. He talked of shame, of a total and unmitigated defeat, of gross neglect and deficiencies, of his country being weighed in the balance and found wanting. He spoke magnificently, a guiding star for the rebels. They were few in number, about thirty, but of considerable standing, men of stature – like the former Foreign Secretary Anthony Eden, Duffie Cooper, Leo Amery, Bobbety Cranborne, Admiral of the Fleet Sir Roger Keyes, Macmillan, Boothby, Duncan Sandys, Harold Nicolson. As Nicolson recorded in his diary, *'Our group decided that it is better for us all to abstain, than for some to abstain and some to vote against. We therefore sit in our seats, which must enrage the Government, since it is not our numbers that matter but our reputation.'*

He was right. The Government was deeply enraged. Even as Chamberlain rose from his seat to acknowledge the wild acclamation from all sides, his mind was made up. The thirty or so rebels had become marked men, every one of them. The reputations which Nicolson talked of with such pride were about to be systematically besmirched.

FOUR

Chamberlain. Chamberlain. Everywhere one went it was that name, Neville Chamberlain. No occasion seemed complete without his presence. His was the name on everyone's lips. Hospital beds were being endowed in his name, the French had opened up a fund to provide him with 'a corner of French soil' in gratitude, while the photograph of him at the Palace adorned the mantelpieces of thousands of homes – *The Times* even offered copies to its readers as a souvenir Christmas card. So great had the public clamour grown that it was in danger of becoming compromising; Chamberlain felt compelled to issue a statement declining the Bishop of Coventry's suggestion that a National Tribute Fund be set up in his honour. This was, after all, a democracy.

'Has he arrived yet?' There was no hint of impatience in the question posed by the Dowager Queen Mary – how could even the King's mother be impatient with a man who was so busy saving the world? But they had missed him. They had gathered at Sandringham in the saloon, a fussy, crowded hall overburdened with family portraits, deer skulls and the paraphernalia of Victorians trying too hard to please. A large stuffed bear stood guard by the staircase. Queen Mary had settled into a chair by the fireplace, glass of sherry in hand, while two men stood by her side, waiting on her and in the process warming themselves by the roaring log fire. The first, Edward Halifax, the Foreign Secretary, was entirely at home in a royal household, for he occupied a position of personal privilege almost unique amongst politicians. He was an intimate friend of the King. They dined frequently and in private, and Halifax had been provided with a key to the gardens of Buckingham Palace so that he was able to walk through them every morning on his way to the Foreign Office. The King practised with his rifle in the gardens and would often waylay Halifax in order to share his views on matters of state, but most of all for the simple pleasure of his company. It could be lonely being an Emperor-King. George VI was relatively inexperienced, a monarch by mistake. He also suffered from a speech impediment so pronounced that his audience often couldn't tell whether His Majesty had paused for thought or was simply stuck on a stutter. As a result, public appearances terrified him, and perhaps that was why he felt at ease in the company of Halifax, who also and so obviously carried with him the misfortunes of his narrow bloodline. The Viscount was exceptionally tall, dome-headed and gangling, slightly stooped, and born without a left hand. The sleeve on his Savile Row suit was filled with nothing more than a prosthesis, a rubber fist. 'Armless Eddie', as the wags called him. And, like the King, the Viscount also suffered from a tangling of the tongue – he was unable to pronounce his 'r's. So the two men walked, talked, stuttered and found support in each other's company.

Theirs had become an uncommon bond between uncommon men.

The other man warming himself by the fire was Joseph Kennedy. The Ambassador was, of course, as common as New England mud and had no right to feel at home in the inner sanctums of the British Royal Family, but he didn't give a damn. Like a presumptuous wine he was *le nouvel arrivé*, acidic, impertinent but, in the view of Queen Mary, excellent value for money. He was irreverent, called her 'Your Graciousness', which brought her out in uncharacteristic smiles, and he shared many of her prejudices.

'Is an American allowed to tell an English Queen she looks radiant tonight?' Kennedy began.

'I think on that matter we might stretch a point, don't you think, Foreign Secretary?'

'Undoubtedly, ma'am.'

A flunkey crept between them bearing a crystal decanter to refill Her Majesty's glass. He was in full royal regalia, stockings, breeches, buckled shoes, ruffs. Kennedy wondered if there was any chance of his borrowing the outfit for Halloween.

'You gentlemen enjoyed yourselves today, I trust.'

'They flew low and slow. Just as I like 'em,' replied the Ambassador who, for all his Wild West hokum, was a poor shot.

'It has been a particularly happy day for us,' Queen Mary announced, patting her thighs with pleasure. 'While you gentlemen were out shooting for your supper I had tea with our nephew, Fritzi – Prince Friedrich of Prussia,' the elderly dowager added for the American's benefit. 'Such a sweet boy. He brought me news and letters from Doorn.'

The American's expression revealed a state of utter ignorance.

'Doorn – in Holland,' Halifax explained. 'It's where the Kaiser has his estates. He's lived there in exile since the end of the war.'

'He's our cousin, you see, Ambassador. We were very close. You can imagine how difficult it's been in recent days.'

Kennedy began to recall his State Department briefings. Family ties were important, sure, no argument from him on that score, but the bloodlines that bound the royal families of Germany and Britain together came close to a genetic noose. Britain had been ruled by Germans for the best part of two hundred years. Called themselves Hanoverians. Some had barely spoken English, all of them had married German wives. Even the dowager seated on the chair beside him was a princess of some place called Teck – and Hesse, and Wuerttemberg, too, come to that, and the exiled Kaiser – the war-mongering, bottom-pinching, mustachio-twirling Wilhelm – was a grandson of Victoria. The British Royal Family was almost Appalachian in its enthusiasm to disappear up its own roots.

'It's inconceivable, war once more. Between Britain and Germany. Cousin against cousin. Isn't it, Ambassador?' Queen Mary demanded.

'Sure, totally inconceivable,' he agreed – although such refined family sensitivities didn't seem to have stopped them last time. When all was said and the dying done, the Great War had amounted to nothing more than one huge family sulk, King against Kaiser against Tsar – until the Americans arrived and banged their inbred heads together.

'Think of the cost,' she continued. 'We couldn't possibly afford it. And the Empire!' For a moment it seemed as though she might swoon; red spots appeared upon her powdered cheeks. 'It would spark unrest throughout the colonies, particularly in those awkward places like the Middle East and India.' She turned on Halifax. 'Edward, you know India, of course.'

Halifax stooped low, bowing his head in acknowledgement. He had been Viceroy of India until a few years previously.

'They are . . . wonderful, yes, quite wonderful, the Indians,' the dowager persisted. 'But they do have a habit of taking advantage every time one's back is turned.'

Her voice grew softer, more conspiratorial. 'No, Herr Hitler may have his faults, but consider the alternative. Either Germany will dominate the continent, or it will fall to the Bolsheviks. And who would you prefer to take tea with, Ambassador? A German traditionalist who at least has the sense to do business with us, or a Bolshevik revolutionary who has one knife at your purse and the other at your throat?'

'Foreign Secretary?' Kennedy enquired, shuffling off the responsibility.

Halifax considered carefully. It was a complex question, one he had debated long and hard with his colleagues and his God. 'I am no fan of Herr Hitler. He is a ferocious bully, a man with blood on his hands. And yet I see no reason why that blood should be British. On the other hand Bolshevism represents a threat to everything this country stands for.'

He began tapping the pocket of his dinner jacket with his prosthesis as if to check that his wallet hadn't disappeared. 'Look at the map, Ambassador. The most substantial obstacle standing in Stalin's path is Germany. Without a strong Reich' – the word emerged most wretchedly mangled – 'there would be nothing to stop Stalin's hordes sweeping through the continent until they stood at our own front door. Personally – and as an aristocrat I have to view such things personally – I take no pleasure in the prospect of being butchered simply because of what I was born. Begging your pardon, ma'am.'

Tiny shudders of sympathy ran through the Dowager Queen, causing the four strands of jewels in her necklace to sparkle. She had long been tormented by the fate of her cousin, the last Tsar, who had been murdered with his entire family in the cellar at Ekaterinburg, led down the steps, repeatedly shot, then finished off with bayonets. No, not a proper fate for a king. Her shuddering became more violent and she moved her hand to the folds of her throat.

Kennedy, meanwhile, was in excellent spirits. The seat of his trousers had been warmed thoroughly by the fire and the bourbon he was sipping was iced and excellent. It seemed an appropriate time for a little fun. 'I agree with you, Foreign Secretary,' Kennedy offered, picking up the thread of the conversation. 'It's a time when we all have to make choices. Tough choices.' A malicious pause. 'Pity no one seems to have told Mr Churchill that.'

The Queen reacted as though she had suddenly found a pin in the cushion of the chair. 'That man!' she gasped with an expression of pain.

Halifax began to clear his throat, loudly, diplomatically, trying to give the Queen the opportunity to withdraw, but she was in her own house and would have none of it. She was, after all, a woman who carried with her the reputation of being a notorious kleptomaniac, and hosts who invited her for dinner would instruct the servants to lock away the best silver in case she took a liking to a piece and stuffed it in her handbag. She was not a woman who had ever been unduly sensitive about other people's feelings, and she had no intention of showing weakness now.

'He crashes around like a bull who hasn't been fed for a week,' she persisted, treating herself to a huge sip of sherry. 'Leaves wreckage everywhere he goes.'

'Ma'am?' Kennedy enquired, wanting more, bending low.

'My apologies, Ambassador, but . . .' For a moment it seemed she had shocked herself by her own indiscretion. Her face had gone pale beneath the powder, like snow-swept granite, and, taking Halifax's hint, she looked for some means of escape. She peered blindly across the saloon. 'Edward, who is that woman? The one dressed like a Parisian actress?'

'Um, the lady by the staircase?'

'The one whose necklace appears to be nudging her navel. They can't be real, surely.'

'The jewels, ma'am? Indeed they can. That is the wife of one of the King's bankers.'

He offered the name and the Dowager Queen's nostrils flared in distaste, as though someone had just thrown a horse-hair mattress on the fire. Not a guest who would have been invited in *her* day. This distraction wasn't working. Anyway, she argued with herself, why should she be seeking distraction? She was old, and with age went all sorts of allowances to indulge her whims, to jump in puddles and rattle the railings and pinch the silver just as she wished. Her husband was dead, she was no longer on parade. Why should she hold back?

'I had forgotten that you are so recently arrived in our country, Ambassador. But since you have expressed an interest in Mr Churchill, it would be rude of me not to advise you on the matter. You will soon get to know Mr Churchill's record. An exceptional one, indeed.' She paused for effect and for breath. 'He has never been loyal to anyone other than himself. He changes parties and friendships whenever it suits him. None of our business, of course, but when he begins blundering into matters of the Crown, that is quite another thing. Oh, it pains me, Mr Kennedy, that my son Edward should have behaved so badly over the abdication. That was terrible enough for any family to bear. But Mr Churchill proved himself to be utterly outrageous. Talked of forming a King's Party. Wanted Edward to stay on the throne and to turn the whole thing into a huge political row. Would have had That Woman as Queen!'

Her Royal Annoyance disappeared into her sherry, unable for the moment to continue, while Kennedy felt forced to stifle a smile in order to maintain the stern face of diplomacy. If only 'That Woman', Wallis Simpson, had been a sour-faced German dumpling, how much easier Edward's path might have been . . .

The Queen's head was up once more, her emotions on the flood. '*Mr* Winston Churchill' – she was intent on putting him in his place – '*Mr* Winston Churchill has done more than any other commoner since Cromwell to bring our family to the brink of ruin. Why, he might as well be a Bolshevik!'

Halifax, anxious that the Queen Mother was diverting down avenues which might prove uncomfortable, picked up the explanation. 'Winston has had many difficult times,' he explained to Kennedy, 'but the abdication row was the worst. He came back to the Commons after what might be termed, um . . . a *considerable* lunch, and would not go quietly. Insisted on rising to make a speech, to argue against the abdication. When the matter was already settled.'

The dowager muttered darkly. Kennedy thought he could make out the words 'dog' and 'vomit'.

'It was, um, an extraordinary scene. He was jeered from all sides, to the point where he could take it no longer. Forced to leave the Chamber. Flogged from his post. His reputation has never recovered. A sad end to a considerable career. Who knows what – um, in other circumstances – might have been?'

Kennedy had to work still harder to contain his amusement at Halifax's soft twisting of the stiletto and the outpouring of tortured 'r's. His entertainment was interrupted by what seemed at first sight to be an ostrich, an apparition in feathers that began to bob slowly up and down. It proved to be one of the guests, the wife of a senior diplomat, who was curtseying – once, twice – trying to catch the Dowager Queen's attention. The attempt failed miserably. The Queen stared unflinching with eyes that could pluck feathers at fifty paces. After all, this particular bird was one of that circle of society women who – like the banker's wife – had taken her son, the once-innocent Edward, under their wings and into their beds, ensuring that the handsome young prince wanted for neither experience nor education. Trouble was, they had also left him with a taste for the exotic which, in Queen Mary's view, had pushed him down the slippery sexual slope that had led to his ruin with That Woman. The Queen chose neither to forgive nor to forget, and the courtier moved on, distraught, flapping her freshly clipped wings.

Kennedy returned them to their conversation. 'So you don't think Mr Churchill has much of a political future?'

'The best is past, and some time ago,' Halifax muttered.

The royal whalebone rattled. 'It is all theatre. He hasn't a smudge of support.'

Kennedy loved this woman and it showed. Fiery, passionate, opinionated. Hell, if only they'd also given the Royal Family a brain, how different history might have been.

'Ah, um, which brings me to another point, Ambassador,' Halifax continued. 'On which the Prime Minister and I would much appreciate your support.'

'You want New York back?'

'Not quite our architectural style any longer, I think. No, it's Paramount, the um . . . picture company. They've put out a news film for the cinemas

which is really – how can one put this? – not *helpful*.
Goes on about what it calls the German diplomatic
triumph and the sufferings in Czechoslovakia rather
than um . . . the peace and security which the agreement has delivered to the whole of Europe.
Censorship is out of the question, of course, I fully
understand that, but I wondered – particularly with
your background in Hollywood – could you have a
word with Paramount? With the owners, perhaps?
Encourage them to bring a little more balance to
their productions?'

'You mean twist a few arms. Break a few legs.'

'I'm sure just a word in the right ear would be
sufficient,' Halifax insisted.

'Hey, but half of Hollywood is run by the sons
of Israel. Fiddling their own tune. What can you
expect . . . ?'

Their discussion was interrupted by a string
quartet starting up. Something Middle European.
Probably Bach. Coincidence, of course, but to the
Queen it seemed like a heavenly fanfare, for at that
moment the Prime Minister himself entered the
room, dressed for dinner with his wife Anne on his
arm.

'Ah, Neville,' the Dowager Queen fluttered,
shaken from her sherry, 'it's Blessed Neville. At last!
Now we can all rest in peace.'

Neville. Blessed Neville. The saintly Neville.
Everywhere he goes his name is on their lips and he
is acclaimed from all sides. Peace – and praise – in
his time. A task completed, a world saved. And a

point proved. How ironic it is that of all the generations of mighty Chamberlains, he should be the one to make his mark, and how grotesque that, after what has been said in his praise, he should still feel insecure. But Neville has been raised in the shadows, almost a political afterthought, the son of Joseph and half-brother of Austen, both more obviously eminent than he. And yet neither made it to 10 Downing Street. But he has. He may not have wits as quick or tongue so lyrical, but what he lacks in natural gifts he has made up for with persistence and hard work – some call it blind stubbornness, a determination that has left him grey and close to the edge of utter exhaustion. His body has arrived at the point where cold iron grips him inside at night, and still lingers there in the morning. He has needed every ounce of that stubbornness and self-belief to enable him to carry on, but carry on he must. The peace of Europe depends upon it. So does the good name of his family.

He is still feeling cold to his core as he drives – rather, is being driven – back from Sandringham House. The applause of the guests is ringing in his ears, the warmth of the King's handshake still upon his palm, but by God it's cold at night in these Fens. He wraps himself more tightly in the car blanket and tries to find comfort on the leather seats of the Austin. He wishes he could sleep, like his wife beside him, but sleep has learned to avoid him. It is dark outside, as it was when he flew back from Germany. He had never flown before but three times now he has made the trip, long and uncomfortable, like being thrown around in a tumbrel as it crosses uneven cobbles. But it has been worth the pain. As he flew back that last time along the Thames towards London, he realized he was following the path the bombers might take. And there below him, in all its electric splendour, had sat London and its millions of men, women and children – his own grandchild included, born just days before he left – waiting. Waiting for him, waiting for Hitler, waiting defenceless for whatever might be thrown against them. But now there isn't going to be a war. And he hopes never to have to go up in an aeroplane again.

He knows there are those who mock him, but only the types who would have mocked Jesus himself. Behind his back they call him the Undertaker, the Coroner, but not to his face, not any more. Even Hitler had shouted and stormed at him, his spittle landing on Chamberlain's cheek, and Horace Wilson had told him that during one of his private interviews in Berchtesgaden the Fuehrer had become so agitated that he had screamed and fallen to the floor in a fit. He is the commonest little dog, the German leader, no doubt of that, but if he is half-mad then there is also the other half, and at least he is a man of business. And he, Neville Chamberlain, has done business with him – 'the first man in many years who has got any concessions out of me,' as Hitler told him – and he has brought back a piece of paper bearing his signature on which the lives of hundreds of millions of Europeans depend. Herr Hitler has given his word.

The visits to Germany have had their lighter moments, of course. When he arrived in Munich and stepped down from the plane, an SS guard of honour had been waiting ready for inspection. With skulls and crossbones on their collars. What, he had wondered, did they signify? Anyway, as they came to attention he remembered that he had left his umbrella on the plane and kept the SS waiting while he retrieved it. The great German army – held up by an umbrella! And they accuse him of having no sense of humour.

He has achieved more than merely an absence of war, he has built the foundations for peace – a peace in which Britain will be at the heart of Europe, with real influence, helping shape its future rather than simply watching in impotence as a resurgent Germany grows increasingly dominant. ''Proaching Cambridge, sir,' the driver announces – God, miles still to go. His thoughts turn to his half-brother, Austen, and the Nobel Peace Prize he had been awarded for his efforts in bringing the nations of Europe together. And he wonders whether two brothers have ever separately won a Nobel Prize before. Not that he has been awarded the Peace Prize yet, of course, no point in jumping the guns (although he has, quite literally). But his brother had never had a poem dedicated to his honour by the Poet Laureate, John Masefield:

> 'As Priam to Achilles for his son,
> So you, into the night, divinely led,
> To ask that young men's bodies, not yet dead,
> Be given from the battle not begun.'

'What was that, darling?' His wife, Anne, stirs, woken from her sleep.

'Sorry, my dear. Must've been talking out loud. Rest a while longer. Still a way to go.'

And what had Queen Mary told him? Over dinner she took his hand – yes, actually touched him – and said she had received a letter from the Kaiser himself in which he had said – oh, the words burned bright – that he had 'not the slightest doubt that Mr Chamberlain was inspired by heaven and guided by God'. It makes him feel unbearably humble. He is sixty-nine, rapidly wearing out, undeniably mortal, yet with the hand of a Queen on his sleeve and his God at his shoulder. Still some, even within his own party, deny him. What would they have him do, for pity's sake? Cast humanity aside and launch upon another bloody war? What in heaven's name would they have him fight with? A French air force without wings? A Russian army with no scruples? Those people, that rag-bag of political mongrels around Churchill – armchair terriers who have urged him to introduce conscription, not just of men but of capital, too. Suggested he should take over the banks and much of business. Control their profits. Insanity! Doing the Bolsheviks' work for them. But what could he expect of Winston, waving around his whisky and soda, desperately trying to obliterate the memories of his own manifold failures as a military leader. They would carve Gallipoli upon Churchill's gravestone, along with the names of the forty thousand British soldiers who were slaughtered there. Herr Hitler had called Churchill and the other warmongers *'moerderen'* – murderers. He had a point.

The car is rolling down the A10 now, his thoughts rolling with it, past the acres of glasshouses that

97

carpet the Lea Valley, approaching the outskirts of Cheshunt. The anger has warmed him inside but he remains exhausted almost to the point of despair. The driver slows to take a bend and through the darkness the Prime Minister can see the outline of a church, and a notice that announces it to be St Clement's. Oranges and lemons, said the bells of St Clement's . . . And St Martin's, the Old Bailey, Shoreditch, Stepney, Old Bow. The candle is here to light him to bed. And here comes the chopper to chop off his head – chip, chop, chip, chop – the last man's dead! In his tormented mind, Chamberlain has a vision. The heart of London has been ripped out by bombers, the church spires are burning like funeral pyres, and in their light he can see Winston Churchill, astride it all, holding the axe! Chip – chop – chip – chop. Oh, but this is no children's game, there is no need for him to run away. Chip – chop – chip. He thinks he can hear the methodical rhythm of the axe as it falls, but it is only the beating of the car engine. His body aches, his mind is swimming with fatigue and a small tear begins to trace an uncertain path down his cheek. He wonders vaguely why he is crying, but arrives at no clear answer. He doesn't make a habit of crying, can't remember the last time he did so. Oh, yes, it was as a young child, when he refused to get out of the bath and his father had punished him . . .

He dwells on memories of yesterday, perhaps because he dare not dwell on tomorrow. Sometimes, at that vanishing point as wakefulness dips into sleep, Chamberlain has a vision that London is burning after all and he has got the whole thing wrong. The crowds are no longer cheering and both God and the Queen have turned their backs. But it is only a dream. As they pass Queen Eleanor's memorial at Waltham Cross, finally he falls into a fitful sleep.

Late nights were spreading like a disease in Downing Street. They disrupted the process of calm thought and careful digestion. They were not to be encouraged.

'I'll follow you in a minute, my dear,' Chamberlain promised as his wife set foot on the stairs. They both knew she would be asleep in her own room long before he made it up to the second floor. There came a point where the body was too exhausted to relax, and he had long since passed that point. He would need a drink and to pace a little before he could think of retiring, perhaps refresh himself from a few of the thousands of letters and telegrams waiting for him.

As he wandered in search of distraction through the darkened corridors, he discovered a chink of light shining from beneath the door of the anteroom next to the Cabinet Room. The elfin grove. Muffled laughter. He was drawn to it like a moth.

The merriment ceased as Horace Wilson and Joseph Ball looked up in concern. 'Everything in order, Neville?' Ball enquired. They were used to the tides of exhaustion that had swept across their master in recent weeks, but the face at the door was more lugubrious, the moustache more determinedly drooped, than ever.

'Things in order? Perhaps you should tell me. You

two always seem to know so much more about what's going on than do I.'

The Prime Minister sank into a chair and held out his hand. It was immediately filled with a glass of white wine. Tired eyes lifted in silent thanks. So often he found there was no need to use words with these elves, they had an uncanny ability to understand his needs – and particularly Wilson, whom he had inherited from the previous administration of Baldwin. At times it seemed to be the finest part of his inheritance. Softly spoken, pale eyes, fastidious by habit, understated but extraordinarily determined. From the start Wilson and the new Prime Minister had been natural colleagues, one the Government's Chief Industrial Adviser, the other a former Birmingham businessman, both seeing virtue in compromise and believing pragmatism to be a guiding principle. Politics were, after all, simply about business, a matter of making deals.

Ball was different. He was a man of fleshy indulgence, which showed beneath the waistcoats of his broad chalk-stripe suits. His fingers were thick, like sausages, and his face was round, an appearance exaggerated by the manner in which his dark hair was slicked close to his skull. His demeanour was often deliberately intimidating – he would take up his position behind his desk, staring inquisitorially through porthole spectacles like the barrister and spy master he once was, stirring only occasionally to wave away the cigarette smoke in which he was half-obscured. Unlike Wilson he was not in the least fastidious, being entirely open about his prejudices, which he promoted through his role as the mastermind of propaganda at

Conservative Central Office, and also through a newspaper he published entitled *Truth*. Truth, for Ball, consisted of destroying the reputations of all opponents – among whom he numbered most Americans and all Jews – and he was liberal only in the means he employed to achieve his ends. He was extremely wealthy and had access to many sources of funds, using them not only to support his own publications but also to place spies inside the head-quarters of the Labour Party and amongst opposition newspapers. He was widely loathed and almost universally feared.

Yet he was even closer to the Prime Minister than was Wilson. Ball and Chamberlain shared a passion for country pursuits and particularly fly-fishing that swept them off in each other's company to the salmon rivers of Scotland at the slightest opportunity, sometimes with unseemly haste. It was widely rumoured that the dates of many parliamentary recesses were set around the fishing calendar. Somehow there always seemed to be time for a little fishing.

'So, how is our ungrateful world?' Chamberlain pressed as he sipped the wine. It surprised him. An excellent hock.

The elves looked at each other with an air of conspiratorial mischief. It was Ball who spoke.

'This will pain you, Neville, I'm sure. But I fear Winston's got himself into a spot of bother.'

'Truly?' A thick eyebrow arched in anticipation.

'More than a spot. An entire bloody bog.'

'Drink?'

'Money.'

'Will he never learn?' A pause. The hock was tasting better by the mouthful. 'How much?'

'More than forty thousand.'

'My God!'

'Forty-three thousand, seven hundred and forty, to be precise. Due by Christmas.'

It was a fortune. More than four times the Prime Minister's own generous salary.

'But how?'

'Been gambling on the New York stock exchange. Losing. Now the banks are calling in his loans.'

'We have him,' Wilson added softly, as though announcing the arrival of a tray of tea.

'Bracken's been trying to help, find an angel to save him. But the angels don't seem keen on saving the soul of a man who wants a war that would ruin them.'

'So what will he do?'

'Sell what's left of his shares. Put Chartwell on the market. Pay off his debts with the proceeds.'

'Chartwell's been a nest of vipers for too long,' Wilson added. 'Time it was cleared out.'

'No, no . . .' Chamberlain was shaking his head, his brow furrowed in concentration. 'That would be *wrong*.'

'Wrong? What's *wrong*?' Ball muttered, as though grappling with a new philosophical concept.

'He loathes you, Neville,' Wilson objected. 'Leads the opposition on all fronts.'

'And he'll do so again, given half a chance,' Ball emphasized.

'Precisely,' Chamberlain agreed, steepling his fingers as though in prayer, urging them on.

102

'But these debts will crucify him.'

'What is to be gained by seeing him crucified now?'

'For the pleasure of it!' Ball cried.

'To clean up Westminster,' Wilson suggested.

'But he can do us no harm,' Chamberlain persisted. 'It would be like stepping on an ant.'

The two elves fell into silence. They hadn't caught on, not yet, but they knew the Prime Minister tied a mean fly.

'Winston doesn't matter, not now, at least. He has lost, we have won. That's the truth of the matter. And if at this moment he were to fall over the edge, no one would even hear the splash. And how should we gain any benefit from that? Those who stand against us would only regroup, find a new leader and we would have to start all over again. No, there's a better way. Not today, perhaps, not this month but sometime soon, there will be another crisis. How much better it would be, when that time comes, that their leader is a man who is on the brink. Vulnerable. Unstable as always. Whom we control and with one small nudge can send spinning into the abyss – if that were to prove necessary.' There was colour in his face again, a spirit that had revived. The tips of his fingers were beating time, pacing his thoughts.

'By God,' Wilson breathed. 'But how?'

'Bail him out. Extend just sufficient credit for him to survive, for now. Play him on the line. Until he's exhausted and we can net him whenever we choose.'

'But he must not realize . . .'

'Of course not. Do we know his bankers?'

'Most certainly.'

'Are they . . . friends?'

Ball snorted, struggling with the concept that bankers might be blessed with feelings more complex than those of black widow spiders. 'Much better than friends. They're the party's bankers.'

'Then they will co-operate. Tell them we want to help a colleague – but quietly, anonymously, to save embarrassment. Underwrite his loan. Let Winston survive – for the moment.'

'Goes against the bloody grain. When they're hooked, pull 'em in, Neville, that's what I say. Don't let them slip the line.'

'You and I are a little too skilful for that, I hope, Joe.'

'You let that forty-pounder go last August.'

'You know very well he tangled the line in the roots of a tree. Winston is considerably less agile and will have much less stamina for the fight. Don't you agree, Horace?'

Wilson had been quiet. He was no angler. He was a negotiator, looking for advantage. 'If we've won and there's no real opposition, as you say, then strike now. Not just for Winston but the whole damned lot. You have the King beside you and the country behind you. Call an election!'

'An election? But it's not due for another two years.'

'There may never be a better time.'

'Joe?'

'It would call Winston's bluff. Maybe get him thrown out in Epping, if he continues to be disloyal. Think of that. What a sign that'd be to the rest of the buggers! And the opinion polls are putting you a mile ahead, Neville.'

'Are they? Are they . . . ?' But Chamberlain was uneasy.

'A referendum on the peace,' Ball encouraged.

'But profiting from Munich?' He looked tired once more, his sentences growing clipped.

'Why not make a little profit?'

'I signed the agreement at Munich. Doesn't mean to say I have to like it.'

'Peace with honour, Neville.'

'Silly phrase. Borrowed it from Disraeli – what he said when he came back from the Congress of Berlin. I shouldn't have. Moment of weakness. Did what I had to do, but how can I take pride in it? I gave my word. To the Czechs. Then I broke it. Sacrificed them to save the world. Not much of a manifesto, that.'

His eyes were cast down in confession, and for a moment silence hung heavily in the room until Wilson spoke up. 'We did what we had to do, Neville. And the world rejoices.'

Slowly the head came up. 'A fine thought to take me to my bed.' Chamberlain rose.

'But does that mean forgive and forget, Neville? Let the bastards off?' Ball called out, evidently exasperated, as Chamberlain made to leave the room.

'I think that's for their constituencies to decide. And the press.' He was standing at the door, leaning on the jamb. The exhaustion had returned and he could fight it no longer. His face was the colour of old linen yet his deep-set eyes still burned with a remarkable defiance and were staring directly at Ball. 'I suspect some of them are going to be given a pretty rough ride, don't you, Joe?'

'Damn right,' Ball said.

The eyes flickered and went out. 'And so to bed.' It was then Chamberlain noticed that he still had his glass in his hand. He drained it before setting it aside. 'Incidentally, an excellent hock. Far better than our usual fare.'

'It's a Hochheimer Königin Victoriaberg, from a vineyard once owned by Prince von Metternich. I thought it would be appropriate for you. Full of subtlety, nobility, audacity . . .'

'And where did you get this liquid jewel?'

'From Ribbentrop. He sent several cases back with us from Munich as a goodwill gift.'

'Always the wine salesman . . . eh?'

Joachim von Ribbentrop, the German Foreign Minister, had until recently been his country's Ambassador to London. He had been a natural choice for the post since he was a Nazi of long standing who knew the British capital well, having run a wine business there for many years and established a reputation as an excellent host. He had been – and in many eyes still was – the acceptable face of Hitlerism, and much of London society had beaten a path to the dining table of his embassy in Carlton House Terrace.

'I was his landlord for a time, you know,' Chamberlain muttered. 'He rented my family house in Eaton Place. After I moved in here. Like clockwork with the rent. Always told me – raise glasses, not guns. Good man, good man . . .' The rest was lost as he stumbled up the dark stairs of Downing Street.

FIVE

Guy Fawkes Night – 5 November 1938.
It was one of those nights that would change everything – although, of course, no one knew it at the
time. And as was so often the case Max Aitken, the
first Baron Beaverbrook, was to be its ringmaster.

They had gathered together at the summons of
the mighty press baron to celebrate the torture and
execution more than three centuries earlier of that
quintessentially British traitor, Guy Fawkes, who had
attempted to destroy the entire Houses of Parliament,
King included, by stuffing a cellar full of gunpowder.
He had been apprehended at the critical moment
with candle in hand, and executed by having his
entrails dragged from his still-living body, burnt in
front of his face, then having his beating heart
plucked out. Sadistic, mediaeval Europe – before the
twentieth century turned torture into a modern science of factories and furnaces.

The weather had relented after weeks of skies filled
with rain and Roman auguries. A full moon hung
overhead, an ideal evening for the lighting of the traditional bonfire which had been constructed in the
grounds of Beaverbrook's country home at Cherkley.
The garden and walkways had been turned into a fairy
grotto by countless candles concealed in old tin cans,

while Boy Scouts from the local troop were on hand to cook sausages and chicken legs over charcoal barbecues and to dispense mulled wine loaded with cinnamon and pepper. They had also erected tents and canvas awnings to provide shelter if the sky changed its mind and turned against them. Beaverbrook, ever the showman, had even instructed that chocolate eggs and sweets should be hidden around the grounds for the children. No one was to be left out of the fun. So to Checkley they had come, the good and the great, the famous and those still seeking fortune, more than two hundred of them wrapped in their furs and astrakhans and silk scarves and hand-warmers, giving thanks for the column inches they hoped they would receive from the *Express* and the *Standard* and putting aside how many of those past inches had been cruel and indecently unkind. Yet press barons have no monopoly on unkindness.

'You are . . .' – the Minister paused for thought, but already it was past thought, too late for anything other than gut emotion – 'being ridiculous, woman. Hysterical. A disgrace to your sex.'

'Only a *man* could be so stupid.'

'Ask anyone. Neville is the greatest Englishman who ever lived.'

'He makes me ashamed to be British.'

'You dare talk of shame!'

'Meaning?'

'God's sake, aren't you tired of climbing into Winston's bed?'

'He might yet save us all.'

'What? The man who's killed off more careers than Caligula. Who's filled the graveyards of Gallipoli.'

'He's a prophet —'

'Nigger in a woodpile with a box of matches.'

'. . . pointing to our mortal peril.'

'All the more damned reason for doing a deal with Hitler, then.'

'You'd deal with the Devil.'

'I support my Prime Minister. Loyalty to my own. Something you wouldn't recognize.'

'I recognize naked cowardice.'

'I resent that, madam. I oppose your silly war because it will destroy civilization.'

'War against Hitler may be the only way to save civilization!'

'Madness. Pure madness. Are you Jewish, or what?'

And all that from colleagues who sat on the same Conservative benches.

It had started with laughter and gaiety and one of Beaverbrook's little jokes. (He had a notorious sense of humour — some argued that it had been developed to compensate for his notoriously absent sense of fidelity.) He had given specific instructions about the making of the guy that was to be burnt on the fire and it had arrived with some pomp, seated on an old wooden chair decorated with flowers from the hothouse and pushed in a wheelbarrow by a groundsman. The guy was large and overstuffed, as all good guys should be, bits of straw and paper sticking out from an old woollen three-piece suit that had been plundered from the back of a wardrobe for the occasion. Particular attention had been given to the face, which was round, bald, with a scowling expression and an open slit for a mouth. The arms were spread, as though making a speech. The guests who were crowding about Beaverbrook in the darkness applauded its entrance and drew closer to inspect.

'So, whaddya think of the villain of the piece, Sam?' The question was delivered in Beaverbrook's characteristic style, with a broad Canadian accent and out of the corner of his mouth.

Sam Hoare, the Home Secretary and one of the four most powerful men in Government, studied it carefully, his wife by his side.

'Guy Fawkes tried to blow up every politician in the land. No wonder they remember him, Max.'

Laughter rippled through the guests. They included diplomats and entertainers as well as politicians and press, all gathered around a charcoal brazier for comfort while they waited for the ceremonial lighting of the large bonfire.

'Fawkes was a foreigner, of course. Spanish,' someone added from the darkness.

'Hey, ain't nothing wrong with foreigners,' Beaverbrook insisted in a theatrical hokey twang.

'Just so long as we can ignore most of them, eh, Max,' Hoare added.

'But we can't ignore them, Sam, that's the whole point.'

The Home Secretary turned, a shade wearily. Even in the darkness he'd recognized the unmistakable trill of Katharine, the Duchess of Atholl and Member of Parliament for the seat of Kinross and West Perthshire. *What was the point?* He didn't want any points, not now, he was trying to enjoy himself. For pity's sake, they all had points, all passionately held and honed to a razor's edge, but surely this wasn't the time or the place. Not here. So the Duchess was a long-standing opponent of the Prime Minister and appeasement, they all knew that, an opponent so venomous she had earned herself the nickname of 'Red Kitty'. She paraded her conscience everywhere, rehearsed her arguments a thousand times before breakfast and again over lunch until her intransigence had pushed her to the furthest limits of the party and, in truth, almost beyond. But Sam Hoare was a party man, loyalty first, and wasn't going to allow her to forget it.

'Kitty,' he hailed his colleague, 'didn't see you there in the darkness. About time you came back into the light and enjoyed yourself with the rest of us, isn't it?'

Kitty Atholl bristled. 'Enjoyment? Is that what it's supposed to be about, Sam? Is that why we gave Czechoslovakia away? For fun?'

'Let's not trespass on Max's hospitality . . .'

'Don't mind me, Sam,' the Beaver interjected. 'Always encourage a healthy disagreement. Except amongst my employees, of course.'

And so it had begun. A discussion that became a debate that transformed into a character-ripping confrontation in the middle of a moonlit field and in a manner that had been matched across the land for weeks, and yet still showed no signs of exhausting itself. As they faced up to each other a squad of Boy Scouts ran around with jugs of mulled wine to top up the fuel tanks.

'Hey, how about a toast to the guy?'

'And death to Ribbentrop. May he die in pain.'

'You callous witch.'

'I'm not the one with my head buried in my red box desperately trying to ignore everything that's happening in Europe.'

'There you go again, fussing about Hitler. Fellow's only digging over his own back yard.'

'Digging graves.'

'He's cleaning up Germany, that's all. He may be a dictator, but he's also a bit of a Puritan. Like Cromwell.'

'Cromwell didn't slaughter Jews!'

'For God's sake, listening to you you'd think that pogroms started yesterday. It's the history of Europe, woman, centuries old.'

'Where's your sense of justice, Sam?'

'Kitty, we all have our consciences. But only you dine out on it.'

'Put yours away in the closet, have you? All wrapped up in tissue paper?'

'Any fool can go to war. And right now, only a fool *would* go to war.'

'Conquest. Bloodshed. That's what you'll get with Hitler.'

'Bugger it, Kitty, it's how we won the Empire.'

'And cowardice is how it'll be thrown away!'

Gradually it had just become the two of them. Others fell by the wayside until it was just Sam Hoare and Red Kitty, and he had accused her of being weak-minded and a xenophobe and every other calumny that came to hand. It had gone too far. Neither could find the words to stop it and their host refused to intervene – hell, he was enjoying the game, every minute of it, one arm waving a huge cigar, the other arm linked through that of Joe Kennedy, another spectator who had stepped out of the fight several insults earlier. Beside them, out of the darkness, appeared the rotund form of Joseph Ball. Hoare saw him, and even though he was Home Secretary, feared him a little. It gave him his cue.

'Loyalty. That's what this is really all about,' Hoare offered, trying to find a way out of the confrontation with a final jibe. 'You go sleep with your strange friends but I'm a party man, Kitty. Always been a party man. And I'll die a party man.'

Her lip twisted in mockery. 'Dying for your principles, that I can understand, Sam. But to die for your party?'

She reached sharply towards him. He swayed back in apprehension, alarm flooding his eyes, afraid she was intent on slapping his face, but she did nothing more than grab the umbrella that was dangling over his arm. With her trophy she walked over to the stuffed guy, stared at it as though it might spring to life, then thrust the umbrella beneath its armpit and with a final glance of dark-eyed derision swept away into the night. Hoare was left standing on his own, suddenly isolated, feeling like an abandoned bicycle.

A gust of English embarrassment blew around the ankles of the onlookers until Beaverbrook was once again centre-stage, demanding their attention, strutting theatrically over to the guy as though on a tour of inspection. He was ridiculously small with a face that would not have been distinguished even on a gnome, but his money more than made up for it. A Napoleon in newsprint and an astrakhan collar. 'So – what do we have here?' he demanded. 'Munich

Man, eh? Not quite what I had in mind.' He retrieved the umbrella and used it to prod the guy. 'Whaddya think?' he addressed the gathering. 'Who is he? Had him made specially, so don't disappoint me.'

'A clue, Maxie darling, give us a clue,' a giggling voice pleaded.

'OK. So he's a little like Guy Fawkes, maybe. Someone who tries to blow up everything in sight. Over-stuffed. Over-blown. Come on, any ideas?'

A brief silence from the crowd and then: 'Mussolini. It's got to be Mussolini!'

'*Signor* Mussolini to you,' Beaverbrook growled. 'Hell, he hears that and he'll confiscate my villa in Tuscany. No, not Pasta Man. Another guess.'

A woman's voice: 'With a stomach like that it's got to be Hermann Goering.'

'No, no, no. And if you're listening up there, Hoy-man' – Beaverbrook swapped his Canadian brogue for a thick Brooklyn accent and raised his eyes to the dark skies – 'we loves ya!'

Amidst the bubbling of laughter other names were thrown in – Hore-Belisha, Herbert Hoover, Generalissimo Franco, even Wallis Simpson ('It's got to be her with the mouth open like that . . .') – but Beaverbrook continued stubbornly shaking his head until: 'Give us another clue, Maxie. Don't be such a tease.'

The diminutive press baron waved his hands for silence, the gleam of mischief in his eye. 'One more clue, then,' he conceded. Taking the large cigar from his own mouth, he inserted it into the slit in the face of the guy, where it remained gently smouldering. 'I give you . . .'

'Cigar Man. It's Cigar Man! Oh, Maxie darling, you're so wicked!'

They cheered Beaverbrook from all sides. Only one or two of those present drifted off into the night, declining to be carried along on the tide.

The smell of sausage and singeing onion that wafted on the breezes of that night had proved irresistible, and the canvas awning erected by the Boy Scouts as a hospitality area was crowded. Brendan Bracken had lingered on the edge for some time, fighting the urge to join their number. He was hungry but it was a question of image and image to Bracken was most of what he had. A workman could eat sausages in public, so could an earl or an actress, but an Irish impostor had to be careful of such glancing blows to his reputation. The English insisted that things be in their rightful place, and the place for a would-be statesman who wanted to be taken so terribly seriously was not on his own in a sausage queue. He imagined them all talking about him – but he always imagined people talking about him, dreamt of it, *insisted* on it, for to be ignored would be the biggest humiliation of all. But not about sausages. So he fought his hunger, feeling weaker with each passing minute, twisted inside by childhood memories of the kitchens of Tipperary until, despite his reservations, he could resist his cravings no longer. He grabbed a sausage and bun with all the fillings and wandered a little way from the other guests to enjoy in solitude the sensation of simply stuffing himself. That, he knew, was where the danger lay. These bangers-in-a-bun were impossible to eat delicately, you had to wolf them down before they turned on you and attacked, dripping grease and ghastliness everywhere. Bracken was notoriously fastidious, a desperate hypochondriac who took meticulous care over his appearance, washing his hands many times a day. This public encounter with a sausage was definitely a one-off, so he prepared himself. He found a spot where he could turn his back on the crowd, place his feet carefully in the sticky grass for security, lean gently forward and –

'Why, is that Mr Bracken hiding over there?'

The sausage turned into a missile, disappearing into the night, leaving the bun limp in his hands and a trail of grease spreading across the front of his starched white shirt. His bow tie drooped in despair.

'You told me you'd call, Mr Bracken,' Anna Fitzgerald said accusingly, ignoring his plight – no, enjoying it! Bracken's arms were spread in dismay, his hair tumbled over his forehead as though trying to get a look for itself at the devastation. 'You offered to show me round London, but you never called,' she continued.

'I . . . I . . . I've . . .' Words suddenly deserted him as he tried to comprehend the mess of slime that was creeping across his chest. His brain and his tongue, usually so sharp and active, had seemingly dived for cover. All he could do was to gaze at her through pebble-thick glasses with the expression of a chastened child.

'You don't like Americans?'

'No, no, please . . .'

'Married or something?'

'No, of course not . . .'

'You've got a jealous girlfriend?'

'Nothing like that.'

Good, she'd got that sorted. She approached much closer; he noticed she had a small dog in tow, a russet-and-white King Charles spaniel trailing from a lead. 'I know, you're an important man. Very busy. Lots of distractions . . .'

She had taken the linen handkerchief from his top pocket and was beginning a clean-up operation on his shirt, gently wiping away the mess, taking control. 'The truth is, Mr Bracken, you're just a little clumsy. And rather shy.'

Anna Fitzgerald was petite, slim, almost boyish, dressed in a dark leather airman's jacket that was a couple of sizes too large for her, and boots up to her knees. She was dressed so much more sensibly than he. The cold, damp grass beneath his feet was turning to mud and already laying siege to his hand-tooled leather town shoes, yet it no longer seemed to matter. She possessed the purest black hair he had ever seen. Her eyes danced and shimmered in the light of a thousand candles. She was different – so very different from other women he had ever met. It had taken her only a few moments to break down the defences of a lifetime and now no one else at this gathering seemed to matter. He wanted the grease stain to last for ever.

'Busy – yes. I have been busy.' At last he had regained some measure of composure, his brain in contact once more with his tongue. Other parts of his anatomy seemed to be gaining a life all their own, too. 'Winston's been making speeches, keeping me running around . . .'

'So no time to show a dumb American around town.'

'Well, it wasn't just that – I mean, not that at all . . .' Bracken began to stammer; bugger, he was making a mess of this. He was almost relieved when she was distracted by the spaniel – whose name turned out to be Chumpers. He had found something in the grass – Bracken's sausage – and was giving it his undivided attention. 'I was worried that your uncle the Ambassador, and Winston, they – how should I put this?'

'Send smoke signals from opposite sides of the blanket?'

'Exactly. Both very passionate people. I thought it might be difficult.'

'You find passion difficult, Mr Bracken?'

'I meant that it might be awkward – for you – if I were, you know, to invite you out. Mixing with the enemy.'

'I'm not so sure about English girls but in Massachusetts they raise us with minds all of our own.'

'Ah.'

'So is it Mr Churchill who would object if you called me? He owns your social loyalties as well as your political loyalties?'

'Of course not!' he protested, before suddenly it dawned on him that this was probably a lie. 'There was also the thought – well, I am considerably older than you. About fifteen years.'

'Why, glory be, Mr Bracken, you are a very ol'-fashioned gen'leman,' she whispered in a voice that reeked of Dixie and seduction on the verandah. She was mocking him, but gently. Her hand was back on his chest, adding improvements to the clean-up operation.

'Not at all. It's just that –' He stopped. Came to a complete halt. No point in continuing. A flush had appeared upon his face that came close to matching the colour of his ridiculous hair and he had an expression that suggested he might be passing kidney stones. 'I'm making a complete mess of this.'

'For the first time this evening, Brendan, I'm inclined to agree with you. So let me simplify things for you. Would you like to see me again? Take me to dinner? Show me the sights of London? Play canasta, or whatever it is genteel English folk do?'

'Of course I would.'

'And you know how to use a phone?'

He began to laugh.

'Hey, Brendan, looks like you're in business.'

She held up his grubby handkerchief and dropped it into the palm of his outstretched hand. 'Bombs away,' she whispered. Then she walked off, dragging the reluctant Chumpers behind her.

It was a night not simply of entertainment but also of encounter and intrigue – just as Beaverbrook had required. He couldn't plan such things, of course, but he understood human nature and knew that the inevitable outcome of mixing alcohol and ego was information. And in his world, information was power.

As he turned to mingle with other guests, he

found himself pursued. A woman, tugging in agitation at his sleeve. Lady Maud Hoare, wife of Sir Sam.

'Maxwell, dear Maxwell . . .'

Whoa, no one called him Maxwell. The girl was nervous.

'I'm so sorry. I hope it didn't cause a scene,' Maud spluttered.

Of course it caused a scene. A splendid one. As Joe Kennedy had just remarked to him, good parties were like battles. They required casualties.

'It's just that Sam is so passionate,' she continued. 'You know that, being such good friends . . .'

Friends? Well, scarcely. Friendship wasn't the sort of game played between politician and press man.

'Like you, he's so loyal to the cause.'

Ah, the cause. The great cause to which he had devoted so many of his front pages in recent weeks. The cause of winning! Winning was everything and Chamberlain had won, for the moment, at least. There was to be peace. It had to be so, the advertisers in the *Express* insisted on it. They wanted a world in which everyone had a little fun and spent a little money, not a world in which every last penny was buried in war bonds or pots at the end of the garden. So far Chamberlain had proved a good bet.

'And Sam's under such a lot of pressure . . .'

'Pressure? What sort of pressure?' Beaverbrook's news instincts were suddenly alert. He laid a comforting hand on her sleeve.

'He'd never complain, of course, not the type. But, oh, Maxwell, the poor man's so torn.'

'Torn?'

'He's a good man, a great man . . .'

Perhaps one day the main man, too. The man to take over the reins. Beaverbrook had a sharp eye for the runners and riders, and Slippery Sam was a man with prospects. In Beaverbrook's judgement Hoare was a man to watch, a man to be – well, all right, to be *friends* with.

'You know what it's like, Maxwell, so many demands on your time, your energies, your . . . money.'

Ah, so there it is. The girl had shown her slip.

'He's not a man of inherited wealth like Neville or Edward Halifax. He can't simply run off on grand lecture tours and *sell* himself like *Winston* does.' She made it sound worse than pimping. 'Sam has to struggle by on nothing more than his Cabinet salary. And it *is* a struggle, Maxwell.'

What – five thousand a year? A struggle for him, maybe, but a fortune for most.

'You know Neville couldn't have done what he's done without Sam's unfailing support – you know that, don't you, Maxwell?'

'Most certainly,' he lied.

'But it's slowly wearing him down, and I've been crying myself to sleep worrying about him.'

'We can't have that, Maudy.'

'Oh, at times I get quite desperate, watching him sacrifice himself. For others. Always for others.' Her voice had fallen to a whisper, but it was soon to recover. 'I scarcely know what to do. These are such terribly difficult times.'

How well she had rehearsed it. How easily the lip quivered, the manicured fingers clutched, how readily the nervous sentiments emerged and presented themselves in regimented line.

'So I was wondering . . .'

Here it comes.

'Maxwell, is there any way you can think of that might just – take the pressure off him? Allow him to get on with that great job of his?'

If you were a few years younger, maybe, Maudy, old dear, and not so hideously ugly . . .

'I'm a woman, I barely understand these things, while you, Maxwell, are not only a friend but such a wise man.'

Oh, Maudy, you think flattery is the way past my defences? When I am surrounded every day by lap-dogs whom I pay to fawn and fumble at every moment in my presence? But present me with a business proposition, that's another matter entirely. Show me a man who is Home Secretary – one of the most powerful men in the land, the keeper of secrets, the charmer of snakes, the guardian of rep-utations high and low, a man who has a reasonable chance one day of being placed in charge of the entire crap game – show this man to me and place him in my debt. How much would that be worth? As a business proposition – and fuck the friendship?

'Two thousand.'

'I beg your pardon, Maxwell.'

'Two thousand a year, Maud. Do you think that might help? We can't have him being distracted, having to work through his worries.'

'No, of course not, you're so right.'

'If I can help him, Maud, be a damned privilege. Ease those worries. Make sure my newspapers are behind him, too – hell, make sure Sam and I are working on the same team, for each other.'

'And the cause.' She was breathless now, red in cheek, like a young girl who had just been ravished and loved every second of it.

'An entirely private matter, you understand. No one must know apart from you and me, Maud. And Sam, of course. Wouldn't want the muck media to get hold of it.'

'Of course, of course . . . I scarcely know what to say, Maxwell. "Thank you" sounds so inadequate.'

'No, I thank *you*, Maud. Sam's a great man. I'm glad to be of some service. Send him to me. We'll sort out the details, man to man.' Yes, send him on bended knee, Maudy, and get him used to the position.

Others were approaching. The moment was over, the business done. He had bought a Home Secretary for less than the price of his new car.

'Be in touch, Maud.'

'Oh, we shall, we *shall*,' she breathed as she wafted into the night.

'And who was that?' his new companion enquired, staring after the retreating woman. His voice was deep, carefully modulated, like that of a bishop.

'A Hoare,' Beaverbrook muttered.

'Oh.'

'But a whore on my White List. For now.'

'Ah.' Tom Driberg sucked his teeth. A tall, dark-complexioned figure in his mid-thirties with receding hair that wrinkled in the manner of a studious maharajah, Driberg was one of the many paid by Beaverbrook to 'fawn and fumble'. To the outside world he was known as William Hickey, the highest-paid gossip columnist in the country, and Driberg was very good at gossip – good at both recording and creating it – although the rules by which he was required to document the misadventures and general muck-ups of the society set were far tighter than those by which he himself chose to live. One of the strictest rules governing the way in which he worked was that he should never, *never*, antagonize his publisher, and the White List contained the names of Beaverbrook's intimates who were deemed to be beyond bounds and who would never find their way into the William Hickey column without the copy first being scrutinized by the press lord himself. Gossip was a powerful political currency, and both Beaverbrook and Driberg were keepers of the keys.

'Busy evening?' Beaverbrook enquired, almost casually, reminding the other man that he was here to work.

'A Minister who appears to be canvassing for the support of a young lady who – how can one put such things delicately? – won't be old enough to vote for several years yet.'

'Looking to the future, eh? Damn fine slogan.'

'And an actress who has just spent the last twenty minutes rehearsing the role of Cleopatra in the back of her car. A magnificent performance, all moans and misted windows. I damned nearly froze waiting for her to take her bow. Then she steps out with her husband. It beggars belief.'

'What is the world coming to?'

'But the night is young.'

'Yeah. Which reminds me. Keep your hands off

the Boy Scouts. None of your nancy nonsense here. My house is off limits. Understand?'

'I shall protect your honour down to my last item of underwear, Your Lordship.'

'Fuck off.'

'With the greatest pleasure.'

'Oh, and look out for Duffie Cooper. He's here tonight, I don't suppose with his wife. He no longer makes the White List.'

'Good. He was once very rude to me when I asked him about a certain Austrian lady with whom he was seen breakfasting on four consecutive days in Biarritz. It only goes to remind one, sir. Always be nice to them when you're coming, because you're bound to meet them again in the morning, that's what I always say.'

'You're full of crap.'

And much, much more. Or would be later. He'd just met this amazing young producer from the BBC.

The climax of the night was drawing near. The guy had been sent in procession around the guests, still with the cigar in its mouth – someone had even sacrificed a homburg to complete the effect – and had now been wheeled to the base of the bonfire, where the groundsman and two young assistants used a ladder to place it at the very top of the pyre. Soon it would be ablaze.

'Fine, fine party, Max.' Joseph Ball congratulated his host and took his arm in a manner that gave clear signals to those around them that the two men intended to talk business – alone.

'You're not drinking that pond water, are you, Joey?' Beaverbrook growled, examining Ball's glass of mulled wine as though expecting to find tadpoles. 'Here.' He produced a large hip flask filled with an exceedingly fine single malt. In return, Ball offered him an Havana.

'Max, old friend, the pleasure of your hospitality never dims. And quite a show you've put on for us this evening already.'

'You mean Sam and Kitty? Sam's a fine chap, damned fine chap, but Kitty . . .'

'Yes, dear Kitty. Not a chap at all. Perhaps that's the root of her problem. Frayed nerves. Mental feebleness. You know, women of a certain age. You saw her tonight: she's lost control, a gnat's wing away from hysterical. Apparently it runs in her family. They say there may be money troubles, too.'

'That so? I'll be damned.' Beaverbrook reclaimed his flask and refreshed himself, all the while never taking his eyes from his guest. Ball was up to his old tricks, putting ferrets down holes and flushing out a few reputations. He'd turned ruination into an art form. 'So what are you going to do, Joey? You've already taken the party whip from her, not much more to threaten her with, is there?'

'Max, we'd never dream of threatening her. You know me better than that. But as for what others might do . . .' – he paused to take a long pull at the cigar and fill the air around them with smoke and mystery – 'I hear on the grapevine that her constituency party is positively rattling with resentment at her disloyalty. Applies to all the rebels, really. In the next couple of weeks most of them are going to come under a deal of pressure to start toeing the line, or else.'

'Else what?'

'There's the whiff of an election in the air – next year, maybe. Time for the party to wipe its boots clean.'

'Throw 'em out?'

'Their constituencies might well decide they'd had enough.'

'Bent over the old ballot box and buggered? I like it.'

'Only one small problem . . .'

'Tell your Uncle Max.'

'The constituencies don't know about this yet.'

'You sly bastard.' It was offered, and accepted, as a commendation.

'Look, you remember that little group of letter-writers you set up at the time of the Abdication non-sense?'

'The journalists I got to write poison-pen letters to the King's bitch?'

'Exactly. It never leaked.'

'Was never going to leak. I told 'em if one whisper of that got out, none of 'em was ever going to work in Fleet Street again. It's one of the benefits of being an authentic Canadian bastard like me – I get loyalty, Joey. I always get loyalty.'

'So what I had in mind was this. Another loyal little group who'll write letters to the main people in Kitty's local association. You know, complaints about her unreliability, saying they'll never vote Conservative again while she's the candidate, time for the party to move on. Talk about her age, her feebleness, imply she's been shagging Stalin. That sort of stuff. See if we can't push her out before the voters do. Have a new candidate in place before the next election.'

'Same thing for some of the others?'

'All of the others, Max. Everyone who was against Neville over Munich. It's not a time for half measures.'

Beaverbrook nodded in the direction of the guy. 'Winston too?'

'Everyone. Most will survive, of course, but it'll shake them. Keep their heads down until after the election. Make them realize there's no such thing as a free shot at Neville. But Kitty's a special case, she's too near the edge. One shove and she'll be over. A few screams, the flapping of petticoats, a bit of blood. Something that will motivate the others.'

A broad smile almost cut Beaverbrook's face in two. 'You want things stirring up a little? My pleasure.'

'I shall be in your debt.'

'Hey, don't you just love democracy?'

As they conferred, other guests kept their distance, the hunched shoulders and conspiratorial tones of the two serving as a warning unmistakable to any but the most insensitive – or young.

'Let's go, Maxie, we're all waiting,' a young woman called out, stamping her feet impatiently against the cold. 'Time to set the night on fire.'

The base of the bonfire had been well soaked in paraffin and tar, and the groundsman was standing by with a burning torch.

'Come on, darling Maxie,' she complained again,

tugging at the fox-fur stole around her neck. It looked new.

'Time for some action,' Beaverbrook muttered. He grabbed the torch, raised it high above his head to the applause of his guests, then thrust it deep into the innards of the bonfire. Soon the flames began to conquer the night and Cigar Man from his lofty throne began to cringe in the heat and turn black, squirming as the flames took hold until finally he slumped forward and disappeared in a storm of sparks. The young woman squealed with delight.

'Bit young even by your standards, isn't she, Max?' Ball chided.

'Hell, Joey, I'm simply growing nostalgic. I once knew her mother.'

Later that week, much of Europe burned, too.

It was called Kristallnacht – Crystal Night – named after the millions of shards of glass that were left shattered in the street after Jewish shops throughout Germany and Austria were ransacked. Businesses and homes were plundered, the synagogues put to the flame. Ninety-three Jews were killed that night. In the ensuing weeks thousands more were to take their own lives. It was to be but a small down-payment on what was to come.

SIX

The eleventh hour, of the eleventh day, of the eleventh month. The moment when the guns had fallen silent on the Western Front and the slaughter had ceased, exactly twenty years before. Armistice Day. Bludgeoned by the ever-lengthening shadow of circumstance, the crowds had gathered in exceptional numbers around Lutyens' stone Cenotaph in Whitehall to take part in the nation's tribute to the dead. Nearly a million of them. Wasted in war. A war that some would have all over again.

It was a sunny day, mild for the time of year, and he had only to walk a few yards from Downing Street, but nevertheless the Prime Minister felt in need of his overcoat. He was feeling every one of his sixty-nine years. His physical resources were not what they once were. He found these ceremonies an ordeal, stirring emotions that he found hard to deal with, particularly the remembrance of his cousin, Norman, who had been killed in France. They had been devoted. Chamberlain had described Norman as 'the most intimate friend I ever had' and still grieved for him, most of all on days like this. Perhaps, too, there was that nagging memory inside Chamberlain that he hadn't fought in that war, that even all those years ago he had already been too old. Past it.

Unfit for Duty. Norman and the others paying a debt which he should have shared. Churchill had fought in the war, of course, seen action at the front and never ceased to remind people of the fact. The Warrior. Hero of the Boer War. And of the Great War. Almost as though Churchill were trying to torment him – no, nothing conditional about it, of *course* Churchill was trying to torment him. Trouble was, so often he succeeded.

They were all there, in formation around the white memorial of Portland stone, to his left the King and the other male members of the Royal Family, opposite him the Bishop of London, beside and behind him the other political leaders. And on all sides old soldiers, those who knew what it was like to bear the guilt of living while they watched their brothers die, all the time wondering why they had been spared the slaughter. There were young soldiers, too, who knew nothing of war – and who would never know, so long as he was Prime Minister.

At nights recently he had often woken, shivering with cold, feeling as though a cold grey hand were clawing at him deep inside. Sometimes he thought he was surrounded by ghosts. Men he had known, like Norman, and who had died, in his place. He heard their voices, whispering, but could never quite make out their words. They would not let him rest.

The band of the Brigade of Guards played their mournful music, then a lone piper took a single pace forward, pulling from his soul the notes of Purcell's 'Lament'. Chamberlain stood, head bowed. No other noise but the champing of a horse at its bit, the crowd fallen silent. At his right shoulder stood Edward

Halifax, tall, gaunt, his large feet splayed out, towering above those around him, casting Chamberlain in shadow and making him feel almost insignificant. He felt the Foreign Secretary bend slightly, like a reed, and whisper in his ear.

'Neville, did you see the papers this morning?'

'The Jews?' Chamberlain nodded his assent, still looking straight ahead.

The piper had finished and there was a short pause as the Bishop prepared to offer the prayers that led up to the two-minute silence. Soon they would be called upon to step forward and lay their wreaths of blood-poppies.

'My God, but Hitler doesn't make it easy for us, Edward.'

'They'll say it makes a mockery of our agreement with him.'

'No! It mocks nothing. It illustrates the dangers. Makes our agreement all the more necessary.' Chamberlain shivered in spite of the sun. 'He gave me his word, Edward.'

'Not on the Jews, he didn't. We didn't ask for it.'

'Is there anything we can do?'

'Do?'

'Yes, get some balance back into the reporting, make it less lurid. Perhaps give the papers another story to get their teeth into.'

'We've given them peace. What more can we do?'

'We need a distraction.'

'So, I suspect, do the Jews.'

'I think Horace and Joe have something in mind. For distraction. Setting up a bit of a fox hunt.' He seemed unwilling – or unable – to continue. He

132

sighed, a long, pained rattle of breath. 'Anyway, Christmas soon. Peace on earth . . .'

Chamberlain shivered once again; this time Halifax couldn't fail to notice. It was almost time. As the clock of Big Ben began to strike the hour, the crash of artillery was heard from Horse Guards. Deep inside, Chamberlain cringed, wondering yet again how he would have withstood the deluge of death, had he fought.

It was after the ceremony had finished and they had marched stiffly behind the King back into the nearby Old Home Office Building that the conversation was resumed. They were drinking tea, warming themselves, relaxing after the parade. The King in particular seemed to find these official occasions a trial.

'It went well?' he asked. The words came at the stumble and in the form of a question. There had been no speech to make, nothing more to do than be a figurehead and set down a wreath of poppies, but still the King-Emperor needed reassurance.

'Quite splendidly, sir,' his Prime Minister replied.

'Thank you, Mr Chamberlain.' He was relaxing, feeling more at ease once he was inside and beyond the public gaze. And among friends. Halifax was his great companion and Chamberlain, too, had grown close. It had been exactly eighteen months since George had been crowned and had asked Chamberlain to assume the highest political office in the land; it had come to seem as if their destinies would be forever intertwined. That was why the King had invited his Prime Minister onto the floodlit balcony of Buckingham Palace immediately on his return from Munich. Some had said the gesture was unwise, even foolish, that it involved the Crown too deeply in politics and too closely with the fate of one Prime Minister, but the King had insisted. Appeasement was the right policy, it was the moral policy, the policy not only of God but also of his wife. He felt no need to compromise.

Around the room other men of matters were gathered, their voices low, respectful, except for one that was raised a shade too loudly, making his point vociferously, not in the manner of a gentle English stream but like a cascade of water running across the carpet. But then Leslie Hore-Belisha was scarcely – well, it wasn't his fault, really, that he hadn't been brought up in the manner of an English gentleman.

Words such as Berlin and Vienna reached out across the room, and the King stiffened within his uniform. 'What is to be done about them, Prime Minister?' he asked softly.

Chamberlain followed his gaze. 'Ah, you mean the Jews, sir.'

'What can we do? We've already given asylum to thousands. Now it threatens to turn into a flood.'

'Halifax and I were just discussing the matter.'

'I read the newspaper reports with distress, of course, but so often it seems as if these people don't help themselves. Look at Palestine. We offer them seventy-five thousand places over the next five years, yet hordes of them try to pour in as illegal immigrants and cause chaos.'

'Of course, sir, Palestine can't be the answer. Too small. And too many Arabs. I'm afraid we were a little rash all those years ago to suggest that it might become a Jewish homeland.'

'Wandering tribes, eh?'

'The Foreign Secretary and I have been giving some consideration as to whether other parts of the Empire might be brought in to help.'

'Other parts?'

'Africa, perhaps. Tanganyika, sir,' Halifax intervened, glad of an opportunity to participate. His height made it difficult to converse with the two considerably smaller men. He bent delicately, like a crane attempting to feed. 'And perhaps British Guiana. It might be possible to make large tracts of virgin forest available for Jewish refugees to settle.'

'At their expense, of course,' Chamberlain added.

'Wouldn't it be possible simply to insist that they remain in their countries of origin? Prevent them from leaving in the first place?' the King persisted. 'After all, it's not just the Jews from Germany trying to invade Palestine but those from places like Poland and Romania. There must be millions of them there. Surely it would be better for everyone if they simply stayed.'

'Quite so,' Chamberlain agreed. 'But Herr Hitler isn't helping, not with his latest nonsense.'

'Damnable man, disrupts everything. But all this fuss. The press always sensationalize and exaggerate these things, don't you think?'

'Perhaps. My lieutenants are already pursuing the matter, phoning a few friendly editors, making sure they don't . . . well, overdo it. Perhaps it will be better by tomorrow.'

'And if any of them decides not to co-operate, you

have our full permission to tell them that we won't have it. Won't have it, do you hear?' The teacup rattled dangerously. 'If those editors ever expect to come and kneel before me at the palace, they'd better mind their . . .' – the King had intended to say 'p's and 'q's but the effect of authority was entirely spoiled by a thunderous stutter.

'Distraction, that's what we need, sir. The Foreign Secretary and I were just discussing it. We thought it might be helpful to give them something else to write about, sir. With your permission, I'd like to announce that Edward and I will be going to Rome to visit Signor Mussolini early next year. He's been difficult, I know, invading Abyssinia and sending troops to Spain. But at Munich he was so helpful, so solid. If we show him the hand of friendship, I think we might get him to lean on Herr Hitler a little. Help tie up some of the loose ends of the peace.'

'A little more of your personal diplomacy. Mr Chamberlain? Another diplomatic triumph?'

'With the help of the Foreign Secretary, sir.' Chamberlain shuffled. He wasn't very good at playing the unassuming hero, least of all would anyone be convinced that he owed anything to the Foreign Office. He ran his own foreign policy, and so blatantly that the last Foreign Secretary, Anthony Eden, had felt forced to resign earlier that year.

'And Ciano's an excellent Foreign Minister, isn't he, Edward?' Halifax bowed in approval. 'Not like that strange man Wibbentrop. You know, when he came to the Palace to present his credentials, he gave me one of those ridiculous straight-arm salutes and shouted "Heil Hitler". Think of it. It was all I could do to stop myself returning the salute and shouting "Heil George"!'

They shared their amusement and drank their tea, while from outside came the muffled sounds of the last of the old soldiers marching past the Cenotaph and fading into the shadows. A final bark of instruction from an NCO and they were gone, taking their memories with them.

'It's no good shouting at the Germans,' Chamberlain continued, 'they simply shout back. So we think Herr Hitler needs a little encouragement, and the Italians could play a vital role in making sure he remains reasonable.'

'Sound man, is he, Mussolini?'

'A necessary man, at least.'

'And the Italians have always been so much more sophisticated than Hitler's type of German. Discussing diplomacy with Herr Hitler and his henchmen is like casting pearls before the swine. But the Italians – their art, their culture, their great history – that must make a difference.'

'They've had a great empire.'

'They understand the advantages of compromise.'

'And so long as he doesn't want to rebuild the *entire* Roman empire . . .'

'Then let us toast him, this great Italian.' The King raised his teacup, pinky on alert. 'To Signor Mussolini.'

'And to Italian culture.'

*　　*　　*

(The Times, Saturday 19 November 1938)

MICKEY MOUSE
REPRIEVED

—■—■—

EXEMPT FROM ITALIAN BAN

—■—■—

From our own Correspondent.
ROME, November 18

The productions of Mr Walt Disney are to be exempted from a general decree of the Ministry of Popular Culture that everything of foreign inspiration is to disappear from juvenile periodicals in Italy by the end of the year.

The decree was prompted by the feeling that an excellent opportunity of inculcating Fascist ideals in the youthful Italian mind was being neglected by allowing pure fancy to run riot in the pictures and 'comic strips' of the coloured juvenile weeklies which are as common in Italy as in any other country. Publishers and editors were accordingly informed that these periodicals must in future be used to exalt the military and heroic virtues of the Italian race. The foreign stuff was to go.

But an exception has now been made in favour of Mr Walt Disney on account of the acknowledged artistic merit of his work . . .

Mac had just come out of the Odeon cinema in Notting Hill Gate. A Noël Coward comedy. He'd laughed and rocked until the tears poured down his face, the first time he'd laughed in ever so long. And he'd not cried since the camps. Good to forget your troubles, to have things touch you. He had stayed on to watch it all over again, hiding for a while in the toilets, dodging the beam of the usherette's torch that swept like a searchlight across the rows of seats, happy to be lost in a world of make-believe. Anyway, it was warmer here than in his small flat. He was economizing, saving on coal, uncertain of what might lie ahead. He might laugh, but still he couldn't trust. And he was beginning to feel the insidious dampness of an English autumn seeping into his bones, even though it was as warm as any summer's day in the camp. He must be getting old.

When finally he left the cinema, he began walking up the hill in Ladbroke Grove towards the church that stood guard at the top. It was a clear night, bright moon, autumn breezes tugging the last of the leaves from the trees. Hard times to come. Barely a light to be seen, but for the moon that hung above St John's, casting long shadows all around, stretching out, pursuing him, like his memories. He buried his hands in his thin overcoat, counting the few pennies of change in his pocket for comfort, and hurried on. He had a coat, and boots, money in his pocket, a bed to sleep on and coal in his scuttle, if he needed it. Why, he'd even treated himself to a chocolate ice at the cinema. A life of ease. But not at ease, never at ease. As he pushed on up the hill he found he was growing breathless – perhaps the unaccustomed laughter had been too much for him – and when he reached the purple-dark outlines of the church he sat down on the edge of a leaning gravestone to catch his wind. His breath was beginning to condense, like mists of ice powder that he remembered would settle round your beard and freeze your lips together, tearing the flesh if you tried to eat, if you had anything to eat. Then you could feel your eyeballs beginning to turn to frost so that they would not close, and your brain began to freeze so hard that you wondered if this was going to be the last moon you would ever see, but you knew that the ground was already too hard for them to bury you, so they would leave you under a thin scattering of rocks, for the foxes.

But this was England! Such things never happened here. The English wouldn't allow it. Mr Chamberlain had promised. An Englishman's promise. We could sleep soundly in our beds, burn our coal, enjoy our little luxuries of chocolate ice and cake, safe in the knowledge that we didn't need to worry and that when we died of very old age they would bury us deep and the tears wouldn't freeze even before they hit the ground. That's how it would be, in England, at least. The Empire would insist on it.

He sat, desperately wanting the world to stand still, but even as he watched, the moon moved on. Dry leaves were caught by the gentle wind and scuttled in waves around his ankles, like the sound of sea breaking on shingle. As it had broken that day on the beach in Solovetsky.

Suddenly the tears were flowing again. He felt weak, and shamed by it, glad there was no one on the street to see him. But why did the opinion of others matter? His was a life alone, cut off from emotion, a life rebuilt only for himself – and why not, when there was no one else there for him? Not after little Moniek had gone. For half his time on this earth his only god had been survival. What happened in the rest of the world and to the rest of the world was for him a matter of complete inconsequence. Another man's rations, his blanket, his work detail, sometimes even another man's name, had on more than one occasion been the difference between death and tomorrow. It had all grown to be so simple, a world in which he would gladly exchange a man's life for an hour of sunshine.

Yet now tears fell, uncontrollably. Tears for the life he had lost. And the lives that he knew would now be lost. The lives of those who had stared at him with those gaunt, awful eyes from the frames of the Pathé News film he had just seen, the fear in their faces made bright by the burning of the synagogues around them. He knew those faces, for he could see himself in every one. He wept, hoping the tears might douse the flames.

'Another brandy, McCrieff.' The proposal was placed with all the subtlety of a German ultimatum to a minor Middle-European enclave.

'That's most obliging of you. Just a wee one, if you insist, Sir Joseph. It's been a splendid dinner.'

'The first of many, we hope.' Horace Wilson reappeared from behind the glow of his cigar.

'That would indeed be pleasant. My club – the Caledonian – next time, if I may insist?' An edge of uncertainty had slipped into the Scotsman's voice – wouldn't these great men find the Caledonian too gruesomely provincial for their tastes? He was uncertain of the tastes of fashionable Westminster; he felt the need to strengthen his hand. 'Their kitchens may lack a little subtlety, of course, but the cellars are filled with some particularly fine single malts that I think might tempt you. Not that I've got anything against the French, you understand,' he reassured them, draining his balloon, wishing alcohol hadn't dulled his wits, 'but I know where my loyalties lie.'

'You fish, McCrieff?'

'I could tie a fly before I could fasten my own shoelaces.'

'Then I think we should arrange for you to join the Prime Minister and me when we next come up to the Dee. Probably at Easter. You could spare a day, could you?'

'I'd be honoured, Sir Joseph, truly. But I'm aware that you're all such busy men, I'd hate to think I might become a distraction.'

'Ah, distractions, McCrieff, distractions. Life is so full of distractions. Wars, revolutions, scandal, strikes, floods – not to mention being forced to follow on behind the Australians. There are so many distractions in politics, so many things that are thrust upon you. Ah, but then there are the distractions you create.'

The Smoking Room of the Reform Club creaked with ancient red leather and history. It was a club created a century before for the singular purpose of celebrating emancipation. One Man, One Vote – or rather, one property, one vote, a twist of the rudder designed to steer a course between the distractions of revolution and repression that were bringing chaos to the rest of Europe.

'But don't you know, McCrieff, I've always regarded the greatest distraction in political life as being women. Don't you agree, Horace?'

'Women? Certainly. Did for Charles Stewart Parnell. Damn nearly did for Lloyd George, too. Should've done for him, if you ask my opinion.'

'Might even do for this Government, if we let 'em.'

McCrieff's brow puckered; he'd lost the thread. He readjusted his position in his armchair by the fire, sitting well back, listening to the leather creak, trying to convey to the others the illusion that he was entirely comfortable inside the maze of high politics. But women? Had Chamberlain got himself into difficulties on account of – no, ridiculous thought. Not Chamberlain, of all people. More likely the Archbishop than the Undertaker. Chamberlain just wasn't the type. So where did women come into it?

'Forgive me, gentlemen, but I'm not sure I entirely follow your –'

Ball cut him off ruthlessly. 'What do you think of your local MP, McCrieff? The Duchess?'

McCrieff retreated from Ball's stare and gazed into the fire. Their invitation had been so unexpected, so urgent in tone – was this what it was about? The Duchess of Atholl? And if so, which way did loyalty lean? Towards her? Or away? No matter how hard he stared he could find no answer in the fire, yet some edge in Ball's tone told him that his answer mattered. He would have to tread with considerably more caution than he had dined. 'As you are well aware, gentlemen, I am what I think it's fair to describe as an influential member of the Kinross and West Perthshire constituency association. I also wish to become a Member of Parliament myself. I'm not sure it would be wise for me to go round criticizing those who I'd like to become my colleagues.'

'You'd sit with Socialists?'

'Of course not.'

'But you'd sit with the Duchess? Support her causes?'

'Well, she has a fair few of those, to be sure. Not all of them to my taste.'

'Nor to the taste of others, McCrieff. Including the Prime Minister.'

'Strange, so strange the causes she adopts,' Wilson added. 'Once heard her make a speech about female circumcision amongst the Kikuyu in Africa. Took up hours of parliamentary time on it, refused to give way. Quite extraordinary performance.' He was shaking his head but not taking his eyes for a moment off McCrieff. 'Not, of course, that as a civil servant I have any views on these matters, but personally and entirely privately . . .'

They were interrupted when a claret-coated club steward produced fresh drinks and fussed around the fire, stoking it back to life and propelling a curl of coal smoke into the room. McCrieff was glad of the opportunity to think. He was a laird, a Scottish farmer, not a fool. He had been invited to dine by two men who knew he had considerable influence in a constituency where the MP was one of the most troublesome members on the Government back benches. He'd guessed they wanted to talk about considerably more than fishing. He swirled the caramel liquor in his glass, where it formed a little whirlpool of alcohol. Suddenly it had all become mixed with intrigue. There was a danger he might get sucked down.

'Yes, speaking personally, McCrieff,' Ball picked up the conversation, 'privately, just between the three of us – how do you feel about the Duchess?'

The revived firelight was reflecting from Ball's circular spectacles. His eyes had become two blazing orbs, making it seem as though a soul-consuming fire were burning inside. This was a dangerous man.

'Gentlemen,' McCrieff began slowly, stepping out carefully as though walking barefoot through a field of broken glass, 'one of you is the most powerful man in the party, the other the most significant man in Government next to the Prime Minister himself. And I am a man of some political ambition.' He paused, holding in his hands both opportunity and extinction. Time to choose. 'How would you like me to feel about the Duchess?'

The lights burned unusually late on the top floor of the *Express* building in Fleet Street. It was well past the dining hour. A group of five journalists, all men, mostly young, had already been closeted in the boardroom for three nights that week, and another night beckoned. The work was tiring and the banter with which they had begun had long since passed into a bleak determination to finish the job. They had been provided with all the tools – sheaves of writing paper, envelopes, twenty-seven separate lists of addresses. The lists had arrived by courier marked for the attention of the deputy editor, who had removed the covering letter and any trace of their origins.

They wrote. Some used typewriters, the others wrote by hand. A total of more than five hundred letters, many purportedly from ex-servicemen, intended for opinion-formers within the twenty-seven constituencies. As the week had passed, any sense of restraint had dimmed, their language had grown ever more colourful, the metaphors more alarming.

The Bolshies are regicides. Is that what you want? I would hazard the conjecture that the Germans, the most efficient fighting machine on this earth, would go through the rag-bag of Reds like a hot knife through butter. Take care you are not standing in the way when it happens!

It was the season for mud and muck, it was inevitable that some of it should spread out and stick. And so they toiled, disturbed by nothing more than the chiming of the clock, the drumming of typewriter keys, the scratching of nibs, the occasional flooding of a handkerchief – one of them had been dragged from his sick bed despite the protestations of his wife. Death and misery were much on his mind.

If you vote for the Duchess there will be war, and your sons will all be killed, like mine were in the last war, butchered by German steel. Can you bear that on your conscience?

There were alternative strategies in use. One of his colleagues preferred to inspire by adulation:

Mr Neville Chamberlain is a saint. He has saved us. There is war in China, in Abyssinia, in Spain. Hundreds of thousands have already died. If Britain goes to war, that will surely be our fate. Yet even though the Prime Minister is an elderly man he has thrown himself into his duties, flying three times to Germany though he had never before flown, hurled himself into the breach, unsparing of his time, uncaring of his health and safety. His one ambition has been PEACE. Peace for this time, peace for all time. He is surely amongst the great men of all time. That is why I will do anything to support him. I trust you will, too, by letting your MP know [underlined twice, in squiggly waves] *of the strength of feeling of the ordinary people in this country.*

He signed it Mrs Ada Boscombe.

It was ten minutes or more after the clock had marked nine when the doors of the lift opened. Two butlers emerged, dressed in tails and stiff wing collars, bearing substantial silver trays. On one was heaped a steaming tangle of brick-red lobsters, all claws and alarmed eyes, accompanied by a large dish of clear molten butter and surrounded by a plentiful garnish of sliced cucumber and tomato. The other tray bore three bottles of chilled Pol Roger champagne and five crystal glasses.

'With the compliments of 'is Lordship,' the first butler informed them, placing his tray on the sideboard, producing knives, forks and linen napkins like a magician from deep pockets inside his jacket. 'And 'e says to make sure you bring the silver trays back.'

*   *   *

147

They had come, in unprecedented numbers. Every seat was occupied, every corner crowded. The Duchess had remarked on the numbers, and on the fact that many of the faces seemed unfamiliar to her, but her agent assured her that apart from a handful of journalists they were all paid-up members of the association. 'The times are very political, Your Grace,' he had explained. What he declined to tell her, and what she was never to know, was how many of those fresh faces had had their membership dues paid in the last few days by William McCrieff. As McCrieff had put it to him, many ordinary voters in the constituency had been galvanized by the events of recent weeks and he had persuaded them to join, urged on by great issues such as war and peace – and, the agent suspected, by an extra pound in their pockets for their trouble in attending a political meeting, not to mention the promise of free hospitality afterwards. Even if many of those gathered together had been members for no more than six days and some for no longer than six hours, there was nothing in the rules to prevent such a show of interest and enthusiasm. In any event it was bound to be a meeting of exceptional significance for it had been convened to decide whom they should choose as a candidate to fight the next election. And the agent, like so many members loyal to the causes of appeasement and a comfortable life, found the Duchess about as comfortable as an ice storm in August. She was always lecturing, hectoring. Not like McCrieff. His methods were different. A quiet word, a dram or two, and the business was done. A good party man, was McCrieff, unlike the Duchess. She not only had her own opinions – so many of them – but insisted on sharing them. A grave fault in a politician, the agent reckoned, perhaps a mortal one. Anyway, the chairman had just called the meeting to order; they were soon to find out.

They had been to see George Bernard Shaw's *Man and Superman* at the Old Vic – a splendid performance, she'd thought, with Valerie Tudor and Anthony Quayle, but he found it a preposterous play, like most of the stuff the old man produced. All those left-wing ideas tangled up in his bloody beard, which were then scraped off like yesterday's lunch. He thought Quayle's role as Tanner had been absurd, and played in the same manner – all this guff about woman being the pursuer and man the pursued. But Anna Maria had warmed to it, said it was splendid and up-to-date, seemed to enjoy wrapping herself in theatrical fantasy. So he indulged her, and for once bit his tongue.

He hadn't wanted the evening to end – he thought about inviting her back for a drink at his home in Lord North Street, which was near at hand, but he didn't know her well enough and was afraid it might sound predatory and she would say no. He didn't know how to deal with rejection from women – his mother had always treated him as nothing better than an inconvenience, and after he had left the family home he had made it a rule in his carefully constructed life never to put himself into a position where rejection might be possible. Yet he did not want to simply say goodnight. So he had suggested that they not drive all the way home, but stop on the other side of the park from where they could walk the last stretch to her front door. She had accepted with a smile.

He had deliberately taken the long way round, leading her through Hyde Park until they had arrived at the Serpentine where the rowing boats were tied up in a miniature armada and little waves lapped at the edges of the ink-black pond. She looped her arm through his, clinging tighter than was strictly necessary. Perhaps he should have invited her back for a drink after all.

'So do you think there will be war, Bendy?' She had given him a nickname. He'd never had a nickname before.

'Hope not,' he replied, not wanting to alarm her.

'But your Mr Churchill says he thinks there will be.'

And he found himself irritated. Churchill was his hero, his political master, yet Bracken was growing to resent the manner in which others treated him as little more than an adjunct to the elder statesman, and no one took him more for granted than the old man himself. 'Don't know what's going on with Winston. Very peculiar,' he muttered. 'He – perhaps I shouldn't be telling you this, but – well, he's got money problems and asked me to help him. To see if I could find a backer, someone to provide him with a loan to get him through. So I've been running around all over London making enquiries and then, just yesterday, he tells me to stop. No explanation. No thanks. Just –' He waved his hands in dismissal.

'Great men are like that. Hope you won't be like

that when it's your turn.' She held him still tighter. 'Uncle Joe's like that. Bit like Mr Churchill, I suppose. Do you think he might ever become Prime Minister?'

So they walked, disturbing the sleeping ducks, exchanging confidences in a manner that was unusual for Bracken with a woman. Churchill's money problems, Churchill's ambitions, Churchill's drunken son and his protective wife. Always Churchill. Anna sensed that Bracken didn't care for Churchill's wife and much preferred the company of his disreputable son. Bracken protested that Churchill still had plenty of time to become Prime Minister – why, Gladstone had been eighty, he insisted – but she thought he protested too vigorously on the matter, as if trying to shout down his own doubts.

And wasn't it strange, he said, that the two of them should be walking arm in arm while their two masters were usually at each other's throats.

'Oh, you mustn't mind Uncle Joe, he's always mad at something. Always plotting, always a little angry. He doesn't think much of the State Department – calls them a bunch of cookie-pushers – and gets quite furious about the White House. Think he'd like to be President himself, one day, just like Mr Churchill. They're a lot alike in some ways.'

'If we value our personal safety I suggest we don't mention it to either of them.'

They stopped in the shadow of a tree, looking at the distant lights of Knightsbridge that sparkled off the water and seemed to find reflection in each other's eyes.

'Don't worry about war, Anna,' Bracken said, tried

to reassure her, holding her shoulders, playing with the ends of her soft hair. 'You Americans worry too much, you go funny at the very thought of war,' he chided. 'Why, just days ago, that fellow – you know, Orson Welles – makes a radio broadcast about "The War of the Worlds" and half the eastern seaboard of America goes into a panic because they think the Martians are attacking. You're not very good at war.'

'Didn't do too badly in the last one,' she reminded him softly. And she kissed him.

Almost before he knew it their bodies were pressing up against each other, their tongues searching, his fingers, too, through the buttons of her fur coat and on her breast, but she drew away. Suddenly he was gripped by shame. He heard his mother whispering in his ear, tormenting him, accusing him of being no better than a prowling dog, and he wanted to scream at himself for being such a fool. 'I'm so sorry,' he mumbled, preparing to flee, but she held him.

'Bendy, no – it's me that's sorry. I'm so very fond of you,' she whispered. 'It's just that – I've got too much Irish and Catholic in me, it makes me feel so, so – guilty. You wouldn't understand.'

Understand? He could write the entire encyclopaedia. Of course he understood. Unlike hers, his Irish Catholic upbringing was entirely authentic. A mud-roofed hut in Tipperary rather than a New England mansion. With dirt floors instead of marble, and only one room. Lying awake, listening to his parents behind the curtain surrounding their bed, his father's ferocious grunts, her pleas for him to be quieter, and more gentle. And always afterwards, while his father snored, his mother prayed, begged that she would have no more children and be released from the hell of her life. Guilt? His very existence was a matter of guilt, of sin, of suffering, and the lesson had been beaten into him every day at seminary school until he had run away from it at the age of fifteen. But it always came back to him, every time he heard a woman pray, or every time he thought of sex.

So, yes, Anna Maria, he knew all about guilt.

Which was why he didn't want anything more to do with the Irish, why he'd tried by all sorts of invention to scrub any lingering bit of Irishness from his voice and his soul, one of the many reasons why he hated Bernard Shaw. Yet Anna Maria reminded him of Ireland every time he looked into her pale green eyes. He didn't even like women – at least, not the hairy, scratchy, unpleasant women who were the sum total of his sexual experience, who smelt so strange and who demanded more money afterwards – yet he was already counting the moments before he could see this woman again. For Bracken, image was everything, yet here he was standing under a tree in a public park with a handful of nipple and a girl almost young enough to be his daughter. He'd never wanted to share his life with any woman, largely because his life was such a fabrication that it wouldn't stand up to any sustained scrutiny, yet suddenly he was breaking every rule in his book.

That's when he came to the conclusion he had fallen in love.

*　　*　　*

'You've gone too far this time. Too wretchedly, damnably far!'

And they had thought they were bringing him the best news of the day.

As soon as they had knocked on the door of the Cabinet Room, Ball and Wilson sensed that their own feelings of elation were misplaced. 'What do you want?' Chamberlain had demanded imperiously, not taking his eyes from the letter he was writing.

Another of those endless missives to his sisters, they decided. He wrote to them in astonishing detail, not only of the facts of his Government but of his ambitions and aspirations, and also of his fears. For him these letters were a cleansing process, like the bleedings insisted upon by a mediaeval physician, except that in his letters he bled feelings and soul. Sometimes the sisters knew more than even Ball and Wilson, and always more than his wife.

'News from the front, Neville,' Ball exclaimed, moving into the room.

'Which of the many fronts that seem to engage my attentions?' the Prime Minister responded. He was always like this when he was tired: overbearing, sarcastic, short. They had learned to ignore it.

'In their manifold and great mercy, our friends in the frozen north have decided not to retain the Duchess as their candidate at the next election,' Ball continued.

Still Chamberlain did not look up. There were livid red spots high on his cheeks. He had just been told that the furniture he and his wife had ordered for the new residence at the top of Number Ten would not be arriving for another two months. Delay upon delay. The incompetence was scarcely believable. How was he supposed to secure the peace of Europe when he hadn't got anywhere to store his clean shirts? He was going to visit Signor Mussolini, who normally appeared in public covered in gold braid. Would the British Prime Minister have to arrive looking like some agricultural worker? 'If this is democracy, I sometimes wonder why we bother,' he muttered.

'Neville, this is a triumph of democracy,' Ball protested.

'What is?'

'The damned Duchess. She's out.'

At last he gave them his attention. 'She's out?'

'Constituency's disowned her.'

'Ah, about time.' He relaxed a little, leaning back in his chair. 'And I suppose if I examined the matter closely I would find your fingerprints somewhere on the death warrant.'

'The lightest of dabs, perhaps.' And they almost tumbled over themselves in their enthusiasm to offer him the details. 'Seems it was quite a lynch mob.' – 'She didn't stand a chance.' – 'The motion was put to the meeting that they should seek a candidate who'd support your position on Europe.' – 'It was overwhelming.' – '273 votes to 167.' – 'The agent says he's never known such a turnout.' There was laughter. 'And the best bit's yet to come. The poor Duchess was so distressed she's resigned her seat. Flown off in a fit.' – 'Intends to stand as an Independent, would you believe?' – 'Yes, there's going to be a by-election.'

'What?' Chamberlain sprang to his feet. The pen

he was using clattered to the table, spraying the letter with wet slugs of ink. 'What?' he demanded again. His entire face had now coloured and his hand was clasping his temples. 'How could you? You fools!'

'Steady on, Neville.' Both men turned momentarily to stone. Something had gone dramatically wrong, this wasn't the script they had brought with them. 'What's the problem? She's turned her back on the peace, now she's turned her back on the party. She's done for.'

'But a by-election. Don't you see what that means?'

Wilson and Ball looked at each other in bewilderment.

'The voters will have to choose.'

'Some choice,' Ball snorted. 'Between war and peace.'

'Between her – and me.' Chamberlain leaned for support on the white marble fireplace, both arms outstretched, gazing into the empty grate, as if faith itself were draining from him. 'You've gone too far this time. Too wretchedly, damnably far!'

'No,' Wilson objected. 'How?'

Chamberlain turned, his voice grown tight, enunciating every word with care. 'But what if she wins?'

'She can't bloody win,' Ball insisted. 'She doesn't have a friend who isn't a Bolshie or can't be made to look one.'

'You're almost as popular as God out there.' Wilson waved a hand in the general direction of the windows.

'The Lord giveth. And He taketh, Sir Horace.' Chamberlain was breathing heavily, struggling to

156

control his mood. 'Something's been going on – out there. I don't know what, perhaps all this nonsense with the Jews, but it's all wobbling.' He picked up a cardboard folder that had lain beside his blotter and threw it down the table. 'Hitler's pogroms have made him look like a criminal. And us like conspirators and accomplices.'

'You can't possibly believe the stupid Duchess will win,' Ball protested.

'The *News Chronicle* has just got hold of an opinion poll that suggests she might.'

'Those polls?' Ball snorted. 'It's a bit of a rebound, nothing more. Like the bride coming back from her honeymoon to find a pile of washing.' He chewed casually at a fingernail. 'Anyway, I've already persuaded the *News Chronicle* to suppress most of it.'

Yet Chamberlain was in no way reassured. He began to stride impatiently around the long rectangular Cabinet table, leaning forward as though into a wind. 'They don't believe Herr Hitler. They don't believe he has no more territorial ambitions. They don't believe in Munich any more.' He stopped, glaring at them, accusing. 'Which means they don't believe in me.'

Ball thumped the table so hard the silver and crystal inkwell jumped in its place. 'You're confusing the issue, Neville. We've never said they've got to like Hitler. I hate the bugger myself. Which makes what you've done with him all the more remarkable. You've extracted a more than reasonable deal from a totally unreasonable man. People understand that. You get the credit for it. And if he goes and tramples all over the agreement and half of bloody

157

Europe, then everyone will know who's to blame. We're not dealing with issues of delicacy here, Neville, we're dealing with the dregs of Europe. With Jews, with jumped-up little Austrian upstarts, with the decadent French who change their governments as often as they change their mistresses and with millions of bloody Bolshies who are sitting just across the border sharpening their knives and ready to slit the throats of everyone who's not looking their way. Europe's a mess. You can't clean it up all on your own, but you have given them the chance to do it for themselves.'

'Cleaning up? Is that what you call the things Hitler's doing?'

'It's omelettes and eggs, and by the time the voters get round to wiping the last bit of grease from their plates they'll be too busy rubbing their stomachs to worry about a few scraps on the kitchen floor. So Hitler's breaking more than eggs, but the muckier it gets the more grateful people are going to be that you've kept this country out of it. Scotsmen don't want to go to war with Germany all over again for the sake of Jews and Communists.'

'The by-election isn't a war with Herr Hitler, it's a war between the Duchess and me. We'll be fighting on her territory. And if I lose, my credibility will be ruined, not just at home but abroad. I would never be able to look Hitler or Mussolini in the eye again. It would be a disaster. All my efforts for peace would be lost and we'd end up embroiled in the most dreadful war mankind has ever known. It's not just my record at stake, it's the survival of civilization. Don't you see? I must win that election.'

'You will, Neville. And when you do, every other rebel in the party will be on their knees either begging your forgiveness or waiting for a bullet in the back of the head. The Duchess is doing us a favour.'

'You can guarantee that?'

Ball looked slowly from the Prime Minister to his colleague, then for a moment examined a badly chewed fingernail. 'Trust me. Your by-election is already in the bag.'

This was A Bad Thing and Churchill knew it. A Very Bad Thing. And like so much nowadays, he knew there was nothing he could do about it. Yet at first it had seemed to be such An Excellent Thing.

The manager of his bank had telephoned most unexpectedly, and after the initial pleasantries – more strained on Churchill's part than was usual – came straight to the point. Had he found 'alternative accommodation' for the loan? Bloody fool. 'Accommodation'? What was the man running, a bank or a bed-and-breakfast place? It wasn't accommodation Churchill needed; his loan wasn't asleep, all gently tucked up. It was very much awake, like an evil monkey, perched on his shoulder. Always there when he looked round. Staring, growing heavier. So, no, he hadn't found anywhere else.

'Then I may have some good news for you . . .'

The manager thought he could get his superiors at the bank to agree to renew the existing loan. 'With the easing of the war threat, Mr Churchill, we are able to take a somewhat longer-term view of such matters. I'm sure you understand.'

Now he was convinced the manager was A Bloody Fool. The threat of war gone away? It hadn't left, it had only become temporarily distracted while it stuck its knife and fork into Czechoslovakia. But what was Churchill to say? He held his tongue, he needed this man. The manager might yet prove to be a Useful Bloody Fool.

No guarantees, the manager had insisted, still only a proposal, but one he would be advocating to his colleagues with great force. And he was hopeful. An Ever Optimistic Useful Bloody Fool. So could Churchill make himself available to sign the relevant documents, perhaps the following week, in London. Not quite sure precisely when, and apologies for the inconvenience, but time was short and they would have to move extremely quickly to make the deadline, otherwise . . .

Yet that following week he was supposed to be travelling up to Scotland to make a speech on behalf of the Duchess of Atholl. The major speech of the campaign. The great by-election rally. Showing her electors and the entire world that she wasn't alone.

But the bank manager was both insistent and inflexible. The documents were indispensable, the signatures vital, the deadline loomed and he was sorry but he couldn't yet say precisely when next week. In spite of all Churchill's pleadings he could find no alternative.

And now he had to tell her.

The phone clicked and cracked and at last he heard her voice. 'Kitty, my darling Duchess, how are things on the battle front?'

But he was unable to listen to her answers. Then

he explained that he could not make the meeting. He had to break his promise. He would send her messages to publish, he would shower her with words of support and deepest affection, but he could not come to the constituency.

'Another one of the walking wounded not up to the long journey north,' she muttered dispiritedly. Her opponent had already flooded the constituency with dozens of MPs and there were more to come in the last few days of the campaign – 'my constituency's beginning to look like the front hall of Conservative Central Office.' Yet it seemed that her own supporters in the Conservative Party, few in number as they were, had encountered any number of impediments to helping her. That was the word she used – impediments. She clearly meant excuses.

But this wasn't an excuse, it was . . . Money. Security. His home. Chartwell. Hadn't he already made enough sacrifices for the cause? Yet if the cause were so vital and urgent then surely . . . ? But his first commitment must be to his family. They had no one else. And what of other families? Those who had already lost their homes, and would undoubtedly lose much, much more? Whichever way he argued the matter, it was of little comfort to him and would be of no comfort whatsoever to the Duchess. He was tired, exhausted by his many burdens, he couldn't carry on being nothing more than a storm in the wilderness. So he had left her with no explanation, merely the excuse of unavoidable commitments.

His darling Duchess was on her own.

*　　*　　*

'You doin' all right down there, ducks?'

Desdemona was concerned. She'd found a right one here. He'd seemed grumpy right from the start, almost angry – and he wasn't much with words. Foreign, she thought, bit of the Wop in him. Still, he was polite – said please, even – and it was her last engagement of the day so she'd thought, Why not? It was rent day on Friday.

It was when he'd taken his clothes off that her concern began to grow. He'd undressed very methodically, not bashfully like some of her clients, nor over-eagerly either, just bit by bit, laying everything out carefully on the chair. Old clothes, neat, but probably second-hand. He was clean, that she liked, and well groomed, but as he took off his vest she saw a body that reminded her of old Bluey, the mongrel collie she'd rescued from the dogs' home who had promptly gone and got himself run over by a milk lorry. Wasn't used to roads, poor thing. They'd tried to stick him back together but he'd just pined, wasted away, all crooked, until his body looked like nothing but – well, like this chap's. Full of ribs and scars.

Then he'd looked at her and asked if she would take her clothes off carefully, too. Like they were going to bed, instead of having a quick one before she had to hand over the room to the night shift. Goodness, she half expected him to suggest they get down on their knees and start to pray. But she rather liked it. He had watched her carefully, appreciating every new area that she exposed, and although her body nowadays left a lot to be desired he seemed to appreciate it. It had been a long time since anybody, including herself, had done anything with her body

162

except use it. Not since Jimmy had come home on leave and she'd told him she was up the spout, and he'd acted all sort of funny, gone quiet, then walked down to the pub one Sunday dinnertime and never come back. She'd burnt the meal to a crisp, waiting for the bastard. He'd even left his naval uniform behind. She burnt that, too.

But because this one seemed to appreciate her, she found herself enjoying it, him getting down to it. Yes, the old torpedo was in the tube, as Jimmy used to say, and his engines were running. So she closed her eyes and listened to the rhythm of the bedsprings and tried to get back in touch with those senses in a woman she thought had been lost with the laundry ages ago.

'You're enjoying it,' he said. And stopped.

'What's the matter, ducks? Have I done something wrong?'

'You're enjoying it,' he repeated, like an accusation. 'I've . . . I've never had a woman who enjoyed it.'

'What, never?'

'Only pretend.'

'What, even your wife?'

'Never been married.'

'Not ever?'

'Who would marry this?' he said, indicating his broken body.

'Hey, don't do yourself down. Hell, I'm not exactly Betty Grable meself.' Then, quietly: 'You always been like that?'

'Since I was very young.'

'You poor bleeder,' she whispered. 'But let me tell

you, ducks, don't let it get you down. I tell you, I've had – well, I know what I'm talking about, know what I mean? And I was really enjoying it with you.'

He stood up, every part of his body looking mournful.

'Now I've spoilt it. Sorry,' he muttered. 'Can't seem to enjoy anything at the moment.'

She couldn't get over it. A punter who apologized. Where had this one come from? And she looked at him and he reminded her of Bluey, someone she wanted to take care of. So she had got down on her knees, but not to pray, ignoring the bare floorboards, and had made sure he enjoyed it after all. She assured him that she had enjoyed it, too – well, only a little white lie, the sort of thing you pretend to a – friend.

'There you are, ducks. Feel better now, do we?'

And he did. Earlier that afternoon he'd been round to his former fiancée's, the nearly-but-never-to-be Mrs McFadden, and asked for the ring back. It had cost him two weeks' wages and he saw no reason why she should keep it, particularly when over her shoulder in the kitchen he could see another man's ironing hanging out to air. He hadn't got the ring, of course, only several lungfuls of abuse. And a few tears. It had been a stupid idea, but he had nothing to lose, not even his pride. He hadn't bothered with pride, not since the camps. But he'd thought of her, the would-be Mrs McFadden, in the middle of his session with Desdemona, because he'd never had sex with his fiancée and had begun to wonder whether it would have been enjoyable getting into her drawers.

Perhaps that's why he had been so distracted. Until Desdemona had . . .

'Can I see you again?' he asked.

''Course, ducks. I do Tuesdays and Thursdays most weeks and –'

'No. I mean – see you. Not just sex. Maybe just for a drink.'

'Why?'

'Dunno. Perhaps because I hate drinking on my own.'

'Full of compliments, you are.'

It seemed for ever since she'd last talked to a man about anything other than tricks and time and money in advance, except for the occasional queer sort who wanted to talk about his wife, and anyway it was the end of her shift. So she had dickered and negotiated for some more money and ended up pushing her way alongside him through the evening crowds that thronged the Market to the King's Head. Just round the corner, very public, where other working girls would be able to keep an eye on her, like they did for each other. She still didn't trust him; maybe he wanted to drag her off into his cave and cook her.

Standing room only in the King's Head. They leaned on the bar. 'You look different,' he muttered across his pint of mild.

She was wearing a simple corduroy dress and a woollen sweater that was probably knitted at home, with low-heeled shoes and only a touch of makeup, complemented by pearl earrings and a ruby butterfly brooch that probably came from Woolies. The push-up and pull-apart gear – her 'working clobber', as she called it – was in a little cardboard suitcase at her side. 'I have another life outside the Market. They don't mix.'

'Am I permitted to ask what?'

'Suppose you'd better, 'cos I ain't going to stand in the middle of the public bar and shout about me Tuesdays and Thursdays, am I now?' She leaned forward, smelling of rose water. 'So Mondays, Wednesdays, Fridays and Saturdays I work as a cleaner. That pays for the rent. Tuesdays and Thursdays is food and clothes for the kids.'

'Kids?'

'You don't think I'd do this unless I had to, do you?'

'Do they have exotic names like their mother?'

She laughed into the froth on her Mackeson. 'What, Desdemona?'

'You are going to shock me and tell me it is not your real name.'

'It's Carol.'

'And the children?'

She hesitated – he'd gone a pace too far. 'I'm so proud of the little blighters. Yet somehow I don't want to tell you their names. Maybe it's 'cos I separate the two parts of my life and there's a long trip in between, and I leave my kids on the other side. They're not the sort of thing I want to talk about with a punter in the middle of the public bar.'

'I see. But if I asked you out for another drink – just for a drink – would I still be a punter?'

A smile caught the edge of her lips. 'Dunno. You're a sly bugger, you are.' But already she was giving her answer, picking a small piece of lint from his lapel, building bridges.

'So, what's it to be? Dinner at the Ritz? Dancing at the Café Royal? Oysters at Wheelers?' He picked up a newspaper that had been left on the counter, folded to the entertainments section. 'Or a cup of tea at Lyons Corner House and an evening at the pictures? Next week. Anything you want to see?' He handed it across.

She pushed it back. 'No, you choose.'

'Can't. Haven't got my reading glasses.'

'Me neither.'

'What, an eagle eye like you needs reading glasses?' Not when she could spot stray fluff on his jacket. He pushed the newspaper back along the bar.

It was as though he had handed her a jail sentence. In a moment the smile melted, the eyes had grown agitated, she no longer wanted to be there. He reached over and touched her arm in concern. 'Carol, what's the matter? What have I done?'

'I . . . I . . .' For a moment there was nothing but an incomprehensible stammer. 'I am so ashamed.' Then the stammer turned to a blubber and she scrabbled in her handbag for a handkerchief, but he was ahead of her, offering her his own, neatly laundered, and soon it was covered in mascara. Then his arm was on her shoulder, shielding her distress from the other drinkers.

'Funny, innit?' she sobbed defiantly. 'Me, in my profession, feeling shamed.'

'But why?'

She glared at the newspaper with a look that

might have encouraged spontaneous combustion. ''Cos I can't bloody read, can I.'

He looked from her to the newspaper, then back again. 'You can't . . . ?'

She shook her head, which hung low in humiliation. He placed a finger under her chin and raised it until he was looking into her eyes.

'We have quite a lot in common, you and me, Carol. I couldn't read English until I was almost thirty years old. And it is not a cause for shame. But if ever you have an evening or two free, would you like me to teach you to read?'

'You would?' Hope had begun to swim alongside the tears once more.

He nodded.

'And what would you like me to do for you in return?'

He roared with laughter. 'Allow me to buy you another drink. For a start.'

'You really are a sly bugger, you are,' she said once again. 'My boy does all the reading for me at home. Letters from the landlord, his school reports, that sort of thing. Even reads books to me at night. We're doing *Lorna Doone* right now. Sounds bloody cold on those moors. And aren't men such tossers? Well, most of them, anyhow.' The words were flooding from her, carrying away her shame. 'But I'd love to learn to read. Maybe get another job, shop work or something. Just a little more money. Get out of this business. Get out of the cleaning business, too. Although I don't suppose I'd have that job if I couldn't – you know, not read.'

Mac was sucking his fingers distractedly – his fresh

pint glass had stuck to the varnished counter and spilled beer over his hand, and he had only half a mind on what she was saying. 'Why's that then?' he asked, buying time.

'Well, I'm a cleaner at the Home Secretary's house – you know, Sir Sam Hoare? Think the only reason I got the job is 'cos they know I can't read – he's a bit untidy with his papers, he is, and doesn't like to have to sort himself out every time a cleaner comes in. Bit of a bastard on the quiet, too. Tried it on when Her Ladyship was away once, dirty sod. After lunch, had a bit too much at his club. 'Course, it would have been different if he'd asked on a Tuesday or Thursday . . .'

Beer was still dripping from his fingers but Mac no longer seemed to care. Thoughts had begun to spin round him like a swarm of under-fed flies. Thoughts about Carol, about Hoare, about his highly polished table and the crumbs that fell from it. And half-formed thoughts about his customer named Guy Burgess who seemed to have an insatiable interest in those sorts of crumbs.

'But one thing I've got to ask,' Carol was saying, dragging him back to the bar. 'Why is it you don't seem to have a problem with – you know, my Tuesdays and Thursdays? Most men would . . .'

'I am not most men. And in my time I have done far, far worse than you – during the war, and after. We all have to find our own ways to live and I long ago learned to live without shame. I remember a story from my childhood. Bible stuff, about the battle of Jericho. Before it started, Joshua sent two men into the city. The King heard of this and gave orders for the men to be captured. So they hid on the roof of a house owned by a prostitute named Rahab. She wouldn't reveal where they were hiding, even when the King threatened to torture her. So when Joshua came with his army of Israelites and all their trumpets and marched around the walls and blew the place down, everyone in the city was killed, except for Rahab. She had gathered all her family in her room and tied a red ribbon on the window as a sign, so every single one of them was saved.' He smiled. 'She was a fine, brave woman. You remind me a little of Rahab.'

'What? She took on two men at a time? Sounds like bloody hard work. I'm a bit old-fashioned, me, strictly a one-man girl.' She was mocking him gently. 'But it's a lovely story. Thank you, ducks. Never realized you were religious.'

He shook his head, almost defiantly. 'Not me. Don't believe in very much at all.'

'I'm C of E. Take the kids every Sunday. Not that I'm particularly religious, either, but it means my boy can go to the church school.'

'I bet Rahab's kid grew up to be Chief Rabbi.'

'But one thing's puzzling me. Why did Rahab need to hide these two men in the first place? Why was the King hunting them? Who were they?'

Suddenly the flies that were swarming inside his brain had stopped buzzing.

'Not a puzzle. Thought you'd have guessed. They were looking for crumbs.'

'What do you mean?'

'They were spies.'

SEVEN

The figure that walks into the midst of a smoky, well-sweated and mostly masculine baiting pit this evening is small and delicate, even elderly. She is not beautiful but certainly striking, almost doll-like in her thick ankle-length skirt. Yet appearances deceive, for Katharine, Duchess of Atholl, has the stomach, the determination and the heedless commitment of an Andalusian bull. She has made a reputation for herself by embracing causes that many deem simply absurd – lost causes, mostly, not only in the fight against female circumcision in Africa but other problems that her male colleagues find difficult or downright embarrassing, like child prostitution and refugees. It is a time when the fashion is for caution, not causes.

Her heart is large and her sympathies are limitless, washing over the narrow banks of party loyalties that so many of her colleagues insist upon. That's why they have never forgiven her. It has been a long and often lonely path that has brought her here, to this congregation packed into the town hall. Her eyes – dark, eloquent, hooded, the most expressive of eyes with their constant shadows of too much caring and too little sleep – move amongst them. There are people here she does not recognize, and more than a few she knows for certain support her opponent, the official Conservative candidate, a local laird named Snadden. His message has been simple. He stands for appeasement, for Chamberlain and for the total destruction of her career.

She is a woman of passion and has no objection to political fervour in others, but enthusiasm in these parts in recent days has turned to ugly obsession. Conservative Central Office, that bastion of victory-before-virtue, has swamped the constituency many times over with MPs, leaflets and newsletters, and in their wake they have left libel and innuendo – rumours that she is a secret Communist, that she is sick, on the edge of a nervous breakdown, is neglecting her husband, that she has an illegitimate child by a Jew.

Letters have appeared throughout the constituency, letters that threaten her supporters and encourage those who cannot make up their minds. No one seems to know who has written these letters, but most of the postmarks appear to come from the London area. Other actions are indisputably local. Traders who have put up her posters in their shop windows quickly find themselves the victims of an unspoken boycott; several windows have been broken. Gangs of small boys have been roaming the streets of the constituency waving placards which proclaim: 'RED KITTY WANTS WAR'. Their leaders have been paid two shillings and sixpence for their trouble.

Most sickening of all is a vicious anti-Communist, Jew-hating, Duchess-baiting journal perversely entitled *Truth* that has been delivered to the doorstep of every household in the constituency. Amongst many other things it accuses her of speaking on Communist platforms and singing 'The Red Flag'. It is false and directly libellous, but her efforts to discover who is behind this publication have failed.

Yet she does not doubt she will win. The people of Kinross and West Perthshire are a little dour and intensely proud. They will not be won over by innuendo and attacks launched from an outpost four hundred miles to the south. These are her people, they know her not as the Red Kitty of the scandal rags but the woman who has served them for fifteen years, often to the point of exhaustion and infirmity. She has fought for their jobs, helped build their schools, saved their houses, often paid their medical bills out of her own pocket. She has wept with them, too.

But it is a pity Winston could not come. This is the major public meeting of her election campaign and his participation has been widely advertised. She bears Churchill no ill will. Several others have also failed to fulfil their promises to speak for her and have offered every sort of excuse. Bob Boothby, at least, has been candid. He has explained that the chairman of his association and half his executive spent an entire evening shouting at him and insisting they would resign if he joined her on an anti-Chamberlain platform. Just an hour before this confrontation he'd received an anonymous letter threatening to make public his relationship with Dorothy Macmillan *'if you insist on sticking your head above the sandbags in Perth. The trenches can be muddy at this time of year. Don't be surprised if the mud sticks.'*

In the circumstances, he had been able to offer her nothing but his best wishes.

Both Churchill and Boothby would have been helpful – oh, so useful. They have gifts of oratory, the ability to capture a moment, gifts which she has never had. They could have transformed a packed audience such as this, turned them all to silk purses, while she can only lecture them and hope to be heard amongst the throng standing at the back.

Yet rapidly it becomes apparent that lectures are not what they have come for tonight. She stands behind a table draped in a Union flag and finds herself battling against a tide of questions that make her feel she is standing not on the familiar wooden stage but on nothing more substantial than quicksand.

'Your Grace, why did you stand and sing "The Red Flag"?'

'I didn't. I beg you to believe me that this is a total distortion . . .'

'Then do you agree that all Communists are scum?'

'Ah, Mr McCrieff. Good evening . . .'

'Please answer the question directly, Your Grace. Do you agree that all Communists are scum?'

'I find name-calling never gets debate very far.'

'Some journalists have suggested that on your recent trip to the United States you vigorously attacked Mr Chamberlain.'

'Lies! I have never said anything that would embarrass Mr Chamberlain personally.'

'But wouldn't your policies have meant that we would have gone to war over Czechoslovakia? That we would be at war with Germany this very evening?'

'Such questions are far too simplistic . . .'

'Then perhaps Her Grace would be kind enough to tell us what questions she would like us to put, because it seems perfectly evident she's unwilling to answer any of the questions she's been asked so far?'

And the rest join in.

'Is the reason ye're so keen on war because ye have no children of your own?' – *'Will you tell the mothers of Perthshire how many British deaths you think would be acceptable in your war?'* – *'Can ye confirm what I've heard, that ye were seen takkin' tea last month wi' the Soviet Ambassador Maisky?'*

On all sides and in many voices, the level of noise and impatience grows. It is helpful to no one, but she is the only one with anything to lose. As the evening draws on, her eyes, increasingly sad and sombre, are torn in many directions in an attempt to identify the sources of the heckling and constant interruptions. Strangers, many of them, but not all. Some are – or were – old friends. The growing clamour is accompanied by the pounding of the gavel with which the chairman is failing to keep order, and soon it has reached the level of *'Get ye back home to Moscow'* and *'Little wonder your husband keeps sending you abroad.'* Her senses are swimming. In the morning she will know what to do, what stratagem or device or words she might use to quell the uproar, but not now.

Then the final moment. McCrieff is back on his feet, pressing another question. She suggests he has already been given more than a fair amount of time but he stands his ground amidst a sea of waving hats and leaflets, insisting on the moment. Many others are pressing his case, too. The chaos has reached such a level that it appears impossible he can be heard but he raises a silver-headed walking stick above his head, like a prophet beseeching the heavens, and all is suddenly quiet.

'Your Grace,' he begins, 'you ask for my support as a Conservative, and for the support of everyone here, most of whom I'll wager are loyal Conservatives.'

She nods. That is undeniably true.

'But is it not a fact that earlier this year you held meetings in Westminster with others to discuss the setting-up of a new party? A breakaway from the Conservatives? That you plotted to split our cause? I have put the question as simply as I can, and I would appreciate a direct answer, yes or no.'

She is dumbfounded, her distress evident. How can he have known that? They had met in private – with only those they knew could be trusted – and had committed nothing to paper. They had talked, they had telephoned, and in the end had failed to agree. There were those who still hoped that the Conservative Party – *their* party – could yet be turned to a new course, once time and the outrageous arrows of events began to bring Chamberlain low. But for the moment they had parted as they had met, in secrecy, and had agreed to wait upon another day.

But McCrieff knows. Which means that there are those at Central Office who know, for he is undeniably their creature. But that is impossible!

And while she ponders the impossibility of it all, her silence rings out most eloquently to every corner of the hall, giving the answer McCrieff wanted and condemning her in the soul of every loyal Conservative in the constituency.

She searches her audience for friendly faces. They are there, but seem to her like fishes in a sea crowded with sharks, their expressions helpless and filled with bewilderment. The Duchess closes her eyes. They are such eloquent eyes. Often they speak of pity, sometimes of anger and exasperation, always of boundless love. This night she walks from the platform with her head held high, her chin raised in defiance above the clamour, but it is her eyes that tell the story. For they have lost something, something that up to this point has always sustained her and provided her with a lifeline between reality and tomorrow.

Hope.

Politics is often a little like seduction: a coming-together of opposing forces. Bracken has planned the seduction of Anna Fitzgerald in the manner of an election campaign, for he knows no other way. He has planned every move, even scribbled some of it down on paper because he finds that whenever he thinks of Anna so many of the channels in his exceptionally febrile brain seem to close down. He grows nervous every time he remembers those parts of her body he has touched, while the thought of those other parts he has yet to touch reduces him to bewilderment. So he goes back to basics. He has overcome all the other obstacles that life has thrown in his path by sheer energy and persistence, and love can't be so very different.

He has thought of taking Anna to the theatre once

more, but quickly discarded the idea – they seem to have such different tastes in playwrights. Instead he has proposed a visit to the National Portrait Gallery off Trafalgar Square, where they have a couple of fine Romneys that he wants her to notice. He has a Romney of his own – above his fireplace in Lord North Street, a portrait of Edmund Burke – which if all other inspiration fails will give him an excuse to invite her back there later. Yet before he gets round to any suggestion that she should inspect his library it would be dinner, at Wiltons in Jermyn Street. This has several advantages. Not only does it have an excellent kitchen but also he is well known there; they will make a fuss, indulge in a little continental grovelling, create a good impression. Wiltons also has secluded booths that offer a reasonable degree of intimacy, yet at the same time enable you to be seen. He's already ascertained that at least three members of the Cabinet would be dining there; they will undoubtedly be drawn by both good manners and the charms of Anna to hover at his table. It will all add to the sense of theatre. Heady stuff for a young girl. So dinner. Then the Romney . . .

He has prepared with thoroughness. A hair trim, a temporary taming of the savage beast, and a shave – he'd mentioned to the barber that a young lady was involved, exchanging male confidences for a liberal dose of eau de cologne. His favourite Savile Row three-piece, four-button, the lucky one he'd had made for the last election campaign, freshly sponged and pressed by his housekeeper to get rid of its faint tang of mothballs. Cartier cufflinks and a diamond tie pin. And silk everywhere against his skin, socks, shirt, vest. But what about his hat? To wear, or not to wear? And which one? What was fashionable amongst young women? He stood in front of the mirror and considered the different impressions. Solid and respectable? A little daring? A cheeky fedora? Confused, he threw away all the hats and decided to place his trust in his barber. Less challenging were the flowers. A single long-stemmed red rose placed on her linen napkin at Wiltons, and a bouquet of hot-house lilies for when he picked her up. And another rose beside the bed, for luck.

Now all the planning and painful expectation have come to their climax. The lights have been set – and reset – in Lord North Street, Edmund Burke is smiling down benignly from above the fireplace, there is champagne in the refrigerator and chocolates beside the sofa, along with a leather-bound copy of his latest speeches. Oh, and clean towels and linen, too. Everything is waiting for her. Lobster at Wiltons, and specially ordered creamy New England clam chowder in case she turns out to be one of those women who are wretched and ridiculous about raw oysters. And at last he is standing in front of her doorway in Knightsbridge, his smile shifting awkwardly as though it's having trouble finding a comfortable position. He's clutching his flowers – too tightly – and feeling fourteen.

He throws away a half-consumed cigarette and rings the bell. Steps back. Shines his shoes yet again on the back of his trousers. Waits. Nothing. More hesitantly, he rings again. Eventually he hears a scuffling from the other side of the door and the sound of a fumbling at the lock. The smile switches places one last time, he shakes the flowers as though to wake them up and he raises his hat in salute – yes, he's changed his mind yet again.

Yet the process of seduction is to prove even more like politics than Bracken has bargained for. For Anna is standing at the door, evidently unprepared, her fingers scrabbling nervously at her chin and her cheeks stained with mascara from her tears.

'My darling, what ever . . . ?'

'It's Chumpers.'

'Chumpers?'

'My dog, you silly man. My devoted little Chumpers.'

'What about him?'

'He's run away!'

And along with the wretched, flea-bitten and sausage-chomping Chumpers had disappeared all of Bracken's plans.

Frost had bitten at the heart of London and a shimmer of mist clung to the waters of the lake in St James's Park. The ducks shivered and huddled together, while the royal pelicans complained from their rock in the middle of the lake. The branches of the plane trees seemed to droop in disappointment. On the pathway that led around the park, the Prime Minister was taking his daily constitutional. Usually on these outings he was accompanied by his wife, but she had been discouraged by a slight migraine, so instead Sir Horace Wilson was with him. A detective loitered in their wake.

Chamberlain stepped out briskly, his pace fuelled

not simply by the cold but also by irritation at the morning's news.

'Next year,' Wilson sympathized.

'Yes, yes, yes, of course next year. But why not this?' Chamberlain's voice sagged with disappointment. 'The Nobel Peace Prize is supposed to go to those who have done most to secure the peace. And who has done more?'

Wilson trod carefully across the slippery path. 'Perhaps the Norwegians thought it would need to go to both you and Herr Hitler. To be even-handed.'

'Wouldn't have minded sharing it. Austen had to share it,' Chamberlain muttered wistfully, almost to himself, nodding curtly as a passer-by smiled in surprise and bowed.

'The Nobel Committee's been led by the nose – taken by the plight of refugees.'

'But even so. I've done my bit, offered to resettle as many as I can in the colonies – Africa. Southern America. They can't get much farther away from Germany than that! Has the – what are they called? – the Nansen International Office for Refugees done more? Do they really deserve the Nobel Prize above me?'

'It's the Scandinavians sticking together. An imagination limited by a diet of dried cod.'

'It's damnable how little gratitude there is in this world. Makes me worried, whatever next? What about the by-election, Horace? You and Joe assured me . . .'

'Joe's pulling out all the stops –'

'Is he? All of them? He knows more about the vices of men than anyone I've ever met. Are you sure he's doing everything he can?'

'In all honesty, there are some things he does I don't want to know about. Or think you should know about, either.'

'A most useful man, brings me all sorts of interesting information. We live in difficult times, Horace. No point in half measures.'

'If the Cabinet were ever to know . . .'

'If the Cabinet were ever to know, then Sir Joseph would have found out first. That's why he taps their phones.'

Wilson looked around awkwardly, breathless. At times Chamberlain set too frantic a pace. Yet suddenly the old man came to a complete halt and pointed his furled umbrella to the sky, demanding silence. His eyes scoured the banks of the lake beneath the trees.

'Ah, a song thrush. I thought I heard a song thrush, Horace. But it was nothing more than a sly old blackbird imitating the tune.' He shook his head sadly. 'A false spring. Sometimes I wonder whether we shall ever see the flowers in bloom again. Sometimes, Horace, in the dark corners of the night, I wonder whether there are some things that I want simply too much. Even peace. Is it possible to want peace too much?'

'I'm not sure I understand. How can you want peace too much?'

'Even Christ turned on the moneylenders.'

Chamberlain resumed his walk, his steps now less rushed, more deliberate, crunching softly through the frost. 'Tell Joe that there is only one thing I want – indeed *expect* – from him this Christmas.'

'What is that, Prime Minister?'

'News. I want news. Of the Duchess. I want to hear that she's been thrown out of my temple.'

From the start Burgess had the suspicion that he had, in Mac, found a diamond. A rough diamond, to be sure, and a man whose shell had been constructed of material so tough that it was all but impenetrable, but a man of quality and great value nonetheless. And a man who played by his own rules. So Burgess took it upon himself to find out what those rules might be. In conversation and over pints of mild, he tried to probe and understand what motivated his new friend, what enjoyments he embraced and what vices he indulged in. Know thy friend, for later he might become thine enemy. Yet all he had been able to get out of Mac so far was little more than a series of grunts and the startling admission that he loved old books. Reliable friends, said the man from Solovetsky. Take them to bed and they're just the same in the morning when you wake up. Never complain. Allow you to travel, to leap over any wall and higher than any watchtower, to go wherever you please. So when Mac called and asked for a meeting, Burgess had suggested a pub in one of the alleyways off the Charing Cross Road amidst the shops and chaotic shelves of the second-hand book trade. They had spent a good half-hour simply meandering amongst the piles of dusty and slightly unkempt books which sat waiting like faithful but discarded dogs, all of whom had once been loved and asked for nothing more than to be loved again.

They made an unlikely couple, the undersized Jew

with the broken body in clothes that were old but carefully kept, and the English gentleman with the drooping Old Etonian bow tie who seemed unable to contain all the nervous energy within him that caused him to chew at his fingers and constantly flick the ash from his ubiquitous cigarette. His clothes were of much finer quality than his companion's yet in poorer condition, as though he had slept in them, which last night he had. He ought to take more care of himself, of course, keep the creases in their proper place, but it was damnably difficult when your trousers had spent half the previous evening lying crumpled on wet grass.

'I thought we might talk about money, Mr Burgess,' Mac muttered when at last they were alone.

'Ah, the green-eyed god,' Burgess responded, not warmly, throwing down a large Jameson's.

'Beg pardon?'

'How much do you want?'

Mac wiped his lips with the back of his hand. 'No, you don't understand. It's not for me. It's for a lady. I think she might be rather helpful to you. But she needs money in return for her help.'

'What sort of lady?'

'A lady who empties the wastepaper bin of the Home Secretary three times a week.'

Burgess made no reply. He held Mac's stare, their dark eyes locked upon each other, struggling for supremacy. They had reached a turning point. Burgess had known this moment must come, for Mac was too intelligent to be fooled for long by the line that Burgess's only interest was in furthering his

184

journalistic career. Anyway, no self-respecting journalist would lower himself to rooting about in another man's rubbish. Mac was testing him, seeing how far Burgess would go. How far he would stoop. His eyes flickered and looked away in search of the barman. He waited until a new drink was in his hands before turning once more to Mac, who was sitting on his stool, sipping his beer steadily and wiping his lips with the back of his hand after every mouthful.

'When can I meet this lady?'

Mac shook his head. 'You don't. She's a friend of mine, a good friend, and if you won't take it as an insult, Mr Burgess, I don't want her business mixing with your business.'

'So how the hell will I know she's genuine?' Burgess replied sharply.

'In the first place because you have my word. And also because you have these.' Stiffly Mac hopped off his stool and reached down for the canvas bag he had been carrying with him. Burgess had thought it was full of clothes or books; instead he found it filled with treasure. Paper treasure. Torn envelopes, a shopping list, expired invitation cards, a note from his wine merchant, a hastily scribbled reminder from his wife about dinner arrangements, two badly chewed pencils and a mummified apple core. The jetsam of a busy life. Yet floating amongst it there were other things. Drafts of notes to Cabinet colleagues. Half-scribbled memoranda. Carbons of exchanges between other Ministers. A polite but firm letter from his tailor, screwed into a tight ball, requesting immediate payment. The first trial run of a submission to the Prime Minister about the handling of enemy aliens during wartime. And a sheet of blotting paper with what looked like an entire day's correspondence reflected in it.

The new whiskey disappeared in a trice.

'As you see, Mr Burgess, he has a very large wastepaper bin.'

'How much do you want for this?' Burgess's eyes were sharp, nervous.

'*I* want nothing.'

'I apologize – how much does the lady require?'

Mac named his figure. It had been based on the research he had conducted one recent Thursday, concealed in a coffee shop within sight of Desdemona's doorway (she was always Desdemona to him when she was working). He knew from personal experience how much she charged. He multiplied that figure by the number of men he saw that day – then doubled it for Tuesdays, too. On top of that he added a premium of fifty per cent for rainy days and the kids. He supped his mild and once more wiped his lips with the back of his hand.

'Damn it, Mac, you strike a hard bargain.'

Burgess scanned the other man's face for any sign of posturing or willingness to compromise. He found nothing but Archangel ice.

'You can keep the sodding apple core, Mac. But as for the rest . . .' Slowly Burgess nodded his head and tried to quell the trembling in his hand.

'That's settled, then. Let me buy you another drink, Mr B.'

*　　*　　*

Intimidation comes in many guises. Around the great estates that dominated the communities of West Perthshire it arrived dressed in a velvet glove. Crofters on the estates whose leases were coming up for renewal at Christmas received letters which proposed unusually favourable terms. The letters were folded inside leaflets demanding 'VOTE SNADDEN'. And when workers on these estates picked up their pay packets they discovered the same leaflet had been stuffed into their brown envelopes, along with an unexpected 'Christmas bonus'.

The vote, on the Wednesday before Christmas, was by secret ballot, but the communities in and around the estates were tightly knit. Generations of deference meant that secrets were not readily hidden and all too easily betrayed – by a lowered glance, an uneasy smile. It was said that the lairds set the price of everything, but most particularly fixed the cost of disloyalty. Lose the sympathy of the laird and you lost your job, your home and with them, perhaps, your family. Not worth the risk.

Bracken had found Anna inconsolable about the loss of her dog. All his careful preparations for her seduction had gone to waste. He hadn't even got past the door. Instead he heard himself promising to scour the streets in search of her precious little Chumpers and she insisted that he start that very night. It was a rash promise at the best of times, made all the more risible when it started to pour with rain. Not much chance of seeing a dog in the dark through the windscreen of a rain-swept Bentley.

Yet it was clear that if he were truly to claim Anna's heart, he would have to find the bloody dog. So the following day Bracken retained the services of two private detectives, whom he commissioned to prowl the streets of Knightsbridge and South Kensington in search of the missing mongrel, offering a reward for relevant information to every postman, milkman and pavement-watcher in the area. Their efforts were to no avail; there was no trace of the thing until, on the second day, a road sweeper showed them an ornate dog collar just large enough to fit around the neck of an overweight King Charles spaniel. The buckle was bent and the collar covered in blood. Bye-bye Chumpers.

Now he had to think of another plan.

It seemed as though the quarrels of men had been taken up by the gods themselves.

Across the sprawling constituency of Kinross and West Perthshire, polling day, the twentieth of December, dawned bathed in ice and adversity. Snow lay on the ground everywhere, blocking gullies and drifting ankle-high in winds that taunted those forced to step out. The constituency was one of the largest in the country, stretching for eighty miles north to south and nearly seventy east to west, and every square inch of it froze. A day for hiding, not for voting. The sort of day when he who drives, wins. Cars were the best and, in all too many cases, the only practicable means of transport, but along with the support of the Conservative Party Kitty Atholl had lost their formidable organizational powers –

their volunteers, their committee rooms, and most of all their vehicles. Tories sat in the back of cars that drove them from door to door with blankets wrapped around their knees, while Kitty's supporters were forced to struggle out on foot into the cruel snow and a wind which that morning had come straight from Siberia. Many refused to leave their young children and their hearths. Many others were forced to turn back.

Four hundred miles further south in London it was less cold, the snow turning to rain that fell in grey, mischievous sheets. It sent most pre-Christmas revellers scurrying for shelter, yet as always Brendan Bracken had an eye for the opportunity.

His mind had become possessed by thoughts of Anna. Ever since she had lost that bloody dog, she had refused invitations and rebuffed his every approach. He had thought he might advance matters by explaining with all the sensitivity he could find that she must accept the sad fact that little Chumpers was, to all intents and purposes, lost. Gone. A fond memory. A tragedy which would sit alongside the fall of Rome and the sinking of the *Titanic*, but which nevertheless would have to be accepted. After all, had he not scoured the streets of Knightsbridge day and night in search of little poochy? Yet his concerns brought him no reward other than a few burbled words of grief and more streams of sobbing down the phone. It seemed she would grieve for ever. Now Christmas loomed, and Bracken knew what he wanted for Christmas. He had it clearly in his mind, and at times it seemed to be the only thing he had in his mind. He wanted Anna. He wanted to possess her, he wanted her body, he wanted to have sex without paying for it, he wanted to enter the New Year with a relationship that people would talk about, with a much younger, importantly connected woman, and without all those knowing smirks that crept across people's faces when they discovered he was thirty-seven and neither engaged, espoused nor actively shagging several actresses.

So, in the rain, he arrived on her doorstep, but he did not knock straight away. First, he stood in the downpour long enough to make sure he looked bedraggled. A man who had made a considerable effort just to be there. And in his arms, in the manner of a baby rescued from the lake, he clutched a puppy, a brown-and-white King Charles spaniel that his chauffeur had that afternoon obtained at kennels. Around the dog's neck was a new collar, and through the collar was threaded a pink silk bow. Bracken stood long enough on the step to make sure the dog was shivering.

When Anna opened the door she was confronted with the pitiable sight. A sad and sodden Bracken, and a puppy – not Chumpers to be sure, but a tiny dog that might perhaps have been Chumpers' best friend or even a skinnier sibling – and both seeming in desperate need of affection and a home.

Irresistible.

He was in.

*　　*　　*

The apartment at 28 Chester Square was already ringing with screams and raucous laughter – early, even by the standards of Burgess's parties. His hospitality was notorious amongst both his friends and neighbours – his friends because he was a shameless collector of people and usually managed to cram into one room a most eclectic grouping, which stretched from Privy Counsellors and press men to male prostitutes and poets (including Auden and Spender), and which embraced multiple politicians, a few female professors and proselytizers of every hue. There was even the odd priest. Their only common denominator was their enjoyments, which by Burgess's strict decree had to be outrageous. It was this aspect that made these gatherings notorious to his neighbours, since inevitably these outrages ended up spilling through the front door and onto the landing where they would frequently dissolve into fights and tearful recriminations. Yet there were few complaints – at least, not directly – since whenever his neighbours knocked on his door they would be cowed by the combination of public figures and dishevelled drag artists who appeared behind his shoulder, and Burgess had the irritating habit of responding to their objections by simply laughing and inviting them in. Invariably they refused.

He would not, however, have invited strangers into his home this evening. In the sitting room the guests had started up a round of Christmas carols, led by a senior Minister, with words taken from a distinctly unauthorized version of the English hymnal, while in the other room an intense and distinctly irregular game of table tennis was in progress.

Burgess's new-found friend, Tom Driberg, was playing against a much longer-established companion, Edouard Pfeiffer, the *chef de cabinet* of the French Prime Minister, Daladier. They were using the dining table as a playing surface and a young delivery boy stretched naked across the table as the net.

The players began disputing a point, raucously demanding that Burgess decide the issue. A smell of singeing varnish came from the sideboard where the Frenchman's cigar smouldered, while from the other room came the sound of carol singers murdering the Three Wise Men one by one. Chaos reigned, yet, for once, Burgess found no appeal in it. Christmas had come, and for a few days the world would stand still. Men would promise each other peace on earth and, for a few hours, might even mean it. Burgess's Christianity was faded but still sufficient to believe in Hell, and to know that it had arrived, here on earth, waiting for them all across the Channel, come the New Year. He was afraid. His hands trembled because he was a lush, but most of all because he could not rid himself of his fear that they were damned, every one of them, and he above all others, that whatever the outcome of the war there would be no hiding place for him. He was doomed, whichever side won. He wanted to close his eyes, to stop the trembling, to believe in something again, apart from Hell. He desperately wanted his Christmas to last for ever.

So he emptied his glass and awarded the point to Driberg.

*　　*　　*

They counted the votes in West Perth that night. Chamberlain had won – by a slim margin, little more than a thousand votes, but it was enough. The Duchess was defeated.

The Times said the result would be a great encouragement to Mr Chamberlain, and hinted that it would come as a dire warning to all those who, like the Duchess, opposed him and his policies. They were on their own.

'Rejoice. Oh, rejoice! Blessed are the Peacemakers.'

The Prime Minister's metallic and echoing voice poured from the end of the phone and so loudly that Wilson held it away from his ear. He could almost sense the gleam in the old man's eye, a rekindling of that inner light which he had carried back from Munich and had worn through all those photographs, yet which in the long weeks since had been dulled by the exhaustion of events. He had lost weight, was in need of recuperation, so Mrs Chamberlain had taken him off to Chequers, his official country retreat, to recharge his batteries. That took longer nowadays.

Chequers was an ideal place for this purpose, a fine red-brick building of Tudor origins tucked away behind long avenues of Buckinghamshire beech. It was a hideaway, not a nerve centre. Indeed it was not a centre of any sort. It had only one telephone, which was regarded as an instrument of the Devil and had been hidden away in the pantry in order not to disturb the Prime Minister – even when he was needed. So Wilson had rung and rung, then rung some more, until in despair he had telephoned the local police constable in Princes Risborough, who had clambered on his bike and ridden through the snow to ask the Prime Minister if he'd be pleased to pick up the phone and 'take a call from Sir 'orace what's been trying to get 'old of 'im all day, sir'. Chamberlain had discovered the phone hiding under a pile of freshly starched table napkins.

Yet now his joy was unconfined. Never mind that the majority was so slim. Mind even less that it had been delivered by snow and storm and outright skulduggery, and mind not at all that it was one of his own colleagues, once a friend, who had been put to the sword. To the elderly Prime Minister it was a victory that seemed inspired by God and, like loaves and fishes, it could be made to go a very long way. He could feed the entire country on this, and in return it would be only right for him to claim the rewards of the peacemaker. His place in history, alongside Disraeli, Wellington, Gladstone. Why, alongside Moses, even, for had he not rescued his nation from the bondage of war? Delivered them from evil? How proud his father and Austen would have been. At last he could show them, show their memories, at least. Oh, but then there were the Churchills, the Attlees, the Edens, the Duff Coopers, the entire ungrateful mess of the vainglorious who had for so long been snapping at his heels. Yes, he'd show them, too, show them all in the new year, in 1939. His Year of Retribution.

Chamberlain slipped away from the pantry in excellent humour, wondering if there was any more of that excellent hock he had been sent by

Ribbentrop. He forgot to replace the receiver on the telephone. He was out of touch for another two days.

The Duchess cancelled her victory celebrations, went home to her ailing husband and spent the evening playing Beethoven sonatas on her piano. Her supporters evaporated into the Siberian night, their tears freezing to their faces.

The following day she received a telegram from a fellow MP, Josiah Wedgwood:

To Socrates they gave hemlock. Gracoleus they killed with sticks and stones. The greatest and best they crucified. Katharine Atholl can hold up her head in good company. Let the victors, when they come, when the forts of folly fall, find thy body by the wall.

Blenheim Palace, Monday 26 December.
Boxing Day. A Black Dog Day. One of those days that came to haunt Churchill and cast him into despair.

Churchill walked stiffly through the grounds that 'Capability' Brown had laid out two centuries earlier to mark the Battle of Blenheim. Brown had landscaped the grounds along the lines of the opposing forces that confronted each other that day; he wanted the memory of that great victory to endure as long as men walked these paths. And Churchill would never forget. Yet there would be no gardens built, no great palaces erected, to commemorate the Meeting at Munich, not in England, at least, nor anywhere in unoccupied Europe. Looking back. He seemed to spend so much of his time looking back. Writing histories. Remembering great ancestors. What else could he do? No one would listen about tomorrow.

Churchill had been born here, at Blenheim. Prematurely, so his mother said, always in a hurry. Seven months after she had married. The palace was the ancestral home of his cousin and great companion, Sunny, the ninth Duke of Marlborough – a dull man, but family – and Churchill had returned to celebrate Christmas. He had also come to hide, to escape from the miseries of today by clinging to the memories of a glorious past that was, well, precisely that. Past. Out of time. Like him.

Churchill had never felt more alone. Clemmie was gone – had been gone for weeks – on a tour of the West Indies designed to restore her spirits and her health. She had recently stubbed her toe against the claw foot of an Empire table in Paris and become debilitated; she needed some time away from the difficulties she was forced to share with him at home. So off she had gone, accompanied by another of her outrageously expensive wardrobes, and was now relaxing beneath the Caribbean sun while he trod the damp, leaf-strewn grass of England. He missed her, needed her. She was the only one who came close to understanding, the only one on whom he could rely without question. Yet even she complained – about his impersonal telegrams, about the letters to her he dictated through others, demanding letters be written in his own hand. If only he had time! But he was out of time.

Her absence had at least allowed him to come to Blenheim to be with Sunny, his chum. Clemmie didn't see it that way – she and the Duke had fallen out over such a silly matter. When Anthony Eden had resigned as Foreign Secretary in protest at Chamberlain's policies she had written kindly to him on notepaper bearing the Blenheim crest. The Duke had objected, and Clemmie had immediately packed her suitcases and left, thereafter finding excuses to see as little of Sunny as she could. So senseless, Churchill mused, to mix personalities and politics, to loathe someone for their rotten opinions rather than their rotted heart. Yet it was a lesson he thought Randolph might never learn. Churchill had arrived at Blenheim with his twenty-seven-year-old son and his youngest daughter, Mary, to be greeted by a host of relatives and close friends, and already Randolph had fallen out with many. It was becoming a habit. Randolph would present himself for dinner, drink, eat, drink much more, then argue and spread insults like salt upon a wine stain. A tongue that hadn't yet understood the difference between irony and pure acid. And the habit had extended to breakfast – Sunny had been forced to order him from the table that morning after he had called another guest 'an inexcusable idiot' for suggesting that holidays in Tuscany were far more pleasurable since Mussolini had sorted out the trains. Randolph playing with his tongue was like a toddler discovering a loaded revolver in the middle of a playground.

And Randolph had asked for another loan. A loan that Churchill, in all honesty, could not afford. The boy would get it, nonetheless. Just as Clemmie had acquired another new wardrobe and Chartwell would gain a new cottage in the grounds. There never seemed to be enough money. He had earned a fortune – several fortunes – and always spent a penny more. He was working tirelessly on his literary ventures, working double shifts, dictating until two or three in the morning, surrounded by secretaries and scurrying research assistants. He was working on the 'English-Speaking Peoples', for which he had been paid the enormous advance of twenty thousand pounds. But that had been in 1933. The money had long since disappeared. Only the work remained.

And Beaverbrook had cancelled his contract with the *Evening Standard*. 'Winston, every time you write about your goddamned war, a hundred thousand of my readers crap themselves and head for the hills.' The contract had been replaced by one with the *Daily Telegraph*, but the money was less. Yet it was the setting aside of friendship that Churchill mourned, as much as the money. Beaverbrook and he had sat together in the Cabinet of Lloyd George, had conspired and cajoled and caroused and got drunk together. Then they would argue. He and Max fell in and out of friendship as frequently as Max clambered in and out of a young woman's bed, and at the moment he was sleeping with appeasers. One day, Churchill felt, Max would finish with them, as he always did, and come back to him.

There were fewer friends this year, fewer than ever. The invitations to dinner were less frequent, requests to speak in a colleague's constituency had all but dried up. A sense of formality rather than friendship surrounded his dealings, even with those like Eden and Duff Cooper and Leo Amery who had sat beside him in protest and abstained on the Munich vote. It was as though they sensed he was a drowning man and feared death by association.

There were some who still supported him, or at least his cause, but they were about as reliable as sunshine in spring. Harold Macmillan rushed around babbling wildly about leaving the party every time he found Boothby in bed with his wife. Not that Macmillan any longer found it impossible to live with his wife's infidelity, but it seemed to provoke in him a need to find other outlets for proving his virility. Boothby himself had been banned from Chartwell by Clemmie for an outburst at the dining table which had concluded in him upsetting an entire decanter and describing Nancy Astor as 'nothing but a fucked-up little fart-catcher'. Clemmie was scarcely a shrew, yet she had scrupulously high standards which allowed forgiveness only for Winston. Bracken, too, was barely tolerated by Clemmie. She had no time for his inventions and fantasies. 'Brendan,' she had once remarked, deliberately unkindly, 'is the type of man for whom two and two make twenty-two.' She endured him only for his dogged loyalty to her husband. Yet even Brendan had begun acting queerly, strangely distracted. All queer folk, these elusive allies.

Churchill passed beneath the towering, bare elms that stood like sentinels by the bridge, disturbing the crows, who flapped away, crying in annoyance. His knees ached in the damp air that clung around the roots of these great trees. Behind him the baroque splendours of the palace had almost disappeared from view, a memorial to times past and ancient victories which now lay hidden in the grey English mist. Yet he felt so comfortable here, like an old relic who had at last found his place. He had already lived twenty years longer than his own father, longer than his uncle, the seventh Duke, longer perhaps than was due to him. Mouldering leaves clung to the end of his walking stick; death seemed to surround him. He had just read in the newspapers of the death of Sidney Peel, a man who had courted Clemmie and almost won her hand. Decent fellow, but his decencies hadn't saved him. So many of those Churchill had known when he was young were dying now, and he himself had reached that age of uselessness when old men run out of time. He prayed he might live as long as the squabbling crows, and die before his faculties decayed and grew dark.

He wrapped the scarf more firmly around his neck and continued on his lonely walk by the shores of the lake. The rest of the company was off hunting, had tried to insist he join them, but today he had no joy in it. Perhaps the chase would exhaust Randolph and the evening would be one of civilized conversation around the dinner table, but usually the excitement only fired him up. By the lake the mists grew thicker, closed in around him. Trees and shrubs appeared like ghosts, until out from the shadows emerged a figure clad in a dark cloak that to his surprise he thought was Kitty Atholl. But it was only a momentary mistake. Soon he realized it was nothing other than Guilt, disguised as a beech tree.

Oh, but he could have made the difference. To lose the seat, to lose all they had fought for, for a thousand votes. Votes which he could undoubtedly have delivered, had he gone, and taken others with him. Had he fallen so far – was he so old, so distracted, so worn out that his entire life's work could have been pushed aside for a half-hour meeting with a bank clerk? He had saved Chartwell, for a while, but what would that be worth if what he feared and what Kitty had fought against came to pass? Nothing but ashes. At times Churchill disliked himself very much. Kitty had offered no recriminations, had died with great dignity, and alone. It only made Churchill feel worse.

His path led him upwards, through the clinging mists to a high point above the lake where stood a small temple in the Greek style dedicated to the goddess Diana. It was here, on the bench thirty years before, that he had proposed to Clementine. She had been in a disdainful mood that day. He had lingered in bed and she had been on the point of packing her bags and leaving. Then they had walked and been caught by a shower of rain, and taken shelter in the temple. There, on the bench on which he was now sitting, he had asked her to marry him and to put up with all his impossible ways. 'Most of them,' she had replied, 'so long as you put up with an equal number of mine.' So it had begun, and continued. It would be a good end, whiling away their final days with each other.

Except . . .

Except that every time he looked ahead, he saw anguish walking arm-in-arm with disaster, and they would not leave him alone to die a graceful death. Hitler attacked him personally and viciously in the

German press, called him a scheming warmonger and a drunkard, while Chamberlain treated him scarcely any better. It was difficult at times to know who posed the greater danger, the mad little Austrian who screamed and spat, or a British leader who sang his songs of silence. 'Do not tie my hands,' the Prime Minister had pleaded to Parliament, justifying his negotiations with Hitler over Europe. *Monstrous idiot.* Didn't he realize that soon the rope would be knotted not for his hands but for his neck? For all their necks?

Churchill knew he was a stubborn old man, and that was an end to it. And yet a beginning, too, perhaps. For besides being obstinate he was also eloquent – those were words that young Burgess had used about him, the day after Munich – and these troubled days were a time for eloquence rather than Chamberlain's songs of silence. He could continue to speak out, to persist. Warn of the dangers in Europe and fight for the right of Britons to be free and fickle, and not just vassals. It might mean tearing his party apart, but what did that matter when the country itself was on the brink of being torn apart? Country before party, always, there was no middle way.

They could bury him with his conscience, at least, and maybe sooner than he cared for. He had been summoned to appear before the executive of his Epping constituency – *to explain himself and his recent positions,* in the words of the peremptory letter. To defend himself against charges of disloyalty, to show why he should not be put aside in the same manner they had cast aside poor Kitty, to argue that loyalty to a party and a misguided leader was not the highest duty of a politician. After all, what was loyalty? A word, an excuse, a shield behind which cowards hid their own nakedness. The party didn't need loyalty, it was suffocated in the stuff, what it needed so desperately was the fresh air of imagination and leadership.

He had received a Christmas card from young Burgess, a hand-drawn cartoon which was crude but which displayed considerable talent. And insight – it had shown the entire Cabinet standing in a circle with their heads embedded firmly up the next man's backside, and although their heads weren't visible, most of the characters were easily recognizable. The figure at the front had a wing collar and was clutching an old umbrella. The cartoon was entitled simply: 'Leadership'. A man of considerable imagination, was young Burgess.

So . . .

He didn't really have a choice. He must fight. Fight on. Then fight some more. Continue to fight until he had neither breath nor words left within him. For what else could he do? It was his nature.

PART TWO

An End to Illusions

EIGHT

(Daily Express, Monday 2 January 1939)

THIS IS WHY YOU CAN SLEEP SOUNDLY IN 1939

There will be no great war in Europe in 1939.

There is nothing in our present situation which affords any ground to suppose that an upheaval can, or must, come.

Nothing is here today that we have not experienced over and over again in our history – at moments when we stood on the threshold of an era of peace.

What is it that makes the prophets of evil quake in their shoes?

They see dictators in Europe. There have always been dictators in Europe. It is the natural form of government for many countries in that continent.

They see rearmament going on at high speed.

We have always had spells of that often before in this island. We have shied at all sorts of fears – and phantom fears . . .

The peddlers of nightmare should pay a little more heed to British history and a little less to their own nerves. They might also consider the following facts in the world today.   .

Britain grows more formidable. Mr Chamberlain tells us that. She is stronger in Europe. When the Singapore base is ready this year, she will be stronger in Asia . . .

There was a danger that there might be a great war over Czecho-Slovakia. If France had kept her word. If Britain had backed France in doing so. All the makings of a cataclysm.

But Czecho-Slovakia is over and done with.

Look forward, then, to a year in which the bulwarks against a general war will grow in strength. Remember that war, now too costly for little States, is also growing more and more impossible for great Powers. The destruction is too great. And the people know it.

Believe in peace – and insist that Britain shall be strong in order to buttress your belief!

Miss Susan Graham examined the newspaper that lay spread out on the floor in front of her with an expression of restrained contempt. The crusader on the masthead of the *Express* had a raised sword and jutting jaw, yet he seemed faintly absurd, almost comic, for his eyes were sightless and he had his back against an advertising box. He seemed to be defending a gargling solution for sore throats.

Instinctively she smoothed out a crease across the newsprint. Hers was a neat and orderly life – as was expected of a postmistress in the sleepy seaside town of Bournemouth – a life spent on behalf of the community, helping others, not indulging her own feelings. Leave that to the French just across the Channel. So she had smiled and never wavered during the hectic weeks before Christmas as an unprecedented flood of letters and cards had poured across her counter. The whole town seemed to have been engaged in mass celebration, an outpouring of relief – no war! – so they did what the British did best. They queued. Queued to take money out of their savings accounts, queued to send telegrams, queued some more to buy postal orders for gifts and stamps with which to send them, then queued in search of string and brown paper for their parcels. The whole of Bournemouth seemed to have formed a perpetual line across her doorstep, yet she had coped, as she always did, and smiled at their expressions of joy and deliverance. Not that Sue believed a word of it. Shouldn't trust a German, not after what they did last time, particularly what they had done to her dad, a postman himself who had come back from the mud and gas of Passchendaele with half a lung and even less of a life. He hadn't complained – well, not much, just wheezed a lot. Sue didn't complain much either, just got on with things, and even as a teenager had taken charge of the post office, served the customers and cared for her dad. Not much time for anything else, until he died, by which time it all seemed a little late. She was thirty-three, had just noticed a grey streak in the hair that she kept swept back in an unfashionable bun, and was as far back on the shelf as a bundle of last year's Christmas cards.

Sue was not the excitable type. Perhaps that was

why she knew the talk of peace was – what would her father have said? – 'a load of bloody old cobblers'. Took two to make a peace, only one to make a war, everybody knew that. Particularly Dr Stern and his wife. They were Jews who had fled from Vienna and hadn't stopped running until they'd arrived in Eastcliffe. Pleasant couple, quiet. He tried to get on with his work as a family doctor as best he could, although truth be told a lot of people weren't too happy about taking their clothes off in front of a Jew, but he was cheap. He didn't insist on living well, he was simply grateful for the chance to live in any condition. Yet the doctor's wife had never quite completed the journey. Her heart and mind were still back home in Austria and her nerves had been lost somewhere on the journey. She rarely opened the door, even for the post, her eyes darting, filled with anxiety, and Sue hadn't seen her at all since the night the synagogues had been torched. Dr Stern had explained that they hadn't heard from her mother or her sister who were still back in Vienna – at least, that's where they hoped they still were. They kept hearing terrible things about a place called Dachau.

But Mr Chamberlain and the *Daily Express* didn't seem to have heard about Dachau. Only a few miles outside Munich, so Dr Stern said, and Mr Chamberlain had been to Munich. But like Mrs Stern, he seemed to have lost something on the journey back.

Sue Graham was used to coping on her own, and didn't make a fuss. She'd cope with Harry Hun, too, if it came to that, and it probably would. In the meantime she would make a few preparations. Take out one of the flower beds – the roses, they were always so difficult in the salt winds – and plant more vegetables in the garden. Preserve a little more of the autumn fruits. And, just for tonight, she would light a fire to keep out the chill that was blowing from across the Channel and into her bedroom.

She got down on her knees and rolled the pages of the *Daily Express* into long spills, which she folded neatly and settled in the grate beneath a few sticks of kindling and a sprinkling of coal. It took her two attempts and half the newspaper before the fire caught – the coal was damp – but at last her bedroom began to warm. That was about the only bit the *Daily Express* had got right. She would sleep soundly, for tonight.

Burgess clung to the darkness, finding shadows, wrapping them around him like a cloak. He was following Mac, at a distance, and was anxious not to be seen.

He had to find out who Mac's informant was. The last batch of contents from Sam Hoare's wastepaper bin had contained a note from Max Beaverbrook that had obviously been accompanied by a cheque – 'a small contribution from an ample pocket' – with the suggestion that the note should not be kept. The sack of rubbish had also contained a sheet of blotting paper on which was imprinted an almost complete replica of a letter from the Home Secretary to the Prime Minister suggesting Beaverbrook should be brought back into Government – 'possibly as Min. of

Agriculture?' The material was so good it made him nervous. Was he being set up? Duped? He had to get nearer the source.

So he had followed Mac for several evenings. He was scarcely a trained pursuer but Mac proved to be a creature of hopeless habit. Every evening he would walk back to his room in Kensington, using the same path across Hyde Park, the same route through the maze of streets in Notting Hill, never tarrying, never stopping to peer in a shop window, never taking time off for a quick pint, the same steady, stubborn step, as though he had established a pattern to his life that he could no more vary than a monk could rewrite the Ten Commandments. But habit was his undoing, for this evening he had emerged from Trumper's carrying a canvas bag – *the* bag, the one that always arrived with the rubbish – and instead of setting off across Hyde Park had turned for the Underground station. He had taken the Tube to Chigwell in Epping, where he disembarked and began walking once again with that steady, stubborn pace. Burgess followed, at a distance, shoulders hunched, feeling faintly ludicrous, until they had reached a small, poorly lit street of terraced Victorian red-bricks. Mac had knocked on one of the doors and stood for a moment bathed in a pool of light before entering with the familiarity of a man who was amongst friends.

Burgess stood for a while in the shadows at the end of the street, his hand cupped around a burning cigarette, while he examined the house. Poor neighbourhood, peeling paint, entirely unexceptional, apart from a children's tricycle that lay abandoned in the rug-sized front garden. So there were children. And he had the address. The electoral register should provide the name of the occupant. The mystery was beginning to unravel. Perhaps next week he would follow Mac's friend to ensure that she was, indeed, a cleaner at Sam Hoare's home. Three times a week, Mac had said. Shouldn't be too difficult. He took a swig from a quarter-bottle of Irish he carried in his raincoat pocket. He had difficulty replacing the top. His left and right hands seemed to be having a difference of opinion, arguing amongst themselves until they began trembling in frustration. At this rate he'd never get the top back on the bottle, so he decided to empty it. Easier that way.

Then Burgess began laughing, mocking himself quietly amongst the shadows, until tears began to roll. What a ridiculous life he led. That morning he'd had breakfast at the Ritz with a senior member of the Labour Party, which had been arranged to discuss whether appeasement was a moral imperative or a doormat for dictators. Instead they'd ended up agreeing to discuss their own personal morality later that week at the Mandrake Club. Lunch had been taken at the home of Rozsika Rothschild – Burgess had been to university with her son, Victor, and she had become so impressed with Burgess's grasp of international affairs that she paid him a retainer to act as her informal investment consultant. 'Put your money into war,' he had advised over the smoked salmon. 'Take everything out of Europe and invest it in Rolls-Royce and General Motors.' She had thought the analysis penetrating and the advice shrewd, but she would not follow it. 'I have half my family in Europe, Guy,' she had explained. 'It would

213

be like turning my back on them and abandoning them to the terror.' He had left her polishing silver photo frames with a handkerchief damp with tears.

And now this. Scurrying around the back streets of London with his hat pulled low over his head, trying to lead a ridiculous double life when it was apparent to everyone that he couldn't even organize a single life properly. Hunting others – they said he was good at it, one of the best, but if that were so, why did he so often feel that he was the one being hunted? It was absurd. That's why he had to laugh at himself, otherwise he might start taking it all too seriously and end his days as messed-up as old Mac. That's why he had to drink, too. Go down with the whiskey rather than all the worries and woe. As for the other . . . Well, no one could accuse him of waving his dick in the dark. He was an outrageous, insatiable, out-and-out queer, the sort of person others expected to skulk around on street corners, and with the kind of habits few cared to investigate too closely. That's only Guy, they would say, you know what he's like. Then they would move on quickly to something else. No one wanted to get too close. It suited him down to the ground.

A brilliant Suffolk morning. Cold, with a sun that sparkled off the flat, frosty landscape. The noises of beaters in the woods carried on the air and filled it with expectation. The killing time had come.

Suddenly the wood erupted in an explosion of indignation and feathers. They flew low and in great numbers, wave after wave of them, mostly pheasant but also French partridge, English partridge, too, although it had been a bad year for the English bird. The damp autumn and cold winter had reduced their number dramatically. After breakfast the head keeper, Turner, had ridden up and down in front of the shooters on his pony, like a general issuing his final orders before the battle. 'Me Lords – and those wanting to be – we ain't be shooting no English partridge today. On account of the fact that there ain't be enough of 'em. Plenty of the foreign type, and pheasant, if you be quick and have woked yoursel's up after last night's fodder. But you leave my English birds alone, and my beaters too, or you answer to me.' He was an original, was Turner, a life form considerably rarer than any partridge and one in far greater danger of extinction. The game birds might struggle through what was waiting for them, but not his kind. When the great estates had been bankrupted and broken up, as they would be, the Turners of this world would be gone for ever.

Chamberlain stood on his peg, a small, gangling figure, narrow shoulders, long arms, his moustache as ever at the droop, his three-piece Harris tweed suit firmly buttoned. His gun was up, his shoulders swivelling. A crack of gunfire, the wooden stock digging into his shoulder. A high angled blast of shot, right and left. It brought down two hen pheasants. They hit the ground with considerable force only yards from his feet. First blood.

And still they kept coming. Reload. Another savage blast of the shotgun. When the smoke had cleared, he looked down at the misshapen and brilliantly coloured remains of a cock pheasant.

So it went on. Feet steady, gun up, swing the shoulders. Kill. Reload. Again! Both barrels. One bird missed, another dying in a graceful arc that ended in a ball of feathers bouncing off the frozen soil. New gun, fresh prey, more bloody feathers.

'All in all it's what I'd call a splendid start to the new year. Don't you think so, Neville?'

Sam Hoare, the Home Secretary, had the peg next to his Prime Minister. Now he approached, holding out a hip flask which they shared as they walked, guns broken, to the next beat.

'A year of achievement, Sam, which will deliver unto us all those things the people need. New homes, new hospitals. A Government committed to the highest moral standards.' Chamberlain's mood was crisp, like the air.

'Sounds like the first draft of an election manifesto.'

'Confusion to the enemy, eh?'

'You seemed to have your eye in early. Didn't see much get past you.'

'You know how I did it, Sam? Know the secret, do you?'

'Tell me!'

'You imagine that the bird in front, the plump one, is Winston. And the one immediately behind and up his arse is Duffie Cooper. I find it inspirational. Never miss!'

The Prime Minister was warming to his task as they walked across the frozen fen, and soon he had unwrapped the scarf which wound in a double loop around his neck. He took another dive into the proffered hip flask.

'Arms, arms and more arms, that's all Winston understands. But unemployment's up again this month. Scarcely the time to be throwing away our budget on bullets.'

'I fear the French may take a different view.'

'How so?'

'They'll demand that we build up the army, Neville. So we can support them if they're attacked. And if we refuse, they'll accuse us of being perfidious allies and hiding across the Channel behind our navy and air force.'

'The French, Sam, the French?' Chamberlain's thin voice rose in indignation. 'Is His Majesty's Government really to build its strategic policy upon the complaints of a nation which has lost every war it's fought in two centuries?'

'They're first in the firing line, Neville. They won't understand if we don't rearm.'

'No, *they* may not understand – but the Italians will.' Chamberlain was shaking with passion. 'I'll make Mussolini understand, you see if I don't. Look, Sam, if we refuse to rattle the sabre, there'll be no need for them to do so, either. I persuade the Duce, he convinces Herr Hitler of the same thing. Result – peace. I can do it, Sam, I know I can. Everyone will be happy.'

'Except Winston, don't you think?'

The eyes turned to steel beneath the dark brows. 'I think as little as possible about that man. Sometimes in politics it's a mistake to think too much. Distracts you from guarding your back.' Chamberlain stepped out purposefully, his boots crunching through the frost, as though crushing bugs. 'And I will not be distracted by anyone. If that means Winston is left bleating in the wilderness, then it's something I feel I shall be able to tolerate.'

'They're all on your side, Neville, the party, the people, even the King. Prayers are said for you in churches up and down the country. There's no need to worry about Winston.'

Chamberlain ran his fingers down the barrels of his gun, as though stroking a cat. 'New Year's resolution, Sam. Time to come out fighting. No more nonsense. Talking of which, I was reading something recently by a scribbler named Waller. One of Max's boys, I believe.'

'Think I know him. Young, irreverent, inquisitive little shit.'

'A piece he'd written about Signor Mussolini. Most unhelpful – would've got him locked up anywhere else in Europe. Abusing his freedom, I'd say.' Suddenly he stopped and turned to face his Home Secretary. 'You've got good relations with Max. Have a word with him, will you? Get him to call off young Waller, transfer him to the sports page. Better still, transfer him to Argentina. Permanently.'

'Hell, you've really got your eye in, Neville.'

'And the sooner the buggers realize that, the better.'

So morning flowed into lunch, then onward into the afternoon. It was as dusk was falling and the first stars appeared dimly in the fading-blue sky that the bag was counted. A total of 818 creatures, and more to come from the pick-up. With five very English and very dead partridges, found near the Home Secretary's peg. They were smuggled into the Prime

Minister's personal bag on the grounds that even Turner wouldn't dare tangle with God's personal representative on earth.

Over dinner Chamberlain expressed his complete satisfaction with the day's expedition. It was an excellent omen, he suggested. Not a single thing had fired back.

Her name was Marie-Noëlle, her age was certainly less than twenty and her naïveté was a delight for him to behold. A featherbrain that had just stepped out into the wind. A country girl, although until recently she'd scratched a precarious living around the garrets of Montmartre as an artists' model. She wanted to be an actress, she said, had an ambition to be dressed like a diva instead of taking her clothes off for a few francs an hour, so in search of her fortune she had thrown herself at London. That was how she'd met Joe Kennedy, during a party thrown by the French Embassy where her cousin was a lowly *fonctionnaire*.

As a seasoned film magnate, Kennedy had an eye for talent – at least, the sort of talent that got young girls bit-parts in B-movies. The hopeful, hungry eyes brimming with inexperience, the unblemished skin, the firmness of a body that had borne nothing but desire and almost excused her crime of being young, the beguiling curve of lips caught long before the age when they would wither and grow taut. To a man of similar age she would be seen as unique, full of feminine mysteries, an object for adoration or at least worthy of a long-sustained siege, but to one of

Kennedy's years and background she was no more than an excuse for dinner at a discreet country hotel near Windsor.

'The problem for France, you see, is that it's surrounded on three sides. Hitler on one side, Franco on the other and the ice creamers down here.' He arranged the cutlery and the vase of flowers to form an enclosure into which he placed her hand. The first touch. 'Where did you tell me your parents lived?'

'Alsace,' she whispered, pointing with a hesitant and totally unwrinkled finger to an imaginary farmhouse somewhere beneath the shadow of her wine glass, the nail circling and leaving a barely visible trace on the linen cloth.

'Pity. No wonder they're concerned.'

'We 'ave the Maginot Line,' she announced, her chin raised, her eyes fluttering in defiance.

'And Hitler has ten thousand brand-new bombers that'll scoot over your Maginot Line like ducks on a frozen pond.' He poured her more champagne. 'I shouldn't say this, Marie-Noëlle – hell, I'm supposed to be a diplomat, but at times I have to be a man, too. You understand that?'

Her lips pursed in acknowledgement.

'And I burn up inside when I think about the English, standing in their puddles and looking down their goddamned noses at the rest of us. Get up and fight, they're always telling the French, get at 'em! Meanwhile they're scratching their feet by their fire this side of the Channel knowing it's no risk to them. Hundreds of thousands of French like your own family at risk, while the English hunt foxes and get

220

young boys to warm up their toilet seats. Jesus H. Christ, what a miserable damn country this can be!'

Her eyes flared in concern. 'So what will 'appen, Joe?' The words emerged stumbling with emotion, her accent all too obvious – delightful across the crackle of the log fire, but this one had no chance outside the silent movies.

'If we can keep the peace – nothing.' He dismissed it with a wave and went for his glass.

'But what if . . .'

'If the Brits screw up, if they start a war and fight it on French soil . . .' – he reached across and wrapped her hand in both of his – 'then France will be caught like a bear in a trap and squeezed until the only thing that comes out will be tears.'

Brutal, but it was the only way he knew. He'd never been a great romancer – it wasn't the fashion on the East Side. Anyhow, he'd never needed it. He had wealth beyond normal avarice and powers that made most men tremble at the knee, and seemed to work with most women, too. Yet some women were so young, so foreign, so unfocused, that they never quite understood how lucky they were. They required a little encouragement. To be deprived of their sense of comfort and security, stripped bare until they jumped straight into his bed for fear of freezing. Marie-Noëlle's eyes had already grown wide with despair, and she was beginning to shiver. She was still holding his hand.

'Hell, after the last time you'd have thought the Brits might have learned their lesson. All those battles, all that blood . . .' She gripped his hand ever more tightly. 'But no need for you to worry, Marie-Noëlle. I can

221

help you, if you want to stay in London. Maybe fix you up with a film part.'

'But I do worry.' She spoke in short sentences, rarely more than a handful of words, often not finishing the thought. Perhaps because she had no thoughts, at least none more complicated than could be contained in a few simple words.

'You care for your family a great deal. That's good. Family's *good*,' he offered, staring at her breasts. 'You must be lonely, so far away from them.'

'You are very understanding, Joe.'

'Because I know what it's like. I get lonely, too.'

'You?'

'Sure. Sometimes feels like I'm the only one fighting the fight. For peace, that is. I care very deeply about peace, Marie-Noëlle. I want the ordinary people of Europe to have the chance to live, be at peace with each other. To put aside the old divisions. One family, just like the US of A, not for ever at each other's throats. Nothing wrong with pouring a little new wine into the old bottles, if you know what I mean.' The delivery was faultless – and why not? It was exactly the same script he had delivered to the Foreign Press Association lunch the previous week.

'Oh, Joe, that would be so wonderful . . .'

'That's why I'm always telling Mr Chamberlain. Jump in a plane, not down their throats. That's why I told him – go to Munich, go to Mussolini.'

'You told him that?'

'Make yourself a hero, I said. But make sure we get peace.'

He leaned forward, his voice rising, as did her

breasts beneath the cotton dress, as though in admiration.

'But it sure does get lonely at times.'

'You cannot be lonely. You are a great diplomat, you 'ave so many friends . . .'

'Not friends I can talk to. They're always looking for the angle, wanting me to talk the Prime Minister into this or that, or telling me I should become President after Roosevelt.'

Breathless – 'You would be a magnificent President.'

'I agree.' He flashed a smile and an expensive Swiss wristwatch as he pushed his glasses back up his nose. 'But sometimes all I want to do is to run away and hide, like here, where nobody knows me.'

'I am lonely, too. So far away from my family.'

'I guessed that. Why else would you come out to dine with an old crock like me?'

'But you are so fit . . .'

'I work out a little.'

'You are so active and virile for an ambassador.'

'Well . . .'

'I think you are – wonderful.' The last syllable was carried on a rush of sweet Latin air, the youthful lips puckered to force out the sound, reaching to him. Oh, Mother Mary, he was in, he was in!

He gazed once more, transfixed by the imprint of nipple under cotton, rosebuds on a dewy morning in spring. She smiled back, ran her tongue gently around her lips, nothing excessively provocative, just enough to drag his eyes back from the molestation of her body. She had him – or soon would. She'd almost starved since she'd arrived in this wet and wretched country, living in a borrowed room at her cousin's, down to her last respectable dress. Now she was about to give a man of power and wealth the most cock-cracking night of his life. Another two hours teasing and, judging by the man, about two minutes copulating. If she played this right, she'd end up with an entire new wardrobe hung up in her own apartment in a discreet central area of London not too far from the American Embassy, and have access to the sort of bubbling social circle that her pathetic little cousin could never provide. Yes, as far as she was concerned, the New World could come and rescue the Old any time it wanted.

The trip was a masterpiece of public relations. A Roman triumph. Everywhere they went, Chamberlain and his Foreign Secretary were greeted with acclaim and waving handkerchiefs. The crowds gathered everywhere, in streets, at country level crossings, roosting in trees and at open windows. They besieged Chamberlain as he went into the Vatican, where the Pope praised him for his efforts to secure peace. Mussolini echoed that praise and on every side the people sang the chorus.

Yet Chamberlain did not understand dictatorships. He did not appreciate that crowds gather only with the Party's permission, and usually at the Party's insistence, that they were well paid for their work and would proceed directly from an outpouring of orchestrated adulation to the nearest bar. Neither did the travelling British press unlock the mystery. They were spun and spiralled until they became giddy and could see nothing other than what was presented to them. They were corralled in the same luxury hotel, provided with cars, ferried through an itinerary so laden with hospitality that it kept them either occupied or inebriated, offered visits to the opera, to the Palazzo Venezia, to any number of archaeological excavations, and all in the company of youthful interpreters who quickly became known as the 'teeth and tits' brigade on account of their readiness to flash both.

So the press had a good time, and said it was a triumph. And, of course, the Prime Minister himself said it was a triumph. Extraordinarily, however, he also seemed to *believe* what he was saying. Reporting back to his Cabinet colleagues, he spoke of the personal bond of friendship he felt he had been able to establish with Il Duce, although he admitted to some frustration in the fact he had been unable to wean the Italian leader away from his unambiguous support for Herr Hitler. Musso and Adolf were still the closest chums. The Cabinet minutes reported Chamberlain as saying that 'at the time he had been somewhat disappointed at this attitude, but on reflection he thought that it reflected credit in Signor Mussolini's character'. Of course, splendid man, just the sort you wanted to see your sister bring home.

Elsewhere it was business as usual. The day the British Prime Minister left for Rome on his high moral crusade was also the day Churchill was to answer the summons of his constituency executive committee. Ball had left nothing to chance. On that same day Churchill received a large envelope which contained no letter, no note, only a cartoon. It was unmistakably in the style of Guy Burgess.

It showed a diminutive and pinned-sleeve figure of Lord Halifax standing on a reviewing rostrum beside Neville Chamberlain. The Foreign Secretary wore a bowler hat and the Prime Minister a wing-collar and a worried smile. Past the rostrum were marching the goose-stepping and heavily armed hordes of the Italian dictator, whom Chamberlain saluted with a furled umbrella, on top of which perched a threadbare dove.

Beneath the picture ran the caption: 'The One-Armed and the Completely Bloody 'Armless'.

St Valentine was the sort of person her dear and departed father would have called 'an irritating old sod'. How she had frowned at the language, scolding him for his frequent departures from decency. But how much she would have given in the long and lonely years since to hear him cussing just one more time. Anyway, right now Sue Graham was inclined to agree with her dad. St Valentine – or at least his representative here on earth – was intensely irri-tating. He had upset her entire day's system by leaving one red rose at the counter of the post office. At first she had tried to persuade herself that it had been left by accident, that someone would be back in five minutes to reclaim it, but five minutes had dragged into half an hour, and anyway its stem had been woven into the counter's protective wire mesh in an act that was unmistakably deliberate. She couldn't think who it might be. She ransacked her mind for the names and faces of those who had been through her post office that morning, but they all turned out to be, in the words of the dear departed, 'an unlikely bunch of buggers'.

Someone was making fun of her. Yet the impostor had succeeded in rousing her, not only with irritation but also with curiosity – just in case. She hadn't been out with one man on his own for – well, she couldn't remember – yes she could, Harry Coxall, that was it, and he'd only done it as a wager with his friends at the pub to see if he could get five new dates in a week. It wasn't that she was unattractive, but Bournemouth was a quiet community where people came to sleep, to rest, and eventually to die – not to mate. They went to London for that, and she hadn't been to London in five years. 'Harwich for the Continent,' ran the line, 'and Bournemouth for the Incontinent.' So she wasn't used to red roses. Must be another one of Harry Coxall's little jokes. She'd have to start feeding his newspapers to his dog, just like she'd done last time.

It was only ten minutes to closing. Last-minute rush to catch the post, some schoolchildren tussling over a bag of sweets, a man in a raincoat taking for ever to decide which size of envelope to buy, a neighbour from down the road buying a savings certificate for her grandson. The shop was nearly empty when at last the man in the raincoat decided on his purchase. She knew him vaguely: tall, aquiline nose, flecks of grey and a scar on his right cheek that lifted the lip and gave him a perpetual smile which, happily, was also reflected in his eyes. He'd been in several times before but had never mentioned his name.

A newcomer, perhaps, whom she remembered particularly because he'd bought a stamp for an envelope addressed to the Right Honourable Winston S. Churchill, MP, everything spelled out formally and in a neat, strong copperplate. About forty, she reckoned. And he was standing awkwardly by the counter, his smile on the wobble.

'Think I ought to apologize, like,' he said in a distinctive Midlands accent, 'fer wasting your time. I don't particularly want an envelope. Got dozens at home.'

'Then . . .'

'I left you a rose this morning. Hope you didn't mind, but – I'd noticed ye've been digging up your rose bed at back. Wondered whether you had black spot or something. Thought you might be in need of – reinforcements?'

'I thought it was a joke.'

'Should've brought you an entire bush, of course, to replace the ones that have gone. But roses are so hard to find –'

'On Valentine's Day.'

'Precisely.'

His smile was returning, she thought he might be mocking her. In return she offered him an expression which reminded him of his schoolmistress after he'd played truant and offered her a sick note which had the wrong date and misspelled 'stomach ache' and 'excuse'. In those days he'd spelt everything with a 'k'.

'But you don't know me.'

'Well, I do, sort of. Know you're competent and organized – frighteningly so, if truth be told.

228

Frightens the 'ell out of me. I'm such a disaster area. My place looks like the trenches at Ypres.'

'Before or after the attack?'

'Didn't make much difference, those trenches were a mess from the moment we'd dug 'em. I was a sergeant. Staffordshire Regiment. Solicitor's clerk now. Jerry White's the name. Anyways, I know you're patient – I've seen you with the schoolkids. I'd have murdered the little perishers while all you do is scold 'em and give 'em an extra half ounce of bull's-eyes. You read newspapers – counts as an intellectual, that does, where I come from. And you love flowers – I'm sorry, got to ask. Why are you digging up those lovely roses?'

'I'm planting more sprouts. And some runner beans and potatoes. For the war.'

'Of course. How sensible.' She was sure now that he was mocking her. 'Anyhow you looked – er, on your own, like. Is that the right term? Me too. Widower. Wanted to ask you out but I haven't the slightest idea where to start. Out of practice. Been in several times, bought more stamps than I'm likely to need in a month, and enough balls of string to get Theseus out of his maze a dozen times over. I've purchased newspapers I've never read and even half a pound of sherbet lemons. But I *hate* them. Never found a chance to talk to you, you're always busy, so thought I'd leave a rose. But of course it's supposed to be anonymous. Bloody silly, if you ask me – how the heck am I supposed to ask you out if you don't even know who I am? Which is why I thought I'd come back, like. And make a fool of myself. Think I'm doing rather well in that regard.'

Perhaps after all he was mocking only himself. 'You wanted to ask me out?'

'That's right.'

'Why?'

He gave her a look of utter disbelief. 'Daftest question I've heard all day. And from a pretty girl like you.' So, he was blunt. Just like the dear departed. 'Can I ask you a daft question in return?' he ventured.

'Go ahead. Two minutes left before closing. They're all yours.'

'Any chance of you accepting the rest of 'em?' From beneath his mackintosh he pulled out a bunch of red roses. She knew there would be eleven. 'Because walking around with these thorny little buggers under my coat is killing me.'

On Valentine's Day 1939, the Leader of the Thousand-Year Reich gave himself a present that was rather more substantial than flowers. He launched the *Bismarck*, the largest battleship ever to have been built in Germany. It had eight 15-inch and twelve 5.9-inch guns, triple propellers and double rudders. It was to cause mayhem in the North Atlantic and would sink the pride of the British fleet, HMS *Hood*, with a single shell. But, in the course of things, it was to prove far less significant than twelve red and very English roses.

'There you are, Dickie. Snifter?'

'Don't mind if I do, Ian. Feeling a bit rattled, to

tell you the truth.' He sank dolefully into the cracked leather of the Smoking Room.

'Yes. Heard you were near that IRA bomb in Leicester Square last night. Ears must still be ringing.'

'No, not that. It's Their Lordships. Our Noble Knob-Heads. You'll never guess what they've been debating.'

Ian looked miffed. He didn't care for puzzles.

'Bastardy,' Dickie continued.

'I beg your pardon?'

'They're debating a Bastardy Bill. Which'll insist on blood tests in the case of disputed paternity.'

'My God, Dickie . . .'

'Yes, can you imagine it? More pricks in us than the madam of a Nairobi knocking shop.'

'They start testing for bloodlines amongst their Lordships and there's no telling what they'd find. Know for a fact that old Buffy's from the wrong side of the potting shed. His ma was a notorious dick-switcher.'

'Not to mention the Royal Family.'

'Precisely. How is the Duchess?'

'Writhing in hell, I hope.'

'Always puzzled me, Dickie, why they insist on having the Home Secretary present at the birth of a royal heir. Supposed to guard against foul play. But you just think about it. Damn-all point being present at the birth. They really ought to be there at the conception.'

'From what I hear, old Sam Hoare's been present at too many conceptions for his own good.'

'Which reminds me – where are those bloody drinks?' He waved once more for a steward.

'You think there will be war then, Ian?'

'Old Mother Chaos? She's come knocking on everyone else's door. Manchuria, Abyssinia, Spain, Czechoslovakia. Now the Arabs and Jews running all over Palestine taking pot-shots at each other. Makes me nervous at times, can't help admitting.'

'But Hitler's promised, given us firm undertakings.'

'His firm undertakings are a little like a work of modern art. Seem to shift every time you look at 'em.'

'Everything's so uncertain. Can't even take a walk through the centre of bloody London without the IRA chucking a bomb at you.'

'What were you doing in Leicester Square anyway?'

A sniff of discomfort.

'Ah, don't tell me – short cut to Soho?'

'What else's a chap supposed to do? Wife's on the warpath again. Caught me canvassing after hours and has cut off the conjugals. Asked me to spend a little less time with the family.'

'Never mind, Dickie. She'll get over it. Always has done before.'

'She goes on about loyalty as though she were the bloody Chief Whip.'

'You'd listen to the Chief Whip.'

'Have to. Don't fancy going the same way as old Kitty. Even Winston's in trouble in Epping, so I hear.'

'A little local difficulty. Actually, more than a little local difficulty – an entire manure heap of it. Epping has a distinctly farmyard smell about it nowadays.'

'Joe Ball turning the screw again?'

'Could teach the Gestapo a thing or two.'

They both contemplated their drinks for a few seconds.

'Should tell Bracken, maybe.'

'Tell him what?'

'About the Bill. Settle his parentage once and for all. He could run off and demand a blood sample from Winston.'

'Pure alcohol. He'd get nothing but pure alcohol.'

'Maybe it runs in the Churchill family, this dubious parentage. His mother was less than eight months married when Winston was born. Always ahead of himself, even then.'

'Married three times, wasn't she? A woman of *considerable* experience, I hear. Perhaps that's why Winston was so keen on supporting the bloody Duchess.'

'What – the Windsor woman? Saw a bit of his own mother in her?'

'He'll end up like his father, too, mark my words.'

'Silly bugger. An avalanche of fine words, yet not an ounce of common sense. Always trying to make up for his disasters in the last war by being first in line for the next.'

'Never knows when to quit.'

'You've got it, Dickie. The Never-Never Man. Just too old.'

Suddenly Ian became distracted, his nose was up, sniffing the air like a beagle. Smoke. Cuban. He swivelled to find the source, suddenly buried in apprehension. The smoke was billowing from behind the wings of a leather armchair whose back was towards them. The next moment a cigar appeared, and the head of Winston Churchill followed.

Ian flushed, then affected a brave face. Maybe the old man had been snoozing, hadn't overheard. 'Ah, didn't see you there, Winston. Did we, Dickie?'

Dickie dived into his drink.

Churchill extracted the cigar from his mouth. 'They tell me,' he spat, 'that competitive examinations are an excellent means of weeding out idiots and imbeciles. It is a monumental pity,' he continued, his blue eyes carving through their defences, 'that elections don't appear to be so discriminating.'

It was a day when the winter rains seemed to have grown exhausted from their relentless efforts and were hovering just beyond the horizon, gathering their strength once more. For the moment it was dry, a good day to get out, even if only to the market. In truth it was something of an experiment, the first time Carol had brought Mac and her kids together. Yes, kids, plural. Not just Peter who read to her and was the anchor in her life but also little Linda, still in terry-towelling nappies. Linda had been a mistake. A silly working practice. An industrial accident. A mop-haired, blue-eyed wonder. There hadn't been any man in Carol's life for six years who measured loyalty in terms that stretched much beyond twenty minutes, yet to one of them, unknown and evidently unprotected, she owed half the happiness in her life. A cause for gratitude, never grief. But for all the joys they brought to her, the kids were a formidable mountain to climb for a potential partner with his mind on anything other than a quick one. Mac had potential, she thought. He'd already proved himself to be remarkable – he had the patience of a hibernating toad – and now she had to find out how good his climbing legs were.

Saturday morning. They had wandered through the marketplace at Epping, purchasing a bag of boiled sweets to pacify Peter, lingering over swatches of dress material, pinching and prodding the offerings of fruit and fresh veg that were laid out on the stalls. They shopped with care, loading their purchases into the baby's push-chair while Linda was carried along, uncomplaining, on Mac's shoulders. She drooled on his hair while he pretended to be a circus ride, swirling her around until she squealed for him to stop. Carol struggled to hide the smile – there they were, the hooker and the now non-paying punter, shopping for cabbages and King Edwards, to all intents like any other Epping family busy with the weekend chores. There was a long way to go up the mountain, but so far Mac's footing seemed remarkably secure.

The market was filled with tantalizing smells and traders' cries. Women staggered like drunken sailors beneath a week's worth of provisions while menfolk muttered at their side, rolling cigarettes from tobacco they kept in little leather pouches and wondering if there'd be enough left to put a little on the two-thirty at Kempton. It was growing busier, the crowd ever more pressing. Carol's little caravan pushed ahead, push-chair to the fore like a battering ram, squeezing, nudging, until Peter dropped his bag of sweets in the crush and it became clear that they were getting nowhere. They had become mixed up in a throng that stretched around an elderly man who was standing on a platform and shouting at everybody. Several of those around were shouting back.

'And so I have decided to bring my campaign to the people –'

'But the people don't want you, Mr Churchill!'

The man on the platform stared at the accuser. 'Some people don't want me, that is true. Some people within my own party don't want me. Want to push me out, like cuckoos in the nest. But it is not the cuckoo class who must decide, it is the ordinary people of Epping, like you, ladies and gentlemen – yes, and even you, young man' – he pointed to the persecutor who was trying to interrupt him – 'even you, sir. Because the rules of democracy insist you should be allowed to vote if you are over the age of twenty-one. Which is only fair and right and decent, in spite of your evident shortcomings, since those same rules of democracy insist that if you are over the age of seventeen and one-half you should be allowed to enlist for your country and be shot.'

There was an outpouring of abuse. Mac turned away, wanting to leave, but Carol tugged his sleeve and held him back. 'It's old Winnie. Hang on a minute,' she whispered.

Another young man, slightly older than the first, had taken up the cudgels. 'You don't know what you're saying. You used to be a bleedin' Liberal.' Others in the crowd joined in with jeers.

'Yes, indeed I was. But we must always be prepared to change. Why, I have changed, I cannot deny it. When the Bo-ers were hunting me throughout the veldts and kops of South Africa, they put up a notice – indeed, many notices. Wanted. Dead or alive! Winston Churchill.' There was a stirring of pride amongst some of the older members of the crowd. 'Twenty-five years old, they said I was. But sadly, and all too evidently, I have changed. Red-brownish hair, they said. That has changed, too – all but disappeared. Small toothbrush moustache, they said. That also has gone – although I notice that such appendages have become rather fashionable in other parts of Europe.' The crowd was chuckling, joining in with him. 'And the Bo-ers accused me in their posters of having an in-different build. Well, just look at me now' – he patted his substantial stomach, which was clearly detectable beneath his overcoat, and there was laughter, punctuated by yet another interruption. Someone was accusing him of living off the fat of the land. 'And the Bo-ers also said – and I quote' – Churchill was shouting now to drown the interruption, waving pages of prepared notes that had become irrelevant – 'that he talks through his nose and cannot pronounce the letter *S* properly. Well, I commend that defect to you, sir, for talking through one's nose is far to be favoured over talking through the back of your head!'

He was getting the better of them now. Others in the crowd were turning on the agitators, trying to shout them down, but Churchill called them to order, waving his hand. 'No, we must respect their freedom. Freedom to disagree, and freedom even to abuse. Freedom that is denied them today in half of Europe, and will be denied in the whole of Europe if dictatorship wins the day. We cannot take our freedom in this country for granted. So let them have their say. Allow them the liberty of making fools of themselves. But I must warn you, young man' – he was pointing at one of the more persistent of his antagonists – 'that if you insist on keeping your mouth open and your ears closed, you'll catch nothing but flies!'

A mistake. Normally a speaker can have the last word, beat the hecklers at their own game but, at the rear of the crowd and out of sight of Churchill, Mac could see a well-suited middle-aged man circulating, whispering in the ears of the hecklers, urging them on, pressing money into the hand of one. The day was not yet done. As soon as the cheers for Churchill had died down, the agitation started once again.

'You talk about liberty. But what about loyalty?'

'Loyalty, yes. To my party, to my leader, to my country. But not necessarily in that order.'

'Loyalty to Mr Chamberlain?'

'I am loyal to Mr Chamberlain. But I am loyal to freedom above all else. And freedom is not divisible. We cannot in this country be free if half of the rest of Europe is cast into slavery. We cannot turn a blind eye, for it will be our turn next. We must look at what is happening to the Jews, and take care, for if we do not I fear that we shall all soon be Jews.'

A rhetorical gesture too far for some in the crowd. 'Send 'em back to Germany. To Austria. Send 'em back to where they came from!' the cries began.

'It would be like throwing Christians to the lions.'

'It's called appeasement.'

'The Christians had another name for it.'

'These ain't Christians, they're Jews.'

'Jesus was a Jew!' Churchill retorted hotly.

'So was Barabbas!'

And Churchill had lost. From all corners of the crowd shouts of derision erupted. Not from the majority, for the British majority has that peculiar habit of preferring to remain silent, embarrassed by confrontation. Placards on sticks had appeared and were being waved around the platform, blocking Churchill off from those he wanted to reach. His tongue was sharper than his opponents' but their number was greater and blunted his edge. They didn't have to win; stopping him from winning was sufficient for their purposes.

It was too much. With a wave of his hand and muted applause from his supporters, Churchill stepped down and disappeared from view. Another day, another battle. He hadn't won this one, but there would be many more to fight. The crowd began to disperse. Carol tugged at Mac's sleeve, time to go – but now it was his turn to be reluctant to leave, looking back over his shoulder to the place where Churchill had been standing. Mac's face was raw. Linda was pulling at his hair and wanting to use him as a hobby horse but he seemed not to notice. The joy they had shared only minutes before had vanished. He was elsewhere, in another marketplace. He remembered youths – just like those here – in Wadowice, except they had hurled not only abuse but rocks, too. He remembered asking his father why. Why us, *tatele*? Why don't we just stop it? 'One day, *kindele*, you will understand,' his father had said, and dragged him away, just as Carol was doing now. But Mac could never be dragged far enough. Throughout his life, wherever he had gone and no matter how hard he had run, he had never been able to escape, not even here, no matter how hard he pretended to be almost English. They would always find him.

Yet he had just seen one man who understood – or understood as much as any *goy tzedek* Gentile could. A man who had stared into the fire that was to come and was crying a warning. Yet his words seemed futile, like birdsong in a thunderstorm.

'Mac, love, what on earth's the matter?' Carol's voice was filled with concern. This was supposed to be such a special day, yet something had gone wrong. She'd lost him, somewhere deep within himself, a place where she couldn't follow.

'It's Yosef Ya'akov. That's the matter.'

'Who the hell's he? And why's he upsetting you?'

'Can't be helped.'

'He'll need bleedin' help after I've finished with him.'

'No he won't.' He had stopped and was looking at her, holding her wrists tight – too tight, he was almost hurting her. His skin was hot, burning inside. He had an air about him that seemed turbulent, a battleground, a territory that had been fought over many times and yet would be fought over again. 'You see – it's me. Yosef Ya'akov. Yosef Ya'akov Farbenblum. My name. I think I just remembered who I am.'

Churchill was in deep trouble. The Chigwell branch of his Epping constituency party voted to sweep all his supporters from their official positions and replace them with Chamberlainites. Then the branch in Theydon Bois declared its unambiguous support for the Prime Minister, and other branches did the same. Such moves were made possible by the sudden influx of fresh members. New names were conjured up as though by magic on the membership lists and their votes were counted in the tally against Churchill, although very few of these new members ever attended a single meeting. And every party gathering within the constituency was reminded that Epping was on the bombing route to London. Yes, Epping was nervous and blamed Winston Churchill, and there were those who wanted to ensure that the entire country knew it . . .

(The Times, Monday 6 March 1939)

MR WINSTON CHURCHILL'S 'INSURRECTION'

A CONSTITUENT'S PROTEST

Mr C. N. Thornton-Kemsley, chairman of Chigwell Unionist Association, speaking at a dinner of the Nazeing (Essex) Unionist Association on Saturday night, said:

'Mr Churchill's post-Munich insurrection was shocking. His castigation of the National Government, which we returned him to support, would in any other party but the Conservative Party have earned him immediate expulsion.

'Loyal Conservatives in the Epping Division have been placed in an intolerable position. I feel that unless Mr Churchill is prepared to work for the National Government and the Prime Minister he ought no longer to shelter under the goodwill and name of such a great party. Most of us in the Epping Division agree that Mr Churchill has overstepped the line.'

NINE

In the gardens of Buckingham Palace it was undeniably spring. Snowdrops were handing over tenancy
of the lawns to daffodils and crocuses while cherry
blossom and early willow buds had begun their
annual dance across a stage of bare bark. Life – and
hope – seemed to be reclaiming the land after a
winter that had seemed endless, bringing with it a
mood of infectious youth that had revived even the
Prime Minister.

'The dawn of a golden age, sir,' he reported. 'I
used precisely that description with the press lobby
this morning. A golden age.'

'You did?' his Monarch replied. It wasn't really
meant as a question, it was simply that all his life
the tongue-tangled 'Bertie' had found it easier to participate in conversations by peppering them with
questions, no matter how pointless, thus relieving
himself of the need to offer comments of either
length or substance.

'Yes, sir,' Chamberlain responded, recognizing the
game. 'Sir Joseph had summoned them to St
Stephen's Club for a briefing.'

'St Stephen's? Don't know it myself.'

'And neither should you,' Chamberlain continued,
laughing gaily. 'A gentlemen's club frequented by

243

many politicians. A place of ne'er-do-wells within the shadow of Big Ben. And ideal for its purpose, I must say. A fine leather chair for myself, a fireplace on which Sir Joseph can lean and survey the scene, and far too few seats for the gentlemen of the press. Most of them have to stand. Keeps them alert, of course – and in their place.'

'I never c-cease to admire your success in that respect.'

'Ball is indefatigable. I didn't know the meaning of terror until I saw him set about a cub reporter who'd arrived for an interview with neither his pencil nor a copy of my latest speech. Dealing with the lobby's like training a pack of dogs, he tells me – split them up, train them one by one, and if they still won't respond, put 'em down!'

'B-bravo.'

'Most of the proprietors, of course, can be counted either as personal friends or at least sensible businessmen. Every time they produce a headline that suggests war and chaos are lurking around the corner, their advertising revenues melt like butter in a bread oven. Seems to focus their thinking, I find.'

They passed beneath the spreading limbs of a graceful willow whose arms bent low with fresh leaf – a graceful contrast to the squat palace with its heavy Germanic overtones that stood behind them. Chamberlain had never cared for the place as a piece of architecture, he found it unimaginative and excessively formal and had been delighted at the suggestion of the King that they should conduct their weekly audience on the hoof. Yet he found these meetings increasingly tiresome, the Monarch and his

First Minister, each beholden to the other, bound by ties that were not only invisible but which also made little sense. To be consulted, to encourage, to warn, those were the rights of a King, so the conventions said – yet at times he stumbled about in the constitutional undergrowth like a lost boy. Chamberlain sighed to himself – he was impatient, intolerant even, and increasingly so. He recognized the fault, of course, but so often the fault seemed more evident in others.

'And Dawson at *The Times* is a brick, a constant delight,' Chamberlain continued, returning to his theme. 'I think it might soon be time to express our thanks to him in the usual manner – with your gracious permission, sir.'

'Sir Geoffrey? Why not, indeed? Halifax is always singing his praises. They hunt together, I understand.'

'And a knighthood for Dawson would act as a clear marker to the others. They've a choice. Friend or foe, elevation – or exile.'

The King nodded his approval and lit his second cigarette in as many minutes, tossing the finished butt carelessly onto the lawn.

'To my mind it's a moral choice. Either you are for peace – or for war. There's no middle ground any more.' Chamberlain was smacking his fist into the palm of the other hand as they walked – the King had rarely seen him so animated. 'The truth is that the future of Europe will be settled by three men – Hitler, Mussolini and myself. That's why I went to Rome, to do everything within my power to deliver one unambiguous message. That we are for peace.

And if that overriding purpose makes life difficult for the whiners and the warmongers . . .' He left the thought unfinished. Royal ears were constitutionally delicate.

'I hear that Mr Churchill may be in a spot of trouble.'

'A large splash of it. But better an outbreak of hostilities in Epping than across the whole of Europe.'

'Like a spinning top, he is. Tremendous energy, of course, dashing off in all directions. But sometimes so' – the stammer grabbed at his tongue – 'irritating.'

They had reached the lake. Two mallards flew overhead before crashing into the water. Chamberlain decided it was time to take the risk he had long pondered of bringing the Monarch into his confidence.

'You see, sir, we have to make every effort we can to ensure that the right message reaches Berlin. I'm sure you agree.'

The King nodded, uncertain of what he was agreeing to.

'So for some months now, Sir Horace has been holding private talks with certain German emissaries. No fuss, no public fanfare. In the strictest confidence, you understand, sir.' Somehow Chamberlain made it sound like a rebuke aimed directly at the Monarch, which was not far from the effect he intended. 'We've offered them a loan.'

'What? With financial crisis on our own doorstep?'

'Allow me to explain, sir,' Chamberlain insisted. 'Germany is spending every mark it can find on weapons. It can't go on like that, not without bank-rupting their entire system. So it will eventually be faced with only two choices. Either they can march the Wehrmacht into neighbouring countries in order to steal the resources they need – which is what we've been desperately trying to avoid . . .'

'Yes, I think I grasped that,' muttered the King, a trifle acidly. He resented being kept in the dark. For months, Chamberlain had said, they'd been talking to the Germans for months. Why hadn't he been consulted earlier? Simply because he'd never had a head for examinations didn't mean he was a feather-brain.

'Or we can provide generous loans – to encourage them to switch from arms to everyday industry.'

'Sort of . . . butter before bullets?'

'Yes. Very well put, sir. I want to tie them in, you see, bring their economy alongside ours.'

'By offering them a generous loan.'

'Precisely.'

'How generous – precisely?'

'Perhaps a billion pounds sterling.'

Suddenly the King started to splutter, over-whelmed by surprise and an inadvertent intake of nicotine. 'My God, so much?' he gasped.

'A small price to pay for saving the peace.'

'Yes, b-but . . .'

'And saving the Empire, sir.'

The Monarchy, too, of course – although Chamberlain was far too delicate to mention the fact. There was little need. George was all too aware that the last war had resulted in the disappearance of Kaisers and Kings in so many corners of Europe, and a new war might beat a path all the way to Windsor. 'I quite agree, war is unthinkable, b-but . . .'

'But, sir?'

'There's one bit of this I don't understand. What's to stop them spending all the money we give them on their air force?'

Chamberlain counselled himself to be patient. Sometimes it seemed he had so little time left, and so very much still to do. But better a King like George who had to be led every step of the way by the hand, than one like his brother, Edward, who couldn't be restrained, no matter how many hands were laid upon him.

'Why on earth should Herr Hitler go to war when he can achieve everything he reasonably wants without it? That was the message I left him at Munich, after all. I've given him half of Czechoslovakia and he didn't have to fire a single shot. Now I want to go another step further and bind him in economically, with all Germans reunited and with Britain at the very heart of Europe.'

George was striding slowly forward, measuring his pace, nodding his understanding and approval. 'I see you are still a businessman to your roots, Mr Chamberlain.'

'And I can do business with Herr Hitler.'

They had come full circle. The sweeping steps that led up to the palace lay before them. They started to climb.

'I hope to make more progress on the matter over Easter.'

'And after that?'

'With your permission – an election, perhaps.'

'Ah, I see.'

'One has to come soon. A chance for the people to decide – a golden age of peace and prosperity.'

'Or Winston and war.'

'That's one way of looking at it. In fact, that's an excellent way of looking at it.' As they strode into the palace, for the first time in days Chamberlain's face bore a smile.

There are moments when a man's life seems little more than a plaything for the gods, something to be kicked back and forth until they tire of the game and leave him to fall where he may.

They toyed with Churchill during that early spring of 1939, abusing him, piling favours upon others. On all fronts, from the continent to his own constituency, his opponents were gaining strength. Another few weeks of the game and it might all have been too late for him, and for all that was to follow, yet the gods are nothing if not capricious. Churchill was to be saved by two outrageous pieces of good fortune, unwittingly manufactured by his most bitter enemies.

The first was one of his leading constituents, Colin Thornton-Kemsley, a thirty-six-year-old chartered surveyor whom Joseph Ball had nominated to lead the opposition to Churchill's reselection in Epping. He was an effective organizer, intriguing and ambitious, yet his talents proved to be all too effective, for on the day after the Prime Minister had briefed the press about the dawn of a new golden age, Thornton-Kemsley was selected as the Conservative candidate for the forthcoming by-election in the distant Scottish constituency of Kincardine and West Aberdeenshire. From that moment on his presence was usually to be found on the overnight sleeper headed north and his attentions lay about as far away from Epping as it was possible to get.

Three days later, a second man came forward to save Churchill's neck. History is a refuse heap of ironies and coincidences, all manner of tangled loops that would leave any editor of romantic fiction writhing in embarrassment, yet the man who stepped out to rescue Churchill was none other than Adolf Hitler. He didn't mean to, of course, it was entirely inadvertent; his objective was not Epping but a location nearly seven hundred miles further east.

Prague, to be exact. The capital of what remained of dismembered and independent Czechoslovakia that had been left over after Munich. A state that was on the point of ceasing to exist.

On 14 March the Czech President, Hacha, was summoned to Berlin. He was kept waiting while Hitler watched a film. At last, in the early hours of the morning, Hacha was marched into the room and told that in a few hours' time the Wehrmacht was going to invade his country. He was told that if Czech troops showed the slightest sign of resistance, the Czech capital would be razed to the ground.

On hearing this, Hacha collapsed, clutching his chest. He'd suffered a heart attack. A doctor was summoned and gave him an injection. The old man revived sufficiently to be able to sign his country's death warrant. Hours later, the Wehrmacht marched into Prague.

Chamberlain's golden age had lasted less than four days.

The old man was up to his thighs in the crystal water that ran off the Grampians and was having difficulty maintaining his footing on the slippery stones. It wouldn't have happened a year ago. He was tired – and ageing, although he refused to admit it. He had escaped for a couple of days' fishing to recharge the batteries, but after dinner the previous night he'd complained of acute stomach pain and had grown grey, refusing a nightcap and taking early to his bed. Nowadays his face could age in a moment, his skin growing thin beneath the scars of strain. Yet his spirit was indomitable and this morning he was dressed in heavy waders and a tweed jacket with flies pinned to the lapels, his hat pulled rakishly over his eyes, casting towards the purple and peaty pool that spread beneath the far bank.

'You know,' Chamberlain muttered as he cast yet again, his words carrying effortlessly in the light Scottish air, 'the skills of fishing are a lot like those of diplomacy.' There was a swish of line as it snaked towards the far bank. 'Patience. Tenacity. Understanding what it is they want. Making sure you have the right bait, the right fly, the right hook. Tempting them. Then more patience. Until they bite!'

His companion, Joseph Ball, offered no reply. His reticence had nothing to do with the logic of the argument, simply that at that precise moment he found himself incapable of speech. His tongue felt as though it had swollen and was likely to make him choke. He was sitting on the bank, clutching the note that had just been brought to him by cycle messenger from the lodge. A note that spelled disaster. That told him Hitler was in Prague, telegraphing to the whole world that he didn't give a bowl of spit for appeasement or agreements and least of all for Mr Neville Bloody Chamberlain. Czechoslovakia gone. Extinguished, without a shot being fired.

Ball lay back on the bank, praying that the ground would open up and swallow him. It didn't, so although it was only ten in the morning he reached for his hip flask.

How to present it? How to ensure that this calamity did less damage than otherwise it might? How to prevent it from destroying not only the Government in Prague but Chamberlain's Government, too? Chamberlain had given his word to defend the independence of castrated little Czechoslovakia, had insisted that the world should trust the word of Hitler, and now it had all fallen apart. Stripped the Prime Minister naked, left his balls dangling for target practice – and in Scotland, miles away from the editors and proprietors who might otherwise help to throw up some sort of smokescreen. They had to rush back to London, of course, but rush back to what? To their execution, perhaps.

The policy of appeasement, Chamberlain's policy, his 'golden age', lay smashed beyond repair at the border posts around Prague. The Ides of March. They should've been on their guard.

'Bite, my dears, bite,' the old man was saying. He looked thin, wasted beneath his tweed, almost pathetic. For a fleeting moment Ball wondered whether he should leave him there, stuck in the water, rush to London and declare his loyalty to Halifax or Eden, the two most likely successors, but the panic lasted only for a moment. There was no way out; he and the Prime Minister were grafted together and they must get through this. Somehow. Appeasement was dead, of course. They would have to embrace re-armament, the policy of the critics, and make it their own. A few telephone calls before they began the long train journey south – to Dawson and Beaverbrook, then James Kemsley with his control of the *Sunday Times*, the *Daily Sketch* and a forest of regional titles. Give them an angle. Emphasize Chamberlain's experience, that his policies had put Hitler clearly in the wrong and handed Britain the moral high ground. Bit like the mouse squeaking as the cat trod on its tail, but the more noise they could create the more confused the public might become as to whose fault this whole mess was.

Then there was also the tiniest, meanest little problem in that only last September Chamberlain had guaranteed the independence of what remained of Czechoslovakia. How the hell did they handle that? The hip flask reappeared. A swig, a moment's thought as in his mind he rode the avalanche, never knowing where it might stop or how long he had before he was buried beyond hope. Then it settled. Of course, they'd argue that Czechoslovakia had signed away its own independence and so no longer existed. They couldn't guarantee something that had ceased to exist now, could they? That would be stupid. Almost suicide.

And there would be more. Get the Whips busy amongst the back-benches. Most politicians were no better than a shoal of sardines, chasing the current, open-mouthed, constantly shifting their position, their whole life torn between hunger and touches of transporting fear.

'Got him!' the Prime Minister cried, reeling in something slippery.

Yes, fear would do it. The fear that grips a politician when he regards a looming election. The fear that haunts an editor when he thinks he might be denied the knighthood he's been promised. The fear infecting bankers and businessmen that if Chamberlain fell they would be cut off from their points of influence. The fear of any decent Englishman that the hordes of Socialism might soon be kicking down their doors and carrying off their daughters. Fear – the motivator of the masses. Ball put away the whisky. There was still all to play for – and much to do.

The Prime Minister was struggling with his catch. The fish was proving obstinate, and the old man's footing was still unsteady. Ball stretched a hand into the clear, chill water and splashed his face.

'Leave it, Neville, we've got to go.'

'Leave? Leave? What the devil do you mean? Why do we have to leave?' the Prime Minister snapped in irritation.

'Sharks,' Ball replied.

Sue Graham was in her bedroom packing away her winter clothes, sprinkling them with moth powder before wrapping them in sheets of tissue paper, when she heard a gentle knock on the back door. She knew that knock – Jerry's.

'Gasping for a cuppa,' he shouted from downstairs. 'Been helping Freddie repair his pigeon loft. Dust's gone right down the old tubes.' The announcement was followed by a clattering of the kettle upon the gas stove. Always doing something, was Jerry. Only the other day he'd loosened up every sash window in the house and cleaned the outsides, paintwork too – she couldn't reach the outsides, not upstairs. He'd come into her bedroom, leather and bucket in hand, looked around him and declared: 'You'll have to get a bigger bed than that, girl. When you grow up.' Suddenly, at the age of thirty-three, she wanted to grow up very fast indeed.

She finished wrapping her sweaters and placed them inside cardboard boxes. These boxes she placed on the top of her wardrobe, alongside her old family bible. It was a huge thing, its spine almost five inches thick – and old, the gilt edging of its pages faded, the heavy leather cover scuffed by more than a hundred years of use. Her grandmother's great-grandmother had bought it from the same shop in London that supplied churches throughout the south of England and it had been passed down to the eldest child of every generation as a wedding gift. The flyleaf bore the signatures of each of its five owners – the last was her dad's – and he had wanted nothing more than to be around when her own was added. 'You married and I can die a happy man,' he'd told her. But she wasn't, and he hadn't.

So the bible had come to her by default. Bit like

Jerry, through the death of his first wife. And through his roses. How she had tended those roses, talking to them – singing to them at times, when no one could hear – taking care to place them out of draughts, giving them half an aspirin to coax every hour of life out of them. One by one they had faded and drooped until only a single bloom was left, and this she had placed between two sheets of clean blotting paper at the centre of the bible. The Song of Solomon, chapter two, verse eleven. 'The rain is over, it is gone: The flowers appear on the earth; The time of singing is come.'

'So what did you do with my roses?' he demanded when next he had come round and spotted the empty vase.

'Threw them out. On account of their being too old,' she had retorted. 'Just like I plan to do with you.'

'That's right, girl, but not before I've had me cuppa.' He was always dying for a cup of tea, was Jerry.

By the time she came down to the kitchen the tea was brewing on the stove and he'd begun to make himself toast, the bread impaled on a toasting fork that he was holding to the glowing coke. He was seated in her dad's old smoking chair, staring into the flame, bent over his work, listening to the radio. A bowl of dripping from the weekend joint stood on the table. She'd only known him four weeks yet already it had become something of a ritual. He would wipe a thick smear of the fatty dripping on his toast, then scoop out the sweet dark brown jelly from the bottom of the dripping bowl to place on top. She'd always hated dripping, loathed the stuff, but now there were three bowls of it sitting at the back of her larder.

Yet today the dripping was untouched. A spiral of smoke began winding upwards from the stove – the toast was burning, practically screaming – yet still he didn't react, staring blindly into the fire. Not until she had shouted in alarm did he jump from the chair and flip the charred bread into the sink.

'It's the only sort of toast fit for dripping,' she muttered as the flames hissed and subsided in a cloud of bitter smoke.

'Buggered that up a bit, didn't I?'

'I think you express it well.'

'I'll make up for it. Cook you dinner, maybe?'

'Great. I'll call the fire brigade.'

'Sorry. Got distracted by the wireless.'

Only then did she focus on the radio burbling in the background. The voice of a news correspondent, fading in and out over the static in the manner of someone who was reporting from a distant land, a country that had woken up to find it no longer existed. A story of tanks rattling down the cobbled streets of historic towns, being resisted with nothing more than snowballs. Of presidential palaces surrounded by troops in strange grey uniforms. Of tiny Czech flags sprouting from the buttonholes of suits. Of arrests. Of a place called Wenceslas Square being washed with tears. Of Mr Chamberlain expressing his regrets. Of the death of a dream.

'It's happening all over again, Sue. Just like last time.'

'But Mr Chamberlain promised . . .'

'So did Hitler. Said all he wanted back was his Germans. But these aren't Germans, they're Czechs. And it'll be only the start.'

She greeted the news without any show of emotion. The dear departed had always reminded her that she was English. 'Emotion's all very well,' he would tell her, 'but first you have to make sure you can cope.' So she picked up the pot of tea from the stove and began pouring; it was thick, dark, stewed, it didn't matter. She handed him a cup and sat beside him in front of the fire. 'Your tea's almost as bad as your toast.'

'You haven't tried my custard.'

'What can we do?'

'About my custard?'

'You know what I mean, Jerry. If there's a war, it won't be like the last one.'

'How's that?'

'The boys fighting over there, the rest of us back here – it won't be like that. Not with the bombers. We'll all be involved. We'll all have something to do.'

'Maybe.'

'So what will you do?'

'I was thinking – while I was making toast, you see – thinking that I might join the Territorials. Become a part-time soldier again. Seems to me that if there's going to be another soddin' war, this time I want to be ready, pardon my French.'

'You'll need your French, Jerry, if there's fighting to be done.'

'Would you mind? You know, me joining up?'

'Does my opinion matter?'

'Very much. You should know that by now, girl.'

'Then I don't mind, seeing as you ask. We'll all have a role to play in the next one, the women included. We'll have to do more than make the tea.'

'Why, what are you thinking of?'

'I'm thinking of quite a lot, actually.' She paused for a moment, lost in her own thoughts about war, and invasion, and how close she was here in Bournemouth to any likely landing ground. And about what might follow from that. 'But first things first.'

'So what is to be first?'

'Onions, Jerry. I'm thinking I shall have to plant a lot more vegetables, and particularly onions. Just in case the French run out.'

In the early part of the year Churchill had been confined to bed by a severe bout of influenza. In the darkest corners of his mind, the parts that he hid even from Clemmie, he hoped at times it might even turn to pneumonia and carry him off, such was his sense of desolation. Yet he proved to be made of sterner stuff. He survived, and now, as jackboots fell upon the cobbles of Prague like a blacksmith's hammer upon steel, Churchill was given back his cutting edge.

He summoned his constituency officers to a meeting, instructing that they be lashed in if necessary – all except Thornton-Kemsley who was distracted hundreds of miles to the north. Never mind, he would hear of it soon enough. Now they sat before him, shifting uneasily, like impoverished relatives

259

waiting for the reading of a will from which they suspected they had been entirely excluded.

Churchill chomped at his cigar, bit it so hard he all but killed it, then saw that the doors at the rear of the hall had been closed. It was time to begin. He rose to his feet, stared at them, said nothing, then glowered at them some more until their shuffling had entirely ceased and you could hear a dead man cry.

'There are people in this constituency, active, influential people, many of whom are in this room tonight, who have gone about complaining that I should have remained silent. That I should not have warned against the present dangers as I did. Mr Chairman, there is an entire nation lying in desolation tonight, crushed beneath the heel of tyranny, the brave and once independent nation of Czechoslovakia, which wishes that the voices of an entire continent had been raised in tumultuous warning.'

There was absolute silence. His eyes roamed about the room, searching their souls, and many of them could not hold his gaze.

'But what could we have done? About *a quarrel in a faraway country between people of whom we know nothing*?' Oh, how they flinched at the cruel echo of Chamberlain's words. 'We could have spoken out. We could have displayed determination. We could have shown the resolution for which this land, the land of Nelson and Drake and Marlborough, is justifiably famous. Instead – we turned our backs. And in doing that, we turned the British spine, which has run long and straight and true throughout the centuries of our history, into a whipping post for the amusement of dictators.'

'Hear, hear!' a woman's voice cried from the hall. They weren't all creatures of conspiracy. As he looked upon them, his shoulders hunched like a boxer waiting to deliver a blow, he found resolute faces scattered amongst the restless eyes. In his dark hours it was easy to convince himself that he was utterly alone, that he had been deserted by the entire world, but it was never true. He always found friends, and usually when he was most in need. He recalled that just a few short weeks ago, lying in his bed, praying that the Black Dog might drag him away from all his mortal misery, he had received a letter: *'Dear Mr Churchill, I hear you are unwell and in low spirits. I could send you flowers, but already you live in such an extraordinarily beautiful place. I could send you wishes for a speedy recovery, but they would only be added to the mounting pile on your secretary's desk. Instead I will remind you of something you once said – something I have read in the book you gave me . . .'*

His audience was waiting, uncomfortable but expectant. 'A young friend recently reminded me of something I had once said. Something about the British people, something which, I admit, I myself had almost forgotten. Here are his words:

'*"You said, Mr Churchill, that historians have noticed all down the centuries one peculiarity of the British people which has cost them dear. After a victory, we always contrive to throw away the greater part of the advantages we gained in the struggle. Our biggest challenges come not from without, you said. They come from within. And they don't come from the cottages and hearths of the wage-earners,*

they come instead from a peculiar type of brainy people
always found in our country, and from the mood of ridicu-
lous self-abasement into which we have been cast by a pow-
erful section of our own intellectuals. They come from the
acceptance of defeatist doctrines by a large proportion of our
politicians who sit round their dinner tables throwing away
freedom as though it were an unwanted scrap, who insist
on a course of inaction and subordination towards Europe
on the grounds that their fate is inevitable . . ."

'But as my young friend reminded me – as he has continued to remind me from the first moment we met – nothing is inevitable. *Inevitable* – it is an ugly word with hideous consequence. To argue that some-thing is *inevitable* is to argue for the end of democ-racy. It is to discard our freedom of choice. It is to close down all our processes of free thought and to cast aside those liberties that have made this country a beacon of justice and fair play.'

Their chins were coming up now. Like fish about to take the bait – no! not like fish. Like Englishmen awaiting the call. But whether perch or patriot, it was still time to play them a little, confuse them with a change of mood.

'Some have argued that I should not be returned as the Member of Parliament for this constituency at the next election. Some of you in this room tonight. To those with whom I have had genuine disagree-ments, let me apologize . . .'

Even those eyes that were still filled with suspi-cion showed an interest. The Old Man apologizing? Never been heard of before, not in Epping nor any other part of England.

'I confess I have been an irritant. A thorn in your

rumps. An obstinate and belligerent old man who has his own mind and the disagreeable habit of sharing it with you. But what is the use of Parliament if it is not the place where true statements can be brought before the people? What on earth is the use of sending Members to Parliament to say what they are told to say by the Government Whips and to cheer loudly every Ministerial platitude? What value can we place on our parliamentary institutions if constituencies return only tame, docile and subservient members who try to stamp on every form of independent judgement? For that is precisely what some have suggested. But let us put all that behind us. Let us not dwell in the dark pits of disaster. Let us move forward, to face the challenges which lie ahead – to face them together – and, if we shall prevail, onward! To the broad sunlit uplands that lie beyond.'

A woman in the front row wanted to applaud, had her hands raised and ready, yet let them fall back to her lap, not daring to break the moment.

'So let us, tonight, resolve to cut out the cancer of confusion and division from within this constituency. Let us look not inwards, but outward to the duties that lie before us and before the entire British nation. The great constituency of Epping should be a beacon, not an object of derision and idle speculation in the columns of the gutter press. So I ask that the issue should be decided – here and now. That we should walk from this room knowing whether I have your fullest confidence, and your unfettered support to continue to speak out, or whether you wish another to take my place. I ask any of you who still have doubts about my beliefs or abilities, to rise so that we may share our differences openly and in amity, as old friends should.'

Not a muscle was moved. Now he dropped his voice, humbled, catching on the emotion of the moment. Just as he had practised throughout the long afternoon.

'And to those who wish me to remain at my task, as your spokesman, I can do nothing more than to promise you my unflinching service, and to all of you, my friends, my heartfelt and most humble thanks.'

His chin fell to his chest, offering a tiny bow of gratitude. They rose as one to applaud. Many of the women were weeping, Churchill too, the tears flooding down his cheeks. There would be no more opposition, no more tittle-tattle about dumping him. There might well be mutterings in dark corners. They would claim that this was entirely unorthodox, a constitutional abuse, that it was not a properly convened gathering of the association and therefore had no powers to impose any decisions. They would argue that it was nothing less than a case of outright bloody banditry, and they would be right. But none of them would dare come out into the daylight and say so.

What had Burgess said, the first time they met, sitting around the table at Chartwell? Words are weapons, sometimes the only weapons left with which to fight, but in the right hands they can prove the most powerful weapons of all. A remarkable and perceptive man, was young Burgess. Churchill thought he rather liked him.

TEN

Chamberlain had extraordinary recuperative powers. He could no longer deny that things had gone wrong – dreadfully, hopelessly wrong – but since most of the rest of the British Establishment had been guilty of precisely the same misjudgements there were plenty of others with whom he could huddle for warmth. There was an excellent chance that their memories – and therefore their desire for recrimination – might fail them completely. Where there was office, there was hope.

He was standing in front of a full-length mirror in his bedroom, fumbling with the collar stud that secured the ruffled collar of his court dress, when there came an apologetic knock at the door. Wilson and Ball stepped forward with a marked degree of trepidation – it had been another wretched day. That morning the Baltic state of Lithuania had handed over the strategic port of Memel to Germany rather than face the threat of invasion and aerial bombardment. The Wehrmacht marched on. And, almost more terrifyingly, in Westminster a posse of women had paraded up and down outside Parliament clad in sandwich boards that carried the single word – CHURCHILL.

'Forgive the intrusion, Neville . . .'

'You're just in time. Tell me, are my stockings straight? The buckles on the breeches?'

They muttered affirmation.

'Got to maintain standards, you know. Damned important, standards.'

'You're seeing the French President tonight –'

'Of course I'm seeing the French President tonight,' Chamberlain snapped, the irritation of the day finally bursting through. 'Why else am I getting dressed up like a bloody tropical parrot?'

The collar stud spat away and rolled across the floor. Wilson scurried to retrieve it, rather too quickly, grateful for the chance to duck out of the firing line. Chamberlain did this when he was exhausted, took it out on those closest to him when it seemed that the whole world was aiming its barbs at him. It helped him to pass on some of the pain. Wilson tried to return the stud to the Prime Minister but he was having none of it, standing to attention, arms by his side, chin held high, expecting Wilson to finish the job like any lickspittle servant. Chamberlain didn't intend rudeness to his friend, it was simply that his moods were at times mercurial. It was also the fact that in recent days he had discovered that his own fingers would no longer bend to his command, his hand had developed a tremor which made things like collar studs almost impossible. He didn't know why; tiredness, perhaps. But when you reach your seventieth birthday, as Chamberlain had the previous week, you stop asking why, because most of the answers you received you simply don't want to hear.

'It's just that the President will press you,' Wilson

purred, swallowing both the slight and the temptation to choke his Prime Minister, 'to send more men to France. We've four divisions there while Hitler has hundreds. The French think it's all a bit one-sided.'

'Of course it's one-sided. Any fool can see that!'

'The Bore-Belisha's been banging the same drum for weeks,' Ball observed.

'As I said, any fool . . .' Chamberlain hissed.

'He's also pushing very hard for conscription. Whispering it in every ear, twisting every arm he can lay his hands on.'

'Then warn them to count their change!' Chamberlain barked, and the collar stud flew away once more, diving under the wardrobe. It was Ball's turn to fall on his hands and chubby knees to retrieve it, accompanied by a series of grunts and wheezes which suggested it had been a long time since he'd bent any lower than an armchair. He handed the stud over once more, and sat down on the end of the bed to recover.

'Won't be easy to rebuff him, Neville. He's even been heard muttering about resignation.'

'Then perhaps the time has come to let him go wander amongst the tribes,' Chamberlain snorted in disdain. Up close, Wilson noticed how spent his eyes were, how fiercely he seemed to have to struggle in order to prise the lids apart. They were red, raw.

'No, Neville, not now,' Wilson responded, his tone soothing but his manner determined. 'Not a time to go making martyrs, not when they're all still so giddy after the Czech nonsense. Leslie has friends.'

'So what am I supposed to do – give in? I'm surprised at you, Horace.'

'Conscription is something we'll have to consider, Neville, like it or not. Perhaps this is one matter on which we should let Leslie have his head.'

'And have him doing his little jig through every watering hole in Westminster claiming he's running the Government? Never – never that!'

'You said yourself that standing still is no longer an option, not with every border post in central Europe having its door kicked in.'

Ball watched from a safe distance, not prepared to get between them. He'd seen it all before, the Prime Minister and Wilson, his *alter ego*, knocking around the strengths of a policy or the flaws of a personality. And when they had settled the matter, together, in agreement, as they always did, he was never quite sure who had won. But as Wilson had told him once, 'It doesn't matter who's won – only that Neville thinks he's won.'

And so it was. 'Very well, Horace. Time to take charge. If Leslie wants to dance, then *we* shall set the tune. If we must have conscription –'

'I think we do.'

'Then let it be done our way.'

'What way is that?'

Chamberlain turned on him, his expression mocking, the collar still dangling loose. 'I would have thought better of you, Horace. Didn't you know I've always thought conscription might be necessary? I'll announce it to the Cabinet next week. Explain that the reason I've held my hand on the matter so long is . . .' – he glanced around the room as though in search of a lost sock – 'why, because of my concern for the sensitivities of the trade unions.'

'Trade unions?' Wilson repeated slowly, unable to hide his disbelief. From the end of the bed, Ball clapped his hands in appreciation.

'Precisely. I want it all on the official record. Cabinet minutes. It's got to be clear. I want you to make sure there's no confusion – no suggestion we've been forced into backtracking. Call in Dawson and the others. Give them a briefing. Why, with any luck Attlee and those idiots in the Labour Party will oppose the whole damned thing and we can blame any confusion upon them.'

'But what do we announce, Neville? What is this plan of ours?'

'Good grief, Horace, what do I pay you for? You must have something locked away in your bottom drawer. Get it out. Dust it down. Just make sure it doesn't sound like Leslie's.'

Wilson was still crouching beneath the prime-ministerial chin, his fingers aching from his exertions. It shouldn't have been such a struggle. Chamberlain had lost weight recently, everything seemed to hang on him a little loosely, even his politics. But at last the collar stud was pressed home and order restored.

'We need something big, Neville,' Ball was saying, picking up the embroidered tail coat that was laid out beside him and preparing to slip it around Chamberlain's shoulders. 'A grand idea that'll really grab them by their balls. We're under pressure.'

'I think Joe's right,' Wilson added. 'Hitler didn't just march into Prague, he stamped all over your parliamentary majority.'

Chamberlain stood to attention in front of the mirror, examining every detail.

'I've spent sleepless nights thinking the same thing. Something to restore our fortunes. Some dramatic gesture that will put the Czech nonsense behind us. Something that will make even Herr Hitler sit up and take notice. I resent what he did, you know, more bitterly than I can express. He gave me his word, said he had no more territorial claims in Europe. He promised me – *promised* me – that he had no further interest in Czechoslovakia. Then he made a fool of me. Can't let him get away with that again.'

He was still staring into the mirror, picking off a stray golden thread and straightening his medals. At last he seemed satisfied. 'You're right. Something dramatic. Demonstrate that he can go no further. Draw a line.'

'Draw a line, Neville – but where?' Wilson enquired, still straightening his aching back.

'Poland. That's what we're going to do. We're going to guarantee Poland.'

Spring was revealing its usual feelings towards the grime-smeared and soul-scratched city of London. It was raining. Not a downpour, more a brisk shower, which Burgess relished. He stood for a while, counting the droplets as they landed on his thick hair and trickled down his face. It had been a long time since he felt so refreshed, almost clean. He loved water – he could swim like a fish as well as drink like one – yet it had been months since he'd found time to visit a pool – well, in truth, since the afternoon the caretaker at the Hackney Metropolitan had taken an active dislike to the amount of time he was spending in the changing rooms and had threatened to call the police. Ridiculous thing was, Burgess hadn't been taking liberties, only an after-lunch nap. It was warm, womb-like in there, a place to curl up and indulge in the make-believe that the world which waited to pounce on him at any moment had simply gone away. He had fantasies at times about the womb, and his mother, and his long-dead father, and the replacement husband who lay between his mother's legs – a place which was *his* space, the first place in this world he had ever known and which had now been taken from him. From the day he had passed puberty he had wondered what it would be like to have sex with his mother. He'd once told his housemaster at Eton, old F.W. Dobbs, about these thoughts, blurted them out over tea and buttered crumpets on a Sunday afternoon. They would pass, came the kindly reply. But they hadn't. He knew it was all a little twisted, but no more twisted than supposedly normal men blowing the entire fucking world apart.

His digressions made him late. He was always late, Mac had got to know that, and the barber was a patient man. He had still only taken an inch off the top of his beer by the time Burgess rushed in, a good forty minutes after he had promised. He sat there dripping, gently steaming, as Mac began his tale about his most recent summons.

'So they tell me to go to the rear entrance.'

'Not the front?'

'No, I said the rear. You think I can't tell the difference? I get my things together, walk down through Green Park and St James's, and half an hour later I'm being taken up to his office.'

'Whose office exactly?'

'Halifax's.'

'*Lord* Halifax?' Burgess responded, startled. 'You're sure?'

"Course I'm sure. How many people do you know about a foot taller than yourself and with only one arm? And I wish you'd stop interrupting me. You want me to feel as though I'm back in bloody Russia?'

'Sorry, Mac.' Burgess took a mouthful of whiskey and tried to swill it around for as long as he could, drowning his sudden impatience. Mac hadn't made it clear on the phone why he'd wanted to meet – couldn't have, of course, he'd been told to say nothing on the phone. But a house call on Halifax?

'So I'm up in his office – huge place, like a palace, all sorts of chairs and bookcases right to the ceiling and marble busts and a table around which you could sit about twenty. There was a massive desk, too, beautifully carved, it was, with a grand leather top, the biggest I've ever seen. Very nice. Lots of papers, but all arranged in neat piles.'

Burgess forgot about his vow of patience and tried to talk with his mouth still full of whiskey. Mac waited for him to finish coughing.

'By the window there's a simple wooden chair, with newspaper spread all around to protect the carpet. Then in he comes, surrounded by lackeys, and it's all *Your Lordship* this and *Your Mightiness* that and *Can I Bring You Tea or Kiss Your Rear End, My Lord*. Don't they realize he whistles and farts the same as anyone? And he'd bleed the same as anyone, too, with a knife in his gut. Saw that in the camps. Blood isn't blue, it's red, even in the snow, same as

272

everyone's. Anyway, he doesn't say anything above "good-day" at first, sits down in the chair with a handful of papers, but soon he realizes he's getting them all covered in hair, so he throws them to one side and starts to relax.'

'Did you see what the papers were about?'

'Only the top one. It was titled "Danzig".'

Burgess swallowed. Mac could see his throat bobbing up and down like a courting pigeon. 'I don't suppose you managed . . . ? No, 'course not. Pity, though . . . Danzig, you're sure? God's bollocks . . .'

The curse brought a snort of abuse from behind his shoulder. 'Shame! Shame on you, sir!' came a female voice. Burgess turned, startled, to find himself staring into the reproachful eyes of a woman in the uniform and claret-and-blue bonnet of the Salvation Army. She was carrying an armful of newspapers. The *War Cry*. 'For he that profaneth in a public place shall surely feel the lash of the Lord,' she intoned ominously.

'Leviticus?' he asked tentatively.

'No, Beryl.' She dropped a copy of the newspaper down on the table in front of him. 'That'll be at least a shilling.'

Burgess smiled in defeat and gave her two. In return she offered a muttered 'God bless' before turning on her way in search of other sinners.

'Didn't realize you were religious, Mr Burgess.'

'I'm not. Just trying to keep my options open.'

'Expensive business, options,' Mac murmured as he noticed that the copy of the *War Cry* Beryl had left behind was priced only a penny. But Burgess never seemed to be short of any amount of change.

'You were telling me, Mac . . .'

'Yes, Lord H. So he starts relaxing and talking to me. Like they all do. Asks me if I think war is likely. *Me*, as if he cares an onion about my opinion. I say it depends, but I could see he wasn't listening, just letting off a little steam. So even before I've finished he starts talking about Czechoslovakia, and what a dreadful pity it all was. Then says it mustn't happen again and that it's time to get Hitler to sit up and take a little notice. So they're going to offer a guarantee to Poland.'

'I'm sorry to interrupt, Mac, truly I am, but please, *please* try to remember exactly what he said.'

'He said they were going to offer a guarantee to Poland. Even asked me if I knew where Poland was.' Mac began muttering into his beer, and Burgess took the opportunity to order two more large Irish whiskeys, which he lined up in front of him like coal barges on the Thames.

'So I said my mother had told me it was out Russia way, and he says – exactly. Stuck between Germany and Russia. And we're going to guarantee its independence. So I ask him what that means. Does it mean that if Germany wants part of Poland, we have to go to war?'

The first of the refreshed drinks had already disappeared. Burgess was chewing his thumbnail, had jammed it right into his mouth like a baby in a desperate attempt to persuade himself not to interrupt and get in the way of Mac's story.

'So he says' – Mac reached for his beer and took a long, slow draught. He was playing with Burgess, they both knew it, not unkindly, but teasing, reminding Burgess that their relationship had changed over the months and he was now in charge – 'he says, not necessarily. That depends. So I tell him I don't understand. So he says it's a guarantee of Polish independence, but not necessarily Polish frontiers. They might be moved, by agreement, and that would be all right. He said it was the principle of the thing that mattered.'

'Principle! What bloody principle?' Burgess spat, unable to contain himself any longer. 'It's not any sort of guarantee if it's not a guarantee of the borders. They'll wriggle out of it again, just like they did with the Czechs. This lot'll have to be dragged by their balls behind a whole division of *panzers* before they think it's time to go to war.'

'You want to go to war, Mr Burgess?'

'No, Mac, I don't. But I think Hitler will insist.'

'I think so, too.' He noticed that Burgess had bitten his thumbnail down so deep into the quick that it was actually bleeding, and back in his mouth. 'But Herr Halifax has got a different view. He said he didn't want to go to war – not that he could anyway, not with only one arm – and that he thought the guarantee of Poland might do the trick. Those were his exact words, that it might *do the trick*. Like a music-hall act. Then the door opened, another stuffed dummy came in, looked important, Halifax called him Rab –'

'Rab Butler, the Number Two in the Foreign Office. The biggest appeaser of them all.'

'So this chap says he wants to talk about the guarantee, says he's got his doubts about it, and that if it goes ahead, then it's got to be made more palatable – is that the right word? – to Herr Hitler.'

'By God, you've got a memory.'

'When you spend years in the camps with nothing to read apart from *samizdat* – and that only comes a page at a time, perhaps weeks apart – you try to remember every little bit.'

'I'm sure you do.'

'Anyway, I go on trimming, trying to make his haircut last as long as I can without leaving His Nibs completely bald, creeping around on the newspaper so as not to make a noise and remind them I was there – while he says to this Rab fellow that he's determined to make sure the guarantee does its job and delivers peace. He says he feels sure Hitler will understand. Then he said something else. You know me, Mr Burgess, I'm a mild man, but what he said made me want to reach for my razor.'

Burgess put down his glass. It was still half full. Mac had never seen him put down a glass that wasn't empty.

'He says to this other chap, Butler, that his work wouldn't be complete until our differences with Germany were settled and he had seen the Fuehrer driving down the Mall at the side of the King . . .'

'Mother Mary,' Burgess whispered.

'Went on to say that Hitler's birthday was coming up in a couple of weeks, and would Reichsleutnant Butler make sure that a suitable message of congratulation was prepared for the King to send.'

There was a long and strained silence. Burgess desperately wanted more.

'And that's it. I suggested I come back in three or four weeks and keep it tidy, then they kick me out into the typists' room while they get on with it.'

'Did you get a look at the papers on his desk, by any chance?'

Mac shook his head.

'Bugger.'

'Could be worse, Mr Burgess. The typists were all on their lunch break, the room was empty, bit messy to tell the truth. So I thought I might do a bit of tidying-up.'

He lifted his barber's case onto his lap and opened it. It was like a leather briefcase lined with pockets which on one side held razors and scissors and combs, while the other side held miniature bottles of lotions that gave off a sweet, perfumed smell. Mac loosened the fastenings that held the lining in place, lowering it just a fraction, allowing Burgess to see. Behind the lining the case was stuffed with thin sheets of paper, carbon copies mostly, the contents of a wastepaper basket, the cast-offs from another busy morning of toil inside Halifax's Foreign Office.

Everyone had an opinion of the Polish guarantee including, of course, Joe Kennedy. Problem was, he was insisting on letting everyone within earshot know about it, and by the time Brendan Bracken arrived at the Ambassador's residence to pick up Anna, Kennedy was well past the halfway mark on a bottle of Tennessee mash. He encouraged Bracken to share the other half in his book-lined den while they waited for Anna.

'So tell me, Bracken,' the Ambassador said, handing him a large crystal tumbler and settling himself back into an overstuffed armchair, 'what the fuck do you Brits think you're doing? Guaranteeing Poland? Like trying to guarantee sun in one of your god-awful summers.'

'I have to admit that Winston and I aren't overwhelming supporters of the Polish guarantee, but since Czechoslovakia turned turtle we decided that Poland was better than nothing.' Kennedy noted the 'we', the reliance on Churchill's name. That had always been his question about Bracken, whether the man could ever stand up on his own to be counted – although, in truth, Kennedy had a hundred other questions about this odd, flame-haired fantasist.

'But Poland's even farther away than fucking Czechoslovakia. Czechoslovakia had its fortified borders and the best damned arms factories in Europe – till you gave them all away. But the Poles've got nothing except a few rusting cavalry sabres and their drinking songs.'

'It's a dam against further German expansion.'

'Yeah, yeah, and Chamberlain gave me the same bullshit about it being a line in the sand. But dams burst. And lines in the sand get blown clean away. Then what are you gonna do?'

'We may have to fight.'

'Fight? With what? And against who?'

'What do you mean?'

'You've guaranteed Poland, old son. Know where that is? Stuck between Germany and Russia. Halfway between Hell and a hard place. Like guaranteeing a chicken in the jaws of an alligator. You're gonna end up fighting the entire fucking world on your own for a bunch of Polaks who can't even piss straight.'

'But America has warned –'

'Hey, let's all stand up and salute,' Kennedy mocked.

'Democracies standing together.'

'Like hookers on a street corner. Look, America has warned about nothing – it's Mr Franklin Duckhead Roosevelt who's been throwing all the words about. And it's because America *is* a democracy that you can bet your last buck we Americans ain't gonna get tangled in another European war. We're done with bringing home coffins. Roosevelt can rattle away all he wants, but there's a presidential election next year. We don't want war, and we're not about to elect a President who wants war, mark my words.' Kennedy rolled his glass between the palms of his hands, gazing at it as though it were a window on all the secrets of tomorrow. 'White House policy's nothing but one grand, over-hyped Jewish production nowadays. And if dear old Franklin insists, well, we might just have to dump him. Replace him with someone more in tune with the mood of the people.'

'Ah – someone like you?'

'Hey, it's an ill wind . . .' Kennedy rose, chuckling. 'Anyway, take some sound advice. You think the Polish deal's a pile of well-rotted horse manure, then put your money where your mouth is. Sell Polish securities short. Like I did with Czechoslovakia.' He refilled his own glass but Bracken declined, covering his glass with his hand. Too late, the bourbon splashed onto the back of his hand. Their eyes clashed – Bracken flushed with impatience, Kennedy with doubt as to what sort of man would refuse a free

279

drink. Not a man for his home, least of all for his private den. The Ambassador, without apology, slumped back heavily into his seat. 'What you doing here, anyway? Don't remember inviting you.'

'I've come to pick up Anna. Taking her out to dinner.'

'She'll be down in a minute. Just finishing off sending some telegrams I gave her.'

'Thank you.'

'Where you taking her?'

'To a play, then dinner at the Savoy.'

'Good. Glad to see you're treating her right. Important that you treat a girl right.' Suddenly he lurched forward in his chair, peering hazily through his round glasses. 'You've been seeing a hell of a lot of her recently, haven't you? Damned if I know what she sees in an Englishman; her father would turn in his grave. You giving her one?'

'I beg your pardon . . .'

'You giving her one? Got to take care of her interests. *In loco parentis* and all that bull. Promised her mother. So, you giving her one?'

'I don't think that's any business –'

'Course it's my fucking business. She's a goddamned American citizen and I'm the goddamned American Ambassador. And maybe more by next year.' The drink was upon him now, and both his logic and words were growing slurred. 'You've been dating her for months. Must be boning her. Only natural.' He waved his glass towards a series of framed posters of well-known actresses that hung above the fireplace. In the centre, occupying pride of place, was Swanson. 'Boned Gloria, I did. Won'erful woman.

Boned all the others, too, every single one of 'em. My little playmates. Gave the one at the end, there, little Ethel, to Duggy Fairbanks. Had it written into his contract. You know at your age, Bracken, I was boning everything in sight. But including the wife, you un'erstand. That's important. Don't neglect your wife. Fellas make that mistake and get a shit-load of trouble. You gotta treat them right, wives included. So, tell me – you treating little Anna right?'

Bracken, unsure whether 'boning' Anna would be a matter for capital punishment or congratulation in the eyes of this Ambassador, reverted to the truth. 'My relationship with Anna is entirely honourable.' Damn it. She was pure, had asked for his patience, had promised so much but nothing too quickly. His ideal woman. One who wasn't soiled, had no history, hadn't done the rounds, whom he could parade in front of other men without their exchanging knowing leers. He had to have a woman – ambition required it of him – and Anna was just about as good as any man could get.

'So *not* boning her?' Kennedy muttered, befuddled, just as his niece's footsteps could be heard scurrying down the staircase.

'No,' Bracken responded, tartly.

'Not boning her. Well, ain't that a thing,' Kennedy muttered into his glass, shaking his head. 'You not boning her. Could've sworn somebody was . . .'

The approach of Easter 1939. Bucketfuls of daffodils. And optimism. Chamberlain's reputation significantly restored by his guarantee to Poland – if for no other

281

reason than that, for the moment, it kept his critics quiet. Having raised Cain about a lack of action on Czechoslovakia, they could scarcely complain when he moved to protect Poland, not with an election in the wind. Life, for some, seemed to have returned almost to normal.

Although what passed for normal in Burgess's life was another matter.

He had his new friend – Tom Driberg – who had a house, a crumbling rectory on a promontory which jutted into the Blackwater estuary in Essex. Driberg had bought the house in an excess of enthusiasm some months before, when he had neither the money for the purchase price nor the means to underpin its crumbling foundations. Yet his was a lucky soul. The deposit arrived in the form of a personal injury claim following a car accident in which he broke both nose and kneecap, and the rest was provided by his reputation as the *Daily Express*'s William Hickey, which secured the overdraft he needed until the legacy he was expecting from his mother, who was dying of leukaemia, came through. In the meantime, he instructed builders to thrust steel girders into the cellar to prevent it sinking still further and to install a central heating system to guard against the chill winds that blew off the estuary. The builders did as they were asked, and within days had rendered the house completely uninhabitable.

So, in the week before Easter, Driberg was to be found motoring towards the far reaches of Essex in order to inspect the progress of the building works, and also to have a little fun. To assist with this latter purpose he had invited Burgess. While both were notorious and indiscriminate sexual highwaymen, they had no particular attraction for each other. Theirs was an entirely disinterested, almost sisterly friendship, but they shared many other passions – politics, journalism, public lavatories, danger and fast cars. They had clambered into Driberg's Studebaker and set out on the journey from London through Essex. They stopped for lunch at a pub just before the village of Steeple and, when they set off again, Burgess, who was driving, had a bottle of John Jameson's on his lap. They were driving too fast and had drunk too long. Disaster was, if not inevitable, then at least likely, but that was the point. They shared a thirst for danger which amounted to a compulsion.

It arrived while they were driving at nearly sixty and approaching the crossroads on the other side of Steeple just as a cyclist wobbled into their path. Burgess swore, then swerved, then skidded, finally coming to a halt nearly a hundred yards further on after having completely demolished a signpost. Driberg wound down the window in order to bellow insults at the hapless pedaller – which proved to be their second slice of misfortune, for the cyclist turned out to be the local policeman.

As he rode up he was greeted with the overwhelming aroma of whiskey. Burgess had dropped the bottle in an attempt to regain control of the car and his clothes were now covered in the stuff. 'You've been drinking,' the constable accused.

'No, officer,' he lied, 'not drinking. But I have been spilling. The waste of a fine and nearly full bottle. I assure you we were doing nothing more than toasting the parents of my friend here. He's Czech, you know, and he hasn't heard from them for weeks. I think in the circumstances you might be a little understanding –'

'You dirty bastards!' the policeman shouted across him. He had now inspected Driberg, who was in the back seat of the car. He was not alone. He was seated beside a young man, a bellboy Burgess had brought along as a housewarming gift. Both Driberg and the boy were in a state of disorder, for they had been struggling to replace the clothes they had only just discarded in order to experiment with sex at seventy over the bumps leading out of the village. Driberg hadn't bothered taking his shoes off and as a result had found it impossible to replace his trousers in a hurry. His underwear was still twisted around his knees.

'You're all going to go down for this,' the constable announced without a trace of irony, allowing his cycle to fall to the grass verge and reaching for his notebook and pencil. 'You – name,' he demanded, pointing at Driberg.

'Ah, my name? William Hickey.'

'How do you spell that?'

'Like in the *Daily Express*.'

'Don't you mess with me, you bleedin' degenerate.'

'No, officer, seriously – I am William Hickey. Of the *Daily Express*. Look.' He thrust that day's copy of the newspaper at the policeman.

'Don't prove nothing,' the policeman said, leafing through.

'Call the office. I can give you the number. And I've got my press card somewhere,' he added, scrambling back into his trousers.

'You're kidding. My mum reads William Hickey all the time.'

'I can tell you everything that's in that column today. I'll even tell you what's going to be in tomorrow, if you like.' Driberg was now out of the car, standing by the constable, at last respectably clad, dealing with him man to man.

'You really William Hickey?'

'Word of honour. And all this, officer' – he flapped his hands at his trousers – 'not what it seems. I'd simply dropped a lighted cigarette and it was burning me terribly.'

'But he said you were from Czechoslovakia.'

'On my mother's side. A countess. But I'm as British and as proud of it as you. And I'm terribly worried about the situation. Aren't you?'

'Looks like war. That's what my mum says.'

'Too right. We'll all be driving tanks soon. Silly to fall out amongst ourselves at a time like this, isn't it?'

The policeman was shaking his head, gripped in disbelief. 'My mum'd die if she thought I'd met William Hickey.'

'I'll happily sign the newspaper for her, if you like. Here, lend me your pencil a minute.'

And suddenly the constable was no longer taking notes.

'The least I can do is pay for the sign we've broken,' Driberg insisted, pulling out a wad of notes with which he had planned to pay his builders.

'So if you're William Hickey, what's going to be in tomorrow, then?' the policeman demanded, still not entirely in command of events.

'Well, you – if you want. I'm moving down to these parts – love it, everyone so kind – and I'd be happy to put in a reference to the friendly local police.'

'What, in William Hickey?'

'I guarantee it.'

'Tell you what, Mr Hickey, no need to pay for a new sign. You give me a couple of quid drinking money and I'll get some of the lads down at the Rose and Crown to fix it. No fuss. Mended by tomorrow.'

'And a signature for your mother? Happy Easter? Something like that?'

'Be really fine, sir. Could you do one in my book?' He ripped out the sheet on which he had been scribbling and offered Driberg a clean page. 'Me mum's going to ruddy well die . . .'

Chamberlain himself constantly attempted to mislead political correspondents in the most calculated fashion, by telling us what later proved to be the most grotesque version of the truth. He persisted in giving optimistic forecasts of international prospects which were lies. In all situations and all crises, however menacing, he always claimed that the outlook was most encouraging, with not a cloud in the sky; he claimed his contacts with Hitler and Mussolini were very good and that the dictators were responding with understanding and promise, and if only the Left-wing newspapers would stop writing critical and insulting things about them, he was confident that Herr Hitler and Signor Mussolini (he was always punctilious in using the Herr and Signor as a mark of respect, and frowned on any off-hand reference to Hitler) would co-operate with him in his peace initiative.

So forget your worries, he would tell us; the world situation has never been more promising; all these war-mongering stories are got up by the Communists, Jewish propagandists and their sympathizers . . .

It was on the eve of the Easter recess that Chamberlain met a group of us (press men) for yet another of his sun-shine tours. Reassure public opinion, he urged us; the worst was over and there would be no more shocks or surprise coups by the dictators – he was convinced of their good intentions. Have a good holiday, he advised us, free from worry and care.

He was, he added for good measure, acting on his own advice and was leaving that night on the Aberdeen express for a salmon-fishing holiday on the Dee.

James Margach, *Abuse of Power*
W.H. Allen, 1978

The next day was Good Friday.

Even before Chamberlain had cast his first fly, before his words of comfort had a chance to grow cool, before the ink on that morning's newsprint had dried, the dictators had struck again. Mussolini's troops marched into Albania.

Yesterday, Albania had been on the far side of the globe; now it seemed as though the whole world had shifted and she could almost hear the firing of the guns. For Sue Graham, Easter was not to be what she had planned. Those plans had included Jerry – indeed, had been entirely focused around him – but now the world talked of nothing but war and, with all the sensitivity that those oxymorons at military planning could muster, they'd sent him away for a week's basic to learn how to fire blanks. It had been pretty basic at Ypres, wasn't that enough?

So, with no post office duties to distract her, she was left on her own, which mattered more than she had realized. She missed him very greatly. The night before she had taken her family bible down from its perch on top of her wardrobe and sat on her single bed – the bed he had told her from the start she must change for something more accommodating, which she had known then and felt with a surprising inner force now meant accommodating him – simply to inspect the rose he had given her. She even found herself wandering around in the sloppy jacket he had left hanging on the back of the kitchen door, just so she could touch and smell him. And she had traced their favourite walk, along the cliff tops of Bournemouth past the Highcliffe Hotel, the breeze riffling through her hair, her face covered in his scarf.

She put her head down into the wind and walked briskly towards the highest point on the cliffs, struggling to convince herself that the tears in the corner of her eyes had been caused by nothing more than the fresh sea air tugging at her cheeks. As she gained the top, she came to a full stop and raised her head, suddenly alert. For carried on the breeze was not only the smell of salt but also the sharp reek of cold, oiled steel . . .

Her tear-filled eyes swept out to sea. It was thick with warships, their guns blazing, landing craft filled with men, disgorging a grey-clad army onto the beach, and bombers with bent wings were falling out of the sky, howling, casting a rain of death all around – at points the sea was churning red. She could see chaos and confusion – and death – on the beaches, and almost all of it was British . . .

Sue shook her head. It was only her imagination, of course. And foresight. She gazed along the beaches with cleared eyes and saw nothing but gently sloping sand and shingle, and a man out walking his dog. And that was about it, wasn't it? A man and his dog, for otherwise there was nothing here, not a minefield, not a pill-box, not a single strand of barbed wire, not a gun nor even an embrasure for a gun. Nothing. Nothing to stop those warships and landing craft and bombers and all the paraphernalia of war that was surely to come. Defences based on nothing more than the optimism of ostriches. Once more unto the breach, dear friends, once more, or close the wall up with our English dead. Starting with Jerry.

They had much to answer for, those men of Westminster, who had sat by irresolutely and thrown away the sacrifices of those who had bled, and suffered, and died in the last war. Like her dad. And now they wanted Jerry, too.

What had it all been about if it hadn't been the war to end the carnage, to stop Jerry and those like him marching to the slaughter, leaving the women behind to weep and the children with nothing more than faded sepia images of men? Well, she'd be no weeping widow, vainly wringing her hands. Her dad had died a proud man who had been buried in his Sunday suit with his medals by his side, and she would be damned before she'd let bloody Huns trample all over his memory as they had trampled over his life. She was the postmistress. She knew things. Above all she knew people – all the people – the sort of things it sometimes took a woman to know. She knew those who were made of steel, and those who would bend. She knew the gossips, the fighters, the compromisers and the outright cowards. Those who might resist and turn bomb-maker or saboteur, and those who would raise their hands and their petticoats at the sight of the first German invader.

It might come to that. And if it were to come to that, there was damn-all point in following the example of Chamberlain and starting tomorrow, the day after it was too late. So she came to a decision. She would start that afternoon. Making her plans, planting more vegetables and sowing a few seeds amongst those who would be forced to stay behind, after all the young men had gone. Seeds of resistance. She owed that to Jerry and her dad.

They sat on the terrace overlooking the river, glad of the chance to take the air. It was musty inside, with all the gas-proofing that had been carried out. Workmen had been busy installing air-tight windows, and there were new double doors and screens in addition to the dark blackout blinds and blast-proof curtains, all of which rendered the atmosphere inside listless, at times almost lifeless.

'Can't cope with all this, Dickie.'

'The ice-creamers in Albania, you mean?'

'All this Grand Old Duke of York stuff. We go off for Easter expecting peace, then get rushed back for war. It's all very well, but there's an election coming up at some point. How the deuce am I to explain all this to the voters when I can't even explain it to myself?'

'Does rather take the plum out of the pudding.'

'It's all very well Neville promising us a green and pleasant land, but he's got to stop covering the whole farmyard in horse droppings.'

'Bit harsh, old boy, isn't it? What was Neville supposed to do? Hitler and Mussolini are hooligans, for sure, so what do you do with hooligans? You let them pass by the front door. Last thing you do is drag them into the parlour and start up a blazing row.'

'But what if they don't simply pass by? What if they want to kick down our door, too?'

'You mean – invade?'

'Walk in. Just like they're doing everywhere else.'

'Ah, but we have the Channel, Ian.'

'Oh, I see. We sit back and pray for bad weather, do we?'

'It's not like you to be so down, old chap. Don't worry, something'll turn up.'

'Like the bloody Wehrmacht, you mean? No, Dickie, we can't go on, not like this. Something's got to be done.'

'First principles, Ian. The time for change is when change becomes inevitable. Not before.'

'We may be getting close.'

'Good God, you can't mean – not Winston. Not in the Cabinet.'

'A testing possibility, I grant you. But a possibility nonetheless.'

Dickie grimaced as though a knot had formed in his lower intestine. 'Not bloody Winston. We need a steady hand on the tiller right now, not some headstrong alcoholic who's still rushing around trying to rescue his reputation from the trenches of Gallipoli. Which is why I thank God for Neville. Even if the whole of Europe goes up in flames, he'll pull us out of the fire.'

'But will he? That's what I worry about. With this Polish guarantee, it means we don't get a choice. If the Germans invade, we have to go to war, whether we like it or not.'

'Neville would get us out of it. Somehow.' The words were brave, but there was a chaotic glint in Dickie's eye. They fell into silence for several minutes, staring out at the coal barges billowing their way up river, the tidal waters of the Thames rushing past as if they had somewhere more important to go.

'You know, from here on a clear day, Dickie, sometimes you can see as far as Clapham.'

'What'll we do, Ian? What on earth will we do?'

'Maybe time's up for the likes of you and me. Our day's come and now it's gone. Politics doesn't seem to have much meaning any more, no common ground left. Perhaps time to head for the hills. Have a word in the Whip's ear, remind him how loyal we've been. Years and years of loyalty, stretched out like a tiger skin. Not like Winston and all the other fair-weather friends.'

'Thought we were praying for storms.'

'Not the point, Dickie. We've still got years of service left to offer the nation, you and me. From the Lords.'

'What, the coma ward?'

'Why not? I wouldn't mind dying a peer. It would make the passage to the afterlife seem so very much shorter.'

There was a glass-covered lean-to at the back of Carol's house, overlooking the small back garden, where she would sew and knit, darning socks, altering clothes, or letting her hair dry in its curlers, while she watched over Peter and Linda as they played. When it wasn't raining and the glass roof leaking, she would sit with Mac at the little trestle table to read and write.

She was making excellent progress, all the letters and sounds falling into place, the words coming to life, and her fingers forming the written letters most deftly – but that came as no surprise to Mac, who knew all about her deft and dextrous fingers and the magic they could weave. Her illiteracy, it seemed, had more to do with childhood abuse than ignorance or inability, and she appeared to have put so much of her past behind her as reading opened up worlds full of new ideas. She often laughed as she read and recognized new words; it was like a great game and at last she was winning. The kids laughed when he was around, too – Peter seemed to thrive simply through the presence of another man who was much more fun to chase and to run with than his little sister, and even little Linda showed her joy. Only that morning she had run up to Mac, put her arms around his leg, burbled 'uvoo' and bitten him.

Yet the attention made Mac nervous. He wasn't used to complications, and babies who expressed their love for him seemed hopelessly entangling. His life had been so simple – eat, work, stay warm, survive – yet love meant being responsible for someone other than himself, and he hadn't been responsible for anyone since the day he'd watched poor Moniek's head being blown apart.

'What's wrong with you?' Carol demanded.

'Nothing,' he replied, 'just can't concentrate. Do your top button up, woman, it's distracting me. And get on with your magazine.'

'OK. Another five minutes. Then I've got to get Peter's birthday tea.' Peter was ten today. Mac had bought him a cowboy hat.

Carol turned the page of the magazine. He'd begun to bring home old copies of the *Illustrated London News* from Trumper's – the combination of pictures and words along with things she'd heard about on the radio seemed to enliven the lessons and fill in many of the gaps. She examined the page in front of her.

'So what's an eclipse, love?' She pronounced the new word firmly.

'It's when the sun disappears during the day. Supposed to be bad luck.'

'Says we're going to get one in a couple of days. You'd better stay in bed with me, then, dearie. Try your luck there.' She laughed again and began playing with the offending button on her blouse, only to stop suddenly. 'And what's this about Musso and his tomato tops?' She examined a photograph of the chaos in Albania and a dockside swarming with troops. '"A column of – kick-lists?"'

'Cyclists,' he corrected.

'"– whose mob-ility was of great assistance during the rapid advance . . ." Sometimes I wish I was back in the old days and couldn't read a bloomin' word.' She turned the page in distaste. 'Oh, bloody 'ell. It gets worse.' She was looking at a page of photographs of Madrid at the end of the Spanish civil war. Twisted statues that leaned at drunken angles. Bombed bridges. Rubble that had been homes. Fragments of torn fabric that might once have been bedroom curtains, or tablecloths, or children's clothes, now blowing hopelessly in the wind. But no people. 'Where have they all gone, Mac, all the people?'

He shook his head, struggling to hide the pain in his eyes. He was back in Poland, standing against a crumbling wall beside a smashed chicken coop, the screams of Ashkenazi still echoing in his ears. Ashkenazi was the youngest in their class. He hadn't screamed at first, simply stood examining the intestines that had fallen into his hands when he'd unbuttoned his tunic. Only after a while had he started screaming, until a Russian had put a bullet in him to stop the racket. There was blood on Mac's uniform, too, someone else's blood, neither his nor Ashkenazi's, perhaps Yitzhak's, and Mac remembered how he had rejoiced when he'd realized that the blood wasn't his own. He also remembered deciding he very much wanted to live, and not to die with

Ashkenazi alongside that battered chicken coop. He remembered it all now, and desperately wished he didn't.

'"*The rava-ges of war in a city for thirty months in the front line.*"' She turned to him, insistent. 'What does it all mean, love?'

'Ravages? It means –'

'I know what the bloody words mean. But all this – the wars, the bombs, the dying. Last month it was Czechoslovakia and now – this.' She pushed the magazine away angrily. 'We was promised, Mac, *promised*. Peace in our time. So what does all that mean?'

He looked away, trying to hide his eyes once more, and saw Peter in his too-large cowboy hat chasing his little sister round the lawn using the garden rake as a rifle. 'I'm ten, I'm ten!' he cried. 'Bang! Bang! You're dead.' Oh, little Peter, don't rush, don't rush, for it will all come soon enough. It had been Ashkenazi's birthday, too. He'd turned sixteen on the day he died.

ELEVEN

A fine evening, overflowing with drink and verbal excess. Churchill carried its full weight in the back of the taxi as it bore him home. He rarely missed a gathering of the Other Club, a dining group he'd set up nearly thirty years earlier along with his outrageous parliamentary colleague, F.E. Smith. Its purpose was simple – to dine, drink, debate and dispute with other men of authority and opinion. 'Nothing in the Rules or intercourse of the Club,' said its constitution, 'shall interfere with the rancour or asperity of party politics.' And it didn't.

They gathered in the Pinafore Room at the Savoy. It was decorated with splendid *trompe l'oeil* reminders of Victorian comic opera, but the discussion that evening had taken a particularly rancorous turn. The sense of order never sat more than lightly on such evenings, and it had begun to fall apart as soon as one of those present reminded the group that it was nearing the third anniversary of Chamberlain's appointment as Prime Minister. On cue and in the manner of a conductor pursuing the Valkyries, Bracken had started throwing his arms about wildly and denouncing 'a Government based on a jumble of old umbrellas and unction'. That had required a response from the only Government Minister present, who had found himself following a route which led him inexorably to the conclusion that Chamberlain's foreign policy, in spite of all its adversities, was above all unambiguously ethical. It was an argument which even the Minister himself suspected went more than a step too far, but alcohol induces politicians to overreach the limits of their own logic and he found himself stuck with it. Having reached the end of his road, he turned to face his accusers and raised his glass in a defiant toast – 'To Neville. Happy anniversary!' – challenging the others to join him. Bracken had begun to shout something particularly rude when, to the astonishment of everyone and not least the Minister himself, Churchill had raised his glass. It was a substantial balloon of cognac, which the old man examined in the light of the candles as though weighing the reputation of his leader. He demolished it in a single gulp. 'Anaesthetic,' he had announced, and belched. The Minister rose and left.

The evening had grown ever more boisterous, and Churchill seemed disinclined for it to finish. 'Celebrating Mr Chamberlain's success exhausts me so. I need your help,' he had informed both Bracken and Bob Boothby as at last the gathering had broken up. His two young friends now accompanied him, squashed in the back of the London taxi as it bore them through darkened streets towards Churchill's apartment in Morpeth Mansions overlooking the Catholic cathedral. It was beyond midnight when they arrived and, with some unsteadiness, tumbled onto the pavement. Churchill made some attempt at searching his pockets for the change to pay the driver, but his fingers had suddenly become those of an elderly man. Bracken had more money than either Churchill or Boothby combined but was notoriously reluctant to part with any of it, so it was left to Boothby to provide a ten-shilling note.

It was while they were fumbling on the pavement that a figure emerged from the darkness, calling out Churchill's name. Startled by the intrusion, Bracken sprang forward, moving protectively in front of his master and placing a hand on the advancing man's chest with such force that the stranger was propelled backwards. The raincoat he wore was old, his hair unkempt, and in the gloom he could easily have passed as a tramp – or worse. IRA bombers had been active since the turn of the year and had left a trail of destruction and fire across the major towns of Britain; it was only a matter of time before someone died. The Churchill family's reputation in Ireland made him an obvious target. So Bracken's caution was understandable, indeed commendable, yet appeared unwelcome on all sides.

'Touch me again and you'll end up on your arse in the gutter,' the stranger growled, showing his teeth like an alley dog.

'No, no, no, Brendan,' Churchill protested, pushing Bracken brusquely aside, 'that's Mr Burgess, I believe.'

Bracken stepped back in embarrassment.

'I'm sorry but – I saw you as I was passing,' Burgess lied. 'On my way home – round the corner. Chester Square.'

Beneath the meagre yellow light of the street lamp Churchill looked into Burgess's eyes and recognized the companionship and hard glaze of a fellow drinker. 'So, are we neighbours as well as fellow travellers, Mr Burgess? Splendid. Meet Mr Bracken, Mr Boothby. You will join us for a nightcap,' he instructed, taking Burgess's arm and leading him energetically up the steps. Boothby followed, stumbling from the excesses of the night, while Bracken appeared reluctant to follow. He was disconcerted by the arrival of this outsider, not only by its manner but also by the enthusiasm with which Churchill had taken his arm and left the others in his wake. Bracken was intensely proprietorial about his relationship with the old man. Churchill had a passion for life and a grasp on all matters political that Bracken knew he would never match, no matter how much he paid his tailor, so he was content to stand close – closer than anyone else – and bathe in the reflected light. It made him reluctant to share such favours with others, even with a colleague like Boothby, and after an evening's indulgence he had no relish for being pushed aside to make way for a complete stranger. The sense of Celtic disgruntlement only increased when, once inside Churchill's apartment, the old man threw his coat across the back of a dining chair and artlessly instructed Bracken to pour drinks for the rest of them. Churchill could inflict many careless insults; tonight, somehow, it mattered.

Soon Churchill stood with a glass in hand, leaning against the fireplace, surveying the scene while the rest sat around like a crew before its captain.

'I miss your columns in the *Standard*, Mr Churchill,' Burgess began.

'So do I, so do my readers. But most of all they

are missed by my bankers.' The words came more slowly and with greater sibilance than usual. 'Bugger Max.'

'Never thought he'd turn out to be an arch-appeaser.'

'He's not. He's an arch-opportunist, nothing more. A wolf in a Canadian winter looking for his next supper. He'll come round, when the winds have changed, bearing his chequebook and wanting to make up again. And we always do.'

'So you're not writing at the moment.'

'Oh, but indeed I am. A vast enterprise. A history of the English-speaking peoples.' The brandy glass performed a wide circle in the air and he seemed about to embark on an enthusiastic sales pitch, but suddenly his brow clouded. 'Sadly I seem stuck in the Middle Ages.'

'The years of invasion and conquest from across the Channel.'

'Ah, you are an historian!'

'Always wanted to finish off the life of Salisbury that his daughter Lady Gwendolen began. I've been in touch with the family. Perhaps one day . . .'

'A fine ambition. And a fine life.' The chin was up, the eyes fixed on a more colourful world. Behind him the army of stiff white invitation cards that crowded the mantelpiece seemed to stand to attention. 'I was first elected to Parliament when Salisbury was Prime Minister. The year before the Queen died. We were still doing battle with those devilish Bo-ers. Nineteen hundred . . .'

The old man was off. Bracken and Boothby, used to the late-night soliloquies and outpourings of nostalgia, settled down with their drinks for the duration, but Burgess couldn't resist the challenge. 'And within five minutes of getting elected you'd deserted him and joined the Liberals.'

'Steady on,' Bracken intervened.

'But he is right, Brendan. I jumped ship. Some men change their principles for the sake of their party. I found it more convenient to change my party for the sake of my principles.' He held out his empty glass. Wearily Bracken rose and attended to it. 'Ah, but they were tempestuous times and the Tory ship had no idea in which direction to sail, whether to run before the wind or to turn and fight its way through the gathering storm. So – I ratted.'

'And now you've re-ratted.'

The old man chuckled. 'No one can accuse me of having a closed mind, Mr Burgess.'

'Mr Churchill, I suspect you are something of a bandit.'

'Indeed I am! We Anglo-Saxons are by our nature bandits and pirates. An island needs stormy seas and a race of adventurers for its protection.'

'Ah, but those stormy seas won't stop the Hun.'

'The French will,' Bracken intervened, eager to reinsert himself into the conversation. In the other chair, Boothby had fallen asleep and was gently snoring.

'The French?' Burgess rounded on Bracken, his tone impatient and dismissive. 'You can't be serious. The French won't fight!'

'Nonsense. They're our allies,' Bracken snorted, repaying the belligerence.

'They'll hide behind the Maginot Line and hunt

nothing but truffles. The smell of rotting fungi's hardly likely to scare off bloody Hitler.'

'The French alliance is fundamental to –' Bracken began, but Churchill cut across him, spurred by Burgess's thought.

'I wonder. I do so wonder,' the old man chanted, leaning with both hands on the fireplace and looking into a grate of grey ashes. 'They have the largest armies in the world. They also have their Maginot Line, the mightiest defensive line Europe has ever known. But whom does it protect? Not poor Czechoslovakia. Nor Albania. Neither will it defend Poland nor any part of the Balkans. I hate to think of it, but what Mr Burgess says has the unhappy ring of truth. The French have been fooled by their own defences. They may shout defiance from behind their fortress walls but unless they can be persuaded to advance beyond those walls and hunt down the Hun, then the Line will protect no one but the Nazis as they fall upon their neighbours in the east. Oh, it has become a cruel deceit. I fear the Maginot Line will not stop this war. On the contrary, perhaps it makes war all the more likely and on a much more vast scale.' He turned to face them, his face grown sombre. 'So what is to save us, gentlemen?'

Burgess took a huge sip of whisky, then another, before muttering: 'Russia.'

Bracken sprang to his feet, like a fisherman striking at a pike, except the drink had made him unsteady and it appeared for a moment as though he were slipping on a muddy bank. 'Russia? Are you mad? Bolsheviks riding to the rescue of Christianity? What planet were you born on? They want nothing but to sweep us into the sea.'

'Moscow's nearly two thousand miles from London, Mr Bracken, they're not in any position to sweep us into the sea. But the Wehrmacht is camped barely two *hundred* miles from the Russian frontier with only the potato fields of Poland in between. Don't you think the Russians might just have other things on their mind than picking the pockets of a few wobbling English aristocrats?'

'Mr Burgess, explain yourself!' Churchill commanded sharply.

Oh fuck, the drink had driven him over the top. Beneath the glass that lay in his lap, Burgess squeezed his own balls. Hard. Anything to stop his tongue running away with his sense. He didn't like Bracken – a mutual and instant antipathy, perhaps a recognition that they were both fantasists and adventurers – and he had allowed his alcohol-sodden temper to get the better of him. He had loitered outside in the freezing cold for more than an hour waiting for Churchill, wanting to get to him, yet now that he was inside his parlour he was about to get himself thrown out. He squeezed again until the pain had given his brain a thorough shaking. He took a deep breath.

'You said it yourself, Mr Churchill. In the book you gave me . . .' Book, what book? Bracken looked between the two in alarm, like a Menshevik who had missed out on a conspiracy – 'Russia is an Ishmael amongst the nations, you said. Yet you also said she is one of the most titanic factors in the economy and in the diplomacy of the world. That's the word you used. Titanic. You painted a lurid picture – I can almost remember your words. *Russia, with her enormous, rapidly increasing armaments, with her tremendous development of poison gas, aeroplanes, tanks and every kind of forbidden fruit; Russia, with her limitless manpower and her corrosive hatreds which weigh heavily upon the whole line of countries, some small, others considerable, from the Baltic to the Black Sea, all situated adjacent to Russian territory . . .'*

'Your memory is excellent.'

'And your geography's bollocks!' Bracken protested, determined to fight his corner against this usurper. 'Poland's one of those adjacent countries that come under the Russian hammer – and we've just agreed to guarantee the bloody place.'

Burgess was shaking. 'And when Herr Bloody Shitler invades Poland – as he undoubtedly will – he'll find himself staring down the spout of all those Russian barrels. Given half a word of encouragement, Russia could be our most awesome ally!'

'Russia – an ally? Not even Stalin trusts the bloody Russians!'

'You don't even trust your own Prime Minister –'

'Gentlemen!' Churchill barked, bringing them both to order. 'What has trust got to do with it? The basis of diplomacy isn't trust, otherwise we wouldn't put the Foreign Office in charge of it. No one trusts the Foreign Office, not even the pigeons. No, what matters is *need*. And I fear we may need Stalin's cohorts more than I would wish. Never turn your back on a Cossack – yet that is what Hitler must do if he is to throw the full might of his armies against us in the west.'

'But you're the most notorious bloody anti-Bolshevik in the business, Winston,' Bracken protested, his pebble glasses misted with emotion. 'The most destructive and degrading tyranny in history, you called it.' Fuck and damnation, if Burgess could quote Churchill back at him, Bracken wasn't going to be left out of the game. 'Why, when you were at the War Office you sent thirty thousand British soldiers into Soviet Russia to strangle the little bastard at birth.'

'And I failed! It turned out to be some bastard. Some birth. And where I failed, do you really think an upstart Austrian corporal can succeed?'

'You'd have us side with murderers?'

'If it would save my own grandmother from being skinned alive – of course! I was in the Smoking Room the other day and Maisky, the Soviet Ambassador, fell upon me with all manner of encouragement and friendship.'

'Untrustworthy little shit –'

'But a *useful* untrustworthy little shit, Brendan. When he as good as promised me lifelong brotherhood, I replied to him thus.' The glass waved in the air, conjuring up the memory of the occasion. 'Mr Maisky, I said, let me be frank. I do not like you. Least of all do I like your Government. But I recognize you – as a fact. And I recognize the uncomfortable fact that I may need you – we may need each other – if Hitlerism is not to snuff out the candle of liberty in every corner of Europe.'

'And what did the useful and untrustworthy little shit reply?'

'He laughed. Then he clapped me on the back and invited me to dinner.'

'Sometimes, Winston, I think you'd dine with the Devil.'

'I dine with the American Ambassador, so I'm scarcely in a position to claim moral superiority.'

'Bob!' Bracken turned on Boothby, his sharp tone rousing the other man from his slumber. 'What do you think of the Russians?'

The Member for East Aberdeenshire raised a heavy head. 'Russians?' he growled in the melodious timbre that, before it had broken and sunk beyond bass, had won him a choral scholarship at Eton. He shifted in his seat. His dark suit was dirty, his collar soft and crumpled, his stomach already over-large and seemingly held in by an enormous watch chain. He looked a lot like a waiter in a restaurant that had been living off a long-discarded reputation. 'Russians?' he repeated, trying to reassemble the various pieces of his mind. 'What've they done now?'

'Nothing, Bob, we want to know what you think of them?'

'Bastards buy lots of Aberdeen herring. Splendid chaps.' With that, his head dropped once more and he was instantly unconscious.

Bracken cleared his throat, not wanting to catch the glint of triumph he suspected he would find in Burgess's eye. He'd lost this one. It was time to retreat. 'It's late, Winston, and Bob needs his bed. I think we'd better go.'

Churchill threw away the stub of his Havana to join the ashes in the grate. 'Fly away to your nests, if you must. Rest yourselves for the fight ahead.'

Bracken shook Boothby's shoulder and Burgess stood, too, but made no move to depart. 'Mr

Churchill, I was wondering – may I have a word? In private?'

'No, no, Burgess, it's very late and Mr Churchill has a full diary in the morning,' Bracken complained, but already the old man was waving him towards the door.

'You young politicians never have enough time, but for historians like Mr Burgess and myself, time is all but immeasurable. Let yourself out, Brendan, dear boy, while Mr Burgess and I settle down for a nightcap.'

Churchill poured the drinks. Huge goblets of cognac. 'You drink cognac?'

'I prefer Irish whiskey.'

'Then you and Brendan have more in common than I had thought.'

'He doesn't like me.'

'Oh, he'll like you well enough, Mr Burgess, when I tell him to. He'll even like your ideas about Russia in the morning, although he'll offer you no credit for them and attribute every detail to himself.' The door downstairs slammed; they were alone. 'He is my parliamentary Puck – a mischievous and at times misguided sprite but, in the end, faithful.'

Churchill handed across the heavy glass. 'Learn to enjoy cognac, Mr Burgess. It's like a good woman. Warm it between your hands and coddle it, don't assault it.'

Burgess took the goblet and wondered what it was like to lay hands upon a woman. Would he – *could* he – even in the service of his cause or his country? He prayed he'd never have to find out. He'd stick to Jameson's.

Burgess had already begun to realize that Churchill's relationship with alcohol was entirely different to his own. Burgess drank because he needed to. It was the only way he'd found to drown out the screams of terror that welled up inside him every time he tried to stop and sleep, and could smell his soul scorching. But Churchill had other needs, drank to sustain his thoughts and his unquenchable energy. Alcohol was his fuel, like a racing car required petrol or a bonfire wood. He ran on the stuff.

'So,' Churchill began after he had spent some time lighting a new cigar, 'you wanted a word. You are a modest man, Mr Burgess, for I normally insist on several, and charge for every thousand.'

'It's kind of you. I may be making a fool of myself . . .'

'I am a politician,' Churchill growled. 'Folly is my second cousin.'

'Then let me be blunt. War is coming – agreed?'

'Indubitably.'

'And when it does every money-man will join in a stampede for the hills?'

'The Appalachians, I suspect, where they will camp and make occasional visits to New York.'

'They like to travel light. And I've been wondering – after what you told me at Chartwell – whether they'll bother carrying your debts with them.'

Churchill looked at the younger man with curious, cautionary eyes. It was one thing for him in a fit of depression to share his woes, quite another for those woes to be brought back to him. 'I had hoped, Mr Burgess, that I would be able to finish my history of the English-speaking peoples before war came and so relieve the situation, but . . .'

'You can't write as quickly as the Wehrmacht marches.'

'Quite so. Hitler's ambitions grow even faster than my needs.'

'I'm an adviser to the Rothschild family – went to Cambridge with the son – the mother seems to think I have a grasp of international affairs. Anyway, I help keep her investments from being squashed under the tank tracks. Haven't mentioned a word of your situation to them but . . . I'm sure, if they heard you were in need, the Rothschilds and some of their friends would be happy to help.'

Churchill drew long on his cigar, considering what had just been said. 'Why should they be willing to act as Samaritans in circumstances when my own bankers might prefer to pass by on the other side? The Rothschilds are bankers, too, and you could scarcely advise them that it would be a good investment.'

'But that's where you're wrong. They're Jews. They know what's happening in Europe. They know what Hitler stands for and how useless it is to turn the other cheek. In every part of Europe that Hitler controls, Jews are being roasted on the spit. They also know one other thing. That the only politician in Europe whom Hitler fears is you.'

'And what would they require in return?'

'Nothing.'

'I consider that most unlikely. In my experience there is always a price to pay.'

'Then we'll make the money available from a

trust. A blind trust. So you won't know who's involved or who's given what. Your hands will be entirely clean and free to get on with the job.'

From his perch by the fireplace, the old man peered down impassively, drifting in and out of the fog from Havana.

'You represent hope to every Jew in Europe,' Burgess continued. 'That's why I think they'd be willing to help.'

'The Rothschilds and their kind haven't built their financial empire on the basis of sentiment, Mr Burgess.'

'Well, it's more than just sentiment. Let's face it, if we lose a war against Hitler, they're buggered anyway. First in line. Any money they might lose on you would be nothing but a drop in a very bloody ocean.' He drained the last of his drink, surprised that he had finished it already. 'They'll rescue you, because you may be the only man in Europe who can rescue them – and their money.'

'You have a very high opinion of my talents, Mr Burgess –'

'I do.'

'Almost as high as my own. And I must admit that your visit is uncanny, like that of an angel in the hour of need. My bankers, as you say, are nervous types who appear to be busy gathering up their mountaineering equipment. I get the feeling that my debts may be a little too burdensome for them to carry on their trek.'

Burgess's hand, the hand on his crotch, was trembling. He desperately wanted another drink. He wanted to toast Rodney, the Dickensian little clerk

311

in Churchill's bank who was all waistcoat and wet lips and whose responsibilities included scurrying around the vaults to ensure that all sorts of interesting records were filed away properly, including the one that covered Churchill's loan, six months, non-renewable. The six months were up in as many weeks. That's why he'd come. And even if the Rothschilds wouldn't help there would be many more who would, once they were instructed to do so.

'A blind trust, Mr Churchill. Leave it to me.'

'You are an *unexpected* man, Mr Burgess. You arrive on my doorstep in Chartwell when all the world is about to fall apart. Then you emerge from the dark in London when we can almost hear the sounds of crashing masonry. And each time you come bearing the gift of hope. What is to become of a man like you?'

'Perhaps one day I'd like to join the Foreign Office.'

'A splendid ambition – one in which I would like to be able to assist, if I could. You want to use your expertise in international affairs?'

'No,' Burgess responded, his task now complete and his defences swept away in the flood of alcohol. He no longer had the energy for equivocation. 'It's simply the job security. You can't get fired from the Foreign Office, not for anything less than goats.'

For some time after Burgess had left, Churchill sat in his armchair by the window looking out across the darkened skyline of London, and brooding.

Eventually he came to a conclusion. He picked up his pen and began to write. An article that would appear in the *Telegraph* under the headline: 'Towards a Pact with Russia'. It spoke of the need for alliance with Moscow, of how the long-held objections to such an alliance had simply ceased to be relevant, about the harmony of interests that now existed with the Soviet Union. And about their common interest – peace.

He didn't believe that last bit, of course, about the Soviet leader having turned from a tyrant into an apostle of peace, but Stalin was needed and such things had to be said.

And he would be paid for the article. Not a fortune, but in his present circumstances every little helped. Sell a few articles, while in corners all across London other men were selling their principles.

'Damn his eyes – damn, damn, damn him!'

'Neville, please –'

'I won't have it!'

'Of course not, but –'

'I'm the bloody Prime Minister. I am! I am! They'd better start remembering that.'

'No one would dare –'

Horace Wilson's attempts at emotional surgery were cut short as Chamberlain's fists pounded on the leather-topped desk in Wilson's room so ferociously that the telephone jumped off its cradle. In an armchair by the fireplace, Joseph Ball shrivelled in alarm.

'No sooner does he drivel on about getting into bed with the Russians than half of Fleet Street goes crawling to his door and demands his return to the Cabinet.' Chamberlain swept up an armful of papers. 'The bloody *Telegraph* again, the *Manchester Guardian*, the *Chronicle* – even the bloody Astors are at it. Look at the *Observer*.' The offending newspaper shook in his hand. 'He must be blackmailing the Astors, there can't be any other reason. What's he got on Nancy, for God's sake, more sexual savagery from those ridiculous weekend parties of hers?' And all he'd got from his weekend with the Astors at their sumptuous home at Cliveden was a game of musical chairs. With an impatient sweep of his arm Chamberlain threw the offending journals into the corner, where they died like throttled chickens.

Wilson took a long moment before intervening, clearing his throat. He wasn't normally discomfited in the presence of his Prime Minister but he had rarely seen Chamberlain in such form. His face was white, the skin like cracked parchment, as though all the blood had drained to his spleen to fuel the rage. 'You have to make a choice, Neville. Is he in or is he out?'

'Out! Out!'

More throat-clearing. 'You ought to know what the Foreign Office is saying. That there are those within the German Government – those who don't want a wholesale war – urging you to include Winston as the only way to show Hitler that we mean business about resisting further aggression. The only way to keep the peace.'

'Which is why I *never* listen to the Foreign Office. Can you imagine that man in Cabinet? May the gods help me – he'd just talk. Take up my time. Endlessly disrupt. Use the Despatch Box like a brawler uses a public bar.'

'Nevertheless, there's a lot of pressure –'

'And have my Government swept away on a tide of whisky and hot wind? Never! You know how he rambles. I sometimes wonder whether he's entirely stable, mentally. Passed down from his father. And all that alcohol over so many years. Must take its toll.'

'But we have to decide. Not just about Winston, about the pressure for an alliance with Russia.'

Chamberlain's eyes stared at Wilson in real pain, the lips thin as razors beneath the sagging moustache. 'With murderers? Regicides? How can I go to the Palace and tell His Majesty that I am to do a deal with the men who butchered the Tsar? What will history say of me?'

'Churchill thinks that if we don't do a deal with Stalin, then the Germans might. Carve up Poland and the rest between them. He's been telling everyone . . .' – it was Ball, re-emerging from the depths of his armchair to come to the aid of his friend. He was waving a sheaf of transcripts. 'I've stepped up the monitoring, you see.'

'But what you don't see – what neither of you seems to see – is that if I do any sort of deal with Russia now it will look as though *he* has set the agenda. And I will not – I will never – have the policy of my Government set by Mr Winston Bloody Churchill!' It was the first time he'd brought himself to mention his adversary's name since the start of the outburst. He spat it out as the hands thumped down on Wilson's desk once more. His starched wing

315

collar had become twisted and was digging into his neck, but he appeared not to have noticed.

Wilson rose to his feet, trying to engage his Prime Minister on the same level, tired of the flecks of spittle that kept falling on him. 'Neville, you must calm down and listen. Half the wretched Cabinet want us to do a deal with the Russians.' It was a lie – the true figure was more like three-quarters – but such figures did not seem to impress Chamberlain, who began to scream.

'They are my Cabinet and they will do as they are bloody-well told!'

The spittle continued to fly, but Wilson would not back down. He held Chamberlain's gaze, calling on their years of friendship, of understanding, of achievement. When finally Wilson spoke once more, his tone was determined. 'The Russians have offered us an alliance. Publicly. We have to give them an answer, Neville. We can't dodge it.'

Chamberlain drew a huge lung-bursting breath which, as it was released, seemed to carry away with it much of the fire that had been consuming him inside. At last the heaving chest grew calm. 'Very well, Horace,' he muttered, straightening his collar. It left a red weal where it had dug into his neck. 'We will offer them talks. We will thank them for their proposal and send a delegation to Russia. But – we will send the delegation by ship. A banana boat for preference. Very slowly. We shall insist that every detail of the discussions is reviewed back here in London. And we shall put in charge a man of such hideous mental dullness –'

'You mean someone from the military,' Ball interjected.

'– that the talks can never come to any clear conclusion.'

'So what's the point?' Wilson enquired.

'It will give us time.'

'Time for what?'

'Time to get Winston off our backs. Time to put a bit of spunk back into the Cabinet. And above all time to pursue our own policies. I still want peace. Even if half of Europe demands annihilation, I still want peace. And I want Hitler to know that. So, Horace, this is what you will do.'

Chamberlain began to pace the small room, three paces forward on the rug, turn, three paces back, his hands clasped behind him, his narrow, sloping shoulders leaning forward.

'I want Hitler to know that he has a way out. That he still has more to gain from peace than from war. So you will continue your negotiations with the Germans about the loans, Horace. Offer them the hand of peace and make sure it's full of cash. Tell them we want to get their workers out of the front line and back into the factories. Arms to agriculture, swords into ploughshares, all of that. You must persuade them of the peace dividend. *Must* persuade them of that. Everything depends on it.' Suddenly he had stopped and was jabbing his finger at Wilson. 'But whatever you do, keep the whole thing out of the reach of the Foreign Office. Nothing to do with the Foreign Office, you hear? I won't have them briefing every journalist they can find in exchange for half a bottle of claret.'

He was standing at the window now, staring out over the park, silhouetted against the early summer

317

light in a manner that left nothing but an outline. From inside the room, it seemed as though the sun itself had rejected him.

'Need to get things back into order on the home front, too,' mused Wilson, picking up the baton once more. 'That's where you come in, Joe. Those security measures of yours.'

'You mean the phone taps.'

'Your watch over Winston.'

'Eden, too. And a few of the others.'

'Make it a few more of the others, eh? Try those within the Cabinet who've got good personal relations with Winston. Give us early warning of trouble. If it's going to happen, let us be the first to know about it – before it arrives on the front page of the *Telegraph*.'

'No problem.'

'Does Sam know about the taps?'

'Not exactly.'

'Meaning?'

'Doesn't know a bloody thing.'

'But he's the Home Secretary.'

'This isn't an official operation, you see. It's more by way of a testing of technical equipment, if you follow my drift. And asking Sam's permission might prove – a trifle delicate.'

'Why?'

'Because he's on the list, too. Thought it best to keep track of the Home Secretary's love life – very little of which actually takes place at home. Dates, times, names – I've got the lot. I think we can rely on Sam's continuing loyalty. Don't know about his wife, though.'

'You disgraceful bastard.'

'Thank you. I'm being scrupulously even-handed. Managed to acquire some friends inside Odhams Press. They do all the printing for the Labour Party – pamphlets, posters, that sort of thing. So we know what they're going to say before even they do. Means we can get our oar in first. Got a couple of chums down at Labour Party headquarters, too.'

'How the hell . . . ?'

'Bit of public indecency here, a drunk and disorderly there. I settle things for them with the Yard – no prosecutions – just leave the charges on the books to ensure their undying gratitude and, of course, enduring indiscretion.'

'Your mother was a vampire, surely . . .'

'Sadly, the black arts don't work every time. Some less good news. Winston's loan. Seems he's got someone to replace it. So no collapse of that particular stout party, at least not yet.'

'Pity. It was only meant to be a little distraction, a chance to twist his tail, but it might have kept the old monster quiet for a while. If only we can get through this summer . . .'

Suddenly, the figure at the window stirred. It had stood impassively, like stone, but now the shoulders heaved, a conductor calling his men to the music. 'There is another way,' he announced quietly, joining them once more. The voice was hoarse, desiccated. He turned. 'Another way, perhaps, to keep him quiet. One he might least expect.'

'We shoot him?'

'We *encourage* him.'

'Neville?'

'If we let him *think* I might reappoint him to Cabinet, make him believe we're considering it, play on his inexhaustible vanity . . . then he might turn the good little nigger.'

The others grew excited as the idea inflated before them.

'He wants office more than he wants breath . . .'

'Vanity's always been his Achilles heel . . .'

'Start the ball rolling with an indiscreet gossip at the bar of the Athenaeum, perhaps . . .'

'Get Dawson and the Beaver to send up a few balloons. See how high they fly . . .'

'Seduce him.'

'Confuse him.'

'Then screw him.'

'Keep him quiet. Just get us through the summer,' Chamberlain urged, 'until the press has got something else to get its teeth into.'

'Like a deal with Berlin.'

'Get Hitler to fly over here for a change.'

'Show who's in charge.'

'Just so we can get through the summer . . .'

'And an election . . .'

'And keep Winston quiet.'

'And then what, Neville?'

'Then? Then we bury the bastard.'

TWELVE

The world entered that exhausting, stifling summer of mistrust that was 1939, and no one was quite certain who the enemy was.

The British emissary was chosen for the negotiations with Russia; he was, as Ball had predicted he would be, a military man, an elongated aristocrat bearing the name of Admiral the Honourable Sir Reginald Aylmer Ranfurly Plunkett-Ernle-Erle-Drax. It was economical, at least, like sending an entire delegation all wrapped up in one name. It isn't clear what the leaders of the great proletarian revolution in Moscow made of him, although they couldn't fail to have noticed that, while Chamberlain had flown at a moment's notice to meet with Hitler at Munich, Sir Reginald was sent the long way round to Russia, by boat. If it took Stalin a little time to work out British motives, much clearer to him was the rattling of the Wehrmacht's panzer treads. Russia had no faith in the ability of the Polish army to stand in the way of the Wehrmacht, for they were armed mostly with obsolete rifles that dated from before the Revolution of 1917. Russia should know – she had supplied them. Meanwhile, Horace Wilson sent emissaries to pursue the prospects of a deal with Germany, even while Germany continued to spit and scream and shake fists of warning in the direction of Poland. German workers bent their backs to the lathe and the production line in order to produce the arsenals for war, while in Britain the numbers of the unemployed rose yet again. So did the level of fear, and, with it, the level of desperate distraction.

Champagne flowed across the nation. It flowed at Wimbledon, where an American, Bobby Riggs, won the men's championship in five sets (all five Wimbledon championships fell to the Americans that year, much to the disgust of the British press who implied that the winner of the ladies' championship, Alice Marble, was a man). It flowed at the Henley Royal Regatta, even though the top rowing prize was carried off by yet more Americans, a crew from Harvard. And the champagne flowed most uninhibitedly during the racing of Cowes Week – dominated by the yacht *Vim* owned by Henry Vanderbilt, who was, of course, American. They were everywhere, the damned Yanks, beating the British at their own games – but, hell, the editors reflected, the British could still show these interlopers something about the greatest game of all, the game of war . . .

Something was rotten in old Albion, yet it seemed to encourage still greater outbursts of escapism. The summer sales were in full force – a Persian lamb fur coat could be bought for the knock-down price of forty-five pounds, while those with less substantial budgets could pick up woven silk and wool underwear for as little as ten shillings. *The Times* encouraged the population to relax and enjoy their summer, stating that 'there seems to be a general feeling that there is no reason why a holiday should not be taken with a fairly easy mind'. Almost business as usual. Meanwhile, marriage banns were read from pulpits in every corner of the country as the number of wedding ceremonies reached a record level. Ordinary people, distrusting every assurance thrust at them by politicians, were rushing to grab any morsel of happiness while they could.

Yet reality insisted on its place. Rumours that Chamberlain was negotiating once more with the Germans, that he was planning another Munich, began to bubble through the cracks of secrecy. In late July the *News Chronicle* reported that Britain had been negotiating a loan of one billion pounds sterling in exchange for some undefined measure of disarmament. The news caused confusion in Britain, but in Moscow the message rang as clear as a newly burnished blade. The British were going to betray Russia yet again. They were planning a deal with Germany; Russia would be left isolated, alone, abandoned once again, screwed by capitalists and imperialists. Just like before. So Stalin made up his mind. He wasn't going to be caught short this time around.

Chamberlain, too, was determined not to be caught. When allegations about the German loan were raised in the House of Commons, he denied any knowledge of the matter. He stood up at the Despatch Box, leaned on it, waved his hand, and lied.

In the same week in late July, less than six weeks before the outbreak of that most catastrophic war, Chamberlain's Government suspended the legal immigration of Jews into Palestine on the grounds that too many immigrants had already arrived illegally. The quota would be 75,000 over the next five years, and not a single Jew more. The Government particularly condemned those Jews who had fled from Poland and whom 'the British public did not regard as coming within the term "refugee"'. After all, Poland was safe; Downing Street had guaranteed it. So they were to stay where they were, all six million of them, and pressure was put on leaders of the Jewish community in Britain to ensure that they co-operated in keeping the Jews in their place.

So when a party of German Jews was discovered concealed and almost suffocated in the airless ballast tank of a small ship arriving off the east coast, the ship's captain was arrested. The Jews were sent back.

The British Government seemed to have no idea who the enemy was. The IRA, at least, suffered no such confusion . . .

It was a mean, worn suitcase, constructed primarily of cardboard, barely meriting the two tin clasp-locks that secured it. The suitcase had been brought to the Left Luggage office at King's Cross shortly before noon by a man in a trilby – the only distinguishing feature anyone could remember afterwards, apart from the Liverpool accent. He'd said he would be back for the suitcase later that evening, so it had been left beneath the counter rather than being moved to the back of the office, where it might have done less damage amongst so many other pieces of luggage. Like sandbags, they would have been. But instead the stranger's suitcase was placed beneath a front counter constructed of wood, which was a terrible pity. Wood turns to fragments like shrapnel that can turn a station concourse into a slaying field, particularly when it is crowded with lunchtime travellers.

Less than two hours after the suitcase had been left, the contacts on a timing device – constructed from the hands of a travel alarm clock – touched. This completed an electrical circuit that was powered by a battery from a bicycle lamp. The circuit ignited a fuse. The fuse was fashioned from gunpowder which had been plundered from rifle bullets, but it had been wrapped too tightly inside the sticks of gelignite, which in turn had been wrapped inside an oilskin, and the fuse burned for longer than intended – more than a minute. The suitcase began to emit wisps of purple-orange smoke. However, it was a busy time of day and none of the cloakroom attendants noticed until it was far too late. When the device exploded it blew out the wooden counter and the glass front of the Left Luggage office and created a blast wall of shrapnel. Many items of baggage were thrown after the shrapnel. Dr Donald Campbell of Edinburgh, newly married, who had just returned with his wife from a trip to the Continent, was queuing for his luggage when the bomb exploded. He was hit with its full force and died within minutes on the floor of the office, surrounded by tattered remnants of other people's holidays. His wife, four cloakroom attendants and ten other people were injured.

Later that same evening, a bomb exploded in the Central Section Cloakroom of Victoria Station. Five civilians were injured. Several more devices exploded at various points around the country.

Just in case anyone had forgotten, the Irish Republican Army were already at war.

Burgess had been drinking – to excess – and why not? The country was moving inexorably towards the embrace of evil, yet no one in authority seemed capable of grasping the fact. As the summer drew on, long and exhaustingly hot, so the intolerance of Germans towards their neighbours seemed to rise, just as the water levels on the great defensive rivers like the Dniestr and the Vistula that protected the plains of Poland began to fall. Men had become nothing more than cogs in an infernal machine that was preparing to devour the entire world. Governments across Europe were now frantically pouring money into weapons for the war that was to come, and Burgess knew that men like him would soon be thrown after them.

So he drank. The hotter it got, the more he drank, and the more he drank, the more he went out and got fucked. He'd never been a man to indulge his sexual tastes with any caution, but now he grew utterly indiscriminate. He fucked to forget, and there was so much he wanted to forget.

He'd spent some time loitering in the public toilets in Grosvenor Gardens near his home, standing with his raincoat over his arm. The raincoat was a signal to others in the fraternity and also a means of hiding a stiff dick, if it came to that. He hoped it would. The man that was to change his evening around – well-groomed, scrubbed skin, not much more than twenty – had walked in and established immediate eye-contact – a slight, nervous flicker, but no smile; this wasn't something you took lightly. They had both tarried – washing hands, combing hair, re-tying a tie, a long inspection in the mirror – waiting to be alone, but it was the time of night when the pubs were closing and the passing traffic was heavy. Two men idling in a public convenience were bound to be the cause of more than an occasional glance of suspicion, so the stranger disappeared into a cubicle. Burgess took the one alongside. They'd exchanged not a single word, only brief glances, nothing that would stand up in court. But the time to strike, to risk, was at hand. Burgess had been at this point so many times before, driven on by what lay deep inside, something raw, rough, chaotically primordial which he hated but which tore at all his senses until he was swept up in it. The thrill of the chase – and of being chased. They'd catch him eventually, he'd always known that. But not just yet. And when they did, he'd still get the last laugh. He'd die with a hard-on.

Burgess sat on the wooden seat and took a small piece of paper from his raincoat pocket on which was written the single word: 'HELLO'. He folded the paper and inserted it in a crack between the thin wooden slats that divided the cubicles. He held it there for a second before it disappeared, pulled from between his fingers. Contact. After that a flushing toilet, a door being unlocked. A pause. A soft rapping on his own door.

Burgess opened his cubicle door to discover himself looking at not one man but two. And suddenly the shy young man, the love of his night, he of the nervous eye, had become an avenging brute.

'You twisted little poof. You're nicked!' the man snarled, his face so close and threatening that Burgess could smell overcooked liver and onion. The other plain-clothes policeman – for that is what they were – caught him by the collar and shoved him over the basin – oh, but Burgess would've bent over anywhere for his blue-eyed young colleague, all he had to do was ask nicely, didn't need to shove or twist his arm so *excruciatingly fucking tight up behind his back*. Then there were handcuffs and a thumping from both of them for good measure, but only in places where it wouldn't show in court.

It became something of a mystery tour for a while. His right eye had caught the edge of the basin and began to swell, while the view from the other eye was distorted by the effects of alcohol. Burgess had got himself tanked up before he'd arrived at the toilets – he always did before he went out on the prowl – and very little of the late-night world around Victoria made sense to him until he found himself staring into the face of the custody sergeant at Rochester Row. That's when it all hit him. Oh, mother, he was really going down. Suddenly Burgess was extraordinarily, desiccatedly sober.

'Drunk and disorderly?' the sergeant enquired of the two police constables.

'Queer and quiet, Sarge. Not said a word since he tried to pick me up in the public convenience.'

'I don't recall saying a word to you at any point,' Burgess snapped, unable to resist a verbal foray. His accent was Eton and Cambridge, not quite what they had expected from the contents of a crumpled mac. Suddenly the officers were more wary.

'Ah, he talks. Name and address,' the sergeant demanded.

'Before I say anything I want to know with what I'm being charged.'

'With being a bleedin' shirt-lifter,' the arresting constable obliged.

Burgess squeezed his balls to try to bring some order to the images that tumbled inside his brain. One of those images was focused around the custody sergeant and suggested he was already damned and condemned. Another centred on the sneering constable – Burgess desperately wanted to smack blue-eyes in his big, fat, succulent mouth and make a run for it. Unlikely to get very far, of course, but at least he'd have the satisfaction of seeing the little bastard bleed. Yet another image told him that the place was in chaos with policemen running in every direction shouting about a bomb at Victoria Station. Burgess had already heard about King's Cross earlier in the day – so, they'd done Victoria, too . . .

Briefly, the constable set out the case before his sergeant. 'Loitering with intent, Sarge, he was. Down at Grosvenor Gardens. Been keeping an eye on the place all evening. I see him go in, I follow 'bout ten minutes later. He's still there, doing nothin', just sort of – staring. At me. So I hang around, wash me hands. He waits. I go into a cubicle, he gets the one beside it. Next I know he's pushing bits of paper through the crack in the wall making lewd suggestions.'

'What lewd suggestions?' Burgess demanded hotly.

The constable spread the piece of paper on the

desk in front of his sergeant. 'Don't matter what it *says*. Only deviants hand round notes in a public toilet.'

There was yet another bout of disturbance as the door to the charge room burst open and a man with a thick Irish accent was dragged in protesting and bleeding.

'You suggesting you aren't a deviant?' the sergeant demanded, returning his attentions to Burgess.

'This is ridiculous!'

'Yes, of course, sir. We've made a terrible mistake. We'll try and find an understanding judge for you. We'll also clean up your grubby mackintosh and find some sort of explanation as to why you spend your evenings in a shithouse. But until then, you're nicked. Now – name?'

So, the time had come – Burgess had to make his choice. Being a queer was a crime, it would mean jail and a criminal record. The rest of his life would hang on what took place over the next few minutes. He grabbed at his balls one final, eye-watering time to stop his world spinning. 'You can't charge me. You have no evidence.'

'We have you setting up shop in a men's toilet. We're halfway there.'

'And I was halfway home.'

'From where? To where?' The sergeant had his pencil poised.

'My name is Burgess. I live in Chester Square, just round the corner. Number 28. I've got nothing to hide. And I was coming' – he drew a deep breath – 'from Victoria Station.'

'What?'

'I was there. When the bomb went off.' A pause; they were listening. 'Knocked me over.'

'Fell off the Christmas tree, did we?'

'I was passing by the cloakroom' – he was guessing, a bit of a gamble, but he was in no position to play things totally safe. Anyway, they always left their bombs in the cloakroom. 'All I could see was smoke.'

'And what time was this little tragedy in your life supposed to have happened?'

It was coming back to him. He'd heard the clanking of bells from emergency vehicles not long before he'd arrived at Grosvenor Gardens. 'About half past nine.'

'OK. So there you were, flat on your back in Victoria Station. How come you ended up in the toilets?'

'I was shocked. Shaking. Hit my head when I was knocked over.' He pointed to his swollen eye, now red and beginning to bruise. The sergeant looked impressed, while the constable started to writhe like a hooked eel. 'And I wanted to get home – Chester Square – but . . . couldn't quite make it.' Burgess made it sound as though being caught short after such an experience was a matter for shame.

'You kept staring at me,' the constable insisted, trying to unhook himself.

'I was dazed. Confused. I wasn't staring at you or anyone else.'

'But we have this little note, sir. You were so confused, apparently, that you tried to proposition my constable here.'

'No, Sergeant!' Burgess switched his tone from shame to bravado. 'That note has nothing to do with me.'

'Your word against his. We'll let the magistrate decide in the morning, shall we?' the sergeant offered, licking the end of his pencil.

'I went into the cubicle –'

'For what purpose?'

'What purpose do you bloody think?' Burgess demanded in disbelief.

The sergeant put down his pencil, looking suitably abashed.

'I . . . settle down, and see a piece of paper poking through the gap in the wooden wall. I assume the paper is' – Burgess turned to point an accusing finger at the constable – 'from him! I'm disgusted. I don't read it. I simply push it back through the wall.'

'You claiming this note isn't yours?'

'I'm stating it as a positive fact. Any handwriting expert in the country will tell you exactly the same thing.' Burgess almost smiled. After the incident in the car Driberg had suggested they swap a dozen or more notes of that sort, just for these circumstances, to give them an edge of deniability. 'The paper was there when I went into the cubicle,' Burgess insisted.

'You suggesting *I* pushed it through the wall?' the constable demanded hotly.

'You saying you didn't?'

''Course I bloody didn't!'

'Then the previous occupant must've done. And left it.'

The constable was floundering, trying to mouth a response for which he had yet to find the words.

'So you say you found it,' the sergeant rehearsed, 'pushed it back through the wall, where the constable finds it and –'

'And starts assaulting me. Next thing I know, this baboon and his colleague are throwing me around the place and beating five types of hell out of me.'

'You didn't, did you, Collins? I've warned you about . . .' The sergeant bit his tongue, but the lash of his eyes was sufficient to make the constable cringe. 'So, sir – Mr Burgess of 28 Chester Square,' the sergeant continued wearily, 'you really expecting me to believe all this cock-and-bull you just coughed up?'

'I swear every word is the truth, Sergeant.'

'It's ruddy nonsense, Sarge . . .'

The sergeant drew a deep breath until the buttons on his tunic strained. At the far end of the room another piece of Irish chaos was erupting – three constables sitting on top of a heaving body in an attempt to subdue it. The charge sheet for tonight was going to end up as long as the grass on his back lawn; it wasn't going to be the sergeant's night. He looked at Burgess – the red, liquid eyes, the trembling hands, the crumpled clothing. A man about the same age as his son, Albert. Albert had recently joined up. The Sappers. Bombs that blew people to bits just as effectively as the one at the station this evening. The sergeant had seen for himself what that meant, in Belgium, twenty-five years before. He'd watched as Sappers had crawled through the mud and tangled wire to defuse unexploded shells. It had been like a music-hall act, one second they had been there, the next – gone. Vanished from the face. Nothing left behind but a stain that'd seeped slowly into the damp, smoking mud of a fresh shell hole. So he and Albert had had a tooth-spitting row. Albert was his only child, the sergeant hadn't wanted him to go, but Albert'd gone anyway, as the sergeant knew he would. He hadn't slept properly since. Now he leaned across the counter until his face was close to that of Burgess, their noses almost touching.

'I have to tell you, Mr Burgess, I don't believe a word you've told me. Not a bleedin' word. In my book, you're a stinking little liar and a queer, the sort that ought to be hanging by his bollocks somewhere behind bars. But you're clever, I'll give you that. No doubt you'd get a bath and a clean collar and some expensive poof lawyer before we got you to court. One thing I want you to remember, though. There's going to be a war soon and the likes of you won't be able to hide in any local shit-house. You're going to be dragged out there, whether you like it or not, along with all the good men and the decent men. And I've got an instinct about you. Believe in instinct, I do. And it's very strong where you're concerned. It's telling me you'll be getting a bayonet up your arse and one twisting in your gut before you know it, and you know what? I'll be there to laugh at your bloody funeral. In the meantime, Mr Bugger-Me-Burgess of Number 28 Sodomy Square, I've got more than enough manure to shovel for one evening. So you get out of my station – and don't you dare play the fairy on my patch again – or, God help me, I'll put the bayonet up you myself!'

He closed the charge book with a snap that sounded like an exploding grenade.

It was one of those days when the air itself seemed to have grown heavy and squatted on the shoulders. The breeze stirred fitfully off a green-bronze sea but it gave up the struggle long before it reached the front door of Sue Graham's post office. This wasn't proving to be one of her better days. Her routine had been shot to hell not simply by the heat but also by the ceaseless flow of people that had presented themselves at her counter. The summer season had started with a vengeance in Bournemouth and every holidaymaker for miles seemed to have crowded into her shop. Some came in search of nothing more than directions, others bought cheeky seaside postcards then queued for stamps in front of the metal grille of the post office section. Alongside them, harassed women waited patiently in the heat to withdraw holiday money from their meagre savings accounts, counting and recounting the coins in their purses as they did so, while their sun-bitten children squabbled in the corner by the sweet shelves or tugged at their sleeves. There was also a steady trade in newspapers – the demand had grown sharply in recent weeks. So had the number of telegrams. The bellboy from the Highcliffe had brought in almost a dozen from the hotel guests that morning, and he was certain to be back before the close of play. Everyone appeared to be in a hurry to finish their business, to get things tied up before . . . well, before the end of this long, menacing summer. Even Sue's vegetables seemed impatient.

She hadn't wanted to be here, not this week. She'd been planning to go away with Jerry, a walking holiday on Dartmoor. They'd both been devouring the Baedeker guidebook in preparation and had already mapped out every day's programme – Sue was good with plans and maps, as good as anyone in Jerry's unit – but then a telegram had arrived. The TA had called him up for a week's training. Their holiday week. Nothing to be done, he had to go, of course, but it had come as a considerable blow. Time was short, they both knew that, and they shared a compelling desire to be alone, to escape the confines of Bournemouth in order to explore each other, to take advantage of each other, while they still could. An opportunity lost. 'Harry Hitler owes us,' she had whispered, kissing him goodbye.

Jerry was sent to a camp near Beaulieu in the New Forest. He kept in touch as best he could. He telephoned from a local pub to confirm that he had been awarded his sergeant's stripes and had been taught how to drop a field radio in the fashion prescribed by Army regulations. The plan was to spend the next few days familiarizing themselves with the operation of the Bren gun, but there was only one of these in the entire camp so the waiting list for training sessions was long, and about to get longer on account of the fact that they'd been sent no ammunition.

So while they waited for supplies, they prepared for war. They sat in fields in front of officers who instructed them on how to fight the last war, then spent hours perfecting the art of digging field latrines and filling sandbags. They also brushed up on their saluting, and finally towards the end of the afternoon lit fires of green twigs and straw in order to brew their tea and inform any enemy for miles around of their precise location. But they never got their tea. It began to rain. Proper pelted. Thunderstorms of quite enthralling proportions struck all across the southern part of the country and seemed to mass directly above Jerry's camp, which was soon awash. At first they scurried to ensure that the side sheets of their tents were weighed down with bricks and stones so that the rain wouldn't seep in, and when that failed they hurriedly wrapped their bedding in groundsheets and began to dig drainage channels to lead away the surface water. When these overflowed they tried to dig still deeper and use sandbags to intimidate the sullen brown puddles that now stretched across the entire camp site, but all in vain. Their bedding was ruined, their command and control structure was soon bogged down and their enthusiasm swept utterly away. At this point the lorry with their missing ammunition arrived, and promptly toppled into one of the drainage ditches that were now invisible beneath the universal covering of water.

Twenty-five miles away, Bournemouth missed all the fun and simply squirmed and stifled in the thick heat. The day had grown ever busier as they came demanding lemonade to quench their thirst and calamine lotion to soothe their burnt skin. The telegraph equipment had been spitting out messages all afternoon with replies for the guests up at the Highcliffe and fresh call-up instructions for those in the TA, so by the time it began to shudder into action once more shortly before she closed the post office, Sue was distracted. It took her several moments to realize the telegram she had just taken down was for her, from Jerry – drenched, devoted, determined Jerry – after which she spent several more moments chastizing him. There was a nine-word minimum charge on telegrams yet he had used only two. Typical male extravagance. It was only then that the words began to squeeze their way through the heat and the collective harassment of her long day.

The telegram read simply: 'MARRY ME'.

Proposals by telegram, love on the run, the world in turmoil, every head in a spin. There seemed so little time for anything that mattered. Hitler had the whole of Europe by the balls, soon he would be reaching for its throat.

Bracken had seen so little of Anna in recent weeks – indeed, almost months, but time seemed to step out faster with every passing day – and it only inflamed his desires. He idolized her. She seemed such a perfect partner for him, showed such interest in his work, fanned his ambitions, and in particular understood how important was his role in everything Churchill thought and planned. She knew him so well.

They had grabbed a few precious hours and were resting beneath a great elm in Hyde Park, seeking shade from the heat that had become so searing that even Bracken, who was fastidious about his appearance, was forced to take off his jacket and unfasten his waistcoat. He had his back to the gnarled trunk while she lay stretched out at his feet. He was sweating, and not simply from the heat.

'Something I want to say,' he started diffidently, 'been wanting to say for some time. I'd like to see more of you, Anna. Much more.'

'Will you be busy this summer, Brendan?'

'Lashed to the mast – but I'd still like to see more of you.'

'Me, too. See more of you, I mean. But lashed to that same mast.' She was playing with a long stalk of grass, stroking it with her fingers. He so much wanted to be that stalk of grass. He wriggled and repositioned his jacket across his lap.

'I've got to take Aunt Rose to the South of France next week,' she continued. 'To join Uncle Joe.'

'Ah, pity.' Suddenly he sounded hurt, defensive. 'I knew he'd gone. Assumed your aunt would be with him already.'

'Uncle Joe's spending a little time on diplomatic work –'

'I was hoping you might be free . . .'

'– before my aunt joins him for their holiday.'

'Ah, I see.' Ever since his arrival in London Kennedy had dedicated himself to the re-establishment of the Entente Cordiale, a diplomatic policy fed by a seemingly inexhaustible supply of young French actresses which led him not to the Elysée in Paris but to a variety of yachts moored off Cannes and Monte Carlo. 'He's not on his own, is he?'

Anna gave him a stare flushed with disapproval – of her uncle, perhaps, or simply the naïveté of his question.

'I really want to see more of you,' Bracken insisted.

'You could come to France for a few days, perhaps – but of course you *can't*, not with everything going on here,' she said, making the suggestion and reaching the conclusion all in the same breath. It was one of the things he admired so much in her, the intensely practical side of her nature, so unlike the silly English debutantes who couldn't find their way out of a powder room without the help of at least three friends. But on this occasion her practicality seemed to raise his hopes, only to dash them down again.

'Anna, we've been going out – seeing each other – for eight months now, since December' – how strange he was, she thought, to remember precisely how long they'd known each other. It was almost a feminine trait in Bracken; most men kept their memory in their underwear and always seemed to be losing it.

He gazed at her, on her back, looking sightless towards the skies, caressing the stalk of grass that lay between her breasts, the print of her cotton frock pressed thinly along her body. He imagined himself as a Zulu king looking down from a high mountain across veldt that stretched and undulated into distant magical mists, and he wanted to possess it all.

'Anna, we'd be able to see so much more of each other if we were married.'

She seemed not to react. Not to breathe, even.

'You'd make such a splendid hostess. A grand house. The finest dinner parties. The social and political centre of London, you and me . . .' His words came in a rush, carried on a breath that seemed to

340

exhaust him. She opened her eyes slowly, rolling over onto an elbow to look at him.

'Was that a proposal?'

'I think so.'

A long silence. She studied the stalk of grass intently.

'Well, will you?' he demanded.

'No, Brendan dear.'

'Why not?'

'Because you have a war to fight. And you're not the marrying kind. Anyway, it would spoil our friendship. And your friendship is so very important to me, Brendan. More important than I can say. So it must be no, don't you see? At least for the moment . . .'

Rejection wrapped up in a tissue of hope. But she underestimated Bracken – he was Irish, accustomed to refusal and rejection, which only served to make him more stubborn, more than ever determined to succeed. He wasn't going to take no for an answer. She was young, impressionable, so he would make the appropriate impression and bring her round. Leave her no option but to change her mind.

Although later he was to suspect that, all along, she had known precisely what she was doing.

Downing Street garden. Brilliant sunshine. A bench beneath the shelter of the shade of the silver birch. Teacups on a picnic table.

'Masterstroke, Neville. Complete masterstroke.'

'Thank you.' Tea, sipped with care. 'Which particular masterstroke did you have in mind, Horace?'

'Tempting Winston with the fruits of office. You

know, we couldn't keep him quiet throughout the spring. Up and down like a jack-in-the-box with a loose catch. But then a couple of rumours dribbled across the right bars and he hasn't made a single speech in the House all summer. Not one. Not even . . .'

'About the German loan.'

Wilson turns for tea. 'Not even that. Like a fish mesmerized by one of your flies.'

A moment spent studying the outline of leaves against the sky. 'It can't last, Horace.'

'Why not?'

'Because very soon he'll realize there is no fly. That it's a mirage. A deception. He'll know I have no intention of giving him a job.'

'So . . . what do we do?'

'Keep him quiet by other means.'

'Other means?'

'We'll send him away. Send them all away. Get them out from under our feet.'

'A parliamentary recess?'

'Busy their giddy minds with foreign travel. Preferably on yachts.'

'At a time like this? They'll kick up a fuss.'

'Oh, but not much of one. The attractions of the Côte d'Azur far outweigh those of Poland. Most of them have ambitions to join up with the bucket-and-spade brigade, nothing more.'

'Digging sandcastles rather than trenches.'

'Precisely.'

More tea.

'Winston, too?'

'Maybe not him. Awkward squad. But at least the summer holidays will deprive him of an audience.'

'True.'

Another pause. An adjustment of the tie, almost a fidget. 'And we should deprive him of other things, perhaps.'

'Such as?'

'You are aware of the new Home Office security recommendations?'

'About the IRA? Of course. Banning suitcases on buses – closing the public gallery in the Commons.'

'And increasing protection for prominent persons who may be at risk.'

'Giving them armed detectives, you mean.'

'More tea, Horace?'

'Thank you.'

A very English pause.

'It's a very long list of names. For protection.'

'Inevitably.'

'Too long.'

'You think so?'

'Needs trimming.'

'How?'

'Winston's name is on the list.'

'I know.'

'I want him off.'

'Taken off? But that means . . .'

'Precisely. We'll leave Winston's fate in God's hands, for the moment, shall we?'

The second of August. A Wednesday. The House had a stale, masculine atmosphere that left tempers frayed and caused rings of sweat to gather around the collars. Time to leave. Already millions of ordinary

Britons were on holiday, their thoughts distracted from the threats that hovered over them, and now MPs were to be sent to join them. In normal circumstances such an announcement would be greeted with an outpouring of ill-concealed rejoicing, but the days of August 1939 were not normal times.

Only the previous week when rumours of the recess had begun to circulate, Churchill had risen to demand that the House should not be sent away to be lost in the mists of autumn, and Chamberlain had responded that such a suggestion was 'hypothetical'. Now hypothesis turned to hardened fact and the Prime Minister rose to inform MPs that they were to be banished until October.

It was a simple and straightforward parliamentary procedure, a motion for the Adjournment of the House, which would normally raise no more concerns than the spillage of tea into the saucer. But this was August 1939. MPs rose to offer their views – almost all were concerned, many hostile. What signal would it give to the dictators if the democracies shut up their stall and ran away to build sandcastles? Was Hitler going to take a holiday, too?

Churchill spoke in opposition – the first time he had engaged in a debate in the House in many weeks. It was not an onslaught – perhaps he was still held back by the enticements of office, but clearly nothing on that front could happen now until October, if it ever did. So his speech was at times jocular, but the wit was often biting. He spoke of 'the danger months in Europe, when the harvests have been gathered and when the powers of evil are at their strongest'. He talked of the two million men already under arms in Germany, and the five hundred thousand who had been called up in recent days and would be added to that number before the end of August, massing along the Polish frontiers from Danzig to Cracow. He said their public buildings were being cleared out on a massive scale – and why? To become makeshift hospitals and reception centres for the wounded.

His wit dug deep into the flesh of his Prime Minister. How could it be, Churchill demanded, that in such awesome circumstances Chamberlain could say to the House: 'Begone! Run off and play! Take your gas masks with you! Do not worry about public affairs.' After all, this Government had such a splendid record in predicting the outcome of public affairs . . .

The smile at the corner of the old man's mouth did little to take the sting from the lash as he laid it across his leader's back. Chamberlain sat, and smarted, and sulked, even more so as others rose to their feet to call on him to be more flexible, to compromise, to bring the House back earlier. To be prepared.

Less than two hours after Churchill had resumed his seat, Chamberlain was forced to rise once more. The mood of defiance was spreading through the House like a toxin, but this was *his* House, dammit. He led the party that had an overwhelming majority in this place. Time to use it. So he made it clear to the House that the vote which lay ahead of them was to be regarded as a vote of confidence in his leadership. This wasn't just a vote for their holidays, this was a vote for him, for Neville Chamberlain, their Prime Minister, their best damned leader and their *only* damned leader – and they'd better not forget it! In the language of Parliament, it was a declaration of war. Anyone in his own party who failed to support him would be taking their political lives in their hands, and with an election due in months, those lives would be short. He'd make sure of that. He had suffered the lash for the last few hours, now he turned it with all his force on his colleagues.

There are many turning points in history. Some arise by chance, and perhaps this was one of them. Or maybe it was bound to happen sooner or later. The claim of a political leader to infallibility was scarcely new, but rarely had it been pushed with such ill grace. Even in pre-war days, politicians liked a little enthusiasm while they were being screwed. Yet here was a man willing to declare war on his own colleagues at a moment's notice when he'd spent months ducking the issue with the Hun. The message was clear – Chamberlain's holidays were of considerably greater value than Czechoslovakia.

It was all too much for one young Member. Ronald Cartland was no typical Tory of his time. He hadn't had enough money to go to university, so he'd begun to work as a research assistant in Conservative Central Office for the stomach-tightening sum of three pounds a week. Tough times which bred independence. He had warned the selection committee in his Birmingham constituency that he would be no mindless weather vane, ready to swing whichever way the wind happened to be blowing, but they liked his fresh looks and selected him anyway.

When Cartland got to his feet in the Commons,

he found his audience less than captivated. They were hot, distracted, and largely indifferent, having already feasted on a diet of Churchills and Chamberlains. In truth, many Members barely recognized him, although none were to forget him.

'I'm sorry to detain the House for a few moments, but I would like to say a few words as a backbencher of the Prime Minister's own party,' he began, almost in apology. The House rustled with distractions as many Members headed in search of refreshment. They stopped when they heard him continue: 'I am profoundly disturbed by the speech of the Prime Minister.'

Those who had already passed beyond the Speaker's Chair in the direction of the Smoking Room turned and retraced their footsteps. Had they heard right? The sharp smack of disloyalty?

'We're going to separate until the third of October,' Cartland went on, 'and I suppose the majority of us will be going down to our constituencies, out in the country, to make speeches. But a fantastic and ludicrous impression exists in this country. That the Prime Minister has ideas . . . of dictatorship.' Oh, God, he'd started, set out, and now there could be no turning back. Suddenly bodies were squeezing back onto the crowded leather benches.

'It's a ludicrous impression, of course, and everybody here on both sides of the House knows it is ludicrous, but . . .' – that awesome little conjunction, but – 'it does exist in the country.'

'Hell, Dickie, who is this little idiot?'

'Buggered if I know, Ian. Digging himself one hell

347

of a hole. Dictatorship be damned. Neville'll have his balls on toast for this one.'

From his place towards the rear of the House, Cartland could see the back of the Prime Minister's head three rows in front of him. Not a muscle moved, not a hair twitched, but it was the very immobility that told its story.

'There is the ludicrous impression in this country,' Cartland repeated, 'that the Prime Minister has these *dictatorship* ideas. And the speech he has made this afternoon, along with his absolute refusal to accept any of the proposals put forward by Members on both sides of the House, will make it much more difficult' – these words delivered more slowly – 'to dispel that idea.'

'Bloody nonsense,' a Tory colleague grumbled loudly from nearby, but there were many more words of encouragement from across the Chamber and a large number of Tory heads that had simply turned to look at him and were nodding. It was like watching the eddies of a rock pool as the tide tumbled in upon it.

'Call yourself a Tory,' the colleague remonstrated once more. 'I call you a disgrace.'

'No, no. I received a letter this morning.' Cartland waved a piece of paper in the direction of the complaint. 'From a constituent of mine. Posted in King's Norton and signed simply: "Conservative". She has been a Conservative all her life, and she writes to me now to say that she is very upset' – he read – '*because so many people think the Prime Minister is a friend of Hitler.*'

'Sit down, you bloody fool!' . . . 'He's drunk, must be.' . . . 'Reading your suicide note, are you?' . . .

'God, what sort of people have we let into this place?' Warnings began to be shouted at him from all along his own benches. One Member tried to pluck at the tail of his jacket to force him to sit down but Cartland wrenched himself free, determined to go on – and why not? There was nowhere he could go back to.

'We are in a situation' – the words were all but drowned by the clamour around him – 'we are in a situation that within a month we may be going to fight. And we may be going to die!'

They tried to mock him, howl him down, to prevent his words ever being heard for the record, waving their Order Papers like toreadors tormenting a bull, but his chin was up and his voice carried over the tumult.

'It's all very well for Honourable Gentlemen who are about to take their leave for two entire months to say "Oh" and to protest. But there are thousands of young men at the moment in training camps, who in the nation's interest have given up *their* holidays.' He gazed in contempt at those who barracked him, yet amongst them, like islands in an ocean, he also found faces of concern and support. His heaving chest grew still, his voice suddenly softer. Now they had to strain to hear him, but strain they did.

'I can't imagine why the Prime Minister couldn't have made a great gesture in the interests of national unity. Surely it's much more important to get the whole country behind you, but . . .' Cartland shook his head in despair and for a moment he seemed unable to continue. Chamberlain, who had been sitting immobile and unmoved throughout the speech, half turned his head to catch sight of his accuser –

a glimpse, a glint of cold and undying enmity in his eye, an old man mocking the young – before once more turning his back. The insult seemed to revive Cartland, who sucked in the stale air of a place he had come so to despise, then launched himself onward.

'It is so very much more important to get the country behind you,' he repeated, his voice rising as the tumult around him returned to do battle – 'than to make jeering, pettifogging speeches which divide the nation. Why can't the Prime Minister ask for real confidence in himself – as Prime Minister – as the leader of the country rather than just leader of the party? I say frankly . . .' – they were baying at him, like hounds, wanting to rip out his throat – 'I say frankly that I despair when I listen to speeches like that which I have listened to this afternoon.'

Cries of treachery erupted all around while from across the House the Opposition roared for more. The Speaker called in vain for order, but Cartland had sat down, the only man seeming unmoved in an ocean of storms. Within minutes the speech had been described by his party colleagues and now-former friends as 'poisonous', but there were others who said it was 'a speech of a kind that will live long in the memory of this House'. It divided, because it had exposed the image of Government unity for what it was – an image.

On one thing they were all agreed. It had been a speech of irredeemable self-sacrifice. As the tumult began slowly to die, the Prime Minister's head bent to whisper briefly into the ear of his Chief Whip. Every one of them knew what was taking place.

Cartland was being condemned. He would not be a Conservative candidate at the next election.

Chamberlain would get his wish, for this was to prove the speech of a lifetime for Cartland. Within a month we may be going to fight, and we may be going to die, he had predicted. And so it was to be.

On 30 May 1940, Major Ronald Cartland, aged thirty-three, was shot through the head and killed during the retreat to Dunkirk, and so became the first Member of Parliament to die on active service.

Ignoring the warnings that had been cast at it by Cartland and Churchill and others, Parliament rose for its summer holidays at the end of the week, on Friday the fourth of August.

It was twenty-five years to the day since the first shots had been fired in the First World War. It wasn't known as that, of course, not then. They had called it the Great War. The Last War. The war to end all wars.

THIRTEEN

(Daily Express, Bank Holiday Monday, 7 August 1939)

Daily Express holds canvass of its reporters in Europe, and ten out of twelve say – NO WAR THIS YEAR

BERLIN EMPHATIC: HITLER IS NOT READY

Daily Express *reporters in Europe believe that there will be no war this year.*

That is the result of a canvass conducted in the principal capitals of the Continent last week. Our reporters were asked to give their views to the prospects of peace or war in 1939 . . . It is significant that the three reporters in Berlin are the most confident of peace. None of these men believe that Hitler is ready to wage a major campaign . . .

Chamberlain left London on Bank Holiday Monday for his holiday fishing for salmon on the River Naver in Sutherland. Four days later his envoy – Admiral the Honourable Sir Reginald Ranfurly etc, etc, etc –

arrived in Moscow after a long sea voyage to begin talks with the Russians about an alliance.

All the while, and with every passing day, the news from the Polish frontier glowed like a river of molten metal. The Poles were accused of terrorism, of torture, of murder. Every troop movement they made to guard their frontier was described in Germany as a preparation for war. Goebbels, who clearly hadn't read the *Daily Express*, made it sound as if the Poles were about to launch an armed offensive on Berlin itself.

Meanwhile Chamberlain waited, and fished, and prayed that Sir Reggie might prove a persuasive suitor, even though he had been sent to Moscow empty-handed and impotent. But others were more active and began to make preparations for what they feared was to come. City firms began to move documents and staff to the country, so that they could continue their work in the event that London was razed to the ground by the Luftwaffe. The priceless mediaeval stained-glass windows of Canterbury Cathedral were taken down and placed in storage. Art treasures from museums around London began to be crated and shipped out, and plans were made to kill the poisonous reptiles in the zoo. London became a city of sandbags – mountains of them everywhere. Where they ran out of sand, they filled the bags with old books and election manifestos.

Joe Kennedy cut short his foray in the South of France and flew back to London. The young aircraft captain saluted as the Ambassador clambered down the steps. 'You think there will be war, sir?'

'You can bet on it. I have.'

'What are our chances?'

Kennedy looked at the young pilot with astonishment. 'About as much as Joan of Arc praying for rain,' he growled, before moving on.

The Ambassador was accompanied by Mrs Kennedy and his niece, Anna. Mademoiselle Marie-Noëlle Rey arrived on the flight immediately behind.

The trial of a full national blackout was planned, and then postponed because of bad weather. Searchlights and barrage balloons began to fill the parks of London. Traffic lights were dimmed almost to extinction, kerbs were painted white to make them visible in the dark, and demonstrations were given of how to convert buses into makeshift ambulances. Even the advertisements changed. Some bright marketing spark grabbed hold of the growing mood of crisis and started to advertise the Terry's Anglepoise as 'the only practical blackout lamp'.

But hope – futile, senseless, barren hope – still sprang eternal. The *Illustrated London News* printed photographs of the Polish cavalry at the charge above a caption which announced: 'Poland's impressive horse cavalry – probably the best in Europe and equipped with sword, lance and machine guns. An arm which has been extensively developed and has far greater mobility in difficult terrain than mechanized forces, besides being able to live off the country.'

They would die magnificently.

In Bournemouth, Sue Graham's wedding plans were made, then postponed. She and Jerry were agreed; there would be war and there was work to be done. So they would wait. Sue had already ordered the material for her wedding dress, several yards of pure white satin. She wrapped the material in tissue paper and placed it in a box, and on top of the cascade of white she placed Jerry's dried rose.

On 21 August Chamberlain broke his fishing holiday and returned briefly to London to catch up on events. Crowds gathered around Downing Street, watching the comings and goings of advisers in ever more sombre mood. Occasionally a cheer would go up if they caught a glimpse of the Prime Minister himself. Everyone still hoped war might be averted, but few believed, and those left with any lingering illusions would have them shattered before they went to bed.

On the evening of Chamberlain's return, the most astounding news was announced. Hitler had done a deal with Stalin. A mutual defence pact. While the Russian leader had been waving Admiral the Honourable out through the front door, German officials had been sneaking in through the back. A Faustian bargain had been struck between the two most awesome dictatorships in the world, reaching out for each other, like a vice around Poland which, when squeezed, would make the whole of Europe bleed.

The next day, Joachim von Ribbentrop, the Nazi Foreign Minister, flew to Moscow for the official signing ceremony, his aeroplane casting a shadow that chilled hearts across the entire continent.

Chamberlain could not sleep. Every time he closed his eyes the night filled with terror. The fist of stone he had felt beneath his heart for so many months now turned into lava, burning into him after every meal and allowing him no rest. He felt exhausted, drained, yet he knew that the trial of his life stretched before him. He lay awake in his bed, sweat soaking into his pillow, staring sightless into the dark and listening to the rustlings of the night, which in his confused mind turned into the voices of his father and brother – mocking him, as they had when he was young.

In the morning he rose and set out on his usual morning constitutional around St James's Park, but turned back well before he got to the bridge across the lake. As he walked through the door of Number Ten, a feeling of enormous apprehension overcame him, which he described later to his wife as being like that of a dying man taking to his bed for the very last time. He went straight to the Cabinet Room and slumped in his chair. Then he issued three instructions. Those of his Cabinet colleagues who were in London were to be summoned, as was his doctor. And he would need to speak to the King at Balmoral.

When, a little while later, His Majesty's voice came on the line, not even the bakelite echo of a trunk line could disguise the fact that the call was an intrusion.

'Should be out at my p-p-peg, Prime Minister. Can't it wait?'

'I suggest that you return to London, sir. Immediately.'

'Return? I can't return. Too much to do up here.'

'You must return.'

'But why?'

'Because I fear there is . . . an imminence of hostilities, sir.' A clumsy phrase, stinking of despair.

'War in Poland, you mean? I doubt that. Poland will have to back down, of course she will. Just like Czechoslovakia. And if she doesn't S-s-stalin and Hitler will tear her to pieces. After that they'll start tearing themselves to pieces, you mark my words. No, this couldn't have come out better for us, Mr Chamberlain. We can sit back and watch all those damned Europeans beat themselves senseless.'

A deep sigh, a cry of exhaustion. 'But, sir, we have guaranteed Poland.'

'Yes, I know that, but . . .' A long pause, to collect both his thoughts and his tongue. 'You're not trying to tell me – are you, Mr Chamberlain? – that we can't get out of the guarantee?'

'We have given our word.'

'Our word, of course, but . . .' More silence. Then a voice stripped of every shred of confidence. 'We can't honour the guarantee. There's no way we can save Poland. It would be suicide to try.'

'Nevertheless, we have given our solemn promise. Drawn a line in the sand.'

'But to what p-purpose? What good would it do anyone if we went to war over Poland? We didn't do it over Czechoslovakia, so why Poland, for God's sake? Doesn't make sense, man.'

Silence.

'W-w-war? What's the bloody point?' the King demanded, beginning to raise his voice. 'It would be nothing more than a futile act of revenge. Leave Europe in ruins. The Empire in chaos.' He made it sound as if it were entirely Chamberlain's fault.

'You know, sir, that I have tried more than any man on this earth to avoid war. If there is going to

357

be a war then at least we have shown that of all the nations under God, we tried to avoid it. No one can doubt who the aggressor is, who is to blame.'

'To risk everything for an Empire, that I understand, Mr Chamberlain, for an entire Empire. But for – Poland?'

'I shall recall Parliament. There are emergency measures to be passed, the Dominions to be warned, ships to be requisitioned, reservists to be called up. And so much more. Your place is in London, sir.'

'This is u-u-utterly damnable, Mr Chamberlain. Hitler has upset everything. For heaven's sake, it's August.'

'My apologies for disturbing your holiday, sir.'

'May the grouse forgive him.'

Carol and Mac lay in bed, the shadow of Ribbentrop's plane lying cold between them. A two-up two-down in Chigwell seemed to be so far away from anywhere that mattered, but even in bed they found they couldn't escape.

Peter had been having bad dreams. He seemed to be reacting badly to the tension he could feel all around. That afternoon he'd got into a fight with a neighbour's kid – scraped the bottom out of his best pair of trousers – and Mac had given him a cuff round his ear. Peter had screamed back something very rude, reminding Mac that he wasn't his dad, and so Carol had given him another cuff for good measure. Everyone had gone to bed miserable. And little Lindy had been ill for several days now, burning up with a fever that was beginning to turn to an ugly rash. The doctor had come but hadn't been sure. Now the rash had grown much worse and the doctor would have to be called back again. More money for trousers, for doctors, for medicines, at a time when the tea caddy under the sink where she kept all the housekeeping held nothing more than memories. The Hoares had gone away for the summer – almost two months of it, could you believe? – so Carol had lost her cleaner's wages. And since she wasn't cleaning, neither was she throwing out the contents of his office wastebin.

Burgess had taken this badly. He'd been badgering Mac, yet Mac had nothing to give. It had been altogether sparse pickings at Trumper's since the middle of July; it was that time of year, and M'Lord Halifax was on holiday, too. There were so few clippings to sweep up. They'd met for a drink even though Mac had told him it would be a waste of time, but Burgess had pleaded, then insisted. Burgess had already been drunk when Mac arrived, and judging by his appearance – sleepless, soiled shirt, agitated – Mac guessed he'd been drunk for days. Never seen him in such a state. But the tongue was still as sharp as ever and when it became clear that Mac was true to his word – that it was to be a waste of time – Burgess had begun to grow abusive, his tongue out of control. Said that Hitler and Stalin climbing into each other's underwear had ripped apart everything he believed in. Your fault, Mac had muttered, for believing in anything in the first place, and Burgess had turned on him, said that belief is what raised them above the level of beasts, had spilled his drink and had called Carol a silly cow for not having any more paper. Mac had got up while Burgess was still in mid-flow. 'I've got a sick baby to help take care of, Mr Burgess. Don't need any of this nonsense.' He'd walked out, leaving his pint of mild untouched.

Perhaps that was the end of it. Perhaps there would be no more meetings, even though that would mean an end to the rest of Carol's income. Just when she needed it most. He'd arrived back at Carol's as she was making plans – sticking blast tape over the windowpanes, first in the shape of a vertical cross of St George, then the diagonal cross of St Andrew, until all the windows in the house were decorated like stars. She told the children it was a game, like Christmas. And she built a special hideaway under the stairs next to the electricity meter, with an old mattress on which Peter and Lindy could sleep and with the stout oak legs of an old table jammed under the roof for additional support. She'd taken down the few pictures, put away the breakables, left a bucket of sand at the top of the stairs. She was resourceful; she'd get through, somehow. There were also yards of heavy dark material to fix across the windows as blackout curtains, and foodstuffs to be got in – sugar, coffee, dried fruit, tins of meat and the rest – just in case. It was a bit of a race, every housewife in the street was entering, and to have any chance of winning she'd have to be out of the front door first. But she had no money.

'Did Mr Burgess offer you any money?' she asked between teeth sprouting the sticky ends of tape and balancing precariously on a stool.

'No.'

'Why not?'

'Didn't ask.'

'You didn't –' She spat out the pieces of tape and jumped down from the stool, advancing upon him. 'Why the bloody 'ell not?' she demanded, her tongue honed by anxiety.

'Because . . .' Because what? Mac couldn't be clear, he wasn't clear about so much in his life recently. It had been so simple when he was on his own and the whole world was his enemy, he could shut off from it, not give a damn, just get on with the task of surviving, all by himself. But since Carol and the kids he'd begun to feel again and feelings, he decided, often hurt. They cut him deep inside, brought back memories he'd rather have left buried in the pit alongside little Moniek and the remnants of his soul. And because he didn't know how to handle these things, he hid inside his cocoon and blamed Carol. It was so much simpler that way, wasn't it? 'Because . . . it didn't feel like the right thing to do,' he explained, without explaining anything.

'God, you can be so bloody impractical at times. You think what Mr Burgess has done for us. Just think, for a change! 'Bout time you joined up with the bleedin' real world.' And the argument had started.

'Real world? What's real about this ridiculous world?'

'Peter and Lindy, they're real. That's my world, Mac. I thought they were your world, too.'

He should have replied, comforted her, but it always took time to emerge from his cocoon.

'I've got to do something, Mac.' A pause, her confidence picked at by a thousand nagging ravens. 'You

. . . ever thought about spending more time with us? Sort of – moving in. Properly?' She knew it was the wrong thing to suggest. She was a woman, it was scarcely her place, and it made their relationship sound almost mercenary. But life was mercenary. It cost. And she had two kids to think of. Mac stood staring into space, avoiding her eyes, pretending he was admiring her handiwork on the windows. Commitment. All he could hear through her words was commitment, a term that rang in his mind like the slamming of a prison door. He'd spent almost twenty years of his life avoiding commitment – the quietest, most tidy, least threatening, most liberating twenty years of his life – and now . . .

'Want a cup of tea, girl?' He'd spent long enough in England to know how people filled the emotional gaps in their lives. He limped off without waiting for her answer. Yet it would take more than two steaming cups to move the matter on – and it needed to be moved on, for old wounds were being scratched raw. They were two incomplete people whose lives had been left shredded by others and who had somehow sewn them back together but in a manner that left them distrusting everyone who came their way, including themselves.

Carol accepted the cup of tea he offered her without thanks and with a downward flutter of her eyes.

'It's not the time,' he said, starting upon some sort of explanation. 'Not with the war and everything. Who knows where we'll be in two months, let alone two years. Can't be certain about anything. Let's give it a little time, eh, girl?'

'Don't matter,' she replied, her voice small and strained, as though something was choking her. 'The kids and me, we'll get by.' Defensive mode. Bloody men. Trying to hide the hurt. What the hell was there not to be certain about? Stupid men and their ridiculous wars. She had no trouble being absolutely sure about all the important things in her life – Peter – Lindy. The fact that they had to be fed and housed and loved, and brought up to have more of a chance than she'd ever had. Nothing uncertain about any of that. So the men could have their bloody war, while she got on with her own private war she called Life.

'Don't matter,' she said once more. 'If there's going to be a war, there'll be plenty of work.'

'Got any plans?'

'No,' she lied, and wouldn't look at him.

So they had gone to bed with shadow lying in the cold space between them. They had been there almost an hour, both pretending to be asleep, when the sound of knocking came from the front door. They tried to ignore it but it came again, insistent.

'I'll go,' he said, grateful to be of use.

He opened the door to find Burgess on the step, his face illuminated by the glow of a nervous cigarette.

'Hello, Mac.'

Even in the dark Mac could tell he was struggling with sobriety.

'Wanted to apologize.' He shuffled forward, his arms laden. 'Peace offering. I was rude. Sorry. Brought some flowers for the lady. And a shawl for the baby. Hope you don't mind. Hope she's feeling better. I'd like to pay for the doctor, if you'll let me.'

'It's very late, Mr Burgess.'

'You know me, Mac. All impatience. And I am sorry.' Burgess smiled. Beneath the trampled hair and crumpled suit he had an infectious and entirely genuine boyish charm that would make a dog cross the street simply to get patted.

Mac stood at the open door in his pyjamas, trying not to let suspicion get the better of him. Burgess was a man who had recast Carol's life, and therefore had recast Mac's, too. He was something of a saviour, and now he was standing at the door, bearing gifts. Wanting to help. Perhaps it was going to work out after all. He could hear Carol stirring upstairs, he'd be able to bring her the flowers, the shawl, the money. Patch things up. Move on. It was going to be all right.

'Still don't have anything for you, Mr Burgess,' Mac explained, almost apologetically.

'That's not why I came.'

'I'd invite you in, but . . .' He gestured to his pyjamas.

'No need, Mac. I just wanted to put things right. You're a friend. It was my fault. I apologize.'

Then, although he had struggled so hard against it, suspicion got the better of Mac. In a world stripped bare of loyalties there were no such things as gifts and good gestures, only bribes – he'd learnt that in the camps. So what was Burgess's angle? Why was he standing here so late at night? On Carol's doorstep? Mac started scratching himself.

'But how . . . how did you know where I was, Mr Burgess? How did you know I would be here?'

Burgess laughed. It was nothing more than an

attempt to fill in the gap in his mind. He'd acted on instinct, not sieved things through his whiskey mind, had simply grabbed these bits and run, needing to sort matters out, to re-tie some of the knots in his life that had come unravelled. He hadn't expected questions, now he was scrambling to fill the hole where the answer should be. But Mac had stopped scratching, he was way ahead of this game. It was, after all, a game he'd spent half a lifetime playing.

'Seems I made a mistake, Mr Burgess, thinking you might be halfway decent. But seems you're just a *mamzer*.'

'*Mamzer?*'

'Another bastard who thinks you own me. Like all the rest. You're just a second-rate secret policeman.'

With that he closed the door, quietly but very firmly, in Burgess's face.

(The Times, Friday 25 August 1939)

DOWNING STREET SCENES

————◆—◆————

CALM AND ORDERLY CROWDS

————◆—◆————

CHEERS FOR MINISTERS

As always at a time such as this, hundreds of citizens were drawn to Whitehall and Downing Street yesterday.

*Many were obviously holiday-makers, and, hoping for
an outstanding snapshot of some important personage,
they had their folding cameras out and set; all were
orderly and calm. There was much quiet discussion as
they watched callers arriving and leaving 10, Downing
Street. Just before noon they were afforded a chance of
giving expression to their feelings, and, accepting it
wholeheartedly, they sped the Prime Minister on his way
with enthusiastic cheers when he left by motor-car to
report to the King at Buckingham Palace . . .*

*As the time drew near for the reassembly of
Parliament large crowds gathered in Parliament Square,
and it was with difficulty that members, whether
arriving on foot or by car, made their way to the
precincts. Again they were orderly crowds, composed of
citizens who were deeply interested but perfectly calm.
The only demonstrators were a score or more of men
and women who walked round and round displaying
posters bearing the one word. 'CHURCHILL'.*

*Once more the cheers rang out when, with Mrs
Chamberlain, the Prime Minister left Downing Street
about 2.40 to drive to the House. The cheer was taken
up by the crowds lining Whitehall and grew in volume
as the dense throng outside the House joined in.*

*A woman standing on a refuge near the entrance to
Palace Yard moved forward as the Prime Minister's car
passed and held against the window a 'Churchill'
placard . . .*

August had been a month of preparation for Churchill.
He spent several days on a tour of inspection along
the Maginot Line in France. It was undeniably a

magnificent structure, impregnable where it stood, but he wondered why it didn't stretch all the way to the sea. Afterwards he had gone to spend a few days painting with an old friend, the artist Paul Maze, at a chateau west of Paris. They toiled for hours trying to capture the subtle magic of an ancient mill that stood near the banks of the River Eure. Churchill much preferred landscapes to portraiture – 'they don't complain'. Others, less kindly, suggested his preference was simply because he couldn't spend longer than a few moments in contemplation of any person other than himself.

So Churchill painted, his world awash with colours and fine cognac, and he would have been happy, had he been able to forget. But Churchill was the last man in Europe able to forget or to ignore the events that were taking shape around him. He searched for fresh colours, but the realities of that August were all greys and browns. Suddenly he had turned to Maze and said: 'This is the last picture we shall paint in peace for a very long time.' Then he packed his oils and returned immediately to England.

He went directly to Chartwell, where he spent his hours laying bricks to complete the kitchen of a cottage he was building in the grounds, and working on his History. On the evening of his return he was joined at Chartwell by a retired Scotland Yard inspector, W.H. Thompson, who had been his personal protection officer when he had last served in Government. Now Churchill felt in need of his services once more, for there were twenty thousand German Nazis in England, organized and potentially dangerous, and Churchill knew that, perhaps above all Englishmen, Hitler hated him. So he and Thompson took turns to sleep, and to be vigilant.

They also oiled his pistols.

'They say that London's in turmoil, sir,' Thompson observed as he removed the top slide and barrel off a Browning 9mm.

'I doubt that,' Churchill replied unhurriedly. He seemed to find satisfaction in disassembling and swabbing the weapons, a timeless ritual of preparation with brush and rod and swab that gave him something to do. 'No, not turmoil, Mr Thompson. Londoners do not so easily lose their heads. They're not chickens. But Downing Street, that may be another matter. I suspect Mr Chamberlain is – at this very moment – sitting with his advisers, wondering how it could possibly be that the Nazis have embraced the Communists across a table which he himself has set.'

'They'll have you back, sir. They must.'

'Perhaps. I understand that several poster hoardings have appeared around London with the message: "What Price Churchill?" Somebody obviously wants me. But I doubt they were put there by Mr Chamberlain.'

They spent several minutes in deep silence, sitting on opposite sides of the desk in the study, swabbing, oiling, reassembling, reloading, treating the weapons with reverence as though they were preparing the Sacrament. Finally Churchill blessed them with what remained of his tumbler of whisky, placed the Browning in the top drawer of his desk so that it would be readily to hand as he worked, then weighed the other weapon, a Colt .45, in his hands. He had carried it in Flanders during the last war, it had served him well, and it seemed to satisfy him still. He rose, tried to stretch the aches and the age from his bones, and crossed to the open window which overlooked the short drive and the front wall that hid Chartwell – none too successfully – from the passing road. It was a glorious summer's evening, a red cast to the sky as the sun began to fall behind the bank of rhododendron bushes. On top of the wall squatted a grey squirrel, eating his evening meal while he enjoyed the last of the day's warmth. Churchill braced his heavy shoulders, stretched his neck until his chin was up, raised his pistol, and fired. The noise inside the study was spectacular, leaving a sour smell of burnt oil, while on the other side of the driveway several fragments of red brick spat out from a new hole that appeared some eighteen inches below the top of the wall. The squirrel scampered away in alarm, entirely unhurt.

'I am not prepared for this war, Thompson.'

'Neither is anyone.'

'Last week as I stood upon those awesome defensive works of the Maginot Line, I saw defiance all around me. The French have erected a great banner that proclaims to the world *"Liberté! Egalité! Fraternité!"* Across from that and in full view, the Germans have erected a still larger banner that screams *"Ein Volk! Ein Reich! Ein Fuehrer!"'* Churchill turned from the window. 'And do you know what we have, Inspector?'

He shrugged.

'We have a sign at Dover that says – "Welcome to England. Please Disembark Quietly in Order Not to Disturb Local Residents".' Churchill shook his head in sorrow, tears welling in his eyes. 'That's the first thing they'll see, when they come.'

During the short time that was left to him, Churchill worked into the night on his History, while Thompson watched over him. In the early hours of the first of September, Churchill retired to his spartan bedroom next to his study, surrounded by its photographs of Lord Randolph. While he slept, Germany invaded Poland. Churchill was roused by a phone call shortly after dawn from the Polish Ambassador who told him that, even as they were speaking, bombs were falling on Warsaw and tanks were rolling through every major crossing on the country's western border. Poles were already dying, soon Poland itself would be dead. He asked Churchill to do whatever he could.

Churchill immediately telephoned General Ironside, the Inspector-General of Overseas Forces. The general in turn telephoned the War Office. No one there had heard a thing.

Still Chamberlain fought for his peace. He would not declare war. He announced that Britain would honour its obligations to Poland and issued a warning to Germany that it must withdraw, but gave no time limit. He took emergency powers which swept away democracy and placed all effective powers in the hands of Ministers and civil servants. He sent messages to Hitler through ambassadors and intermediaries and hoped for a reply that offered even the dimmest chink of light. There was talk of Italian mediation. If only the Germans would withdraw, then anything was possible.

Chamberlain pitched for peace while Britain prepared for war. The evacuation of three million children began from the cities. Blackouts were imposed across the land. Church bells were silenced, held in reserve for the invasion that everyone feared would come. The crowds which only days beforehand had cheered and waved, now stood silent.

And while Poland suffered and bled, Government MPs packed the Smoking Room and distracted themselves with drink. 'I have never seen so much drink being consumed before,' wrote one veteran civil servant . . .

'Bugger! Bugger! Bugger!'

'Quite agree, Ian, old boy.'

'How the hell did we get ourselves into this mess?'

'How did Neville get us into it, don't you mean?'

'Damn it all, don't you remember Neville last year? Going on about quarrels in faraway places between people of whom we know nothing. That's what he said about Czechoslovakia. And Poland's even farther away.'

'Bloody suicide to get involved with Poland. Ivan one side, Adolf the other.'

'He hasn't declared war – yet.'

'Be thankful for small mercies and large drinks. Another?'

'Bloody fool question.'

He waved at a harassed steward. 'Trusted Neville, don't you know. Relied on his word that there wasn't going to be any bloody war. He promised, Ian. So I've gone and done a damned fool thing. Kept all the money here. In Blighty.'

'All of it?'

'Patriotic duty – well, most of it's the little woman's, anyway. Tried to have a word with her about it once but – well, you know how it is. One of those damned times we weren't exactly talking.'

A short silence dedicated to drink.

'Anyway, so it's all still sitting there. In the bank and in investments. Shot to buggery, most of them. Should've got out while I could. Now it's too late, all these exchange controls and everything.'

'And conscription.'

'Don't be so mournful, Ian, we're far too old for that bloody nonsense.'

'I was thinking of Cecil, my son. He's twenty-two.'

'Poor sod.'

'Already got his call-up papers. I've asked my solicitor to look into it. Perhaps an exemption on medical grounds. He's got a gammy elbow, you know, can't fire a gun. Couldn't hit a pheasant if it came up and kissed him.'

'What, Cecil?'

'Yes.'

'But I thought he got a rowing blue at Oxford a couple of years ago . . .'

More silence.

'Damn Neville.' Said softly but with passion.

'But we're not at war yet, Ian. Maybe Neville's got something up his sleeve.'

'And Winston banging on the door.'

'I hear that half the Cabinet are up in arms, can't understand why Neville hasn't declared war already. There's talk of a coup.'

'Caesar is to bleed? And who's supposed to be playing Cassius?'

'They say Leslie's the ringleader.'

'Hore-Belisha! Well, that's fine, just dandy. We're going to war on the say-so of little Leslie.'

'He's Minister of War.'

'He's a bloody Levantine, so he can scarcely lay claim to being objective. Probably got investments in Poland. Some bakery he owns with a second cousin. And we're expected to go to war to pull his assets out of the oven? I think not.'

'It's one monstrous mess, Dickie. What do you think we should do?'

A period of silent contemplation.

''nother drink?'

As German troops began their mutilation of Poland, Chamberlain had at last summoned Churchill. He explained that he had long been thinking of recasting the Government and asking him to join, and now that time had come. Would he consider a seat in the War Cabinet? Churchill had offered both his thanks and his acceptance, and had even shed a tear. Chamberlain instructed him to remain on hand to await developments.

So Churchill returned to his London home in Morpeth Mansions to 'await developments', but they stubbornly refused to present themselves. There was no declaration of war, and no War Cabinet. For two days he waited for a summons that failed to arrive, struggling to believe he had not been systematically cheated.

Others were less hesitant in reaching a judgement. Bracken burst in, blood in his cheeks and Boothby in tow.

'Monstrous! Two days now they've been bombing Poland and still Chamberlain hides. The lobbies reek of rebellion.' He helped himself to a drink without asking, downed it in a gulp, then refilled it to the brim.

'Still no call, Winston?' Boothby asked, following Bracken's example with the whisky.

The cigar glowed in impatience.

'No matter. The people are with you. They're marching outside the gates of Palace Yard right now, waving their "Churchill" posters.'

'Then let us pray their enthusiasms prove infectious.'

'Listen to yourself!' Bracken exploded. He began striding around the room, throwing arms and words about in the wildest manner, his soul swept up in a hurricane. 'How can you wait for Chamberlain? It'll never happen, Winston. The rumours are everywhere. He's still trying to concoct some deal with the Germans – Horace Wilson pulling every string – Neville down on his knees again. Can you imagine? Another Munich? Is there no end to their shame?'

'The bottom of that barrel is deeper than any of us could have imagined.'

'It's treason.'

'He has a certain lust for peace. Doesn't make him evil.'

'We've been talking with some of the others,' Boothby joined in, gravel in his throat. 'We all agree. You must break him, Winston. Go to the House. Straight away. Gather our colleagues. March on Downing Street and demand –'

'That is ridiculous. No one but the wretched

Wehrmacht is going to march on Downing Street. You don't discourage an invasion by starting a civil war.'

'We can't fight with him at the helm.'

'He is the leader of our party.'

'The party? The party?' Bracken's turn again, almost shouting in contempt. 'The party won't do a bloody thing. It's rotten to the core. The more mistakes he makes, the more blunders he commits, the more opportunities he throws away – the more they plead that we must pull together. Unity. Discipline. Follow my leader. Like Gadarene swine wallowing in their own muck.'

'Brendan – you must stop! You must learn to harbour your hate. Don't spread it around. Save it for Hitler and his Huns, not Mr Chamberlain. The time will come when we shall need him.'

'Did Jesus need Judas!'

'Chamberlain is exhausted –'

'By ambition!'

'He has given me his word.'

'What, the same word he's hawked around half of Europe?'

'Nevertheless . . .' For once, Churchill seemed to struggle for words. 'Nevertheless, I shall wait for his call.'

Boothby was no less emphatic. 'Winston, it's no good jumping over the sty wall and wallowing alongside him. You've got to sweep him aside.'

'Be a butcher?'

'Not a butcher, a bloody patriot!'

'You dare to doubt my patriotism, Bob?'

'No, Winston, just your appetite for power. For

Christ's sake – and I mean for Christ's sake – someone has to lead us into this bloody war!'

They had pierced him, had set his ambition against his duty, and for once he found the two difficult to reconcile. Angered at them, and even more at himself, he chewed silently on his cigar. But Boothby would not wait. He swept up the jacket he had thrown casually over the back of a chair and made for the door, turning as he was about to disappear.

'OK, you wait, Winston. Go ahead and be patient. And pray to God above that the Poles will find some way of understanding.'

'Understanding what?'

'How you could trust the word of a man like Chamberlain. And how you could remain so ridiculously serene while the bloody Luftwaffe is slaughtering their wives and children!'

Then he was gone.

A blanket of embarrassment fell over Churchill and Bracken as they heard Boothby pounding out of the front door.

'Over-excitement,' Bracken apologized. 'There's a lot of it about this evening. Two Members were physically sick in the Chamber.'

'Not simply from excitement, I suspect.'

'Well, there's a lot of that, too.' Bracken put his glass down; this was a night to keep his wits about him and he'd never been able to match Churchill's capacity for alcohol.

'Go after Bob,' Churchill instructed. 'Calm him. This is not a night to fall foul of our friends.'

Bracken picked up his own jacket, relieved at the excuse to leave. 'All he needs is a little fresh air.

We'll go and join the protesters. Wave a few of your banners,' he joked, heading for the stairs. 'You don't mind, do you? The banners, I mean.'

'Why should I?'

'That's a relief. I couldn't ask beforehand – you were away in France – so I . . .'

'That is your work?'

'Yes,' Bracken lied. 'Had a word with a chum in the advertising industry.'

'You are always full of wonders, Brendan.'

'It was nothing.'

Churchill knew it was precisely that – nothing, at least, so far as Bracken was concerned. The posters had been placed by an admirer. Not Bracken's work – but Bracken always wanted so desperately to be included. He was an outrageous chancer who lied – no, that was the wrong word, for he had never engaged in harmful deceit so far as Churchill was concerned – who invented things almost without knowing he was doing so. Churchill had always known he could rely on Bracken's loyalty, and that counted for far more than any occasional 'evidential economy and frugality with the facts', as he'd described it to Clemmie. Anyway, such inexactitudes were nothing compared to those that had been poured down upon them in such abundance from on high.

'Bob didn't mean it,' Bracken offered, trying to reassure, but Churchill waved him on into the night with a sweep of his cigar.

Boothby was right, of course – indisputably, ineluctably right. There was no reason to believe Chamberlain's promise. But the Prime Minister was faced with circumstances which overshadowed all personal considerations and previous slights. Churchill had watched him that afternoon in the House, borne down and made grey by the weight of his cares. War was at hand, surely this was a time when a Prime Minister could be trusted to deal straight. So Churchill would wait.

'Ah, my Praetorian guard.' Chamberlain offered a thin smile as Wilson and Ball entered the Cabinet Room. His face, always finely drawn, looked spectral beneath its tight covering of pale, drawn parchment. On the table in front of him stood a glass of effervescent liver salts.

'Pains?'

'Are you surprised – on the diet of disloyalty I am fed?'

'Leslie?'

'He says he cannot support a policy of – I quote – pusillanimity and indecision.'

'Upstart and intriguer, like all his kind.'

'That may be, Joe, but he is not alone. He came with others.'

'There's Winston, too.' Ball waved a folder. 'He won't stay quiet much longer. Been telephoning everyone to say we must be at war by midday tomorrow, or else.'

'Or else what?' Chamberlain snapped at his acolytes, grimacing as though in physical pain.

'Else you'll find him right outside the bloody door. And he'll have company.' Ball waved the file again. 'They're organizing, Neville.'

'How many?'

'Too many.'

'Horace?'

'I think, Neville' – a breath, a final pause for thought, a moment of history – 'that if you don't declare war tomorrow, then someone else will.'

'Ah, so it's come to that . . .' For a moment Chamberlain seemed to have forgotten the business in hand. He took a long draught of his liver salts and used it to wash down a couple of pink pills he took from a circular box. 'Thank you for your honesty. Both of you. I swim in a sea of deceit, and you are my rocks. I don't express my gratitude enough.'

'Not necessary.'

A pause, his mind wandering.

'They'll know it's not my fault, won't they – the people? I've done everything I could to avoid this outcome – they'll say we've taken the ethical course?'

'Without doubt they will.'

'We must be up there with the angels, but . . .' A lengthy pause, hanging on to a half-hope which withered even as he grabbed at it. 'If there is to be war' – another silence, more painful – 'then I will have to include him. Won't I?'

'War requires sacrifice.'

'He bombards me with letters – two since this morning. As if I have time to read them, on a day such as this.'

'Perhaps better inside the tent . . .'

'Keep him busy.'

'Distracted.'

'At the Admiralty, I think.'

'Magnificent! His post from the last war.'

'So no promotion.'

'Duties that will keep his attention a thousand miles from Poland.'

'So once the Polish issue is settled . . .'

'A quick war –'

'And a much-praised peace –'

'You, Neville, once again the man of the moment.'

'And Winston lost at sea.'

'Britain at the heart of Europe, rather than at its throat.'

'With an election. Maybe even before Christmas.'

'Oh, praise God! We may yet overcome . . .'

The broadcast was made in a thin, reedy voice at precisely 11.15 a.m.

'I am speaking to you from the Cabinet Room at Ten Downing Street.

'This morning the British Ambassador in Berlin handed the German Government a final note stating that, unless we heard from them by eleven o'clock that they were prepared at once to withdraw their troops from Poland, a state of war would exist between us.

'I have to tell you now that no such undertaking has been received, and that consequently, this country is at war with Germany.

'You can imagine what a bitter blow it is to me that all my long struggle to win peace has failed. Yet I cannot believe that there is anything more or anything different that I could have done and that would have been more successful . . .

'Now may God bless you all. May He defend the

right. It is the evil things that we shall be fighting against – brute force, bad faith, injustice, oppression and persecution – and against them I am certain that the right will prevail.'

It was the voice of a man dragged to the point of exhaustion by disappointment, the words of one who sought self-justification even at the height of the nation's peril. We are at war but, please, it's not my fault . . .

When he had finished, he found further speech difficult. His mouth was dry, his eyes damp. He gathered his papers into a neat pile and screwed the top carefully back onto his fountain pen. Finally he turned to Horace Wilson, who had been standing guard at the door, and nodded as though the movement of every muscle threatened to tear him apart. The words would not come at first, and when they did, they had an edge like shattered glass.

'Send for him.'

PART THREE

The Limits of Loyalty

An elderly statesman with gout,
When asked what the war was about,
In a Written Reply,
Said, 'My colleagues and I
Are doing our best to find out.'

(A limerick popular in the
Foreign Office at the outbreak of war)

FOURTEEN

September 1939.

It took four weeks – twenty-nine days of extraordinary late-summer heat and crushed spirits, to be precise – before Warsaw succumbed in flames. By that time two hundred thousand people and an entire nation had bled to death. It was the start of what someone in America dubbed 'the Phoney War', a phrase that seemed as remote as hope for those trapped in the rubble of the Polish capital during that endless month of September 1939, when orphans screamed in terror and the flies feasted and grew fat.

It was only the beginning. And not even the end of the beginning.

During the very first hour of war for the British Empire – an empire that was doomed to extinction as surely as was Poland, but simply didn't know it – the air-raid sirens had sounded across London, only minutes after Chamberlain's thin aristocratic voice announced that the battle had begun. Churchill and his wife, Clemmie, had climbed to the top of their house by Westminster Cathedral to observe the silver-grey barrage balloons rising into the sky above the rooftops and spires of London. 'Bloody punctual, the Hun,' Churchill had observed, before leading her down to the nearest air-raid shelter clutching a bottle of brandy to his chest and trailing cigar smoke. The shelter proved to be nothing more than an open basement; it had no door, no sandbags, no seating. As he looked along the deserted street, Churchill imagined the carnage that he had been warned would follow an air blitz. He knew that the Government had already made its preparations, in secret, digging huge lime pits and stockpiling 100,000 cardboard coffins for the casualties their experts had predicted would be inflicted upon them within weeks. But, on this occasion at least, it proved to be a false alarm, sparked by a solitary – and friendly – French plane. Yet the two squadrons of RAF fighters sent up to engage what they thought might be the first wave of the Luftwaffe somehow managed to engage each other in a dogfight above the Thames, and in the ensuing mayhem two fighters were shot down. It became known as the Battle of Barking Creek.

That evening a German U-boat torpedoed and sank the outward-bound passenger liner *Athenia*. One hundred and twelve lives were lost, including twenty-eight Americans who were fleeing home. And two weeks later, as the sun set on the evening of 17 September, the aircraft carrier *Courageous* turned into the wind in order to allow her aircraft to land upon her deck. In so doing, she unwittingly turned into the path of the U-boat she and other ships had been hunting. A single torpedo struck her amidships and sent her to the bottom. More than five hundred of her crew, including her captain, drowned with her.

On that same day the fate of Poland was sealed

when Soviet armies swarmed across her eastern and all but undefended frontiers and stabbed her in the back. It was what had been agreed in the secret protocols of the pact signed by Ribbentrop and Molotov. Poland was to be wiped from the map of Europe.

And yet . . . hadn't Britain and France guaranteed Polish independence? Declared war on Germany for the crime of invading Poland? So what now of the Soviets? Didn't honour, justice, consistency, simple humanity *demand* that they now turn their wrath on this new locust from the east? Ah, but this is diplomacy, and diplomacy is not the art of innocence, nor does it strain to be either ethical or consistent. So, as German and Soviet armies met and embraced at the Polish town of Brest-Litovsk – in comic opera fashion, the same place where in 1917 Russia had concluded its humiliating peace with the armies of the Kaiser – the statesmen in London and Paris drew in and held their collective breath. They would wait.

But patience is for those with full stomachs.

The first night of the war finds Carol Bell in tears, trying to focus through salt-smeared eyes on the needle she is prodding through Peter's jacket. It has gone the way of his trousers. He and the other boys in the street have been using the top of an Anderson shelter to practise parachute jumps, and the elbows of his jacket are now ripped to buggery on the bolts. It is his only jacket. And he is leaving tomorrow. She wants so desperately for him to look smart at that moment in the morning when she will try to find a smile and wave him goodbye, perhaps for the very last time.

She has spent the afternoon filling sandbags and her back feels as though she's been taking care of a football club on tour, including a full set of reserves. Not that she ever did that, of course, strictly a one-punter girl. She's been hoping to spend every last minute with Peter but he said he wanted to play with his friends and she thought it best he should feel as normal as possible – no tears, they can wait for tomorrow – so she let him go with an instruction to be back by teatime. He's always been restless, could never keep still, even when she was carrying him, impatient little sod. Gets that from her. Anyway, he went to play and she couldn't just sit and wait for him, practising her false smiles and her goodbyes, so she put the sleeping Lindy in her pram and pushed her to the park where they were filling sandbags. Wasn't much, so far as the war effort goes, filling sandbags, but there isn't much else a single mother can do – or is allowed to do. So she filled sandbags. And heard them gossiping behind her back.

Chigwell is supposed to be a fresh start, away from all those vicious tongues that surrounded her in her last street, but even in Chigwell a deserted wife is viewed with suspicion no matter what excuse for her circumstances she invents. The gossip is lurid, as gossip always is; she might as well have put an advertisement in the church magazine announcing she does tricks for a fiver a time. It's the way of the world, which sees something very wrong with any woman who isn't up to keeping a man. All men are unreliable bastards, but any decent woman finds *some* way of coping . . . So Carol keeps up appearances, helps others – when they allow her to – steers well clear of their husbands and today she fills up sandbags. Something to bridge the gap between now and the moment Peter leaves home.

He scurries in through the back door, filthy, scratched, radiant – and in tatters. She gives him a clip around the ear – it's what he would expect, a fair exchange for the good time he's had – then she digs out her last shilling to send him round to the bakers for his favourite cherry tarts and lemonade. He goes to bed smothered in love and crumbs. And as the light fades, Carol sits alone, her world no larger than the tiny back room, hemmed in by blackout curtains as she tries to repair all the holes that have suddenly appeared in her life. She struggles desperately to forget about tomorrow, for tomorrow is when she's going to lose her son. She will send Peter to school with nothing more than his gas mask, a small bag and a large label around his neck, at which point he will be swallowed up by the Great Plan. He will be evacuated. Lined up in the playground along with all the other children and taken away – to a place of safety, the Great Plan insists, but where that place of safety will be, the Great Plan doesn't know and can't yet say. Somewhere in the country. With new parents. No longer hers. With people who know nothing about Peter, who don't understand his sense of mischief, who won't know how much he adores cherry tarts and lemonade, who might abuse him, or use him as some form of cheap labour. Peter will be little more than a refugee, another frightened face from the pages of *Picture Post*.

All this she can do nothing about – but she is

determined that at least he will be a refugee with sound leather patches on the elbows of his jacket. So she sews beneath the light of a bare bulb and fights the dread rising inside her which tells her that, after tomorrow, she might never see Peter again.

She struggles on. Got to keep herself strong, for the children. Send him off with that smile. She reminds herself that she still has Lindy, that it could all still be worse. That's when she raises her eyes and spots their rubber gas masks on the table. Peter and Lindy have been playing with them at teatime, chasing each other, screaming in muffled voices, pretending to be bug-eyed monsters from another planet. Which is exactly what the war had already made them. Unrecognizable. No longer hers.

Even before the first bomb has fallen on London, her entire world has been blown apart.

Halifax had expected to find the Prime Minister working in the Cabinet Room, but it was deserted. The long, elegant room had grown claustrophobic, with tape masks pasted across every window-pane, cutting out the view and the light. At its far end the French windows were open and the lace curtain was shimmering, as though someone had made a hurried escape. Halifax followed the route, which led him out onto a sun-scorched patio from where he could see Chamberlain, down on his knees beside the roots of the silver birch, chatting animatedly with the gardener. Judging by the arch of his back and the earnest movement of his hands, it appeared to be a matter of considerable importance.

'Ah, Edward!' The Prime Minister looked up, his expression full of unaccustomed enthusiasm. 'Have you seen the autumn crocus? Just breaking through.'

The Foreign Secretary gazed down from an imperial height. Poland was in flames, Warsaw being reduced to rubble, and yet . . .

'Planted them myself. Last year,' Chamberlain continued. 'Makes you think – doesn't it? – that things will get back to normal.'

'Hope – and the crocuses – spring eternal.'

'Then perhaps you might persuade your friend Dawson to take that view,' Chamberlain observed, his voice grown suddenly taut, rising awkwardly with the aid of a stick. He was beginning to suffer from the early symptoms of an attack of gout.

Halifax couldn't escape the hint of accusation. *Your* friend Dawson . . . One editorial in *The Times* that was only a couple of degrees less than adulatory and the Prime Minister had taken personal offence, seeing enemies on every side. 'You know Geoffrey is one of *our* greatest friends,' Halifax insisted, 'and continues to be. He's given over his editorial columns to us these past months.'

Chamberlain sniffed.

'But he – like so many – feels . . .' Halifax searched for the word. He was going to use the expression 'let down' but decided it was too ambiguous and open to misinterpretation by an overly sensitive Prime Minister. 'He feels *deflated*.'

In fact, what Dawson had told him as they had shared a compartment on the train journey down from Yorkshire was that he felt almost *betrayed*. 'Left standing bloody naked in the park, Edward, I can tell you. I've backed this Government, you know I have. To the hilt. Let you write more of my leader columns than I have myself. And Neville *promised*. That appeasement would work, that there would be no war. Right up to the very last minute. Now I look a complete fool. All of a sudden my editorial meetings are chaos, everyone's arguing – I've even got the wretched lift man telling me where I got it wrong. Not much fun being an emperor with no clothes, I can tell you.'

Halifax sympathized. He knew precisely how Dawson felt. He'd never liked Munich, had described it as 'a hideous choice of evils' even while Chamberlain was promising peace and honour and claiming his place in history. At the end of the day Halifax had gone along with it because there seemed to be no other choice. He didn't like Hitler and so he didn't trust him. He was also more than a little afraid of him. Halifax had three sons of military age and he found the thought of losing them almost unendurable, and he feared that was what Hitler might demand. And it would all be his fault – *their* fault, his and Chamberlain's. Somehow they'd got this thing wrong, terribly wrong, yet this morning he found Chamberlain in no mood for self-flagellation. The Prime Minister took him by the arm and began to lean on him as he set off around the garden.

'Tell Dawson this. What is clear is that our cause is the moral cause. There has never been a clearer case in Christendom of such an unnecessary war. History will show this. What we have succeeded in doing over these last months is showing that we are the innocent party, the crusaders for peace. We have God on our side and I take great comfort from that. So should Dawson.'

Halifax felt uneasy. He was a High Anglican and spent more time on his knees than any of his Cabinet colleagues, yet at this moment he felt no more capable of laying claim to being a Christian crusader than he did of pronouncing it without sounding ridiculous.

'I think Dawson is struggling – many are, I suspect – to explain why on the one hand we go to war with Germany when they invade Poland, yet on the other barely lift a finger of protest when the Soviettes' – Halifax refused to call them *W*ussians – 'do exactly the same thing.'

'Our guarantee was aimed against Hitler, not Russia.'

'There's not much of a difference, so far as Poland itself is concerned . . .'

'So far as Poland is concerned, nothing will make much of a difference, since in all probability in a matter of days it will no longer exist!'

Halifax came to an abrupt halt as he stumbled over the sudden appearance of Realpolitik amidst their contemplation of morality. Meanwhile Chamberlain thrust his head forward and continued alone, as though trying to leave all this sophistry behind.

'Have to say, Neville, it's not the easiest intellectual argument we've ever put forward,' Halifax ventured.

'Forget intellectual, think *survival*. We send an expeditionary force to Poland, it would never make it off the beach. Get shot to pieces, along with you, me and the entire Government.'

'Then . . . what?'

'We wait. Bide our time. The war can't last – Hitler's over-stretched himself, not got the resources. I have a fair suspicion that by the spring the German people will be calling for an end to all this nonsense.'

'What – glutted with their victories?' Halifax couldn't hide the scepticism.

Chamberlain shook his head as though bothered by mosquitoes. 'The war is a temporary distraction, Edward. A diversion. Hitler has ransacked the German economy, it can only be a matter of months before it collapses. War can only lead to starvation and disaster, just like last time. But . . .' – he turned to his Foreign Secretary, tired eyes glinting with defiance – 'if we can limit the conflict, confine it to Poland, then by the spring Germany will have grown thin and weary, and we can get out of this awful mess with our prestige and our Empire intact.'

Halifax wanted to be convinced, yet if it came down to an economic contest between Britain and Germany, it might prove to be a damned close-run thing.

'That's why we've got to keep the lid on it,' Chamberlain continued. 'No bombing of the German mainland, no excuse for them to retaliate and for the war to spread. We must make sure they understand that we *still* – even at this point – have no desire for an all-out war. My conscience couldn't live with that.'

'But it could live with Hitler?'

'That's for the German people to decide. And by

the spring, God willing, the war may be settled and the British people can make their decision, too.'

'An election?'

'Why not?'

'Oh, but what a bloody place Europe is.' And what a bloody art is the art of politics, Halifax thought, when a war is viewed through the lens of electoral advantage. Sometimes democracy stank.

As if to confirm his thoughts, he spotted Wilson and Ball crossing the lawn in their direction. He had developed a growing antipathy for these men who served Chamberlain so ferociously – 'the Iron Triangle at the heart of Government', as they were sometimes called. What was it, why did his missing arm seem to ache whenever these two were near? Was it a question of class? Ball was the son of a bookstall clerk and Wilson that of a Bournemouth furniture dealer – although from the point of view of an hereditary Viscount, Chamberlain himself might be viewed as little more than a provincial metal basher. Or perhaps it was much simpler to understand than the English class system, perhaps it was no more than naked jealousy. Wilson was altogether too mighty, had accompanied Chamberlain to Munich, had been used by Chamberlain for all sorts of unorthodox dealings with ambassadors and others that should rightly have been within the fiefdom of the Foreign Office. Yes, it was a little of all of these things. But mostly it was because Halifax knew that in justice Wilson should bear the lion's share of the blame – blame for promoting appeasement so blindly, for pushing Chamberlain too far, blame which, because Wilson operated from the shadows, Halifax would have to shoulder in public.

Wilson approached, waving pieces of paper. 'Here's another two.'

Chamberlain groaned. 'Not more helpful hints from Winston,' he pleaded.

'He hopes you don't mind' – Wilson started to read – '"*my drawing to your attention the enormous wastage of paper involved in the daily conduct of Government business. Might I suggest that you consider issuing instructions to all departments that, henceforth, all envelopes used on official business should, wherever practicable, be pasted up and re-directed again and again rather than dismissed from service? Although this seems a small thing, the savings over the months and years ahead might prove to be substantial and it will teach every official – of whom we now have millions – to think of saving . . .*"'

'No more, no more,' Chamberlain sighed, leaning heavily on his stick. He turned to Halifax. 'He bombards me with his ideas without pause for breath. I feel as though I'm part of his own personal *blitzkrieg*.'

'You think you're being picked out for special treatment?' Halifax enquired. 'Why, he does it with everyone.'

'You, too?'

'Only this morning. Comments on Foreign Office telegrams. Somehow Winston's comments sound like divine commands even while they reek of port and chewed cigar.'

'I had my doubts. Remember discussing it with you, Horace. Would Winston cause more chaos inside the Government than out? I'm still not sure I made the right choice, bringing him back. It's like competing with a brass band.' He stabbed his stick into the turf. 'So what is the subject of his second commandment?'

Wilson waved the piece of paper. 'Mr Churchill desires to express his concerns that our Army and the Air Force are not of sufficient size to meet the current threat –'

'What?' Chamberlain exploded, shaking his stick as though trying to thrash the offending letter from Wilson's hand. 'Winston is Navy. I gave him Navy, nothing more. Got nothing to do with the others. Not a bit of it. Damn him and his insolence!' He grabbed at Halifax's sleeve with surprising energy, the fingers digging in like claws. Vivid crimson spots had erupted on Chamberlain's cheeks although the face remained as pale as parchment in spite of the sun. 'Two minutes back in Government and already he seems to think he can do my job better than I can. But I won't have it, Edward, won't have it at all. That man will never become Prime Minister so long as I have breath.'

'So long as you have breath, Neville, there won't be any need.'

'I agree with you, Edward. But if that day ever comes when I feel I should step aside, I can tell you without hesitation that you are the only man I want as my successor . . .' He brushed aside Halifax's predictable mutterings of humility. 'No, I know that occasionally you and I have our differences, but that's mere emphasis rather than objective. You've stood by my side faithfully over these last dangerous months, and I want you to know how much that loyalty means to me.'

'That's very generous of you, Neville.' Halifax bowed his domed head.

Chamberlain's voice rose, he turned as though addressing an invisible audience that lurked amongst the flower beds and stretched into the farthest corners of the large garden, his hand waving to command their attention. 'And if that means cutting an ungrateful upstart like Winston back down to size – well, I'm just the man to do it!'

Suddenly Chamberlain had grown tired. His proud back was bent like a bow, and he leant heavily on the arms of both Ball and Wilson as he climbed the short flight of steps that led back to the tiled patio outside the Cabinet Room. His feet had grown heavy, his step uncertain. Halifax followed, his head bowed, his countenance severe, like some cleric from ancient times processing behind saintly relics. All that was missing from the picture was a bell and a bishop's crook.

Chamberlain gasped. The fire in his heart was spent; for the moment it had fled to the joint of his big toe. He began to complain, of the war and of its torments. He began insisting that the burdens should be borne equally. Equality of suffering.

Wilson and Ball remained silent, uncertain how to deal with this sudden outpouring of high moral tone. Sometimes, at moments of extreme exhaustion, Chamberlain appeared to have left them and to be talking to some distant spirit or ancestor. At such times they found it best to leave him undisturbed and not to attempt to follow the meandering pathways of his private morality. After all, they were fixers, not philosophers.

Chamberlain said that if Germany were to be starved into submission, then there could not be those who grew fat. He insisted they devise some arrangement – 'taxation, restriction, duties, whatever is required' – to ensure that the profits of those who would do well out of the war were capped.

Wilson and Ball seemed suddenly stiff. They half-led, half-carried the Prime Minister to his chair at the Cabinet table. A trickle of sweat ran like an ant from his brow down towards his stiff collar. The acolytes fetched him liver salts and muttered about Socialist confiscation, but it had no effect. Chamberlain appeared deaf. More strongly, they urged that it was the great weapons manufacturers who had suffered cruelly during the years of appease-ment, that it was only right that they should restore the balance, but still Chamberlain did not hear. Then they reminded him that the great industrialists were donors to party funds, the oceans of money which kept his Government afloat.

'I only wish to be fair,' he insisted.

'But how?' they demanded.

He smiled weakly. 'That is for you to tell me. You, my advisers, my loyal elves. Something from your bottom drawer. You always have something in your bottom drawer, Horace.'

Ah, the bottom drawer. At last Ball and Wilson relaxed. They would take care of things.

They left Chamberlain, whose head had dropped in the heat. Before the door had closed he had already fallen asleep in his chair.

26 September 1939.

The Prime Minister gets up to make his statement. He is dressed in deep mourning relieved only by a white handkerchief and a large gold watch-chain. One feels the confidence and spirits of the House dropping inch by inch. When he sits down there is scarcely any applause. During the whole speech Winston Churchill has sat hunched beside him looking like the Chinese god of plenty suffering from acute indigestion. He just sits there, lowering, hunched and circular, and then he gets up. He is greeted by a loud cheer from all the benches and he starts to tell us about the Naval position. I notice that Hansard *does not reproduce his opening phrases. He began by saying how strange an experience it was for him after a quarter of a century to find himself once more in the same room in front of the same maps, fighting the same enemy and dealing with the same problems. His face then creases into an enormous grin and he adds, glancing down at the Prime Minister, 'I have no conception how this curious change in my fortunes occurred.' The whole House roared with laughter and Chamberlain had not the decency even to raise a sickly smile. He just looked sulky.*

Harold Nicolson, *Diaries and Letters 1930–1939*
edited by Nigel Nicolson, Collins, 1966

The thirtieth of September. One month since the war began. Horse Guards Parade lit only by the intermittent moon and the glow of a single cigar at a window in the Admiralty Building.

Churchill is alone, despondent. His staff have all fled before the howl of the Black Dog that all day has been circling and that finally late at night has fallen upon them. Unfair of him, of course, to take it out on his staff, when the real problem lies out there, on the other side of Horse Guards, in Downing Street, but in the morning they will all be back, eager for more, just like old times.

So many memories. First Lord of the Admiralty. Again. An office from which he had been dismissed nearly twenty-five years before. 'Winston is back!' they had telegraphed every ship in the fleet on the day the Prime Minister had reappointed him. It had been a magnificent day. He had known exactly where he was going the moment he stepped through the entrance of the Admiralty Building, marching pell-mell down the corridors, his heels clipping along the mosaic floor, the officers and staff struggling to keep pace, until he had burst in upon his old room to find it so little changed – his chair, desk, the same half-panelling of finest English oak, and the map box concealed behind it. When he had thrown back the shutters on the map box he had found the same charts he had left behind in 1915, with pins still showing the positions of every ship of the Imperial German Navy on the high seas of Europe. A search had been undertaken of the cellars and store rooms to unearth the lamps and other office furniture that had served him so well in his previous incarnation. All was soon as it should be – except for the war.

One month. In which both Poland and with it, British honour, have been wiped from the map. While Poles have been fighting and dying in their tens of thousands, their bodies strewn across a landscape of despair, what have their British allies done? Nothing. Not a bomb has been dropped in earnest nor a bullet fired in anger. Instead of bombs, the RAF have been dropping leaflets. Chamberlain's little bits of paper. Propaganda – even copies of Chamberlain's speeches – assuring the Germans that the British have no wish to fight them – as if there could be any doubt of the fact! After a month of supposed hostilities there has been only one reported German casualty – an unfortunate soul who was hit by a bundle of Chamberlain's speeches that had been thrown out of a Whitley bomber and had failed to separate, striking the man dead from sixteen thousand feet. This is not war as Churchill knows it.

Bombing – real bombing, designed to fire savagery from the air and bring the enemy to his knees – has been forbidden. 'We cannot bomb their munitions factories,' the Secretary of State for Air, Sir Kingsley Wood, has informed the Cabinet, 'because they are private property.' Anyway, if the British start bombing, the Luftwaffe might retaliate. The courage of mice. So the strategy appears to be to bore the Germans to death. And bludgeon them with leaflets.

On the Western Front even less has been happening. Eighty-five French divisions face no more than thirty-four divisions of the Wehrmacht. The French march and counter-march, and peer out from behind the Maginot Line, but will not go to war. Perhaps they are waiting for their British allies, who have sent only four divisions to France. All along the front the Germans have placed loudspeakers through which they constantly taunt the French – *'Ou est l'armée anglaise?'* Where are the British? No, this is not war as Churchill knows it.

And while he tries to fight and to encourage others to do so, Churchill meets with nothing but resistance. Just today he has received a letter from the Prime Minister – in belated response to several of his own – which tartly points out that his responsibilities stretch so far as the Royal Navy and no further. It rebukes him for interfering in other domains and draws to his attention 'the remarkable similarities between what is contained in your confidential memoranda to Cabinet colleagues and what subsequently appears in the newspapers'. Of course, that much is true, Churchill leaks like a rusting Thames dredger, but only from frustration and in an attempt to focus the minds of others on winning this war – a task which, in his less-than-humble opinion, can be achieved only by fighting it.

The war. One month old. Already soaked in blood. And another anniversary, twelve months ago to the day, when Chamberlain was being saluted by an SS honour guard, young Bavarian women were weeping with joy outside his hotel and he was concluding his pact with Hitler. Twelve months of failure, of deceit, of frenzied death as Hitler's war machine marches on all but unopposed while in London the Government covers its face in shame. It is like his map box, as though time in this place has stood still, as if the lights have gone out and all the clocks have been stopped.

Well, bugger that. He swears softly beneath his breath, throwing the stub of his cigar through the open window. There will be no stopped clocks on his watch. He resolves to give Time a little nudge.

'Oi! Can't you bleedin' read? It says *reserved*. This shelter is *reserved*.'

The ARP warden in his tin helmet and dark uniform grabbed at Mac's arms as he was trying to squeeze between the sandbags that formed the entrance to the air-raid shelter off Mayfair's exclusive Berkeley Square, a couple of hundred yards from Trumper's. The sirens had just sounded – perhaps another false alarm, but who was to know? It was hot, his leg hurt and Mac was running short of patience.

'Reserved? For who? Got a list?'

'Reserved for officials and the like. So's they can carry on working even while there's a raid on. That's why only the list get allowed in – you follow?'

'How do you know I'm not on your little list? Show it to me,' Mac demanded, but the warden ignored him, shoving him out of the way as a woman carrying a fur coat and wearing a hat full of fruit approached the sandbag battlements. It was a scorcher, eighty in the shade, but the woman clung to the fox as if it were about to come back to life. The ARP warden saluted: 'Afternoon, Mrs Studely-Grimes.' In exchange he received a curt nod that threatened to spill the entire contents of her hat into the gutter.

'Officials, eh? So who's she, then, the head of MI5?' Mac asked, his voice the echo of innocence.

The warden's eyes narrowed. The headquarters of

the security service were only around the corner but that fact was strictly need-to-know. This little oik clearly didn't have a need and wasn't supposed to know. 'Don't get smart with me, matey. You just run along to the next shelter up the road,' he instructed, ignoring the fact that, quite evidently, Mac was incapable of running.

'And tell me, Mr Warden, do the Luftwaffe bombs have little reserved notices on them, too, or can we all share them?'

'Take a word of advice from me, sunshine – and bugger off!'

'Two. That's two words.'

The warden's face drew close to Mac's, threatening. Then he sniffed. 'Oi, you reek of drink. Right, that's it. I'm having you. Drunk and disorderly. You bloody wait . . .' The warden began gesticulating to a policeman patrolling on the other side of the street, but his shouts were drowned by the sirens as they started wailing once more to sound the all-clear. Another false alarm. The constable passed by.

Disappointed and denied, the warden pulled himself up to his full height, bounced in his boots and glowered at Mac. '*Next* time, matey . . .' His finger wagged ferociously as if it had suddenly caught fire. '*Next* time . . . well, you just better bleedin' watch it!'

'Put them in uniform and they all become Nazis,' Mac sighed as he hobbled off, loud enough to make sure the warden heard him.

But it was true. He did reek of drink. Bloody Burgess again.

Burgess had called, badgered, pleaded with Mac

to meet with him once more, even gone to the lengths of booking another hairdressing appointment to deliver the summons in person. He had seemed so genuinely contrite that finally Mac had succumbed and agreed to meet.

It was clear that Burgess had been in the pub – a dark, untidy place in a back-street mews not far from Victoria Station – some time before Mac arrived. The blue eyes were like melting ice, the hair seemed to have been put on back to front, the sensuous and almost feminine mouth that on other occasions broke so easily into a smile seemed cemented to his glass. Strange, thought Mac, it was almost as if Burgess had a double personality, for while the hand that held the cigarette trembled like a leaf in a Siberian storm, the hand that clung to the glass was as steady as stone. His mind seemed to reflect the hands, at one moment faltering, uncertain, the next a model of insight and conviction – but always unpredictable. Mac sat with his pint of mild, and had little option but to listen while Burgess led him on a tour around a tormented heart.

'Thanks, Mac. And sorry. About tracking you home. Should've asked. Not sneaked. Sorry. Apologies. Castrate myself in the morning.' Suddenly his eyes were dragged from his glass to confront Mac. 'Anyway, what you so pissed off for? Got the love of a woman, beautiful family, yet still you're pissed off. What the hell you pissed off about?' But before Mac had the chance even to consider the question let alone his reply, Burgess was off again. 'Don't know how lucky you are, Mac. To have someone special. Be in love. I'll never be able to have someone special. To trust.

Least of all a woman.' He gulped in a huge lungful of air as though he'd forgotten to keep breathing, then continued, gazing into his glass. 'Was eight, I was. Asleep in my bedroom. Heard these screams coming from my parents' room. Rushed in. Well, you would, wouldn't you? Mother's screams, an' all. Found her underneath my old man. Been poking her, giving her one, he had – know what I mean? – then had a heart attack. On the job. On top of my bloody mother.' His voice sounded bitter and he gulped down more Jameson's to placate it. 'She couldn't get him off. My old man, on my mother . . .' A silence, then: 'Know what? Ever since then I can't look at a woman without thinking of my mother. And my old man. Dead. Fucking her. Doesn't seem – well, somehow doesn't seem natural. Can't do it. Don't know how bloody lucky you are, Mac. Can't love a woman. I can't love anything, really. No ties, you see. Sent away. Boarding school. Like a trunk, not wanted on voyage. Not belonging anywhere. Try to love my country, of course, but . . .' Another silence for an enormous pull of nicotine. 'Russia. Terrible place. Dark, bleak, god-awful. But they share the misery, you know. Equal shares. Of misery. Misery all round. Pity they had to share it with Poland. You ever been to Russia, Mac? 'Course you bloody have. Solovetsky Academy of Higher Learning. One of Stalin's students, you are. And survived. More than I'm likely to. They'll take me out 'n' shoot me one day. Or hang me. A traitor, like you, in the eyes of the System. Love my country, I do, Mac, seriously I do. Cricket. Crown. Christmas pudding – what more could a man want? Home his castle. Except scratch away and behind every bush you find

407

a bunch of little Francos. Bothers me, it does, this love and hate business. Done all right out of it, personally. Eton and the Cambridge all-comers. Top shelf. Born to rule. Me. Guy Burgess.' He shoved a grotesquely bitten fingernail into his chest, raising his voice in what seemed to Mac an almost contemptuous tone. 'Guy *Bloody* Burgess!' he shouted, to the curiosity of those seated at nearby tables. Then the moment had passed. 'But somehow . . . I hate it all. At times – most times – hate myself. So stupidly superficial. Whistle "Rule Britannia" out your arse and they all applaud. Kick hell out of the Establishment and no one complains, so long as you kick it from the *inside*. And I'm an insider. But you – damn it, people like you – this country'll freeze you out like it's Solovetsky every damned day. So you know what I do? I get stupid. I care. I ask my conscience and it says – sod 'em. Sod 'em all. And the System. Smash it, no matter what it costs. "My conscience will bring me to my dying place, 'tis only cowardice that has kept me away so long." Auden, I think. Friend of mine. Led me astray in every corner of Cambridge, he has. And – that's just it – comes a time when you have to decide. Country. Conscience. Or a stiff cock.' He broke into liquid laughter that dissolved into tears and began to pour down his face. 'You know, Mac,' he sobbed, 'in the end you can only betray one thing. That's yourself. And I do it all the time.'

He pushed his empty glass across to Mac, who noticed with some astonishment that his own glass was also empty. He rose and refilled them both.

Burgess made even less sense after that, except to insist that Mac should forgive both his drunkenness and the intrusion upon Mac's private life. 'Keep in touch, Mac, keep in touch.' And Mac promised he would. As he left the pub and walked slightly unsteadily down the cobbled mews, he wondered why he had agreed to that. After all, he was so different from Burgess. He didn't believe in country – he had no country, and it spared him the torment that open-eyed patriotism inflicted upon Burgess. Neither did he believe in conscience. Hell, look what conscience did to *goy tzedek* – righteous gentiles like Burgess. And he had no doubt that, deep down, Burgess was righteous – or believed himself to be righteous. That's why he hurt so much. He was falling to pieces, swept away in alcohol and self-abuse, while Mac had always been brought up to confront problems in a different way. He remembered his uncle, Moshe, the cobbler, a huge man with delicate fingers and a ready grin. 'You behaves, you be good, little Yosef Ya'akov,' he had bellowed one day when Mac had returned from the market-place bearing a black eye inflicted by a policeman's fist, 'but if you finds yourself in troubles with the law, this is what you do. First you fast. You fasts till it hurts, 'cos nothing in this life comes without a little pain, you hear? Then you prays to God. You recites your Psalms, you call upon the Almighty. And if your shovel still full of shits – well. That's the time you bribes the *mamzer* magistrate.' During his years in the camps, Mac had learned to short-circuit the system. He'd gone straight to bribery. Several times it had saved his life, and his conscience had disappeared with the sun.

So no country, no conscience. Which left only . . .

well, Carol, that first time. And now Peter and Lindy and things that had begun to matter to him. He cared. He hated caring, it complicated his life, but he had fought that battle and knew that he'd lost. He had begun to feel again. And remember things, like his roots, and Uncle Moshe, and that bloody policeman in the marketplace. And the ARP warden. Half a lifetime later and half a continent away, so little had changed. There were still those who enjoyed giving him a good kicking, just for the hell of it. And now, because he belonged, had a home, it had begun to hurt. For the first time since he had been marched out of his school playground in Wadowice, Mac was truly afraid. He had something to lose. So if Burgess wanted to kick back, he could do some kicking for Mac, too, and for Carol and Peter and Lindy. So Mac would do as Burgess asked and keep in touch – after all, apart from a hangover, what had he got to lose?

FIFTEEN

October 1939.

'Turn it up, dammit – up, up, up. Can't hear a bloody thing.'

Beaverbrook's voice echoed around the marble walls of the bathroom before erupting through the open door into the outer room, and anxious fingers scrabbled at the dials of the wireless set. 'Not that there'll be any damn thing worth listening to, just Winston's usual windbagging,' the Canadian added.

'It's starting,' a discomfited and evidently junior voice announced.

This observation was followed by a series of gruntings from within the bathroom that sent a ripple of embarrassment amongst the four men gathered around the desk outside. They were all over-paid executives, and one of the functions they were over-paid to endure was their boss conducting meetings from the john. Beaverbrook liked to shock, keep men guessing, and usually he succeeded. The men continued to shuffle uneasily until the voice of Churchill, sibilant, slightly crackling and lacking in bass but nevertheless totally distinctive in its lilting tones, at last gave them merciful distraction.

'*The British Empire and the French Republic,*' the First

Lord began, *'have been at war with Nazi Germany for a month tonight. We have not yet come at all to the severity of fighting which is to be expected, but three important things have happened. First, Poland has been again overrun by two of the Great Powers which held her in bondage for a hundred and fifty years but were unable to quench the spirit of the Polish nation. The heroic defence of Warsaw shows that the soul of Poland is indestructible, and that she will rise again – like a rock.'*

Ungracious noises emerged once more from the bathroom, followed by a flushing of water.

'What is the second event of this first month?' Churchill's voice continued. *'It is, of course, the assertion of the power of Russia. Russia has pursued a cold policy of self-interest. We could have wished that the Russian armies should be standing on their present line as the friends and allies of Poland, instead of as invaders. But that Russian armies should stand on this line was clearly necessary for the safety of Russia against the Nazi menace . . .'*

'God's name, Winston, wake up! The Russians are there 'cos they're two-faced goddamn Communists.' A diminutive figure now followed the voice out of the bathroom door. The First Baron Beaverbrook emerged, slipping his braces back over his shoulders. The flies of his trousers remained unfastened and flapped like sails in a squall.

'I cannot forecast to you the action of Russia . . .'

'Raping the rich!' snapped Beaverbrook, throwing himself into his chair behind the desk and plucking a cigar from an elaborate humidor.

'It is a riddle wrapped in a mystery inside an enigma . . .'

'Hey, cute phrase, Winnie, grant you that.'

'But perhaps there is a key. That key is Russian national interest. It cannot be in accordance with the interests or the safety of Russia that Nazi Germany should plant itself upon the shores of the Black Sea, or that it should overrun the Balkan States and subjugate the Slavonic peoples of south-eastern Europe. That would be contrary to the historic life-interests of Russia. But here these interests of Russia fall into the same channel as the interests of Britain and France . . .'

'You have got to be kidding!'

'Through the fog of confusion and uncertainty, we may discern quite plainly the continuity of interests which exists between England, France and Russia . . .'

'Damn his eyes. The Bolsheviks are only just through screwing the Polaks and he wants to bend over for the bastards. Enough!' Beaverbrook exclaimed. He leaned across and switched off the wireless.

'Overblown nonsense,' one of those on the other side of the desk laughed, trying hard to sound confident. Meetings in Beaverbrook's sumptuous art-deco office in the *Express* building often had the effect of transforming grown men into nervous teenagers.

Beaverbrook turned on him. 'Nonsense, is it?'

'Jumping into bed with Joe Stalin? It's just too fantastic.'

'Is it? Dunno about that. For the first time in his entire mess-strewn life old Winnie might be right. Do a deal with the Russians and this whole war thing might just turn around.'

'But we hate the Russians,' another voice suggested diffidently.

"Course we hate the bloody Russians. Not sure I like you too much, either, but that don't stop you working for me.'

The voice retired hurt.

'But that's not the issue for today – which is not *war*, so much as *peace*,' Beaverbrook continued. 'Hitler's offered an end to it all. Got what he wants in Poland, now says he wants to be a good boy again and will never darken our door. What do you gentlemen think? What does the *Express* think?' He was testing them. He enjoyed acting the inquisitor, probing. He had so very few fixed views himself that he enjoyed scouring for fresh ones, hoping to bump into something he liked.

'You had lunch with Horace Wilson today – what does he think?' enquired Heale, the editor, who was standing a little apart from the rest, sucking at a large briar pipe and toying thoughtfully with an antique globe.

Beaverbrook's boyish eyes sparkled, delighted that at last someone else was playing the game. 'Simple. Poland is lost. So if we continue the war, we won't be saving Poland. It can be nothing other than a war of retaliation and of revenge which will result in the pointless slaughter of thousands of innocent Englishmen.' He didn't say so, but the inflection in his voice made it clear he was quoting directly.

'And the Prime Minister?'

'Since when did Horace allow as much as a cigarette paper between himself and the PM?'

'So – Churchill wants war. While Chamberlain doesn't. An unfortunate dilemma.'

'And the *Express* – what does the *Express* want?' Beaverbrook demanded, the eyes now more serious, casting across the editor.

Heale paused before replying. 'We've been pretty consistent these last couple of years. Kept to our creed. *Blessed are the peacemakers*. Why should we change now?' It was a subtle tactic, turning to the scriptures. Beaverbrook was an industrial magnate and former Cabinet Minister from the First War, a man of extraordinary ruthlessness who liked to suggest he'd be happy to do a deal with the Devil so long as he was offered a percentage of the approach road to Hell, but he was also many other things, including being the son of a Presbyterian minister from middle-Canada. He kept a Bible on his desk and another on the glass shelf inside his private/public bathroom, and any opinion that was served to him wrapped in a biblical context would never be treated with scorn.

'Yeah, sure – *blessed are the peacemakers for they shall be called the children of God*. But God also said, and I think rightly' – he paused, waiting for a reaction, running his hand through his untidy mop of thinning hair – 'Oh, for pity's sake, you guys, it's a joke, a bloody joke . . .'

They all looked at each other, wondering if it was too late to laugh.

'But God also said – something like this. Ezekiel, I think . . .'

In the corner, Heale smiled to himself. Beaverbrook had a memory like a coal dredger that would dig up a biblical quote for almost any occasion, and usually word-perfect. All it required was an audience.

'"*Thus saith the Lord God: Behold, I will bring upon you Nebuchadnezzar, king of Babylon, a King of Kings! From the north, with horses and with chariots, and with horsemen, and companies, and much people. Who shall slay thy daughters in the field."*' The smouldering tip of his cigar was thrust forward like a bayonet. '"*And make a fort against thee, and lift up the buckler against thee. And he shall set engines of war against thy walls, and with his axes he shall break down thy towers!*" Some crap like that, anyway. So what do you think? Do we stay on our knees in praise of peacemakers? Or would you gentlemen prefer we find a warlord to slay a few virgins?'

'Keep the virgins,' one man offered. 'We'll need them later. And Churchill as the King of Kings? I scarcely think so.'

'The rationing of newsprint is killing us,' another executive ventured. 'Advertising shot to hell. We'll never make any money while the war carries on.'

'Excellent point – excellent,' the magnate agreed. 'Unless, that is, we stir up a bit of controversy. Use a few gutsy headlines to sell the paper.'

'The war's not controversy enough?' a voice asked incredulously.

'War? What bloody war? You seen the latest communiqué? Poland's dead and gone and it's all quiet on the Western Front – again. Like watching grass grow.'

'What sort of controversy were you thinking of?' Heale enquired.

Beaverbrook smoothed his lips around the end of his cigar. It was usually a sign he was just about to pull the pin from a grenade. 'Well, what do you think about jumping into bed with Winston?'

'Over Chamberlain's dead body!'

'Precisely my point. Get a good few headlines out of a "Chamberlain-must-go" campaign.'

'But the *Express* has always been an appeasement paper. In Chamberlain's corner.'

'Except he's lost the plot. He wants peace, but can't say so because he knows that Jack and Jill in the street won't have it. Hitler's stuck his finger up their collective arse once too often. If Chamberlain announces he wants to go to Munich again to sign another peace deal, chances are his plane'll be shot down by our own guns.'

'But Hitler's serious. What did he say he wanted the other day?' An executive began scrabbling round for a two-day-old newspaper and quoted from its front page. '". . . *the liquidation of the present war between Germany on the one hand and Great Britain on the other.*" That's what he's proposing. Sounds to me like the best offer we're going to get.'

'OK, Hitler wants peace, Chamberlain wants peace. Let's assume Jesus Christ still wants peace and so, I suspect, does the Dalai Lama. And *we* want peace. But our readers, God love 'em, the men and women who keep us in martinis and mistresses, they in their abiding wisdom *don't* want peace. They're mad as hell. Want us to go and beat the crap out of the Krauts. So how do we bring them around to some sort of peace deal?'

He had set them a test. It was important they should respond. Ideas began to stumble forth, then gathered pace. Letters from irate correspondents already weary with war, they suggested. Lurid columns about how many businesses were about to go bust, how children might soon be reduced to begging in the street, how the blackout had turned roads into a death trap. How conscription was already wrenching families apart, how separation was undermining both public morale and private morality. And how the traditional pleasures of women would be wiped away by rationing, how they were being forced from the kitchen and into the factories, making bullets instead of babies. And perhaps, they suggested, the paper should carry interviews with the blind, the halt, the lame, the heroes and victims of the last war, the war that should have ended all wars . . .

And so a campaign was born, not so much out of confidence but out of naked convenience. Behind a smokescreen of cigar fumes, Beaverbrook hid a broad grin of satisfaction. He had brought them exactly to the point where he wanted them to be – and where Horace Wilson, over lunch, had told him they should be. By the time pudding was served there had even been mutterings about a Ministry in a reformed post-war Government for Beaverbrook himself. All in all, a good day's work.

'Then let us propagand! Distribute the pieces of silver and run up the white flag,' Beaverbrook instructed.

'And if no one salutes?'

Beaverbrook considered the point for a moment, then smiled.

'Why, *then* we jump into bed with Winston.'

*　　*　　*

For centuries the park of St James's that backs onto Whitehall has been a leafy retreat in the heart of London. In Tudor times, when Westminster was a sprawling and deeply unsanitary mediaeval place, the people poured forth from their hovels beside the noxious waters of the Thames to enjoy the pleasures of fresh air and the jousts that were held in the park. There were also other entertainments – bear-baiting, cock-fighting, the imported French game of pall-mall or bowls, and 'cooing' or 'coupling' seats for those who preferred more sedentary sport. After dark, many a young girl would emerge from the cobbled alleyways of Mayfair to earn a living propped up against the trunk of one of the trees as a drunk took his pleasure while she, as often as not, relieved him not only of her fee but also the rest of the contents of his pocket. St James's Park, for all its genteel and neatly trimmed appearance, has always been – and remains – a field of many follies.

It was where the paths of Churchill and Kennedy crossed in the early afternoon, on the narrow bridge that stretched across the lake. They had both been busy at lunch, consuming a volatile mixture of intrigue and alcohol – Churchill during a barnstorming performance before an all-party group of backbenchers at the Reform Club, while the American had lunched amidst the more restrained but no less conspiratorial atmosphere of the royal palace that stood at the park's western end. Kennedy was on his way to Downing Street on the other side, accompanied by Anna and a man in his mid-thirties.

'Ah, Mr Ambassador,' Churchill growled, raising his hat. Bracken, who was beside him, did the same.

'Mr First Lord.' The hatless Kennedy nodded in his direction. There was no warmth in the exchange, Churchill having difficulty deciding whether the American's odd form of greeting was merely an example of his crassness or an attempt at being comic. 'You know my niece Anna,' Kennedy continued, 'and this' – he indicated the tall and blue-eyed man to his right – 'is Mr Bjorn Svensson.' There was no further explanation; it seemed the minimum to satisfy the requirements of politeness. Bracken was ignored by the Ambassador, a slight which he put down to familiarity and provincialism. Even Anna only managed a coy, nervous smile.

Churchill turned towards the Swede. 'Mr Svensson and I have met. Over dinner at the ambassadorial residence a year ago, I think. Businessman, eh?'

The Swede nodded, revealing a thinning head of hair. 'We didn't get much opportunity to talk on that occasion, Mr Churchill.'

'Indeed. Seem to remember I walked out – eh, Joe?'

'So you did, Winston. So you did.'

'Heard about you, Mr Svensson. Spend a lot of time in Germany. You run messages.'

'Not at all,' the Swede protested, his manner mild and elegant. 'I simply like to keep both sides . . . informed. Aware of what each other is thinking, as well as saying. These are difficult times for everyone, Mr Churchill, and I try to help.'

Churchill sniffed.

'Just come from Buck House, Winston. The King was eager as an alley cat to hear what Bjorn here had to say,' Kennedy continued, embarking on a little game of one-upmanship.

Churchill sniffed again, more consciously. Lunch at the palace – and neither Kennedy nor the Swede was wearing a hat. 'I trust you found His Majesty in robust condition.'

'Excellent, thank you, Mr Churchill,' the Swede responded, his elegance standing in contrast to the Ambassador's brusqueness. 'He was most interested in Herr Hitler's offer of peace talks.'

'Can't have this Phoney War getting out of hand, Winston,' Kennedy interjected.

'I prefer to call it the Twilight War, Joe. The twilight that comes just before the descent of darkness.'

'Come on, Winston, this is the chance for you guys to get out of the hole. It was madness to guarantee Poland when you had no chance of defending it. But it was a little local conflict a million miles from here. For God's sake keep it that way.'

'And when the next little local conflict erupts . . . ?'

'Who gives a damn? Nothing to do with us. Let 'em play their damn-fool games – nothing says we have to go in and bat for them.'

'This is not a *game* –'

'Call it what you will, still wasn't worth a single dead American or Brit. Not then, not now. Think the King agrees. Prefers to shoot grouse rather than his first cousins.'

'We restock the grouse out of season. Sadly, war is a little more uncompromising.'

They were sparring, but their punches were grazing ever more closely by, tugging at the thin veil of civility that covered them. Their voices were growing louder, more intransigent, and the others in the group drew imperceptibly back, like seconds at a duel.

'Which is why, Mr Ambassador,' Churchill continued, returning to formality to cover the nakedness of their feelings, 'we shall be grateful when your country resolves to provide us with the materiel to prosecute this war to the limit.'

'We're neutral.'

'Yes, but your President assures me of his fullest sympathy . . .'

If it had been intended as a riposte in their game of contacts, it failed, for although Churchill had his own open line to the American President – as much as it seemed Kennedy had to the Royal Family and Downing Street – the Ambassador responded with a barely disguised snort of contempt. 'Sure, sure, sympathy's everywhere. It's a commodity traded openly in Washington right now. And it's going cheap. Trouble is, the sort of stuff you want for your war is going at a hefty premium.'

'We hope for more than sympathy. Favourable terms – even open support.'

'Nuts. This war has nothing to do with America.'

'Mr Roosevelt assures me –'

'Old Rattle Brain –' Kennedy couldn't restrain his impatience. 'Believe me, he's got more than enough on his plate to bother pulling Europe's chestnuts out of the fire. New Deal on the rocks, twelve million unemployed, a re-election campaign this time next year. If he wants to get involved in your mess it's only because he's got so much to cover up.'

'This is not about gaining advantage in some election campaign, this is about the survival of democracy itself.'

'Wanna know what I think about democracy, Winston? I think what Dr Gallup thinks. That ninety-six per cent of Americans want nothing to do with your war – not a damn thing. And if Rattle Brain forgets that, he'll find plenty of others at the nominating convention next year who'll be more than ready to wipe the salt off his peanuts.'

'Your ambitions burn bright.'

'And your ambition could end up wiping out half of humanity!'

They stood astride the bridge, two Horatios unwilling to give quarter, surrounded by expectant ducks. Churchill had his left foot planted forward, as though waiting to deliver a punch, while the taller American stretched to his limit so he could gaze down from an imperious height. He was breathing heavily, battling with contempt.

'You start a wider war, Winston, and you're gonna get whupped. Look around you,' the American demanded, waving his hand towards the extraordinary roofscape of minarets and ornate bell towers that rose above Whitehall. 'All this is going to get laid flat the first week of any real war.' He leaned closer, almost conspiratorial. 'You haven't got the planes or the guns to stop it – and between you and me, most of your Cabinet colleagues haven't got the guts, either. You got guts, Winston,

I give you that – I put that down to your being half-American. But you still haven't understood. The only winners of that little war will be the Communists and Jews.'

'Oh, spare me your confounded conspiracies! You see Jews in every corner.'

'Yeah – and in the Supreme Court, in the US Treasury, in the State Department, and most of all in the White House. Rattle Brain's found hideyholes for them everywhere – Baruch, Morgenthau, Lehman, Frankfurter. They're running the shop. And they've got their hands in the pockets of every arms manufacturer in the business.'

'We hold these truths to be self-evident,' Churchill quoted, his voice carrying across the lake. 'That *all* men are created equal. That they are endowed by their Creator with certain unalienable rights, that among these are Life, Liberty and the Pursuit of Happiness.'

'Sure. And there's another self-evident truth which the Founding Fathers didn't bother scribbling down 'cos it's so damned obvious. That you don't go guaranteeing a ridiculous country like Poland which you can't defend and which no longer exists.'

'Honour insists that we continue.'

'Jesus H. Christ, even George the Third knew when the game was up – and he was a raving lunatic!'

Churchill turned away, gripping the railing that ran along the bridge, head bowed, afraid for a moment that he might lose control of himself. Overhead a fist of starlings suddenly turned the sky dark, screaming as though they had just been hatched in hell.

'Winston, for God's sake listen. Bjorn here was in Berlin three days ago, saw half the Nazi big-hitters, even Goering. Hitler wants a peace. He's got Poland, doesn't want any more – well, maybe a few chunks of Africa as colonies, but nothing he's not willing to negotiate on. You can have peace inside a week. All you got to do is ask.'

Churchill turned slowly, his round face suffused with rage, his hands tight bundles of knuckles. 'Hitler is a hyena who has broken every rule of justice and common decency. He has waylaid one country after another, and like a hyena he will be back for more until there is nothing left on the continent of Europe but bleached bones and memories. You talk of democracy and the will of the people, Mr Ambassador. And I tell you that it is the will of this mighty nation of freedom-loving peoples that we shall never cease or desist until the disease of Hitlerism has been purged from this planet – not by promises, not by pieces of paper, not by asking Mr Hitler nicely if he will be so kind – but by fire! War is very cruel. It goes on for so long. But that is the price of liberty. And we shall so bend ourselves to our task and withstand any sacrifice until the governance of Europe is returned once more to its free people, and we Britons can once again sleep soundly in our beds.'

Kennedy was silent for a moment, shaking his head. 'Winston, if words could win a war, old Adolf'd be signing surrender documents by sundown. But they don't – and he won't either. And until he does,

I'm going to take Mr Svensson here off to have tea with the Prime Minister and see if there isn't another way.' He smiled, a twisted, scornful effort, and stepped past the hunched figure of Churchill, followed by Anna and the Swede himself, who gave Churchill a severe bow like a passing priest handing out penance. As they reached the far side of the bridge, Kennedy turned. 'Must do this again sometime, Winston. Enjoyed it, dammit!' With that he was gone.

Churchill stood motionless for many moments, his whole frame trembling slightly, tears in his eyes, until in a movement of explosive energy he snatched off his hat and threw it to the ground. It rolled off the bridge and into the lake. The ducks scattered in alarm.

When he turned, she was naked down to the waist, had slipped the shoulders of her dress, letting it fall, exposing the breasts, with nipples that were small and made of pink coral. She appeared almost child-like.

'For you, Brendan,' she whispered, a catch in her voice.

They had argued, his temper frayed by frustration, and now he felt racked with guilt, as though his mother had caught him with his hands down his own trousers. His relationship with Anna was going nowhere, had advanced scarcely at all since the day he had stumbled into his proposal of marriage to her and she had said no, not yet. That was what she had said, wasn't it? Not yet? Since that moment they would meet, would dine, would laugh, would whisper endearments and devotions, and then not see each other for a week and often two. Her duties to her uncle would not allow more frequent encounters – as, in truth, his duties to politics and particularly to Churchill were also formidable obstacles – and they had remained little more than kissing cousins, and she would laugh gently and move away every time he, in his own awkward fashion, tried to pursue the matter. During their encounter on the bridge she had as good as ignored him. Understandable in the circumstances, perhaps, but no eye language, no little secret sign of intimacy; it was almost as though she were ashamed. It had rankled.

His patience had snapped, not so much because he felt driven by any animal urge to possess her – he'd been mercifully relaxed about those sort of lusts, perhaps the monks in Tipperary had beaten much of that nonsense out of him – but because he knew he was not in control. So he had shouted. Raised his arms and his voice. Said he could not respect her as a woman if he could not respect himself, as a man. The ridiculous thing was that he didn't particularly want to throw her onto the sofa and ravish her, but he wanted to know that he'd be allowed to if that's what took his fancy. A matter of being in control. So he had lost his temper – the effect was impressive, with his eyes magnified and made wild by his bottle-bottom glasses, the hair erupting down his forehead, the hands flailing, his bad teeth placed on prominent display – and she had begun to sob. He had no idea how to handle a woman in distress so he had ranted some more, just to ram home the point, and moved away to find another cigarette.

When once again he turned to face her, she was half-naked and trembling. Had made herself defenceless. His to devour. As he moved towards her, she raised her hands to cover her breasts. 'For you, Brendan. Only for you.' She was sobbing, as though in fear.

He embraced her, put his arms around her, didn't touch her breasts but kissed her and pulled the cotton dress back over her shoulders. Because he knew that was what she wanted, and because this time it was his choice. She whimpered with relief and kissed him all the more eagerly and thanked him. 'Soon, darling Brendan, soon,' she breathed into in his ear.

'I was worried,' he began in half-apology. 'Thought, on the bridge, that you were embarrassed to have me near. Almost ashamed.'

'Embarrassed only by Uncle Joe and Mr Churchill. And a little angry. They make it so difficult for you and me.'

'Two of a kind.'

'They seem to enjoy fighting each other.'

'Those two would be going at each other even if there were no war.'

She ran her fingers through the hair that had flopped across his forehead, trying to push it back into some semblance of order. 'Brendan, do you think . . . there might be peace soon?'

'Not if Winston has his way.'

'He seems to enjoy fighting.'

'Too true. And sometimes too much.'

'Really?'

'He's a great man, of course, don't get me wrong, but sometimes . . . Hell, he even wants to fight the Irish. As if Hitler wasn't enough.'

'I don't understand, darling.'

'The Irish won't let us use their naval bases. Winston's furious with them. Claims they're legally bound to do so. And if they don't agree we – well, he says we should simply occupy them.'

'Take them by force?'

'Chamberlain and Halifax say it's madness. And probably it is. We'd never get another Irish volunteer. And it would have about the same effect in America as sailing a gunboat up the Mississippi.'

'Your Mr Churchill has a lot of ideas. And a lot of enemies. According to Uncle Joe, Halifax told him that the first thing Mr Churchill did when he got to the Admiralty was to order a bottle of whisky, and the second thing . . .'

'Was to drink it. Hah! It's probably true. But I doubt if the Ireland nonsense will come to much, anyway. Winston's got other fish to fry.'

'Like?'

'Well . . .' Bracken hesitated. This was a sensitive area. Absolutely need-to-know, but then he shouldn't really know, either. Winston could be such a gossip. And Anna was gazing up at him, her dress falling forward, exposing herself once more, trusting him.

'He wants to send a task force to the Baltic.'

'That would make sense, I suppose.'

'But they can't get the battleships through the

narrows between Denmark and Sweden, you see. Less than two miles wide at some points, no depth. So . . .' He swallowed, sounded awkward, glanced down her dress once more. 'He wants to float the fleet across. Put caissons – huge floating balloons – around them so they can get through the shallows and . . .'

'Sounds . . . exciting.'

'Bloody dangerous. Half the Admiralty thinks it would be a nightmare. Winston's always full of ideas. Sometimes gets ahead of himself.'

'And what do you think about it, Brendan?'

'Think about it? I'm not even supposed to know about it – and neither are you.'

'Then I shall forget about your silly ships right this moment.' She kissed him, pressing herself into him. 'And don't let others make us join in their ridiculous battles. Let's just keep it like this, Brendan, you and me, until the time is right.'

Entwined in her arms, he couldn't help but agree. He'd won, he was master in his own house and of their relationship. When it came to the physical stuff, he was content to be patient – after all, it was much more important that she should believe in him than that she should climb into bed with him. He was happy. And in his happiness, he had failed utterly to realize that, once again, Anna was in control.

'Had no choice, Ian. No option but to move into this place.'

Ian looked around the grand dining room of the

Dorchester Hotel on Park Lane. 'We're at war, Dickie. We all have our sacrifices to make.'

'You're telling me. Cookie buggered off to join the Army, damned fool. Old enough to know better, I told him, but what can you do? The man was determined to go and get his bollocks shot away. I told him straight, I did. He was leaving me in most unfortunate circumstances and he shouldn't expect his job back afterwards.'

'Man's propensity for selfishness never ceases to amaze.'

'So I'm cook-less. Without cook. Completely cooked up. I was faced with this awful dilemma. Move into the Dorchester – or go back to Deirdre in the country. Well, I can tell you, it'd take one of Fritzi's bayonets to get me back with her outside of weekends and holy days, so I'm afraid it's this place. For the duration.'

'I've known worse foxholes.'

'But you see, Ian, you see,' Dickie insisted, waving a loaded fork, 'it's the perfect place. Magnificent cellars –'

'Can't complain,' Ian muttered, raising his glass. 'What is it? Lafite or Latour?'

'Even better. A Léoville-Las-Cases, 1899, when they still knew how to make the stuff. Drink up, old fella. 'Nother on its way.'

'Be a shame to see it all disappear down a German gullet, I suppose.'

'But that's what's so wonderful about the cellars. Even got a place to sleep in during an air raid, sheets and all. So if Goering pops over, the gong goes, we disappear into the cellar, enjoy a bottle of something or other, then sleep like babes. They've even got somewhere reserved for Halifax. He'll be my neighbour. Play my cards right, could end this war with a job in Government.'

'Only if we win.'

'Bit old-fashioned, isn't it, Ian, this idea of winning or losing? Seems to me Uncle Adolf had it just about right. Time to draw stumps. Otherwise we all lose.'

'Neville seems to have other ideas.'

'Winston's ideas, you mean. I tell you, Ian, my postbag was jam-packed with letters saying we should grasp the offer, stop it right here and now. And if he wants a few hundred miles of fly-blown Africa, let him have it, I say. And let 'im suffer. After all, what's Africa ever done for England?'

A sommelier interrupted, proffering the second bottle of claret. Dickie declined to try it and waved for him to pour.

'But then, Dickie, I think of Cookie. And the others like him. The ordinary folk, the type that perhaps don't write letters.'

'*Can't* write. Cookie could barely make out a shopping list.'

'Perhaps. But there's a lot of Cookies out there who seem determined to fight this one to the bitter end.'

'You know why, Ian, do you know why? 'Cos they've got nothing to lose. Remember 1917? One minute Russkies are at war with Fritzi, next thing they've got a revolution on their hands. Could happen here, mark my words.' He dived into his glass. Silently Ian calculated his companion had just sunk two weeks' wages for Cookie and his kind.

'This isn't Russia, Dickie.'

'Isn't it? Isn't it, by Christ? They had Trotsky the Jew in charge of their army, and we've got Horab-Elisha. Destroying the War Office he is, my soldiering chums tell me, turning everything on its head.' A sudden burst of English mustard caused him to gasp, and he quenched the fire in yet more ancient claret. 'Know what they sing as they march, Ian? The British Army?' He began to chant gruffly, conducting himself with his fork and growing louder with each breath.

> 'Onward Christian Soldiers,
> You have nought to fear,
> Israel Hore-Belisha
> Will lead you from the rear.
> Clothed by Monty Burton,
> Fed on Lyons pies,
> Die for Jewish freedom
> As a Briton always dies . . .'

He snatched the starched napkin he had tucked in his collar and began to wave it in the air. 'Christ, Ian, might as well run up the white flag straight away. Sometimes you've got to ask yourself what the hell we're fighting for.'

The sommelier, attracted by the noise and the flapping napkin, scurried to their side. 'May I get you anything else, gentlemen?'

'Well, what d'you think, Ian? Got time for Number Three?'

*   *   *

433

The man from Romford sucked his teeth and sighed. He'd come about the piano. He said he needed it for his local TA unit, 'to entertain the boys', and there wasn't enough in the kitty. But Carol knew it was lies. He was simply trying to con her.

From the back garden came the sounds of screams and laughter. Peter was back. After weeks of waiting for Armageddon from the air, London's mothers had begun to tire of false alarms. They wanted their children back, and their hosts in the country had been only too pleased to oblige. Perhaps the war would get sorted out after all. And Carol had her own Anderson shelter now, which Mac had dug into the back garden and which had become a fort, a ship, a prince's palace, a store room, a place for them all to hide from Red Indians and elephants. And from Mr Goering.

She had wanted only forty quid for the piano. An upright, decent condition. Superficial scratches. Forty quid. To get her through Christmas. It had been her grandmother's, a sort of heirloom, the only thing she had left of her childhood. As a kid she had sat and learned to play, and to escape, particularly from her father, when he was around. Tunes like 'Nellie Dean' and 'On Mother Kelly's Doorstep'. Her mother used to cry. It had a couple of wonky notes but nothing which, to Carol's mind, at least, lessened its enormous value as an instrument of pleasure and distraction. The man from Romford disagreed. He kept banging down on the key which produced no sound at all, and sighing.

With Peter back, she was determined that this Christmas should be special, that the children shouldn't go without. Nowadays you couldn't rely on Christmas – couldn't rely on anything. But forty quid would get them through. Food. A few presents. Perhaps a fiver left over for the tea caddy. Dinner today had been a small tin of sardines, stretched to cover their pieces of toast by mixing in a handful of oats. As if they were horses. Forty quid would make all the difference, but the man from Romford was sucking his teeth fit to swallow. And offering only twenty-five.

She didn't mind haggling, was used to it, knew more than most about the marketplace, but she needed the money more than Romford Man needed a second-hand piano with a couple of dodgy keys. From outside came the sounds of banging on the metal sheeting of the shelter, reminding her that they would be running back inside and demanding to be fed in a couple of hours. And they would want more than oats.

She had to sell the piano, get through Christmas. And after that – well, she knew what she had to do. The thought of it made her hate herself, men even more, and Mac most of all. Elusive, mysterious, silent, non-committing Mac, the man with a soul so sensitive that she was only occasionally allowed to touch. And what she hated about him most of all was the turmoil he had brought into her life, changing everything around. Giving her hope. She could never forgive him for that.

The money had dried up. Mr Burgess had become unreliable, Mac said, always drunk, not been sober since the start of the war. And when he was drunk there was no money. So she sold whatever she had left.

Now Romford Man was dragging the piano through the doorway. She told him to be careful, not to tear the linoleum, but already it was too late. She had twenty-eight pounds in her hand. It had just been announced that food rationing would begin at Christmas – butter, bacon, sugar, ham – and more would follow. So now she could rush down to the shops, stock up, while she could. On sardines.

Happy Christmas, Mr Hitler.

It had to be resolved, this stand-off between the two most powerful men in the country, a circumstance that was sapping the will of the Cabinet and sowing confusion throughout the by-ways of Government. They both knew it had to be brought to an end – but how? They were of one Government, but two entirely different worlds, these sons of Birmingham and of Blenheim.

They had just finished Cabinet. A tetchy affair. The gout had got to Chamberlain and he could no longer walk without considerable pain. He had been forced to use the service lift to descend from his attic bedroom, and two policemen called from duty outside Number Ten had carried him into the Cabinet Room, placing him like a rag doll in his chair. After that, the Prime Minister's notorious lack of patience with his colleagues had been distributed widely without any obvious sign of favour, and they all seemed keen to gather their papers and scurry off to their next engagement. It seemed an inappropriate moment, perhaps, to invite the Prime Minister to dinner, but that is what Churchill had done. In all their long years serving together in Parliament they had never once broken bread or shared anything other than business, and neither of them could mistake Churchill's invitation as being other than an offer of peace.

'If you feel up to it, Prime Minister,' Churchill had added, perhaps incautiously.

Chamberlain's steely eyes had flashed – in pain or irritation? – and he had mumbled his acceptance. He could scarcely refuse.

So they had come together in Churchill's apartment in Admiralty House, he and Clemmie with Chamberlain – still leaning heavily on a walking stick – and his considerably younger wife Annie, who was as socially competent as Neville had always proven stiff. It was she who threw the regular Downing Street parties for the good and the great, three nights in a row in order that the flowers and hired crockery could be made to stretch, keeping everyone circulating between the state rooms in order to enhance the social value of the occasion and to avoid undue strain on the weak floors. Yet, while both kitchen and floors creaked and strained, Chamberlain would remain working in his study. A serious man. Not good at the small-talk required of social occasions and, with gout, even worse at drink. He declined Churchill's proffered whisky.

'Ah, twenty years serving arm-entwined-in-arm in the great chamber of Parliament, Neville, and never before dined together. How foolish of us to allow so much time to slip by,' Churchill enthused, ushering Chamberlain to his seat at the table.

Chamberlain refrained from reminding Churchill that much of those twenty years had been spent not so much arm-in-arm as at each other's throats. He took his seat and grabbed a soup spoon.

It was during the soup that they were interrupted by a flush-faced lieutenant, hot foot from the War Room below. 'Pardon the interruption, ladies, gentlemen, but beg to report latest intelligence.' For a moment he seemed a little uncertain to whom he should reveal his news, First Lord or Prime Minister. Unable to decide on the etiquette, he stared at the blackout curtains and offered a crisp, sightless salute. 'U-boat sunk on the western approaches to Ireland forty minutes ago.'

'In your honour, Prime Minister!' Churchill exclaimed, jumping from his seat. His eyes were moist. 'My dear Neville, I feel at this moment almost overwhelmed with emotion. You and I . . . we haven't always seen eye to eye, but they were such petty differences compared with the awesome task which now confronts us.' More tears welled. 'And I must tell you that I have never felt so much honour in service as I feel tonight, serving in your Government.'

Chamberlain offered a nod of acknowledgement, inwardly mortified at such an unmanly display of emotion, and immediately Churchill was transformed into a whirlwind of activity. He began pacing the room, demanding details of the officer, issuing messages of congratulation, refilling glasses and raising a toast to the Royal Navy, insensible to the fact that the Prime Minister was drinking only water.

'Prisoners, Lieutenant?'

'No survivors reported, sir.'

'Oh, dear,' murmured the Prime Minister's wife into her napkin.

'Ah, the sea, my dear Mrs Chamberlain, tumbling with tempest and vicissitudes –'

'As I know to my cost,' Chamberlain cut across him, concerned that Churchill was about to launch upon a panegyric that would take him through any numbers of odysseys and all the way to pudding.

'Do you, Neville? But I thought you were a Brummie, born and bred.'

Chamberlain was never the most sharing of men when it came to personal details, but he resolved on this occasion to make an exception – it was, at least, an opportunity to listen to something other than Churchill. He cleared his throat. 'Sisal,' he ventured.

It had the required effect. Churchill remained silent, a look of bewilderment spreading across his face. Chamberlain grabbed his opportunity.

'When I was a young man, barely twenty, my father got it into his head that we should make a fortune growing sisal. In the West Indies. Concocted this great plan. Found an island about forty miles from Nassau – barely inhabited, he thought it was ideal. You know he was always an Empire man, my father. Insisted it should be a family business – but my brother, Austen, was already in Parliament and so . . . it fell to me, the youngest son. Off I went. The place was called Andros. Built a harbour, even a little railway to carry out all the sisal we were going to produce. Spent the next five years stripped to the waist, up to my knees in every kind of manure, fighting hurricanes, salt spray, dysentery, mosquitoes, sunstroke – and, of course, the local native labourers.

439

Robber barons, I always called them. Almost went native myself, half naked most of the time, washed in the sea. Cut off from civilization. One year when the supply boat was late because of the storms we survived on coconuts and fish for a week, then when the boat finally turned up we drank a month's supply of beer in a single weekend. A hard life – but a fine one, battling the elements. Made a man of me.'

The room was silent. It was the longest personal statement Churchill had ever heard him make and he was loath to interrupt, wanting more. Chamberlain's chin was up, his eyes fluttering as they gazed at the pictures of a distant past, reliving the dream. But he would say no more, until Churchill urged him on.

'Five years,' he whispered in awe.

'One did one's duty.'

'And still to this day. But what happened, Neville? Pray tell us.'

'Ah, of course, you would want the conclusion. Sea won, of course. Always does in the end. One night there blew up the vilest of storms and washed away half the crop and two of the native boys – me, too, almost. Rest of the crop went rotten, and the labourers with it. Wouldn't work any more, even when I threatened them with a lashing.' He sniffed. 'They were right, of course. No place for sisal, let alone a white man. Always being cut off by the sea. Should have realized that when we discovered no one lived there in the first place. Anyway, I came back to England, confronted Father – not best pleased, I can tell you. Fifty thousand pounds wasted, he shouted. And five years of my life, I reminded him. No, that wasn't wasted, he said, you must learn from your failures. In which case they will no longer be failures.'

'I know what he means,' Churchill mumbled softly.

'So instead of a pioneer . . . I became Prime Minister.' Chamberlain smiled, affecting modesty, and the ladies laughed accommodatingly.

'Such an inspiration,' Churchill barked, banging the table and spilling his wine. He took no notice; he was a disgracefully untidy eater.

'Well, you've scarcely done badly yourself, Winston. In other circumstances, you might have become Prime Minister instead of me. Not enough failures to build on, that's been your problem.'

Clementine choked on her wine but Churchill hadn't even noticed the slight. Neither had Chamberlain, it had been entirely unintended.

'No, Neville, your story of the sea. Being cut off. That's the inspiration. For the first time, thanks to you, I think I see the way ahead.'

'For what?'

'For the war. For beating Germany!' He swept aside his plate and, despite the sternest of Clemmie's looks, began dipping his finger into his glass of fine Burgundy in order to draw a simple map on the linen tablecloth. 'Norway!' he announced with pride.

Chamberlain seemed thunderstruck, almost as if he had suffered a stroke. It was his wife who revealed what was in all their minds. 'But I don't understand, Mr Churchill.'

It was his cue, and the performance began. 'This stain here' – he indicated an unpleasant mark on the edge of the table – 'is Germany and this' – he grabbed a salt cellar and banged it down on his map – 'is the Swedish iron workings at Gallivare and Kiruna. Now they are vital to the German war effort, Hitler's war machine obtains almost nine out of every ten parts of its iron ore from here. So . . .' His right hand slapped down firmly on the table. 'This is the Baltic Sea and this' – the left hand came down, spilling much of the contents of the salt cellar – 'is the Atlantic Ocean. During the summer, the iron ore for Germany sails through the Baltic, but for almost five months every winter it's frozen solid. So then the iron ore has to come across to the Norwegian port of Narvik – on the Atlantic. And is sailed south until it falls into Hitler's maw.' Churchill's face glowed with pride as if he had just unravelled the secrets of the atom.

'But I'm still not sure . . .' Annie Chamberlain ventured.

'My Navy controls the North Atlantic. If we can force the iron ore ships out from the coastal seaways of Norway into open water, we shall be able to blast them into the deep, and with them will founder any hope Hitler has of winning this war!'

'But how do you expect to do that? Force the ore ships out of Norwegian waters?' Chamberlain prodded.

'By mining 'em! I'll get the Navy mine-layers to sow the coastal seas as though it were springtime in Suffolk.'

'But . . . But . . .' Chamberlain's lower lip began to quiver in astonishment. 'Norway is a *neutral* country. It would be an act of war.'

'An act of survival! Hitler couldn't last more than two months – three months at most – if we did the job properly.'

'First Lord, I think I must remind you that we went to war in order to protect the integrity of neutral countries.'

'And I venture to suggest, Prime Minister, that the only way we shall succeed in that task is by *winning* the war.'

They had slipped into official mode, rehearsing the arguments that they knew eventually would erupt across the Cabinet table.

'The Queen of Norway is our own King's aunt,' Chamberlain protested.

'Which is why they will understand. Even support us.'

'Let me get this straight,' Chamberlain insisted, pushing his pudding to one side. 'You expect Norwegians to support an unannounced attack on their own country?'

'It's the stuff of diplomacy. We have a Foreign Secretary, set him to work! And glory in the victory that by next spring could be ours – a victory inspired by your own story tonight.'

That much, Mrs Churchill knew, was tosh. She had heard Winston rehearsing the argument in his bath that afternoon. She suspected the entire evening had been set up precisely for this purpose, but her musings were interrupted by a second officer, this time a Lieutenant Commander, who arrived to declare that another U-boat had been reported sunk.

'An omen, an omen,' Churchill declared, rising to perform a little jig of joy and insisting on yet another toast. He could be so like a schoolboy. Chamberlain did not join in the toast. He would not be bullied into aggravating his gout by a man who was merely the newest member of his Government, even less would he be bullied into launching a full-scale war by him, either.

'If we were to attack Norway, the consequences could be incalculable,' Chamberlain declared, returning to his theme.

'And if we don't mount such an attack, there will be no doubt about the consequences. Hitler will get every bit of iron ore he needs for his war machine, which he will then turn in its fullest might upon us.'

'We don't need an all-out war to beat Hitler. They can't hold out for ever. They can't eat iron ore. There are reports coming out of Poland of people already starving.'

'The Jews are starving, Neville, no one else. And if he ever goes short of anything, Hitler will do what he's always done. Invade another country.'

'Perhaps.' Chamberlain placed his napkin on the table, folding it neatly to indicate that the evening was over. Churchill's was still tucked firmly into his collar. 'Since it is . . .' Chamberlain scratched away at his trousers for the right word – 'an *inspiration* of yours, you will undoubtedly wish to give the matter prolonged thought.' It was meant to indicate an idea that had not found its day.

'I shall expect the entire Cabinet to give the matter prolonged thought, Prime Minister,' Churchill growled defiantly. 'I shall circulate papers forthwith.'

'If you insist.'

'I insist . . .' Suddenly Churchill's nerve seemed

to fail him, or perhaps he realized that the evening was not working out in the way he had planned, that there never had been a chance of beguiling Chamberlain on board, that he must take the long route. His life seemed such a succession of long routes. 'I insist only that you and your lovely wife shall come again soon, Neville. It has been a most outstanding occasion.'

The pleasantries of departure were undertaken and it was as Churchill was helping Chamberlain and his wife into their coats that they were disturbed for yet a third time by an officer scurrying from the War Room.

'This time they have sent us a full Commander,' Churchill exclaimed, 'a sure sign of good news. I have found that if ever the accounts are unpalatable, they send nothing but a midshipman with a scribbled note.'

'Beg to report a third U-boat sunk this evening, gentlemen,' the Commander offered. 'Caught on the surface near the Northern Approaches. Thought you'd want to know.'

'This is truly exceptional! Nothing like this ever happened in a single day before. The Royal Navy does you honour, Prime Minister.' Churchill offered the lines with typical enthusiasm, even though he knew that flattery as well as alcohol had been wasted on the Prime Minister this evening.

'Are you sure you didn't arrange all this on purpose, Mr Churchill, for our benefit?' Mrs Chamberlain ventured coyly – and with singular insight.

'Madam, if you would do me the honour of

445

bringing your husband to dine with me every night, I venture that the war would be over within weeks. He brings me good luck.'

What Chamberlain thought his First Lord brought him, for the moment he kept to himself. Gout was more than enough for him to be getting on with.

So they wandered into the night, the two old men, one a son of Birmingham, the other a scion of Blenheim Palace, from different quarters and still set upon their separate ways. One headed home. The other, in his mind's eye, was already in Norway.

'His Navy. He called it *his* navy, Horace. Damned if he didn't.'

'He thinks it's his war, too.'

'First he wants to invade Ireland. Now bloody Norway.'

'War, whatever the cost.'

'Must get his ideas from comic books.'

'Not a gentleman.'

'I thought sending him to the Admiralty might keep him at arm's length. Busy in distant places. A second-hand war.'

'Instead we got a first-hand fool.'

'But I'll not let him destroy it all, Horace. He killed enough good Englishmen in the Dardanelles. Would destroy half of England in pursuit of his vanity.'

'And sell the other half to the highest bidder.'

'I'll not have it, Horace, not have Winston playing his games of war. I'll make you one vow.'

'Neville?'

'I swear to you. I will sink the First Lord. Long before he ever gets close to sinking a single German ore ship. Sink Winston, before he sinks us all.'

SIXTEEN

November–December 1939.
War comes in many different colours.

In late November, a black taxi was driven round the West End of London during the blackout. In its wake it left several acid bombs, four of which exploded in and around Piccadilly Circus. The IRA was blamed. No one was hurt.

That same weekend, in the forbidden city of Prague and after days of civil unrest, the German security forces raided the homes and dormitories of 'intellectuals', in truth high-school and university students. Some were killed as they tried to flee, the rest were dragged from their beds and taken in their thousands to Ruzyn barracks and the Sparta football stadium. Cold water was flung over them and they were left in the open until the evening. Then 124 high-school and university students were paraded in front of the others, and shot.

In occupied Poland, the Lord Mayor of Warsaw was arrested and sent to Dachau. Three hundred thousand Polish prisoners had already been sent to labour camps. The German authorities announced that: 'The Pole is a servant here and must only serve. Blind obedience and ruthless fulfilment of orders must be enforced. No sentiment is permissible and no exceptions, no consideration, even for any particular Poles whom we know and esteem. We must inject a dose of iron into our spinal columns and never admit the idea that Poland may ever arise again.'

Hans Frank, the Governor-General of German Poland, decreed that 'all Jews more than twelve years old must constantly, under severe penalties for default, wear an armband with the Shield of David whenever they go out of doors.'

It had begun.

Off the coast of Iceland the converted P&O cruise liner *Rawalpindi* intercepted the two battle-cruisers *Scharnhorst* and *Gneisenau*. The *Rawalpindi* had four elderly six-inch guns, the Germans a huge array of armaments, including six eleven-inchers. The *Rawalpindi* did its damnedest, but it was like trying to stop an express train with a pea shooter. Soon all her guns were reduced to twisted metal, her whole bulk was ablaze. Still she pushed home her attack, trying to ram the enemy with the last of her strength. She sank in flames. Only thirty-eight of her crew survived.

On the other side of the Baltic Sea, the Russians made increasingly threatening gestures aimed at their tiny neighbour, Finland. Soviet propaganda accused the Finns of committing atrocities against Russians and planning to mount an invasion of Russia itself. It was eerily reminiscent of the accusations made by German authorities shortly before the Wehrmacht descended upon Poland.

And the Germans themselves sowed mines in abundance, sinking many ships, not only British but also those belonging to neutral nations. It was precisely this threat on which Chamberlain chose to concentrate in the first broadcast he delivered to the nation since he had declared war on Germany. It was delivered, on a Sunday, in his typical precious, reedy voice. It began in a mire of platitudes.

Up to the present, the war has been carried out in a way very different from what we expected. We need not attribute the reluctance of the Germans to begin a great land offensive, or to attempt a series of mass attacks from the air upon this country, to their humanity. We have had plenty of evidence that no considerations of humanity deter them from any form of warfare that they think will bring them some advantage. They must, therefore, have come to the conclusion that at present they would lose more than they would gain by such attacks, and they have preferred to use methods which they think can be employed without serious loss to themselves.

Only then did platitude turn to passion.

The latest of these methods – as you all know – is the sowing of a new kind of mine – indiscriminately in our home waters. It matters nothing to them that what they are doing is contrary to international agreements – to which they have subscribed. It matters nothing to them that they are daily blowing up neutral ships as well as British, and thereby drowning or mutilating citizens of countries with which they are not at war. They hope by these barbarous weapons to cut off our supplies from overseas and so squeeze or starve us into submission. You will have no fear that this attempt will succeed.

At a time of challenge and sacrifice, no one but the most desiccated of cynics could have imagined that his words were aimed at anyone other than the Germans. But, at the end of the broadcast, Sir Horace Wilson was seen to be smiling broadly and exchanging private words of satisfaction with the Prime Minister. And on the day Churchill circulated his paper on Norway to his Cabinet colleagues, they also received copies of the Prime Minister's broadcast. No one could be quite certain who circulated them, but the section concerned with sea mines and neutral countries was underlined in red.

'Fine, fine speech, Ian – bless 'im. Pity about the missing crown. Not sure he was right to swap it for his naval uniform. Even Kings have to keep up appearances, you know.'

'Simple. Austere, I thought. Entirely appropriate for a State Opening of Parliament during wartime.'

'And mercifully short. If he'd run into one of his stutters we could've been there all day.'

'Steady on, Dickie. Appearances and all . . .'

'Got to face up to it, Ian. He's scarcely the fattest cock in the Windsor farmyard.' Dickie shrugged. 'Not his fault, he wasn't born to it. Not his fault his brother's a traitor.'

'Dickie, please!' Ian looked around the House of Commons Dining Room in alarm, fearing they might be overheard.

'Well, it's true. Why d'you think they sent Windsor back to France?'

'To . . . help, I assume.'

'To get him out of the way. To get *her* out of the way. Apparently he tells her everything, then she tells everyone else. Hairdresser, skirt-maker, manicurist, anybody who'll offer them a free dinner.'

'You can't be serious.'

'Look here, old chap, he's a wrong 'un. Always told you that. So when the war breaks out and he says he's coming back from exile in France, they all panic. Won't send him a plane, hoping he'll simply rot in a French bordello or get lost somewhere on the way back – till bloody Winston sends a destroyer to pick him up at Cherbourg! So the Duke comes back and gets the old cold-shoulder treatment. Queen Mary refuses to see him – her own son. Imagine. Maybe their last chance, and still she won't see him. Tough as old boots, she is. Anyway, there's no car for him, no curtsey for his wretched wife, and nowhere to stay. Even Chamberlain keeps putting him off while they decide what to do, until Winston – always bloody Winston, isn't it? – takes him off for a lunchtime tour of the wretched Admiralty War Room. The whole shebang's there – you know, top-secret charts, the entire fleet's positions. All laid out for him.'

'But the Duke is an Admiral of the Fleet, Dickie.'

'Yes, a Field Marshal and all the rest. That's the bloody trouble. They realize they've got to find him something to do, but as far away from London as it's possible to get. So they get old Bore-Belisha to tell him it's back to France to play mud pies with a reduction in rank to major-general. Nice touch, I thought, getting old Elisha to do it. The commonest little man in the Cabinet. You know, if ever I get dumped on by the System, Ian, I want it done properly – wigs, gowns, ermine, the whole damned caboodle. But a firing squad of one common little Jew?'

A moment of silence as they contemplated a future of mixed fortunes.

'Extraordinarily fine burgundy, Dickie.'

'Romanée-St-Vivant '65. Very best of the bunch.'

'Didn't know the Wine Committee was up to this.'

'They're not. It's a little private supply of mine. Had a word with the Serjeant-at-Arms and asked if he could find me a corner of the cellar to take care of the really good stuff. Can't leave it in the cellar at home, not deep enough, and damned if I'll leave it for bloody Adolf. So I thought we might celebrate the opening of the new session of Parliament with a little treat. After all, might be the last Parliament we're ever going to get.'

'That bad, eh, Dickie?'

'Worse. Did you hear the other news today?'

Puzzled brow.

'Russians. Denounced their neutrality treaty with Finland. And you know what that means.'

'Oh, Christ.' A stretched, half-strangled sigh. 'Pass me the bloody bottle.'

The Russians invaded Finland on the last day of November. No longer was Russia a riddle wrapped in a mystery inside an enigma. It was ravenous, rapacious, despicable, a universally loathed power which preyed on its neighbours and which had no common interests with England and France, no matter what Churchill had said. As Dickie announced in the Smoking Room, in a voice that was intended to carry to its farthest corners, there was nothing in the least bit enigmatic about another bloody *blitzkrieg*.

Burgess choked. He couldn't move without pain. He'd been drinking for a week, an entire days-and-nights week, couldn't even remember when last he'd made it home. It drowned the physical feeling, but inside he ached with torment and humiliation. He felt as if Joe Stalin and the entire Red Army had been stamping across his soul. First Poland, now Finland. Russian tanks once again making war on perambulators.

He didn't understand why, so he'd got drunk. He hadn't dared go to the Reform or the Garrick, even with their relaxed approach to the rules of engagement, not after a week of sleeping in the same suit. And it had been raining, soul-drenching rain that had lashed down for days as though God himself was joining in the misery. Eventually he'd made it to the Mandrake Club in the basement off Dean Street, his hideaway in Soho where they'd only throw you out if you threw up over people, but he'd got sick with them instead, all these writers and intellectuals pontificating about war and conscience and sacrifice – as if they knew a damned thing about it. Brain-fuckers. No wonder they were the first to get shot in any good revolution. So he'd insulted everyone and stumbled on to a pub in Covent Garden, which had thrown him out after just one whiskey until, by and by, he had found himself beside the river. He gazed down into its angry waters, where flowing tide did battle with storm waters tumbling downstream, and in it seemed to have found something which resembled his soul. He had wanted to get closer. So he had clambered up on Hungerford Bridge, the pedestrian walkway that backed onto the railway line into Charing Cross. He had no thoughts of suicide, in truth had no thoughts at all, but he was in the mood to throw himself off the bridge simply to find out what it felt like. Falling. Drowning. So much like life.

It had stopped raining for the moment, but the scudding clouds suggested it was nothing but a temporary respite. He was on his own, in the middle of the long, narrow bridge, swallowed up by the night. He reached into his pocket for a cigarette but found only a soggy tobacco stick that refused to light and quickly crumbled in two. Maybe he'd kill himself after all. 'And you can go fuck yourself, too,' he muttered, as suddenly he realized he'd been joined by a stranger, some intruder upon his private misery. He turned, to discover a police constable.

There is something extraordinarily instinctive about the reactions of some homosexuals, a trigger that goes off inside when they meet, an understanding which requires no words, no exchange other than a glance. Burgess thought the constable gave him one of those glances. He was far too drunk to have any reliable instincts, but then again he was also far too drunk to care. If he was going to fall, and drown, maybe he should do it around the cock of a complete stranger. *This* stranger. Hell, if he'd got it all wrong, he could always throw himself off the bridge after all. Go down . . . well, going down. Maybe he was about to make the greatest mis-judgement of his life. He knew in twenty minutes' time he could be in police custody and wouldn't come out for another ten years, but somehow it didn't seem to matter. It was a solution of sorts, would simplify things. Take away the pain. Suddenly the policeman had become a private angel for Burgess, someone who would take all those impossible decisions out of his hands, and resolve them, one way or another, and he didn't much care which.

Within thirty seconds of telling the policeman to go fuck himself, Burgess was down on his knees, tearing at the other man's trousers, gambling his life. Within two minutes he was finished.

They knew they would never meet again – at least, not like this. The policeman buttoned up his fly, straightened his tunic.

Then he kicked Burgess in the guts, just once, but viciously, and Burgess thought he would never be able to breathe again.

'One day you're going to get your stupid head beaten in,' the other man muttered, and walked off into the darkness, leaving Burgess clinging to a bridge support.

As the policeman's footsteps faded into the

distance, Burgess was overwhelmed with a sense of self-loathing. He was drunk, grovelling on his knees, in a stinking puddle, nowhere to go, and had little idea where he'd been. He was a man who viewed much of the rest of humanity with contempt, who derided their values, yet who had just valued his own life as nothing more precious than a wet-lipped fumble in the dark. He'd always thought he was a man who might help transform this sick, pathetic world, yet right now he was a man who couldn't even help himself – and in the process thought he might have fouled himself, but couldn't even be sure of that. Disgust was welling up inside, bending his body in two, as though he were trying to escape from himself. Suddenly he was retching into the river.

It was only much later that he was able to pull himself to his feet and stagger home.

It was the opening days of the worst winter in centuries, when the ice gods attacked on all fronts. Rail points seized, diesel turned solid, coal went short and water pipes froze and burst, bringing misery to millions. Not that anyone was supposed to notice, since weather forecasts were subject to the strictest censorship. Ice was an enemy, like the Nazis, to be ignored. Britain was shrouded in misery, in frost, and in darkness. The number of deaths on the road rocketed to nearly a thousand a month, and the unemployed still totalled nearly one and a half million.

Businesses affected by the war were closing or making desperate appeals for support. The Orchard

Hotel at Marble Arch ran advertisements proclaiming: 'Hitler must not sink this ship, or put the crew out of commission. Rally round! Terms made to suit all nice people.' Elderly matrons pleaded through the classified columns for domestic help – housemaid wanted, good references essential, not over forty-five, any nationality, but no Germans . . . Everything was for sale or for barter, not just pianos.

And rationing began to bite – meat, ham, bacon, sugar, petrol . . . although restrictions on electricity and gas were temporarily lifted to fight the cold. They simply put the price up.

It was, perhaps, an unfortunate time to release a new set of carefully posed photographs of the Queen, taken by Mr Cecil Beaton, which captured her amongst the marble columns, silk-clad sofas and glittering crystal chandeliers of Buckingham Palace, resplendent in 'a gold dress embroidered with pearls and diamonds', as *The Times* reported. The Queen is in good heart, they proclaimed. It might have been better to imply that the suffering was, at least, being shared.

After a hundred days of war, Britain seemed to have lost the will to fight. The RAF was largely grounded by the weather, the British Expeditionary Force in France did battle armed with shovels in fields that had frozen to rock. Only the Royal Navy seemed keen to pursue the issue of war in the distant grey seas beyond the shores.

And the United States, it seemed, had no will to fight at all . . .

*   *   *

(The Times, Tuesday 12 December 1939)

MR KENNEDY'S ADVICE
TO U.S.

------◆------

WARNING TO KEEP OUT
OF THE WAR

From our own correspondent
NEW YORK, December 11

Mr Kennedy, United States Ambassador to Great Britain, speaking yesterday at Boston, earnestly warned the United States against getting into the war.

Speaking extemporaneously at a parishioners' meeting in the church where he was once an altar boy he said: 'As you love America don't let anything that comes out of any country in the world make you believe that you can make a situation one whit better by getting into the war. There's no place in the fight for us. It is going to be bad enough as it is.

. . . He said that one of the chief influences that might involve the United States in the war was the American people's 'sporting spirit' in 'not wanting to see unfair or immoral things done', but he reiterated: 'This is not our fight.'

But it was Churchill's fight and, at times, it seemed exclusively Churchill's fight. When he presented his proposal to mine the Norwegian coastal waterways to the Cabinet, it was turned down flat. Halifax expressed his horror at the violation of international law implied in an attack on neutral territory, and there was no sign of support for Churchill's eagerness to extend the war. The word 'Dardanelles' could be heard muttered in every corner. The most he was able to squeeze from his colleagues was their approval to submit the proposal to the military chiefs for 'further study', a Whitehall euphemism for being told to bugger off. He was isolated and overruled.

Yet not for the first time, it was Hitler and his war machine that came to Churchill's rescue.

In early December the pocket-battleship *Graf Spee* arrived in the southern Atlantic intent on preying upon the rich traffic in the sea lanes off the River Plate. Instead of discovering defenceless merchantmen, however, she ran straight into a British task force. The *Exeter*, the *Ajax* and New Zealand-manned *Achilles* were much more lightly armed than the *Graf Spee*, but they confronted her nonetheless. On the early morning of 13 December a battle began in which all four ships fought and manoeuvred inside thick clouds of camouflaging oil smoke. An hour and twenty minutes later, the *Exeter* was crippled. She had been hit more than a hundred times by the *Graf Spee*'s huge guns, her bridge was destroyed and her forward guns out of action. She was burning fiercely amidships; many of her crew were dead. The other British ships had also been hit, but so had the *Graf Spee*. Her commander, Captain Langsdorff, decided to withdraw to the neutral port of Montevideo, three hundred miles away, only to discover that the battle was not yet over. The British ships, despite their serious damage, limped in pursuit like bloodied hounds.

In Montevideo, the *Graf Spee* faced a desperate dilemma. She could stay only seventy-two hours – otherwise under the rules of neutrality she would be interned for the duration of the war. Yet outside the port lay a British pack, wounded but still desperately dangerous. And by seeking refuge in Montevideo, the *Graf Spee* had thrown away all element of surprise and manoeuvrability. She would run headlong into the waiting enemy.

As Langsdorff deliberated, the world took the battle to its heart. The harbour at Montevideo was mobbed by crowds, the world's media flew in journalists to report on the hour-by-hour developments, radio links were set up. The Battle of the River Plate was about to become the first modern media battle.

For the first time in weeks, the headlines in the British press were dominated not by doom and depression but by news that the Germans were at bay and the British flag was flying tattered but high. For four days the nation watched, and waited.

As soon as Langsdorff had unloaded his wounded, he tried to squeeze more time out of the Uruguayans. He failed. Seventy-two hours was it, and all of it. He would not allow his ship to be interned, to wallow in some foreign backwater as a rotting symbol of Nazi failure, yet neither would he risk having the pride of the German Navy blown to pieces before the mocking eyes of the world. There was only one way out – which was not a way out at all. At sunset on 17 December, with only a skeleton crew, the *Graf Spee* weighed anchor and made its way six miles into the estuary of the River Plate. Spotter planes flew overhead, reporting back to the waiting ships of the Royal

Navy. A resumption of battle seemed imminent but, before the British ships could engage her, Landsdorff himself decided the fate of the *Graf Spee*. Scuttled her. Blew her guts out. Destroyed her with his own hand. She burned, then listed, and finally sank.

Two days later, in the privacy of a Montevideo hotel room, Captain Langsdorff blew out his own brains.

The Royal Navy – Winston's Royal Navy – had won the first great engagement of the war.

Chamberlain flew back to Heston and into a world that was the colour of cold steel. It was the same airport he had used on his return journey from Munich, but this time there were no crowds, no cheering throng tussling to lay palm leaves in his path, no summons to share the spotlight on the palace balcony. There was only Horace Wilson, struggling beneath his overcoat to retain some trace of body heat.

'You heard it?' Wilson enquired as the Prime Minister stepped down the ladder from the De Havilland. No pleasantries.

'Why didn't you stop him?' Chamberlain snapped.

'I was in the country, knew nothing about it until I turned on the radio. Winston's like Hitler. Mounts his attacks at weekends.'

'While my back is turned. How dare he? Damn him! I freeze for days in French fields inspecting the front line and he wallows in his glory like a pig in his sty.'

'Nevertheless . . .'

'He made it sound as if he'd fired the guns himself. Sunk the *Graf Spee* all on his own.'

'Nevertheless . . .'

'Lies. He lies through his teeth. One whisky and he's away, exaggerating, inventing. Conjuring up mythical U-boats he claims to have sent to the bottom.' The shallow breaths came forth in swirling clouds of condensation as they walked the short distance to the terminal. Chamberlain's pace was slower than was normal, as though he were afraid of slipping on ice.

'Nevertheless,' insisted Wilson, 'we can't retract a word he said. The press and public loved it.'

'What?'

'And his announcement that the first Canadian troops had arrived.'

'The Devil take him! What's that got to do with the Admiralty? Did they swim here, for God's sake? Can't he keep his interfering fingers from grabbing any morsel of good news?'

'Not in his nature.'

Chamberlain was white, a mixture of fury and exhaustion. The intense cold of France had dogged him, cut to his bones, he wasn't a young man any more and his resistance to physical hardships was noticeably on the wane. Yet he had persevered, motoring hundreds of miles along the front over several days to greet the troops and consult with his generals, uttering no word of complaint, only to discover he had been stabbed in the back – because that was what it felt like. The body of an exhausted politician is sustained by praise, yet now Winston had stolen it, grabbed it all for himself, and the applause still clung to the ice in the wind.

'I can't stand this any longer. He's got to go,' Chamberlain declared, his breath escaping in a rush, as though it were his last.

Wilson considered this for a moment, then stopped. They had not quite reached the terminal building and the frost had climbed right through the soles of his feet and was eating every one of his toes, yet something more important than his comfort seemed to have gripped him.

'We can't. Not now. Not yet, at least.'

Chamberlain turned on him but Wilson continued, cutting off the inevitable protests.

'We're at war, and so far as the general public is concerned Winston appears to be almost the only Minister fighting it. In Whitehall he may be something of a joke, but in the country he's a figure of defiance. Destroy him, and you destroy any chance of continuing the fight.'

'But don't you understand, I don't want to fight!' Chamberlain exploded.

'But you can't make a peace either, not now, not if you want to survive in office.'

'Sometimes I wonder whether –'

'So you need to reassert your authority. Not a direct broadside aimed at him, but perhaps more of a shot across the bows. Get him to think twice, watch his back. Let him know he's living on borrowed time.'

'And how do you suppose I am to achieve that considerable miracle?' Chamberlain demanded from the middle of a swirling, frost-nipped cloud of anger.

'Send for Leslie.'

*　　*　　*

Oh, but what a convenient target Leslie Hore-Belisha would prove to be. Ebullient, unorthodox, obnoxious, frequently insensitive, openly ambitious and inexcusably innovative. Innovative – the Secretary of State for War! And always with a smile for the cameras.

And, of course, he was Jewish. Not that Chamberlain particularly held that against him, or even disliked him for it. The Prime Minister's anti-Semitism was not of a vigorous kind, he really didn't care too much about the whole issue, it was rather like his antipathy for twentieth-century symphonies – except you could never switch Leslie Hore-Belisha off, or even turn down the volume. Yet for others, the Minister of War was a white nigger. An undesirable, a man of different orientation, an outsider who had forced his way past the palace guards and had erected his cooking pots in the marble hallways of the mighty. In the words of *Truth* (proprietor: Sir Joseph Ball), he was 'a minor man whose most conspicuous talent is for getting his photograph into the newspapers' – and particularly those newspapers run by his co-religionists which operated in the 'Jew-owned gutters of Fleet Street'.

He had made other uncomfortable enemies, particularly amongst the Army General Staff. They had spent weeks bickering more and more venomously about the concrete pill-boxes necessary to extend the defences of the Maginot Line across the unfortunate gap behind Belgium which the British Army had to defend. Hore-Belisha said that a pill-box could be constructed in three days; the General Staff said it took three weeks and were incandescent when he refused to believe them. So around the mess tables of the British Expeditionary Force in France, the name of Hore-Belisha was spat out like pips in the pudding. And many of the pips landed on the table of the King. He was, after all, the most senior military figurehead in the land. He had a role, a right to intervene – a duty, even. And the King would not tolerate a War Secretary who had sided openly with his brother Edward during the Abdication crisis, and who had added error to that insult by being the first to visit the Windsors in exile. Damn him. George wasn't anti-Semitic, of course not. He just didn't like the man. Anyway, George was fed up with the muttering suggesting he was colourless and weak.

So the King summoned the Prime Minister. He complained, and suggested that a man like Hore-Belisha was not appropriate for his office. In doing so, he was out of order – the monarch's job was to be seen but rarely heard – yet what was the point in being King if he couldn't take a view about His Own Ministers? And there were plenty of other voices nagging Chamberlain. So, in turn, and just before Christmas, the Prime Minister summoned Leslie Hore-Belisha.

'How are things, Leslie?'

'Magnificent.'

'Any problems? Worries?'

'Nothing that a few more millions for my Army couldn't sort, Prime Minister.'

So, he didn't know, hadn't caught on. Poor sap. But Chamberlain was not a man to be bullied or hectored into any action he thought unworthy; he liked to take his own good time for such things.

'Just wanted you to know how grateful I am, Leslie. Difficult – almost impossible task you've got. Admire your dedication, truly I do.'

'Why, that's . . . extraordinarily kind of you, Prime Minister.'

'Yes. Just wanted to let you know. Before you disappeared.'

'Disappeared?'

'To celebrate Christmas. You do celebrate Christmas, don't you, Leslie?'

The boiler was called Beelzebub. Covered in soot, he carried on in life largely unappreciated, squeezed into the airless basement of the old school and surrounded by a puddle of coke. Beelzebub had been one of West Bromwich's finest, circa 1890, but those days were long since past. He had a personality all his own. He stood no nonsense. He grumbled, groaned, strained, he indisputably did his best, yet still he was asked to do more. That happened when there were ten degrees of frost outside. He began to feel unappreciated. He had a pressure gauge at the very top, like a Cyclopic eye that watched all the comings and goings in the basement of the old school, and when the caretaker approached for the fourth time that day with a frown and a large spanner, Beelzebub shuddered. The caretaker poked him in the eye, then poked him again and still didn't seem to care for what he saw, so in frustration took his large spanner and hacked at Beelzebub's main steam pipe – at which point Beelzebub decided he had finally had enough. A large slug of calcium that had been clinging for years to the inside of his pipework broke loose and fell into the main regulator valve. Beelzebub shuddered, and then he died.

Which was great news for Jerry. The old school – near the main Royal Signals depot at Blandford Forum – had been requisitioned as a temporary home for Jerry's battalion, and with the passing away of Beelzebub and the lack of immediate alternatives amongst the crowded but frozen camps in the Dorset countryside, his entire company was given two days' leave, the first in more than two months. Five hours later, still in his army fatigues with his new sergeant's stripes fresh upon his sleeve, he was sitting with Sue at a table in the Royal Gardens restaurant in Bournemouth. He'd called to make the reservation as soon as he had heard of the leave, and his timing had proved immaculate – it was Friday, three days before Christmas, and the entire community of Bournemouth seemed to want to celebrate its survival in the Phoney War. He'd got the last table.

So they sat and held hands by candlelight, exchanging lives. Jerry talked of how in the morning he was being trained to be a radio operator, and how every afternoon he was being instructed to yell and stick his bayonet into bales of straw lying motionless on the ground. He said this greatly heartened him. During the last war he had never known a German to lie still on the ground while a British soldier stuck a bayonet in his guts, but perhaps Army Intelligence had discovered a new way of simply terrifying German soldiers to death. It was a considerably more comforting thought than the alternative – that the War Office still couldn't tell a bayonet from a butter knife. Then Sue began to talk of what she termed her stay-behind plans, of how, in the event of an invasion, she wanted to organize a group that would continue the fight behind the lines. Ordinary folk, with everyday jobs and duties, who would spot the opportunity for a little havoc in the event of an occupation. The Cock-up Club, she called it with a coy smile. Jerry was concerned, but she explained how she had already identified several possible resisters. Harold, the postman, a veteran of the Boer War as well as the last, who could carry messages without suspicion. The lady doctor, who knew not only how to cure but many different ways to cause acute discomfort, even to kill – she claimed to be able to put an entire regiment out of action for forty-eight hours if she could get near their water supply. The garage mechanic who reckoned he could make a working rifle out of a rusted bike.

'People get shot for that,' Jerry whispered.

'I'm told that in Poland and Czechoslovakia people are getting shot for doing nothing at all.'

'It won't come to that.'

'It will if your Army can't tell the difference between a bayonet and a butter knife,' she retorted. 'If there's an invasion, Jerry, this place will be one of the first to be occupied. And if that happens' – she squeezed his hand – 'well, I suspect it means you probably won't be around any more. That's what goes on in war, isn't it? There aren't any simple or safe options. We all have our different battles to fight.'

'But even so, my love –'

'It's too late, Jerry. I've already got Mr Woolton –

you know, the local builder? He's putting up a new clubhouse at the football ground. I've already persuaded him to build a little hiding hole between the changing rooms – a sort of store room cum safe house. The football crowd would give us excellent cover. He's done all the work himself, poor fellow, and he's over sixty with bad lumbago, so I can't go and tell him it's all been a waste of time and blisters, can I?'

'You are a remarkable lady.'

'You forget, I'm a postmistress. I see them all. They come to my counter and talk. Those who gossip and complain about rationing or the blackout and the fact that Harold was an hour late with the post the other day in the middle of a blizzard. And those who simply get on with things. Who get ready.'

Jerry sucked at his pipe, but it was dead, had died as he had listened, fascinated and not a little frightened. 'You know, Sue, I love you very much. But you shouldn't be telling me this. Need-to-know, and all that.'

'And it's the last time I'll ever mention it to you, Jerry. But you do need to know. Just in case.'

'Just in case of what?'

'Well . . . just in case.'

She squeezed his hand once more, very tightly.

Suddenly, the head waiter was at their elbow, hopping distractedly from one foot to the next, crouching low. 'Ah, the menu. Time to order, darling,' Jerry announced.

'No, sir. I'm sorry, sir, but . . .' the waiter began, in an accent that suggested something south of Rome. Behind his shoulder hovered two officers, a captain and a colonel. Ordnance Corps. Backroom boys. Waste-bin wallahs. 'This is the last table, sir, and these two gentlemen – two officers . . . I'm afraid I must ask you to let them have it.'

'Why?'

'Rank, dear chap,' the colonel barked. 'One of the perils of war.' He smiled beneath a thin moustache.

'But I booked. Made a reservation. Did you make a reservation?'

'Don't be insolent, Sergeant.' The smile had disappeared, the moustache shot out like a sharpened pencil. The officer turned to Sue. 'I beg your pardon, miss, but we're on war duty – I assume your companion is on leave? We've got to be back in the office in an hour, very little time to eat, hate to do it, but war is damnable. Have to hurry. Perhaps we might buy you a drink to sort of . . . smooth the passage?'

'I don't think so, Colonel.'

'Well, as you will.'

The waiter was bent almost double in humiliation. 'I'm so sorry – miss – sir.'

Jerry rose from his chair, fire in his eyes. 'If you think –'

Sue cut him short. 'Other battles to fight, darling. Eh?'

'Double up, Sergeant. Time's wasting,' the officer barked.

Jerry was going to hit him, Sue knew that, so before he could react she had taken his hand and squeezed it once again, still harder, digging in her nails until they hurt. 'We're going, Colonel, but one question first, if I may?'

'Of course.'

'Do you know the difference between a butter knife and a bayonet?'

'A butter knife and a b . . . ? Not sure I understand the question.'

'No, that's what I thought.' She gathered up her handbag. 'Oh, and by the way, Colonel, one final, very feminine thought.' She drew herself close to him, so close he could feel her breath on his face. 'Real men don't pull rank. They pull magnificent women. Like me.'

'Well, I never . . .'

'Doesn't surprise me. Too busy, I suppose. With all those battles in the office?' She offered the most coquettish of smiles before turning to Jerry and rubbing her fingertips over his new stripes. 'Come on, darling. Your night still has a very long way to go.'

Mac trudged back through the park, his footsteps breaking unevenly through the new frost. It had been dark for several hours, and London had an eerie, desolate look in the blackout with only the half-moon to guide him on his way. He should have been heading home, but instead it was back towards Trumper's. He had just finished an evening shift at Kensington Palace, giving some Duke or other a seasonal trim. Not his usual beat, the Palace, but the young man who generally did for the Duke was off to the war and Mac had been drafted in at the last minute to take his place. Mac hadn't taken to the Duke – His Royal Hairnet, as Mac had quickly dubbed him – largely because HRH seemed to be blissfully unaware of Mac's presence, even while he was at his work. At one point he had taken a phone call from a general during which he had talked about 'our favourite Jew' and 'HM putting on the pressure'. Must have thought Mac was stupid as well as deaf. And it was selfish, Mac thought, summoning a barber on the Friday evening before Christmas, although the Duke's secretary had proffered a generous tip in compensation. It meant Mac could take some fresh fruit to Carol's for the kids. But in the rush to answer the summons to the Palace, Mac had forgotten to bring with him the small can of paint he needed to finish off Lindy's rocking horse, so now he was trudging his way back to Trumper's. It wasn't a new horse, of course, nothing more than a rescue case from the church jumble sale with a busted leg, a scratched saddle and no reins. So, in the evenings of the last few weeks, slowly he had been whittling away at a new leg, repairing, polishing, varnishing, gluing on a new mane – a lick of paint across the saddle this evening and Lindy would never notice the difference. Tricks of the trade, learnt during his service in the camps of the great proletarian industrial revolution. He'd take the rocking horse with him when he went to Carol's on Sunday. And a jigsaw puzzle for Peter – of the Flying Scotsman pulling through clouds of steam, a new one. You couldn't repair old jigsaw puzzles.

He'd been thinking about a special present for Carol. Jewellery, perhaps a bracelet, but it was time to be practical, needs not niceties – her phrase, which she repeated more frequently with every passing week of war – so he'd found several yards of fine satin in her favourite eggshell blue for her to run up into whatever she wanted. And a modest pair of earrings in imitation turquoise to match. The pair she already had he found too large, almost vulgar, like candle wax dripping off her ear. Funny how, a year ago, when they first met, he didn't give a damn what she looked like or dressed in, yet now . . .

A funny old year. Of digging inside, unearthing things, of rediscovery. And his year was about to get much stranger still.

As he approached Park Lane he put a white armband around his sleeve and another thick white band around his hat. Park Lane was in almost complete darkness but it was also wide and busy, while Mac hobbled only slowly, and the white bands might give him a sporting chance of being seen in the dribble of light that the single car headlamps were allowed to produce. He waited for his chance then scuttled across like a crab being pursued by gulls, and soon he was wandering through Shepherd Market towards his place of work. Everything was dark, a world of shadows, but he could hear the hum of conversation and chinking glasses from behind the blacked-out windows of restaurants and even a piano playing somewhere inside the Grapes. As he cut through the tiny square between the Victorian alleyways he saw the glow of a cigarette in a distant doorway. A man, conversing with a woman – no, haggling with her. He was wearing a raincoat and carried a briefcase, constantly swapping it from one hand to the next. Nervous. A new recruit, perhaps. But he was making progress and soon the deal was done. The girl took him by the arm and began to lead him upstairs to where Mac knew the rooms were. And as she opened the door, a brief crack of light fell across the side of her head. In that light, Mac saw the glint of a garish, candle wax earring.

How much had changed in a year. When first they had met, he could not have felt this anger, indeed he had hardly felt at all, but now – and because they had met – he felt eaten up inside. Cheated. Her fault. Mac waited until the children had gone to bed that Sunday, Christmas Eve, before telling her what he knew, only to discover that his anger was like a spring breeze compared to the whirlwind that was hers. Men, she cried, had been the cause of all the miseries of her life. Her anger and fear descended like an unrelenting storm upon him, because he was the only man to hand – and because he was the man she had so fervently hoped would be different to all the rest. But he wasn't, he was even worse. This was a man's world, a man's war, and Mac was as responsible as any one of them, she screamed – for turning the world to chaos, for leaving her with two children to keep from hunger and hurt, for condemning her for sins which men themselves initiated. He walked in and out of her life when it pleased him, while at least the men in the Market had the decency to pay her.

Most of her didn't mean it, of course, but Carol was a fighter, always had been, and something had changed in her over this last year, too. In spite of the war she had been touched deep inside by something new in her life. Hope. Hope that had arrived with a funny accent and a thickening waist in the form of Mac. Hope that had kept her warm at nights, even when he wasn't there. Yet he was a man who lived so much inside himself that he rarely seemed to have anything left over to share. And did he really think she would have gone back to all that bestiality in the Market if there had been any alternative, any choice – if he'd been a proper man and moved in, started caring for her and the kids the way normal men were supposed to?

And it was true. He knew it was true. The camps had left him scarred and secretive, and confronted by her anger he once again drew back into himself, just like he had learned of old. Don't argue. Don't confront. Just walk. Which is what he did – in spite of knowing that it was the wrong thing to do. He walked. Couldn't help himself. Couldn't deal with all this emotion. Something so deeply ingrained inside he couldn't help himself, any more than she could help herself.

As he walked out of the front door of the miserable little house in Chigwell and into the freezing night of Christmas, he heard Lindy's rocking horse shatter onto the pavement behind him.

SEVENTEEN

January 1940.

It turned out to be a winter of remorseless betrayal,
even by the weather. The temperatures dropped
lower than anyone could remember and the Thames
froze for the first time since 1888. Less than two
weeks later the worst storms of the century
descended upon the country. War was made impossible. The RAF was unable to fly and all available
troops were put to clearing the snow and ensuring
that the country somehow kept moving. Only
Churchill's Navy seemed able to escape the grip of
winter and continue the fight, patrolling seas that,
though wild, had not yet frozen.

Jerry was on the move, transferred to the King's
Own Yorkshire Light Infantry and sent to continue
his training near Thirsk, where the moors fought him
every step of the way. One five-man patrol froze to
death; he'd been drinking with them in the pub the
night before. A spotter plane sent to search for the
missing men crashed and couldn't be found for three
days. Jerry's radio, which had been intended for use
in India, followed the example of the boiler in
Blandford and stubbornly refused to work.

Meanwhile Carol, far to the south in London,
spent her days in her dark, freezing attic trying to

persuade the water pipes to thaw before Peter came home from school. Every day – somehow – she managed, and every night they froze solid again.

Yet the weather was not to be the only source of betrayal. Beaverbrook was at it. Again. Even as he was pressing his case to be brought back into the Government through his house-trained Home Secretary, Sam Hoare, the *Express* proprietor was using his stable of newspapers to complain and to carp about every wartime restriction. He even called upon the Duke of Windsor in an attempt to persuade him to lead a peace movement. Even the Duke had more sense than this, for any move like that would undoubtedly have wrecked not only the war effort but the British Monarchy, too. Chamberlain, when he heard about it, couldn't decide whether Beaverbrook was being a fool or a villain, but decided that Hell as well as Heston Airport would have to freeze before 'Dear Max' got his snout back into the ministerial trough.

To add to the despair, Ambassador Kennedy was back. He'd returned from a Christmas break spent spreading gloom and defeatism in America to continue his work around the Ministries of Whitehall. Meanwhile in Birmingham two IRA men walked to the gallows and were hanged side by side for planting a bomb in Coventry the previous August – although on which side of betrayal those two stood, and swung, depended very much on the accident of your place of birth.

Perhaps it was the presence of so much frozen misery that kept people's minds turning to what was happening in the snows of Finland, where day after day reports came back of how the gritty Finns were resisting and even pushing back the Russian invaders. While Britain grew morose and grumbled, the gallant Finns showed the world what war and resistance were truly about. And the feeling began to grow that maybe Britain should be doing something to help – after all, hadn't they gone to war to defend the innocent against aggression, and what was going on in Finland was surely no less terrible than what had taken place in Poland? It was even discussed enthusiastically in Cabinet, which talked about sending a force of volunteers, particularly after the Finns began to push back the Russians behind their own frontier. But that's all the Cabinet did – talk. As with Poland, not a finger was lifted, not a bullet fired in her defence. Betrayal had become something of a habit.

Then, of course, there was the matter of Leslie Hore-Belisha . . .

Chamberlain rather liked him, really, didn't share in all that prejudice. After all, he couldn't help what he was born, could he? But Leslie did so want to fight – with the Germans, with his own General Staff, with everybody, it seemed. Anyone, so long as Leslie could fight. He was so much like Winston.

In early January Hore-Belisha was summoned to the Cabinet Room in Downing Street. Chamberlain liked conducting such business there, in the formal surroundings; it seemed to de-personalize the whole thing. And Horace Wilson played doorman, which further enhanced the effect. Leslie bounced in while Chamberlain was writing. The Prime Minister continued with his letter.

'Leslie, I've been thinking things over during the Christmas break.' Still he did not look up.

'Thinking what, Neville?'

'About the Board of Trade.'

'For what?'

'For you.'

'I beg your pardon . . . ?'

At last Chamberlain was forced to raise his eyes and meet the other man's suddenly troubled gaze. 'I was thinking – merely a proposal, you understand – that you might move to the Board of Trade.' Actually, Chamberlain had been thinking of sending Hore-Belisha to the Ministry of Information, a more senior post than Trade, but that morning he had discussed the matter with Halifax who had been adamantly opposed. 'A Jew? At Information, Neville? How would that look to the Neutrals? His methods are so vulgar, he would let down British prestige.' So that idea had been dropped. Leslie, dear Leslie, was to be asked to move from the War Office to the Board of Trade. From being in control of the entire British Army at war to commanding divisions of paper clips.

'But, but . . .' Hore-Belisha stammered, trying to unravel the chaos that had suddenly become his life. 'Two weeks ago you were telling me I had your complete confidence. You gave no hint you were thinking of a change.'

'I've thought it over. I think it would be in your best interests. To move on from the War Office.'

'I'm not sure I agree with your proposal.'

'It's a little more than a proposal, Leslie.'

'But you said –'

480

'Only to be kind. To soften the blow. In the hope that you would agree to accept the offer.'

'Is there any other offer?'

'No.'

'May I think it over?'

'I fear it might leak out.'

'I assume you and I are the only two who know about this.'

'Correct.'

'Then how can it leak out?'

God, the wretched man was going to be difficult. Chamberlain went back to his letter. 'War calls for sacrifices, Leslie. Don't be bitter. Take Trade.'

'Time. I need time,' Hore-Belisha had gushed, stumbling from the room and unable to give the Prime Minister the reply he wanted, or indeed any other form of reply. Outside, the bracing air of Whitehall quickly brought him to his senses and he stumbled off in search of advice and of allies – allies who had independent minds, who would be willing to stand up to the Prime Minister alongside him. He went in search of Churchill, but he found only Bracken.

'I need to talk to Winston,' the War Secretary spluttered.

'You can't. He's in Paris. Flew there this morning.'

'But I must,' he groaned, collapsing into Churchill's chair and demanding a large brandy.

It was only later that evening that the two were able to make contact. Over a telephone almost overwhelmed by static and electronic crackling, the War Minister tried to explain his predicament. 'Help me, Winston, help me. They're hanging me out to dry like a gutted herring.'

'What?' Churchill demanded. 'Can't hear a bloody thing.'

So they tried shouting at each other, and across each other, but little of it made any sense until Churchill said: 'Take information, Leslie.' Then the line finally went dead.

Take information – what the hell did that mean? It didn't make sense – nothing made sense to him any more. So, after a few hours of growing despair, Hore-Belisha decided to take his reputation and growing resentment to the back benches. He told Chamberlain he would not accept Trade. 'I don't deserve such a demotion. I am a relatively young man, Neville. Time is on my side.'

Chamberlain had expressed his sorrow, and sniffed. So, His Majesty had been right. Leslie was not a team player.

It was only some days later, when the outpouring of public support which he had expected failed to materialize and a dispirited Hore-Belisha began to hear the rustlings on the grapevine, that it began to make sense. Churchill hadn't said 'take information' but instead 'take *Information*'. He had known that Hore-Belisha was going to be kicked out of the War Office yet had done nothing about it. Not warned him. Betrayed years of friendship. Left Leslie to hang. Been part of Chamberlain's conspiracy . . .

Well, not exactly. Before Churchill had left for France he, too, had been summoned to Downing Street, where it had been explained to him that no Minister was inviolable, that there had been growing resentment about Hore-Belisha's attempts to promote himself at the expense of his colleagues – as there would be about any Minister who placed his personal reputation before that of the Government as a whole. And Chamberlain was determined to remind everyone in Government – 'everyone, Winston' – precisely who was in charge. It was a testy, ungracious performance. 'I will not have any Minister, no matter how capable or seemingly popular, rocking my boat. They'll be overboard before they know it. I know you'll understand.'

Rocking *my* boat. Chamberlain had added the emphasis, just as had been agreed with Wilson. And there was Winston thinking that all the boats belonged to him . . .

So Churchill had left for France believing that Hore-Belisha was to be offered Information – and knowing, but for the grace of God and Neville Chamberlain, that the First Lord of the Admiralty was as entirely disposable as any Secretary of State for War. Not so much as a shot across the bows but an entire broadside aimed just above his head. So, with some reluctance and even a passing flash of guilt on Churchill's part, Leslie Hore-Belisha was hung out to dry until every trace of moisture, and of life, had completely disappeared.

When Mac had walked out on Carol and their Christmas, he had gone and got drunk. For an entire week. Wobblingly, pukingly, where-the-hell's-home drunk. And when at last he had sobered up, he went in search of Guy Burgess.

He found Burgess, late at night, striding along with hunched shoulders and long, loping gait, cigarette cupped in his hand, towards his home in Chester Square.

'Evening, Mr Burgess.'

'Bugger my old granny, what are you doing here?'

'Waiting for you, of course.'

'And how the hell d'you know where I live?'

'You think you're the only one who plays those games?'

For a moment it silenced Burgess. 'You. A cripple. Followed me?'

'Of course not, how could I? But the last time you came into Trumper's, I took your jacket to hang it up. You had an envelope in the inside pocket.'

'Sneaking bastard. You look frozen. Now you're here, s'pose you'd better come in for a drink.'

'That would be nice.'

'Don't have any draught mild.'

'A whiskey would be fine.'

Burgess gave him a strange stare, as though looking at him for the first time, before opening the front door. In the communal hallway, a profusion of letters lay spread out on a side table. Burgess grabbed those with his name on, and inspected several of the rest. He examined one of these with particular care, held it up against the light, turned it, then ripped it open. 'Ah! Old Tweedie in trouble with the landlord. Behind with his rent again. But I ask you, Mac – Tweedie knows he hasn't paid, it's not the sort of thing you forget, so why the hell do they bother writing to tell him what he already knows?' He screwed up the letter into a tight paper ball and threw it into a large modern Chinese vase that stood in the corner of the hall. 'Spoil a man's day, that might. No point in that, is there?'

He then proceeded to bound up the stairs, laughing. Mac lurched behind him.

As Burgess swung open the door to his rooms, Mac couldn't stop himself letting out a breath of surprise. His senses seemed under assault – the red carpet scorched and stained, the white walls several years past spotless, the squalid scattering of unwashed plates and glasses, the profusion of artefacts and antiques crammed into every available corner, the rest covered in a chaos of paper and despairing books. A stuffed cock pheasant stood in what had once been a glass case. The glass had been broken and lay around the feet of the pheasant, who looked on in bright-eyed disgust. A decaying banana skin hung over its beak. Everything reeked of tobacco.

'Aren't you supposed to say something like "excuse the mess"?' Mac suggested.

'What do you mean? I only cleared up last week. You want a drink or a debate about personal hygiene?'

'I'll stick to the whiskey.'

Two huge tumblers appeared and Burgess sat down at the harmonium which stood outside the bedroom, layered in a guano of old candle wax. He began playing, not with any great skill, and accompanying himself in a voice that had more of the qualities of the jungle at dusk than the concert hall. Soon there came a banging from upstairs. 'Tweedie,' Burgess advised. 'Old Scots army buffer. From Perth. Hates music you can't march to. But it'll take his mind off his troubles.' He took up the music once more. More protests. Suddenly Burgess began playing the National Anthem and singing at the top of his voice. The protests from beyond the ceiling stopped. Burgess played all six verses of the anthem – Mac had only ever believed there to be one – including the final phrase at full volume: *'May he sedition hush/ And like a torrent rush/ Rebellious Scots to crush/ God save the King!'*

With a final flourish Burgess slammed shut the harmonium's lid. 'Ha! It always gets him. That old bastard Tweedie'll be by his bed, standing to attention with his pyjamas tumbling round his ankles and his cock limp as lettuce, not knowing whether to salute the King or reach for his claymore.' Burgess reached for his drink. 'It's bollocks anyway, all this God-Save-the-King nonsense. Written by a Frenchman, sung for a Royal Family that are all sodding Germans. Wonderful, ain't it?'

'What is?' Mac asked from the chair he had commandeered after sweeping it with his sleeve. He still had on his overcoat.

'Why, patriotism. Kicking foreigners. Knowing that we Brits are best and that all foreigners are second-class wops.'

Mac sipped his whiskey. Even with his new-found drinking habits he couldn't keep pace with Burgess. The other man was clearly trying to provoke him, but Mac chose to rise to a different challenge. 'Tell me something, Mr Burgess. Why do you punish yourself so much?'

An uncharacteristic silence.

'You mock your neighbours, your country, your King – but most of all yourself. I wondered why.'

'Who the hell are you, Freud's brother?' Burgess snapped.

'No, a Jew,' Mac replied placidly. 'We make an art of punishing ourselves. Four thousand years of practice. And also I punish myself because I hate to love, and when I throw love back in the faces of those that offer it I hate myself even more. The camps did that, I suppose. Teach you to survive, on your own, only Number One. But you aren't a Jew, Mr Burgess, haven't been to the camps . . . yet sometimes I think you are on a mission to torment yourself. Why?'

'You wouldn't understand. You never went to Eton.'

'Ah, but I went to a different finishing school.'

'Yeah. Long live the revolution.' Burgess threw back the remains of his glass and reached for the bottle.

'You always seem to be fighting – but for what?'

'For what I believe in.'

'That is good.' Mac nodded like a schoolmaster in class. 'Every man should have beliefs. I miss not having beliefs, very much. Sometimes I find myself missing not having a country, either. I never used to miss anything except breakfast, but so many things have changed for me over this last year. Would you miss not having a country, Mr Burgess?'

'Totally.'

'Yet you mock your King and country.'

'Not my country, Mac. As countries go, this isn't a bad one. Dammit, I even go to bed in my MCC tie.'

'MCC?'

'Cricket. Love it. And the rest – Shakespeare, Dickens, Constable, strawberries and summer evenings in Kent. Love my country, I do. What I hate is the stinking system.'

'Ah, the System. I know all about the System. Learnt all about that at Solovetsky. But in this country I thought Eton *was* the System.'

'Precisely. Now you know why sometimes I hate myself. And why I drink to forget.' Burgess wrapped his arms around himself tightly, and began rocking backwards and forwards. The words of a refrain began to stumble through his lips. *'So I called to the barman to pour me another/ Me soul was fair bleeding for want of a wet/ And the good resolutions I made to my mother/ Are the good resolutions I drink to forget.'* He smiled self-consciously. 'Something I picked up at Cambridge. Amongst many other things. Somehow seemed to make a habit there of breaking resolutions, along with my mother's heart. But it all seemed so simple then. The young would rise up and overthrow the stinking self-serving system, there'd be liberty and food for all, and we could get first-class degrees in fornication. God, but it seemed simple. That's why a lot of my friends went off to fight in Spain. Damn few of them came back. And you know what the rest of us did?' He took a huge slice off the top of his drink. 'Absolutely nothing. Fuck-all. Sat on our self-contented arses and did absolutely nothing. Could have done, could have stopped it. But we were too busy scratching ourselves and bickering about who was going to be our bloody king. So now it's happening all over again, in Poland.'

'And Finland.'

For a moment Burgess faltered. 'I think maybe that's different. But I take your point.'

'You think there's a difference?'

'Of course there is!' Burgess replied heatedly.

'Russia is being pig-ignorant, but that's nothing compared with the barbarism that Hitler is promising. Not just inflicting it through a war but promising it as a deliberate act of policy. Read it. It's all in *Mein Kampf*.'

Mac shrugged. 'Perhaps you're right. I know what's happening in Poland, Mr Burgess. Particularly to the Jews. I read they are being rounded up and put on trains. Just because they are Jews. Sent to work camps, where they will be purified through their work. I, too, have been on cattle trains that took me to work camps. Believe me, they were not pure. But perhaps you're right, perhaps there was a difference between then and what's happening now. Me and most of the other pupils, we were sent to the camps not so much because of what we were, or even for what we had done. I was never charged or tried, I simply got caught up in things. It was almost as if we were sent there by accident. I don't think what is going on in Poland is an accident.'

'So, we are on the same side.'

'Perhaps. I have been wondering about that. And I've been wondering why you're in what we might call – the *information* business.'

'Journalism, you mean.'

'Mr Burgess. I am a barber, not an imbecile. I've read some of the material I supplied to you from the Home Secretary's bin. You would have been arrested if you had published it, and I should almost certainly be arrested for providing it.'

Burgess held his tongue and, uncharacteristically, didn't reach for his glass.

'I worry that this information – forgive me, I

search for my words carefully – might not be helping the war effort.'

'War effort? What bloody war effort? That's the whole stinking point!' Burgess had leapt to his feet, unable to contain his emotions. 'Don't you see, Mac, it's all happening again. That . . .' – he spat out the words – 'provincial ironmonger we call a Prime Minister tries to beat his blasted umbrella into a flaming sword while the Nazis are planning to turn this country into a footnote of the Thousand-Year Reich. My God, if only there *were* a war effort.' Burgess wrung his hands in unmistakable anguish. 'I drink myself to sleep, I fuck myself to sleep, I do anything I can to take my mind off what's going on in Europe. But I can't, Mac, even in my sleep. I have nightmares. I see the bodies. They're all being piled up like a factory of death – the women, little children, babies, even my mother. She always comes into it. They're all broken, like dolls. And at the bottom of this huge pile there are my friends from Spain, barely more than boys. And somewhere, buried right in the centre, I know I'm there. Except I'm not dead like the rest, I'm just slowly suffocating under their weight . . . Then I wake up and discover it's not a dream after all, it's happening right now. And to stop that, Mac, I'd do anything. Anything it takes.' His blue eyes had dissolved and were openly weeping. 'It seemed so much simpler when I was at Cambridge. The world was black and it was white – yes, and a little red, too – and it was all going to get sorted out the day after tomorrow. But now I foul my own pants because I'm so very afraid that the day after tomorrow we'll wake up and discover that the whole of Europe is nothing but one huge pile of broken bodies, and that stupid prig Chamberlain won't care a damn so long as he's got someone to help him straighten his wretched collar.'

'So what is the answer?' Mac asked softly.

'I don't know, Mac – God, wish I did!' He slumped back into his chair, exhausted. 'All I know is that I've got to do what I can, as best I can.'

'Which is?' But Mac provided his own answer. 'Information.'

Burgess wiped his eyes with the back of his hand. 'You *are* Freud's sodding brother. What's this all about, Mac?'

'It's about a lot of things, I suppose. My own fears, like yours, my own inadequacies. Not knowing what I want, and what I ought to do. There's the lady you know about. I like her very much, you see, and she likes me, too. Couple of great kids. I ought to be very happy but somehow I just don't seem able to . . . It's commitment, that's the problem. That's what lies between me and her. And between me and you, Mr Burgess. Loving something or someone so much more than myself. Something I've spent my whole life running from, like it's a plague that's pursuing me from my past. Yet you? You embrace it with such passion. I wanted to try to understand your commitment. To see whether it's infectious.'

'And is it?'

Mac considered the question for a long time. 'You asked why I came, what this is all about. It's about this.' From beneath his thin overcoat Mac drew out a briefcase. 'Belongs to my last customer this evening. Left in a hurry to get ready for a formal dinner.

Haven't opened it, but . . . You see, about a hundred yards down the road from the barber's shop in Curzon Street is the headquarters of MI5 – regular customers, they are – and my customer this afternoon is a very senior officer. He's off at his dinner this evening and may not notice his briefcase is missing until he gets back – perhaps not even until tomorrow morning. Then he'll panic. And eventually he'll think of Trumper's. He'll be waiting outside the front door as soon as we open at nine.' Mac held out the briefcase. 'It's yours. Until seven tomorrow morning. If you want it.'

'Do you know what you are doing, Mac?'

'I think it's called commitment. Thought I might give it a try.'

She lay back, the smell of leather filling her nostrils, looking up at him with a mixture or bewilderment and growing fear. The evening had started out so positively, all the sort of things that satisfied her about being with him. Bracken had been so attentive. Drinks at the Savoy's American Bar – in her honour, he had announced with a flourish – and dinner in the Grill, where he had strolled between the tables, acknowledged by everyone – although some had expressions that suggested they had just bitten on a chunk of pure gristle. Since the outbreak of war 'dear Brendan' seemed to have grown in stature. Still in the shadow of his master, of course, but that master now bestrode the world from port to far-flung port. At times Bracken was genuinely short-sighted and had difficulty recognizing those who paid him court, at other moments his short-sightedness was entirely deliberate, repaying old scores. One dining table was occupied by a banker who had once refused Bracken a loan. The banker's face beamed, his hand shot out. Very loudly, so that other tables as well as the banker's guests could hear, Bracken had told him to bugger off. And he had wandered on, a prodigal's progress, discussing affairs of state and of finance and of war, while Anna clung to him and smiled.

He had been particularly unrestrained in his descriptions of the resignation of Hore-Belisha, how the War Secretary had come to his room – well, Mr Churchill's room, if one insisted on being pedantic – and the great matters of the moment were resolved. He had not been flattering about H-B's manners and emotions, Bracken's arms flailing with every new exaggeration, but no one seemed to mind or wished to contest the matter. Their attentions seemed to give him an exceptional energy, as though he occupied the spotlight on a stage, the meal becoming one sustained monologue, and as the last formalities of dinner were washed down he had suggested that they drive to Hyde Park and watch the moon above the Serpentine. Bracken was driving himself, in the Bentley, and the Savoy had provided a bottle of Pol Roger for companionship. Soon they had found their way through darkened and largely deserted streets to the lake that spread like a tongue across the centre of the park. They were alone, the world seemed entirely theirs.

And he had started once again on his story of 'little Leslie', as he called him, elaborating to the point where H-B was in tears and vowing to rip the Government apart, had it not been for Bracken's own wise counsel. By the time the bottle of Pol Roger was half empty, almost entirely courtesy of Bracken, it sounded as if he had saved the civilized world single-handed from the depredations of the vengeful Jew. His tales were largely nonsense, everyone knew that, but he imparted them with such relish and self-conviction that by the time he was finished most people almost believed him, and those who couldn't somehow didn't seem to care.

'But Brendan, darling, what does this all mean, Mr Belisha going?' Anna asked.

'Mean? It's bloody obvious. Apart from Winston he was the only man in Cabinet with the balls for war. That's why they got rid of him. That and his propensity for antagonizing everyone from the King to the Archbishop. But my God, if only we could have set him at Hitler, what damage he might have done!' The window was open so that he could flick the ash from his cigarette, allowing the cold air to pour in. Soon the windows were completely misted and the moon was nowhere to be seen. 'What it means, dear girl, is that so long as Mr Neville Chamberlain is our leader, this country will never fight. He'll duck and dive and avoid a conflict so long as Hitler leaves him any half-open exit. Sometimes I think he only declared war so as to throw everyone off the scent. We thought the world was about to come to an end, yet here we are almost six months later and still we've done nothing but try to bore the bastards into submission. Oh, but that won't last long, though.'

'What won't last, Brendan dear?' She nibbled his ear as though this were of far more interest to her provincial American taste than the fate of the world.

'Peace. This Phoney War. The public don't like it, the French don't like it.' Another pull on his cigarette. 'Something's got to be done. I was discussing it with Winston just this morning. It's going to change.'

'But how? Where?'

'Norway! Somehow we're going to start a war in Norway. About the iron ore.' His hands were waving once again. The remnants of the bottle were knocked over but he either didn't notice or didn't care. 'Chamberlain doesn't want it, Halifax hates it, but Winston is determined. Cut off the iron ore then throttle the Hun into submission!' And suddenly his waving hands were upon her, at first over her blouse, and then inside, searching hungrily.

She tried to protest but he was kissing her, his mouth full of the taste of tobacco and champagne. She tried to move away but succeeded only in falling back across the large leather bench seat and he threw himself at her in a way he had never done before. It was something to do with the war, with the drama of public affairs and the way that everyone now listened to him, looked up to him, even as he was looking down on them. As though he were leading a cavalry charge, and taking no prisoners.

Even as she fell back, he pursued her, his lips and tongue upon her, his hands, too, and he seemed deaf to her protests. One breast was uncovered, the draught of cold night air cascading across it, and she could feel him firm, pressing into her. He was muttering stupid endearments, fumbling with himself as well as with her, then his hand was between her legs and she could feel him forcing himself ever closer. She could scarcely catch her breath, pressed down by both his weight and the surprise, telling herself this couldn't possibly be happening to her, until she felt him naked pushing up between her thighs. Flesh upon flesh.

It was the point at which she broke. She forced out a low scream and with surprising strength pushed him away from her, yet his hand was deep inside her blouse and, as she forced him away, she heard the sound of ripping silk. 'Brendan, no!' she screamed, all restraint gone, and suddenly found herself running from the car and into the night. She ran with relief, knowing that her home was no more than five minutes away across the park. But also, as she ran, Anna was pursued by the jeering of owls and a growing dread, for she knew that in the morning, or sometime very soon thereafter, she would have to go back to him.

As the car door slammed behind her, Bracken was left feeling befuddled and angry, and not solely from the drink. He had been in mid-performance, one of his best and most intense, yet suddenly his audience had got up and left. It was perplexing, deeply hurtful, yet Bracken was not a man to allow such irritations to stand in his way. The show must go on.

Shepherd Market was but a short walk from the fringes of the park, still closer if you were driving a custom-built Bentley, no matter how erratically, and it was not long before Bracken was there. He had been to this place a couple of times before – there was something about the danger of getting recognized or being found sinning in public that spurred him on – but he found the Market engulfed in the blackout with every doorway so dark he could scarcely have recognized his mother. And when, at last, he had found what he was looking for and she had taken him up the stairs to her squalid room, he expressed no surprise when he discovered that she had a figure that was almost matronly, a little like his mother's. He would always remember that day as a ten-year-old when he had run back home to tell her of some unmerited punishment from his swine of a schoolmaster, tearfully wanting her comfort and affection, and had burst in only to find her standing naked on the hearth, drying herself off from her bath, all dark nipples and sagging flesh and repulsive hair-hidden secrets. Instead of comfort and affection he had received the soundest thrashing she had ever given him, still naked, which had left welts like tram tracks across his back until he had run back out through the door where she could not follow him.

This woman's body reminded him of his mother. In truth, every woman's body did. And when he removed his shirt and she noticed a scratch mark upon his back, and mentioned it, the obsessive memories came flooding back. She offered an ointment to help it heal, and something that might help the spots on his back, she said, but Bracken hadn't known – didn't want to know – that he had spots on his back! He felt humiliated. He had always been anxious about his personal cleanliness, something of a hypochondriac, which made visits to a whorehouse all the more stressful, and to be told that he had spots made him realize what a terrible mistake this had been, how all women deep down were the same, all wicked, unclean, just like his mother.

So he hit her – punched her, with his fist. On the side of the face, which would leave her with a swollen and blackened eye and which broke the vulgar and utterly charmless blue-stone earring that dangled across her cheek. It cut her cheek, badly, and the blood began to trickle between her fingers, but Bracken noticed none of this as he ran down the stairs and once again tried to flee from the memory of his mother.

EIGHTEEN

February–March 1940.

Dickie had suggested tea, for which Ian had expected little more than crumpets. Instead he got Welsh rarebit washed down with the finest bottle of Yquem he had ever tasted. Someone was certainly taking this war seriously.

'Thought we should relax from the rigours,' Dickie insisted.

'Always glad to help out.'

'Damned war's proving to be something of a struggle.'

'Pity about the poor Finns.'

'Got to help 'em, old boy, just like Neville said. Thought his statement yesterday was masterful. Absolutely masterful. The PM at his most perspicacious. Had the House in the palm of his hands. What were his words? "Proceed immediately to send the Finns all available resources at our disposal." A leader, indeed.'

'You haven't heard, then.'

'Heard what?'

'As I was coming in. Unfortunate timing.'

'What is?'

'The Finns. Capitulated. Bent the knee. Done a deal with the Russians. Given them what they wanted.'

'Oh . . .' Dickie considered this for a moment then muttered an exceptionally rude word. Then he turned his attention to his rarebit, picking up what was left in his fingers and swallowing it in one jaw-grinding mouthful. 'Still, got to look on the bright side,' he suggested through a cascade of crumbs.

'Bright side?'

'Well, all those troops and equipment we were planning to send. Would've been a fiasco if they'd just arrived there and the bloody Finns caved in. Think of it. First shooting match of the war and we're on the losing side? No, better we were never there at all.' He brushed away the crumbs that had settled on his stomach. 'In fact, I'll bet you a shit to a chateau that's what Neville's been up to. On the quiet. Delaying. Making sure.'

'The Finns have been fighting for fifteen weeks, Dickie.'

'Precisely my point. And we managed to keep clear of the whole mess. I think we'll look back on this as a minor triumph.'

'So we offer all assistance short of actual help?'

'Live to fight another day. Take a leaf out of Winston's book. If at first you don't succeed, dig another hole. Been the motto of his entire career.'

'As we never cease to be reminded.'

'So you got that little letter, too, did you? Can't imagine who sent it – but the point's perfectly well taken. He's swapped parties more often than I've swapped wives. Loyalty's never been his game. Never truly been a Tory, has Winston.'

'He's delivered the best news of the war.'

'No, there is no good news in this war, Ian.' Dickie,

his plate now empty, sat back with a disappointed air. 'Nothing but torment and troubles everywhere I look.'

'Troubles, Dickie?'

'As if I didn't have enough on my shoulders. You going to finish that rarebit?'

'No appetite.'

'Excellent,' Dickie announced, picking up his colleague's left-over toast and devouring it before returning to his theme. 'Yes – troubles,' he sighed.

'What's her name?'

'Myra. My sister-in-law.'

'Bloody hell, Dickie, your sister-in-law? You go too far!'

'No! Not like that, you fool. But . . .' – he shook his head distractedly – 'seems she got herself into a bit of a pickle the other night. Well, one does, what with the stresses of war 'n' all.'

'Pickle?'

'Well, sugar, if you want to be entirely accurate. She's overwrought. Was driving back home, bit unsteadily, so the boys in blue pull her over. Pure working-class malice, you know, simply because she's in the Rolls.'

'Drunk?'

'More done-in and distracted. Nothing that a good silk couldn't fix.'

'So what's the problem?'

'They ask to inspect the car. Open the boot. And find a load of sugar.'

'That's not a crime.'

'Actually it is. Turns out the silly cow had gone and bought nearly three years' worth of ration on the black market and was taking it back home.' He sighed dejectedly. 'Three hundred yards from her bloody front door. Damned bad luck.'

Slowly Ian pushed his wine away. He had lost all his appetites.

'Local press'll go wild if they catch on she's one of mine,' Dickie rattled on. 'Smuggling three years of cakes and puddings in the back of her Rolls-Royce. They'll make her sound like Marie-Antoinette without the sense of humour. She's up before the magistrates next week, and wants my help. Wants to know if there are any strings I can pull. Can't think what to do.'

'I can,' Ian offered quietly.

'Can you, old boy?'

'Tell her to go to hell.'

Somewhere on the Moors.

My Daring and Darling Sue,

Miss you. Bournemouth is so far away.

Here everything seems endless – the moors, the weather, the training. The north wind doesn't stop and we still have great floods of snow. Do you? Temperatures below freezing at night but we get sent out on exercise all the same. We get back to our billet in the local village hall and the boiler's no better than Beelzebub. Now you know why I really want to marry you – just to keep warm!

Thought we were being trained for Finland, but that's now gone. So where? Never much fancied fighting Russians, too many of them. We're still training hard

*in the snow. The tracks on the moors are sheer ice and
I slip all over the place on my BSA. Came off twice yesterday. Still, the bike's better than Shanks's pony which
is all the others have got. At last we've got our radios
to work – they were fitted with the wrong valves. Food
indescribable, but local beer and natives friendly. We
haven't drunk them out of house and home yet, but
we're trying. All rather spartan.*

*Some of the wives have turned up in lodgings in the
town, and the rest of us are pretty jealous. If only . . .
But there's a sense of something about to happen. More
weapons and equipment have been arriving, and yesterday we got a new 2/Lieutenant who's an interpreter.
Name of Petch – foreigner. Anyway, we plan to take him
down to the town tonight and get him thoroughly drunk
so we can find out where he comes from. Chances are,
that's where we're going.*

*The Yorkies are tough, but that's good. If we ever get
down to fighting anything other than boredom and
chilblains, I want their sort around me. I think we'll
be able to give a good account of ourselves, wherever it's
going to be.*

*How are the changing rooms progressing? Miss you
terribly. Hell – transport for the pub run's just arrived
– must dash. I'll write when I can. Promise.*

Love you always. Can't wait.
Jerry.

It was a soldier's letter from the more relaxed,
uncensored times than would follow later. It was a
letter she would cherish for the rest of her life.

The bathroom was filled with dense clouds of steam.

'That you, Burgess? Come in, come in!' Churchill lay back in the soapy water, a cigar clamped defiantly between his lips. 'Don't mind me in my bath. So little time for anything nowadays, have to double up. Come, sit down on the guest chair.'

Precariously, and somewhat diffidently, Burgess perched where he was instructed while Churchill continued to splash in the vast enamel tub of his Admiralty apartments. Moisture ran from the walls and the mirrors.

'Strange note you sent, asking to see me. Scribbled on the back of a cartoon. Why?'

'I'd written a couple of other notes suggesting we meet, sir. Hadn't got a reply. Thought perhaps there was a hiccup in the system – that maybe you didn't have the time. Can't loiter outside your door any more now that you've moved into the Admiralty so – thought I'd give it one last go. Try something a little more eye-catching than a letter.'

'Almost didn't see the damned note, I was laughing so much about the drawing. You're good, very good.'

The cartoon had consisted of a destroyer named HMS *Britannia* which had been transformed into the unmistakable features of Churchill, cigar thrust forward like a blazing muzzle, straining to be unleashed upon the open seas while a sheet anchor consisting of several other members of the War Cabinet – and most notably the Prime Minister himself – was clinging to the rear, holding him back and threatening to capsize him from behind. On its reverse Burgess had scrawled a cryptic note – *'May we meet?'*

'You say you'd written before? Hadn't seen 'em.'

'A hiccup in the system,' Burgess repeated.

'Hah! Brendan, you mean. Handles a lot of my diary. Doesn't like you, I suspect.'

'The feeling may be mutual.'

'Not his fault. He feels very protective about me. Doesn't care for people who just wander off the street and into my parlour – or my bathroom. Sees you as something of a threat.'

'A threat?'

'To his position. He's rather proprietorial. Even Clemmie thinks so. Says he arrived with the furniture and never left. Tiresome at times, but he is totally loyal, serves no other master than me.'

'How can you be sure?'

'Think about it. Who else would have him?'

Burgess had several thoughts on the matter, but shared none of them, while Churchill searched around the farther reaches of the bath for the soap.

'So, young man, you wanted a word. You seem to have a habit of wanting words with me at particularly confused and troubled times. Take care not to become an expert in such matters, otherwise Mr Bracken will like you even less.'

'Confusion brings opportunity – eh, Mr Churchill?'

'Yes, but confusion for whom?'

Burgess leant forward, his elbows on his knees, growing increasingly damp amidst the steam. He wasn't a great poker player, had trouble controlling his features, humour and contempt came too easily to him, and he was about to take a considerable gamble. He wanted to feel entirely comfortable, yet didn't. 'As a journalist I have all sorts of contacts. Some unorthodox and some indiscreet. The nature of the job.'

'You still haven't answered my question. Confusion for whom?'

'For Mr Chamberlain, I suspect, and his cause.'

'Which is my cause.'

'No it's not!' – said with too much emotion.

'You contradict me?'

'He's a nut and bolt manufacturer to the roots of his soul. Doesn't understand men, only machines. Has no idea in which direction to march and is surrounded by those who don't want to march anywhere. Who'll buy peace at almost any price. His heart isn't in it, never has been.'

'Mere tittle-tattle.'

'We can never win the war with Mr Chamberlain. And he's sick. That's what I've been told, on very good authority.' Well, on the authority of the folders he'd found in Mac's briefcase. 'He's got a bad ulcer, perhaps worse.'

'The war is a strain on us all –'

'He's seventy-one tomorrow. An old man in a hurry.'

'Some might suggest that would also prove an excellent description of myself.'

'But he's a sick old man, can't sleep, can't eat. And he's facing the biggest threat this country has ever confronted. Cause for concern, I'd say.'

Churchill lowered himself beneath the waters, like

a hippo on a hot day. 'You said you had this on good authority. Whose authority?'

Burgess shook his head. 'Journalistic sources, Mr Churchill, you know I can't share them. But it doesn't matter where I got it from, what matters is whether it's true. You see Mr Chamberlain practically every day, you can make your mind up for yourself.'

Churchill brooded, playing distractedly with the soap. 'Suppose it is true – what would you have me do with this information?'

'Use it. This country can't afford to have a sick man as Prime Minister.'

'I cannot use it.' Churchill shook his head heavily. 'Why not?'

Churchill's blue eyes scolded the guest. 'Precisely because he is the Prime Minister.'

'But you must!'

'Cause chaos and give Hitler the opportunity he's been waiting for? To catch us off our guard, destabilized and leaderless?'

'Which may be precisely what occurs if Chamberlain staggers on.'

'You would have me be the assassin in the Senate?'

'Certainly.'

'And then what?'

'You replace him.'

'And what example would that be, pray, for other assassins when it came to my turn? No, Burgess, Mr Chamberlain has asked for my loyalty and I have given him my word.'

'You place value on promises? Even when his lackeys distribute poisonous letters about you?

Undermine you at every turn? You know they're only waiting for the right moment, just like they did with Hore-Belisha.'

'Nevertheless!' Churchill held up his hand to stay the onslaught. His instincts were at war inside himself, loyalty charging full tilt against ambition, and he couldn't hope to resolve this in the bath. He needed time to consider what he had just heard.

'There's something else.'

'You ration your blows like a ship's master-at-arms.'

'Daladier, the French Prime Minister.'

'Our prime ally.'

'Practically your only ally.'

'You argue savagely.'

'I'll remind you these are savage times, sir. I have a friend, he's the *chef de Cabinet* –'

'Ah, the estimable Monsieur Pfeiffer.'

Burgess blanched; in the heat of the moment he'd given too much. 'It's his belief that the Daladier Government will fall at any moment. He has failed to deliver, just as Chamberlain has, and his enemies are gathering. There could be chaos in France.'

'And perhaps renewal. A stronger leader in his place.'

'Which is what should happen here!' The logic was unimpeachable, but it was getting lost in the swirl of raw emotion.

'No, no, no!' Churchill sat in his bath, scraping the thin hair away from his eyes. 'I will not have mutiny.'

'It's not mutiny, it's simply charting a different course. Or would you prefer to spend your time rearranging deck chairs?' Oh, dear God, he'd gone too far . . .

'Bloody insolence!' Churchill stormed, but Burgess held his eye without flinching. This was a determined if hot-headed young man, just like Churchill himself had once been, and rather wished he were once more. Suddenly the fire waned. Churchill shook himself. 'Be so kind as to bring me my towel,' he instructed Burgess.

Burgess did as he was told. There was an enormous parting of the waves, like some miracle at the Red Sea, and Churchill stood naked, very pink, a huge dripping Nautilus surrounded by steam and slopping water.

'Tell me, Burgess, are you a sheep-shagger?'

'What?' Burgess almost choked.

'You know what I mean – a Jennie Wren, a queer. Do you deal from the bottom of the deck? I don't care what you call it, but I require an answer.'

Burgess stood mummified. It was some sort of test; what the hell was he to say? He decided on the truth, for no better reason than that it would at least be novel.

'Put it this way, Mr Churchill, I wouldn't suggest you consider me material for an ideal son-in-law.'

'You'll have to forgive the impertinence, Burgess,' Churchill continued, wrapping himself in the folds of the towel, 'but I've heard of Monsieur Pfeiffer's proclivities and your sharing them would explain a lot about your connections. I have to make a judgement, you see.'

'About whether you like my type?'

'About whether I can trust you.'

'Whether you can trust a homosexual?'

'Good God, man, don't be an idiot, I went to Harrow. I merely want to ascertain whether I can trust your honesty – and your information. You are, after all, a man who deals in information. That makes you potentially dangerous.'

'You're beginning to sound like Bracken.'

'Ah, but there's the difference.' Churchill was now sliding into underwear of pure silk and splashing cologne generously over himself. All this he managed to do without once removing the cigar from his mouth. 'I've learned in my life to value men of information – during my years in the wilderness, such men saved me more than once. But also to suspect them, for information is power and men of information are often manipulators. This town is crawling with such people.' He was looking directly at Burgess, frowning. 'I need to make a judgement about you, about whether you are being honest with me.'

'And?'

'I suspect you may also have contacts with the intelligence services.'

It was another test. Damn, this was a man who knew too much about – well, knowing too much. Burgess felt sick. He'd overplayed his hand.

'Informal contacts,' Burgess replied. It was about as close to the truth as ever he could get – and seemed sufficient to cover the larceny of an MI5 briefcase.

'So whose interest do you really represent, I wonder?'

'Yours, I hope.' But he knew the cards had fallen badly.

'Ever since we met you have shown a commendable desire for me to succeed – promoted me, encouraged me. But I sense you have your own agenda, like Cassius and his conspirators. I will not be your Brutus.'

'Then get used to havoc and the dogs of war.'

'Once I said you were an unexpected type of man, Burgess. A man who turns up when my world is falling apart. Somehow, I wish I needed to see a lot less of you.'

'Joe!' Horace Wilson hailed. 'Welcome back to these shores. How fares the land of the free?'

'Preparing for dictatorship. Roosevelt wants a third term and'll cut a deal with the Devil to get it.'

'Seems to be uncommonly fashionable, dictatorship.'

'Which, in my none-too-humble opinion, Horace, may be no bad thing. Say what you like about Adolf, he's cleaning up a lot of the mess in Europe. Doing your dirty work for you.'

'His methods leave something to be desired.'

'Hey, it's *Lebensraum*. Everybody does it some time. What's your Empire if not *Lebensraum*? Hell, the United States of America itself is nothing but the mother of all experiments in *Lebensraum*. You guys should ease up on Adolf, while you can.'

'Ah, Joe, you do know Margot? The wife of the Minister of –'

'Sure I do.'

The Ambassador held out his arm affectionately – perhaps almost a shade too intimately, considering the occasion – but she ignored it and returned only a glance of cold fury before disappearing into the depths of the Pillared Drawing Room in Downing Street, where guests had gathered to celebrate the Prime Minister's birthday.

'Memory of a she-elephant, Margot has. I always say forgive and forget.' He took another glass of champagne from the proffered silver tray. 'Not a bad policy when it comes to Hitler, if you ask me.'

'The country's not in a mood to dabble with this forgiving and forgetting business, Joe. You know we just had the first civilian killed by a German air raid – up near Scapa?' His voice was quiet, his eyes roamed the room like a sentry on guard duty, even while his full attention was on Kennedy.

'First of millions, if you guys insist on it.'

'We scarcely insist upon it, it's more a matter of finding the appropriate way to avoid it.'

'My niece, Anna, keeps telling me the rumour is Norway.'

'Ah, the millstone of democracy – public opinion. Insists that we do something, but not in our own back yard. So there we have it. British public opinion wants something to be done far away across the sea, while French public opinion with equal vigour insists that something be done well away from France. The answer? Norway.'

'The answer is a horse's ass.'

'Well, without wishing to be accused of disloyalty, I have to acknowledge that the main enthusiast for fighting amongst the ice floes is Winston.'

'I repeat. A horse's ass.'

'But with a considerable streak of good fortune.

Refuses to be kept down. My God, have we tried, but . . .'

'I took a trip to Arizona last year. Was thinking of buying a stud farm. Took me round on a horse that got uppity. They shot it.'

'Sadly, breeding statesmen is a less precise science than breeding horses.'

'Not in Germany, it ain't.'

Wilson declined to respond but instead acknowledged a passing guest.

'So, it's Norway,' Kennedy persisted.

'It's a possibility. The French want it, Winston wants it. And the Norwegians exposed their own throats with that nonsense over the *Altmark* – left the Foreign Office arguments about the need to respect neutrality in shreds.'

'Then you'd better be prepared.'

'Joe, I can assure you, we've had plans, assessments, committees, evaluations, reports and new plans until we can scarcely –'

'No, I meant you better be prepared – for failure.'

'You doubt our ability?'

'You tumble into Armageddon with barely an ally in the world –'

'We have the French.'

'Not even the French have the French! Yet you take on this war without enough planes or guns or tanks or soldiers – and now you want to go fishing in the fucking Arctic.'

'Even so . . .'

'All I'm saying is be prepared, Horace. If you win, fine and dandy – get ready to claim the credit for Neville as a great warrior. But if you don't, if it all goes belly up – then you'd better get yourselves prepared to pour every ounce of sewage that'll be coming your way straight over the head of Winston Churchill, just like you did at Gallipoli. Just be prepared, that's all I am saying.'

'Mr Ambassador, it's always so refreshing . . .' Wilson began, but suddenly seemed to startle. His roving eye had snagged elsewhere in the room. 'Joe, forgive me. Something I need to attend to.' And with undiplomatic haste he disengaged himself from Kennedy's side and was threading his way through the throng until he was at his Prime Minister's shoulder.

'Neville, I hate to spoil your birthday, but you look done in,' he whispered. Chamberlain's features had turned the colour of old wax, the eyes to glass. His back was rigid, his hand slightly trembling.

'I feel as though someone has just walked across my grave,' the Prime Minister replied softly and with effort.

As unobtrusively as he could, Wilson began manoeuvring his master towards the door.

'Just heard, Horace. Got a note,' Chamberlain was saying, his voice grown hoarse. 'Daladier's gone. They kicked him out. His own people turned on him in the Chamber of Deputies and they kicked him out. Claimed he wasn't up to running a war.'

'That's his grave, not yours, Neville.'

'Reynaud's taken over. He'll insist on Norway. It'll happen now. The war's coming closer, we'll not be able to resist it.'

'We can handle it, Neville. You don't have to worry.'

514

'It's just that . . . this is what Winston wanted. Been demanding for months. Like a Catholic at his creed. Norway, Norway, nothing but Norway. Everywhere I look there's always bloody Winston.' He clutched feebly at Wilson's sleeve. 'I have this tearing pain in my gut, you see. Finding the pain really rather difficult. Think I need to go and lie down for a while.'

Yet war does not allow for relaxation and rest. The Prime Minister's doctor was summoned and prescribed a period of recuperation and medical tests, but Chamberlain declined. There was no time, too much to do. The public and the French insisted – something must be done! Anyway, there were too many enemies who would take advantage of the slightest sign of weakness. No one must know. And he wouldn't be the first man to struggle on with ulcers. So the doctor increased the strength of the medication, gave strict instructions about his diet, and Chamberlain forged stubbornly, bravely and distractedly onwards.

And in early April Chamberlain made a speech, full of confidence and vitality – his powers of physical recovery proving to be quite remarkable. He went to a party meeting in Westminster and told them he was ten times more confident of victory than he had been at the start of the war. The audience of party faithful loved it – and loved him, that's the whole point of being faithful. They applauded his every breath. Encouraged by such enthusiasm and borne along by their unquestioning allegiance, he went on to announce that Britain was stronger than ever and all but unassailable – 'Hitler has missed the bus!' he proclaimed in triumph, words plucked from the overheated air of blind loyalty inside the hall that were to find new life in headlines everywhere. Not quite as many as 'Peace for our Time', perhaps, but words which would come back to haunt him nevertheless.

Chamberlain knew about missing the bus – indeed, he and his colleagues had developed a considerable facility in the matter. They'd been considering military action against Norway since before Christmas and, with Churchill's bullying, had on several occasions almost decided to act. Yet there was always some reason for delay. Norway was neutral. Norway might be pushed into alliance with Germany. So might Sweden. What would the Americans think? How would the Germans react? What if it snowed, what if it thawed, what if the Norwegians resisted, and (more softly) what if it turned out to be another of Winston's Dardanelles. What if, what if, what if . . . ? Norway might be the right place but it was never the right time, not until Daladier had been blown away and procrastination had become not salvation but a mortal sin.

So in the end, it all became a bit of a bugger's muddle. It descended to the point where, in the middle of an inspection of maps in the War Cabinet, Halifax had even mistaken the frontier between Norway and Sweden for a railway line. But it only went to show that, in Europe, frontiers weren't what they used to be.

*　　*　　*

Churchill was standing by the black marble fireplace, leaning on the mantelshelf, glass of whisky to hand, studying the flames in the hearth, when Bracken with his customary lack of reticence burst into his Admiralty office.

'Ah, Brendan!' he greeted, his eyes rising from the fire. 'Just in time. It's started. Norway!'

Bracken rushed over to the drinks table to fill his own glass. 'So the old bastard buckled.'

'He has, as you so say, flagged down the bus and agreed to climb on board.'

'So what are we sending?'

'Mine-layers first. Then troops. Half the fleet.'

'To victory!' Bracken toasted. 'By the weekend!'

'Don't be so bloody impetuous,' Churchill scolded. 'You think Hitler's going to take this lying down? Marching into Norway's like pouring iodine on a porcupine's arse. He'll scream and shout. And fight.'

'Is that what Chamberlain thinks?'

'*Is that what Chamberlain thinks?*' Churchill repeated the words, not attempting to hide his scorn. 'My God, if he thought this operation would lead to a shooting match he'd be shoving horse shit down the muzzle of every gun we possess.'

'So . . . ?' Bracken continued, baffled.

'Don't you see? Hitler will respond, he will fight. He knows no other response but war. And soon we shall be in the midst of chaos. Oh, it will be tough, a most terrible war, but it is the only way. Instead of devouring everything around him piece by piece, we shall force him to try to do it wholesale – and in attempting that, he will devour himself.'

'Sounds pretty bloody desperate.'

'We must have war, Brendan. It is the only way we shall beat the tyranny of Nazism.'

'Mother,' was all Bracken could think of offering, and poured himself another, considerably larger drink.

'It has started.' There was a peculiar light in Churchill's eyes, a glow of swirling energy remarkable in a man of his age. 'Which is why we must prepare ourselves. I have a mission for you, Brendan, one of the highest importance. Sit down and pay attention.'

It was like school all over again, with Bracken desperately trying to understand what was going on.

'War will soon be upon us.'

'The Prime Minister says he's ten times more confident.'

'And so he might be – if we had ten times the men and ten times the arms! But we don't. We have a mighty navy, and an air force that at last is growing. I've seen the new aeroplanes – the Spitfires and the Hurricanes. They are few but formidable. Yet our army finds itself in desperate circumstances. Millions of conscripts flood to the flag but they are raw, untrained – and in many cases unarmed. Do you know, Brendan, recruits are being forced to drill with pitchforks, even broomsticks? We can't fight the Bosche with broomsticks!'

'You have a plan. You always have a plan.' Bracken made it sound like an accusation.

'We must have rifles. Our factories can't produce them quickly enough, but I think I know of factories which do.'

'Where?'

'In Germany. And you shall get them for me.'

There was a stunned silence.

'Isn't it brilliant, Brendan?'

'Correct me if I've got any part of this wrong. But you want me to go . . .'

'To Europe. To the borders of the Reich itself. Belgium I suspect would be best.'

'And ask for a few thousand rifles.'

'Several hundred thousand. For which we will undoubtedly have to pay hard cash.'

'But don't you expect the Germans might be a trifle suspicious, even a little *unco-operative*, if I turn up on their doorstep and start buying all their rifles?'

'Well, I can't do it. So you'll have to. Look' – he began stabbing his finger around the map that hung on his wall – 'Germany is surrounded by a host of neutral countries which trade with the Reich in every sort of goods. So go to one, make suitable enquiries, and do a deal. You're a businessman, you know the ways of these things.'

'But if it's so easy, why don't we send the Minister of Supply?'

'Don't be an imbecile! The Germans would never sell arms to the British. So you must maintain the subterfuge that you are dealing on behalf of a neutral country, Brendan. But most importantly it must be done quickly. Today. Tomorrow, I beg you. Before the storm is upon us.'

Bracken examined Churchill intensely. The First Lord seemed sober, and sounded in deadly earnest. 'It may come to nothing, of course, but unless we try . . .' he was saying, pursuing his theme.

'Brilliant,' Bracken applauded softly, 'absolutely brilliant. But it cannot be me.'

'Why, pray?'

Why? Because it sounded crackpot. And bloody dangerous. Wasn't that enough? But also because Anna had telephoned, repentant, in tears of remorse for creating such a scene in the car, pleading with him to see her again, suggesting they might go away for a few days in the country to put it all behind them. He'd been feeling bad, out of sorts about that night, even a little embarrassed, but now her call smoothed through all those creases and happiness could be his again – if only he could find the time.

'Because of Norway, Winston, that's why. There'll be statements, debates, questions, all sorts of things going on in the House, just at the time you'll be tied down here in the Admiralty. You'll need me more than ever around the Tea Room and Smoking Room. So we send someone else, someone we can trust.'

'Who?'

'Why not Bob Boothby? He's perfect. Political nous, a business background. Totally loyal to you. Speaks fluent French, I believe, Italian, too, and a bit of German.' Bracken was making it up as he went along – in truth he had no idea about Boothby's competence with languages, but his enthusiasm seemed more than adequate for the situation.

'Then find him, Brendan. Get him here this instant!' Churchill commanded. 'Let's brief him and send him on his way.'

So the call went out. Bracken briefed Boothby.

And as he did so, neither of them could have been aware that every word of their conversation was being taken down in shorthand, and the transcript placed at the very top of Sir Joseph Ball's daily file.

NINETEEN

April 1940.

In early April Jerry's battalion had been moved from its training area at Thirsk to a staging post in Scotland where they became part of the 146th Infantry Brigade. Word was that they were going to see action – real action – before long, and to most of them the prospect seemed considerably more pleasing than the tedium of training on the moors. Other units joined them, most of them Territorial units rather than regulars. That made them wonder if this was, after all, going to be simply another exercise rather than the real thing.

Late in the evening, as the light was fading, they were moved in a convoy of trucks bristling with camouflage to the port of Rosyth. The docks were full of barely controlled chaos as supplies of every description were being loaded on board two cruisers – vehicles, crates, sacks of food supplies, even live donkeys. Jerry also noticed a few fishing rods and sporting guns finding their way on board. So, it was definitely an exercise, but a huge one judging by the massive concentration of men and the impatience of their officers.

By early the following morning Jerry's battalion had been transferred aboard one of the cruisers and, after more than a little bad temper between the quartermasters and the civilian dock workers, the last of the supplies had been crammed within its hull or piled high on every spare yard of deck. In the noise and confusion, one of the donkeys panicked. It began struggling violently in its cradle as it was being loaded, braying fearfully and swinging around many feet above the deck. Loading came to a complete halt as dockers and soldiers shouted recriminations, until the quartermaster drew his Webley and shot the beast as it swung. He announced he would not hesitate to draw his weapon again if there were any further delays. He did not limit his threat to donkeys.

As dawn broke, everything was loaded and accounted for. Six hundred soldiers waited on board in a state of high expectation. Then new orders arrived. Disembark! With all possible speed! German ships had been sighted heading for the North Atantic and the Royal Navy was needed elsewhere. In their haste the supplies on deck were thrown back – literally *thrown* back – onto the dockside, the cruiser's decks were cleared for action and, one hour after the order was given, the Royal Navy sailed. No time to unload the heavy equipment stacked in the holds; it was all still inside when the cruiser squadron steamed out of port.

Norway was an enigma of neutrality. It didn't have a foreign policy, or at least anything that could be mistaken as one. Its Government was made up of socialists, anti-militarists and former Bolsheviks who clung grimly to the belief that the power of neutrality and international law would be sufficient to see them through. It was a country grotesquely ill-prepared to become the focus of foreign intrigue. It had no standing army to speak of, no submachine guns, no grenades and no anti-aircraft guns. It was saving up for a tank so the soldiers might have the opportunity of at least seeing one, but it hadn't yet arrived. The air force existed in theory only – they had negotiated to buy a few trainers from Italy in exchange for supplies of dried cod – and the navy possessed the two oldest ironclads in the world, the *Norge* and the *Eidsvold*, which hadn't left port since 1918. In military affairs it lacked any clear leadership – its Minister of Defence had once been arrested on a charge of spreading pacifism amongst Norwegian soldiers. It seemed that Norway could do little to prevent the British occupying its key strategic ports, no matter how badly equipped the invaders were when they came.

Trouble was, the German High Command had reached exactly the same conclusion.

Edward Halifax was a man steeped in the traditions of public service. He enjoyed the authority of ministerial office but he also firmly believed that it was accompanied by obligations. One of those obligations was to bring to his work a set of strong moral values, and to that end he had already visited his local parish church in South Audley Street that morning to pray quietly in the corner pew that had been reserved for him. Another obligation was to ensure that his appearance always lent authority to his work, and today he expected to need every inch of that authority since many ambassadors would be knocking at his door and some even pounding on it. The Norwegian Ambassador, Colban, would undoubtedly be the first to arrive, bearing yet another note of protest. The Norwegian was a perfectly amiable man but today he would be grim-faced and stripped of his customary light humour. Behind him the Italians, Danes and Swedes would form an anxious queue. It was certain to be a difficult day, so in order to prepare himself for it, the Foreign Secretary had summoned not only God but also Mac. While Halifax sat at one of the huge windows overlooking the park and read through a formidable pile of notes and telegrams, the barber trimmed his hair.

So it was that Mac was in place to watch as the duty clerk stumbled and stuttered his way across the room. The Foreign Secretary's office was so vast that Mac had time to study the flush on the clerk's cheek, the despairing look in his eye and the inane droop of his lower lip that seemed to prevent him from uttering a single comprehensible word. A sheet of paper was trembling in his hand, which was thrust out in front of him, like a blind man groping towards a new obstruction.

There is a majesty about the office of the British Foreign Secretary. It is by far the most splendid and awe-inspiring of any Ministerial office in Whitehall, larger than the Cabinet Room itself. In such a venerable place, normal men seem scarcely to matter, and someone like Mac to matter not at all. So Halifax did not dismiss him as he read this latest note, and seemed barely to remember that Mac was present.

Instead, as he read, he muttered to no one in particular – perhaps to himself, or to his God – a long list of names. Oslo. Narvik. Trondheim. Bergen. And as he read, from over his shoulder Mac could see that Halifax's hand had begun to tremble, too. His voice was barely audible, strained with anxiety, but Mac was close enough to hear the Foreign Secretary's words with total clarity.

'Dear God. They've got there first. The Germans have invaded Norway,' he whispered. 'Now we can never win.'

It wasn't all going the Germans' way.

They had achieved complete surprise, smuggling units of the Wehrmacht into Norwegian waters hidden beneath the hatches of apparently empty ore ships, while the Luftwaffe controlled the skies, but the German Navy encountered unexpected obstacles. An armada of Kriegsmarine ships appeared shortly before midnight sailing up the Oslo fjord. The entrance to the Norwegian capital was guarded by a single fortress armed with nothing more than two obsolete guns that were as old as time and – in honour of their almost biblical origins – had been christened 'Moses' and 'Aaron'. The commander of the fortress was understandably cautious – the guns took for ever to reload, and in any event his searchlights were out of action so he could barely see the invasion force. He decided to gamble. He would hold his fire until the largest ship, the *Blücher*, one of the newest and most powerful vessels in the German Navy, was only a few hundred yards away. It was a gamble that was to pay spectacular rewards. The shell fired by 'Aaron' hit the ship just below the bridge, wrecking its anti-aircraft control centre, while the shell from 'Moses' hit a starboard store room and ignited the aviation fuel, setting the *Blücher* alight like a Roman candle and making it a target almost impossible to miss. Soon the ship's engine room was flooded, her magazines had begun to explode and she was sinking. The *Blücher* was carrying the entire command staff designated by the Germans to take over the administration of Oslo and a thousand of them were killed as the ship disappeared beneath the dark waters of the fjord, delaying by several hours the German occupation of the Norwegian capital. When at last they entered Oslo, led by a marching band, they discovered that the King and most of the leading members of the Government had taken advantage of the delay and fled.

So it wasn't all going the Germans' way. But most of it was.

It was morning yet they sat in the dark, the three of them, around a sulking coal fire, the blackout curtains still not drawn back, as though they wanted to believe this day had never arrived.

'How could it happen? How *could* it have happened?'

'Coincidence, Neville?'

'With all my heart I want to believe –'

'Head, Neville, head – not heart,' Wilson argued. 'Not at a moment like this. Does your head let you believe that it was coincidence which made the

Germans invade on the very day we planned to send our own forces in?'

'I cannot,' he whispered, staring into the coals.

'Then the bloody Germans knew!' Ball shouted, pounding the arms of his chair.

'But . . .'

'Someone told them, Neville. Someone who knew and who let it slip. Or who simply handed everything over.'

'Negligence.'

'Treachery! Unless you've got a better name for it.'

'My God, has it come to that?'

'Neville, it always comes to that. Someone driven by malice or ego. Who puts himself above everyone else. Who'll switch sides for personal advantage.'

'But who?'

A lengthy silence while they shared their souls and the wispy smoke.

'I do not believe – I *will* not believe,' Chamberlain insisted, 'that Winston could do such a thing. Not with the Germans.'

'He's changed parties often enough.'

'Nevertheless.'

'Then someone close to him. You know Winston can never keep his mouth shut. He'd sooner brag than breathe.'

'And he's been acting very strangely recently, Neville.'

'Has he, Joe?'

'Asked Bob Boothby to go to the continent, apparently with some mad-cap plan to buy rifles.'

'Rifles? From whom?'

'There's the rub. From the Germans.'

'You can't be serious.'

'Winston is. In most deadly earnest, apparently.'

'From the Germans? This is madness.'

'Or much, much worse.'

'I shall confront him.'

'Patience, Neville. Better to watch him for a while.'

'That's best, Neville. Watch him. See where he leads us. Find the others . . .'

Chamberlain sighed as though he were giving up a small fragment of his innocence. 'Very well. Tap his phone, Joe, if necessary – tap all their phones.'

'Already have.'

'Oh, Winston . . . But why?'

'How many reasons do you want? Malice. Ego. Hard cash, even.'

'For money? You think he'd sell us for money?'

'As you never cease to remind us, Neville, there are some who will try to profit from anything, even war.'

'And remember the loan, Neville? He repaid it all. More than a mere trifle. Come to think of it, we never did find out where he got it from.'

'Then we shall. We must!'

'It was enough to save Chartwell.'

'And enough, perhaps, to sink a Churchill.' Chamberlain's hands were clenched into tight fists of frustration. 'I want to know what's going on – I *must* know.'

'And so you shall. But there's more, Neville,' Wilson interjected. 'If the Germans have been told – whoever has told them – we have to assume they know everything. Know where – and when – we plan to strike.'

'They'll be waiting for us, all prepared.'

'It'll be a bloody disaster, Neville, Gallipoli all over again.'

'Then, by God, we must change our plan of campaign. Something they're not expecting.'

'Something their informant is not expecting.'

'That Winston is not expecting.'

'Or else . . .'

The damp coals spat, a spark flying onto the hearth tiles where it struggled for life and slowly starved. Chamberlain tried to rub the ache from his eyes.

'Winston pushed me into this adventure in Norway. I always considered the risks were too great, everyone knows that. If it all goes wrong –'

'It is,' Ball interrupted, 'it's already going wrong.'

'*If* things turn out badly,' Chamberlain continued doggedly, 'there is something we must never forget, or allow anyone else to forget about this chaos in Norway.'

'Yes, Neville?'

'This was Winston's war.'

The 146th hadn't seen or sniffed an enemy, but already it was in turmoil. They'd lost half their supplies and with them much of that veneer of organization which separates an army from the rabble. They'd also lost Jerry's long-range radio equipment. By the time they eventually sailed two days later, very few of the lost supplies had been replaced. Jerry asked the quartermaster about new radio equipment. The quartermaster had stared back with raw-red eyes. 'I'll do my best,' he replied stiffly, his lower lip bitten deep with frustration.

Doing their best. Somehow, it didn't feel like it.

They knew now that their destination was Norway – Narvik, they were told, the iron-ore port in the distant north. And they were well underway when new orders arrived for Jerry and the 146th. A different objective – change of mind at the top – the very top, lads. They were being diverted to a place called Namsos in central Norway, in order that the 146th could lead an attack on the old capital city of Trondheim further south. They were informed this was part of a bold new plan to outwit and outflank the enemy. It met with immediate success in the case of the 146th's commanding officer, who remained stuck on one of the ships still bound for Narvik. Much of what remained of their equipment went with him.

No one seemed to know precisely where Namsos was, or what they were supposed to do once they got there. They hadn't a single map of the town. Still, they would Do Their Best. And it had to be better than Narvik, didn't it?

Yet, in the midst of the chaos that accompanies war, some were able to find contentment. Bracken sat opposite Anna and rejoiced in the attention he was being shown – by the waiters, by other diners at the Ritz, but most of all by Anna. Her appearance was stunning and her apology had been generous – and he, too, acknowledged that he might have been considerably more sensitive about the matter of that night by the lake. Carried away with the moment, with the passion of the events of war all around them, he explained. She had reminded him that she was Irish Catholic – enough said, he muttered to himself – and she implored him to be patient, backing her plea with an army of supporters from the Virgin Mary to the memory of her own poor mother. Anyway, she admonished through lips which puckered and moved him all the way to his roots, Uncle Joe says he'll break your legs if you get out of hand . . .

So they had sat very publicly and she had shone as bright as any chandelier while those around looked on in admiration and more than a little envy. He could see them whispering. Most of the other diners already knew who he was, and the rest would undoubtedly be told by the end of the evening.

She understood these things. Unlike so many other women, this one seemed truly to have come to terms with the stresses that stretched him to his limits and occasionally, like the other night, took him beyond. Living in the eye of the storm, bearing the weight of a man such as Churchill, guiding him, supporting him, sometimes scolding him, and being at his side when things went wrong – like now. Winston had thought the Norwegian adventure would be spectacular, that it would end this wretched phase of Phoney War, but instead it was all falling apart and the others were doubting him, overruling him, changing the plans. Narvik fjord was occupied – not through any fault of Winston's but because of the prevarication of others. Yet, incredibly, they tried to blame him. One Cabinet colleague had even dismissed

Churchill's plans for a full frontal assault down the fjord as being like another Charge of the Light Brigade.

She held his hand, and told him she understood. Then she kissed him and told him she would always understand.

Namsos, when they arrived, appeared like a small brown smudge against the snow-swept highlands lying beyond. Lumps of floating ice bounced off the hulls of the ships as they approached and a steady wind threw sharp crystals of ice in their faces. No one on board knew much about this spot other than it was already freezing their lungs. Back in London the planning staff of the War Office had sent out to the Norwegian tourist office for brochures and photographs of as many parts of the Norwegian coast as possible, but none of them featured Namsos. No one in their right mind would normally want to visit. It was a town of fewer than four thousand souls, built almost entirely of wood, whose main occupations were timber and fishing. The fish in particular left their mark. The town stank.

'You'll like it more than Narvik,' the quartermaster had told Jerry. 'Narvik's up in the bloody Arctic Circle. This place'll be warmer.'

But warmth along the Norwegian coast in April is a relative concept, and as dawn arrived the early sun brought precious little relief from the cold, only a glare that scattered off the frozen snow and blinded them. Perhaps that's why they missed the first air raid until the planes were almost upon them. A brief and indecisive confrontation took place before the Heinkels of the Luftwaffe left.

'Ran off before the RAF arrived, I suppose,' Jerry observed.

'Shouldn't expect too much from our boys in blue,' the quartermaster muttered. 'Too far from home. Think we're going to have to handle this one on our own.'

So there was no air cover, which might have been tolerable, except for the fact that there were also no anti-aircraft guns. So they were forced to disembark at night, which at this time of year lasted barely four hours. A race against time.

They landed at various points along the coast, at night and in the middle of a snowstorm. Some of the supplies made it ashore safely, but some simply fell into the sea, and they had to leave much of the heavy equipment in the holds of the transport ships.

It came as almost comic relief when the French *Chasseurs Alpins* disembarked at Namsos in the wake of the 146th. They were specially trained mountain troops, snow men, but this was an academic point since the straps for their skis had been left behind in Scotland along with their mules and all their vehicles. Their commander purloined a British jeep and set off to find his British counterpart to sort things out, but had travelled less than a hundred feet before he was involved in a head-on collision. The British and French drive on different sides of the road, even in war.

Sue knew Jerry was in Norway. He'd been training for weeks on the freezing moors, so they weren't about to send him to the Sahara. She hadn't heard from him, not since a final note from Yorkshire saying they were 'on their way', but it had to be Norway. Yet she was reassured. According to the British press, the landings in Norway were akin to the march on Waterloo. 'Brilliant work,' *The Times* crowed, 'British troops have made a rapid thrust into the heart of Southern Norway. Germans retreating!' The Phoney War was over, and an historic British victory seemed as imminent as it was inevitable.

Still she worried. That, too, was inevitable. After all that's what women in war were supposed to do. Wait at home and worry, while the men sorted things out. And Mr Chamberlain said he was sorting it out. During the day she kept the post office open, putting up posters which proclaimed 'Walls Have Ears!' and which denounced the dangers of gossip. People did gossip, of course – you might as well tell them not to breathe – and with so many husbands away for long periods in the armed forces there was so much to gossip about. She had also been instructed to make preparations for handing out things like war widows' pensions, which somehow sounded less confident than the official communiqués. Perhaps things weren't so certain after all. So in the evenings, just to be on the safe side, she made plans for the 'stay-behind' group. Maybe it wouldn't be necessary any longer, if what the press and the Prime Minister said was true – but on the other hand, if what they said had been true, there wouldn't have been a war in the first place. She visited a farmer. His wife had been in the post office explaining how one of their calves had been lost, suddenly disappeared, all they could hear were her moans of complaint coming from beneath the ground. Eventually they discovered the beast had fallen into an all-but-invisible hole beneath the field, remarkably dry and surprisingly expansive. A network of natural tunnels. And Sue suggested that if it could hide a cow then it might hide – well, almost anything. Or anyone. The farmer agreed not to fill in the hole. Just in case.

It was exhausting, working and worrying that way. Then, the very last thing at night, she would lift her box from the top of her wardrobe and lay it gently on her bed, smoothing the counterpane, placing the lid to one side, turning back the tissue paper, running the tips of her fingers across the transparent white lace of her wedding veil, as though brushing snow, being with him. She would say a little prayer, and place the dried red rose to her lips. It became something of a ritual, to keep her in touch.

Jerry assumed that his first night in Norway had to be the worst. He'd made an inauspicious entrance well after midnight, disembarking from his destroyer on his backside as his hobnails hit ice on the gangway and threatened to dump him and the crate he was carrying into the oil-black waters below. It would have been almost welcome – he'd been so violently seasick on the passage from Scotland – but in the end he lost nothing more than his dignity. The quartermaster stood screaming at the bottom of the gangplank, issuing Jerry with specific instructions as to what he could do with his sodding crate and sodden arse. Didn't seem to matter what was in the various crates being manhandled ashore, for the moment the priority seemed to be to get the stores offloaded. Other vessels were waiting and by daylight in a couple of hours' time they'd be transformed into nothing better than targets on a turkey shoot. Jerry and his crate staggered uncertain into the night. He found the tiny dock at Namsos enveloped in a biting snowstorm and lit only by the headlamps of a couple of jeeps, and no one knew where they were going. In the end he stacked his crate on top of the hundreds of others that were being dumped outside a foul-smelling fish-gutting shed. The stench was so powerful it made him want to heave once more. There was no food, no mess facilities had yet been set up, but for the moment he couldn't give a damn.

The arrival of an insipid, washed-out dawn sent them scrabbling in the snow looking for their supplies. Soon crates lay strewn along the dockside, their sides ripped open as increasingly anxious soldiers prayed that the contents had been mislabelled and inside were the snowshoes, maps, searchlights, mortars, medical supplies and rangefinders they so desperately needed. Jerry kicked open one crate marked 'Signals Support' to discover it was crammed with typewriters. The one next to it contained nothing but bicycles.

'They forgot the picnic hampers,' someone muttered.

Back in Britain, the operation was declared to be a triumph. While Jerry stood with frozen slush slopping over the ankles of his boots, almost every editor in Fleet Street seemed to be stepping out to the sound of beating drums.

Carol had read the newspapers, as many of them as she could borrow, even if they were days old, and as she read she remembered Mac. Stubborn, considerate, vulnerable, mysterious Mac. She couldn't read a thing without being reminded of him, and that morning Peter had looked up from his toast and asked once again where Mac was. She couldn't tell him, she didn't know. Bloody man. But learning to read had changed her life – one of the many ways Mac had changed things. She read reports of the heroic battle for Norway, how to make the Anderson shelter more comfortable, and how she and the other women left at home should be 'doing their bit' to help win the war. It led her to the door of Mrs Marjorie Braithwaite.

Marjorie Braithwaite was what they appropriately termed a pillar of the community. Early fifties, stout, with a considerable voice that she used to dominate most proceedings in which she was involved. These proceedings were many, since her husband was a magistrate and she was chairman of the local WI and Red Cross. Marjorie Braithwaite was a public figure, at least in her own mind. She was also a regular worshipper at the local church, and it was at church that Carol had on occasion exchanged a few passing words with her. They could scarcely claim to know each other well, yet Mrs Braithwaite, Carol thought, would be just the woman to help.

She walked up the short gravel path that lay behind the Braithwaites' front hedge. She was nervous. She had learned to deal with most types, but the likes of Marjorie Braithwaite went considerably beyond her experience. As she approached the door of the large Victorian semi, the gravel made a sharp scrunching sound beneath her feet, as if complaining that she was trespassing. After some hesitation, she knocked.

Mrs Braithwaite answered. 'Yes?' She was breathing heavily as stout women do. A second woman peered over her shoulder. Carol had interrupted them at tea.

'Mrs Braithwaite, my name is Carol Bell. From the church,' the visitor began.

'We know who you are, don't we, Agnes?'

The woman at her shoulder nodded. Mrs Braithwaite was examining Carol intently, as though searching for freckles, until Carol realized she was looking for signs of the bruises left by her beating. The scar at the top of her cheek caused by the smashed earring still hadn't fully healed, and perhaps it would never heal completely. She'd tried to hide the marks, of course, would have stayed at home for a week by choice, but she couldn't, not with two kids. She hadn't been to church while her face was cut and certainly hadn't seen Mrs Braithwaite, but clearly the word had got round. She was a woman with a black eye and no husband. Enough said.

'What do you want, Mrs Bell? It is *Mrs* Bell, isn't it?'

'I was wondering . . .' Carol faltered, flinching beneath the intensity of the other woman's gaze, 'I read this article in the newspaper, you see. "Knitting for Norway". You know, gloves, balaclavas, socks,

that sort of thing. For our soldiers over there. I . . .
I wanted to help, but I don't have no wool.'

'You don't have no wool?' Mrs Braithwaite
repeated solidly, while Agnes tittered.

'So I was wondering . . . d'you know anyone who
might be able to spare some wool? Old wool?
Anything I could . . .'

'Mrs Bell' – the title was stretched out as though
Mrs Braithwaite was projecting from the back of the
Old Vic – 'this is a respectable neighbourhood. We
don't encourage begging at the door.'

'I'm not begging, Mrs Braithwaite. I'm only trying
to do something for the boys.'

'Ah, yes, the *boys*.' The pillar of the community
inflated and drew herself up to her full five foot two,
causing her shoes to squeak. 'I want to tell you, Mrs
Bell, that we have standards in our little community.
Don't we, Agnes?'

'Most certainly we do,' the other pillar simpered.

'Sickens us, doesn't it, Agnes? The way some
people try to take advantage while the rest of the
country is fighting for its life.'

'Take advantage? I was only asking for a little wool.'

'I understand you're a busy woman, Mrs Bell –
yes, a Very Busy Woman. So let me not beat about
the bush. We are fighting this war for the survival
of common decency and family values. Regular families, where the husband goes out to war and the
wife stays home to cook. That's why Mr Chamberlain
has told us to fight the Germans, because the
Germans are degenerates. So this war is a war against
all forms of degeneracy. God's war, if you like. Do I
make myself clear?'

'What's that got to do with a bit of wool?' Carol asked, perplexed.

'I have no wool for you. Nor do I know anybody who is likely to have wool for you. And I would recommend you give some thought to why we are fighting this war before you come disturbing respectable people in their own homes. Come, Agnes, we mustn't waste any more time. We have tea to attend to!'

And with that, the door was closed firmly in her face.

Carol stood at the doorstep for some while, struggling to control her grief. She had always known it would come at some point – as it had come in every place she had ever lived – where the gossip started and spread and eventually forced her from her home. Risk of the job. But here she had hoped it would be different, with Peter settled at school, with little Lindy growing so fast, and with Mac . . . She had been so careful, until the beating gave her away. The scar on her cheek was throbbing and she wanted very much to burst into tears, but she refused. She wouldn't give Mrs Braithwaite the satisfaction. She would wait until she got home.

Brussels, the capital of neutral Belgium, emerged beneath a sprawling mat of cloud as Boothby's plane flew in. Soon the war that had erupted in the skies and seas around Norway would stretch even to this part of Europe, but for the moment all was quiet and Brussels lay oblivious to the arrows of reality that already had been set aside for it.

Immediately upon his arrival Boothby sought out the head of British military intelligence in the city. He had expected to find him at the centre of a hub of frenetic endeavour, but instead found him eating lunch with another officer who, it turned out, was the only member of his staff. Yet they were as helpful as they could be in the circumstances. They advised him to travel to Liège. From the top of the cathedral spire there, he was told, you could see clean over the German border and into the Ruhr, if the exhaust fumes from the panzers cleared for long enough. But don't stay there long, they warned him, in fact don't stay anywhere in this part of the world too long. All these exhaust fumes were enough to give a man a cough that was likely to end up killing him.

They made two phone calls on his behalf and that afternoon Boothby caught a train to Liège. A man clasping a bunch of daffodils met him beneath the station clock, and by teatime Boothby had been told what they could supply. Nine thousand rifles, more than a hundred machine guns and a thousand light automatics.

Boothby remained unconvinced. Daffodils? Beneath the clock at the railway station? Could it be that easy? Boothby peppered them with questions. Were all the arms new? He was assured they would be delivered still in their factory wrappings. What form of payment did they require? Why, a banker's draft, made out in US dollars, of course – what did he think they were running, a fruit stall? And delivery, could they arrange immediate delivery, Boothby demanded? At this point his contacts sucked their teeth. *Immediate* delivery would not be possible, they apologized – the guns had to come all the way from Cologne, which was a drive of seventy miles, and there were customs officials to be bribed. Could he wait until breakfast?

But still he was not satisfied. Nine thousand rifles were nowhere near enough, he had instructions to purchase many, many more. They explained that this would be difficult, even in exchange for US dollars, but if he could persuade his masters to deal in uncut diamonds then anything might be possible.

They directed him to Amsterdam.

He left the following morning, nursing a slight hangover and unaware that he was being followed every mile of the way.

'There is some treachery here, I think.'

'Hard words, Horace.'

'For hard times, Neville.'

'There must be an innocent explanation. Has to be.'

'Negotiating for thousands of rifles and wanting hundreds of thousands more?'

'We are desperately short of rifles.'

'German rifles, Neville? They're German. There can be no innocence in that.'

'For the Home Guard – why not for the Home Guard?'

'They would then be Winston's Guards.'

'A Fifth Column?'

'A Quisling Column. Armed. Worse than Norway. To do Winston's bidding.'

'It seems utterly incredible.'

'So was leaking the date of the invasion. Yet it happened.'

'And then there's the money, Neville.'

'You've found out where he gets it from, Joe?'

'A blind trust. The tracks extraordinarily well hidden.'

'*Secret* money?'

'And a lot of it.'

'Can there be an innocent explanation?'

'As innocent as a Mauser pointing at your chest.'

'We must find out where the money comes from.'

'Spare no effort, Joe,' Wilson encouraged. 'Break a few bankers' legs.'

'It'll be a pleasure.'

'Rifles? Hidden gold? Invasion secrets?' The Prime Minister's voice grew tight. 'Perhaps I should have him arrested.'

'Not yet, Neville. Let's dig over the ground a little first. Discover more about the money. We'll go through his diaries. Find out who he's been meeting. See how many worms we turn up.'

'Ambition, envy, impatience – those things I can understand in Winston. But not this.'

'Perhaps he is mad, like his father, or simply riddled with greed, but whatever the disease it makes him dangerous.'

'A pity, perhaps, we could not have arranged for him to be in Namsos. That would have put an end to his suffering.'

Peter had at last been put to bed, and Lindy had long been asleep. Quiet time. Carol sat beside a lamp with tears trickling slowly down her cheeks. But these weren't tears of humiliation. These were tears of pride. She had decided that Mrs Braithwaite and her kind weren't worth the blubber from which they were built. Carol knew that what she was doing wouldn't make the slightest bit of difference to the war, but it would make a difference to her. A tiny, insignificant act of defiance. Yet if that defiance were repeated a thousand times over and a hundred thousand times more, then an entire nation might defy the whirlwind that was about to be hurled at it.

Carol sat with her favourite woollen jumper on her knee, unravelling it thread by thread. When she had finished, she picked up her needles and started to knit.

The clerk at Churchill's bank had told him. Rodney, that honey-lipped creature who kept Burgess informed of all the comings and goings around Churchill's financial affairs. Rodney told him there was competition. Other people making enquiries. Official-type people, who wanted to know where Churchill got his money. He knew they were official types and that it was urgent because the branch manager had jumped on him from a great height after lunch, which was unusual because on most days after lunch the manager suffered from sleeping sickness. He had demanded that Churchill's files be brought from the archives, and now they were locked in his desk.

Burgess didn't like the questions, because he knew that those asking them wouldn't like the answers when they found them, as eventually they would. Burgess hadn't made the arrangements himself, but knew that the money would have been 'washed' several times, passing through a series of different accounts. Washed carefully, because it was dirty money. Not Jewish, as he had suggested to Churchill, but Russian money soaked in blood, the blood of Tsars and peasants and Poles and Finns.

It might take them time to get to the bottom of it, but they were still digging, so Rodney had said. Digging Burgess's grave. And Churchill's, too. Suddenly he was afraid, more afraid than he had ever felt in his life. Too scared even to drink, at least for that first night. But by Christ he made up for it on the second, and every night thereafter. Yet in spite of it all, he couldn't sleep. Every time he closed his eyes, he had dreams filled with silent, faceless men who were getting ever closer.

TWENTY

Bob Boothby's train to Amsterdam was remarkably punctual, considering the atmosphere of uncertainty that was growing throughout Holland. From the station he walked to the Amstel Hotel, a nineteenth-century gingerbread confection on the banks of the city's main river. He gave his name as Brown to the receptionist, which he hoped he pronounced as Braun, and was escorted immediately up the rear stairs to a private room at the back of the hotel on the second floor. He found four men sitting round a green-baize table. He appeared to have interrupted a languid game of cards. There were only four chairs, but as soon as Boothby entered one of the men rose and took up position by the door. The others introduced themselves with nothing more than a handshake.

Thirty-five minutes later, he had been offered four hundred thousand new German Mausers, with one thousand rounds of ammunition each. He was told delivery could start the following week and could be completed in a maximum of three. The bulk of the rifles were still in Germany, but they could be swiftly moved to any port in Belgium he required. Payment was to be in uncut diamonds, on delivery in Belgium.

However, for a surcharge of twenty-five per cent they would also accept payment in dollars through a nominated bank in the United States. Boothby suggested a European bank, but they shook their heads.

'Not even the Bank of England.'

'You doubt its word?' Boothby enquired.

'No. Simply its future ownership. It would not be comfortable for us if the records of this transaction fell into German hands.'

'Impossible!'

They simply shrugged.

'Tell me – how can I explain to my masters how these weapons found their way out of Germany? How can you guarantee their delivery?'

'Many Germans hate the Nazis – industrialists, customs officers, even some within the Wehrmacht itself. And even those who don't hate the Nazis have an extraordinary affection for dollars. There are so many military vehicles moving every hour of every day just across the border in Germany that no one notices the odd truck which disappears in the darkness. More trucks than ever are on the move right now, that's why the quantities we can offer are so large. And why the time we have is so short.'

'Then on behalf of my Government –'

'Your *neutral* Government,' they emphasized, toying with him. They knew.

'I accept. I'll return home to confirm the details and you shall hear from me forthwith.'

'Then go now, and go swiftly. Time is not on your side.'

'You said three weeks.'

'Maybe less. And remind your Government of one thing.'

'Which is what?'

'If you don't use these rifles, then the Germans will.'

The British press, fed by Government communiqués, would have none of it. Retreat? Impossible! So they announced that it was the Germans who were retreating, abandoning aerodromes. On the twenty-third of April they claimed that British forces had made a rapid thrust into the heart of central Norway and were enjoying considerable success. On the twenty-sixth they claimed that 'anti-aircraft artillery had been landed at Namsos in time to protect still further Allied landings'. Yet by then the Government had already decided to abandon the campaign.

Well, it was only a secondary objective anyway, the main priority had always been Narvik to the north. Hadn't it? And it wasn't really the Government's fault that the operation had been delayed time after time. Not the Government's fault that the officer placed in charge of the campaign in central Norway had suffered a stroke on the Duke of York's steps on the very night he had been appointed and been found senseless. Or that his successor's plane had crash-landed, injuring everyone on board, while flying north to visit the embarkation points in Scotland. It wasn't Neville Chamberlain's fault that the campaign had turned into a fiasco, not his fault that the Wehrmacht had got there first or that within days the Luftwaffe had reduced the wooden port of Namsos to smouldering ash.

Yet still the 146th pressed on. They were spread along a front many scores of miles long in their eagerness to get to Trondheim, but now the ice that was supposed to protect their flank was melting and the Germans were outflanking them, threatening to rip them to pieces. Yet they pressed on, because no one had told them that their campaign had already been abandoned.

Churchill had not favoured the attack on Trondheim; his interest had been focused on Narvik, further north, from where the iron ore was shipped. He had agreed to Chamberlain's insistence on the Trondheim campaign only with reluctance. Yet now Chamberlain had changed his mind. It wasn't working. Time to run. It left Churchill feeling powerless, almost humiliated. 'If we must withdraw,' he told his Cabinet colleagues, 'then let us at least throw our full force at Narvik. Hold back the iron ore. With a little good fortune we might achieve that within days. Salvage something.'

It seemed sensible, indeed possible; the Germans were much weaker in the isolated port so far beyond the Arctic Circle. So, incredibly, they had gone back to Churchill's original proposal, dismissed all those months ago.

Chamberlain issued the orders. Pursue the campaign against Narvik with full speed. Forget Trondheim.

'But don't tell the French, not yet. I fear they will leak it,' Chamberlain instructed. 'And don't tell the

Norwegians anything at all. They'll think we are abandoning them and refuse to help.'

Churchill cleared his throat; something unpleasant was sticking in it.

'And tell our own troops to hold their positions, not to evacuate for a few days more,' Chamberlain continued.

'But why?' Churchill demanded, startled. 'There are no military reasons I can think of for delaying the withdrawal.'

'Political reasons, First Lord, political. We have a home front, too, remember. If we announce we are . . .' – he reached once again for that ambiguous, shameful word – *'withdrawing* from central Norway, it will have a terrible effect on public opinion. No, let us hold on for a few days longer and see whether we can temper the news with a victory at Narvik. Perhaps present the picture that we only went into central Norway in order to gain time for our real objective. Narvik.'

'We are to instruct our troops there to hold their positions – their untenable positions – in the hope of . . . better headlines?'

'We must never allow ourselves to forget that morale on the home front is the key to winning any war, First Lord,' Chamberlain responded testily. 'As I'm sure you agree.'

The key to winning a war. And to winning elections and staying in power. Furious thoughts about casting down the lives of brave men to save one's own were beginning to frame themselves in Churchill's mind, but he knew any such expression would have to be handled with the greatest care. In any event it was too late – Chamberlain had closed his folder, the War Cabinet was over. The pretence of success was to be maintained.

And so it was. Two days after the decision to evacuate had been taken, the *Times* correspondent proclaimed that *'the Allied war machine is working smoothly and efficiently along the front north of Trondheim – all the British and French troops we encountered were confident and cheerful'*. The following day he wrote that *'there is no truth whatever in the statement issued by the German Headquarters claiming a serious defeat of the Franco-British forces. In fact, real fighting has not yet begun round Trondheim, the Allies being busy preparing bases for operations.'*

Of course the real fighting had not begun. It was never going to begin. The same day as *The Times* published their confident explanation of 'the truth', a flotilla left Scapa to begin the evacuation.

The spring had arrived, clothed in a cloak of many colours that was as vivid and inspiring as most Londoners could remember. Yet Burgess saw none of it. His world was drained of light and of hope. His eyes told the story – raw, rimmed with fatigue, staring back at him from a filthy mirror. There was stubble on his chin and his hair was soaked with sweat. He had tried it every way, going to bed sober, going to bed drunk, and getting so utterly obliterated that he had no idea where his bed was. Yet no matter how or where he lay, every morning his life still stank of fear. Rodney, the bank clerk, had told him they were still at it. Digging.

He knew what he was supposed to do – it had been drummed into him a hundred times. Do nothing. Act entirely normally, that's what the manual said. But there was so little that was normal about Burgess, he was a man to whom the rules simply didn't apply.

So he decided to act. To do something. To see Churchill – in person, face to face. He had to warn Churchill, to save him from the consequences, and if he could do that then perhaps, Burgess thought, he might also save himself. But he couldn't get to Churchill. Churchill was at war, a man who ate, slept and worked in the most closely guarded building in the country, a building crawling with watchers who, presumably, were now suspicious of their First Lord, who would be monitoring his mail and telephone calls, would see every move Churchill made and who would mark down everyone he talked to. Burgess couldn't get to him there, not in the Admiralty, it would be a potential death trap.

The face glared back at him from the mirror. He rubbed a finger across his teeth and dug the knuckles deep into his eyes, then he pulled at his hair, but nothing changed. He was still afraid. But it was as he was tugging at his sweat-soaked hair that the idea came to him. Mac. Of course, bloody Mac. The man who was always full of surprises, the worker of minor miracles. Whose empire was Trumper's, the barbers to kings and courtiers, statesmen and spies, almost everyone in the land who mattered.

'Mac, listen,' Burgess barked moments later down the phone. 'Mr Churchill. He one of yours? At Trumper's?'

'Not one of mine, exactly, Mr Burgess. He belongs to Alfred.'

'Churchill's a regular, then?'

'We don't encourage casual relationships.'

'So when? When is he coming in next?'

Burgess heard the pages of a thick ledger being shuffled.

'He's overdue. Seems to have cancelled twice in the last ten days. There must be a war on or something.'

'Mac, you bastard —'

'Wednesday. He has a new appointment for Wednesday, Mr Burgess.'

For a few moments, on Wednesday, the First Lord would be emerging from his shell . . .

And so, as Churchill stepped out from Alfred's chair, he found Burgess at the counter of Trumper's, seemingly engrossed in the study of a range of hair lotions.

'Somehow you don't strike me as much of a hair-lotion man, Burgess,' Churchill growled in greeting.

'Ah, Mr Churchill, what a coincidence.'

'Coincidence, Burgess, is for novelists and composers of operas, not historians like you and me.'

'You're right. But since we've bumped into each other, it would be a pity not to take advantage of the opportunity. Do you have a moment?'

'Ah! Why do I sense that another of our little talks is about to commence?'

Alfred was hovering, stooping, holding forward a hat and cane for Churchill, who took them.

'Brendan wouldn't approve, of course,' he continued, moving towards the door, 'but for once he isn't looking. So let us take advantage of the sunshine. Walk with me. I need the distraction.'

They stepped out into the bright daylight. Churchill's personal detective, Thompson, hovered a few yards to the rear, smothered in a drift of cigar smoke. Churchill set off at an extraordinarily brisk pace for a man of his years, almost at the charge as he threaded his way through the narrow and bustling alleyways of Shepherd Market. At first he didn't speak, his mind was elsewhere. In Norway. Not until they had reached Piccadilly and were waiting for the traffic to part did Churchill pay any attention to his companion.

'Burgess, you look bloody awful,' Churchill snapped as they stood at the side of the broad road.

'Not been sleeping well. Been worrying. About the war, I suppose.'

'You always strike me as a man with something on his mind – something *else* on his mind. As though the agenda is never quite complete. The rest of us get round to Any Other Business and you've only just started. Can't be good for the nerves.'

Burgess was startled by the insight and concerned where it might lead, but already Churchill was off, racing across the road at the charge, his silver-topped cane demanding that the traffic make way. Burgess followed, dodging delivery vans and bicycles.

'It's going well, I hope, the war,' he offered as they gained the safety of Green Park on the far side.

'Which war is that?' Churchill sniffed. 'The one I'm trying to fight against the Nazis, or the one I am forced to fight every day against my own colleagues?'

'I sense I'm not the only one with something on my mind.'

'I apologize. Shouldn't have spoken like that. But . . . damn it, you know what war is like. Sometimes we're forced to wonder whose side we're on. Who the real enemy is.'

'Amen,' Burgess whispered.

'How will history judge us, Burgess? Will they say of this time that we were bold and brave? Or that we were craven and sometimes downright cowardly?'

'History is often blind. I suspect it will judge us on our results – on what we do, not our motives for doing it.'

'My contemporaries have always judged me on what they deem to be my results. Gallipoli. The Gold Standard. I hope history will be more kind.'

'History is written by the victors. I hope you'll end up writing every word yourself.'

'A splendid idea! One I shall endeavour to follow.'

'If only all my ideas were as acceptable.' There was an edge in his voice that made Churchill stop and face the younger man.

'Burgess, you have something on your mind, and you've waylaid me in order to tell me about it. Pray get on with it.' And he was off again. They were passing in front of the Palace; Churchill raised his homburg in distant salute.

'Mr Churchill, it's about the money. The loan. A blind trust, of course, you not knowing where the money came from. And me, neither. It turns out that some of the money I managed to raise is foreign money.'

'Foreign money? From where? From whom?'

'I don't know for sure – there were intermediaries

– but it seems to me that at times like this any sort of foreign money might be . . . uncomfortable.'

'How much foreign money?'

'Too much. Sorry, I should have been more careful.'

'Bloody right you should have been more careful. Have you any idea what they'll do if they find out I'm living in some foreigner's pocket?'

'I'm aware –'

'So whose money is it, Burgess?'

'I don't know.'

'From where, then? If you know it's foreign you must know from where.'

'I can't be certain.'

Suddenly Churchill had stopped again and turned on Burgess. 'Damn you. Who the hell are they?'

'I don't know, I can't tell you. That was the whole point of setting up a blind trust.'

'And I must have been blind to have trusted you.'

'I was only trying to help.'

'Help your bloody self!'

'No, you! You, Mr Churchill. A most remarkable man, perhaps the only man for these times.'

'So why do you seem intent on throwing me to my enemies?'

Churchill's fists were clenched, as though he were about to hit the younger man. Thompson, the detective, hovered a yard closer.

'You expect me to believe that you raised money without knowing where it came from?' Churchill continued, his face flushed with anger. Burgess stood his ground.

'And do you, Mr Churchill, expect history to

believe that you put money in your pocket without knowing where it came from?'

'Damn your insolence!'

Thompson drew still closer but Churchill waved him away.

'How dare you, Burgess.'

'I dare because I have no choice. If this matter ever becomes public and causes you embarrassment, it will be no more than a drop in the ocean of difficulties it will cause me. I know that in the scheme of things, what happens to me is unimportant, but whether you like it or not, Mr Churchill, you and I are in this together.'

The old man was breathing heavily, chewing at his cigar. Then, once more, he was off, striding through St James's Park towards Whitehall. Burgess raced after him.

'What will you do, sir?'

'Do? *Do?*' His cane flew out in front of him as though scything through unseen enemies. 'I suppose I could go to the Prime Minister. Explain the situation. Pray he will understand. Then we shall both dig a bloody huge hole in which to bury you, Burgess.'

'He'll shove you in after me. You know that, don't you? You'd better have an alternative.'

'You have any suggestions?' Churchill spat.

'Return the money. Replace it from another source. Shouldn't be too difficult. When you took that money you were an outcast with nowhere else to turn, but now you are First Lord. I suspect such things weigh heavily in a man's bank balance.'

'It might provide me with a measure of protection.'

'And if anyone enquires you'll be able to swear on a stack of bibles you have no idea where the original money came from.'

'You've already thought all this through, haven't you, Burgess? Part of your wretched agenda.'

Burgess said nothing. He was afraid Churchill saw clean through him. They were now at the bridge across the lake. The clock tower of the Admiralty rose in the distance. Churchill faced him once more.

'This is the point at which we must part, Burgess.'

Burgess hung his head, uncharacteristically contrite. 'I am so sorry.'

'So am I, so am I. And now I fear Mr Bracken will like you even less.'

'You can taste the blood. Straight from the battlefield,' Beaverbrook muttered, swirling the caramel liquid round in his glass until it caught the light from the candles. 'It's Napoleon, the real McCoy, you know, Joe. From the Imperial cellars. Hell, the French know a thing or two about living.'

'And dying.'

'Christ's sake, you're not going to spend the whole goddamn evening crowing, are you? All that "I-told-you-so" crap? You know I'm with you on this lousy war.'

'It's gonna get worse before it gets terrible, Max. Know the latest thing I heard? Remember the anti-aircraft guns they sent to Namsos and made such a fuss about? They had no predictors, no aiming sights on them. To use a technical term, they're Totally Fucking Useless. Takes a truly half-assed military

brain to take months planning the invasion of a
pathetic country like Norway and still screw it up.'

'Not just Norway. You hear about the Brits in
France? Got just seventeen light tanks between 'em.
Hitler must be quaking in his boots.'

'Time to do a deal. Quit while they're not too far
behind. Leave Europe to work out its own thing –
you know . . .'

'Destiny?'

'You always were a man with words, Max. Yeah,
let 'em work out their own destiny. No need to get
involved.'

'That's what Neville's always wanted. Still wants,
I suspect.'

'But what Neville wants and what Neville gets . . .'
A prolonged silence.

'You been hearing the noises, too?'

'A lot of fluttering in the chicken coop. They're
expecting a fox.'

'Who do you hear crowing loudest?'

'The glamour boys. Duff Cooper, Hore-Belisha. All
those moaners and martyrs who drag their discon-
tent behind them like a cross.'

'Neville will be OK, though.'

But there was a question mark hovering somewhere around the end of the thought, an inflexion
of uncertainty.

'It's not possible. Daladier – *and* Neville?'

'It's all falling apart. Just like I said it would.'

'Yeah, yeah. So what happens next?'

'The Brits get fucked.'

'Can I persuade His Excellency to be a little more
precise?'

'OK, so Neville might get fucked, too.'

'Not brilliant timing for me. The *Express* has backed him all the way. I've always thought it inconvenient to change horses while you're getting your ass shot at.'

'Better make sure you choose the right horse, then.'

'So if not Neville . . . ?'

'Pray it's not Winston. Get down on your knees and pray! How much damage can one man do in a single lifetime? This fiasco in Norway – it's like Gallipoli and the Dardanelles all over again. Will the Brits never learn?'

'You'd think he'd have enough experience to avoid another disaster.'

'It's been Winston's game all along. For months now. Norway and nothing but Norway. Like a cracked record that can't switch itself off.'

'Practically bullied Neville into it, so I heard. So my newspapers will be saying.'

'Spreading the shit.'

'There'll be more than enough of it to cover them both.'

'So who comes out from this one smelling like roses?'

'Why, Halifax, of course.'

'God's doorkeeper?'

'He's solid. Sound. The man who didn't want British troops traipsing around Norway in the first place and had the sense to let everyone know it.'

'Give me strength. And more cognac.'

'What's wrong with Edward?'

'Nothing that a couple of centuries of careful

breeding with mates other than his first-cousins couldn't cure.'

'Can't all be as genetically prolific as the Kennedys.'

'I'll drink to that.'

'Which reminds me, Joe. That little French ally of yours I've been hearing so much about. D'you have her under exclusive contract – or might you be interested in a little lease-lend?'

Chamberlain had heard the mutterings – well, some of them, at least. Whispers don't usually travel as far as Downing Street. But a tide of concern was washing at his door that could no longer be ignored. Some were even saying that the war was being lost. So he instructed the Whips to put it about that it was all the fault of Winston – another one of his dismal failures – while he himself decided to make a statement to the House of Commons. To show them that he, Neville Chamberlain, was still very much in control. Still the silly rumour mill.

It was, even by his own high standards, a masterpiece. The House was packed, anxious. They hung on his every word, knowing that disaster and defeat were knocking at their door.

'We decided last week that we must abandon any idea of taking Trondheim,' he began, 'and that we must therefore withdraw our troops.' (Ah, that was fine, then, *we* had decided, not the Germans with all their wretched air superiority and outflanking manoeuvres. So long as we were still in control of things . . .)

Chamberlain's tone grew more sombre, and the House hushed to hear him.

'The operation of withdrawal in the face of the enemy is one which has always been recognized as amongst the most delicate and difficult of operations.' Wise heads nodded in understanding. 'And the action of Sir John Moore at Corunna, although accompanied by heavy loss of life, including the commander, has taken its place among the classic examples of British military skill.' (Skill? More like a bloody disaster. A British army which had retreated through the freezing ice and slush of Galicia, hacked to pieces along every mile of the way until the pursuing army of Napoleon had grown too exhausted to continue the mutilation. What was left of the British force had been allowed to steal away by ship. My God, he's preparing us for another Corunna . . .)

A prolonged silence. Chamberlain demanded they be silent. He stared around the House, his dark eyes alighting upon friend and foe alike, insisting they be still before he would tell them more. And they obeyed. His head fell towards the notes in front of him.

'We have now withdrawn the whole of our forces from central Norway.'

So there it was. Retreat. Defeat. It was said softly, as though to cushion the blow, but what was this? Chamberlain raising both eye and voice to meet the challenge of those around him. 'We have now withdrawn the *whole* of our forces – from under the very noses of the German aeroplanes – without, so far as I am aware, losing a single man in this operation!'

Not a single man? Could this be true? Then this

was no Corunna, it was deliverance from the jaws of death and despair. Those crammed onto the Government benches around him fought to express their enthusiasm more loudly than the next.

No, this was no defeat. The Germans had lost so many ships during their operations that it had altered the entire balance of naval power, he told them. A victory, by any other name. And there was still Narvik, too. 'The balance of advantage still lies with us,' he enthused, 'it is far too soon to strike the Norwegian balance sheet yet.'

Chamberlain stood at the Despatch Box, his fingers searching for the comforting touch of wood polished by a thousand hands, his chin high as his gaze swung around the crowded House – *his* House. He felt that surge of excitement that made all the travails of his task worthwhile – and that nowadays seemed to be the only thing capable of dulling the pain. It had been getting worse, more insistent, and soon he would listen to his doctors, slow down, find time for recuperation. But when brave British soldiers were dying in Norway, how could he rest? When the fate of a nation, of an Empire, of the whole globe perhaps, lay in his hands, how could he think of himself? History was in the making, and history would not wait for an old man's lower intestine to catch up with his breakfast.

Cries of support were coming from behind him. He gave a small nod of appreciation, two bright red marks high on his cheeks. It had been a masterclass, one of his best. He was back in charge.

Yet as he sat down, his whole being went cold. His legs gave way and he hit the leather bench with a sharp bump. A sudden thought had entered his mind, a thought that seemed to drain him of his composure. The thought that, somehow, he might just have made the most appalling mistake.

Across the nation they heard Chamberlain's message through a filter of relief, fear, confusion and shame. In his polished wooden cubicle in Trumper's, Mac discovered them all. Retired soldiers who understood, and who because of their understanding seemed suddenly to have grown much older; bankers who understood only money and who thanked the Lord for his mercy, and one of the Lord's own men – a vicar from Bayswater – who, in the instant that Mac had turned from him, was suddenly reduced to weeping. Rivers of shame trickled down his apple-red cheeks. 'To have invaded a neutral nation was a mistake,' he pronounced. 'But to have abandoned it is monstrous. I am English. I was proud of that fact. Now no foreigner will ever be able to trust an Englishman's word again.'

Burgess heard Chamberlain speak, but was too frozen by fear to weep. It was Spain all over again. And Austria, and dismembered Czechoslovakia, and Albania and Poland. Where would it end? He no longer knew. Not with Norway and Denmark, of that he was certain. Perhaps this hell had no end.

Sue Graham shared the tangled emotions of many. What was going on in Norway had no obvious or immediate impact on the genteel pace of events in Bournemouth, but in spite of the posters plastered around her post office, tongues wagged. A military campaign which one day had been a headlong rush to victory was now presented as triumph in retreat. You didn't need to be Albert Einstein to figure out the holes in that. But, for the moment at least, Sue was content to bathe in the relief that the men were on their way home. Better they be back with their tails between their legs than not be back at all. So that night she lit a candle in her bedroom and lifted down her box from the top of the wardrobe. She took out her wedding veil, smoothed out the creases with her fingertips and put it on. Then she walked around the bedroom in a pair of Jerry's old shoes, just so she could touch him. Silly, really. Part of her wanted to scold herself – she was supposed to be Miss Practical – but even Miss Practical had to take an evening off occasionally. She re-read Jerry's last letter, as she had done a hundred times before, and suddenly her mind was filled with all sorts of images – dangers, hazards – that might have happened to him since he had written those words. Her thoughts disturbed her. She replaced the veil in its box and held the dried rose to her lips before tenderly placing it on top of the white lace. Only then did she realize how much it seemed like the colour of blood.

Carol, in her tiny house in Chigwell, did what a woman had to do. She fed her children, cleaned and cared for them, and prayed they wouldn't have to grow up as quickly as so many children in central Europe. Nothing formal about most of these prayers, just incantations muttered as she stood at the sink. And when she had finished praying, she knitted. She even knitted when she went to church, throughout the sermon. Mrs Braithwaite scowled until she took on the appearance of an over-boiled potato, muttering darkly about disrespect. Carol simply smiled.

Anna provided a comforting breast on which Bracken was able to pour out many of the troubles he saw surrounding him. She listened patiently to his graphic stories of the growing chaos both in Norway and in Westminster. This was a man's war. And what else could women do but listen, and weep, and knit?

Yet this was Germany's war, too, and the Germans listened more carefully to Chamberlain's words than most. About the difficulties of withdrawing an army. About the evacuation. About how it had all been carried out right under the Germans' noses. It rankled, of course, to have been cheated of their victory-at-arms. Who could have guessed that the British would simply turn tail and run? And who could have known that the remorseless snows of Norway would have hidden the entire operation from view? Right under their very noses! For a short while – for a very short while – the German High Command could only stamp their feet in frustration at what seemed a hollow and somehow devalued victory.

Then the stormclouds broke and a spotter plane returned with astonishing news. Namsos was still burning brightly from the bombing, and the flames cast a new light on events. The evacuation was not yet complete. Stragglers were still making their way to the harbourside. British destroyers were lying off the coast waiting to pick them up. It wasn't yet over.

Chamberlain had been caught in a silly, pointless boast. A parliamentary deceit designed to generate a few cheers and buy a little time. But that time had already run out, for now the Germans clapped their hands in delight. They could now ensure not only their enemy's defeat but also his humiliation. Make Umbrella Man look ridiculous. From that moment on the Germans poured all their awesome attentions at their enemy's most vulnerable point.

Namsos.

Jerry had little idea how he had made it to the hills above the port. Hunger. Cold. Fear. The Luftwaffe. With every uncertain, stumbling step he took they hounded him. When the sky above hadn't been dark and freezing, it was full of planes. German planes. In all his time in Norway, Jerry hadn't seen a single British aircraft. He felt deserted, betrayed.

He had been part of the lead unit of the 146th as it had pushed south in a convoy of requisitioned buses and trucks, expecting to be in the vanguard of the assault on Trondheim. Yet suddenly Germans were everywhere, not only in front of them but also behind, shelling them, shredding the company to pieces. It was the first hostile fire that most of the 146th had experienced; for some it was to be the last. The attack on Jerry's company lasted less than twenty minutes, but in that time the advance of the 146th was turned to rout.

There were many injured and no transport, which had slowed the retreat. As Signals, Jerry had been sent ahead to make contact with other units and request support. But the other units were also retreating. When at last he made fleeting contact on his short-range radio, he was told that no help was available. 'Return RV1,' he was instructed, 'return RV1.' Retreat to Namsos. It was official. Every man for himself.

A dozen times on that retreat, Jerry thought he would die, either from the bullets of the Luftwaffe planes that pursued him every stumbling mile of the way or from the still more remorseless cold. A dozen times he had almost succumbed to the temptation to lie down in the snow and sleep, to dream of home and of Sue. Yet it was precisely those thoughts that kept him from faltering, lashing him onwards.

Until at last he was there. Above Namsos. This place had a chilling, almost savage beauty to it. Before him in the moonlight stretched the fjord which, now it was no longer filled with the biting snow of his arrival, was magnificent. Away to his right he could see the mystical, swirling colours of the aurora borealis, the Northern Lights, as though Heaven itself had been waiting to greet him. And beneath him lay Namsos. Not the Namsos he had left less than two weeks before, but a Namsos without shape or form, a town that retained nothing but its name, a wasteland illuminated by the flickering of yellow fires that still clung to the wreckage of what once had been homes and churches and schools and wharves. And beyond the town, out in the fjord, he began to make out the shapes of ships skulking in the dark. British ships, evacuating the troops.

It was a sight that appeared terrible to him. But it meant he would soon be home.

*　　*　　*

They had gone to pray. To beseech the Almighty. It had been Halifax's suggestion, a moment spent with their Maker before they went their respective ways to the Houses of Parliament, and Chamberlain had accepted with alacrity. He had the sense that unrest was mounting around him, and it would be no bad thing to remind God on whose side He was fighting. So they had stopped by St Margaret's, across the road from the parliament buildings.

Ball and Wilson had accompanied them, and knelt a few rows back. Ball was in bad humour – a little bending of the knee had been an idea which carried with it considerable publicity potential, but it had also been made at the last minute and he hadn't been able to contact the picture desks in time. There was almost nobody to witness this act of homage, except for God Himself, and Ball had doubts whether He was playing at home nowadays.

'How bad is it, Joe?' Wilson whispered.

'When did you last see me down on my bloody knees?'

'I don't like the smell of it myself. Did you see the *Guardian* this morning? All that claptrap about Neville's "capacity for self-delusion", how it had become a "national peril"?'

'They're getting out of line. I'm calling in all sorts of favours, but those parasites don't seem to understand the concept of loyalty.'

Wilson's nostrils flared, taking in the lingering aroma of candle wax and spent incense. 'The troops will return from Norway dragging disaster behind them. Someone will have to pay a price.'

'Then it had better not be Neville. Or you and me.

It's our necks on the line, too, you know.'

'If not us, then who?'

Ball chewed a pudgy knuckle. 'We take the high ground. As decent men. Start by blaming the Norwegians. Quisling and all the rest, who let us down just as we were risking everything to come to their aid.'

'For God's sake, Joe, not even Neville could swallow that. We need stronger meat, I think.'

An archdeacon from the neighbouring abbey came scurrying in. He had heard of the arrival of the two eminent guests and was now busy offering them a blessing.

'Dammit it, we'll be here all day,' Ball snapped.

'There's always Winston, of course.'

'Yes, always Winston.'

'Norway was his baby.'

'And all those bloody rifles, too.'

'What news?'

'Boothby's come back saying he's found enough for an entire army. All he needs now is the money. Winston's demanded that we pay.'

Chamberlain and Halifax had now risen from their knees and were talking quietly to the archdeacon. Wilson and Ball crossed themselves and stretched the ache from their legs.

'Talking of Winston and money, Joe . . .'

'Almost there, Horace. Almost there.'

'For heaven's sake,' Wilson snapped, his impatience bursting through, 'how long do these things take?'

'Ah, that's the beauty of it. The reason it's proving difficult is because it's foreign.'

'Oh, dear God, if that's so then we have him . . .'

'Not quite yet, Horace. The money was passed through an obscure trading company called Omni-Carriers. Bank in Geneva, mistress in Vienna, usual sort of thing. We can't touch it directly, so I've got the SIS boys digging away. See what Omni's really up to.'

'But foreign. Don't you see what that means?'

'I see what it *might* mean.'

'He's hiding something.'

'Of course he's hiding something. But what? We can't go coshing the truth out of the First Lord of the Admiralty in the middle of a bloody war. We need some other names for that.'

'His diaries. You've checked?'

'While he was in Paris. But nothing out of the ordinary, apart from his multitude of arse-wipers like Boothby and Bracken.'

'You checked his office diaries?'

'Of course his office diaries.'

'But he wouldn't be stupid enough to meet anyone in his office, would he?'

'Where else? He goes nowhere now except for the House and the Admiralty. And we tap all of his telephones.'

'But is there another diary? A personal diary? For his appointments outside the office?'

'What personal? He doesn't have the time. He lives in the bloody Admiralty, remember, the flat above the shop?'

'He lives in the Admiralty,' Wilson repeated slowly, his lips moving as though reciting some half-forgotten prayer. 'Of course. So all of his visitors, even the personal ones, would have to go through the Admiralty reception. Past the doorkeeper. Be recorded in the doorkeeper's daily log.'

'So what?' Ball asked cautiously, not yet up to speed.

'So find the doorkeeper's log. Today! Now! Check it against his diary. See if he's had any other visitors.'

'Visitors? What sort of visitors?'

'Those who didn't make it onto the first list. Who had no official or obvious personal reason for being there. The one-off callers. Those he saw on his own. You check it out and come up with a list of names. Shouldn't be more than a handful – as you say, he doesn't have the time. Unless he deliberately made some. If there are any devils at our elbow, that's where we'll find them.'

'Then what?'

For the first time in days Wilson allowed a thin smile to replace his frown.

'You come up with a name, Joe. And that, I strongly suspect, will be an end to Winston's little war.'

It isn't clear how Jerry can make it to the dockside. For a man whose physical resources have been consumed by fatigue, it seems impossible to cover nearly ten miles in under two hours. But fear carries him, and thoughts of home, every step and stumble of his way down the mountainside, pushing him, forcing him on, picking him up when he falls. He thinks of Sue. Where the drifts of snow lie thick, her smile gives him strength; when he becomes disorientated and lost, she whispers to him, guiding him towards the glow in the night that is the burning of Namsos.

As he draws closer, Jerry knows he is no longer alone. He begins to find abandoned buses, broken trucks, redundant supplies, on all sides the wreckage of retreat that has been cast aside by those who have gone before. And every time his path leads him up to a vantage point, he sees with ever more clarity the signs of the evacuation below him – the outlines of men scurrying between the fires, of small boats leaving the makeshift wooden quays, the shadow of a destroyer lurking at anchor beyond. He knows they won't wait for him, for soon daylight will arrive and death waits for any ship stuck motionless in Namsos fjord. By dawn, they will be gone. Jerry stumbles on.

He passes more abandoned vehicles. A baker's truck, several private cars, even cruelly bent bicycles. And gun emplacements where, until perhaps only minutes earlier, the British rearguard watched and waited for the order to fall back on the port. It seems they were armed with nothing more substantial than Bren guns – they have left the tripods behind, along with boxes of unused ammunition. They were all taking part in a race against time, a race in which Jerry started several laps behind.

Now he can see them. Clearly. Less than two miles away. Can even hear an occasional shout of command, but it's drowned out by the thudding of the engine of a crowded trawler as it disappears into the darkness. Jerry shouts back, waves his arms, but it is useless. His legs feel on fire, as though he's being burned at the stake. He wants it to stop. His body and his mind are screaming at each other, insisting the other give way. He drags himself forward.

Now he is in the town, or where the town has been. Nothing left but smoke, moving like banks of fog across his path, burning his throat, trying to suffocate him. Half-collapsed walls that look down on him in reproach. The front of a church, windows blown out, staring sightless, like a skull. Fires flickering everywhere, marking the gateway to Viking hell. He will soon be there. But as he catches glimpses of the dockside, it seems there are now only a few men left, and only one boat.

Still the stench of rotting fish pervades the place, fighting its way through the choking dust, taking him back to the time when they arrived, so full of hope and expectation. The memory fills him with anger, for what has happened has been no accident of war but raw, bloody, inexcusable incompetence. Incompetence that has killed so many of his mates and has all but done for him. But not yet.

Then he is there. He stumbles onto a quayside that is full of equipment of all kinds – vehicles, a dozen trucks, heaps of rifles, boxes, oil drums, stores, some abandoned, others only recently arrived and never touched. There are even two Bofors anti-aircraft guns, waiting for their orders to go to war. But Jerry is no longer interested in war, he's interested in nothing but survival. And now he is at the water's edge.

But they are gone. He is alone on this dockside, but on the water in the distance he can see a turbulent wake, and he follows that to a point where he can just make out the ghostly outline of a small tender rapidly disappearing into the dark. He shouts, but his cries echo back unheard. Shouts again, waves his arms, but it is pointless. Armies in retreat don't look back.

Yet Jerry is not done. Nearby, lying in the snow, is a motorbike, a Norton, thrown to the ground and forsaken. Jerry hauls it upright and sits astride, pointing it out to sea. He kicks the engine into life, switches on the headlamp, flashes it at the retreating boat. Nothing. He flashes again, blows the horn – it must be so difficult to see against the fires of a burning town, but it's all he's got. Then it seems to him that the boat is no longer disappearing but is hovering just on the edge of his vision. He flashes again. And again. 'SOS – SOS.'

At last a lamp flashes in response. 'IDENTIFY'. They've seen him!

'SGT WHITE B COY KOYLI.'

But they are cautious, fearful of a ruse by the German mountain troops they know are in hot pursuit.

'MOTTO,' they demand.

Oh, but they know what they're about, these boys. His legs begin to tremble as relief floods through and overwhelms his body. His fingers are trembling, too, on the light switch.

'CEDE NULLIS.'

Smoke is blowing across the quayside, blotting out the lamplight. They ask him to repeat. He flicks the switch.

'NEVER BLOODY YIELD.'

Then an interminable pause, before they respond: 'RETURNING.'

And the distant shadow is moving once more, but this time growing larger. It all seems too slow for him, but the sea has its own pace. Jerry is off his bike, standing in the snow, staring out to sea from where his rescuers are coming, waving his arms in welcome.

The British are abandoning Namsos, and leaving behind their honour. Under direct orders from London they have failed to inform the Norwegians of their withdrawal, and are leaving their allies hopelessly exposed. Consumed by a sense of personal shame, the commander of the Namsos operation has written to his Norwegian counterpart, apologizing for the impossible circumstances they both find themselves in. He has also tried to find some token, some mark of recompense, which might in some small part make up for the sense of betrayal the other man inevitably feels. 'We are leaving a quantity of material here which I hope you can come and take, and know it will be of value to you and your gallant force.' The material he speaks of now lies abandoned on the quayside all around Jerry.

Yet in the confusion of retreat, objectives are inevitably compromised. No one has told the captain of the destroyer about the intention to leave supplies for the Norwegians. As far as he can tell, anything that is left behind will soon fall into the hands of the pursuing Germans. So as soon as he hears that the last boat has left the quay, he issues orders for it all to be destroyed. It is the early hours of 3 May 1940. The guns of the British destroyer rain down their fire upon the dockside until everything is destroyed. In the process, they kill Sergeant Jerry White.

The last British blood to be shed in Namsos, spreading out across white snow. Like a rose upon lace.

TWENTY-ONE

7 May 1940.

'Christ, bit savage, didn't you think, Ian? All that claptrap in the press?'

'Going for the jugular, that's for sure.'

'Don't care for it. So damned unfair.'

'Even the *Mail*'s calling for a change.'

The pair of old warriors are forcing their way through the crowded House in search of seats, trying to avoid the knots of colleagues and conspirators that seem to have gathered at every point.

'*Mail*, too?' Dickie shakes his head. 'Vultures! Only a few months ago they were singing his praises. Hitler's too. My God what has happened to this place?'

'Defeat.'

'So we've been in a scrap. Got a bit of a bloody nose. But it's not as if London's being bombed.'

It is a gentlemen's club, full of old leather and tradition, but today the House is not a place of comfort. A mustiness hangs in the air, a combination of late nights, anxiety and male bodies too closely packed. But Ian has found a small gap in the crowd, the suggestion of a space on the final row of leather benches at the back of the House. It will give them an excellent view of proceedings. They squeeze themselves in.

'You really think it's possible?' Dickie presses when, after much pushing and apology to either side, his ample trousers finally make contact with green leather.

'What?'

His voice falls to a whisper. 'You know – Neville.'

'Something's got to happen. We can't go on as we are,' Ian replies.

But further discussion is cut off as, beneath them, the Prime Minister makes his entrance, emerging from behind the Speaker's Chair to pick his way carefully like a crane across the outstretched legs of his colleagues who have already gathered on the front bench. A chorus of support rises from the Government benches, organized by the Whips, but Ian notes that very few of his colleagues get to their feet in order to welcome their leader. A secure seat seems to command a greater value.

Chamberlain, too, notes the restraint. In a fickle world a Prime Minister is only as good as his last performance and Chamberlain has acknowledged – privately and only to himself – that he misjudged his performance of the previous week. He presented the matter of the withdrawal from central Norway in a positive light, but now the troops are back and in their wake have come crawling the military correspondents with their wails and woe. They are like the camp followers of old, these satirists and cynics, wandering across the battlefield after the danger has passed in order to rob the bodies. He despises them. He had despised them even when he controlled them. Now that they are proving to have an appetite for carrion, he despises them all the more.

He knows this will be a day of significance. He has dressed carefully. A fresh wing collar, as always, and the tie that his wife bought for him to celebrate the birth of their first grandchild. He wants to present his best appearance, but beneath the silk shirt and tailored jacket he can't help noticing how thin he has grown, how advancing years have begun to wear him away. Not the man he had once been. But neither is the country what it had once been, even twenty months ago, when he returned from Munich and they had all – yes, *all* of them – hailed him and his works. Now they display the gratitude of sea gulls.

He has driven the short distance to the House. He wanted to walk, but there were crowds, some of them displaying unhelpful placards, and he has to keep his mind focused, to rise above them, so high that their slings and arrows will simply never reach. And as he settles into his seat by the Despatch Box he acknowledges the cheer of his colleagues – a self-conscious sort of cheer, perhaps, but enough to drown the inevitable heckles. He can't help noticing that the House is exceptionally crowded, packed tight. The thought crosses his mind that it looks like an evacuation ship, but he quickly dismisses such nonsense.

The cheering and waving of Order Papers along the Government benches has subsided now. Slowly the House begins to settle, preparing itself. As it does so, a voice with a deep Lancashire accent penetrates to every corner.

'There 'e is. The fella who missed the bus.'

And the House once more is in disorder, the Opposition benches roaring their approval, all the careful work of the Whips undone. Chamberlain bows and smiles at the Member, gracefully acknowledging the thrust, and silently vowing vengeance by whatever means he can bring to bear. But now the floor is his. The debate on the operations in Norway gets underway, two days of it. His walk with destiny is about to begin.

He grips the Despatch Box with both hands, steadying himself, like an athlete about to leap. He starts by praising the magnificent gallantry of the British troops. A facile point to make and one that is impossible to oppose. Nothing gained but a little time. So they wait, and watch, like crows strung out along telephone wires, hoping for carrion.

The withdrawal from central Norway, he acknowledges, has created a profound shock both in this House and in the country.

'All over the world!' someone cries.

God, is he to be interrupted before he's begun? He scowls at the Speaker, who pretends to be looking at his notes.

Some have suggested that Ministers are to blame for the shock of the withdrawal, and he acknowledges that Ministers must expect to be blamed for everything. His tone is slightly condescending. He stands tall, braces his shoulders in order to show that he is big enough to take any amount of blame.

'What's he doing – waiting for the bus?' Lancashire cries out again.

Not that tired jibe again . . . Inside he wriggles with rage, but presses on. If anyone is to blame, he declares, it is not Ministers but those who raised expectations about the venture in Norway which were never justified. Expectations that were so ridiculous they might indeed have been invented by the enemy. Expectations that were completely unfounded and certainly never endorsed by Ministers.

Such side-stepping of responsibility causes uproar. Outrage sweeps along the benches of Opposition members in front of him. Catcalls ring in his ears, while from behind he can sense only a dull silence. They are being slow, his own men, perhaps languid after too good a lunch, but languid's no bloody good to him. His eyes fasten on to the Chief Whip seated at the end of the Front Bench, whose hand begins to beat on the back of the bench, like a galley master beating time for the slaves. Tumult erupts and the Speaker is at last dragged from his torpor. 'Don't you want to listen to him?' the Speaker demands in rebuke. 'We've heard all the excuses before,' a shout comes back.

It's time to pursue them. At moments like this Chamberlain sometimes wonders who the real enemy is. Don't exaggerate our difficulties, don't you *dare* exaggerate our difficulties, he scolds them, don't do the Wehrmacht's work for them. Heavens, it's nowhere near as bad as Gallipoli!

Ah, that eternal, irresistible comparison. Gallipoli. All eyes on the Opposition benches float towards Churchill, seated beside his Prime Minister, brooding.

No, this time, Chamberlain continues, our losses have been really quite light. Very well, so we've suffered a certain loss of prestige, and perhaps a certain colour has been given to the legend of German invincibility. And I grant you that our enemies are for the moment crowing. The Prime Minister spreads his hands, nothing to hide, indicating how reasonable he can be. But reason never won the day in the House, and he's beginning to lose control. Press on quickly.

So, you ask, why did we set our sights on Trondheim, knowing how difficult and how hazardous the task would be? Well, how many reasons do you want? But the most important reason is that we were asked to do so by the Norwegians themselves. Brave Norwegians, extraordinary courage, resisting the German bully – who would deny them? Anyone here? Stand up and identify yourselves if you would have dared refuse!

So why did you run away, then? a voice demands.

We went to their assistance because we are decent men who respect the freedom and right to neutrality of small nations (very well, so we invaded their neutrality and laid a few minefields ourselves, but that was nothing compared with what the Germans have done . . .).

So why *did* you withdraw . . . ?

He ignores the repeated jibe. If we hadn't gone to their help, he insists, what would that have looked like? They would have said we were only interested in the iron ore! Which, of course, is so far from being the case!

Out of his sightline Churchill's large head, resting on his chest, remains motionless, except for one eyebrow which suddenly arches in – in what? Disagreement? Mockery? Gentle surprise? To the Opposition it looks as though the truth is struggling to get out.

Understand our strategy, Chamberlain insists.

584

Germany has vast and well-equipped armies. She could attack us at any time and at any place. We must be ready to meet that threat!

Pardon me, they shout, but isn't that what Winston has been saying all these years? Isn't that precisely why you let him starve in the wilderness?

Churchill's head, eyebrow, jaw, every muscle of him, remain like stone beside his leader.

Chamberlain waves his arms in contempt. Some of you are always full of cheap jibes. Accusing every Minister of being either complacent or defeatist. Me, I've always tried to steer a middle course.

You couldn't steer a bloody bus, they cry.

Look, unlike some, I've never sought to raise undue expectations . . .

Tell that to Joey Ball!

. . . or to make the people's flesh creep by painting pictures of unmitigated gloom.

Missed the bus, they cry again.

That's it. He's had enough. Time to deal with these vermin . . . Don't twist my words. I used those words in totally different circumstances. *Before* the invasion of Norway. *Three days before!*

Oh, bugger, he knows he's lost. Got too bloody sensitive for his own good, let them get under his skin. And what's worse, he's allowed it to show. Get back – get back to where you need to be, Neville. Mountain top, lofty visions, not down in the sewer with the rats.

He forges on, piling clichés around him for protection. No time for bickering, for division amongst ourselves. Time for closing ranks, for setting our teeth. For unity. For party loyalty. For friendship!

He even appeals to the Labour Party for help. No, no! they cry – as he knew they would. What? You won't help with the war effort? he sneers.

They erupt in frustration. He grips the Despatch Box. The eyes of the Whips travel like cattle prods around the House, goading, inciting, compelling. Mixed amongst the chaos there are cries of shame. Some of them are coming not from in front of him but from behind, from his own benches.

He has almost finished. Run out of clichés. I don't claim to be infallible, he tells them. I'm not above receiving help and advice from others. For I recognize an overriding national objective – as every true Englishman does – to prepare for the trials that lie ahead. We must put all our strength into preparing for these great trials, and so steadily to increase our strength until we ourselves will be able to deliver our blows, wherever and whenever we will!

It's not great, so far as perorations go, scarcely the stuff of Shakespeare, but he's never had Winston's skills. Yet he has confronted the whirlwind and not been swept off his feet. At last he can sit down, to the applause of his own men and to shouts of consternation from the rest. He is satisfied. He is also utterly exhausted.

Of all the many perils that lie in wait for the statesman, the greatest are his friends. As Chamberlain sat down matters were still, perhaps, in the balance. The first to offer a response was Clement Attlee, the leader of the Labour Party, who in his clipped public-school tones taunted Chamberlain

with being the man who had an almost uninter-
rupted career of failure and who had missed every
bus of the last ten years. Then it was the turn of Sir
Archibald Sinclair, the Liberal leader, who described
at length the failings of the Norwegian campaign –
Territorials, ill-trained boys sent to do men's jobs, and
dying for the privilege.

Yet such taunts were of little account. It is difficult for Opposition leaders to shine in such an arena,
for grand words of denunciation are no more than
is expected of them. So Chamberlain was still free
and in control when the next speaker rose to his
feet. A Government stalwart, a senior backbencher,
a knight of the shires and a brigadier-general all
rolled into one. Sir Henry Page Croft was a veteran
of the Somme campaign who had witnessed the
spilling of much blood. He was about to inflict praise
upon his leader from which Chamberlain would
never recover.

The brigadier drew himself up to his full height.
From where he was looking, the rows of the
Opposition benches stretched out before him like
enemy trenches shorn of their barbed wire – my God,
but he was used to this, had seen it all before in
France and the fields of Flanders. In his mind he carried the orders of the day, delivered by the Chief
Whip himself, and in his hand he held a few notes
which like a bayonet he would soon be plunging
repeatedly into the breast of the enemy. A few short
breaths to fill the lungs, a licking of dry lips, and he
was over the top . . .

First he thrust at Attlee, followed by a lunge at
Sinclair, but these were minor skirmishes. His sights

were trained upon a target he described contemptuously as 'our own Quislings' – the treacherous and treasonous scribblers of the press who 'have enrolled themselves under Dr Goebbels'. These creatures, he accused, have turned 'a minor technical mishap into a great disaster for British arms'.

A minor technical mishap. Well, there it was. The difficulties in Norway were really nothing worse than a broken fan-belt. From two rows behind him, Dickie could be heard offering voluble support.

Yes, the brigadier continued, the Quislings in our press were defeatists – but where was the defeat? There had been no defeat, nothing but glorious victory! (Even Dickie had to pause in order to get hold of this one.) Hitler had been lured into one of the great strategic blunders of all time, Croft insisted. 'He has done the very thing which the whole of the German staff have preached against for the past one hundred years. He has extended his right flank by over one thousand miles. He must keep at least one hundred thousand men in Norway until the end of the war . . .' The statistics were thrown around the Chamber like grenades, the noise was deafening. 'Who can doubt,' he thundered, 'that Hitler, with his right flank stretched out one thousand miles, subject always to possible attack by sea power, has entered upon a road which is a departure from all military reason and strategy?'

Why, it was clear. Hitler would collapse under the weight of his own success. Give him Belgium, give him France, give him anything he wanted, and soon he would be utterly vanquished . . . The brigadier's colleagues sat stunned, but the smell of blood was in his nostrils and he knew from his experience in the trenches that once you'd started you never dared stop or you'd end up with your balls hanging on the wire. No chance of that. On to Berlin! 'And I shall say to all my friends, whatever may be their different shades of opinion,' he exclaimed, pointing to his Prime Minister, 'that if you are convinced you can find a better man, then put him there!' It was only the first half of the thought, of course, merely setting up what he intended to be the *coup de grâce*, but the saviour of the Somme had unwisely paused for breath in the middle of his onward charge. Suddenly he was caught in the middle of no-man's land. Stuck in the mud. Bugger. He struggled onward, ever more recklessly, trying to dodge the enemy fire that was bursting forth on all sides, determined to bury his blade to the hilt. 'But if you believe that this kind of attack in the Press, this sabotage, is wrong, if you still believe in democracy, then do not let those of us who are fighting for democracy take our orders from the biggest dictator of all – the Press!'

What – bigger than Hitler? Bigger even than Joe Stalin? Well, it was a point of view, and one that was to prove extraordinarily effective in having the brigadier's name removed from the *Telegraph*'s Christmas card list. He resumed his seat, breathless. Below and in front of him, Chamberlain did not stir, dare not move. His mind froze. Was this the best they could do? Was he to find himself defended not by valiant knights but by court jesters and fools?

The House of Commons was being turned into a stage for the playing-out of an historic masterpiece, and from the wings entered Sir Roger Keyes, dressed for the part in the full uniform of an Admiral of the Fleet, six rows of medals gleaming at his chest. The Admiral's military record was long, impeccable, indeed heroic; this was a man who knew war. He was also a parliamentarian who had considered carefully the part he must play in this drama. 'I have come to the House of Commons today in uniform, for the first time, because I wish to speak for some officers and men of the fighting, sea-going Navy who are very unhappy.'

Friends, Britons, countrymen, lend me your ears, for I come to talk of honourable men, whom we shall then devour. And with forensic ability Keyes proceeded to rip the heart out of Chamberlain. He talked of damned insults. Of a shocking story of ineptitude. Of things that ought not to have been allowed to happen. Of a battle which should have been a triumph but a battle which had become, instead, an historic tragedy – yes, he used that word. Tragedy. No duplicitous nonsense about the balance of advantage still lying with this country and how it was no worse than a broken fan-belt. The House reeled. Not in living memory had a Prime Minister's arguments been so ably dissected to expose the cancer within.

Then he spoke of Churchill.

'I have great admiration and affection for my Right Honourable Friend the First Lord of the Admiralty.'

What was this? Another honourable man to be thrown to the mob? But no, Keyes had an entirely different purpose. He talked of Churchill's brilliant conceptions, of the unfairness with which in the past he had been treated, and he also spoke of the future. 'I am longing to see proper use made of his great abilities. But I cannot believe it will be done under the existing system.' The existing system? But the existing system was . . .

Chamberlain. Who sat as though iron had entered his soul. Then, presently, when he had found the strength to move, he left the Chamber to faltering cheers from some on his own side. He would listen to no more of the debate that evening. And so it was that he was not present to witness the final drama of the day played out by a fellow Member from Birmingham. Leo Amery was one of those nearly-nearly men, a politician who had enjoyed high office but never the highest. He was diminutive, almost Napoleonic, and always had a little too much to say for his colleagues' comfort. But this was a day of discomforts, so when later that evening he caught the Speaker's eye and gained the floor of a sparsely attended Chamber, other Members began to drift back from the dining rooms and bars. The House was still only half full by the time he declared that 'there are no loyalties today except to the common cause', but the benches filled steadily as, for nearly forty minutes, he shredded his own Government for its failures in Norway. 'It is a bad story, a story of lack of provision and of preparation, a story of indecision, slowness and fear of taking risks.' Damning criticism by any measure, but . . . 'If only it stood alone. Unfortunately, it does not.' Then he mocked his own Prime Minister's words about Hitler having missed the bus. He said such claims were very far from the truth – which was about as close as a Member could come to calling Chamberlain a fool and a liar.

'We cannot go on as we are,' he declared. 'There

must be change. Believe me, as long as our present methods prevail, all our valour and all our resources are not going to see us through . . .'

What? We might lose this war? Yet as he flung his unpalatable truths at them, not a single voice was raised in contradiction.

Parliament itself is on trial, he told them. And recalling another occasion when Parliament had been put to the test, he reminded them of the words of Oliver Cromwell in denouncing the failures of his own companions when it seemed that all might be lost. *'Your troops are most of them old, decayed, serving men and tapsters and such kind . . . You must get men of spirit that are likely to go as far as they will go, or you will be beaten still.'*

Chamberlain's Government – Old? Decayed? Serving men and tapsters?

Even as the House reeled from the insults, Amery was back.

'We are fighting today for our life, for our liberty, for our all. We cannot go on being led as we are. I have quoted certain words of Oliver Cromwell.' He hesitated, for until this moment he had not known whether he would use the words that he was about to use, but as his eyes hovered over so many of those self-serving men and tapsters in front of him, his last doubts were swept aside. 'I will quote certain other words. I do it with great reluctance, because I am speaking of those who are old friends and associates of mine, but they are words which I think are applicable to the present situation. This is what Cromwell said to the Long Parliament when he thought it was no longer fit to conduct the affairs of the nation.'

The House was motionless, more than silent. They were witnessing one of the great parliamentary speeches and were about to be part of its final act.

'"You have sat too long here for any good you have been doing. Depart, I say, and let us have done with you! In the name of God – go!"'

Terrible words. And suddenly they all knew that a new game had emerged. This was no longer a debate about Norway, but a debate about Chamberlain and all his works, and on that debate would depend not simply one man's life but perhaps the lives of an entire country. They hung their heads in shame, in sorrow, in anger, and some in fear, but whatever their motives or loyalties, when the day's business had finished they rushed from the Chamber to their cabals and to their corners, and they plotted. And chief amongst the plotters were the Labour Party. Since the start of this war they had been forced to sit impotent, never certain when to support and when to oppose, but that uncertainty had been swept away by the tide of abuse that had begun to sweep along the back benches and which might yet rise so high as to sweep this Government clean away. So they decided to turn what had begun as a matter of debate into a matter for absolute decision. When they returned on the following day, the Labour leadership announced that at its end, in five hours' time, the Labour Party would force upon the House a vote of confidence. Lose it, and Chamberlain must go.

Wearily the Prime Minister rose to his feet. Must he fight enemies on every front? But he was owed – so many of those in this House owed him – and it was time to call in their debt. 'This is a time of national danger, and we are facing a relentless enemy who must be fought by the united action of this country. It may well be that it is a duty to criticize the Government –'

'Disgraceful!' a voice barked. It was Dickie, jabbing his finger at the Opposition. 'Who are they working for? The Wehrmacht?'

Chamberlain waved his hand gratefully in the air. 'I don't seek to evade criticism. But I say this to my friends in the House – and I have friends in this House.' He smiled thinly as voices of support were raised around him. 'No Government can prosecute a war efficiently unless it has public and parliamentary support. I accept the challenge. I welcome it, indeed!' He looked across his own benches, an edge of menace in his eyes. 'At least we shall see who is with us, and who is against us. And I call on my friends to support us.'

So, they would be flushed out of their corners, these men of whispered conspiracies, into the scorching light of day, where they could be identified. And dealt with. Perhaps the Labour Party had done him a favour, after all. And there was no chance of the Government losing the vote. The Prime Minister resumed his seat, content.

Prime Ministers cling to their office with tenacity and, when they are no longer in office, cling with even more ferocity to their reputations. Sometimes a reputation is all they have left. One former Prime Minister still sat in the House of Commons, a politician with a reputation that eclipsed every other man of his age. David Lloyd George had been the victorious Prime Minister of the last war and had brought the country through its time of peril with a mixture of nerve, energy, imagination, insult, gentle corruption and blinding Welsh oratory which had transformed him into a parliamentary legend. He was now elderly, seventy-seven, and increasingly frail, yet his country was at war once more and everything he had achieved was under threat. As he rose unsteadily to his feet, clad in his ubiquitous blue suit with his mane of white hair falling around his temples, his voice was low – so low they had to ask him to speak up. But when he did, they heard words they would remember for the rest of their lives.

'I intervene with more reluctance than usual in this debate. I hesitated whether I should take part in it at all, but feel that I ought to say something, from such experience as I have had in the past of the conduct of war. In victory, and in disaster.' He praised the gallantry of the country's fighting men, his voice rising and his arms spreading wide, drawing in every single man and woman present. 'We are all, all of us, equally proud of them. It thrills us to read the stories.' They were nodding their agreement on the Government front bench, it seemed that he was reaching out for the common ground. He had, after all, been an appeaser, he hadn't wanted this war either. Yet he was reaching out only for their throats. 'All the more shame, then, that we should have made fools of them.'

The pack began to growl at him, tried to intimidate him, but he had been far too long in this place to care. He brushed aside their interventions.

'Everybody knows that what was done was done half-heartedly. Ineffectively. Without drive, and unintelligently. For three or four years I thought to myself that the facts with regard to Germany were being exaggerated by the First Lord' – he wagged a bony finger in the direction of Churchill – 'because the Prime Minister told us they were not true.' He shook his head in sorrow, his white hair falling like a shroud about his face. 'But the First Lord was right.'

Churchill, sitting beside Chamberlain, steadfastly examined his socks. The old Welshman was handing out compliments as though offering grubs to fish; years of experience had taught Churchill that, when it came to Lloyd George, there was usually a barb hidden in there somewhere.

'Then came the war,' the old statesman continued. 'The tempo was hardly speeded up. There was the same leisureliness and inefficiency. Will anybody tell me that he is satisfied with what we have done?' His eyes roved around the House, challenging them, demanding a response. 'Is *anybody* here satisfied with the steps we took?'

No one would take him on.

'So, nobody is satisfied. The whole world knows that. And here we are, in the worst strategic position in which this country has ever been placed.'

Chamberlain, seated at Churchill's side, slapped his knee with irritation, and Lloyd George saw the sign of weakness in his old foe. He pounced.

'The Prime Minister is right when he says we must face this challenge as a people and not as a party, not as a *personal* issue. So the Prime Minister has no right to make his personality inseparable from the interests of the country.'

'What do you mean?' Chamberlain snapped. 'I did

no such thing. Personality ought to have no place in these matters.' Other objections were hurled from the Government benches, to which Lloyd George responded with nothing more than a smile until their fury had been spent and he could be heard once more. His voice rose to the ancient timbers of the roof.

'The Prime Minister said: "I have got my friends." Yes, he has got his friends. But it's not a question of who are the Prime Minister's *friends*,' he mocked. 'It is a far bigger issue than that.' From a distance of no more than a few feet, Lloyd George caught Chamberlain's eye and held it as a hook holds a leaping salmon. 'The Prime Minister must remember that he has met this formidable foe of ours in peace and in war. He has always been worsted. He is in no position to appeal on the grounds of *friendship*. He has appealed for sacrifice. The nation is prepared for sacrifice – so long as it has *leadership*.'

Now the Welshman's voice had dropped, grown soft once more, sad, like a lover's farewell. 'I say solemnly that the Prime Minister should give an example of sacrifice, because there is nothing which can contribute more to victory in this war' – and here a breath, a pause, a fraction of time which seemed endless while they waited for the words – 'than that he should sacrifice his seals of office.'

The old man was finished, so unsteady that several hands had to help him regain his seat. There were no helping hands for Chamberlain.

And so it continued. Hours of torture. The Government swung like a man in a noose, legs kicking in desperation, slowly dying. For many it was a hideous sight and they sought refuge in the bars, killing their pain. Yet as ten o'clock approached, they were all back in their places. One final rescue attempt was about to be launched. The case for clemency and for cutting down the prisoner was to be put by none other than Winston Churchill himself.

Churchill sat back against the leather bench and smiled wistfully. How ironic, he thought, that he, a man who had been accused of ratting and re-ratting all his political life, should have jumped aboard a ship that was so clearly foundering. He had spent most of the last two days listening to the debate and there was no doubt that this ship of state was listing so perilously that it would require no more than the gentlest of ill-winds to push it over. He had watched as the Tory Whips had moved among the Government benches, urging, imploring, at times impugning, but few would help man the pumps and those who did, like Croft, would have helped more simply by jumping overboard.

They all knew his position was faintly absurd, that Chamberlain and his Ministers should be defended by a man they had shunned, a man they had kept out of office for so many years and who had perhaps so much to gain from their failure. Temptation enough for most men to pull their punches, but the House was to discover once again what it already knew. Winston Churchill was quite unlike most men.

It was already past ten. The last Opposition speaker, Alexander, was drawing to a close and ridiculing the Prime Minister's appeal to friendship, as so many others had done. Damn his friendship, what of victory, he demanded? What of the years of folly based on endless ignorance? And Churchill had less than an hour to pick up the pieces. They were all looking at him, every one of them knowing that in his heart Churchill agreed with almost every word of criticism that had been hurled at the Government.

It was almost time. Alexander was mounting one final and deeply personal assault upon the Prime Minister. Chamberlain was seated beside his First Lord, shoulder to shoulder, and so cold Churchill could feel it even through the clothing. He thought the Prime Minister might be trembling – or was it he who was trembling? Always a final flush of nerves, never take this place for granted. It was a rowdy House, poured neat from the bottle, and Alexander was struggling through his final words. Churchill scribbled a line, made a final shuffle of his notes, searched nervously in his waistcoat pocket. It was the first time he had summed up a debate for a decade – a decade in which those on the Government benches around him had been his implacable foes, and those in front of him had not been the enemy but his only allies. For a moment he felt like a fighting cock confronting his own image in a mirror, confused, uncertain where or whom to attack.

No more room for doubts. He was on his feet, surveying the House, demanding its attention. As he did so, Lloyd George offered him a broad and unmistakable wink.

So Churchill began. He defended the Government's actions in Norway, not only in detail but with more eloquence than all the other Government Ministers combined, telling them of the evacuation of twelve thousand British soldiers which 'was accomplished with very great skill and, I may also add, with very good luck'. He refused to imply that a great victory had been scored; instead he spoke of results that 'were very bad and very disappointing'.

Yet through his very reason he began to establish his argument. The expedition was far from perfect, might have been better, but remember the circumstances. 'If Sweden had come to the rescue of Norway, if her troops had entered, and if her air bases had been at the disposal of the Royal Air Force, very different positions might have been established.' But what had the Swedes done instead? 'Nothing but criticize' – he gazed around him – 'like so many others.'

He explained, he castigated, painted vivid scenes with words, told them of bouquets of torpedoes, of waters where squadrons of transports might be cut to rags, of the rapacious Nazi empire of Hungryland, and brought home to them the awesome realities of combat, particularly upon the Germans.

'I said the toll on the enemy would be heavy, and heavy indeed it has been. There has been a ghastly success – seven thousand or eight thousand men have been drowned, and thousands of corpses have been washed up on the rocks at the entrance of Oslo. At the foot of the lighthouse, the most frightful scenes have been witnessed. But what does the loss of seven or eight thousand men matter to a totalitarian state? What do they matter to a Government such as that which we are fighting?'

He did not mince his words or dull his blade. Looking into the eyes of the Opposition from the distance of only a few feet, he asked what they had been doing during the very long story of these past years when he and a few others had warned of the perils that lay ahead. Where were you? he demanded. Standing alongside the Government that they now attacked – in the appeasement lobby!

But, in the same breath, he thanked them for the great and valuable aid they had given in more recent times. Like a stern parent, scolding, but making sure the infant knew of his enduring affection.

He mesmerized colleagues who had grown thin on a diet of pinched views and lean rhetoric. He made them laugh, wince, then he made them serious before lifting their spirits once more.

'In the brown hours, when baffling news comes, and disappointing news, I always turn for refreshment to the reports of the German wireless' – the words emerged hissing like steam from a locomotive. 'I love to read the lies they tell of all the British ships they have sunk – so many times over – and to survey the Fools' Paradise in which they find it necessary to keep their deluded serfs and robots. The Germans have claimed to have sunk or damaged eleven battleships.' He leaned forward on the Despatch Box, as though confiding in them. 'Actually, two have been slightly damaged – neither of them withdrawn for a day from the service.' Then he shook his head as though imparting grave news. 'We have, unhappily, lost eleven trawlers in the Government service at one time or another – and that explains all these "battleships" in the German accounts!'

And while he twisted and turned their emotions like battle flags in the wind, they played into his hands. Some Scottish Labour Members, clearly the worse for excitement which they had attempted to subdue in whisky, began to interrupt him, rising unsteadily to hurl irrelevant points of order at him just as he was dealing with losses to the British and French merchant marine. And when he scolded them, they tried to suggest that he had sworn at them and used unparliamentary language. Yet every sober and sentient being in that place knew that Churchill had been using words the like of which had rarely before been heard in this place. Most on the Labour side writhed in embarrassment, almost every man and woman in the House was with him. So he turned to the most important issue of the moment, the Vote of Censure.

The Labour Party he dismissed as nothing more than opportunistic mongrels – there were no votes to be gathered in on those benches. It was on the benches of his own side that this issue would be resolved, and he turned to face them, leaning on his elbow.

'Exception has been taken because the Prime Minister has appealed to his friends. Well, he thought he had some friends, and I hope he has some friends.' He tried to catch their eyes, measuring their individual mettle. Not all of them would return his stare. 'He certainly had a good many friends when things were going well,' Churchill observed, goading them one by one.

But the clock was ticking, almost eleven, his time was running out. He turned to face the whole House.

'Let me say,' he told them, 'that I am not advocating controversy. We have stood it for the last two days, and if I have broken out, it is not because I mean to seek a quarrel with Honourable Gentlemen. On the contrary, I say, let pre-war feuds die: let personal quarrels be forgotten, and let us keep our hatreds for the common enemy. Let party interest be ignored, let all our energies be harnessed, let the whole ability and forces of the nation be buried into the struggle, and let all the strongest horses be pulling on the collar . . .'

The rhetoric was, perhaps, beginning to get the better of him, but almost no one could hear as the tumult around him rose at the end of the most momentous debate any of those present had ever witnessed. Churchill's arm was waving, conducting to the last, until above the cacophony could be heard the voice of the Speaker.

'The Question is: "That this House do now adjourn." All those as are of that opinion say "Aye" . . .'

Aye, they roared.

'To the contrary.'

And the noise in response was deafening.

'Clear the Lobbies!' the Speaker commanded.

And so they divide, and are divided. Men and women, Tories, Liberals, Labour, the tapsters and the men of conscience. A whole nation will divide on this night, some of them old friends who will never speak to each other again, and some of them young men who are soon to die.

They crush together, intense, intoxicated, those

filled with passion and others motivated by nothing more than a sense of confusion through which the Whips have helped guide them. False smiles, smiles of courage and confidence, are exchanged amongst Ministers. But no one is certain. Chamberlain knows his support will be diminished, yet with a majority of more than two hundred he has fat enough to spare. After Munich, some twenty of his own men had abstained, not a single one had voted against him. How much worse can it get?

Behind him, good loyalists like Dickie rise from their trenches to do battle on his behalf. 'Typical bloody Winston,' Dickie complains, 'can never tell whose side he's on. Half of it complete bollocks. Scarcely understood a word at times.'

'But magnificent words nonetheless,' Ian replies.

'Can't fight a war with words, Ian.'

'Then what shall we fight with?'

Dickie's brow furrows in incomprehension. Perhaps he has misheard in the crush. 'Whips tell me that some of our chaps will actually vote against us. Can you believe that? In time of war? Bloody shooting offence.'

'How many?'

'Oh, not enough, if you're worried. Can't be that many fools in the Tory Party. Whips think the majority'll be well over a hundred. I say well over a hundred and fifty.'

'How sure are you?'

'Put ten pounds on it. Interested?'

But Ian shakes his head. It does not deter Dickie. As they mingle on the crowded floor of the Commons waiting to file into the Division Lobbies, he finds other colleagues willing to lay bets on the outcome.

They begin to make their way towards the doors which lead into the Division Lobbies. Very quickly it becomes apparent that, unlike Munich, many in the Conservative cause are now intent not on simply abstaining but on actively voting against their Government. One MP joins the file that leads through the Opposition lobby; it is the first time in his life he has voted against his own side. He is in tears.

As more Tories join the Opposition ranks, the cries of 'Quislings!' and 'Rats!' follow them. Yet as the confusion of a crowded House begins to sort itself through, their number seems to grow. Most visible amongst the rebels are those in military uniform – not just Admiral Keyes, but a brigadier-general and also colonels and captains and majors and wing-commanders. Almost every serving officer in the House is voting against the Government. Some of them are giving the last vote they will ever give. Joining them are those, like Amery and Harold Macmillan and Duff Cooper and Hore-Belisha, who over the years have been spurned by the Prime Minister. Their moment for retribution is at hand. Revenge will be taken as a feast.

Yet even as they file through to vote, Chamberlain's goblins are at work, grabbing elbows, whispering in ears, suggesting that the Prime Minister will see them the following day, is about to reconstruct the Government, that he understands their concerns – and their ambitions. That one final act of loyalty will be enough to propel them into ministerial office. The Chief Whip has his arms around the shoulder of one Member even as he is about to enter the Opposition Lobby. He puts forward arguments, offers inducements, but to no avail. Then, on the very threshold, a name is whispered, that of a young woman who is far too young to be the Member's wife and far too exotic to be his daughter. The Member turns, there is a nervous tic at the corner of his mouth. He looks into the eyes of his Chief Whip, and tells him that at least the Nazis are honest. They herd the Jews through the doors with rifles and bayonets. Right now I'd rather be a Jew in Germany than walk behind you, he says. Then he turns his back and continues on his way.

Dickie is encouraged by a colleague to double the size of the bet they have just agreed, but he declines. Too many from his side of the House seem to be disappearing into the wrong Lobby. 'Judas! Rot in hell!' he shouts as a familiar form disappears through the wrong door. They shuffle forward. Ian's head hangs in exhaustion.

'Time to show them what loyalty's all about,' Dickie mutters as at last they reach the point of no return. 'Eh, Ian?'

Suddenly Ian's head is up, meeting his old friend's eye. 'Goodbye,' he says. Then he turns his back.

Ian is one of forty-one Members on the Government side who vote against Chamberlain. In addition, more than sixty abstain, yet still it is not enough to overcome the mountainous majority of more than two hundred that the Prime Minister holds. As the Whips line up before the Speaker to announce the result, the Government tellers stand to the right – the traditional place of victory.

For the Government – 281. For the Opposition – 200.

A majority shrivelled to eighty-one.

Chamberlain has won the vote, but in doing so has lost every shred of credibility. His moral authority hangs on him in rags.

Stupefaction fills the air, which is almost too heavy to breathe. Then a chant begins to rise, one or two voices at first but it spreads like a plague and soon it has swept through half the House. 'Go! Go! Go! Go!' they are shouting. Even on the Government side, feet can be heard pounding in time to the chant. Harold Macmillan, who has just voted against his own Prime Minister, gets to his feet and through the tumult begins to sing 'Rule Britannia'. Screams of abuse are hurled at him from his own side, and before he can finish he is physically hauled back into his seat.

Chamberlain is the first to leave. He looks thoughtful and sad. As he makes his way to the door his supporters rise and cheer him, but they stop as soon as he disappears.

Twenty months earlier he had returned from Munich and been greeted as a messiah. Now, outside in the dark, there are no crowds to cheer him. There is nothing but endless shadow. He is on his own.

'Max! Glad I've found you. Could do with a little help.'

Beaverbrook's face split into a huge grin of welcome as Ball drew closer. 'Evening, Joe. And quite an evening, too.'

'Yes. Stormy waters. Need you to provide a bit of ballast. Steady the ship.'

'What did you have in mind?'

'Front page of the *Standard* tomorrow. A bit of scene setting. You know, how the country needs Neville's experience more than ever. How the rebels are doing Goebbels's job for him.'

'I see.'

'Give a lead to the others. Steady nerves, cool brows. The usual stuff. Before they start to panic.'

Beaverbrook drew on his cigar and examined the glowing tip. 'They're already panicking, Joe.'

'All the more reason to calm them. Pour oil on troubled waters.'

'Seems to me Neville's not in troubled waters but in deep shit. Right up to his wing collar.'

'Meaning?'

'I don't see the point of jumping in after him.'

'For God's sake, you're not joining them, are you?'

The press man shrugged. 'Hey, today's rebels, tomorrow's rulers.'

'After all we've done for you.'

Slowly, and with a growl: 'What – exactly – have you done for me?'

'Given you the sort of access and stories your competitors would give their right testicle for.'

More cigar smoke. 'Joe, my old friend, I see it entirely the other way round. It's me who's been giving you – front pages, editorial columns, opinion pieces extolling your non-existent virtues and attacking everyone you didn't like. Seems to me I've already done my bit.'

'One last push, Max, that's all I ask.'

'And one last push is all it's likely to take, Joe. Neville's as good as dead.'

A pause riddled with uncertainty. 'So . . . what are you planning to do?'

'Consider my options. Very carefully.'

'You can't mean Winston. Whatever you do, don't think Winston. He's up to no good, Max.'

'Tonight I thought he was terrific.'

'But he's up to something, Max.' Ball bit his lip, uncertain how far he should go. 'All sorts of questions coming through about his money. It's dirty.'

'Same thing could be said of half the Cabinet. You dig deep enough and you'll uncover all kinds of skeletons. Your Government's squatting on a damned graveyard.'

'But Winston's pushing to be PM. Number One. We can't have him in Downing Street and not know where he gets his money from.'

'He doesn't get it from me, Joe, that I promise. Not any longer. I fired him, remember? At your suggestion.' Beaverbrook examined the other man while he ground out the stub of his cigar until it was nothing but scraps. 'Just one of many things I suspect I'm going to live to regret.'

TWENTY-TWO

9 May 1940.
Churchill was the king of the night, but the nights are long in Westminster.

After the vote Chamberlain had picked his way around his colleagues' knees and withdrawn to his office immediately behind the Speaker's Chair. Even with the doors closed he could hear the uproar that was continuing outside – laughter, outrage, euphoria, open drunkenness. Inside there was nothing but emptiness. It was the emptiness and its silence that did it for him, screaming at him that it was over, that he'd have to go, tender his resignation and let someone else try to dig his way out of the stables. Yet even as his hand reached out for a tumbler of whisky he found other voices in the night, urging him to hold fast, to wait and see how the pieces fell, even to continue pushing at a few pieces himself. It wasn't simply the humiliation of rebellion that angered Chamberlain – disloyalty, after all, is scarcely novel to any leader – but what seemed to grate inside until it made him raw was the contrast that had been created by Churchill's dazzling performance, more pantomime than parliamentary, which if it had been designed to show up the rest of them could not have been delivered to more telling effect. Bloody Winston at it again, performing his own play. A man they could never truly trust.

Yet a majority of eighty-one was just that. A majority. Many Prime Ministers had survived on less – a point which Wilson and Ball hammered home when at last they arrived. Resignation, they insisted, was simply not an option. But he was aware that they had their own interests to promote. They needed him, lived in his shadow, could never survive the full glare of daylight where they would wilt like lettuce. There were other considerations, too. If he were to go, there would be the manner of his going. If it came to that, it must be in his own way, not simply pushed out by ingratitude and music-hall posturing.

But not yet. And, extraordinarily, Churchill seemed to agree. The previous night, after the vote and hot on the heels of Ball and Wilson, Churchill had stormed into the Prime Minister's office, wafting cigar smoke and excitement, to insist that Chamberlain should carry on. Full speed ahead. No turning back. And why had he done that? What was his *real* motivation? You always wondered that about Winston. Was it just the passion of the moment, Churchill's unquenchable thirst for battle – any battle? Or was he, perhaps, trying to force Chamberlain out on a limb? So far out that he would drop? Yes, with Winston you always wondered.

Chamberlain listened to others, and plotted his own course. By the time Edward Halifax and Churchill presented themselves in the Cabinet Room the following morning, Chamberlain was able to tell them that he had determined to form a coalition

Government which he would lead. Bring in others to help shoulder the responsibility – and the blame.

'Embrace Attlee and his cohorts?' Churchill muttered, his brow creased in concern. 'Rather share my bed with fleas.'

'It's my bed we are talking about,' the Prime Minister reminded him.

'Have they indicated they would be willing?'

'Not yet.'

'And what if they won't?' he pressed.

'Then I suppose it must be someone else. You or Edward,' Chamberlain replied.

Somehow the creases of concern seemed to disappear, and in Chamberlain's eye there was no mistaking how much brighter Churchill's brow seemed to grow with the news.

Damn him.

Burgess hadn't made it to bed that night. He'd been trying to drown his anxiety by celebrating 'The Downfall' with Driberg. After a series of increasingly lurid toasts he had made it only as far as his over-stuffed armchair. Now he woke with the bells of Armageddon thundering in his ear, a shirt that stared back at him in disbelief and a bladder that threatened to relieve him of the last vestiges of his dignity. The bells were still ringing even after he had relieved himself. Someone must want him very badly.

He picked up the insistent telephone and shouted something very rude, hoping it might be his stepfather, who was a steadfast Chamberlain man.

But it was Mac, who told him he needed a shave – insisted on it. And there was something in his tone which told Burgess that his morning of celebration was finished before it had even begun.

Everyone knew Leo Amery had been made bitter by disappointment, explained Wilson. Relieve him of his disappointment and suddenly he would remember that Cromwell was nothing more than a passing demagogue, a tyrant whose body had been dragged from its grave and its head stuck on a pike until it rotted, warts and all.

'Let's raise his sights,' Wilson encouraged.

'How far?' his Prime Minister enquired.

'As high as is necessary. If we can get Amery to climb on board the others might follow.'

'And if not?'

Wilson had no answer for that. And it was unusual, Chamberlain reflected, for Wilson to have no answer.

So Amery was summoned. He appeared disgruntled to find Wilson present, and discomfited to be facing his leader so soon after his mighty words had come between them.

'I meant what I said, Neville,' he began, almost before he had set foot inside the door, 'about old friends and associates. I realize it will be of little comfort to you in present circumstances, but I have never been more distressed in my parliamentary life than having to speak against you.'

Chamberlain steepled his fingers. 'Old friends and associates,' he repeated softly. 'Leo, I firmly hope that we are. And it's in that sense that I wanted to speak with you.'

He looked through the window – it was a perfect spring day. A day of renewal. As it should be. 'We have had our differences, genuine on both our parts, and nothing would please me more than if we could resolve them.'

'Certainly. But how?'

'Not with glib words, not with any sudden discarding of principle – we have both been too long at the front for that. But perhaps by working together, in the common cause, we might yet gain a better understanding of each other's point of view.'

Amery looked sharply at Wilson. These were his words, not Chamberlain's. Wilson smiled through thin lips – he was standing by the window, his back to the daylight, in silhouette, a little bent. A dark figure from a children's fairy tale, Amery thought.

'I hope to construct a new Government, Leo, in the common cause. A Government of all the parties and all the talents.' A pause while it sank in, waiting for a reaction. 'I would like it to include your talents, too.'

'In what capacity?'

'What capacity would you like?'

'Depends what's available.'

Chamberlain looked at Wilson before replying.

'Everything is available.'

'Everything?'

'Anything beyond this desk.'

'Air Secretary. Home Secretary,' Wilson added for clarification, trying to pitch it right.

'Chancellor? Foreign Secretary?' Amery pressed, raising the stakes.

A long silence. Chamberlain looked once more towards Wilson.

'Do I take it that the Foreign Secretary's post might be available?'

'If needs be.'

'And Halifax?'

'He repeated to me less than two hours ago that I have his complete support.'

'And less than two hours later you offer up his job . . .'

'These are hard times, Leo.'

'And how hard will the times have to get before in turn you offer up my job?'

'I'm sure it would never come to that . . .'

Amery remained silent for a while, until the silence began to hurt. Indecision? Calculation? Amery's face revealed nothing.

'What are you thinking, Leo?'

'I was wondering, Prime Minister, how you could so misjudge a man. And so misjudge a country.'

Then he turned and left, dragging Chamberlain's dreams behind him.

Burgess examined himself in the mirror. He looked awful. 'Mac, I'm sorry.'

'So, I suspect, is your liver.'

'We can't all survive on half a pint of bloody mild, you know.'

'So long as we survive, sir.'

Survival. It had come down to that, hadn't it? All

615

the idealism and nobility had at last been shoved aside as the world focused on only one thing. Survival. And Mac was giving him a hard time about his bloody shirt.

'Look, I was up all night wandering around Westminster, watching history being made.'

'Bit like a bed, is history. One minute it's made, next minute it's an awful mess.'

'What are you going on about? Why the hell am I here?'

So Mac told him of his morning's work on two customers. One had said he'd been offered the job of Secretary of State for Air, and promptly fallen asleep. So a reshuffle was in the offing, a last desperate throw of the dice.

'Won't work,' Burgess concluded defiantly. 'Chamberlain's got to go.'

'Which is what made the other customer so interesting. A senior Whip, he was, hadn't slept. Like you, in desperate need of a bit of smartening up. So how is our Mr Chamberlain? I asked him. Been up all night trying to save him, he replied. Then he said: "A complete bloody waste of time. Party's full of incomparable cretins."'

'Told you so. Chamberlain's for the taxidermy department.'

'So I told him how sorry I was to hear that, and asked if we might be seeing more of Mr Churchill. Hold your chin up, please, Mr Burgess.'

Mac tilted the chin up with a finger in order to expose the neck, and started scraping.

'So what did he say?' Burgess demanded through gritted teeth.

'Not a lot, sir. But thought it was interesting. That's why I had to call you. For which I apologize.'

'Don't apologize, just bloody explain.'

'He sat just where you're sitting. Neck up in the air like a Christmas turkey. Had a bit of trouble making out what he was saying, to be honest. But I think I got it.'

Burgess could do little more than grunt in frustration.

'But I think he said Mr Churchill would become Prime Minister over his dead body.'

Churchill was taking his regular afternoon nap at the Admiralty when the phone rang. Had to be something important, his staff had strict instructions otherwise. Wanted at Downing Street, he was told. The pace was hotting up. He dressed quickly and strode across the parade ground at Horse Guards, the gravel crunching beneath his feet, his silver-topped stick flying out in front of him. Marching towards the sound of gunfire.

He still felt the effects of his amusing lunch. Carlton Grill. A splendid occasion full of dark humour and outrage, entirely worthy of such a day. Kingsley Wood had been insistent that Churchill should give him a little time, and such had been his passion that Churchill found himself feeling not so much imposed upon as intrigued. Wood was normally a man of endeavour rather than outrage, the type who formed the backbone of the party, an unimaginative loyalist who as Secretary of State for Air held one of the key posts in the Government – at least, so Wood himself had thought until he had discovered that his prized Cabinet post had been offered to others on at least three separate occasions since ten o'clock that morning. Through mouthfuls of bloodied beef and horseradish he had grown incandescent, the veins on his temple matching the colour of the wine. Churchill found himself in the unusual position of being reduced to the role of spectator, so he sat, ate and watched the Prime Minister's support being carried away on a tide of injury and excellent claret. He couldn't deny that he had rather enjoyed the experience.

And now a summons. The policeman at the door offered a crisp salute and – was it Churchill's imagination? – an extra broad smile. The staff always seemed to be the first to know. Churchill continued his march down the long corridor that led from the front hall to the Cabinet Room. He was just about to reach for the polished brass handle when, as if from nowhere, Horace Wilson appeared at his elbow.

'My dear Winston, a moment of your time?'

Wilson had a disagreeable habit of making his requests sound like papal edicts. Churchill was about to pull rank and excuse himself on the grounds that the Prime Minister came first and in any event Wilson was an irritating office junior, but it would have been a pointless gesture. Downing Street was a magical fortress, a castle of intrigue, and Wilson was its ferocious gatekeeper. Not even one of Goering's thousand-pounders could get to Chamberlain without first obtaining clearance from Wilson, so it was said, and today was not the day for Churchill to kick over the established order, not when so many others were doing it for him. Puffing smoke, he followed Wilson into his gatekeeper's lodge. He found Ball already there.

'Problem, Winston,' Wilson began after Churchill had taken a seat in one of the low armchairs. Wilson leant against the mantelpiece, ensuring that he towered over the other man. Churchill, encased in the leather arms, suddenly felt stuck. He offered no more than a grunt in reply.

'Guns,' continued Wilson.

'Guns?'

'Yes, you know, the things you shoot people with?'

Churchill had never cared for Wilson. He liked men of passion, of exuberance, even men of occasional folly, but Wilson was altogether much too self-contained, a civil servant to the core. Cut him and you'd find nothing but ink. 'Don't bugger around with me, Horace, I'm not in the mood for it and I've got a lot to do. What bloody guns?'

'Four hundred thousand rifles.'

'Ah, those. Been waiting to be collected for a week or more.'

'Mausers.'

'When are you going to pay for them?'

'*German* Mausers.'

'Snatched from under the nose of the enemy.'

'Did you ever pause to think, Winston?'

'Think? About what?'

'Why the Germans would let you have four hundred thousand of their newest rifles?'

Churchill glowered from his seat. 'What are you trying to say?'

'It's not what *I* want to say, it's what others will

say if ever they hear of this . . .' – he searched for the words – 'extraordinary affair.' He paused to light a cigarette, chasing the smoke away with a slowly flapping hand. 'Did you ever consider that the enemy might know about it – *must* know about it? And why they would let you continue with it? The whole of the Western Front is buzzing with agents and spies, and into that cauldron you sent – who? Boothby? Not a trained agent or negotiator, merely a – well, in all honesty, merely a parliamentary crony of yours. A notorious drunk. And, incidentally, a sworn opponent of the Prime Minister. Voted in the Opposition Lobby last night. Nothing clearer than that. And you expect people to believe he went to Europe to help Neville's cause?'

'Some very fine men voted in that Lobby last night.'

'So you say. So we would expect you to say. After all, it's only a matter of office that kept you out of it yourself.'

Churchill's clenched fists pounded the arms of his chair. 'How dare you! What in blazes are you trying to suggest?'

'I dare,' said Wilson softly, 'because others will dare.'

'What – *others*?'

'Berlin, for God's sake!' Ball snapped, joining in at last, reminding Churchill that he was outnumbered. 'Anyone who wants to do the British cause harm. Boothby trampled around the German border like a hog through bamboo. Everybody heard him, all the way to Amsterdam. They were waiting for him.'

620

'With four hundred thousand brand-new Mausers? I scarcely think so.'

'You don't think for one moment we'll get them, do you? We might pay for them, of course, get a few crates as a first shipment. Then Goebbels will release his dogs. Announce that he's made fools of the British yet again. Duped them into a desperate bid to buy Nazi rifles – and why? Because Nazi rifles are the best – even Winston Churchill says so. And because the British are weak, haven't got enough weapons of their own. He'll play it like a fiddle in every neutral country in Europe.'

'You can't be certain –'

'Certain enough to give you Boothby's itinerary for every hour he spent on the continent,' Ball spat back. 'Every place he visited. Every seedy little railway room and hotel corridor he prowled doing your business. *Your* business, Winston. Which is something else Dr Goebbels is likely to pick up on.'

'What has that club-footed degenerate got to do with me?'

'Winston, Winston,' Wilson sighed, intervening again as patronizingly as he could. 'Think about it. Out of Government you were Neville's fiercest critic. In Government you have been his biggest thorn. You are the country's most ambitious and, many would say, most reckless politician. The makings of a dictator – even some of your own Admiralty staff say so. You send a renowned opponent of the Prime Minister abroad to buy German arms – without discussing it with any of your colleagues first.'

'Action! Action this day!'

'Yes. But you can see how it might look. Wouldn't

need a master of propaganda like Goebbels to make mischief with that. He'd have you walking in the Fuehrer's footsteps before the first crate had been unwrapped.'

'You cannot believe I could be capable of treachery . . .' Churchill insisted, his voice cracking with passion.

Wilson paused. Treachery? They would know, very shortly, in a few hours, perhaps. Where he had got his money from. But until then . . .

'Of course not. But others would, all over Europe. And perhaps quite a few in this country, too. The madness of the Churchills, they would say.' He'd been waiting to use those words, knowing that if ever he could talk of such things in Churchill's presence then the argument was already won. He watched his victim writhe with misery in his chair. Churchill was panting, short of breath as though he'd been kicked in the stomach. He hadn't been prepared for this. Of course he hadn't discussed it, but neither had he made a secret of it, even asked the Treasury to pay for the damned things. But they'd been stalling. Now he thought he understood why.

Ball cut through his misery. 'If a word of this gets out, you'll be ruined, Winston.'

Churchill hadn't seen it like this before, hadn't even thought of such possibilities – yes, hadn't thought it through, had rushed ahead, borne along by the excitement and passion of war, like a cavalry charge, only to find himself entirely cut off and surrounded. As a young man in such circumstances he would have let forth a great yell and charged, content to die in the heat of battle. But he was no longer young and he didn't want to die, not yet. And not in this way, not sliced to the meanest of slivers by tongues rather than by swords.

'Who . . . knows of this?' Churchill asked with difficulty, as though his jaw had been severely broken.

'All of it? Only a handful,' Wilson replied. 'And Neville has told them all, face to face, that it must go no further.'

'No one doubts your abilities in fighting and winning this war, Winston,' Ball added, 'so long as you remember who the enemy is.'

'The Prime Minister is very mindful of your loyalty to him in recent months.'

'Then I am . . .' – Churchill was about to say 'his hostage', but the words would not come – 'as always, overwhelmed with gratitude.'

Churchill found his way to the Cabinet Room through a mist of confusion and despair. Halifax was already there, the Chief Whip, too.

'Ah, Winston,' he heard Chamberlain greet him as though from a profound distance. He heard more words. About Chamberlain's continuing hopes of re-forming his Government as a coalition. But also about inevitable difficulties. Of being prepared for the worst – 'the worst' appearing to mean any Government other than his.

'There is one point of considerable relevance,' Chamberlain was saying in his clipped, prissy voice. 'As we all know, there are some who have put Edward's name forward as a potential successor . . .'

Even in despair, Churchill found his brain digesting the red meat that was being thrown to him. *So, the idea of a Chamberlain coalition is sinking even as they try to launch it. No surprise there.*

'There are also some who suggest that his position in the House of Lords would make this difficult. Remove him from the centre of the stage, as it were. It is, after all, nearly forty years since we last had a peer as Prime Minister . . .'

Chamberlain was playing with his pen, turning it over and over. His fingers seemed stiff, awkward, those of an old man. Or was it simply Churchill's mind that had suddenly grown clumsy?

'Quite irrespective of other names I might put forward, Winston,' the Prime Minister was saying, 'I need your thoughts. If events dictate that I must recommend to His Majesty that he should call upon someone else to form a Government, would a seat in the House of Lords be an automatic bar?'

So, he wants Halifax, but isn't sure he can manage it from the Lords. Wants my approval. Wants Churchill to say it's not a problem, so no one else can say it's a problem. Yet if I say it is *a problem, I will be branded the most ungracious of colleagues, the most self-serving of men. A man who would say or stoop to anything to meet his ambition of becoming Prime Minister. A man who would . . .* Suddenly he had an image of Horace Wilson. His thin face with the lizard-like eyes was laughing at him. And as he laughed, as his mouth came open and the teeth were exposed, the face slowly transformed itself into that of Josef Goebbels. The same, soulless mask . . . And he was waving a brand-new Mauser rifle.

From somewhere in the distance, Churchill could hear a voice talking about a cardinal constitutional issue. Asking to know whether he could think of any reasons why a peer's name should not be considered. Putting him to the test. With the Chief Whip as witness. But all he could think of was guns, hundreds of thousands of them. And why a man as grotesquely incompetent as Chamberlain could have presided for so long over so much folly. Why ineptitude had flourished while a Churchill was once again to be denied the role for which he had been born, for no better reason than the jealousies and intrigues of lesser men. The Churchills' fatal flaw. To be too good for the job.

He couldn't give an answer. Then he found himself in the garden, with Halifax. Drinking tea. Being civil. So terribly English.

Thank God it was a quiet day for war. There were endless meetings. The front door of Downing Street swung on its hinges so many times that the doorman told his wife it was like running a brothel in Marrakesh. And everything at the rush. No sooner had their tea begun to cool than Halifax and Churchill were summoned back to the Cabinet Room, where they found Attlee and another senior Labour figure, Greenwood, sitting opposite the Prime Minister. Few formalities, no small-talk. Chamberlain stiffened. 'Will you serve in coalition under me?'

'No,' came the blunt reply.

'Why not?' Chamberlain was hurt, unaccustomed to the lack of subtlety.

'Because we don't like you, Mr Chamberlain. We detest your leadership, think it's been evil,' they said.

In other circumstances, Churchill might have enjoyed this joust, but not now. There could be only one winner of this tumble. Halifax.

The Labour Party was a beast burdened by its own overdeveloped sense of fair play. Revolution had to be pursued strictly by the rule book; after all, if you were going to ransack the pockets of the rich, it was only fair that it be carried out in a systematic and orderly fashion. So the Labour leaders informed Chamberlain that they were only giving their personal opinions, and they would have to consult their party executive for a formal decision. By chance, the executive was gathering in Bournemouth for the start of the party's annual conference. 'But take it from me,' Attlee said, 'Hell will freeze before they agree to serve under you.'

'Then someone else, perhaps,' Chamberlain had offered mournfully.

It was gone seven before Churchill and Chamberlain found themselves alone. How rarely, Churchill thought, that they had ever been alone, man to man. 'Neville, we must speak. This nonsense about the rifles,' he began, but Chamberlain's hand waved him into silence – no need to explain, no desire for an explanation, either.

The Prime Minister expressed his sorrow for the confusion: 'You must see how this might be made to look, Winston. But I for my part have never had cause to doubt where your loyalties lie.'

'Neville, something I must ask. All this has been a rude shock. Such an unexpected blow. But still . . .

If events were to conspire to propel my name to the fore once more as your successor, would you stand in my way – refuse to recommend my name to His Majesty?'

'Why, of course not,' Chamberlain lied. 'But I'm afraid the control of events is now out of my hands. The general view is that the Labour Party must be brought in around the Cabinet table and they have already made it clear they will not tolerate me. I fear they will say much the same about you. You gave them such a terrible pasting in the House last night, your mockery is still ringing in their ears.'

'All that I did, I did in your name, Neville.'

'And for that you have my undying gratitude. But tonight, Winston, it seems that we shall both be sitting alongside our fathers. Men of broken dreams.'

In every corner, in every crevice of political life that night, there was conspiracy. At the Carlton Club, at the Beefsteak and Travellers, in both Houses of Parliament, in all the salons and saloons of Westminster, they plotted and argued until it became clear that Chamberlain was already as good as gone. Yet who was to replace him?

The name of Lloyd George was mentioned in some quarters, but only to be quickly dismissed as too absurdly romantic. In any event he was too old. Some talked, too, of Leo Amery, but only his friends. The clear popular choice was Churchill, the man of the people whose pugnacity had persuaded a nation to fight the war and whose words had given them the will to win it. Yes, Churchill was undoubtedly the people's choice, but it was not the people who would decide. At the end of the matter it would be the voices of no more than a hundred men that would be decisive, men of authority and power – and all of whom, it seemed, had at one time or another been crossed by Winston Churchill.

The Conservative Party were traditionalists, men who put form before substance. They would not forget that as a young man Churchill had deserted them and joined Lloyd George and his Liberals, and even in his old age he still hadn't lost his passion for showering them in mud.

Many in the Labour Party, too, remembered the long and tortuous route of Churchill's career. The Home Secretary who had sent in troops to break the General Strike. The Chancellor of the Exchequer who had returned the country to the gold standard and so helped bring hunger to the doorstep of millions. The imperialist, the instinctive parliamentary pugilist. The man who couldn't meet a Socialist without raising his kneecap in welcome. The man they feared. There were those in the Labour Party who loathed the thought of an hereditary aristocrat like Halifax taking the reins, yet on reflection – not all of it sober – many of them concluded it would perhaps be excellent if the Tories had a Prime Minister locked up in the Lords. Yes, let the Tories leap back a hundred years, and leave the future to Socialism.

Joe Kennedy, too, was part of the piece. He could be seen in his chauffeur-driven car circling Fleet Street with a bottle of iced champagne under his arm, muttering the name of Halifax in every editorial ear. Don't risk Winston, he warned, and don't expect America to pull your fingers out of the fire . . .

All these voices were raised for only one purpose – to recommend to His Majesty, King George, someone whom at his pleasure he might ask to become Prime Minister. But, when it came to it, George wasn't very interested in their recommendation. He'd already made up his mind. If his good friend Chamberlain had to lay down the seals of office, then he knew who he wanted to pick them up. His still greater friend, Edward Halifax.

The King and noble courtier met, by arrangement, that evening in the gardens of Buckingham Palace as Halifax walked on his way back home. No one else to see, entirely private. One friend to another.

'Edward, I think the time has come.'

'In all honesty, sir, I seem to be less certain about the matter than almost anyone I speak to.'

'You are too modest.'

'You know me better than that.'

'Then what?'

'It's simply . . . I'm not sure I'm up to the task.'

'What? Of being Prime Minister? A man of your experience?'

'Oh, being Prime Minister would be a joy, an honour, a task I would embrace with relish, but we are talking of something quite different.'

'Different?'

'Being a war leader, sir. I hate war. I don't understand its means and I'm confused by its morality. For all his faults, I believe Winston might be the man.'

629

'Because he has no morality whatsoever!'

'Perhaps. But morally these are the most mean of times. And Winston has a burning desire inside to do the job while I . . . I burn inside with uncertainty.'

'Good grief, Edward, you're a man who ruled India as Viceroy. Who's become one of the greatest Foreign Secretaries of all time. Who has my trust and the trust of all decent men. I can think of no one better to lead us through these times.'

'But even so . . .'

'Duty, Edward. We cannot shrug off our duty, no matter how at times we might wish otherwise. Your duty, Edward, is much like mine . . .' A pause. 'Anyway, there are other considerations.'

'Such as?'

'How the devil could you tolerate serving under that man?'

Burgess was beginning to panic. Ever since he had left Mac's chair, he'd spent the hours scurrying around Westminster, lurking in its many corners and listening to the sounds of history being rearranged. Even a deaf man could hear the pieces beginning to fall off the Chamberlain Government, but you needed a keener ear to detect the stirrings of what might replace it. The Whip in Mac's chair had evidently meant it – over his dead body – and everywhere bodies were being piled into the breach to prevent the advance of Winston Churchill. His unsound judgement, his undeniable failures, and above all the fact that he was not 'one of us'.

Churchill owed most of them nothing. And that's precisely what they feared they would get.

As the day lengthened and the speculation was reinforced by alcohol and uncertainty, so their insecurities grew more lurid. By early evening, Burgess found himself in the Strangers' Bar listening to a journalist who was proclaiming to all around that Churchill's father hadn't died of syphilis at all but from some inherited condition of madness that had been handed down to his son. It was why all his appetites were indulged to excess – why he drank, why he gambled, why he prowled the Admiralty late at night, dragging the Chiefs of Staff behind him, why his notorious temper was growing ever more corrosive, and why Clemmie had left him. Yes, at this decisive juncture in Churchill's life, even his loyal wife had fled. Where she was, no one seemed to know, and if anyone had heard that her brother-in-law was dying and she had gone to sit by his deathbed, then none cared to say so. They believed such nonsense largely because they wanted to. And because in so much of it there was an acorn of truth. Churchill had never been an easy bedfellow.

And so Burgess grew ever more alarmed. Events were at the melting point and it seemed that every man's hands were on the bellows other than his own, and he couldn't even get near the action. For the first time in his life he began to envy those friends who'd gone off to fight in the civil war in Spain, even those who'd been buried there. At least they had played their part. But he had been marked out to fight a different war. Not for him the simple fulfilment of picking up a rifle and aiming it at the enemy. His enemies were all around him, right at his elbow, yet all he could do was smile and buy them another bloody drink while they closed in.

He didn't know what to do, so with little idea of any purpose had gone in search of Churchill. But Churchill was not to be found – didn't want to be found. The closest Burgess got was to discover Bracken and Boothby on the far reaches of the terrace of the House of Commons where it overlooked the river. The night was chill, lit only by a crescent moon, but they took no notice of the cold. Bracken was even in his shirtsleeves. Both he and Boothby were extraordinarily drunk.

Bracken was stumbling up and down, shouting at his colleague with a savageness that comes only from alcohol and fear. It was *his* fault, Bracken was shouting, the most monumental of blunders, the stupidity of Sodom. Boothby didn't demur. He sat at a wooden table with his head bowed, jowls on his waistcoat, moving only to drink. Bracken's arms flailed the night air and at one point it seemed as though he was about to strike the other man, but it was only the prelude to yet another outpouring of Boothby's shortcomings. These were Churchill's men. And they were in despair.

'I was looking for Mr Churchill,' Burgess interrupted, moving closer so they could recognize him.

'So are the hounds of Hell,' Bracken spat.

'Better you didn't find him,' Boothby added mournfully.

'What's happened?'

'*He's* happened,' Bracken stormed, waving a fist at Boothby and turning his back on them both.

'I've ruined it. Everything,' Boothby was mumbling into his glass.

'But how?'

Two dark eyes rose from the alcohol. 'That's the point. Buggered if I know. Only did as I was told. But Winston says I've bollocksed everything up. Ruined it. Never known him in such a rage. So violent. Said he was going to take the bloody Mausers and shove every one of 'em up me. Every single one of them. Can't say any more. Mustn't.' The effort seemed to have been too much for him and Boothby returned his attention to his glass.

'Mausers? I don't understand,' Burgess began, but Bracken was on him.

'Oh, so *you* don't understand. Stop the world while we take that one in. Mr Burgess doesn't understand. Understand? Who the devil are you to understand? Leaping out of shadows – what the hell are you up to, Burgess?'

'I want to help.'

'Oh, forgive me. I mistook you for one of those freeloading shits who spend their time attaching themselves to people of importance and sucking them dry. Well, about the only decent thing to have come out of this mess is the fact that you, Mr Burgess, have been wasting your damned time. You'll get nothing. No one is going to get anything, not Winston, not me, not Boothby here – and you are last on the list. Right at the very bottom.' Bracken's arm swept out dramatically in front of him, intended as a melodramatic gesture of dismissal, but he succeeded only in connecting with a bottle that stood on the parapet. It flew off into the darkness. Moments later, it splashed dully into the river below.

'I'm sorry you don't like me, Bracken . . .' Burgess continued.

'Funny. I rather enjoy not liking you.'

'But I do want to help Mr Churchill. If I can.'

'And how do you propose to do that? When Chamberlain wants Halifax. When the Whips want Halifax. When practically every spaniel in the Tory Party wants Halifax. When I suspect the blessed King and the bloody Archbishop of Canterbury want Halifax, and when it's a racing certainty that most of Fleet Street want him, too. Oh, but perhaps that doesn't matter any longer, because Mr Burgess has come to help.'

'Stop being a prick, Brendan,' Boothby growled. 'Not his fault.'

'And you know what that gormless idiot Chamberlain has done?' Bracken continued, undeterred. 'He can't make up his mind what to do – never could. So he's asked the bloody Socialists to decide for him.'

'What the hell have they got to do with it?'

'Everything! That cretin in Downing Street has asked the Labour Party to join a coalition and tell him who they'd prefer as his successor. The day after Winston tore them to shreds in the Chamber! Like asking Stalin who should be bloody Pope.' Bracken searched around for his bottle. Only slowly did he remember that it had gone. He picked up Boothby's and splashed what was left of its contents into his own glass, before sending it after the first. 'So unless you're a worker of miracles – or at least know who most of the Labour leadership are shagging on the side – there's not much you can do. So, Mr Burgess, I'd be obliged if you would do what you appear to do best, and bugger off.'

Burgess turned away – there was no point in lingering. Bracken was beyond him and Boothby seemed to be losing a private battle with coherence. He left them by the river. What was the point? He couldn't work miracles, and didn't know anything of the nocturnal practices of the Labour leadership. But as he walked away, he remembered somebody who might.

Driberg was in Bournemouth for the Labour Party conference. Burgess even knew which hotel he was staying at. But when he telephoned, Driberg wasn't there. And probably wouldn't be there until breakfast time. The most expensive hotel in the whole of Bournemouth, and he preferred to spend his nights under the bloody pier.

Bournemouth wasn't the only location where the night was full of activity. On a front that stretched more than two hundred miles, from the Dutch border near the North Sea to the forest of the Ardennes in the south, the mighty divisions of Hitler's Wehrmacht were on the move.

TWENTY-THREE

(Evening Standard, Friday 10 May 1940)

NAZIS INVADE HOLLAND, BELGIUM, LUXEMBOURG: FRENCH TOWNS BOMBED

BRITISH TROOPS MARCH: R.A.F. BASES IN FRANCE ATTACKED

Total war burst into the greatest conflagration in history to-day as Hitler smashed his way into Holland, Belgium and Luxembourg, and bombed many towns in France. Bombs were also dropped on Switzerland.

A series of simultaneous air raids was made on points in a ring around Paris. Nancy, Lille, Lyons, Colmar, Pontoise, Luxeuil, Maubeuge, Valenciennes and Villers-Cotterets were also bombed. Sixteen people were killed at Nancy alone.

Other reports say that Calais and Dunkirk were attacked. The airport at Lyons was raided for two hours.

Brussels has been 'bombed terrifically', according to a New York message. Antwerp, too, has been bombed.

Swarms of warplanes bombed all the Belgian airports and many in Holland. Parachute troops landed at many points. R.A.F. bases in France were also attacked . . .

They held the first emergency Cabinet meeting at eight. It was intended to discuss the outbreak of war across a massive front. It was also the meeting at which most of his Cabinet colleagues expected Chamberlain to announce his resignation. But he didn't. Not a mention.

Neither did he touch on the subject when they met again at eleven-thirty. The discussion was all about the future direction of the war, how they would resist the onslaught of the Hun – until someone, no one was later quite sure who, raised the far more sensitive subject of the future direction of the Government.

But Chamberlain's plans had changed. As Ball had told him earlier that morning when the first reports of the new German onslaught were coming through, every puff of artillery smoke has a silver lining.

'Government?' Chamberlain responded stiffly. 'I would have thought that such a matter would be the last concern in anyone's mind this morning. The situation seems to me to be clear. Whatever might have been the difficulties occasioned by Wednesday's vote, the German advance has rendered them all irrelevant.' He cleared his throat, betraying his nervousness. 'Wednesday was Norway. Today we are dealing with a threat of far greater enormity and much closer to home. My responsibility is to get on with the task of meeting that threat. There's a job to be done, and I intend to get on with it. In doing that I feel sure I shall enjoy the overwhelming sentiment both in Parliament and in the country. And, of course, around this table.'

He stared at them, trying to catch their eyes, but no one was looking at him, except for Winston, who seemed on the verge of tears. They sat stunned. *Taceo consentire* – in silence, consent. So, they weren't going to change horses after all, not in the middle of a stampede . . .

'Therefore, gentlemen, if we can turn to the matter in hand.'

Then someone cleared his throat. Broke that silence. Someone wanted to speak. Suddenly all heads were up, staring. It was Kingsley Wood, the Air Secretary.

'Before we proceed, Prime Minister, may I impose upon our many years of friendship?'

Chamberlain nodded his assent. Wood was a party man, a loyalist. No harm in him endorsing the sentiment. Make sure we're all rowing in the same direction. But Wood was a man who had changed – or been changed. He didn't want to row in the same direction as his leader any longer, not after he'd learnt that Chamberlain was about to toss him out of the lifeboat to appease the sharks.

'As a friend, Prime Minister, may I say . . .' – he was fiddling with his pen, eyes downcast, like Brutus with his knife – 'I disagree. Disagree as a colleague, as a member of your Cabinet, but most of all as someone who respects and admires you beyond measure. The events of this morning only emphasize the need to ensure that the changes in Government which are required are implemented all the more swiftly. This war may go on for years. If now is not the time, when will it be?'

Suddenly Chamberlain found all their eyes were on him; none were flinching. He had to speak, but for a moment couldn't find his voice. The words, when at last they appeared, had an edge like tearing sandpaper. 'Does that reflect the view of you all?' he asked slowly.

No one spoke. *Taceo consentire*. The gamble had failed.

He had known it might. That's why he had another plan.

'Edward?'

'I'm sorry, Neville, but how could I have spoken up? They know I'm your most loyal colleague. They would have discounted anything I said, seen it as self-serving, wanton.'

Chamberlain regarded his Foreign Secretary, uncertain of what he saw. A friend? A loyal lieutenant? But how far did such things stretch, what were the limits of his loyalty? They would soon discover.

But Halifax had already read his mind. 'I don't want it, Neville, not in these circumstances. I don't want to step into your shoes.'

They were sipping tea and eating a sandwich lunch in the garden. It was the most glorious of spring days, the bulbs and buds bursting forth in a competition of many colours. How ironic, Chamberlain thought, that the English sun came out only to illuminate disasters.

'Why not? Why don't you want it?' he demanded peremptorily.

'I'm not sure. Doesn't feel right. Don't think I deserve it.'

'Deserve? It's not a prize, Edward! Not some little trinket to be handed out on sports day, for God's sake. It's a damned duty. *Your* damned duty!'

'That's what the King said.'

'It's going to come to you, whether you like it or not.'

'Not Winston?'

'How can I recommend Winston?' He banged his cup and saucer down on the table. 'Even if I were forced to make way for him, how long do you think he would last? How long before he tested his liver or the patience of his colleagues to the very limits of destruction? Within a few months at most we'd be back at the starting point, looking for a new Prime Minister. Which sooner or later must be you, Edward.'

'Then let it be later.'

'Now! Today! I'm afraid the gods of war insist.'

'Even so, let it be later,' he repeated. 'Let Winston make war. Let him exhaust himself. If I am to take over, how much better it would be if Winston had already failed and had stopped tilting at every windmill.'

'And how much damage would he have done in the meantime while he turns the whole of Europe into some rerun of the horrors of Gallipoli? No, there has to be a better way – *is* a better way, Edward. You. As Prime Minister. Winston can still make war, serving under you, while you plan the peace – a peace that must come, whether this war is won or lost.'

Halifax offered no response, busying himself with his cup. Chamberlain forged ahead.

'Ambition is a foul condition in an Englishman, Edward, and Winston has suffered from it ever since he could crawl. Never been a party man, it's not in his nature. A would-be tyrant who totters from one crisis to the next. My God, at times I fear him almost as much as I do Hitler.'

Still Halifax remained silent.

'Ambition. And avarice, too. He has his hands in so many pies, and somehow they always seem to emerge soiled and clutching money. Listen to me, Edward, I can't tell you the details – don't know them all myself, not yet – but Winston can't be trusted. With power or with money. You know that.'

And Halifax's silence screamed consent.

Chamberlain's mouth had run dry with passion and he very much wanted his tea, but he feared his hand would tremble too much and betray him.

'I have already made an appointment to visit the Palace, Edward.'

Halifax looked up sharply. 'So soon? Are there no decencies?'

'Six o'clock. In less than five hours I shall hand in my seals of office. It's not what I want, but it seems I have no choice. When a rabbit like Kingsley Wood turns weasel, you know the world has begun turning too fast. I have only one duty left, and that is to offer the King my advice about who should be my successor. It must be you. In Downing Street by tonight.'

'But I keep asking myself, am I up to it?'

Chamberlain stretched forward, taut as elastic. 'There are only two men who don't want you as Prime Minister. One is Winston Churchill, the other Adolf Hitler. It's in your hands, Edward. Will you leave the fate of our country to them?'

Slowly, as though weighed down by blocks of stone, Halifax began shaking his head, but so stiffly it wasn't clear whether he was indicating rejection or consent.

'Edward, I shall be there for you,' Chamberlain urged. 'We've guided this country of ours together, you and I. A team. Always a team. Prime Minister and closest of colleagues. You in the Lords, me in the Commons. Never on our own. We can still make it so.'

Halifax let forth the most miserable of sighs, which ended in what was little more than a mumble.

'Very well.'

Two words. But they were enough for Chamberlain. He knew that in a few hours' time a van would draw up at the rear of Downing Street and begin loading all of his personal effects. It would be cruel enough, creeping out of the back door, without the thought that Winston was at the front door kicking it down. A Churchill taking over from a Chamberlain. It could not be. This wasn't simply personal, it was family, generations of it, a matter of honour.

But there was more. What if Halifax succeeded him? Respectable, competent Edward. Yet vulnerable. His empire was the House of Lords, isolated from the centre of events. He would have

Chamberlain as an elder statesman, of course, yet Halifax would also get Winston, who would fight him to a standstill just as he had fought every one of the Prime Ministers he had served, not so much because he chose to but simply because he knew no other way, driven by that most foul of conditions – ambition. And when the two of them, Halifax and Churchill, lay exhausted and unable to continue, who would there be with the experience and background to restore the country's shattered purpose in its hour of need? Why, none other than Neville Chamberlain.

He shook Halifax's hand. This game wasn't over yet.

Attlee rapped his pen on the table to call the meeting to order. He was a small, dapper man from an elitist background who was, without argument, even from his mother, the least charismatic leader in the history of the party, yet he was a master at steering his comrades through the procedural chicanes of Standing Orders and getting things done. They had much to do. They heard Attlee's insistent rapping, and gradually fell to silence.

The members of the National Executive Committee had gathered in the smoke-filled basement of the Tollard Royal Hotel in Bournemouth in order to resolve two outstanding questions. Would they serve in a coalition under Chamberlain? If not, would they serve under anyone else?

They dealt with the first question in the most summary of fashions, using language which would more naturally have been heard in the washroom of a Welsh coalpit after the pipes had frozen. Neville Chamberlain was a man who had treated them with disdain and who had taken meticulous pleasure in taunting them across the Despatch Box. What was more, he was also a manufacturer, practically a Victorian mill-owner, an arch-Tory who had sat back while the forces of Fascism plundered Spain and who now had contrived to bring war and suffering to their own front door. And the bastard wanted their help.

There were some on the NEC who took an intellectual approach to their Socialism. Some others had it bred into them, while more than a few had had it beaten into them by the troops and mercenaries who had broken up the General Strike. Yet from whatever point they travelled, they all arrived at the same conclusion.

Sod him.

Yet it wasn't as easy as that. There was also other business to conduct. There was a war going on, a hideous, headline-grabbing war which was about to flatten Belgium and make their conference ridiculous. The agenda was a fantasy of aspiration and idealism that called for, amongst many other things, an immediate negotiated peace with the Germans, yet Hitler's panzers had turned everything on its head. What yesterday had seemed aspirational and idealistic now seemed simply asinine. So the motions set down for debate had to be buried along with the Prime Minister but, according to the rule book, each burial ceremony required a separate vote.

It was almost two o'clock before they'd finished

the interment proceedings, and still they hadn't dealt with Chamberlain's second question. It was getting stuffy; Attlee called a short break.

The comrades repaired to the bar upstairs where they discovered Driberg. The man from the *Express* was not in the best of conditions. The fresh out-pourings of violence just across the Channel had ter-rified him, and he was not a brave man, not when he had no newspaper to hide behind. So he had responded as he had always done, by spending the night trying to obliterate himself. He had returned to his hotel well after breakfast time to be greeted by a telephone call from Burgess. Driberg's head was thick, his throat raw from the night air, his chilled back killing him, and he couldn't for the life of him understand why Burgess was so agitated about a meeting of the bloody National Executive.

'I don't get it, Guy. Why's what the bloody Labour Party says suddenly so important?'

'Because there's a war on at last, a proper one, and now the Government needs the Labour Party inside the tent. So they're allowed to set the terms for crawling inside the tent.'

'Sure. Chamberlain or not Chamberlain. They'll tell Chamberlain to go jump without his parachute, and we'll get some other bloody Tory.'

'Not some other bloody Tory, you fool. It'll be either Halifax or Churchill. Can you imagine Halifax? That armless idiot? How long would it be before he throws in the towel? Does a deal? Invites the Wehrmacht to stroll up the Strand and stick a bay-onet halfway up your arse?'

Driberg shook his head in confusion. 'But Attlee

can't tell the Tory Party who their leader's going to be . . .'

'Tom, if they can refuse to serve under Chamberlain they can refuse to serve under Halifax, too. Which'll leave the Tories with only one practical option. Winston. All the knives are out for Churchill right now, and the Labour Party might be the only friends he's got.'

'Strange bloody bedfellows.'

'It might be his only chance – *our* only chance. Everything might depend on this, even our lives. You've got to get them to decide, Tom. For Churchill.'

So the befuddled Driberg set about his task in the bar of the Royal Tollard. Pinching elbows, whispering in ears, smiling and cajoling. They knew Driberg well, liked him, for behind the hard-faced veneer of a Beaverbrook apparatchik he was one of them. He had helped many of them, suppressing embarrassments, warning them of impending exposures, joining with relish in their cabals. They knew he was up to something – Driberg was always up to something – but they listened. And when, twenty minutes later, after they were called back to their posts in the basement and Driberg had fallen beneath the largest whisky he had ever held, they remembered his words as they began to argue the merits of the case. About how they had a veto. About how that veto amounted to a decision. About how they could decide who was going to be the next Prime Minister.

They chose Halifax.

*   *   *

Burgess had been struggling all day to contain his growing sense of dread, but when he received the telephone call from Mac the last traces of resistance crumbled. Mac – calm, perceptive, ubiquitous Mac – had called to say he'd just been summoned to the Foreign Office. His Lordship wanted a trim. Straight away.

'And?' Burgess demanded.

'And what? What more did you want, Mr Burgess? His Nibs wants a haircut in a hurry. What does that sound like to you? He's going to a wedding or a funeral? In my experience, men get buried in an old suit and nobody bothers much about the length of their hair.'

'You sure? You sure about this, Mac?'

'All I'm sure about, Mr Burgess, is that if I don't get over there right now I lose my job. It's been nice talking to you.' Then the phone went dead.

That's when Burgess began to lose the battle to prevent fear overwhelming him. It made him feel sick – then he was physically sick, and violently so. He seemed to have run out of options. He was going to be forced to make the most terrifying gamble of his life – to gamble *with* his life – on the basis of a bloody haircut. It seemed all too ludicrous, yet events were careering out of control like a runaway truck and he had no choice but to place himself in its path, to throw his body beneath its wheels in the desperate hope that he might divert it just sufficiently from its course. If only he could save Churchill . . .

Now he knew why he hadn't gone to Spain. The thought of pain, of death, petrified him. He could feel tears falling from his cheeks. Coward's tears. Yet the thought of failure terrified him even more. He didn't even have time for a drink.

'Oh, Mother, save me.'

At almost the same moment, a blue file fell across Horace Wilson's desk. It was emblazoned 'Top Secret' and 'Immediate' and marked 'Prime Minister Only'. In the peculiarly opaque language of the civil service, that meant Horace Wilson too. The file itself was slim, containing only a single sheet of paper, and was from Ball. It was the result of his investigation into the discrepancies between those persons signed into the Admiralty visitors' log and those names recorded in the First Lord's official diary.

There were more names than Wilson had expected – almost two dozen. Most of them were entirely predictable – some of Clemmie's relatives and one or two of Churchill's own; several close personal friends of long standing; his son Randolph and his new wife; his tailor, an Italian who had called on three separate occasions (perhaps something there?); and Churchill's doctor. There was also a single entry for Guy Burgess.

Ball wrote that it was unclear why Burgess had made a personal call on Churchill rather than going though official channels, and even less clear as to what might have been the purpose of the visit. Burgess was a journalist, a seeker after scraps and indiscretions. Although he was not known personally to Ball, he was a young man who appeared to be exceedingly well connected and to be developing something of a reputation for notoriety in his social life. A subject worth kicking about a bit. Along with the tailor.

Which is what Ball had ordered from the security services. Most urgently.

It was shortly after three when Attlee hurried away from the gathering of the NEC. The issues had been resolved, the decisions made, and the momentous consequences of those decisions would be played out in Westminster, not Bournemouth. He was anxious to get back. The Labour Party was an open book, congenitally incapable of retaining secrets for long, and they had already issued a press release declaring their willingness to join in a coalition Government, but an innate caution and sense of personal decency within Attlee insisted that they make no public announcement about the matter of the prime ministership until those involved had been informed. They should be the first to know; it was only decent. Told formally, confidentially and in writing. Everything by the rules.

So on his way to the railway station, Attlee instructed the taxi driver to stop at a post office. From there he sent a telegram to Downing Street. On the buff-coloured form, he constructed a message in language that was intended to be understood only by its recipient.

'TO + THE + FIRST + QUESTION + NO + STOP + TO + THE + SECOND + YES + UNDER + H + STOP + RETURNING + LONDON + IMMEDIATELY + ARRIVING + FIVE + FIFTEEN + STOP + ATTLEE'

Economical, as was Attlee's habit. Less than two

dozen words. He didn't refer to Churchill – it would have cost an extra penny a word, and some on the NEC didn't think Churchill was worth that. Attlee, on the other hand, was genuinely undecided. He sensed a trap. He knew the Tories, knew they couldn't be trusted, not until they were buried. He thought it better to leave the door ajar. Just in case. He handed across one shilling and seven pence, asked for a receipt, then hurried back to the taxi. He was anxious not to miss his train.

Sue was startled. It wasn't every day that a famous man walked into her post office and asked to send a telegram to the Prime Minister. If she hadn't recognized the Labour leader's dark features and neatly trimmed moustache she might have thought it was a practical joke.

When he had gone, doffing his cap and bidding her good-day, she settled down in a tiny, airless room to the rear of the shop which she reserved for valuable items. It was here she kept the safe with its store of stamps, postal orders, savings books and the petty cash, and alongside it was a bookshelf stacked with the many manuals and circulars of post office procedure. It was also here that the Creed teleprinter had been installed. The teleprinter was a machine that translated its messages into perforations on a paper tape. The tape then passed through an automatic transmitter which directed the message to its intended destination, where it would be printed out on more paper tape and pasted onto a telegram form.

As Sue shuffled her chair closer to make herself

comfortable in front of the keyboard, the teleprinter began to tremble into life. A telegram was coming through. As the tape and its message slowly stuttered forth, she realized with some surprise it was addressed to her. She bent over, passing the paper tape through her fingers and reading as the machine continued to chatter and produce its message word by word.

'REGRET + TO + INFORM + YOU + THAT + SGT + J + WHITE + KOYLI + IS + REPORTED + BY + HIS + UNIT + AS + MISSING + BELIEVED + KILLED + IN + ACTION . . .'

Her eyes stared unblinking, held immobile by the lengthening ribbon of paper, and what more it said she could no longer see. A paralysis began to move throughout her body, from her eyes to her neck, arms, fingers, legs, every muscle. She sat hunched over the machine, uncomprehending, unmoving.

Some time later she was found. Two concerned customers discovered Sue Graham still bent over her machine. They could get no sense out of her, and with some difficulty moved her to her father's old smoking chair in the back parlour. They closed the door to the security room and locked the front door of the post office, then sat by her side sipping tea while they waited for the doctor to arrive.

There are times when even a man of prodigious appetites, who has spent a lifetime swimming without a care on a tide of alcohol, relaxes his restraint and gets drunk. It has little to do with quantity, much more to do with deciding to let go and simply sink. Churchill had decided to let go. He no longer cared, content to drown amongst memories and a multitude of regrets. His companion at lunch was Bracken – loyal, dogged Bracken, who could be relied upon later to return his master to wherever was appropriate, no matter what his condition.

They hadn't even made it through the first bottle of claret yet already the old man had run the gamut of his dark emotions. What was at first merely maudlin soon became misery, regret turned to recrimination, anger to outrage, until none of it made too much sense. He grew tearful, sobbing that he had failed. 'I am a Churchill. I was born to fight this war, Brendan, to lead us through it, but it is lost. Lost! We shall be destroyed, a thousand years of English independence swept away.'

'But we've scarcely started . . .'

'He will not fight! Halifax will not fight! He will run, like the wretched foxes he pursues, until we shall all be hunted down. Nothing to stand in their way, no hiding places. Oh, if only I had the rifles . . .'

'But that's why you're here,' Bracken began to object, but was waved into silence as Churchill's voice and emotions began to climb.

'They said I wanted them to fight my own war – my own war. As though it were a war of an entirely different character to *their* war. Damn them, perhaps they were right. Perhaps my war might have been different – no, indeed, Brendan, I tell you that my war would most certainly have been different, fought without mercy and without respite until the victory was ours! And yet there is always that most dangerous of foes, Brendan – no, not those in front of you in the moment of battle, but those treacherous bastards who attack you from behind. They are the real enemy, the enemy within. Oh, perhaps we should have used those rifles after all!'

Bracken began to stutter in alarm but his protests were swept aside in the onslaught.

'Cromwell purged this kingdom with four hundred cavalry, so just think – think what a Churchill might have done with four hundred thousand Mausers?' Then his voice flooded with apprehension. 'And what, now, will Hitler do with them? There's the question.' Tears began to glisten on his cheeks.

The enemy within. Did he mean Chamberlain? Halifax? The party? Or those ghosts within himself which continually haunted him. Bracken had never seen the old man in such misery.

'But you'd never have used the rifles, not for yourself. Would you, Winston?'

'Marlborough would've. He would have fought.'

'Yes, but surely . . .'

'If I could raise an army of stout-hearted Englishmen, what could I not have done? Most surely I would have used them.'

'But . . . against whom?'

Churchill responded with nothing but an expression of exquisite pain, a man at war within himself and with a world that had brought him low.

They were now halfway through their second bottle, but they were not to finish it. A messenger had arrived. There was to be yet another meeting of the Cabinet. The Prime Minister's apologies, but would the First Lord mind presenting himself forthwith?

'My firing squad,' Churchill bellowed, throwing his napkin to the floor. He stumbled out without a backward glance or word of thanks.

At almost precisely the same moment that Churchill returned once more to Downing Street, a messenger from the Secret Intelligence Service also arrived. He was carrying two additional files for the small, neat pile that was mounting on the in-tray of Wilson's desk. Both were no longer than a single paragraph and were marked with a yellow flag for the exclusive attention of the Prime Minister. The first related how, at a recent diplomatic reception in Berlin, a drunken Russian well into his cups had been overheard telling his German counterpart that Chamberlain was ill. Deeply unwell. Stomach trouble. Knew it for a fact, so he claimed. Because buried deep inside the Kremlin they had a copy of the Prime Minister's personal medical report.

The second file was more detailed. It was headed 'MR. CHURCHILL', in capital letters and underlined. It stated that following recent investigations into the First Lord's personal finances, it had been discovered that the majority of his income during the past twelve months had derived from a single payment. Although nominally the payment had come from a British-based trust, the trust received all its monies from a single source, a privately owned trading company named Omni-Carriers. Omni's only known office was in Bucharest and its bankers were in Geneva, but almost every other detail of its activities was shrouded in deliberately manufactured mystery. Yet SIS had got there eventually (with the assistance of an embittered and impoverished former employee, although this detail was omitted from the report to the Prime Minister). For Omni had begun its life trading not in its customary raw materials but in antique works of art. Enormous quantities of them, and every one of them Russian. The sort of supply that could not have continued without official sanction. And when, like so many other companies, it had nearly gone under during the great crash of 1929, Omni had been able to survive only through an emergency injection of funds. These funds, so the former employee swore, came from the Narodny Bank. Of Moscow.

All the strands of an extraordinary noose were now present in the files on Wilson's desk. They required nothing more than a little threading together, and one sharp tug.

Burgess arrived at the club only minutes after Churchill had departed, having wheedled from the old man's secretary the location of his lunch. As he leapt from the back of the taxi, he almost bowled into Bracken who was coming down the sandbagged steps into St James's. Bracken scowled.

'Bugger off, Burgess.'

'I have to see Mr Churchill.'

'Never ceases to surprise me how often you seem to need to see Winston. And it never ceases to astonish me how, in spite of it all, he manages to struggle on without you.' Bracken didn't bother to break his stride.

'I have to see him!' Burgess repeated breathlessly, not bothering to hide his anxiety.

'Can't!' Bracken sang out merrily. 'Gone!'

'Where?' Burgess grabbed the other man's sleeve.

Bracken turned, his eyes filled with loathing. 'Get your filthy hands off me!'

'Not until you tell me where Mr Churchill is.'

'Rot in hell,' Bracken spat, moving off again.

'Then I'll share damnation with you. And Anna Fitzgerald.'

Bracken pulled up sharply. 'What's your stinking little game, Burgess?'

'Did you think you could keep your affair with her secret?'

'Never been a problem. I'm happy to be associated with her,' Bracken responded, his words growing clumsy through surprise. 'If you think I have something to hide –'

'Sorry. I was forgetting. It's Miss Fitzgerald who's got the problem. On account of the fact that she's also having an affair with a Swedish gentleman. Name of Svensson. Bjorn Svensson.'

Bracken prayed that his face remained inscrutable behind his bottle-thick glasses, but there was no disguising the flush of astonishment and torment that had begun rising in his cheeks. 'You miserable bastard. You repeat one word of that and I'll break you. I'll make sure you never work again. And when I've finished breaking you into pieces I'm pretty sure Joe Kennedy will be standing in line to feed what's left of you back into whichever sewer you crawled from. I'll destroy you, Burgess. And it will give me the most immense pleasure.' He turned his back and was off again, striding forcefully down towards the park.

His total destruction. Yes, there might be many people standing in line for that pleasure, but it was a risk Burgess knew he had no option but to take. To destroy himself, if that's what it took, in order to get to Churchill. Oh, God, this was it. No turning back. He began to run after the retreating figure of Bracken.

'Then we'll go down together. She'll destroy you, too, Bracken.'

Still the other man did not stop, striding out ever more impatiently, pushing his way along the crowded pavement and leaving looks of irritation in his wake.

'Do you know she tells the Swede everything. Everything you tell her.'

A slight faltering in the step, but still Bracken pressed onwards. Burgess had almost caught him, was up to his shoulder.

'Do you know that's how the Germans found out the invasion date for Norway? Because you told her.'

Bracken stopped but did not turn, as though he had walked into an invisible wall.

'Thousands of British lives lost, Bracken. Because of you. And her.'

At last he turned, his face a battlefield of rage and misery.

'Lies,' he whispered. 'Lies! Absurd lies!'

'Face it, Bracken, why the hell d'you think she hangs around with a character like you? To get tips from your hairdresser?'

Bracken grabbed the lapels of Burgess's crumpled suit. 'Svensson's nothing more than a friend of her uncle!'

'A very well-connected man, is Mr Svensson. Lots of business interests in Germany. Trades all sorts of things, he does. Currencies. Timber. Rubber. And pillow talk.'

Their faces were only inches apart.

'Know what she does, Bracken? Goes directly from your dining table to his bed. Takes your bloody roses with her.'

That's when Bracken hit him, lashed out and connected with Burgess's chin so forcefully he sent him sprawling in the gutter. Bracken stood towering over the fallen figure, ready to do it again.

Burgess felt his chin, then managed a smile through a lip he knew had split. 'That's nothing to what they'll do to you, Bracken, when they find out about your little love triangle. Beat bloody hell out of you, I expect. But that'll be kids' play compared with what they'll do to your career. And that of Mr Churchill. Everything destroyed, because you got up the wrong piece of skirt.'

The foot went back, ready to kick the insult out of him, but something snapped in Bracken's memory. The Swede in the company of Anna and Joe Kennedy, at dinner when he'd first met Anna, then their encounter walking through the park. A man of many contacts, Kennedy had called the Swede – Christ, they'd just come from the Palace. And Anna had been so remarkably, irritatingly coy.

'How do you know about Anna?'

'Because I know about Svensson.'

'He's a spy?'

Burgess clambered gingerly to his feet, still rubbing his chin. 'They'll have difficulty proving it. After all, he's done nothing you haven't done – done no more than repeat gossip. Except you knew it wasn't gossip, you knew they were state secrets. Yet still you passed them on. Anna Fitzgerald whispered sweet nothings in your ear and you – well, you whispered everything in hers. They'll have a much easier time making the case stick against you.'

'But, but . . .'

'Know what they'll do, Bracken? They'll conclude that you're either a fool or a traitor. They'll go digging about, looking for something in your background that might have made you turn against us, turn anti-English. Something you've hidden away and buried all these years.'

Bracken's Irish cheeks, which had been burning with torment, turned to ice.

'If they find you've been holding out on them, fabricating, hiding your tracks, then you'll go down as a traitor. If not, you're simply another infatuated fool who got led on by a much younger woman and just happened to be responsible for the military disaster in Norway. Oh, wouldn't Chamberlain just love to pin that on someone else? Someone so close to Mr Churchill?'

'You cannot be serious.'

'Deadly.'

'I don't believe you,' Bracken whispered.

'Then why are you still standing here? Or maybe you want me to tell you when Miss Fitzgerald and Svensson last met? Hyde Park Hotel less than a week ago. They spent the night there, and much of the next morning. Big "Do Not Disturb" notice swinging from the door knob.'

The lips moved, but no sound emerged.

Burgess pushed home his advantage yet again, but this time there was an edge of pity in his voice. 'That was the night after you last saw her, wasn't it?'

Slowly, the words formed. 'You mean to destroy me.'

'Funnily enough, Bracken, I intend to save you. Because that's the only way I can save Mr Churchill. You go down, he goes down for being such a monumental bloody fool as to have you as a friend. That's why I need to see him. Must see him. Immediately.'

'But you can't. He's in Cabinet.'

'Oh, my God,' Burgess gasped, as though he'd just been hit again. 'Then it's probably too late. But we have to try.'

They began running down the street in the direction of the park and Downing Street which lay beyond. Until Bracken came sliding to a halt.

'Wait!' he insisted.

'No time.'

'Then make some.' Bracken was staring angrily at him, all signs of wretchedness gone. 'How the hell do you know all this? Who are you, Burgess? *What* are you?'

Burgess simply stared, still panting from the chase.

'A traitor or a fool, you said. And you're no bloody fool, Burgess, I'll grant you that.'

They stood eye to eye, of similar height, with hair seemingly ruled by the same laws of chaos.

'A traitor trying to save Mr Churchill?' Burgess demanded. 'Bizarre definition of treachery.'

'How would you know about Svensson? About Anna? About me? Unless . . .'

His bluff had been called, and Burgess had run

out of excuses and explanations. He was also desperately afraid he might have run out of time.

'Christ, you're not just a queer, you're the same sort of creature as Svensson, aren't you, Burgess? But for which side?' And slowly, as memories of late-night conversations about the qualities of Russia began to tumble through his jarred brain, a smile began to form a slow path across Bracken's face, twisting as it went. 'Oh, I think I can figure out which side. Can't I, Commissar?'

'I'm English, Bracken. As English as any man on this earth.'

'You're a Communist.'

'I'm not the one who betrayed thousands of British troops. Let's remember that, shall we?'

And the smile was gone. 'You can prove nothing.'

Suddenly Burgess began to laugh, mocking.

'You can prove nothing!' Bracken repeated, trying to bluster, but Burgess's eyes were colder and more sober than Bracken had ever known.

'Can't you see, Bracken, how ludicrous all of this is? Neither of us can prove a damned thing. We can kill each other off with accusation – but we can't prove a bloody thing. I admit I've got friends in some pretty low places – you've got that much on me and I suppose you might use it to make my life distinctly uncomfortable. But nowhere near as bloody uncomfortable as I promise I will make things for you, if I have to. Because what have you got against me? Russia? We're not at war with bloody Russia! We want Russia as an ally, on our side – Winston Churchill's been making broadcasts about it for months. No, they'll not care much about me – hell, if I'm half as good a friend of the Russians as you suppose, they might even find me useful. Whereas you . . . You have blood on your hands, Mr Bracken. British blood. They might find many uses for you, too, but none which will allow you to sleep at night.'

Bracken shook his head.

'No matter how much you might loathe me, Bracken, we're in this together. Oh, yes. Sort of a team, we are, you and me. Tied to each other like the Devil to his tail. And we both might burn in Hell – but if we do, it'll be *together*. Because if I go down I shall have to insist on taking you with me.'

'You threaten me like some cheap bully.'

'Wake up, Bracken! This isn't about you and me. It's about a world that's grown insane and wants to destroy itself, a world in which you and I count for nothing more than a piss in the park. We have a choice, you and I, to make right now. We can stand here and pick over our mutual lack of merit while the world annihilates itself – or we can take the only chance we've got of doing something about it.'

'Which is?'

'Saving Mr Churchill. When we've done that we can sit down over a crate of champagne and talk about our shortcomings until we are both old men. But in the meantime – unless you have some unnatural desire to form a queue for the nearest scaffold – may I suggest we get on with it?'

And they were both running, hurling themselves across Pall Mall, into the park and towards Downing Street.

*   *   *

Four-twenty p.m. Ten minutes before Cabinet.

'You say Mr Attlee's on a train?' Wilson was demanding into a bakelite telephone.

At the other end, a secretary struggled to explain.

'Telegram? But we haven't received any telegram,' Wilson insisted. 'For heaven's sake, what sort of operation are you running down there?'

The secretary was tempted to explain that she wasn't running any sort of operation and the Labour Party in conference was both constitutionally and temperamentally incapable of 'being run', as he put it, no matter how hard the leadership tried, but she sensed he wasn't interested in the democratic niceties.

'Is there anyone there I can talk to?' Wilson demanded, as if she were no one.

They'd all gone off to the Winter Gardens where the conference was being held. She offered to run there herself and get back to him.

'How long will that take?'

Thirty minutes, if she hurried.

'But we only have ten! What am I to tell the Prime Minister? Have you no idea what was in Mr Attlee's telegram?'

There was hesitation at the other end of the line.

'If you know, for the sake of sanity, you have to tell me,' he insisted. 'There's a war on out there, you know.'

Silence.

'Please . . .'

Ah, the magic word. At last. Well, not the telegram, that was up to Mr Attlee. But she had typed out a press release and stencilled a hundred copies for distribution later that evening. They were sitting in a pile beside her. She supposed it could do no harm to let Wilson have the gist of it. About the unanimous National Executive decision to be a full partner in a new Government.

'Yes . . .'

Under a new Prime Minister.

Ah, so there it was. To the first question – no. But to the second they had responded in the affirmative. Wilson replaced the phone without thanks or formalities.

Chamberlain was standing at his shoulder. Wilson looked up.

'It's as we expected, Neville.'

Chamberlain nodded slowly.

'Would it have made any difference? If they'd had other thoughts?' Wilson pressed.

Chamberlain seemed lost in another world. He stood tall for a moment, his shoulders braced. 'We shall never know,' he replied. Then he picked up his slim folder and marched into the Cabinet Room.

'Sorry, sir. Cabinet's already started. Five minutes ago. No one's allowed in.'

'Heavens, man, I'm Mr Churchill's Parliamentary Private Secretary.'

'I know full well who you are, Mr Bracken. But you are not a member of the Cabinet and no matter how loud you shout at me and wave your arms about, I can't let you in.' The Downing Street doorman stood firm, doggedly obstructing their path down the corridor to the Cabinet Room.

'I – we – have to get a message to Mr Churchill,' Burgess interrupted, his tone deliberately more conciliatory but the effect disrupted by a split and freshly swelling lip. 'The message is vital to what they are discussing. Surely you can –'

'You'll forgive me, sir,' the doorman replied, looking askance at the dishevelled and panting stranger with a rip in the leg of his trousers, 'but I doubt that very much. I happen to know there's only one item on the agenda for this meeting, and that's by way of being a personal matter. Anyhow, I'm still not allowed to pass in papers.'

'But that's . . .' Impossible. Disastrous. An end to it all. Burgess turned away in despair, only to be confronted by another exasperated figure shuffling across the threshold. It was Kingsley Wood.

'Can't stop, can't stop, late for Cabinet,' he insisted as Bracken tried to wave him to a halt, but Burgess stood resolutely in his path and was clearly not intending to let him past.

'You must, please, give this to Mr Churchill,' Burgess insisted. From out of his bulging jacket pocket he produced a book.

'What the hell is this?'

'It's one of Mr Churchill's own, some of his old speeches,' Burgess responded, flashing the cover. 'It has words in here which he thought might be very important for your meeting. He left it behind, asked if we could fetch it for him . . .'

'If ever you should need me, send me this book and I shall remember our conversation . . .'

It had been intended merely to get Burgess past the porter's lodge at the club and to summon

Churchill from his lunch table, yet now it might serve another purpose. Bewildered, Wood shook his head in impatience, offended at being asked to be bloody Winston's messenger boy. Yet, on an instant's reflection, it was perhaps a better fate than being Neville's sacrificial lamb. He grabbed the book and bustled towards the door.

Chamberlain sits down in his chair – the only one around the Cabinet table with arms – and begins his meticulous preparations. Moves the silver inkwell that once was Gladstone's no more than half an inch, straightens the folder in front of him, runs the damp palms of his hands across the baize tablecloth. One last inspection of the room, one lingering glance. Everything is ready, even if he is not and could never be. He nods to the Cabinet Secretary standing by the door.

They file in, subdued, none of the normal pleasantries, glancing at him, scurrying to find their seats. Winston is sitting second on his left – strict order of seniority should place him immediately by his side, but Chamberlain could never endure him so close and from the start has contrived some constitutional excuse to have at least one man's body between himself and the First Lord. One other seat is still empty – Kingsley Wood hasn't arrived, damn him, no doubt detained by the blasts of war coming from across the Channel. The others assemble in silence, waiting for Chamberlain's cue. On the mantel behind him, the clock strikes half past the hour.

'Gentlemen, thank you for attending. My apologies

if I have disturbed . . .' – he is going to say lunch, he knows that Winston has been at lunch, can see it in those watery eyes – 'your duties. But it is my duties, those as Prime Minister, which I'm afraid this afternoon must come first.'

Shuffles of discomfort around the table.

He starts again, but suddenly the door bursts open and in rushes Kingsley Wood distributing apologies. 'Your pardon, Prime Minister. I am so sorry. Unavoidable duties . . .'

Chamberlain nods in condescension and Wood takes his place. He is carrying something in his hand – a book – which he slides down the brown baize tablecloth to Churchill. The First Lord sits up sharply, as though woken from slumber, but says nothing.

'Gentlemen!' Chamberlain once again calls them to order, irritated by the interruption. 'As soon as this meeting of the Cabinet finishes, I shall be going to the Palace to tender my resignation to His Majesty the King.'

Ritual murmurs of regret, but no surprise. They all know what's been going on. Churchill, meanwhile, has opened the book. Damn his eyes! What the hell does he think he's doing?

'You all know that this is not what I would have wanted,' Chamberlain continues, 'but events dictate that the present uncertainties about the future direction of Government must be brought to an end. My energies, my enthusiasm for the tasks of being His Majesty's First Minister remain undiminished . . .' – (or will be, after a little rest, a chance to deal with this damned ulcer that's been bothering me so) – 'and I would like to think that my service to the country has not yet come to an end . . .' – (why, give you gentlemen a little time, a few months to mess things up without me, and I might yet be back sitting in this chair) – 'But I have a responsibility to you, and through you, to the country at large. I have been Prime Minister for very nearly three years, and during that time we have been through many trials and tribulations. The responsibilities of this office are awesome, as you all know –'

But Churchill is no longer listening. He cannot fathom why a book, one of his own, has been thrust at him during this Cabinet of all Cabinets, and he's not in the mood for mysteries. He tries not to be distracted by it, but he flips the cover and discovers the inscription he himself has written. To Burgess. Why, oh why, has he resurfaced here? Now? To what purpose? Damn him.

Chamberlain is intoning that he cannot leave office without taking the opportunity to thank them all personally for what they have done for him. Some of those present imagine that his gratitude is a little ironic, almost spiteful. Churchill isn't one of those, for he is no longer listening. Tucked inside the pages of the book he has found two sheets of paper, folded down the middle. In the circumstances, they are irresistible.

Chamberlain is talking about the one responsibility that still lies ahead of him, that of advising the King whom he should appoint as successor. A ripple of anticipation washes around the table, but the expression on the face of Halifax is set in stone, his head bowed, as though in expectation of laurels. Churchill reads on.

'I have done my best,' Chamberlain is saying, 'and my duty is to ensure that I pass on the mighty burdens of this office to someone who, I know, is more than capable and worthy of bearing them . . .'

'Prime Minister!'

A voice is raised; a collective breath of outrage is drawn. It is monstrous that Chamberlain should be interrupted during his valediction. They stare accusingly. It is Churchill.

'It is an unpardonable offence, I know, to intervene at such a moment, but I fear that you might end this meeting in your characteristic humble and modest manner without allowing any of us to express what we all so fervently wish to express to you. Which is our thanks.'

Churchill has stood up. No one stands up to speak at Cabinet, but Winston has always been outrageously theatrical and this is not, after all, like any other Cabinet meeting. If he insists on making a tribute – and who better? – let him be seen.

And as he stands, he slips across the two sheets of paper towards Chamberlain.

'I have had the honour of serving many Prime Ministers,' Churchill recalls, 'both in war and during times of peace. Yet you, sir, have been unique, both in the breadth of your vision and the determination with which you have pursued your objectives. And your greatest objective, of course, has been peace.' He has prepared nothing, is speaking entirely off the cuff, but it's what is expected at such moments when assassins gather round the body to praise their victim's virtue.

Chamberlain is reading. No one notices, all other

eyes are on Churchill, who is extolling the integrity of their fallen leader. 'Never has a nation gone into battle with such reluctance, having done so much to secure the peace, and having established in the eyes of the entire world its credentials as being blameless. Never has so much been owed by so many in our community of nations to just one man.' An awkward phrase, Churchill concludes, but one which might bear a little polishing.

And now Chamberlain's eyes are up, levered from the paper like limpets from a rock. He knows.

From the first sheet of paper he knows that a small British concern named Chiltern Investments has active shareholdings in foreign companies. These companies include several of the most significant German steel and arms manufacturers – Blohm und Voss, Daimler-Benz, Junkers, Krupp and Messerschmitt. Individually these holdings are not huge, but collectively they amount to a tempting portfolio. With grim irony, one of those companies in which Chiltern Investments figures as a shareholder is the Mauser Works at Oberndorf, the manufacturers of the rifles Churchill has attempted to acquire.

The other page that has been taken from Burgess's book is of slightly thicker paper. It is a photo-stat. Of the Certificate of Incorporation of the company known as Chiltern Investments. Joint proprietors: H. Wilson and J. Ball.

Who have become Chamberlain's hangmen.

His eyes overflow with betrayal and memories of how Wilson and Ball argued so fiercely against the profits tax on British arms manufacturers. He had told them to find an alternative. Evidently they have.

He feels numb, except for that part of his stomach where the pain cuts through him like a ragged sword. Only slowly does he begin to hear the words that come pouring forth from Churchill.

'. . . those who have served with you know of your courage. They know of your dedication. Above all, they know of your sense of public duty, passed down from father to sons, which has long illuminated the great name of Chamberlain and which will continue to do so, so long as I have any part to play in matters.'

What? What is he saying? My family's good name – in his hands?

'A reputation is a fragile thing. In our modern and pitiless world, a reputation such as that of the Chamberlain family carries with it the envy of lesser men – men who always seem ready to cast stones and to bring the mighty low.'

Is he praising me – or trying to intimidate me?

'But you, Prime Minister, can leave office today, not only with our gratitude and – if I may use such terms – our love, but safe in the knowledge that your place in the annals of our country will be fixed this very day not only by your own merit but by the merits of those who you have carried with you on your great journey.'

Now Chamberlain knows. To others it sounds no more than an outpouring of emotion perhaps bred and brought forth by a good lunch, but Chamberlain knows better. These are no idle words being used by Churchill. They are a warning, and a terrible threat.

'I pray the indulgence of our colleagues a moment longer if I finish on an entirely personal note. No man's life is lived in isolation. It is carried out in the company of others . . .'

That point again, so loudly beaten that no one but the meanest of fools could miss it.

'Great Caesar travels with many troops and I, for one, give boundless thanks to be here with you today so that I may express the hope that what you have given to us will be repaid an hundred-fold, and to ensure that the tributes which will be raised to you will do nothing but honour to the great name of Chamberlain.'

To most of those present in the room it seems a rhetorical gesture almost too far, yet eulogies are built not on morsels of emotion but on vast buckets of the stuff, and if the room is awash with it, then no one will complain. As Churchill resumes his seat they beat their hands upon the table in approbation until their palms begin to sting. Yet to Chamberlain, the noise sounds like the beating of drums on his path to his place of execution.

'Is there nothing to be done, Mr Chamberlain?' the King demanded in his clipped tones, clearly vexed.

'I'm afraid not, sir.'

'I was rather hoping . . .'

'Edward. Yes, a fine man. But not a man for this war. It is a wretched and terrible conflict which I fear will cover Europe in much blood. It needs to be fought by a man who understands such things.'

'I take your point.'

'So does Edward.'

The King rose, there was no point in prolonging

the audience. Chamberlain gazed out through the long windows at the palace forecourt and railings beyond, where only twenty months before a crowd of tens of thousands had stretched as far as the eye could see in order to acclaim him as their saviour. Now there was no one, nothing but sandbags and khaki.

'I think you have been most cruelly treated by those around you,' the King concluded.

'Perhaps,' Chamberlain acknowledged. 'But it seems that it is by the merits of those around a man that, in the end, he is judged.'

The telephone rang. It was the King's private secretary. Churchill was instructed to be at the palace at six. Not until the moment he replaced the telephone was he certain that he had won.

Clemmie had returned earlier that day from the deathbed of her brother-in-law and was there to wave him off. The drive from the Admiralty to Buckingham Palace would take no more than two minutes and Churchill, too, noted that there were no crowds. There was, however, considerable resentment in many corners of Whitehall. Later he would hear that in the Foreign Office they had broken out champagne to toast not the new Prime Minister but the old. The King across the water, as they dubbed Chamberlain.

But Churchill did not worry about such things. Indeed, he felt nothing but relief. The crisis which now lay before him – before them all – was the challenge for which he had thirsted all his adult life and which would sweep aside the petty posturings. He was walking with destiny, and others would follow as they might.

His detective, Inspector Thompson, held the car for a few moments. 'Want to make sure Mr Chamberlain has got away, sir. Wouldn't be proper to pass him, you on your way in before he's even properly out.'

'No. These things must be done properly, Thompson.'

Churchill sat silently in the back of the car, waiting, thinking of Chamberlain. The man who had fought so hard, with such intensity and passion, yet who had finally been felled. As they were mostly all felled, these Prime Ministers, hacked, stabbed, scratched, kicked, dragged from office. As he, too, in all probability would be. The only question was its timing.

Tears brimmed in his eye. He would never know another moment like this, not unless somehow he could conjure victory out of the tragedy that was taking place beyond the Channel and would soon sweep across it. A moment to relish, to stir around the palette and splash upon life's extraordinary canvas, even if at its end it meant he was to be put up against a wall and shot. At least he would have something to tell his father, when they next met.

It was time. Thompson was climbing into the car beside him.

'Just like to offer my congratulations, sir,' the inspector said as the car began moving off across the gravel of Horse Guards Parade.

'Thank you. Thank you very much.'

'You've deserved it.'

'No, Thompson, I fear I have not. But I hope by the time this awful ordeal has been met, that I shall have deserved it.'

Ball was not a fool. His time was at an end, but he might still decide the manner of his going. He knew that if the file he had left in Downing Street marked for the attention of the Prime Minister came into Churchill's hands, the manner of his departure would be as violent as the old man could devise. Better to go quietly and in one piece.

It had not been a day for processing paperwork in Downing Street. The file remained unopened. Before Churchill had returned from the palace, Ball had ensured that it was removed and destroyed. No one would know he had been prying into the new Prime Minister's private diaries.

The Secret Intelligence Service faced a similar dilemma. After all, there was no absolute proof that Churchill's money had come from Moscow, and even if it had, it wasn't necessarily illegal. And digging around in his bank account was scarcely going to be the best way to impress an incoming Prime Minister, particularly one with a notoriously sharp temper. So the file with the yellow flag disappeared, too.

Only the file concerning the personal medical records of Neville Chamberlain remained on Wilson's desk. Eventually it found its way, as instructed, to the Prime Minister. Churchill read it several nights later as he was catching up on paperwork. So, the news that Burgess had brought to him about

Chamberlain's medical condition had found its way to Moscow . . .

'Brendan, what do you really think of Burgess?'

Bracken turned from pouring drinks.

'Strange man. Not as bad as I first thought, perhaps. But there's something about him which makes me – uncertain. Arm's length, I think. And a very long arm at that.'

'I agree,' said the old man, initialling the note and tossing it back onto the pile.

Mac limped up to the front door in Chigwell. He was carrying a small bunch of flowers.

Carol showed only a moment of surprise. 'Hello, stranger. What you doing here?'

'Mr Burgess sent me.'

Her face scarcely fell. 'What does he want? Can't give him any more papers, I can't. Don't do cleaning any more.'

'No, I don't mean it like that. It's . . . well, he was in my chair yesterday and we were talking. He was very upset about things.'

It was raining very gently, forming a sheen of dew on his hair, but she made no move to invite him in.

'He was crying. Real tears. So I asked him why he cared so much about everything. He said he doesn't care about everything, that the only thing he loved was his country. He has no family, you see, says he never will, and he misses that. So his country is all he has.'

'Sounds a nice man, that Mr Burgess. Compassionate. I'd like to have met him.'

'It's just . . . I don't have a country, not like Mr Burgess has. It got me to thinking what I do care about – or have ever cared about. And there's only ever been one thing. You. That's why I got so upset to think of you with the other men. Because I have changed, I can truly care about something at last – your fault, that. So . . .'

'So you walked out on us.'

'What I've come to say, Carol, is that I care about you – and the kids – very much. I'm sorry for getting angry. About the Market.'

'Don't do the Market any more. Not cleaning, nor the punters. There's plenty of jobs now. There's a war on.'

His face lit up. 'That's wonderful, Carol. I'm so happy for you.'

'Me, too.'

'How are the children?'

'In bed.'

'And . . . you?'

'Bit like Mr Burgess. Done a lot of thinking. And crying. About the things I care for.'

'I'm sorry if I –'

'You? Well, I must admit I had a little sniffle at the time. But that was four months ago, Mac.'

'I'd like to try to make up for it. If you'll let me.' He moved forward, to the very threshold, holding out the flowers. Burgess had said he should take flowers, had insisted. Nothing elaborate, just a few stems and a lot of sincerity. He'd even left a particularly large tip to cover the cost.

'We're moving, Mac. Going away.'

'But why?'

'Because like you and Mr Burgess I care more than my life about something. The kids. Too much to keep them in London, not now there's a proper war.'

'Not too far –'

'Somerset. Nothing there but cows. Nothing that Mr Hitler wants to bomb.'

He was silent for a moment, nodding his head in understanding, and offering a prayer – the first time he had prayed, sincerely prayed, in more than twenty years, since the day he had watched little Moniek floating away. 'That is such a pity. I was hoping . . .'

'Yeah. Me, too.'

'A second chance?'

'No second chances in a war, Mac. Sorry.'

Burgess had told him she wouldn't have him back, not after four months, but he'd had to try.

Then she closed the door, crushing the flowers.

Mac turned up his collar and hobbled off into the rain.

EPILOGUE

In extraordinary circumstances and against the odds, Churchill became Prime Minister instead of Halifax, and that one decision changed the course of history. If Halifax had succeeded Chamberlain, he would not have fought, and Britain would not have won.

Yet even after 10 May it was still a damned close-run thing. The following day Jock Colville, a memorable diarist who served as private secretary to both Chamberlain and Churchill, wrote that *'there seems to be some inclination in Whitehall to believe that Winston will be a complete failure and that Neville will return . . . Seldom can a Prime Minister have taken office with the Establishment so dubious of the choice.'*

Colville's view was, to Chamberlain, great hope. Only at the very end of his life did the former Prime Minister finally release his hold on the belief that, one day, he might return to Downing Street. The cold grey hand he had felt inside him was not an ulcer but gnawing, inconsolable illness. Within weeks of leaving Downing Street he underwent exploratory surgery followed by a major abdominal operation. It was cancer, from which there would be no recovery. In his diary of 9 September 1940 he recorded: *'I have still to adjust myself to the new life of a partially crippled man, which is what I am. Any ideas which may have been in my mind about possibilities of further political activity, and even a possibility of another Premiership after the war, have gone.'*

In October he was told he had not long to live, and wrote: *'this is very helpful and encouraging, for it would be a terrible prospect if I had to wait indefinitely for the end, while going through such daily miseries as I am enduring now. As it is, I know what to do, and shall no longer be harassed by doubts and questions.'* He died on 9 November, less than six months after leaving office.

Halifax continued as Foreign Secretary, but his time at the heart of things was rapidly drawing to a close. He opposed Churchill's insistence that Britain would fight on no matter what – Halifax, true to his appeasement roots, preferred a negotiated peace to the 'blood, toil, tears and sweat' which was offered by Churchill, and before the end of May he came to the point of threatening resignation. But Churchill would accept neither negotiation with Germany nor the splitting of his Cabinet. He took Halifax for a private walk in the garden of Number Ten. They talked man to man, and Halifax behaved like the true English gentleman that he was. The crisis passed, and so did the Foreign Secretary. At the end of 1940, Churchill despatched Halifax across the Atlantic as Ambassador to the United States.

Sir Horace Wilson met a more brutal fate. When he arrived in his office on 11 May, he found Brendan Bracken and Winston's son Randolph sitting on his sofa. They stared at him but not a word was spoken or a smile exchanged. He left, never to return – and never to be forgiven. His belongings were thrown into the corridor after him. He was retired from Government service completely in 1942.

His fellow elf, Joseph Ball, resumed a business career. He ended up controlling the industrial concern Lonrho, which he later sold to the controversial tycoon, Tiny Rowland, who had once been a member of the Hitler Youth.

Fortune smiled on others. Max Beaverbrook did not have long to wait before realizing his dream of being invited once more back into Government. Despite the press baron's vigorous and at times vicious anti-war campaigns, Churchill invited him to become Minister for Aircraft Production. Casting aside his former views without so much as a blush, the newspaper peer made an outstanding success of the task.

His employee on the *Express*, Tom Driberg, soon gave up his role as 'William Hickey' in order to become a Member of Parliament and eventually Chairman of the Labour Party. He also became an agent for the KGB and was one of the most notorious homosexual pick-up specialists of his age – and that in an age when homosexuality was usually punished with the full might of the law. His biographer wrote that 'anyone with less influence would have ended up in jail, Driberg went to the House of Lords'. He lived much of his life in a lavatory and died in the back of a taxi on his way to Parliament.

Bracken remained a figure who somehow always lived on the edges of reality, even though he served loyally throughout the war as Minister of Information and eventually First Lord of the Admiralty. But he knew that with Burgess he had made a deal with the Devil which would make it impossible for him to continue once the war finished and the alliance with the Soviets had crumbled. He could have been blackmailed at any point. After 1945 he never again held office and eventually he retired as an MP, becoming the First (and last) Viscount Bracken. He never married and in later life became something of a recluse, spending his last years giving away to good causes the large amounts of money he had accumulated from his ownership of the *Financial Times*. He died in 1958, leaving instructions that all of his papers should be burnt.

Bob Boothby remained Dorothy Macmillan's lover, and was believed to have been the father of her youngest child. Harold Macmillan knew of this. In 1957 Macmillan, who proved to be a far more ruthless operator than many had expected, became Prime Minister. The following year he elevated Boothby to the House of Lords. After Lady Dorothy died, Macmillan, by then frail, in his eighties and almost blind, tried to burn a large number of letters in his garden incinerator. He made a mess of it and was discovered stumbling around the garden chasing after half-burnt pieces of paper. They turned out to be Boothby's love letters to Dorothy.

Leo Amery, one of the undoubted authors of Churchill's succession, suffered perhaps the most cruel blow of all. His son John was a vigorous anti-Communist and was in France when it fell to the Nazis. Thereafter John spent much of his war in an anti-Communist crusade, which included trying to organize a British unit to fight the Russians. He also made several broadcasts from Berlin urging the

British to make peace with Germany. After the war he was arrested and charged with treason. He pleaded guilty and was executed in Wandsworth prison six days before Christmas 1945. His brother, Julian, became a senior and much respected Tory MP.

Mac's fate was the most ironic. In the tense and occasionally hysterical atmosphere of the times, many fears were expressed about the possible existence of a Fifth Column in Britain waiting to assist with the expected Nazi invasion. Within days of becoming Prime Minister, Churchill ordered a massive round-up of foreign aliens and those regarded as politically unsound. Mac was one of many thousands interned under Regulation 18B of the Emergency Powers Act. He spent three weeks in an internment camp on the Isle of Man, into which were thrown many Jewish refugees alongside genuine Nazis, until Halifax intervened to establish his *bona fides*. He was released and returned to London, where he was knocked down by a newspaper delivery van in the middle of the blackout and killed.

Towards the end of the war Carol met a GI and went to live in Idaho.

Joseph Kennedy became a pariah and was eventually recalled from his role as Ambassador in November 1940, soon after the Blitz began. By that time he had become widely disparaged as a defeatist – and also a coward for his propensity to endure every air raid on London from a 'funk hole' near Windsor, usually in the company of a French model. He became known as 'Jittery Joe'. When finally he left England, he took with him an air-raid siren which he said he intended to install at Hyannis to summon his children from their sailing.

Kennedy's reputation was further tarnished by the discovery in August 1940 that all manner of anti-British information had been leaking from within his own embassy and finding its way to Germany. A senior American diplomat was charged with espionage and imprisoned. No mention was made of Anna, who was allowed to disappear quietly from Britain.

Then there was Guy Burgess. He was one who would not disappear quietly. His career led him from the BBC to the Secret Intelligence Service and later still to the Foreign Office, where he was posted to the United States – all the time in the service of Russia's KGB. Yet no man can live for ever on the edge. He became increasingly notorious for his drunkenness and flamboyant homosexuality, and was ordered back from the United States in disgrace and under suspicion. On 25 May 1951, he suddenly vanished in the company of another senior diplomat and Cambridge friend, Donald Maclean. They turned up several years later in Moscow. Their defection caused a world-wide sensation and started a hunt for other Soviet spies within the British Establishment which lasted for many years.

Clearly Burgess had been warned of the authorities' interest in him, and there was much speculation about who tipped him off. Such information could only have come from the very highest level yet neither Churchill nor particularly Bracken, who had much to lose from his exposure, ever fell under suspicion. Indeed Churchill, who became Prime

Minister for the second time only weeks after the defection, did his best to ignore the whole episode. As Jock Colville wrote in his diary: *'I don't think he (Churchill) was much interested. In fact I had to press him to ask the Cabinet Office to provide a Note on the incident. I think he merely wrote them off as being decadent young men, corrupted by drink and homosexuality.'* Churchill was happy for the passage of time to fade the traces of the many friendships and liaisons that Burgess had formed with so many powerful people – including, of course, Churchill himself.

Burgess died in Moscow in 1963, still wearing his Old Etonian tie. As he had requested, his ashes were returned to Britain and buried in a Sussex church-yard.

Many other things passed. Czechoslovakia, the country whose fate had been one of the prime causes of a war that was to spread around the world, was never to recover. After the German surrender it fell under the tyranny of Communism and didn't become an independent state again until the Berlin Wall fell in 1989. Then, at the first opportunity, it voted to pull itself apart. Today the state of Czechoslovakia no longer exists.

Neither does the British Empire for which Churchill fought with all his heart.

And no one believes what they read in the news-papers any more.

ACKNOWLEDGEMENTS

As I emphasized at the beginning of this book, *Winston's War* is not a history. It is a novel that takes all the dramatic liberties required of a work of fiction. However, reality can be every bit as appetising as fiction and I have attempted to stick as closely as I could to the events of the twenty-month period covered by the book.

Some of those events are well known, others less so – the meeting between Churchill and Burgess at Chartwell that forms the basis for so much of what follows in the novel did take place and is described at length in a book written by Tom Driberg. Yet most of the histories of the period don't mention this meeting and therefore draw no significance from it. It's not difficult to understand why. Many diaries and personal memoirs of the appeasement period were thoroughly gutted after the War, and by the time Burgess was exposed as a Soviet spy, those wishing to recall any kind of connection with him were as difficult to find as orchids in Hyde Park. Churchill was just one amongst many with good reason to forget his relationship with the young BBC radio producer.

So there are gaps in the historical record, and I have tried to fill them. Perhaps even the slightest meddling with the facts will upset those who regard themselves as serious historians, but on the other hand I hope that many readers will have their appetites whetted and their imaginations fired by the deliberate intertwining of fact and fiction to the point where they will want to dig deeper and find out for themselves what really happened.

They might also be struck, as I have been, by the coincidence between the issues that Churchill faced at the time and those that continue to baffle us more than seventy years later – such as whether we should appease or confront the forces of terror, and whether a politician owes his prime loyalty to his party or his conscience. We tend to think of spin doctors as being a very recent invention but they were as mischievous and as amoral in the service of Neville Chamberlain as they have been for any modern prime minister, while the English still seem to be struggling to sort out their relationship with Europe and 'Johnny Foreigner'.

And how many of today's leaders in Europe and the United States can be found echoing Chamberlain's plaintive words that their world had been turned upside down by 'a quarrel in a far-away country between people of whom we know nothing'?

Researching and writing this book has given me as much fulfilment and personal pleasure as any I have written, and the debt I owe to those who have guided me and inspired me are as deep as ever. The entire project was set on its road by Laurence Marks and Maurice Gran, who treated me to an excellent lunch and finished it with some half-remembered and irresistible thought about a missing telegram. Rob Shepherd, a colleague of many years, allowed me to plunder his own great knowledge of this period and I have relied heavily on his splendid book, *A Class Divided*. Joe Shattan is another great friend who, in a different life, might have been Mac and is the main reason why the character was able to come to life, and I am also most grateful to Monty Park and to Trumper's, that exceptional gentlemen's barbers that has changed so little since Mac's day and where Monty maintained the highest of standards for many years.

Sue Graham, Carol Bell and Jeremy White gave a very special kind of support. With their backing I have been able to raise many thousands of pounds for the Spinal Injuries Association, even before the book was published.

So many others have helped, particularly my beautiful god-daughter Eugenia Vandoros, and others who deserve a big hug of thanks are Tim Hadcock-Mackay, Ian Patterson, Christopher Burr, Anthony Browne, Sherard Cowper-Coles, Kate Crowe and Glenmore Trenear-Harvey. Angela Neuberger found for me a press cutting that was especially inspirational.

I am also grateful to the following for permission to reproduce extracts from their publications and material: Miss Christine Penney at the Library of Birmingham University for permission to quote from Neville Chamberlain's letters; Hodder and Stoughton Limited for permission to quote from *The Fringes of Power* by John Colville; WH Allen Ltd.

for permission to quote from *Abuse of Power* by James Margach; HarperCollins Publishers Ltd for permission to quote from Harold Nicolson's *Diaries and Letters, 1930–1939*, edited by Nigel Nicolson.

There is little need to offer an extensive bibliography for those wishing to read further about this period since the sources are generally extremely well known, but I don't want to miss the opportunity to express my thanks to the staff at the London Library and to Phil Reed at the Cabinet War Rooms. The International Churchill Society and its magazine, *Finest Hour*, never cease to provide insights, and I am also grateful for the cheerful help provided by the archivists at Churchill College, Cambridge.

So I hope you will read and enjoy – and, while doing so, will remember that had the story of Winston Churchill found another ending, as it so easily might have done, our world today would have been a place of shadows and dark despair, stripped of the freedoms and decencies we too frequently take for granted. The debt we owe to Winston Churchill, and to those who helped him, is beyond measure.